I AM RUNNING AWAY TODAY

I AM RUNNING AWAY TODAY

AWAY TODAY

LISA DESIMINI

HYPERION BOOKS FOR CHILDREN

NEW YORK

Jessica Katz

FOR MY FRIENDS...

Andrew Goldstein

Library of Congress Cataloging-in-Publication Data
Desimini, Lisa.
I am running away today / Lisa Desimini.
p. cm.
Summary: Having decided to run away from home for
a host of reasons, but most of all because his best
friend moved away, a cat changes his mind when he
discovers a new friend moving in next door.
ISBN (trade) 1-56282-120-2. — ISBN 1-56282-121-0 (library)
[1. Cats—Fiction.   2. Runaways—Fiction.]   I. Title.
PZ7.D4505Iam 1992 [E]—dc20 91-25341 CIP AC

The artwork for each picture is prepared
with layers of oil glazing on bristol paper.
This book is set in 24-point Antique Olive Light.

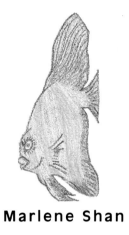

Marlene Shan

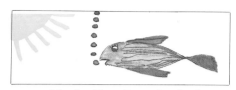

Natalie Desimini

Charlene Wetzel

Maureen Meehan

Katherine Murphy

Giavanna Bruno

Jerome Boxley

Frank Gargiulo

I am running away today.
My house is cold and creaky.

These trees are old and broken.
I've found their secret hiding places.

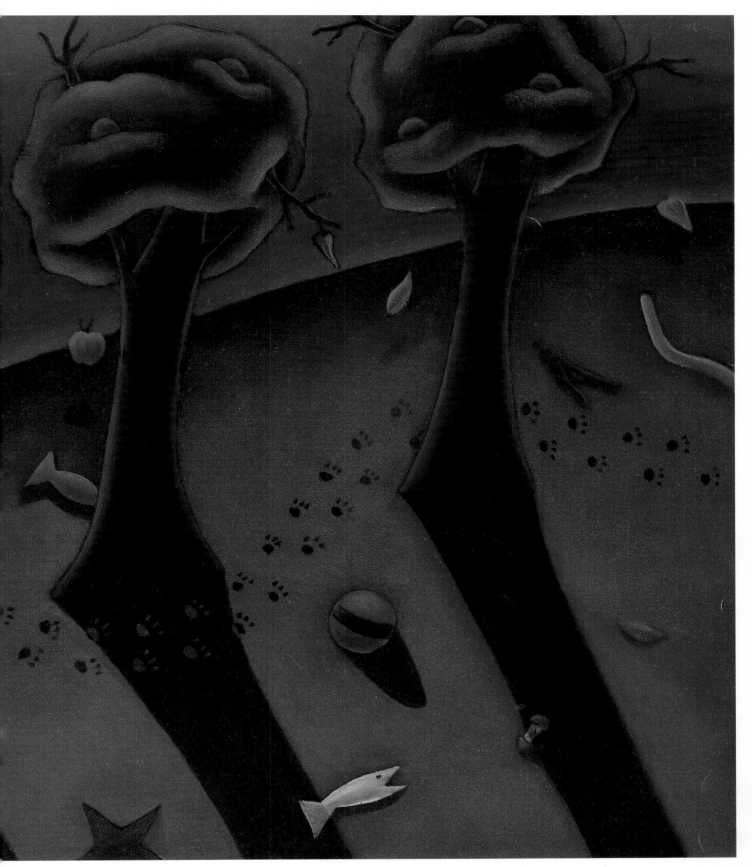

I've played with the same toys
day after day.

And now my best friend

just moved away.

So I'm off to look

for a new house.

I want a big house to play in,

but not too big. I might get lost.

It can't be too small
to stretch out my paws

or too tall
to climb to the roof
for a nap.

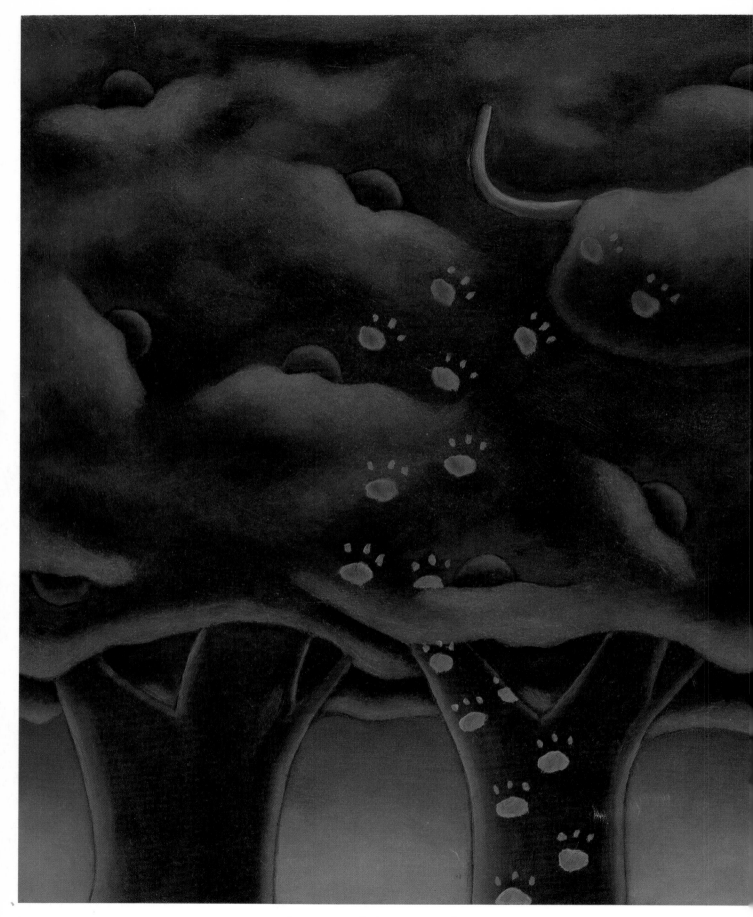

I need trees to

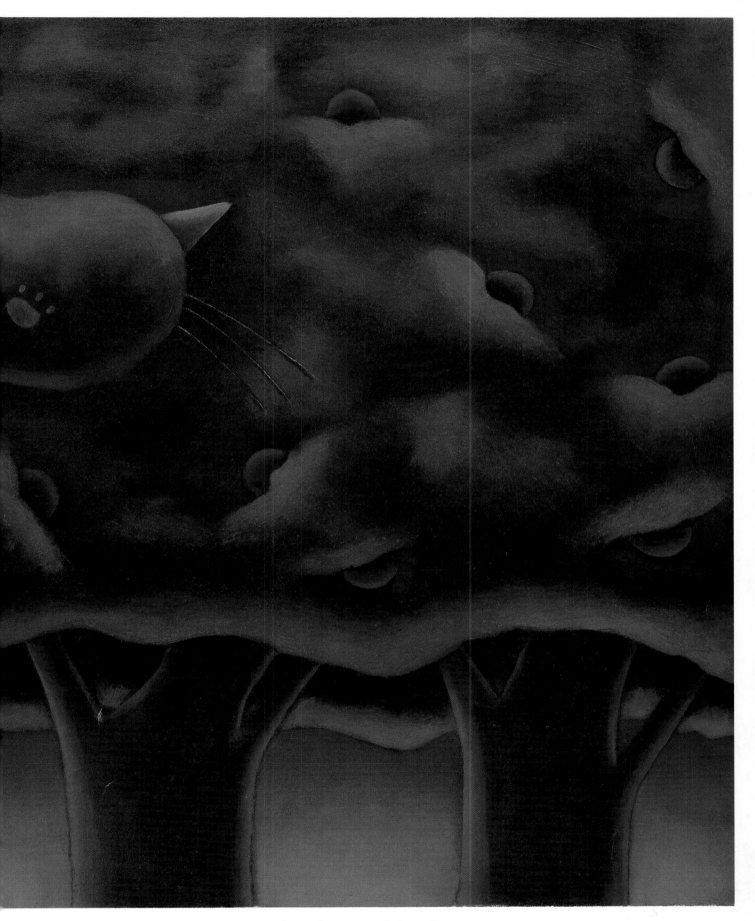

climb and hide in

and very big windows
so the sun can shine through.

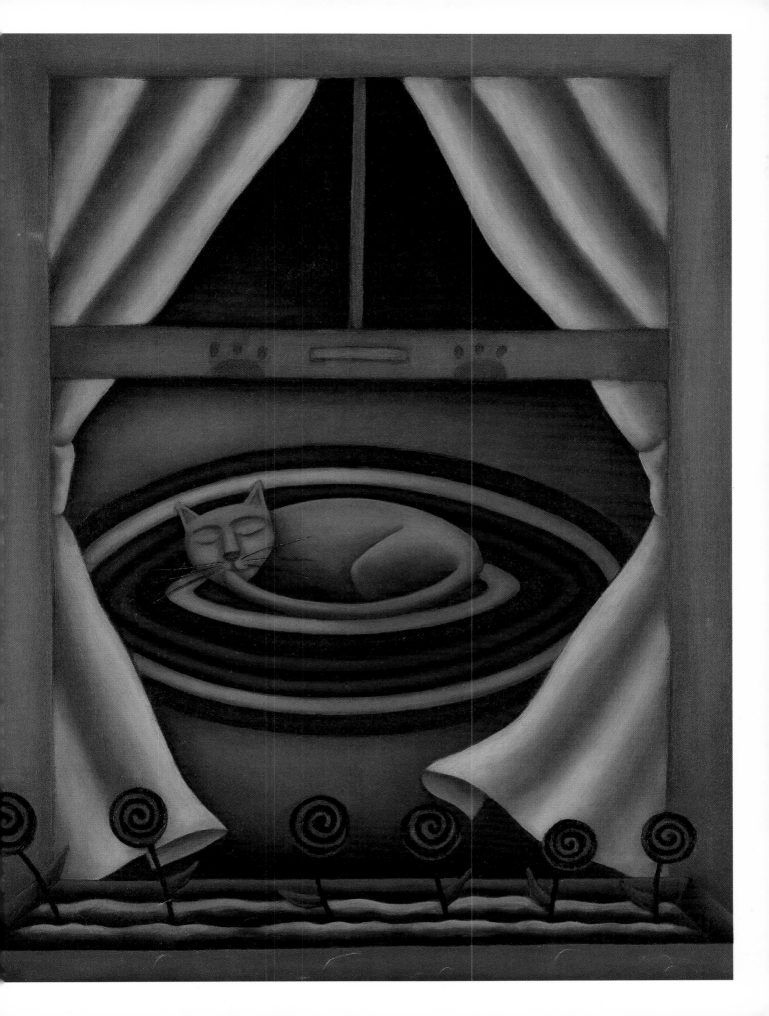

With toys shaped like mice and cars
and fish that are blue.

My new house can be any color but pink—
pink doesn't match my coat.

At the top of that hill
is a crooked little house.
It's not too small or too tall.
It's cozy and bright,
the trees are just right,

and someone to play with

is moving in next door.

I think I'll stay.

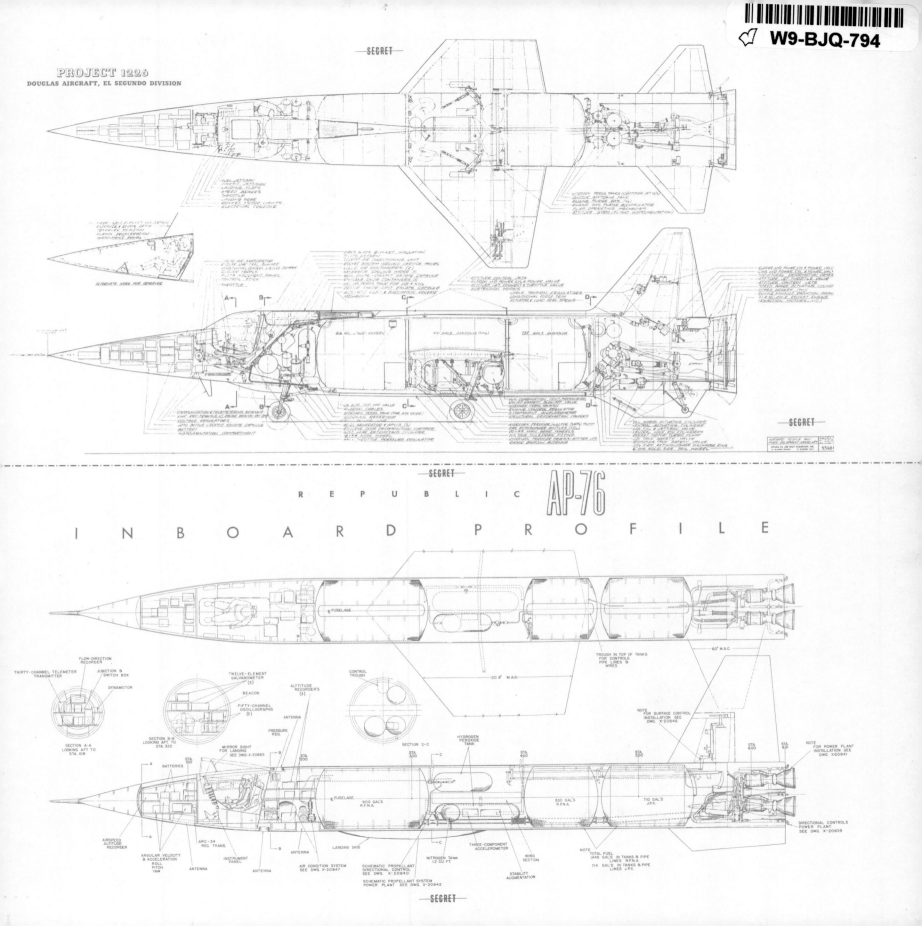

HYPERSONIC

The Story of the North American X-15

Dennis R. Jenkins
& Tony R. Landis

ISBN 1-58007-068-X

specialtypress
PUBLISHERS AND WHOLESALERS

39966 Grand Avenue
North Branch, MN 55056 USA
(651) 277-1400 or (800) 895-4585
www.specialtypress.com

Printed in China

Distributed in the UK and Europe by:

Midland Publishing
4 Watling Drive
Hinckley LE10 3EY, England
Tel: 01455 233 747 Fax: 01455 233 737
www.midlandcountiessuperstore.com

Library of Congress Cataloging-in-Publication Data

Jenkins, Dennis R.
  Hypersonic : the story of the North American X-15 / by Dennis R. Jenkins and Tony R. Landis.
       p. cm.
  Includes bibliographical references and index.
   ISBN 1-58007-068-X (hardbound)
 1. X-15 (Rocket aircraft) 2. Airplanes--California--Edwards Air Force Base--Flight testing--History. 3. Aerodynamics, Hypersonic. I. Landis, Tony. II. Title.
TL789.8.U6 X55297 2003
629.133'38--dc21
                    2002151144

On the front cover: *The modified X-15A-2 just prior to Flight 2-45-81 on 1 July 1966. Uncertainty over propellant flow from the external tanks would cause Bob Rushworth to make an emergency landing at Mud Lake. This was Rushworth's last X-15 flight; what a way to go.* (AFFTC History Office)

On the front dust jacket flap: *Bob White made the first flight above 300,000 feet on 17 July 1962. This flight (3-7-14) qualified White for an Astronaut rating under Air Force regulations and set an FAI altitude record of 314,750 feet that still stands at the end of 2002.* (AFFTC History Office)

On the frontis page: *The NASA hangar at the Flight Research Center on 30 August 1966. The three X-15s are lined up on the right with X-15-1 in the foreground, followed by X-15-3 and then the modified X-15A-2. Note the wingtip pods and tailcone box on X-15-1. The other side of the hangar shows some of the manned lifting bodies (nose of the HL-10, M2-F2, and M2-F1), an F4H-1 (BuNo 145313), F5D-1 (BuNo 142350/NASA 802), JF-104A (55-2961), and the NASA Gooney Bird (R4D, BuNo 17136/NASA 817).* (NASA Dryden)

On the title page: *The X-15-1 is towed across Rogers Dry Lake after Flight 1-21-36 on 7 February 1961. Bob White had reached Mach 3.50 and 78,150 feet during the last flight powered by the interim XLR11 engines.* (NASA Dryden)

On the back dust jacket flap: *Yes, it is a pink X-15. The Martin MA-25S ablator used on the X-15A-2 for the maximum speed flights was a natural pink color; a white wear-layer was subsequently applied that provided protection against liquid oxygen spills and moisture. This photo is dated 21 June 1967, shortly after receiving the complete ablator application for the first – and only – time.* (NASA Dryden)

On the back cover: *On 24 February 1961 Bob White aborted a flight (2-A-25) before launch because of an altitude gyro failure in the stable platform. The X-15-2, in addition to other experiments, carried an experimental infrared emission coating proposed for use on the B-70 bomber. The flight was ultimately launched on 7 March, becoming the first Mach 4 flight for any aircraft when White reached Mach 4.43 and 77,450 feet. Note the original The Challenger nose art on Balls Eight.* (AFFTC History Office)

The Neil Armstrong quote on the back cover is from his foreword in Milton O. Thompson, *At the Edge of Space: The X-15 Flight Program*, (Washington and London: Smithsonian Institution Press, 1992), p. xii.

On the front endsheet: *The four competing designs for Project 1226. Clockwise from upper left: Bell D171, Douglas Model 684, Republic AP-76, and the winning North American Aviation ESO-7487.* (Courtesy of Benjamin F. Guenther)

On the back endsheet: *A circa 1958 drawing showing the placement of most major electrical components in the X-15. Note the detail in the upper left corner showing the removable instrumentation elevator.* (NASA)

First Printing: December 2002

Contents

FOREWORD

Scott Crossfield

The research airplane lore from days of yore has long hungered for a history of the dedicated fervor of the body of talent who dared the X-15. It was a program that initially suffered emotions ranging from skepticism to disdain within much of a production-oriented industry. Even at NACA/NASA its early advocates were certainly not legion.

Hanging in my den is a sign of the times harking to the humble beginnings of the challenge of actually building the airplane. It reads "Home of the X-15, Building No. 20 – The Garret." The "Garret" was a loft above the cafeteria at North American Aviation, Inc,,

at the Los Angeles International Airport in December 1955. We had yet to prove our mettle.

The X-15 was the product of the courage that came out of the generation of the Depression, World War II, and the post-war technology explosion, as well as the professional talent of a very special group of the engineering fraternity who used judgment many times in lieu of hard knowledge. To typify this group I name a select few of the many: Walter Williams, the man of the 20th Century most responsible for the Nation's operational successes from the X-1 through the Space Shuttle; John Becker, of great technical acumen who had the conservative intuition to rein in those of us who overstrained at the bit; Harrison Storms, peerless imaginative innovator of the entire United States mission to space; and, of course, Charles Feltz, the flywheel of common sense engineering who educated the world with the X-15, Apollo, and the Space Shuttle.

Such were typical of those who felt victory when a previously unenthusiastic President of the North American Los Angeles Division proudly erected a huge neon sign on the top of our factory: "HOME OF X-15." So those humble beginnings were the forerunner of the proud success of our first real foray beyond the Earth's atmosphere.

Dennis Jenkins and Tony Landis have blended a triumph of the technology and the evangelistic spirit of its perpetrators into lore of historical moment. I commend this summary here to students of aerospace history and all interested.

The X-15-1 in front of the North American Aviation facility in Inglewood, California. The X-15s were small enough to be transported over the open roads; the only disassembly required was removing the dorsal rudder. Note the large neon sign on the North American building proudly proclaiming its involvement with the X-15 program, a source of pride to those involved. (Boeing via the Gerald H. Balzer Collection)

Scott Crossfield
Pilot, First X-15 Flight
North American Aviation, Inc.
8 August 2002

FOREWORD

William H. Dana

Scott Crossfield came early to the rocket airplane research program. He flew the Douglas D-558 Phase II in 1950 and the X-1 in 1951; by 1955 he was helping design the X-15. He was especially contributory to the cockpit design, including the sidearm controllers, whose designs were a concept far from mature in 1955. By 1959 Crossfield was flying the X-15, making 14 flights – including the first flights of airframes 1 and 2.

As a fledgling NASA engineer, I watched the final two flights of the X-1 in the fall of 1958. During the entire time from my arrival at NASA, through my participation in the rocket airplane program, to the present, there have been scores of persons – myself included – from both the Air Force and NASA who have tried to "sell" various rocket research airplane programs to their managements. These offerings ranged from a subscale space shuttle (a vision by X-15 pilot Milt Thompson) to the Mach 5 X-24C, a hypersonic version of the Air Force X-24B high-fineness-ratio reentry shape. Many of these research vehicles – including the subscale shuttle and the X-24C – had much to commend them in terms of knowledge to be gained for application to production aircraft. But none of the post-lifting body advanced propulsion research airplanes ever reached flight (if the Space Shuttle is accepted as a production vehicle and the reader is able to overlook one flight of the unmanned X-43A.)

There are many reasons why this is so: inter-center rivalries, a "not invented here" climate among some potential participants, and an ever-higher threshold of technical knowledge – part of it gained from the flight research programs of the past – that made some flight research aircraft unnecessary. Those of us who are uninformed of activity in the "black" world often wonder if the high-performance research airplanes are out there but not apparent to the uninvited.

NASA's most recent "best chances" for a rocket research airplane lay in the unmanned arena. The X-33 and X-34 held great promise for lowering the cost of payload into orbit. Both vehicles were cancelled short of flight, as NASA and contractors struggled with lessons learned from previous research airplanes.

The track record for rocket research aircraft since the mid-1970s is abysmal. Still, the X-43A brings the promise of an unmanned advanced-propulsion research airplane, and the hope of a later, manned version.

Perhaps then the Scott Crossfields of the 21st Century will make contributions similar in magnitude to those made by the 20th Century Scott Crossfield.

William H. Dana
Pilot, Last X-15 Flight
NASA Dryden Flight Research Center
3 September 2002

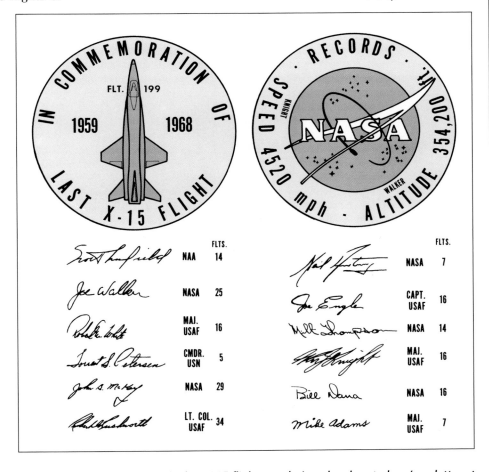

This plaque commemorating the last X-15 flight was designed and pasted up (one letter at a time) by Roy G. Bryant. The original layout has all twelve pilot signatures on frosted acetate that were taped onto the page. (Roy Bryant Collection)

AUTHORS' PREFACE

The Grand Experiment

Déjà vu. At the dawn of the 21st Century there seems to be a great interest in hypersonic flight. For the most part this is related to a new generation of missiles – air-to-air and air-to-surface – that are being proposed as the next logical increment in weapons, although the designers of the forever-in-development replacement for the Space Shuttle also have a vested interest in hypersonic research. If you read the popular press – indeed, even most trade journals – you would think that hypersonics was a new science discovered in the closing years of the 20th Century with the creation of a few "black" weapons and the stillborn X-33 and X-34 programs. It isn't so.

Few people remember that almost 50 years ago there was an earlier hypersonic project, one that resulted in a remarkable manned vehicle. A team of NACA researchers developed a concep-

Not surprisingly, this book highlights the efforts of a few individuals who designed and flew the X-15. But the program was the result of a massive team effort, and we extend our admiration to all of those who made it possible. Here is a representative sample of the people involved when all three X-15s flew in a single week (16, 17, and 19 July 1962). Cockpit: Edward "Ed" Nice; Ladder: Thomas "Tom" McAlister; Standing: William Clark, Edward "Ed" Sabo, Donald "Don" Hall, Billy Furr, Allen Dustin, Raymond "Ray" White, George E. Trott, Alfred "Al" Grieshaber, Merle Curtiss, LeRoy "Lee" Adelsbach, Allen Lowe, Jay L. King, Lorenzo "Larry" Barnett; Kneeling: Byron Gibbs, Price "Bob" Workman, Ira Cupp, unknown, and John Gordon. (NASA Dryden)

tual design, the Air Force and Navy funded the effort, and North American Aviation turned the idea into three small black airplanes. Over the course of ten years and 199 flights, pilots from the Air Force, Navy, and NASA would spend 85 minutes at hypersonic velocities and fly to the edge of space.

There had never been anything like the X-15; it had a million-horsepower engine and could fly twice as fast as a rifle bullet. The airplane and its pilots set records that stood for years. Twelve men flew the X-15. Scott Crossfield was first; Bill Dana was last. Pete Knight went more than 4,500 miles per hour; Joe Walker flew more than 67 miles high. But the airplane and the pilots who flew it were quickly overshadowed by the astronauts and ballistic missiles at Cape Canaveral. The grand experiment in the high desert was soon forgotten.

There was little doubt that a hypersonic vehicle could be built, but nobody was exactly sure what problems would be encountered along the way. When the program was initiated in 1954, the X-planes at Edwards had just broken Mach 2, and the X-2 was expected to break Mach 3 – eventually. The space age was still the work of science fiction. The aircraft that would become the X-15 was designed to exceed Mach 6 and to fly outside the sensible atmosphere. Neil Armstrong, who would pilot the X-15 seven times before he went to the Moon, later described the concept as "audacious."[1]

In addition to high-speed and high-altitude flight research, the program provided the first prolonged experience in a weightless environment, the first opportunity to blend aerodynamic and reaction controls, the first biomedical data under boost and reentry conditions, the most extensive pilot-in-the-loop simulation to-date, and invaluable aerothermal data for both Apollo and Space Shuttle. The X-15 has often been called the most productive flight research program ever undertaken, yet most of the general public has never heard of it.

The X-15 would ultimately exceed all of its performance goals. Instead of Mach 6.5 (6,600 fps) and 250,000 feet, the program would record Mach 6.7 (6,629 fps) and 354,200 feet. It was not easy. Several pilots would get banged up; Jack McKay seriously so, although he would return from his injuries to fly 22 more X-15 flights. Two of the three airframes would be rebuilt following serious accidents. Almost unbelievably, given the large increment in performance achieved by the airplanes, the program suffered only a single fatality: Mike Adams would be killed on Flight 3-65-97.[2]

John Becker, arguably the father of the X-15, once stated that the project came along at " ... the most propitious of all possible times for its promotion and approval." At the time it was not considered necessary to have a defined operational program in order to

DEDICATION

To Betty J. Love

Everybody who knows her understands why.

Joe Walker prepares to ignite the two Reaction Motors XLR11-RM-5 engines during Flight 1-5-10 on 19 April 1960. This flight recorded Mach 2.56 and 59,496 feet altitude. Note the frost around the liquid oxygen tank and the NACA instrumentation boom on the nose. (NASA Dryden)

conduct basic research and there were no "glamorous and expensive" manned space programs to compete for funding. The general feeling within the Nation was one of trying to go faster, higher, or further. The X-15 certainly accomplished the first two; the third was never in the cards.[3]

The most frequently quoted X-15 history was originally written in 1959 by Robert S. Houston, a historian at the Air Force Wright Air Development Center. This narrative, unsurprisingly, centered on the early Air Force involvement in the program, and concentrated – as is normal for most Air Force histories – mostly on the program management aspects rather than the technology. Dr. Richard P. Hallion, later the Chief Historian for the U.S. Air Force, updated Houston's history in 1987 as part of Volume II of *The Hypersonic Revolution*, a collection of papers published by the Aeronautical Systems Office at Wright-Patterson AFB. Hallion added coverage of the last nine years of the program, drawing mainly from his own *On the Frontier: Flight*

Research at Dryden, 1946-1981 (Washington DC: NASA, 1984) and a paper written in 1977 by the Air Force Academy's Ronald G. Boston entitled "Outline of the X-15's Contributions to Aerospace Technology." These historians did an excellent job, but unfortunately their work received comparatively limited distribution.

Needless to say, many people assisted in the preparation of this work. Foremost was Betty J. Love who spent many long hours gathering data from Roy G. Bryant and others, checking our lists, researching data to assemble the most authoritative flight log yet produced, and to identify individuals in photos. Some holes still exist, but they are generally of very ancillary data and unimportant to the principle story. We are terribly indebted to Betty for her efforts.

There was correspondence with many individuals who had been involved with the program: William P. Albrecht, Colonel John E. "Jack" Allavie (USAF, Retired); Colonel Clarence E. "Bud" Anderson (USAF, Retired), Johnny G. Armstrong at the AFFTC (the famous

The phenomenal performance of the X-15 was due largely to the Reaction Motors XLR99-RM-1 rocket engine. Often described as a "million horsepower engine," the engine did not quite live up to that billing. Nevertheless, producing over 57,000 pounds of thrust, it was the first large throttleable and restartable man-rated engine ever built and could push the X-15 to over 4,500 miles per hour. (NASA Dryden via the Terry Panopalis Collection)

"Armstrong Memorial Library"),[4] Neil A. Armstrong, Bill Arnold (RMD/Thiokol), John V. Becker, Colonel Charles C. Bock, Jr. (USAF, Retired), Jerry Brandt, A. Scott Crossfield, William H. Dana, Brigadier General Joe H. Engle (USAF, Retired), Charles H. Feltz, Richard J. Harer, Robert G. Hoey, Colonel William J. "Pete" Knight (USAF, Retired), Gerald M. Truszynski, Alvin S. White, and Major General Robert M. White (USAF, Retired). Johnny Armstrong, Bob Hoey, and Dick Harer, in particular, went far beyond the call of duty in assisting.

In addition, Jack Bassick at the David Clark Company, Michael H. Gorn and J.D. "Dill" Hunley at the Dryden History Office, Stephen J. Garber and Dr. Roger D. Launius at the NASA History Office in Washington, Michael J. Lombardi at The Boeing Company archives, Air Force Chief Historian Dr. Richard P. Hallion, Dr. James H. Young and Cheryl Gumm at the AFFTC History Office, and John D. "Jack" Weber at the AFMC History Office all provided excellent support for the project. Friends and fellow authors Gerald H. Balzer, Robert E. Bradley, Rob Goodwin, Benjamin F. Guenther, Scott Lowther, Mike Machat, Michael Moore, Terry Panopalis, and Mick Roth also assisted.

Others that contributed include Lynn Albaugh at Ames, Jack Beilman, Rodney K. Bogue at Dryden, Anita Borger at Ames, John W. Boyd at Ames, Russell Castonguay at the JPL archives, Erik M. Conway at Langley, C. Roger Cripliver, Larry Davis, Mark L. Evans at the Naval Historical Center, Matt Graham at Dryden, Fred W. Haise, Jr., Wesley B. Henry at the Air Force Museum, T.A. Heppenheimer, James B. Hill at the John Fitzgerald Kennedy Library, Bob James at Dryden, Frederick A. Johnsen, Jack Kittrell (DFRC, Retired), Christian Ledet, F. Robert van der Linden at the National Air and Space Museum, Marilyn Meade at the University of Wisconsin, MSgt. David Menard (USAF, Retired), Peter Merlin at the Dryden History Office, Roger E. Moore, Claude S. Morse at the AEDC, Karen Moze at Ames, Dr. Valerie Neal at the National Air and Space Museum, Doug Nelson at the AFFTC Museum, Anne-Laure Perret at the Fédération Aéronautique Internationale, Colonel Bruce A. Peterson (USMCR, Retired), Charles E. Rogers at the AFFTC, Mary F. Shafer at Dryden, Erik Simonsen at Boeing, Bonita S. Smith at Glenn, Colonel Donald M. Sorlie (USAF, Retired), Henry Spencer, and Glen E. Swanson at the JSC History Office.

From Jenkins

Given that the X-15 is usually touted as the most productive flight research program ever undertaken, it struck me odd that no large-scale history of the program had ever been written. There were several books penned while the program was on-going, but none were true histories. A couple of monographs – the Aerofax one by Ben Guenther, Jay Miller, and Terry Panopalis in particular – provided good high-level treatments of the program, but still no serious history.

When I decided to write this book, I started a journey that would ultimately put me in contact with many of the program principles. It was a fascinating experience. Everybody I interacted with was – more than 30 years later – still thrilled with having been involved with the program, and most consider it the highlight of their professional careers. The enthusiasm was contagious. It has been a privilege and honor to talk to the people that accomplished so much in a relatively short period of time. I hope you find the story as interesting as I did.

I owe a particular thanks to Jay Miller, author of the popular *The X-Planes: X-1 to X-45*, (Hinckley, England: Midland Publishing, 2001), among many other works. Anybody interested in reading about the other X-planes should pick up a copy of this book. Jay was responsible for the first photograph I ever had published, and also published my first book – a short monograph on the Space Shuttle – well over a decade ago. Somehow, I feel he is to blame for the quagmire of aerospace history I find myself embroiled in. I truly appreciate the help and friendship from Jay and his lovely wife Susan over the past 20 years or so.

But most importantly, my mother – Mrs. Mary E. Jenkins – encouraged me to seize opportunities and taught me to write and type, such necessary attributes for this endeavor. As for so many things, I owe her a great deal of gratitude, along with my everlasting love and admiration.

My friend Tony has only himself to blame …

From Landis

When Dennis first approached me about assisting with this project I was both thrilled and honored. Thrilled that I could contribute in some small way to telling the history of such a magnificent program, and honored to be working with Dennis who is not only a talented writer and researcher, but has become a close friend as well. I also feel privileged to be part of a project that will continue, and expand upon, the works done in the past on the subject by authors such as Martin Caidin, Scott Crossfield, Jay Miller, and Dick Hallion.

I owe a special thanks to the staff at the AFFTC History Office at Edwards AFB. Chief historian Dr. Jim Young, deputy historian Cheryl Gumm, archivist Freida Johnson, and historian Ray Puffer have always been helpful, professional, and generous to my many and sometimes overwhelming, requests for assistance. I also owe a debt of gratitude to Ms. Betty Love who spent tireless hours tracking down the names to many of the individuals pictured in the accompanying images as well as getting little known facts and information when all hope seemed to be lost.

Most of all, the best part of this project has been the chance to talk with the people who were actually there and made it happen. Getting a first hand, personal account is by far the best way of reliving the history that we now only get to read about. This book is for them.

The X-15 was designed to go high and fast, but it could not take off under its own power. A pair of early Boeing B-52 Stratofortresses were used as carrier aircraft for the program, usually taking the X-15 to between 40,000 and 45,000 feet and Mach 0.8 to begin each flight. Here is X-15-3 under the NB-52B during the carry for Flight 3-50-74 on 12 October 1965. (AFFTC History Office)

As it turned out, we had too many illustrations to fit into this book. However, the publisher, an aviation enthusiast himself, agreed to publish the *X-15 Photo Scrapbook* (ISBN 1-58007-074-4) as a companion volume. This 108-page softbound 9x9-inch book contains approximately 400 additional X-15 illustrations from all phases of the program. You might find it interesting.

It was not until the X-15A-2 came along midway through the flight program that the maximum speed potential of the design was achieved. Here the airplane is on display at Edwards during a visit from President Lyndon B. Johnson on 19 June 1964. Note the dummy scramjet under the ventral stabilizer and the open skylight hatch and nose-gear scoop door. (NASA Dryden)

CHAPTER 1

Antecedents

Right: *The first of the high-speed X-planes was the Air Force-sponsored Bell XS-1, shown here in September 1949, some two years after Chuck Yeager's history-making flight. From the left, Eddie Edwards, Bud Rogers, Dick Payne (crew chief), and Henry Gaskins.* (NASA Dryden)

Below: *The Navy also sponsored high-speed research airplanes, culminating in the Douglas D-558-II Skyrocket. Initially both the D-558-I and D-558-II took off from the ground under their own power, but eventually the D-558-II moved to air launch using a modified Boeing P2B-1S.* (NASA Dryden)

History is a series of small occurrences that, in themselves, usually seem insignificant at the time. Occasionally, however, a larger event sneaks in, something that marks a turning point. In the world of aviation, one of these occurred in the skies over Muroc Army Air Field on 14 October 1947. It was announced, as many were in those days, by an almost cryptic telegram:[1]

> "XS-1 BROKE MACH NO ONE AT 42000 FT ALT PD FLT CONDITIONS IMPROVED WITH INCREASE OF AIRSPEED PD DATA BEING REDUCED AND WILL BE FORWARDED WHEN COMPLETED PD END"

Air Force Captain Charles E. Yeager – Chuck to those who knew him – had taken a small, bullet-shaped airplane very slightly above the speed of sound in level flight. It was a milestone. Yeager and the rocket-powered Bell XS-1 were not the first to attempt breaking the so-called "sound barrier" – Geoffrey de Havilland had been killed a year earlier during an attempt in the jet-powered de Havilland DH.108 Swallow. But Yeager was the first to live to tell about it.[2]

THE SOUND BARRIER

Supersonic. Adj. (1919). Of, being, or relating to velocities from one to five times the speed of sound in air.[3]

Contrary to general perception, the speed of sound was not a discovery of the 20th Century. Over 250 years before Chuck Yeager made his now-famous flight, it was known that sound propagated through air at some finite velocity. Artillerymen in the 17th Century determined that the speed of sound was approximately 1,140 feet per second (fps) by standing a known large distance away from a cannon and observing the time delay between the muzzle flash and the sound of the discharge. Their conclusion was remarkably accurate.[4]

The first person to recognize an aerodynamic anomaly near the speed of sound was probably Benjamin Robins, an 18th Century British scientist who had invented a ballistic pendulum that allowed the determination of the velocity of cannon projectiles. As described by Robins, a large wooden block was suspended in front of a cannon, and the projectile was fired into it; the momentum of the projectile was transferred to the block and the force could be determined from the amplitude of the pendulum. During these experiments Robins observed that the drag on the projectile seemed to increase dramatically as it got closer to the speed of sound. It was an interesting piece of data, but no practical or theoretical basis existed to further investigate it.[5]

Like the speed of sound itself, the concept of shock waves also predated the 20th Century. German mathematician G. F. Bernhard Riemann attempted to calculate the properties of shock waves during 1858, but a lack of theoretical basis made the results largely meaningless. Twelve years later, William John Rankine, an engineering professor at the University of Glasgow, correctly derived the proper equations for the flow across a normal shock wave. Independently, French ballistician Pierre Hugoniot came up with similar equations in 1887. Today these are known as the Rankine-Hugoniot equations in their honor. This work was expanded to include oblique shock waves by German aerodynamicists Ludwig Prandtl and Theodor Meyer at Göttingen University in 1908.[6]

During this same period, Austrian physicist Ernst Mach took the first photographs of supersonic shock waves using a technique called a shadowgraph. In 1877 Mach presented a paper to the Academy of Sciences in Vienna where he showed a shadowgraph of a bullet moving at supersonic speeds; the bow and trailing-edge shock waves were clearly visible. Mach was also the first to assign a numerical value to the ratio between the speed of a solid object passing through a gas and the speed of sound through the same gas. In his honor, supersonic velocities are expressed as "Mach numbers." The concept of compressibility effects on objects moving at high speeds was established, but little actual knowledge of the phenomena existed.[7]

None of these experiments had much impact on the airplanes of the early 20th Century since flight speeds were so low that compressibility effects were effectively nonexistent. However, within a few years, things changed. Although the typical flight speeds during World War I were less than 125 mph, the propeller tips, because of their combined rotational and translational motion through the air, sometimes approached the speed of sound – dangerously close to the compressibility phenomenon.[8]

To better understand the nature of the problem, in 1918 G. H. Bryan began a theoretical analysis of subsonic and supersonic flows

The first of the X-planes and the man who made them famous. On 14 October 1947 Chuck Yeager took the first Bell XS-1 to very slightly above the speed of sound in level flight – the first time somebody had done so. Yeager named the airplane "Glamorous Glennis" after his wife. At this point the X-1 was overall orange; the original name is shown at left, while a repainted (and more visible) version of it is shown with Yeager in the posed shot at right. (AFFTC History Office)

The D-558-I was never intended to go supersonic. Instead, the design was meant to gather data in the high transonic regime in support of future supersonic programs. (Museum of Flight Collection via Jay Miller)

for the British Advisory Committee for Aeronautics at the Royal Aeronautical Establishment. His analysis was cumbersome and provided little data of immediate value. At the same time, Frank W. Caldwell and Elisha N. Fales from the Army Air Service Engineering Division at McCook Field in Dayton, Ohio, took a purely experimental approach to the problem.[9] To better investigate the problems associated with propellers, in 1918 Caldwell and Fales designed the first high-speed wind tunnel to be built in the United States. This tunnel was 19 feet long with a 14-inch diameter test section that could generate velocities up to 465 mph, considered exceptional at the time. This was the beginning of a dichotomy between American and British research. Over the next two decades, the major experimental contributions to understanding compressibility effects were made in the United States – primarily by the National Advisory Committee for Aeronautics[10] (NACA) – while the major theoretical contributions were made in England. This combination of American and British investigations of propellers constituted one of the first concerted efforts of the fledgling aeronautical community to investigate what would become known as the sound barrier.[11]

Within about five years the scope of the problem had been defined and practical solutions had been found. New thin-section blade designs were developed that minimized the effects of compressibility, and were made practical by using metal instead of wood for their construction. But interestingly, most of the solution was to simply avoid the problem. The development of reliable reduction-gearing systems and variable-pitch constant-speed propellers eliminated the problem entirely for airplane speeds conceivable in 1925 by rotating the propeller at slower speeds. At the time the best pursuit planes (the forerunners of what we call fighters) were only capable of about 200 mph, and a scan of the literature of the mid-1920s showed only rare suggestions of significantly higher speeds in the foreseeable future. Accordingly, most researchers moved on to other areas.[12]

But progress in aviation occurred much more rapidly than had been anticipated. For example, on 29 September 1931 a highly streamlined Supermarine S.6B flown by Flight Lieutenant George H. Stainforth set a world speed record of 401.5 mph – Mach 0.53. Suddenly, it looked like the effects of compressibility might extend to the entire airplane much sooner than had been expected.

The public belief in the "sound barrier" apparently had its begin-

ning in 1935 when the British aerodynamicist W. F. Hilton was explaining to a journalist about some high-speed experiments he was conducting at the National Physical Laboratory. Pointing to a plot of airfoil drag, Hilton said, "See how the resistance of a wing shoots up like a barrier against higher speed as we approach the speed of sound." The next morning, the leading British newspapers were referring to the "sound barrier" and the idea that airplanes could never fly faster than the speed of sound became widespread among the public. Although most engineers knew differently, the considerable uncertainty about how significantly drag would increase in the transonic regime made them wonder if engines of sufficient power to fly faster than sound would ever be available.[13]

Since the beginning of powered flight, wind tunnels had proven to be useful tools, but there were several problems associated with them relating to compressibility research, not least of which was that it appeared in the 1930s that the transonic regime could not be adequately simulated due to the physical characteristics of the test sections. So, on a spring morning in 1940, John V. Becker and John Stack, two researchers from the NACA Langley Memorial Aeronautical Laboratory in Hampton, Virginia,[14] drove to a remote beach to watch the first attempt to obtain supercritical aerodynamic data on an airplane in free flight. A Navy Brewster XF2A-2 had been instrumented to measure the pressure distribution at an inboard wing station and was flown into a steep dive over Chesapeake Bay. After it reached its terminal velocity – about 575 mph – the pilot made a pullup that was near the design load factor of the airplane. The flight was completed without any undue difficulties and some data were obtained, but the general feeling was that diving an operational-type airplane near its structural limits was not the best way to acquire high-speed research information.[15]

X-PLANES

As it happened, John Stack had already considered other alternatives. The idea of a modern research airplane – one designed and built strictly for the purposes of probing unknown flight regimes – can most likely be traced to a 1933 proposal by Stack. On his own initiative, Stack went through a very preliminary design analysis "for a hypothetical airplane which, however, is not beyond the limits of possibility" to fly well into the compressibility regime. Stack calculated that a small airplane powered by a 2,300 horsepower Rolls-Royce engine could obtain a maximum speed of 566 mph in level flight – far beyond that of any airplane flying at the time. Ultimately the NACA did not pursue the suggestion, and it would be another decade before the idea would come of age.[16]

The next proposal for a high-speed research airplane was made by Ezra Kotcher at the Army Air Corps Engineering School at Wright Field. In 1939 Kotcher pointed out the unknown aspects of the transonic flight regime and the problems associated with the effects of compressibility. He further discussed the limitations of existing wind tunnels and advised that a full-scale flight research program was an appropriate precaution, but no immediate action was taken. By the time the United States entered World War II in December 1941, John Stack had confirmed that data from wind tunnels operating near Mach 1 were essentially worthless because of a choking problem in the test section. He again concluded that the only way to gather meaningful data near the speed of sound was to build a vehicle that would fly in that regime. In the meantime, determining the effects of compressibility on airplanes remained a largely theoretical pursuit.[17]

The real-world intervened in November 1941 when Lockheed test pilot Ralph Virden was killed after he could not pull a Lockheed P-38 Lightning out of a high-speed dive that penetrated well into the compressibility regime. By 1942, it was apparent that the diving speeds of the new generation of fighters would quickly exceed the choking speeds of the wind tunnels then in use. Researchers increasingly leaned toward the idea of a specially configured and instrumented airplane capable of safe operation at high subsonic speeds. Those involved do not remember that this idea was specifically promoted by any single individual. Rather it took form gradually, manipulated and developed in innumerable lunchroom conversations and other contacts. Nevertheless, John Stack was a central figure in these discussions, and soon became the chief Langley proponent of the idea.[18]

Researchers at Langley concentrated on a design capable of speeds up to about Mach 0.9 – it is important to note that there was little interest in pushing through Mach 1. It appeared likely that one of the early turbojet engines could provide Mach 0.9 in a small airplane; the idea of a rocket-powered airplane was considered too risky by the NACA. The Army, however, wanted a supersonic airplane and appeared willing to accept rocket propulsion. In fact, Ezra Kotcher had listed this as an option in his 1939 proposal, and it was increasingly obvious that a rocket engine was the only hope at that time for achieving supersonic speeds in level flight.[19]

Possible Navy interest in a high-speed research airplane also began to stir in the 1942-44 period. Interestingly, some significant differences of opinion were voiced at a 15 March 1944 meeting of Army, Navy, and NACA personnel. The NACA tended to think of the airplane as a device for collecting high-subsonic speed aerodynamic data unobtainable in wind tunnels, while the Army thought of it as a major step toward a possible supersonic combat aircraft. The Navy supported both views, wanting to dispel the myth of the impenetrable sound barrier, but also interested in gathering meaningful high-speed data. Despite the NACA objections, the Army soon announced its intention to develop a rocket-powered research airplane.[20]

The NACA continued to emphasize the assumed safety aspects and relatively long-duration data-gathering flights possible with a turbojet engine compared to the very short flights of any reasonably sized rocket-plane. Furthermore, the turbojet would have obvious applicability to future military aircraft while the rocket propulsion system did not. This apparently unreconcilable difference was easily resolved; the Army was putting up the money and they decided to do it their way.[21]

What became the XS-1 program was likely initiated during a visit by Robert J. Woods from Bell Aircraft with Ezra Kotcher on 30 November 1944. After discussing the basic specification for the aircraft, Kotcher asked Woods if Bell was interested in designing and building the airplane. Woods said yes. In late December the Army began contract negotiations with Bell to design and manufacture the XS-1.[22]

Melvin N. Gough, the chief test pilot at Langley, condemned the rocket-plane concept, "No NACA pilot will ever be permitted to fly an airplane powered by a damned firecracker." When it had become clear in early 1944 that the Army was likely to insist on rocket propulsion, John Stack began an effort to interest the Navy in procuring the kind of airplane NACA wanted. The Navy was more receptive to the turbojet-powered airplane envisioned by Langley, and in September 1944 the Navy Bureau of Aeronautics (BuAer) began procurement

The X-1A glides in for a landing on Rogers Dry Lake. The second-generation X-1s were meant to investigate the aerothermal environment at Mach 2.5, but – unfortunately – the X-1A made only a single flight above Mach 2. (AFFTC History Office)

activities; Douglas was subsequently selected to build the D-558 Skystreak in early 1945.[23]

These were the beginnings of the cooperative NACA research airplane program that would last through the end of the 1960s. In reality – until the advent of the X-15 – there were two distinct programs, one with the Army and the other with the Navy. Just because the Army had elected to pursue a path that the NACA did not necessarily agree with did not keep the agency from fully-cooperating with the service during the development of the XS-1. The same level of cooperation was provided to the Navy and the D-558. The NACA always knew who was paying the bills, and chose to emphasize the positive factors, passing over any early controversies. An example was in 1951 when John Stack noted that, "the research airplane program has been a cooperative venture from the start … The extent of the cooperation is best illustrated by the fact that the X-1, sponsored by the Air Force, is powered with a Navy-sponsored rocket engine, and the D-558-I, sponsored by the Navy, is powered with an Air Force-sponsored turbojet engine."[24]

Initially, the primary justification for a manned research airplane was the inability of wind tunnels to operate above Mach 0.8, but as it turned out, this limitation was overcome prior to the beginning of high-speed flight tests. Although some researchers felt this largely eliminated the need for the X-planes, it is unlikely that the rapid progress in the transonic ground facilities would have happened without the stimulus provided by the XS-1 and D-558. Additionally, although slots and perforated test sections solved the choking problem for the tunnels, and allowed transonic tests to be conducted, the wind tunnel data between Mach 0.9 and 1.1 was – and still is – often questionable. This is the speed range where the largest discrepancies are usually found between the wind tunnel results and flight testing; the X-planes helped sort this out. Clearly there was an important two-way flow of benefits. Stimulated by the problems of the research airplanes, new ground facilities and techniques were developed which, in turn, produced vitally needed data in time for the design and safe operation of the aircraft.[25]

A principal value of the research airplanes lay in the comparison of the ground-based techniques with actual flight results, and the fact that the first transonic flights showed nothing particularly unexpected was of great relief to the researchers. The most basic result, however, was dispelling the myth of the "sound barrier." The fearsome transonic zone had been reduced to an ordinary engineering problem, and the design of operational supersonic aircraft could now proceed with much greater confidence.[26]

THE HIGH-SPEED ASSAULT

When people think of the X-planes, what generally comes to mind are the record-setting vehicles like the X-1 and X-15. In reality, most of the X-planes were dedicated to much more mundane flight regimes, and there were only a handful of high-speed manned experimental aircraft, built mainly during the late 1940s and early 1950s. Specifically there were five designs – only three of which carried X designations – intended for the assault on high-speed flight. Of the five, one was intended to probe high subsonic speeds; two were supersonic designs, and one was intended to push the envelope to Mach 3. The fifth design would go much faster.[27]

Douglas D-558-I Skystreak

This was the aircraft that John Stack and the researchers at Langley envisioned when they began thinking of a dedicated high-speed research airplane. During the course of the design process, the D-558 project was divided into two separate phases: phase one was a

A group photo of the X-1A test force on the ramp at Edwards along with much of their equipment. By modern standards the entire operation was very simplistic, but it got the job done. (AFFTC HIstory Office)

straight-wing turbojet-powered airplane and phase two was a swept-wing design with turbojet and rocket propulsion.

Douglas manufactured three D-558-I airplanes that flew 229 times between 1947 and 1953. The airplanes were 35 feet 1 inch long, spanned 25 feet, and were 12 feet high. They were powered by a single 5,000-lbf Allison J35-A-11 turbojet engine. The Skystreaks took-off from the ground and collected data about stability and control, loads, buffeting, and handling qualities in the transonic region.[28]

Douglas pilot Eugene F. May made the initial flight on 14 April 1947 at Muroc Army Airfield. On 20 August 1947 Navy Commander Turner F. Caldwell flew the first D-558-I to a new world speed record of 640.663 mph. Five days later, however, Marine Major Marion E. Carl surpassed the record, flying the second aircraft an average 650.796 mph. Unfortunately, on 3 May 1948, NACA pilot Howard C. Lilly was killed when the J35 engine disintegrated, severing the elevator and rudder cables; Lilly was the first NACA research pilot killed in the line of duty.[29]

Ultimately, the D-558-I proved somewhat disappointing despite the speed records. If the D-558-I would have arrived in the early 1940s it would have been timely; but coming as it did in 1947, it was largely unnecessary. Contemporary service aircraft with equal or better performance became available in the same period and could have been instrumented and used for most of the research conducted by the D-558-I. For example, the North American F-86 Sabre regularly exceeded Mach 1 in dives beginning in the summer of 1948, some time before the D-558-I inadvertently exceeded Mach 1 for the only time on 29 September 1948. Marion Carl's speed record fell on 15 September 1948 – barely a year had passed – when an F-86 recorded 671 mph. Nevertheless, it was the D-558-I and not the service aircraft that were used for extensive flight research by NACA, complementing coverage of the higher transonic speeds by the X-ls.[30]

Bell X-1 Series

The X-1 program ended up being a bit more extensive than Ezra Kotcher and John Stack had envisioned. Bell built three X-1s and the first aircraft made its initial glide flight on 25 January 1946 with Bell test pilot Jack Woolams at the controls. Eventually the first two airplanes completed 151 glide and powered flights.[31]

The original X-1s were 30 feet, 11 inches long, spanned 28 feet, and were 10 feet, 10 inches high. Each aircraft weighed approximately 6,800 pounds empty and 12,000 pounds fully-loaded. They were powered by a single Reaction Motors XLR11 rocket engine that used liquid oxygen and alcohol propellants. The first two airplanes had 5,000-lbf XLR11-RM-3 engines that used pressure-fed propellants, while the third airplane used a 5,900-lbf XLR11-RM-5 engine equipped with a turbopump.[32]

The turbopump-driven engine in the third airplane was expected to allow Mach 2.5 speeds, but it was not to be. Although the aircraft made a single glide flight on 20 July 1951 with Joseph Cannon at the controls, it was destroyed during a ground accident on 9 November 1951 before its first powered flight.

It is interesting to note that the original plan was for the X-1s to take-off from the ground, but the limited propellant supply forced Bell and the Army to adopt an air-launch technique in order to maximize flight time. Normally, a Boeing B-29 (45-21800) was used to carry the first two X-1s; the third X-1 used a B-50A (46-006) for its only glide flight, and B-50s were also used to launch the first two aircraft on occasion. Nevertheless, on 5 January 1949 Chuck Yeager tried a ground takeoff, reaching 23,000 feet before the propellants were exhausted.[33]

Yeager took the first X-1 to Mach 1.06 (700 mph) on 14 October 1947, marking the first supersonic flight by a manned airplane in level flight. The feat remained classified for two months until *Aviation Week* made it public in a short article on 22 December 1947. The NACA made its first supersonic flight when Herbert H. Hoover accelerated to Mach 1.065 (703 mph) on 10 March 1948. The fastest flight of the original X-1s was on 26 March 1948 when Yeager took the first airplane to Mach 1.45 (957 mph). On 8 August 1949 Major Frank K. Everest Jr., flew the same airplane to an unofficial altitude record of 71,902 feet.[34]

Almost as soon as Yeager broke the sound barrier, the Air Force had contracted with Bell for four second-generation airplanes. These were intended for research at speeds in excess of Mach 2 and altitudes above 90,000 feet. The X-1A and X-1B were dedicated to control and stability investigations, while the X-1D was intended for heat transfer research. The stillborn X-1C was a high-speed armament and fire control testbed, but was cancelled just after the mockup stage.[35]

The second-generation airplanes were 35 feet, 8 inches long, spanned 28 feet, and were 10 feet 8 inches high. They had an empty weight of approximately 7,500 pounds and a gross weight slightly over 16,000 pounds. Power was provided by a turbopump-equipped XLR11-RM-5 engine.[36]

The first powered flight of the X-1A was on 21 February 1953 with Bell test pilot Jean Ziegler at the controls, and the X-1B followed on 8 October 1954, piloted by Air Force Major Arthur "Kit" Murray. The X-1D completed one successful glide flight on 24 July 1951, but was destroyed by an in-flight explosion on 22 August 1951 during launch preparations for its first powered flight; fortunately nobody was injured in the incident.[37]

Compared against their intended purpose, the second-generation X-1s were a disappointment. Only a single flight by the X-1A exceeded Mach 2, taking now-Major Chuck Yeager to Mach 2.44 on 12 December 1953. The flight nearly proved disastrous as the airplane tumbled out of control for over a minute, losing nearly 10 miles of altitude. At subsonic speed, the aircraft finally entered a conventional spin from which Yeager managed to recover and land. On a brighter note, Kit Murray flew the X-1A on several flights to high altitudes, eventually reaching 90,440 feet on 26 August 1954.[38]

Unfortunately, the X-1A was lost due to an in-flight explosion on 8 August 1955 having completed only 25 glide and powered flights. Eventually, engineers discovered that the problem that had destroyed the third X-1, X-1A, and X-1D was related to the use of Ulmer leather as a sealant in the liquid oxygen tanks of the airplanes. One of the chemicals (tricresyl phosphate) used to cure the leather had a violent reaction to liquid oxygen under certain circumstances. This would also lead to the destruction of the second X-2. Although Ulmer leather is the generally accepted cause of these accidents, there were other theories. One was that the use of 400-series stainless steel in critical joints in the liquid oxygen pressurization system became brittle at low temperatures, allowing them to catastrophically fail while being pressurized.[39]

The X-1B had an even less distinguished career, apparently never achieving its Mach 2 or 90,000-foot goals. Nevertheless, the X-1B was used for at least one significant experiment: a set of hydrogen-peroxide powered reaction controls was installed for three flights in December 1957 and January 1958. These provided some initial experience using reaction controls, although the 60,000-foot altitudes were not the best test conditions. The airplane was permanently grounded in 1958 after a crack was found in its liquid oxygen tank.[40]

There was one other X-1, at least sort of. After the loss of the third X-1 and X-1D due to Ulmer leather explosions, the NACA was left without any high-speed research aircraft. A decision was made to modify the second X-1 into an interim research aircraft until the arrival of the X-15. An ejection seat, turbopump-equipped XLR11 engine, and a new thin-section wing were installed with the resulting airplane redesignated X-1E. The airplane was 31 feet long, spanned 22 feet, and was 10 feet 10 inches high. It had an empty weight of 6,850 pounds and a gross weight of 14,750 pounds. The first powered flight of the modified airplane took place on 15 December 1955 with Joseph A. Walker at the controls and the airplane eventually recorded Mach 2.22 and 73,458 feet (on separate flights).[41]

Despite all of this, the X-1s had made history. Yeager's first supersonic flight will always be remembered, and on 17 December 1948, President Harry S. Truman presented the Collier Trophy jointly to three men for "the greatest aeronautical achievement since the original flight of the Wright Brothers' airplane." The Trophy was the highest possible recognition for the accomplishments embodied in the X-1, and was presented to John Stack, Lawrence D. Bell, and Captain Charles E. Yeager.[42]

Things were much the same for the X-2, although the airplane was designed to go three times as fast as the original X-1s (and another half-Mach number over the X-1A). (AFFTC History Office)

The X-1E mainly provided personnel at the High-Speed Flight Station continued experience with rocket-powered aircraft while waiting for the X-15 to arrive. Nevertheless, the X-1E provided a great deal of aerodynamic heating and other data. Here the X-1E conducts an engine run on the HSFS ramp. (Tony Landis Collection)

Douglas D-558-II Skyrocket

This was the second phase of the NACA-Navy program begun with the D-558-I Skystreak. Douglas manufactured three airframes that eventually flew a total of 313 flights between 1948 and 1956. Although not as well known as the X-1 series, in many respects this program had greater success, logging more flights and total flight time.

The Skyrockets were 42 feet long, spanned 25 feet, were 12 feet, 8 inches high, and had a gross weight of approximately 15,000 pounds. The wings were swept back 35 degrees, a radical departure from the straight wings used on the D-558-I and X-1 series. The three aircraft gathered a great deal of aerodynamic data on the characteristics of swept-wing aircraft at transonic and supersonic speeds. The effect of the rocket exhaust plume on lateral dynamic stability was also examined throughout the speed range since plume effects were a new experience for aircraft. The third aircraft also collected information about the effects of external stores in the transonic region.[43]

The first aircraft made its initial flight on 4 February 1948 with Douglas test pilot John F. Martin at the controls. The first two aircraft were powered by 3,000-lbf Westinghouse J34-WE-40 turbojet engines and were configured only for ground take-offs. These were later modified to use 5,900-lbf Reaction Motors LR8-RM-6 rocket engines and switched to air-launch using a Boeing B-29 (P2B-1S, BuNo 84029, in Navy service). The third airplane was somewhat different, using both J34-WE-40 turbojet and LR8-RM-5 rocket engines.[44]

On 15 August 1951 William B. Bridgeman set an unofficial altitude record of 79,484 feet using the second airplane with the LR8 engine. Marine Lieutenant Colonel Marion Carl bettered this with 83,235 feet on 21 August 1953. For the most part, the NACA was not in the business of setting records, and most of the record flights were left to the contractor and military test pilots. However, in late 1953 Hugh L. Dryden and Walter Williams made an exception for Scott Crossfield. Once the Skyrocket was turned over to the NACA, technicians at the High-Speed Flight Research Station (HSFRS)[45] installed nozzle extensions on the LR8 to prevent the exhaust gas from affecting the rudders at supersonic speeds; the extensions also increased thrust by 6.5 percent at Mach 1.7 and 70,000 feet. Crossfield planned to take the Skyrocket to Mach 2 – somewhat faster than it had been designed to go.[46]

In preparation, the team at the HSFRS waxed the fuselage to reduce drag and chilled the propellants to increase their density. It worked. Crossfield made history on 20 November 1953 when he flew to Mach 2.005 (1,291 mph), becoming the first pilot to exceed twice the speed of sound. This was the only time the Skyrocket flew that fast, and it beat Chuck Yeager and the X-1A to that milestone by less than a month.

Bell X-2

The X-2 was easily the most tragic of the X-planes. Conceived in 1945, the swept-wing Bell Model 37 was intended to investigate the aerodynamic and heating effects of flights over Mach 3 and 100,000 feet. Two X-2s were eventually built, but between them logged only 20 glide and powered flights between 1952 and 1956.[47]

The X-2s were 45 feet 5 inches long, spanned 37 feet 10 inches, and were 11 feet 9 inches high. They had an empty weight of approximately 12,000 pounds and an all-up launch weight of almost 25,000 pounds, making them somewhat of a strain for their EB-50 carrier aircraft.[48]

The program suffered significant delays during development, many of them related to the Curtiss-Wright XLR25-CW-1 powerplant. This advanced regeneratively cooled two-chamber rocket engine was one of the first to be throttleable, leading to many of its problems. The thrust of the 483-pound engine was continuously variable between 2,500-lbf and 15,000-lbf at sea level. The two-chamber aspect of the engine was a bit unusual. The 8-inch diameter upper chamber could produce up to 5,000-lbf; the 12-inch diameter lower chamber produced up to 10,000-lbf. The full 15,000-lbf could be sustained for 175 seconds using the onboard liquid oxygen and ethyl alcohol propellants, while a 2,500-lbf rating could be sustained for 560 seconds. The Curtiss-Wright engine ran seriously behind schedule, finally arriving about three years late.[49]

While waiting for the engine, the second airplane made its first glide flight on 27 June 1952 with Jean Ziegler at the controls. Two more successful glide flights would be made before the airplane exploded in the bomb bay of an EB-50A while testing the propellant jettison system in preparation for the first powered flight. Jean Ziegler in the X-2 and Frank Wolko in the EB-50A were killed in the accident; the remains of the X-2 fell into Lake Ontario. It would prove another instance of the Ulmer leather used to seal the liquid oxygen tank causing the loss of an X-plane.[50]

The first X-2 finally made its initial glide flight on 5 August 1954, and its first powered flight on 18 November 1955, both with Captain Frank Everest at the controls. Over the course of the next year the program gained momentum and soon Everest recorded Mach 2.578 (1,701 mph) while Captain Iven C. Kincheloe, Jr., flew the airplane to 126,200 feet altitude, both new records. It was beginning to appear that the X-2 might be a useful – if late – research tool after all. Unfortunately, on 27 September 1956 Captain Milburn G. Apt was killed during his first X-2 flight after he reached Mach 3.196 (2,094 mph), becoming the first person to fly at three times the speed of sound, albeit briefly. Apt lost control of the X-2 due to inertial-coupling, resulting in diverging angular rotations about all three axes. At 40,000 feet Apt activated the nose-capsule escape system; the capsule separated cleanly, and the drogue chute deployed normally. The X-2 pilot was expected to jump free of the capsule and descend using his normal parachute; Apt was killed when he either was unable, or did not have time, to do so. This was the 20th and last flight of the X-2 program.[51]

…he contributions of the early X-planes were questionable, and … the subject of great debate within the NACA and the aircraft …try. How successful the early high-speed X-planes were depends …ly on who was doing the evaluation. The academics and labora- …researchers – and a couple of aerospace industry designers – are … cord indicating the contributions of the X-planes were minimal. …e other side, however, many of the hands-on researchers and …, are certain the programs provided solid real-world data that …ly accelerated progress in the design and manufacture of the … 1 and Mach 2 combat aircraft that followed. Trying to sort out …etailed story is nearly impossible.[52]

…or instance, the X-1 was the first aircraft to purposely break …ound barrier in level flight, but other aircraft were doing so in …ow dives very soon afterwards.[53] The first combat type designed … the start as a supersonic fighter – the Republic XF-91 Thun- …eptor – made its first flight only 19 months after the first super- …flight; how much the X-1 experience contributed to Alexander …eli's design is unknown.[54]

…he same thing happened at Mach 2. By the time Scott Crossfield … the D-558-II to twice the speed of sound, Clarence L. "Kelly" …son at Lockheed had already been developing what would …ne the F-104 Starfighter for over a year. Again, it is unlikely that …ocket-powered X-planes actually assisted Johnson very much, …thing he would make very clear during later deliberations.[55] …he X-1E complemented the heating research undertaken by the …, but the F-104 was already flying and could more easily acquire … at Mach 2. Even at the Flight Research Center there was debate … how appropriate this exercise was; FRC research engineer Gene …anga later recalled, "We could probably fly the X-1E two or three … a month, whereas Kelly [Johnson] was flying his F-104s two or … times a day into the same flight regimes, so it really didn't make … for us to be applying those kind of resources to [obtain] that … of information." It is likely, however, that the major purpose of …-1E was simply to keep a cadre of rocket-powered experience at …RC in anticipation of the upcoming X-15 program.[56]

…y 1950 it had become clear that combat vehicles of much high- …rformance would soon be required. In some cases, these took the shape of missiles – the Navaho cruise missile being a p… example. Development of the Navaho had been initiated in 1946, … the large intercontinental cruise missile would be propelled to … speed by a rocket booster then continue to cruise near Mach 3 u… power from two jet engines. The Bell X-2 was designed to investi… phenomena at Mach 3, but this tragic effort did little to help … Navaho or any other program.

Even John Becker recognized the dichotomy represented by … experience: "… the cooperative research-airplane program pur… by the Air Force, NACA, and Navy had not been an unqualified … cess. … Some had lagged so seriously in procurement that … designs had become obsolescent before they were flown. In a few …es tactical designs superior to the research aircraft were in … before the research aircraft flew." It wasn't anybody's fault – tech… ogy was simply changing too fast.[57]

The results of the programs – from a historic perspective – … ironic. When first envisioned by John Stack and Ezra Kotcher the … mary mission for the research airplanes was to investigate a f… regime that the wind tunnels could not achieve. But some cre… wind tunnel design had allowed those facilities to get to the f… regime before the X-planes could be built. In the end, the X-pl… provided a way to validate the wind tunnel (and theoretical) res… But the need to keep up with the ever-increasing performance o… X-planes forced the wind tunnel researchers to continuously imp… their facilities and methods. There will always be a difference of … ion between the researchers that believe wind tunnels (and now, … puter models) are more than adequate and the engineers and … who believe the final proof is always in flying a real airplane.

Still, the concept of a dedicated research airplane held s… promise, but researchers decided that the next design would ne… offer a significant increment in performance to leap-frog the co… types then in development. Chuck Yeager's October 1947 assau… the sound barrier ignited a billion-dollar race to build yet faster … craft, and directly affected every combat aircraft design for … next two decades. However, there had been a few aerona… researchers who had always been certain that the sound barrier … simply a challenge for the engineers, not a true physical limita… Chuck Yeager had proven it was possible for man to fly super… cally. The next goal was so much faster.

…ell X-1B, Douglas D-558-II, and Bell X-1E pose …gers Dry Lake. The X-1 series used straight …, while the X-2 (not pictured) and D-558-II …swept wings. (NASA Dryden)

This 1952 photograph shows the X-2 #2 aircraft mounted on its steerable transportation dolly. This airplane (46-675) was lost on 12 May 1953 during a liquid-oxygen top-off test. (NASA Dryden)

The Bell X-1B with an innovative reaction c… system installed. Although only limited tests … conducted, this gave some of the first real-… experience with such a system. (NASA Dryde…

New Science

Above: *The 11-inch hypersonic wind tunnel at the NACA Langley Aeronautica Laboratory was the first facility in the world capable of hypersonic research anc was instrumental in the development of the concept that became the X-15* (NASA Langley Photo L57284)

Left: *Generally considered the father of the hypersonic research airplane concept, NACA Langley researcher John V. Becker.* (NASA Langley Photo L-70-5770)

Between the two world wars, hypersonics had been an area of theoretical interest to a small group of researchers, but little actual progress was made in defining the possible problems. And even less in solving them. The major constraint was power. Engines, even the rudimentary rockets then being experimented with, were incapable of propelling any significant object to hypersonic velocities. Wind tunnels also lacked the power to generate such speeds. Computer power to simulate the environment had not even been imagined.

As is always the case, war increased the tempo of technological development. By the mid-1940s – just as the supersonic programs were being initiated in the United States – it was becoming apparent that it might finally be possible to build a flight vehicle capable of hypersonic speeds. Indeed, the Germans had already briefly toyed with a potentially hypersonic aerodynamic vehicle, the winged A-4b version of the V-2 rocket. The only "successful" A-4b flight had managed just over Mach 4 – about 2,700 mph – before apparently disintegrating in flight.[2]

An English translation of a technical paper by German scientists Eugen Sänger and Irene Bredt provided by the U.S. Navy Bureau of Aeronautics (BuAer) in 1946 further stimulated interest in hypersonic flight. Expanding upon ideas conceived as early as 1928, Sänger and Bredt had concluded during 1944 that a rocket-powered hypersonic aircraft could be built with only minor advances in technology. Although there were numerous paper studies exploring variations of the Sänger and Bredt proposal during the late 1940s, no hardware construction was undertaken.[3]

A SMALL STEP

Hypersonic. Adj. (1937). Of or relating to velocities in excess of five times the speed of sound.[1]

One researcher who was interested in exploring the new science of hypersonics was John Becker, then the assistant chief of the Compressibility Research Division at Langley. On 3 August 1945 Becker proposed the construction of a "new type supersonic wind tunnel for Mach number 7." By now the choking problems that had originally plagued the wind tunnels had been solved, and a few small supersonic tunnels in the United States could achieve short test runs at Mach 4. Nevertheless, the large supersonic tunnels under construction at Langley and Ames had been designed for Mach numbers no higher than 2. Information that the Army had captured from the German missile research facility at Peenemünde had convinced Becker that the next generation of missiles and projectiles would require testing at much higher Mach numbers.[4]

As the basis for his proposed design, Becker extrapolated from what he already knew about supersonic tunnels. He discovered that the compressible-flow theory for nozzles required a hundred-fold expansion in area beyond the sonic throat for Mach 7 operation. Becker used normal shock theory to estimate pressure ratios and found that at Mach 7 the compressor system would grow to impractical proportions.[5]

Hope for alleviating the compressor problem had first appeared in the spring of 1945 when Becker obtained a fresh understanding of supersonic diffusers from a paper by Arthur Kantrowitz, who had designed the first NACA supersonic wind tunnel, and Coleman duP. Donaldson.[6] The paper focused on low Mach number supersonic flows and did not consider variable geometry solutions, but it was still possible to infer that changing the wall contours to form a second throat might substantially reduce the shock losses in the diffuser. The potential benefits from a variable-geometry configuration were fairly inconsequential at Mach 2, but calculations indicated that they might be quite large at Mach 7. Unfortunately, it appeared that this could only be accomplished after the flow had been started, introducing considerable mechanical complexity.[7]

In the tunnel envisioned by Becker, the peak pressure ratios needed to start the flow lasted only a few seconds and would be provided by flow from a 50-atmosphere tank into a vacuum tank. The second throat would then be deployed – reducing the pressure ratio and power requirements – allowing a continuously running compressor to be phased in to provide longer test times. It was an interesting concept, but a number of uncertainties caused Becker to suggest building a small pilot tunnel with an 11x11-inch test section to determine experimentally how well the scheme worked in practice.[8]

Not everybody agreed that such a facility was necessary. The NACA chairman, Jerome C. Hunsaker,[9] did not see any practical urgency for the facility and Arthur Kantrowitz did not believe that extrapolating what little was known about supersonic tunnels would allow the successful construction of a hypersonic facility. The most obvious consequence of the rapid expansion of the air necessary for Mach 7 operation was the large drop in air temperature below the nominal liquefaction value. At the time there was no consensus on the question of air liquefaction, although some preliminary investigations of the condensation of water vapor suggested that the transit time through a hypersonic nozzle and test section might be too brief for liquefaction to take place. Kantrowitz, head of Langley's small gas dynamics research group, feared that "real-gas effects" – possibly culminating in liquefaction – would probably limit wind tunnels to a maximum useful Mach number of about 4.5.[10]

Nevertheless, the estimated $39,500 initial cost of the pilot tunnel was rather modest, and Dr. George W. Lewis,[11] the Director of Aeronautical Research, advised Becker, "Don't call it a new wind tunnel. That would complicate and delay funding," so it was referred to as "Project 506" instead. The facility was quickly approved.[12]

In September 1945 a small staff of engineers under Charles H. McLellan began work on the facility, which would be constructed inside the shop area of the old Propeller Research Tunnel. This group soon discovered that Kantrowitz's predictions had been fairly accurate – the job required more than extrapolating existing supersonic tunnel theory. The pilot tunnel proposal had not included a heater since Becker felt it could be added later if liquefaction was found to be a problem. However, it became increasingly clear that the ability to control air temperature would greatly improve the quality and scope of the research. By the end of 1945 approval had been obtained to include an electric heater that could maintain air temperatures at about 850°F, resulting in Mach 7 temperatures well above the nominal liquefaction point.[13]

The first test run on 26 November 1947 revealed uniform flow at Mach 6.9, essentially meeting all of the original intents. An especially satisfying result was the performance of the variable-geometry diffuser; McLellan and his group had devised a deployable second throat that favored mechanical simplicity over aerodynamic sophistication, but was still very effective. The benefit appeared as greater run duration – in this case increasing from 25 seconds to over 90 seconds.[14]

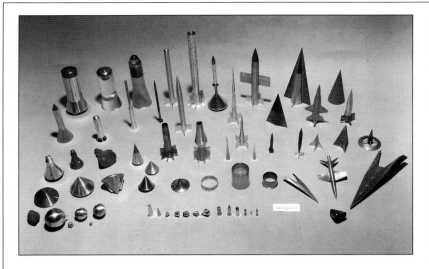

Researchers at Ames tested a wide variety of shapes, as indicated by these wind tunnel models. At the lower left are shapes representing the Mercury, Gemini, and Apollo capsules. Several delta wing shapes are at right, and the X-15 shape is in the upper right corner. (NASA Ames photo A-41445-1)

For three years the "11-inch" would be the only operational hypersonic tunnel in the United States – and apparently, in the world. Several basic flow studies and aerodynamic investigations were made during this period that established the 11-inch as an efficient research tool, giving Langley a strong base in the new field of hypersonics. Without this development, Langley would not have been able to define and support a meaningful hypersonic research airplane concept in 1954. Throughout the entire X-15 program the 11-inch would be a principle source of the necessary hypersonic tunnel support.[15]

Despite the fact that it had been built as a prototype, the 11-inch hypersonic tunnel would operate until 1973 when it was finally dismantled and donated to the Virginia Polytechnic Institute in Blacksburg, Virginia. During that time, over 230 publications resulted from tests and related analysis conducted in the tunnel – about one paper every five weeks for its 25 years of operations. Few major wind tunnels have equaled that record.[16]

As the 11-inch was demonstrating that it was possible to conduct hypersonic research, several other facilities were also being built constructed. Alfred J. Eggers, Jr., at the NACA Ames Aeronautical Laboratory at Moffett Field, California,[17] began designing a 10x14-inch continuous-flow hypersonic tunnel in 1946; the resulting facility became operational in 1950. The first hypersonic tunnel at the Naval Ordnance Facility was constructed largely from German material captured from the uncompleted Mach 10 tunnel at Peenemünde; it also became operational in 1950.[18]

A continuously running hypersonic tunnel incorporating all of the features proposed in the 1945 Becker memo was not authorized until 1958, although the design Mach number was increased from 7 to 12 by incorporating a 1,450°F heater. Initially, Mach 12 was attained in a few tests, but severe cooling problems in the first throat could not be solved satisfactorily and most subsequent work was conducted at Mach numbers less than 10. The enormous high-pressure air supply and vacuum tankage of the Gas Dynamics Laboratory provided blow-down test durations of 10-15 minutes. Together with improved instrumentation, this – ironically – virtually eliminated the need to operate the tunnel in the "continuously running" mode and nearly all of Langley's hypersonic tunnel operations have used the "blow down" mode rather than the compressors.[19]

UNMANNED HYPERSONICS

Not surprisingly, during the early 1950s the top priority for the hypersonic tunnels was to support the massive development effort associated with the intercontinental missiles then being developed. Initially it was not clear if the resulting weapon would be a high-speed cruise missile or a ballistic missile (ICBM), so programs were undertaken to develop both. Much of the theoretical science necessary to create a manned hypersonic research airplane would be born of the perceived need to build these weapons.

Long-range missile development challenged the NACA researchers in a number of ways. The advancements necessary to allow a triple-sonic cruise missile were relatively easily imagined, if not readily at hand. The ballistic missile was a different story. A successful ICBM would need to be accelerated to a velocity of 15,000 mph at an altitude of perhaps 500 miles, and then precisely guided to a target thousands of miles away. Sophisticated and reliable propulsion, control, and guidance systems were essential, as was keeping structural weight at a minimum. Moreover, some method had to be found to handle the new problem of aerodynamic heating. As the missile warhead reentered the atmosphere, it would experience temperatures of several thousand degrees Fahrenheit. The heat generated by shock-wave compression outside the boundary-layer, and which was not in contact with the structure, dissipated harmlessly into the surrounding air. But the part that arose within the boundary layer, and was in direct contact with the missile structure, was great enough to melt the vehicle. Many early dummy warheads burned up because the engineers did not yet understand this.

During this time, H. Julian Allen was engaged in high-speed research at Ames and found what he believed to be a practical solution. In place of the traditional sleek configuration with a sharply pointed nose – an aerodynamic concept long since embraced by missile designers mostly because the V-2 had used the shape – Allen proposed a blunt shape with a rounded bottom. In 1951 Allen predicted that the blunt shape, when reentering the atmosphere, would create a powerful bow-shaped shock wave that would deflect heat safely outward and away from the structure of the missile. The boundary layer on the body created some frictional drag and heating, but this was only a small fraction of the total thermal load during deceleration – most of which heated the atmosphere through the action of the strong shock wave. As Allen and Eggers put it, "not only should pointed bodies be avoided, but the rounded nose should have as large a radius as possible." The "blunt-body" concept was born.[20]

Allen and Eggers verified the blunt-body concept by studying the aerodynamic heating of miniature missiles in an innovative supersonic free-flight tunnel – a sort of wind tunnel-cum-firing range that had become operational at Ames in 1949. Their classified report on these tests was published in August 1953. The Air Force and aerospace industry, however, did not immediately embrace the concept since it ran contrary to most established ideas and the report languished in the archives. Engineers accustomed to pointed-body missiles remained skeptical of the revolutionary blunt-body concept until the mid- to late-1950s, when it became the basis for the new ICBM warheads and all of the manned space capsules.[21]

In the meantime, a new interest in hypersonic aircraft was stirred up by Robert Woods from Bell Aircraft. In a letter to the NACA Committee on Aerodynamics dated 8 January 1952, Woods proposed that the committee begin to address the basic problems of hypersonic and space flight. Accompanying the letter was a document from Dr. Walter R. Dornberger outlining the preliminary requirements for a "ionosphere research plane" powered by a liquid-fueled rocket engine that would be capable of flying at 6,000 feet per second (fps) at an altitude of between 50 and 75 miles.[22] It was apparent that Dornberger was still intrigued by the concept for an "antipodal" bomber that had been proposed near the end of the war by his colleagues Eugen Sänger and Irene Bredt.[23] According to the Sänger-Bredt study, this aircraft would skip-glide in and out of the atmosphere and land halfway around the world.[24] Dornberger's enthusiasm for the concept had captured Woods' imagination, and he called for the NACA to develop a manned research airplane capable of hypersonic flight in support of it. At the time, the committee declined to initiate such research, but took the matter under advisement.[25]

Undeterred, at the January 1952 meeting of the Committee on Aerodynamics Woods suggested "that the NACA is the logical organization to carry out the basic studies in space flight control and stability" and that the NACA should set up a small group "to evaluate and analyze the basic problems of space flight." Woods went on to recommend that the NACA "endeavor to establish a concept of a suitable manned test vehicle" that could be developed within two years. Again, the matter was taken under advisement.[26]

Others joined with Woods with the same requests at the June 1952 meeting of the Committee on Aerodynamics. This time the committee took action, passing a resolution recommending "... that (1) the NACA increase its program dealing with the problems of unmanned and manned flight in the upper stratosphere at altitudes between 12 and 50 miles, and at Mach numbers between 4 and 10, and (2) the NACA devote a modest effort to problems associated with unmanned and manned flight at altitudes from 50 miles to infinity and at speeds from Mach number 10 to the velocity of escape from Earth's gravity." The resolution was ratified by the NACA Executive Committee on 14 July.[27]

The concepts put forth by Woods and Dornberger inspired two early unsolicited proposals for research aircraft. The first, released on 21 May 1952, was from Hubert M. "Jake" Drake and L. Robert Carman of the HSFRS calling for a two-stage system where a large supersonic carrier aircraft would launch a smaller manned research aircraft. The 100,000-pound carrier aircraft would be capable of Mach 6.4 and altitudes up to 660,000 feet, with a duration of one minute at a Mach number of 5.3. The carrier would launch a research airplane the size of the Bell X-2 at Mach 3 and an altitude of 150,000 feet, attaining Mach numbers up to almost 10 and an altitude of about 1,000,000 feet. The report went into a fair amount of detail concerning the carrier aircraft, but surprisingly little toward describing the heating and structural problems that would be encountered by the smaller research aircraft.[28]

The second report was released by David G. Stone, head of the Stability and Control Branch of the Pilotless Aircraft Research Division (PARD), in late May 1952.[29] This report was somewhat more conservative and proposed that the Bell X-2 itself could be used to reach speeds approaching Mach 4.5 and altitudes near 300,000 feet, if it were equipped with two JPL-4 Sergeant solid rocket motors.[30]

Contrary to Sänger's war-time conclusions, by 1954 it was generally agreed within the NACA and industry that hypersonic flight would not be possible without major advances in technology. In particular, the unprecedented problems of aerodynamic heating appeared to be so formidable that it was viewed as a possible "thermal barrier" to sustained hypersonic flight. Fortunately, the perceived successes enjoyed by the X-planes had increased political and philosophical support for a more advanced research airplane program. At the same time, the large rocket engines being developed for the missile programs were seen as a possible method to provide power for a hypersonic research vehicle. It was now believed that manned hypersonic flight was feasible – but it would entail a great deal of research and development. The time was finally right for launching a hypersonic flight program.[31]

The origins of the hypersonic research airplane program most likely came during a meeting of the NACA Interlaboratory Research Airplane Projects Panel held in Washington, D.C., on 4-5 February 1954. The panel chairman was Hartley A. Soulé, and the panel consisted of Clotaire Wood from NACA Headquarters, Charles J. Donlan from Langley, Lawrence A. Clousing from Ames, William A. Fleming from Lewis, and Walter C. Williams from the HSFRS. Two items on the agenda led almost directly to the call for a new research airplane: discussion concerning Stone's proposal to modify the X-2, and a propos-

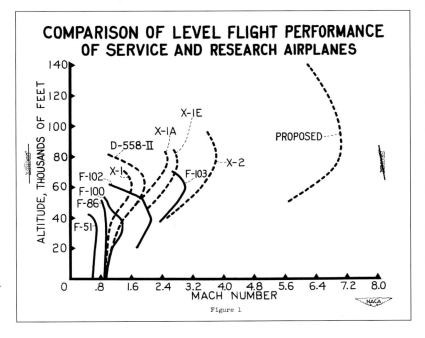

The hypersonic research airplane proposed by NACA Langley was a huge leap forward in terms of performance in level flight. The solid lines indicate service aircraft, while the dotted lines are the high-speed X-planes. The performance listed for the F-102 is that expected of the F-102B, which became the F-106. Of interest is the performance that was expected of Alexander Kartveli's Republic XF-103 interceptor, which unfortunately ran into severe funding and technical problems and was cancelled before its first flight. At this point the X-2 was still expected to contribute to the understanding of high-speed flight, shown here exploring speeds up to Mach 4. (NASA)

al to develop a new thin wing for the Douglas D-558-II. Ultimately, the panel concluded that it was not desirable to fund major modifications to the X-2 or D-558-II since it was felt their research utility was largely at an end. Instead, the panel recognized that a wholly new manned research aircraft was needed, and recommended that NACA Headquarters request detailed goals and requirements for such a vehicle from each of the research laboratories. This action was, in effect, the initial impetus for what became the X-15.[32]

THE NEXT FRONTIER …

Around this time, the military became involved in supporting hypersonic research and development. During 1952, for example, the Air Force began actively sponsoring a study of Dornberger's manned hypersonic boost-glide concept at Bell as part of Project BoMi. This project (and subsequently, RoBo) advanced the Sänger-Bredt boost-glide concept by developing, for the first time, a detailed look at the potential thermal problems and possible concepts to overcome them. Among the concepts investigated were non-load-bearing flexible metallic radiative heat shields ("shingles") and water-cooled leading-edge structures that protected the wings, while passive and active cooling systems kept the cabin temperature within human tolerance. NACA researchers read the periodic progress reports of the Bell study – classified secret by the Air Force – with great interest. Although most were skeptical, a few thought that the project just might work.[33]

All of the NACA laboratories set up small *ad hoc* hypersonic study groups during March 1954 and a comparison is interesting because of their different approaches and findings. The Ames group con-

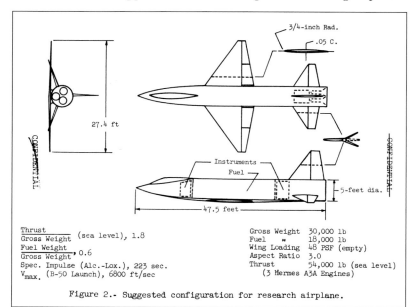

Figure 2.- Suggested configuration for research airplane.

One of the 1954 NACA Langley concepts for a hypersonic research airplane. This version was powered by three Hermes A3A rocket engines, something that would quickly be identified as the principle shortcoming of the design. At this point the wings are still fairly large and the tail surfaces have not adopted the wedge-shape that would become a characteristic of later concepts. Still, the overall size and weight were pretty well defined. (NASA)

cerned itself solely with suborbital long-range flight and ended up favoring a military-type air-breathing – rather than rocket-powered – aircraft in the Mach 4-5 range. The HSFRS suggested a larger, higher-powered conventional configuration generally similar to the research airplanes it was familiar with. The staff at Lewis questioned the need for a manned aircraft, arguing that hypersonic research should be accomplished by ground studies and expanding the PARD rocket-model operation.[34] Lewis believed that previous research airplane programs had been unduly burdened by anticipated military applications; there was no reason to think that anything different would happen in the hypersonic research aircraft program.[35]

On the other hand, Langley had been interested in hypersonics since the end of World War II and chose to deal with the problem in greater depth than the other laboratories. After the 11-inch tunnel became operational in 1947, a group headed by Charles McLellan had been formed to conduct limited hypersonic research. Langley also organized a parallel exploratory program into materials and structures optimized for hypersonic flight. Led by John Becker, the intentions of the Langley study differed substantially from those at the other three facilities. Besides the obvious high-speed aspects, it was decided to investigate the possibility of a 2 to 3-minute excursion out of the atmosphere to create a brief period of weightlessness in order to explore the effects of space flight. Hugh Dryden would later liken this excursion to a fish leaping out of water, and the term "space leap" was coined.[36]

During the late 1940s and early 1950s the overwhelming majority of engineers thought very little about manned space flight. With its "multiplicity of enormous technical problems" and "unanswered questions of safe return," most believed that manned space flight would be "a 21st Century enterprise." It proved to be a very short-sighted view. By 1954, a growing number of American researchers felt that hypersonic flight extending into space could be achieved much sooner, although very few saw it coming by 1960.[37]

By the end of April 1954, Langley had finished a tentative design of the winged aircraft it had in mind. The configuration was kept as conventional as possible to minimize the need for low-speed and transonic development without endangering its hypersonic research utility. Acknowledging what would become one of the program's major challenges, the group did not believe that any of the rocket engines then under development was entirely satisfactory for the airplane. In the absence of the rapid development of a new engine, hypersonic velocities were to be provided by a combination of three or four smaller engines.[38]

While performing the original heating analysis of the proposed reentry from the "space leap," Becker and Peter F. Korycinski ran into a major technical problem. At Mach 7, reentry at low angles-of-attack appeared impossible because of disastrous heating loads. New tests in the 11-inch tunnel provided a surprising solution to this problem: if the angle-of-attack and associated drag were increased, deceleration would begin at a higher altitude. Slowing in the thinner (lower-density) atmosphere would make the heat transfer problem much less severe. Thus, by using "sufficient lift," the Langley researchers had found a way to limit the heat loads and heating rates of reentry.[39]

On reflection, it became clear that sufficient-lift was a "new manifestation" of Allen's blunt-body concept and was as applicable to high-lift winged reentry as to the non-lifting missile warheads studied at Ames during 1952. As the group increased the angle-of-attack in order to dissipate more of the kinetic energy through heating of the atmosphere (and less in the form of frictional heating of the vehicle itself), the configuration became increasingly "blunt."[40]

Throughout 1954 the heating problems of high-lift, high-drag reentry came under increasing scrutiny from Langley researchers. However, the ever-increasing angle of attack brought a new problem – making the configuration stable at the reentry attitude. The researchers did not know the exact hypersonic control properties of such a configuration; no one knew. Nor did anyone know whether a structure could be found that would survive the anticipated 2,000°F equilibrium temperatures.[41]

The HSFRS had forewarned Langley of potential stability problems. In December 1953 the X-1A had developed large and uncontrollable lateral oscillations as it accelerated toward Mach 2.5 – well beyond its expected top speed.[42] This led to a systematic reinvestigation of the stability characteristics of the X-1A and, by mid-1954, the findings indicated that the problem was caused by the loss of effectiveness of the thin-section horizontal and vertical stabilizers at high speed. A similar inertial-coupling phenomenon was encountered by the first generation of supersonic fighters, such as the North American F-100A Super Sabre. The obvious answer was to make the tail surfaces larger, a fix quickly applied to the F-100 series.[43]

A Mach 7 airplane faced a potential stability problem that was several times more severe than that of the X-1A. Preliminary calculations based on data from X-1A wind tunnel tests indicated that the hypersonic configuration would require a vertical stabilizer the size of one of the X-1 wings to maintain directional stability – something that was obviously impractical. Ironically, the thin sections first developed to help the early propellers in the transonic speed range were now detrimental to the first supersonic airplanes. This was largely because of a rapid loss in the lift-curve slope of thin airfoil sections as the Mach number increased. In a radical departure, Charles McLellan suggested changing the thin section to a thicker wedge-shape with a blunt trailing edge. Some time before, McLellan had conducted a study of the influence of airfoil shape on normal-force characteristics; his findings had been lying dormant in the NACA literature. Calculations based on these findings indicated that, at Mach 7, the wedge shape "should prove many times more effective than the conventional thin shapes optimum for the lower speed."[44]

A new series of experiments in the 11-inch tunnel verified that a vertical stabilizer with a 10-degree wedge shape would allow an aircraft with a reasonably-sized tail to achieve the range of attitudes required by heating considerations for a safe high-lift, high-drag reentry. Researchers predicted that the wedge shape would eliminate the disastrous directional stability decay encountered by the X-1A.[45]

On the structural front, two basic design approaches had been debated since the initiation of the Langley study – a conventional low-temperature design of aluminum or stainless steel protected from the high-temperature environment by a layer of assumed insulation; and an exposed "hot-structure" where no attempt would be made to provide protection, but where the materials and design approach would permit high structural temperatures.[46]

An analysis of the heating projections for various trajectories showed that the airplane would need to accommodate equilibrium temperatures of over 2,000°F on its lower surface. At the time, no known insulating technique could meet this requirement. Bell was toying with a "double-wall" concept where a low-temperature structure was protected by a high-temperature outer shell with some insulator in between. This concept would undergo extensive development in support of BoMi and RoBo – and would be proposed by some competitors during the X-15 competition – but in 1954, it was in an embryonic state and not ready for real-world applications[47]

It was not initially obvious that the hot-structure approach would prove practical either. The design temperature for the best available material – Inconel X – was only about 1,200°F. It was clear that some form of heat dissipation would have to be employed, either direct internal cooling or absorption into the structure itself, but both would likely bring a substantial weight penalty. During mid-1954, Norris Dow at Langley began an analysis of an Inconel X structure; concurrently, Peter Korycinski conducted a detailed thermal analysis. In a happy coincidence, it was discovered that the skin thickness needed to withstand the expected aerodynamic stresses was about the same needed to absorb the thermal load.[48]

This meant that it was possible to solve the structural problem for the transient conditions of the Mach 7 research aircraft with no serious weight penalty for heat absorption – an unexpected plus for the hot-structure. Together with the fact that none of the perceived difficulties of an insulated-type structure were present, the study group decided in favor of an uninsulated hot-structure design.[49]

Unfortunately, the hot-structure approach soon proved to have problems of its own, especially in the area of non-uniform temperature distribution. Detailed thermal analyses revealed that large temperature differences would develop between the upper and lower wing skin during the pull-up portions of certain trajectories, and the unequal heating would result in intolerable thermal stresses in a conventional structural design. To solve this new problem, wing shear members were devised that did not offer any resistance to unequal expansion of the wing skins. The wing thus was essentially free to deform both spanwise and chordwise with asymmetrical heating. Although this technique solved the problem of the gross thermal stresses, localized thermal-stress problems still existed near the stringer attachments. Researchers thought, however, that proper selection of stringer proportions and spacing would produce an acceptable design free from thermal buckling.[50]

There were additional concerns. It was discovered that differential heating of the wing leading edge produced changes in the natural torsional frequency of the wing unless some sort of flexible expansion joint was incorporated in its design. The hot leading edge expanded faster than the remaining structure, introducing a compression that destabilized the section as a whole and reduced its torsional stiffness. To negate these phenomena, the leading edge was segmented and flexibly mounted in an attempt to reduce thermally induced buckling and bending. Similar techniques would be used on the horizontal and vertical stabilizers. The structural concept was coming along nicely.

On the other hand, there was still the issue of potential propulsion systems. The most promising configuration was a grouping of four General Electric A1 Hermes rocket engines.[51] At the time, rocket engines could not be throttled – even today, most rocket engines can not be. Throttling a rocket engine may be done several different ways, and each takes its toll in mechanical complexity and reliability. However, there was a crude method of throttling that did not actually involve changing the output of the engine – if a number of smaller engines were grouped together, they could be ignited or extinguished in such a manner that the thrust could be varied. For instance, if three 5,000-lbf engines were clustered, then available thrust levels (or "steps") would be 5,000, 10,000, and 15,000-lbf. This allowed a much more refined profile to be flown, so the idea of "thrust stepping" or throttling the engine would largely define the propulsion concept for the hypersonic research airplane.[52]

At this stage of the study, the vehicle concept itself was "little more than an object of about the right general proportions and the correct propulsive characteristics" to achieve hypersonic flight. However, in developing the general requirements, the Langley group had created a conceptual design that served as a model for the eventual X-15. The vehicle was "... not proposed as a prototype of any of the particular concepts in vogue in 1954 ... [but] rather as a general tool for manned hypersonic flight research, able to penetrate the new regime briefly, safely, and without the burdens, restrictions, and delays imposed by operational requirements other than research."[53]

It is interesting to note that while the hypersonic research aspect of the Langley proposal enjoyed virtually unanimous support, the space leap was viewed in 1954 with what can best be described as cautious tolerance. There were few who believed that any space flight was imminent, and most believed that manned space flight in particular was many decades in the future, probably not until the 21st Century. Several researchers recommended that space flight research was premature and should be removed from the program. Fortunately, it remained.[54]

By the end of June 1954, after three months of investigations, the Langley group reached a point where they could make a convincing case for the feasibility of a hypersonic research aircraft. The preliminary specifications for the research airplane were surprisingly brief: only four pages of requirements, plus six pages of supporting data. As John Becker subsequently observed, "... it was obviously impossible that the proposed aircraft be in any sense an optimum hypersonic configuration."[55]

On 11 June 1954 Hugh Dryden sent letters to the Air Force and Navy formally inviting them to a meeting scheduled for 9 July 1954 at NACA Headquarters. At the meeting Dryden reported that the NACA believed a new research airplane was desirable and outlined the reasons for this. Because the Langley study was the most detailed available, it was used as a starting point for further discussions. All in

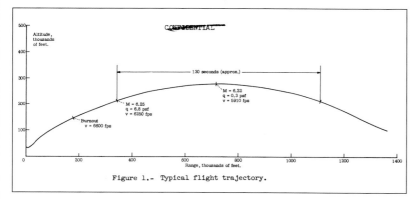

Figure 1.- Typical flight trajectory.

The flight trajectory developed by Langley in 1954 came pretty close to approximating the final X-15 performance. A maximum speed of Mach 6.5 (6,600 feet per second) and a maximum altitude of almost 300,000 feet were called for. The expected range of 265 miles would be the impetus behind developing the High Range. (NASA)

attendance were in general agreement that a new project should be undertaken. The group also agreed that the performance parameters discussed by the Langley study represented an adequate increment over the existing research airplanes, and that a cooperative program would be more cost effective and more likely to provide better research data at an earlier time.[56]

Unexpectedly, it was divulged at the meeting that the Air Force Scientific Advisory Board (SAB) had been making similar proposals to Air Force Headquarters, and that the Office of Naval Research (ONR) had already contracted with the Douglas Aircraft Company to determine the feasibility of a manned hypersonic aircraft capable of achieving 1,000,000 feet altitude. It was stated that the configuration evolved by Douglas "did not constitute a detailed design" but was only a "first approach to the problem of a high-altitude high-speed research airplane." Representatives from the NACA agreed to meet with their ONR counterparts on 16 July to further discuss the results of the Douglas study.

THE DOUGLAS MODEL 671

The "High Altitude and High Speed Study" by the El Segundo Division of the Douglas Aircraft Company had been funded by the ONR as a follow-on to the D-558 series of research airplanes. Although the "D-558-III" is generally mentioned – briefly – in most X-15 histories, what is usually overlooked is how insightful it was to many of the challenges that would be experienced by the X-15 a few years later.[57]

One interesting aspect of the Douglas Model 671 was that the contractor and the Navy had agreed early on that the aircraft was to have two flight profiles – high speed and high altitude, with the emphasis on the latter. This was in distinct contrast with the ongoing Langley studies that eventually led to the X-15. Although the Becker group was very interested in research outside the sensible atmosphere, there was a great deal of skepticism on the part of others in NACA and the Air Force. Douglas did not have this problem – the ONR strongly supported potential high-altitude research.[58]

Excepting the Langley work, the Douglas study was probably the first serious attempt to define a hypersonic research airplane. Other companies that were delving into hypersonics were oriented toward producing operational vehicles – BoMi, ICBMs, etc. – and were concentrating on a different set of problems; frequently at the expense of a basic understanding of the challenges of hypersonic flight.

The proposed Model 671 was 41.25 feet long (47.00 feet with the pitot boom), spanned only 18 feet with 81 square feet of area, and had an all-up weight of 22,200 pounds. In many respects, it showed an obvious family lineage to the previous D-558s. The fuselage was built around a set of integral propellant tanks, and dive brakes were located on each side aft, as in most contemporary fighters and research aircraft. "A conventional configuration was deliberately chosen for the study, and no benefits have yet been discovered for any unconventional arrangement. Actually, for the prime objective of attaining very high altitudes, the general shape of the airplane is relatively unimportant. Stability and control must be provided, and it must be possible to create sufficient lift for the pullout and for landing; but, in contrast to the usual airplane design, the reduction of drag is not a critical problem and high drag is to some extent beneficial."[59]

Douglas had some interesting observations about drag and power-to-weight ratios: "The function of drag in the overall performance

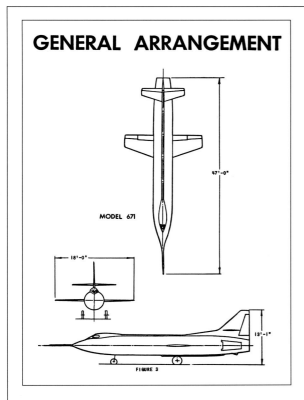

GENERAL ARRANGEMENT

MODEL 671

47'-0"

18'-0"

13'-1"

FIGURE 3

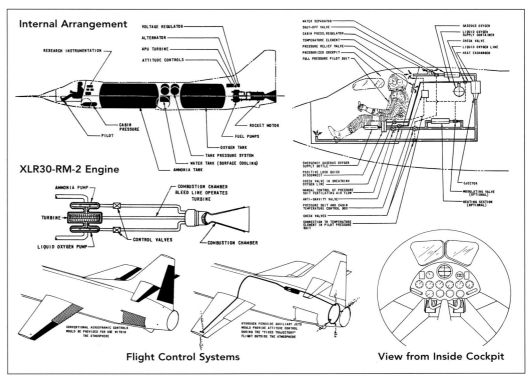

Internal Arrangement

VOLTAGE REGULATOR
ALTERNATOR
APU TURBINE
ATTITUDE CONTROLS
RESEARCH INSTRUMENTATION
CABIN PRESSURE
PILOT
ROCKET MOTOR
FUEL PUMPS
OXYGEN TANK
TANK PRESSURE SYSTEM
WATER TANK (SURFACE COOLING)
AMMONIA TANK

WATER SEPARATOR
SHUT-OFF VALVE
CABIN PRESS. REGULATOR
TEMPERATURE ELEMENT
PRESSURE RELIEF VALVE
PRESSURIZED COCKPIT
FULL PRESSURE PILOT SUIT
GASEOUS OXYGEN
LIQUID OXYGEN SUPPLY CONTAINER
CHECK VALVE
LIQUID OXYGEN LINE
HEAT EXCHANGER

EMERGENCY GASEOUS OXYGEN SUPPLY BOTTLE
POSITIVE LOCK QUICK DISCONNECT
CHECK VALVE IN BREATHING OXYGEN LINE
MANUAL CONTROL OF PRESSURE SUIT VENTILATING AIR FLOW
ANTI-GRAVITY VALVE
PRESSURE SUIT AND CABIN TEMPERATURE CONTROL BOX
CHECK VALVES
CONNECTION TO TEMPERATURE ELEMENT IN PILOT PRESSURE SUIT
EJECTOR
MODULATING VALVE (OPTIONAL)
HEATING SECTION (OPTIONAL)

XLR30-RM-2 Engine

AMMONIA PUMP
TURBINE
LIQUID OXYGEN PUMP
CONTROL VALVES
COMBUSTION CHAMBER BLEED LINE OPERATES TURBINE
COMBUSTION CHAMBER

Flight Control Systems

CONVENTIONAL AERODYNAMIC CONTROLS WOULD BE PROVIDED FOR USE WITHIN THE ATMOSPHERE

HYDROGEN PEROXIDE AUXILIARY JETS WOULD PROVIDE ATTITUDE CONTROL DURING THE "FIXED TRAJECTORY" FLIGHT OUTSIDE THE ATMOSPHERE

View from Inside Cockpit

The proposed Douglas Model 671 bore an obvious resemblance to the earlier D-558 aircraft, and quickly earned the unofficial title "D-558-III." Note the short, straight wing planform. Like all of the rocket-powered X-planes, the fuselage was essentially filled with the large propellant tanks, leaving just a minimal amount of space for the pilot and research instrumentation. Of interest is the water tank in the mid-fuselage used to cool parts of the skin. (Courtesy of Bob Bradley)

---

must be reconsidered. The effect of drag is practically negligible in the power-on ascending phase of flight (for a high altitude mission), because of the very large thrust-to-weight ratio. Throughout the vacuum trajectory, the aerodynamic shape of the airplane is completely unimportant. During the descending phase of flight, a large drag is very beneficial in aiding in the pullout, and the highest possible drag is desired within the limits of the pilot and the structure. In fact, during the pullout it has been assumed that drag brakes would be extended in order to decelerate as soon as possible. However, because of excessive decelerative forces acting upon the pilot, it is necessary to gradually retract the brakes as denser air is entered, until they are fully retracted in the later stages of flight."[60]

Despite the inertial-coupling problems experienced by the X-1A, the empennage of the Model 671 was completely conventional, looking much like that of the D-558-II that had preceded it. However, Douglas realized that this was one of the greater unknowns of the design. "The tail surfaces are of proper size for stability at the lower supersonic Mach numbers, but there is some question of their adequacy at very high supersonic speeds. Further experimental data in this speed range are necessary before modifications are attempted."[61]

Preliminary investigations at Douglas indicated that "extremely large tail surfaces, approaching the wing area in size, are required to provide complete stability at the maximum Mach number of about 7." Engineers investigated several methods that could be used to increase the area of the vertical stabilizer for improved stability if it was

deemed necessary. The most obvious was simply increasing the size of the vertical stabilizer. However, it was thought that placing additional area above the fuselage might introduce lateral directional dynamic stability problems due to an unfavorable inclination in the principal axis of inertia and the large aerodynamic rolling moment due to sideslip (the dihedral effect). The preferred arrangement was to add a ventral stabilizer and to keep the ventral and dorsal units as symmetrical as possible.[62]

Douglas conducted an evaluation of available powerplants, wanting an engine that produced about 50,000-lbf with a propellant consumption of about 200 pounds per second. The only powerplant that met the requirements was the Reaction Motors XLR30-RM-2 rocket engine using liquid oxygen and anhydrous ammonia propellants. The high – 245 lbf-sec/lbm – specific impulse (thrust per fuel consumption) was considered desirable since it provided "a maximum amount of energy for a given quantity of propellant." The high density of the propellants allowed a reduction in tank size for a given propellant weight, allowing a smaller airframe. However, the fact that the engine had been developed for an unmanned missile was a drawback.[63]

Douglas recognized that high temperatures would be a major design problem, although they indicated that "it is impractical in the present study to make a complete survey of the temperatures expected on the airplane [since] the calculations are quite complicated and tedious to obtain reasonable estimates." They continued that "it is unfortunate that the largest contributing factor to the high tempera-

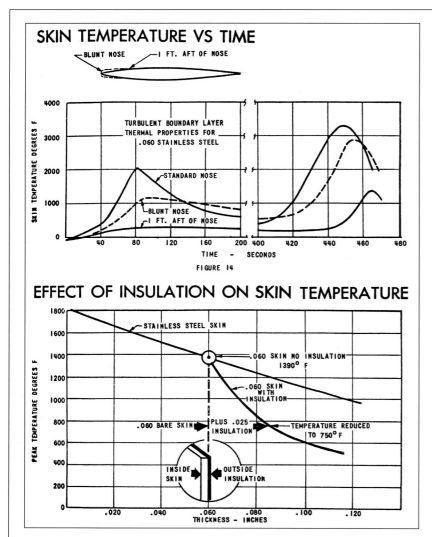

SKIN TEMPERATURE VS TIME

BLUNT NOSE — 1 FT. AFT OF NOSE

TURBULENT BOUNDARY LAYER THERMAL PROPERTIES FOR .060 STAINLESS STEEL

STANDARD NOSE

BLUNT NOSE

1 FT. AFT OF NOSE

SKIN TEMPERATURE DEGREES F

TIME – SECONDS

FIGURE 14

EFFECT OF INSULATION ON SKIN TEMPERATURE

STAINLESS STEEL SKIN

.060 SKIN NO INSULATION 1390° F

.060 SKIN WITH INSULATION

.060 BARE SKIN

PLUS .025 INSULATION

TEMPERATURE REDUCED TO 750° F

INSIDE SKIN   OUTSIDE INSULATION

PEAK TEMPERATURE DEGREES F

THICKNESS – INCHES

Douglas did a considerable amount of research into the effects of high-speed flight on various materials, although the study team made it clear that they had reached no solid conclusions in the limited time available to them. These charts show the relative merits of various leading edge shapes, and also the effects of insulation on skin temperature. (Courtesy of Bob Bradley)

tures of reentry, the convective heating from the boundary layer, is the one about which there is the least knowledge." Nevertheless, they took some educated guesses.[64]

The average heat level was expected to approach 1,400°F, with peak temperatures above 3,300°F on the wing leading edges and nose. "It would be impossible to design a structure for this temperature which satisfies both the stress and weight requirements ..." To overcome this Douglas recommended the use of some as-yet undeveloped "good insulating material." The assumed properties of this material were a density of 20 pounds per cubic foot and an insulating value of 0.20 Btu per pound. For the purposes of the study, Douglas used a C-110M titanium alloy structure and skin protected by an unspecified ablative coating. The wing leading edges and nose area would be

cooled by spraying water into a stainless steel section, allowing the superheated steam to remove unwanted heat to keep those sections below their melting points. The study noted, however, that "none of these systems have yet been proven by practical application."[65]

Not surprisingly, Douglas chose an air launch configuration. What is interesting is that the launch parameters were Mach 0.75 at 40,000 feet – well beyond the capabilities of anything except the Boeing B-52, which was still in the very early stages of testing. Douglas summarized the need for an air launch, "The performance is increased, but the prime reason for the high altitude launch is the added safety which 40,000 feet of altitude gives the pilot when he takes over under his own rocket power." Trade studies conducted by Douglas indicated that an increase in launch altitude from sea level to 40,000 feet resulted in a 200,000-foot increment in maximum altitude on a typical high-altitude mission. Additional benefits of a higher launch altitude diminished rapidly above 40,000 feet since most of the initial improvement was due to decreasing air density.[66]

Some thought was given to using "braking thrust" during descent where a small amount of propellant was saved and used during reentry – either a mechanical thrust reverser would be installed on the rocket engine, or the airplane would reenter tail-first. This technique would have allowed slightly higher flights by reducing the stresses imposed by the pullout maneuver although less propellant would be available for the ascent. The idea was not pursued too far since the mechanical complexity of a thrust reverser was undesirable and entering tail-first seemed risky.[67]

The high altitude profile would use "flywheels, gyroscopes, or small auxiliary jets" for directional control outside the atmosphere, with Douglas favoring hydrogen peroxide jets in the wingtips and at the rear of the fuselage. Flywheels had been rejected because they were too complex (for a three-axis system) and gyroscopes since they were too heavy. Each of the hydrogen peroxide thrusters would generate about 100-lbf and use one pound of propellant per second of operation. A 25-pound supply of propellant was arbitrarily assumed since no data existed on potential usage during flight.[68]

The theoretical maximum performance estimated for the research airplane was 6,150 mph and 190,000 feet for the speed profile and 5,200 mph and 1,130,000 feet for the altitude profile, but actual performance would be somewhat less due to structural and physiological considerations. Landings would be at Edwards AFB because of its "long runways and considerable latitude in the choice of direction and position of touchdown." The study noted that there would be little opportunity to control either the range or the heading by any appreciable amount after engine burnout. "Since the airplane must land without power at a specified landing site, it is obvious that it must be aimed toward the landing site at launch." The figures presented indicated that a misalignment of 5 degrees in azimuth at burnout would result in a lateral miss of over 45 miles.[69]

One of the concerns expressed by Douglas was that "rocket thrust will not be sufficiently reproducible from flight to flight, either in magnitude or in alignment of thrust." It was noted that a thrust misalignment of less than one-half of a degree could impart 500 pounds of side force on the aircraft, causing it to go significantly off course. The engineers investigated several possible solutions to thrust misalignment, including using a larger rudder, using the reaction control system, installing moveable vanes in the exhaust,[70] gas separation in the nozzle,[71] and using a gimbal to mount the rocket engine. All of the meth-

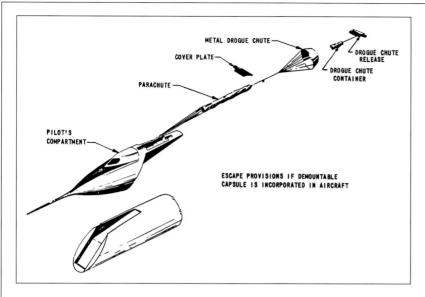

One of the controversies that would surround the early development of the X-15 was whether to equip the airplane with an escape capsule. Scott Crossfield argued vigorously for an ejection seat as being the simplest and best solution. Others disagreed. Although acknowledging that the decision was premature, Douglas opted for an encapsulated ejection system on the Model 671, much like the ill-fated Bell X-2 had. (Courtesy of Bob Bradley)

ods were rejected for various reasons. It was finally decided that thrust misalignment was largely a non-issue since early low-speed flights would point out any design/installation deficiencies which would then be corrected before beginning high speed flights.[72]

The estimated landing speed was 213 mph, with a stall speed of 177 mph. This relatively high speed was deemed acceptable "given the experimental nature of the aircraft and the high skill level of the pilots that will be flying it." The study noted that the speeds could be decreased by using high-lift leading-edge devices or by increasing the area of the wing. However, the increased weight and/or the resulting complications in the leading-edge cooling system appeared to make these changes undesirable.[73]

Considering the short time span they had to work on it, the Douglas engineers contemplated a wide variety of details. For instance, they considered the chances of the aircraft being hit by a meteor. "For a projected area of 225 square feet, the chances of being hit by a meteor capable of penetrating more than 0.08-inches of aluminum are about one in 450,000 in any one flight." Given that there was no data on the number or size of high altitude micrometeorites at the time, exactly how the engineers arrived at this probability is uncertain.[74]

According to the Douglas representative at the 16 July meeting with the NACA and ONR, the next step was a more detailed study that would cost $1,500,000 and take a year to complete. With a new joint project about to be undertaken, the ONR declined to further fund the Douglas study, and the company began concentrating its high-speed efforts on the Model 684 that would be proposed for Project 1226.

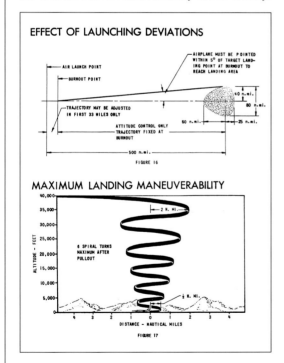

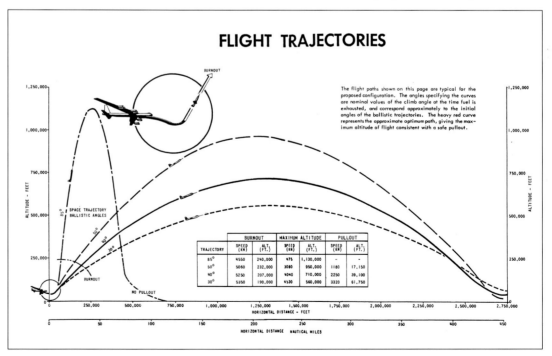

The Douglas study was way ahead of its time in some respects. For instance, the proposed research airplane was launched from a Boeing B-52, several years before the eventual X-15 program adopted such a change. The expected performance of the Model 671 was phenomenal, with a maximum altitude of 1,000,000 feet. One of the things Douglas engineers worried about was the effects of thrust misalignment or other launch deviations that would cause the research airplane to miss its intended landing site at Edwards. Fortunately, the X-15 program never experienced these problems. Nevertheless, many of the operational aspects investigated by Douglas, such as the landing profiles, mirrored the X-15 program. (Courtesy of Bob Bradley)

Project 1226

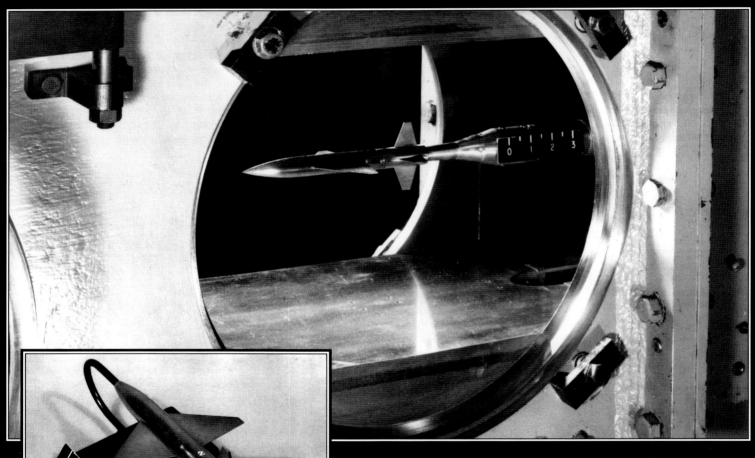

This was the Langley hypersonic research airplane configuration when the Project 1226 competition began. The model is shown (above) in the 11-inch wind tunnel at Langley, the facility that conducted most of the early testing on the various X-15 designs. Note that the stainless steel model is only a few inches long. (NASA Langley photos L86712 and L87998)

It did not take long for the Air Force to identify the principal shortcoming of the Langley study – the apparent lack of a suitable rocket engine. The Power Plant Laboratory at Wright Field pointed out that "no current rocket engine" entirely satisfied the NACA requirements, and emphasized that the Hermes engine was not man-rated. As alternatives, the laboratory investigated several other engines, but finally suggested that the selection of an engine be postponed until propulsion requirements could be more adequately defined.[1]

COMPETITION

The Wright Air Development Center (WADC) evaluation of the NACA concept was submitted to the Air Research and Development Command (ARDC) on 13 August 1954. Colonel Victor R. Haugen, director of the WADC laboratories, reported "unanimous agreement" that the idea was technically feasible; excepting the engine situation, there were no adverse comments. The evaluation also contained a cost estimate of $12,200,000 "distributed over three to four fiscal years" for two research airplanes and necessary government-furnished equipment. Somewhat prophetically, one WADC official commented informally, "Remember the X-3, the X-5, [and] the X-2 overran 200 percent. This project won't get started for $12 million."[2]

The four-and-a-half page "NACA Views Concerning a New Research Airplane" was released in late August 1954 giving a brief background on the problem, and attaching the Langley study as a possible solution. The paper listed two major areas of investigation: "(1) preventing the destruction of the aircraft structure by the direct or indirect effects of aerodynamic heating, and (2) achievement of stability and control at very high altitudes, at very high speeds, and during atmospheric reentry from ballistic flight paths." The paper concluded that the construction of a new research airplane appeared to be feasible and should be undertaken at the earliest possible opportunity.[3]

On 13 September, Major General Floyd B. Wood, the ARDC Deputy Commander for Technical Operations, forwarded an endorsement of the NACA proposal to Air Force Headquarters and recommended that the Air Force "… initiate a project to design, construct, and operate a new research aircraft similar to that suggested by NACA without delay." Echoing the conclusions of several earlier meetings, the ARDC emphasized that the aircraft should be purely a research airplane and should not be considered a prototype of any potential weapon system or operational vehicle. The ARDC estimated that about three and one-half years would be required to design and build the airplane, and forwarded the WADC cost estimate without change.[4]

On 5 October 1954, the NACA Committee on Aerodynamics met in executive session at the High-Speed Flight Station (HSFS) to come to a final decision on the desirability of a manned hypersonic research airplane. During the meeting, historic and technical data were reviewed by various committee members including Walter Williams, De Elroy Beeler, and NACA research pilot Scott Crossfield. Williams' support was crucial. Crossfield would later describe Williams as "… the man of the 20th Century who made more U.S. advanced aeronautical and space programs succeed than all the others together. … He was a very strong influence in getting the X-15 program launched in the right direction."[5]

Surprisingly, Clarence L. "Kelly" Johnson, the Lockheed representative to the committee, opposed any extension of the manned research airplane program. Johnson argued that experience with research airplanes had been "generally unsatisfactory" since their aerodynamic designs were usually inferior to tactical aircraft designs by the time research flights began. He felt that a number of research airplanes had developed "startling performances" only by using rocket engines and flying essentially "in a vacuum" (as related to operational requirements). These flights had mainly proved "the bravery of the test pilots," Johnson charged. A great deal of data on stability and control at high Mach numbers had surfaced as a result of the test flights, Johnson admitted, but aircraft manufacturers could not use much of this information because the designs were "not typical of airplanes actually designed for supersonic flight speeds." He recommended instead that an unmanned vehicle should be constructed to obtain data on structural temperature and control and stability characteristics.[6]

Various members of the committee took issue with Johnson. Gus Crowley, the associate director for research at NACA Headquarters, explained that the NACA had developed its proposal convinced that the new research airplane should be based on the "X-1 concept … to build the simplest and soundest aircraft that could be designed on currently available knowledge and put into flight research in the shortest time possible." In comparing manned research airplane operations to unmanned, automatically-controlled flights, Crowley noted that the X-1 and other research airplanes had made hundreds of successful flights, experiencing on numerous occasions excessive loading and buffeting and equipment malfunctioning. It was the human pilot that permitted further flights exploring the conditions experienced; in Crowley's opinion, automated flight could not be depended upon in similar cases. It is possible that the reputation of the X-planes was greater than their actual accomplishments, but Johnson was the only committee member that seemed to be concerned over this.[7]

After some further discussion – and despite Johnson's objections – the committee passed a resolution recommending the construction of a hypersonic research airplane. The "requirements" of the resolution conformed to the philosophy developed at Langley, but they were made sufficiently general to encourage fresh approaches. Appended to the specification under the heading of "Suggested Means of Meeting the General Requirements" were the key results of the Langley study.[8]

Kelly Johnson was the only member to vote "Nay." Sixteen days after the meeting, Johnson sent a "Minority Opinion of Extremely High Altitude Research Airplane" to Milton Ames, the committee secretary, with a request that it be appended to the majority report, which it was.[9]

In the meantime, Hartley Soulé and Clotaire Wood held two meetings in Washington on 13 October. The first was with Abraham Hyatt at the Navy Bureau of Aeronautics (BuAer) to obtain recommendations regarding the specifications. The only significant input was that provisions should exist to allow an "observer" to fly in place of the normal research instrumentation package. This was the first (and nearly only) request from the Navy regarding the new airplane. In the second meeting, Soulé discussed the specifications with Air Force representatives at the Pentagon, with little in the way of changes being suggested.

On 22 October, Soulé met with representatives of the various WADC laboratories to discuss the tentative specifications. Perhaps the major decision reached was to have a group of experts at BuAer and the Power Plant Laboratory prepare a separate specification for the engine. In effect this broke the procurement into two separate, but related, competitions – one for the airframe and one for the engine. During this meeting, John B. Trenholm from the WADC Fighter Aircraft Division suggested that three airplanes be procured – it was the first time this had been proposed; previously two had been most often mentioned.

Also on 22 October, Brigadier General Benjamin S. Kelsey and Dr. Albert Lombard from Air Force Headquarters, plus Admirals Lloyd Harrison and Robert Hatcher from BuAer met with Hugh Dryden and Gus Crowley at NACA Headquarters to discuss a proposed Memorandum of Understanding (MoU) for conducting the new research airplane program. Agreement was reached with little discussion and only minor changes to a draft that had been prepared by Dryden. The military representatives told Dryden that a method of funding the project had not been determined, but that the Air Force and Navy would arrive at some mutually acceptable agreement. It should be noted that it was normal during the late 1940s and 1950s for the military services to fund the aircraft that the NACA used in its flight research programs; this was how the X-1 and D-558 had been managed.[10]

The MoU provided that technical direction of the program would be the responsibility of the NACA, acting "… with the advice and assistance of a Research Airplane Committee" composed of one representative each from the Air Force, Navy, and the NACA. The design and construction phases were assigned to the Air Force, with the NACA conducting the flight program. The Navy was left paying part of the bills with little active roll in the project, although it would later supply biomedical expertise and a single pilot. The NACA and the Research Airplane Committee were charged with disseminating the research results to the military and industry as appropriate based on various security considerations. The concluding statement on the MoU was: "Accomplishment of this project is a matter of national urgency."[11]

On 30 December 1954 the Air Force sent invitation-to-bid letters to 12 prospective contractors; Bell, Boeing, Chance-Vought, Convair, Douglas, Grumman, Lockheed, Martin, McDonnell, North American, Northrop, and Republic. The letter asked those interested to notify Wright Field by 10 January 1955, and to attend a bidder's conference on 18 January. This was the largest invitation-to-bid list yet for an X-plane, but many contractors were uncertain about its prospects. Since it was not a production contract, the potential profits were very limited and, given the significant technical challenges, the likelihood of failure was high. Of course, the state-of-the-art-experience and public relations values were also potentially high. It was a difficult choice. Grumman, Lockheed, and Martin expressed little interest and did not attend the bidder's conference, leaving nine possible competitors.[12]

During the bidders' conference, the airframe manufacturers were informed that one prime and one alternate proposal (that might offer an unconventional but superior solution to the problems involved) would be accepted from each company. It also was noted that an engineering study, only, would be required for a modified aircraft where an observer could be substituted for the research instrumentation (per the stated Navy preference); that a weight allowance of 800 pounds, a volume of 40 cubic feet, and 2.25 kilowatts of power needed to be provided for research instrumentation; that the winning design would have to be built in 30 months; and that the aircraft needed to be capable of attaining a velocity of 6,600 fps and altitudes of 250,000 feet.

ENGINE OPTIONS

The engine situation was somewhat more complicated. Given that the Hermes engine was deemed unacceptable, the Power Plant Laboratory listed the Aerojet XLR73, Bell XLR81, North American NA-5400, and the Reaction Motors XLR10 as alternatives that the airframe competitors could use in their designs. In reply to one contrac-

tor's comment that three of the four engines appeared unsuitable since they lacked a throttling capability, it was pointed out that the government would undertake any necessary modifications to the engine selected by the winning contractor.[13]

The Aerojet XLR73-AJ-1 used white fuming nitric acid and jet fuel as propellants and its single thrust chamber developed 10,000-lbf at sea level, although a new nozzle could raise that to 11,750-lbf. The engine could be restarted in flight using electrical ignition and was infinitely variable between 50- and 100-percent thrust. Multiple units would need to be clustered to provide the 45,000-50,000-lbf needed by the new research airplane.[14]

The Bell XLR81-BA-1 was being developed as part of Project MX-1964 – the Convair B-58 Hustler – and was usually referred to as the Hustler engine. The B-58 was a supersonic bomber that carried its nuclear weapon in a large external pod; the XLR81 was meant to provide the pod with extra range after it was released by the bomber. A single thrust chamber used red fuming nitric acid and jet fuel as propellants, and the engine developed 11,500-lbf at sea level with 15,000-lbf available at 70,000 feet. The existing XLR81 was not throttleable and could not be restarted in flight. Again, the new research airplane would need at least three engines.[15]

Although listed by the Power Plant Laboratory, it appears that the NA-5400 had little to offer the program. North American was using the engine as the basis for component development, with no plans to ever assemble an entire engine. If they had, it would only have developed 5,400-lbf at sea level, hence its company designation. The turbopump assembly was theoretically capable of supporting engines up to 15,000-lbf, again suggesting that at least three engines would be required. The engine could be restarted in flight by a catalyst ignition system but was not throttleable. Propellants were hydrogen peroxide and jet fuel, with the turbopumps driven by decomposed hydrogen peroxide.[16]

The Reaction Motors XLR10 Viking engine presented some interesting options, although further development of the powerplant had largely been abandoned in favor of the more powerful XLR30 "Super Viking" derivative. As it existed, the XLR10 produced 20,000-lbf at sea level using liquid oxygen and alcohol propellants; the XLR30 produced 50,000-lbf using liquid oxygen and anhydrous ammonia. The Power Plant Laboratory's enthusiasm for the engine was shown by the fact that over two pages of the original four-and-a-half page engine report was dedicated to the XLR10/XLR30. Interestingly, as designed the engine was not throttleable or restartable.[17]

Between the time of the airframe bidder's conference and the 9 May submission deadline, Boeing, Chance-Vought, Grumman, and McDonnell notified the Air Force that they did not intend to submit formal proposals. This left Bell, Convair, Douglas, North American, Northrop, and Republic. It would seem that Bell and Douglas would have the best chances, given their history of developing X-planes. On the other hand, Convair, North American and Republic had no particular experience developing X-planes, but were in the process of either studying or developing high-speed combat aircraft or missiles. Northrop had little applicable experience of any sort.

During a meeting with Air Force personnel at Wright Field on 17 January 1955, the NACA was informed that the research airplane was identified as Air Force Project 1226, System 447L, and would be officially designated X-15.[18]

On 9 May 1955 Bell, Douglas, North American, and Republic submitted proposals to the Air Force; nothing was received from Convair or Northrop. Two days later the technical data was distributed to the WADC, NACA, and Navy evaluation groups with a request that results be returned to the X-15 Project Office by 22 June.[19]

Given the amount of effort that Langley had put into the study configuration, one might have expected that each of the contractors would use it as a starting point for their proposals. This was not the case. The Air Force had made it clear from the beginning that the Langley concept was a "suggested means of meeting the general requirements." John Becker agreed with this; he in no way felt that his was an optimum design, and the bidders were encouraged to look into other configurations that could meet the requirements. As it turned out, each of the four proposals represented a different approach to the problem, although to the casual observer they all appeared outwardly similar. This is exactly what the government had wanted – industry's best responses on building the new airplane.[20]

THE BELL PROPOSAL

Bell would have seemed a logical choice to develop the new research airplane since they had developed the X-1 series and X-2 high-speed airplanes had ushered in a new era of flight research. They were also doing studies on much faster vehicles in search of the BoMi boost-glide bomber. The company had direct experience with advanced heat-resistant metals and with the practical issues of powering manned aircraft using liquid-fueled rocket engines. In fact, Bell had an in-house group that built rocket engines, including one under consideration for the X-15. Lawrence Bell and designers such as Robert Woods and Walter Dornberger were already legends. Somehow, all of this was lost in the proposal.[21]

Unsurprisingly, Bell selected the XLR81 as the baseline; however, the XLR30 was carried as an alternate. The XLR81s were arranged in a triangular pattern with one engine mounted above the others, and each engine was a complete package that could be removed independ-

The Air Force constructed small scale models of each Project 1226 competitor. A few photographs of the models remain; this is the Bell D171 design. Note the three XLR81 nozzles in the aft fuselage. (Courtesy of Rob Goodwin)

ently of the other two. Bell believed that the ability to operate a single XLR81 at its 8,000-lbf "half-thrust" setting was an advantage because "a high percentage of the flight testing would be conducted in the lower speed and altitude ranges." Why they believed this was not clear.[22]

The engine thrust was regulated by a throttle lever in the cockpit that actuated a series of engine firing switches arranged so that thrust increased as the lever was pushed forward in the conventional manner. The initial switch fired the first engine at its 8,000-lbf half-power setting. The second switch caused this engine to go to 14,500-lbf full power. The next switch fired the second engine at full power, resulting in 29,000-lbf thrust. The last switch started the third engine, resulting in full-thrust of 43,500-lbf. The slightly asymmetrical thrust provided by the triangular engine layout under partial power was not considered a problem.[23]

One of the unfortunate consequences of selecting the XLR81 was that red fuming nitric acid required a great deal of volume, causing the oxidizer to be stored in two tanks, one on either side of the wing carry-through structure. This was necessary to maintain the center of gravity within acceptable limits. Bell investigated attaching the wing directly to the oxidizer tank, or passing the structure through the tank, but this was avoided "since it would present a hazard in the form of a possible fatigue failure as the result of the combination of localized wing loads and tank pressurization loads."[24]

The fuselage was broken into six major parts: the forward section (containing the pilot's compartment, nose gear, and research instrumentation), forward oxidizer tank, center section (wing carry-through, main landing skids, and pressurization systems), aft oxidizer tank, fuel tank, and the aft section (containing the engine and empennage). Much like the original X-1, the canopy was smoothly blended into the fuselage to avoid discontinuities in the airflow resulting in thermal shocks on the glass. The main wing had a leading edge sweep of 37 degrees to obtain the benefits of reduced heat transfer to the leading edge and moderate center-of-pressure shifts at subsonic and transonic speeds.[25]

Approximately one-third of the vertical stabilizer area was located under the fuselage but still provided sufficient clearance for the D171 to be loaded into the B-36 carrier aircraft without resorting to a folding or retractable design. The ventral stabilizer would be jettisoned prior to landing and recovered using a parachute. Bell selected a conventional tricycle landing gear arrangement, with a nose wheel and two main skids located mid-way aft on the fuselage.[26]

Based on a launch at Mach 0.6 and 40,000 feet, Bell estimated that the D171 could exceed the basic performance requirements. Velocities in excess of 6,600 fps were projected for altitudes between 85,000 and 165,000 feet, with a maximum of 6,850 fps at 118,000 feet. The maximum altitude capability during the "space leap" was estimated to be 400,000 feet.[27]

Reaction controls were provided using eight hydrogen peroxide thrusters, one pointed up and another down at each wingtip for roll control, one up and one down at the tail for pitch control, and one pointing left and one right at the tail for yaw control. The thrusters were linked directly to the aerodynamic control systems and were operated via the same control stick in the cockpit. Bell noted that "no criteria are available for the design of such controls," and the company arbitrarily expected the X-15 to need the reaction controls for about 115 seconds per high altitude mission and provided 550 pounds of hydrogen peroxide. If all of the nozzles were operated at full thrust for the entire 115 seconds (something that obviously would not hap-

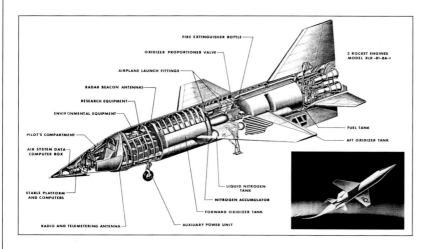

The interior layout of the baseline D171 shows that the oxidizer tanks were split, with a large tank ahead of the wing and a smaller tank behind the wing. The tank just ahead of the rocket engines is the fuel tank. Note the stacked XLR81 engines in the aft fuselage. (Courtesy of Benjamin F. Guenther)

---

pen), 49 percent of the available propellant would be used; Bell felt that this provided a comfortable margin for error.[28]

In a fuzzy look at things to come for the Space Shuttle, Bell investigated a structure protected by external insulation. "Ceramic materials would seem attractive for insulation, except that the present state of development for this application is not well enough advanced …"[29]

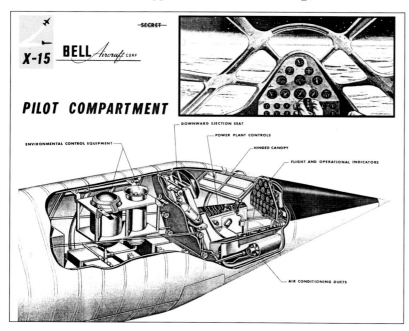

The individual proposals were very detailed. Here is the cockpit of the D171, including an insert showing the expected visibility out of the greenhouse canopy. Note that the ejection seat was arranged to fire downward, much like the Lockheed F-104. (Courtesy of Benjamin F. Guenther)

Instead, Bell decided to use a variation of a "double-wall" concept they had been investigating for BoMi. In this concept a thin outer wall absorbed the airloads but transferred most of the thermal load to an insulator behind it. An inner structural wall absorbed what little thermal load got through the insulator. Surprisingly, Bell found a much more efficient insulator than the best fibrous material could be used – air. The outer wall consisted of a 0.005-inch-thick Inconel X skin panel, approximately 4 inches long and 8 inches wide, welded to a corrugated sheet of Inconel X. The panel was held in position by an outside retaining strip of Inconel X running along each edge of the outer skin panel. The outer wall was slightly separated from the inner structure to provide the necessary air space for insulation.[30]

Thermal expansion of the outer skin was accommodated by separating the skin into elements only 4 inches wide. To prevent the free edges of this very thin skin from being lifted by aerodynamic forces, the edges of adjacent panels were interconnected by "Pittsburgh" joints. This was a standard sheet metal joint, but in this application was made with "considerable clearance" so that the adjacent panels were free to move relative to one another to permit thermal expansions.[31]

The wing and empennage used double-wall construction with a fairly conventional underlying structure and aerodynamic qualities. Since the ventral was only required for high-speed stability, its double-wedge airfoil section was optimized for that condition. The maximum thickness of the double-wedge was at the 50 percent chord line; during supersonic flight the spilt trailing edge opened, forming a single wedge with a 10 degree included angle.[32]

The leading edges of the wings and empennage surfaces were of unique construction. Bell noted "it cannot be assumed that the optimum design has been selected since the evaluation … requires a greater time than afforded in this proposal period." Bell did not believe that the heat transfer coefficients could be predicted accurately, but noted that the equilibrium temperature could approach 2,500°F. At this temperature Bell was not sure that a metallic alloy could be employed, or whether a ceramic material had to be used. Lacking any better information, Bell proposed a leading edge filled with a heat sink – lithium, beryllium, magnesium, and sodium were listed in descending order of preference, with magnesium ultimately being selected.[33]

At first, Bell selected a Boeing B-50 Superfortress for its carrier aircraft, mainly because it had experience with this bomber from the X-1 and X-2 programs. It soon became apparent, however, that the B-50 could not carry the D171 to the desired altitudes. Therefore, Bell switched to a Convair B-36. A comparison of the two aircraft showed that the B-36 had a much better rate of climb, and could launch the D171 at Mach 0.6 and 40,000 feet compared to Mach 0.5 and 30,000 feet for the B-50.[34]

Along with the baseline design, Bell proposed two slight variations. The first was the D171A two-seat version in answer to the Navy's desire to carry an observer on some flights. The observer would be seated on an upward firing ejection seat in a modified equipment compartment, and would have two small side windows to look out of. The gross weight and performance was unchanged since the weight of the observer and his ejection seat exactly matched the research instrumentation load normally carried.[35]

The second variant was the D171B powered by a Reaction Motors XLR30. The D171B had an empty weight about 200 pounds greater than the baseline configuration, but it had a launch weight some 1,000 pounds less. Bell listed the fact that the XLR30 used liquid oxygen as its

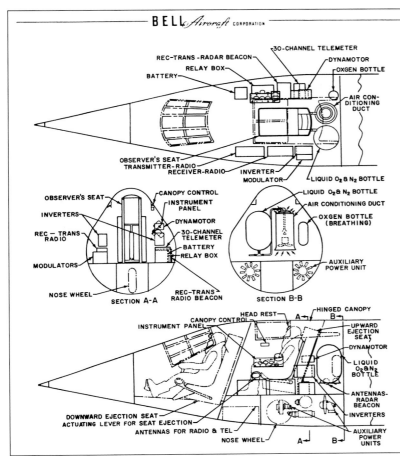

BELL *Aircraft* CORPORATION

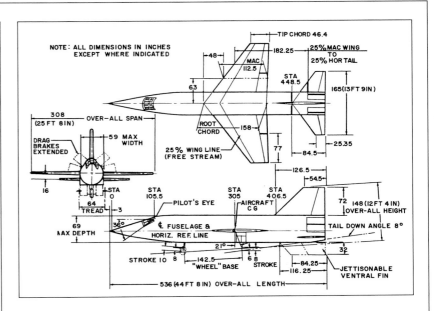

NOTE: ALL DIMENSIONS IN INCHES EXCEPT WHERE INDICATED

Above: *The D171 was a conventional appearing research airplane, with obvious lineage back to the X-1 series. Since the propellant tanks were not integral, there was no need for external tunnels to carry plumbing or electrical lines. There were six speed brakes around the aft fuselage, two on each side and two on the bottom.* (Courtesy of Benjamin F. Guenther)

Left: *The D171A two-seat version had the observer seated on an upward firing ejection seat in a modified equipment compartment. The observer was given two small side windows to look out of. Note how cramped the second cockpit seems compared to the first.* (Courtesy of Benjamin F. Guenther)

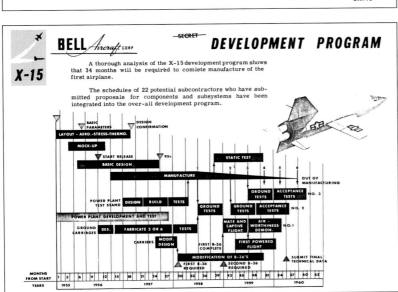

BELL *Aircraft* CORP   ~~SECRET~~   **DEVELOPMENT PROGRAM**

X-15

A thorough analysis of the X-15 development program shows that 34 months will be required to comlete manufacture of the first airplane.

The schedules of 22 potential subcontractors who have submitted proposals for components and subsystems have been integrated into the over-all development program.

This was the schedule Bell included in their proposal. Bell did not believe they could meet the government's requirement to fly the first airplane within 30 months of contract award. Of interest is the mention of needing two B-36 carrier aircraft. (Courtesy of Benjamin F. Guenther)

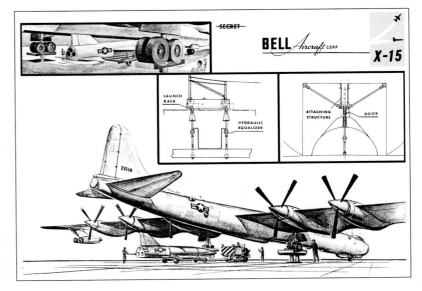

~~SECRET~~   BELL *Aircraft* CORP   X-15

Loading the D171 in the B-36 carrier aircraft looked much like loading a Republic RF-84K parasite fighter into a GRB-36D, something that was done operationally for a short time during the big bomber's career. Note the hydraulic lifts used to raise the bomber. (Courtesy of Benjamin F. Guenther)

oxidizer as its greatest disadvantage since this would require a top-off system in the carrier aircraft, which Bell felt would add "considerable greater weight" to the B-36.[36] Bell also felt that the minimum thrust capability of the XLR30 (13,500-lbf) was unsatisfactory compared to the Hustler engine (8,000-lbf). On the positive side, the internal propellant tank arrangement for the XLR30-powered airplane was much superior since only a single oxidizer tank would be needed.[37]

Bell expected to have the basic design parameters established 6 months after contract signing, and the design would be frozen at 18 months. The first airplane would be available for ground tests 34 months after contract start. Bell indicated that they attempted to compress the schedule into the required 30 months, but were unable to do so. The first glide flight was expected at 40 months, and the first powered flight at 46 months.[38]

THE DOUGLAS PROPOSAL

The Model 684 was a conceptual follow-on to the successful D-558-I and D-558-II research airplanes that Douglas had built under Navy sponsorship beginning in 1944. It also benefited from the experience Douglas gained designing the Model 671 during the "High Altitude and High Speed Study."[39]

Douglas took a unique approach to the structure of the Model 684, somewhat following the hot-structure concept developed at NACA Langley, but adding several new twists. The most obvious was that instead of Inconel X, Douglas chose a magnesium alloy "of sufficient gage that the structure [sic] temperature will not exceed 600°F." The leading edges would be constructed of copper to permit temperatures approaching 1,000°F. All of the proposed structure could be manufactured using conventional methods.[40]

A single Reaction Motors XLR30 was expected to allow the Model 684 to exceed the performance specifications, and Douglas noted that "it appears possible to explore altitudes up to approximately 375,000 feet without exceeding the structural limits of the airplane or the physiological limits of the pilot." The maximum 6,655-fps velocity was expected at 110,000 feet altitude.[41]

The most controversial aspect of the Douglas proposal was the material selected for the hot structure. In advance, Douglas defended this action: "a careful study was made of all the various metals that have satisfactory strength properties at elevated temperatures" which caused Douglas to eliminate everything except Inconel X and a thorium-zirconium alloy of magnesium called HK31.[42]

Douglas noted that the structural properties of Inconel X and magnesium HK31 fell off rapidly as the temperature approached 1,200°F and 600°F, respectively. "Since we are concerned with heating of short duration, not with stabilized temperature, the specific heat[43] of the material becomes a very important factor." The study showed that HK31 had twice the specific heat of Inconel X and since the strength-to-weight ratios of the two metals were roughly equal, Douglas felt that magnesium was a better choice. "One must realize that less heat will be re-radiated by magnesium because of its lower temperature" allowing less internal insulation around critical components such as the instrumentation and cockpit. Douglas estimated that a magnesium airframe would weigh approximately 25 percent less than an equivalent Inconel X airframe.[44]

Nevertheless, the HK31 skin was thick throughout the vehicle. Skin gages on the upper half of the fuselage varied from 0.38 inch

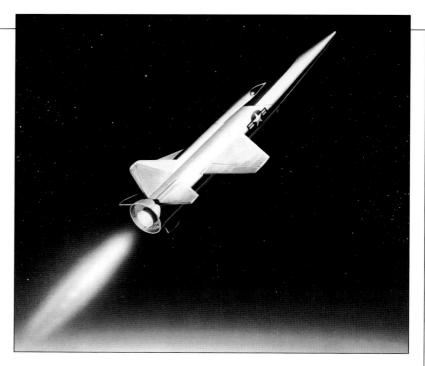

An artist concept of the Model 684 climbing out of the atmosphere. The fuselage tunnel looks larger than other drawings. (Terry Panopalis Collection)

near the nose to just 0.12 inch at the end of the ogive. On the lower surface the gage varied from 0.92 inch near the nose to 0.25 inch at the end of the ogive on the bottom centerline. The upper surface of the wing used skin 0.35 inch thick over the entire exposed portion, and 0.25 inch thick where the wing crossed inside the fuselage. The lower surface of the wing tapered from 0.64 inch near the leading edge to 0.43 inch four feet aft of the leading edge.[45]

The forward part of the fuselage consisted of the pressurized instrumentation compartment and the cockpit. If desired, the instru-

The Douglas Model 684 models. Note the offset location of the XLR30 exhaust in the aft fuselage. (Courtesy of Rob Goodwin)

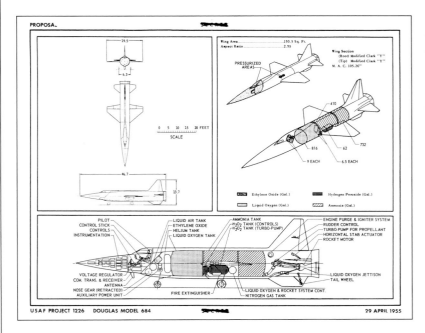

This "Standard Aircraft Characteristics" data was submitted with the Douglas proposal and shows the interior arrangement of the airplane and its overall configuration. (Courtesy of Benjamin F. Guenther)

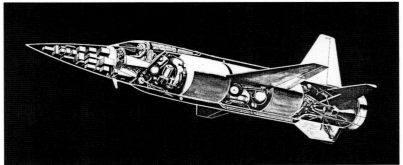

The interior arrangement of the Model 684 shows that every available space is used for either equipment or propellants. The main landing gear folded inside a compartment under the wing carry-through. (Courtesy of Benjamin F. Guenther)

mentation could be removed to allow an observer to be carried, although the accommodations were cramped, the observer had no visibility, and he sat in an awkward position. In case of an emergency, the entire forward fuselage could be separated from the rest of the airplane. Explosive bolts freed the nose and a JATO bottle located near the center of gravity of the nose section would fire to cause the initial separation. Douglas hedged their bets: "It is too early to determine whether this escape system will be satisfactory in the event of an emergency at extremely high altitudes, but no other system will be

as good. … The jettisonable nose will be the most satisfactory system for escape under the high Mach number, high Q, and high G conditions at which this airplane is most likely to get into trouble." As events with the X-2 would later show, the capsule concept did not significantly alter the chance of survival. Of course, the Model 684 system did an advantage over the X-2 – the entire nose would descend to the ground, at which time the pilot would unbuckle and walk out of the capsule. In the X-2, the pilot was expected to unbuckle and jump out of the capsule after it separated but before it hit the ground.[46]

Unlike the other competitors, Douglas proposed a fairly conventional landing gear consisting of two main wheels, a nose wheel, and

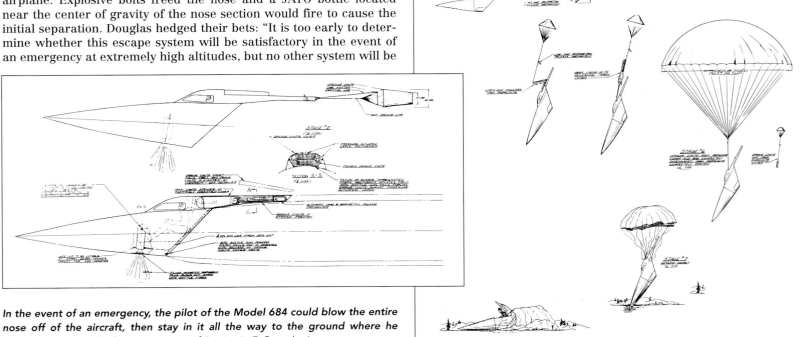

In the event of an emergency, the pilot of the Model 684 could blow the entire nose off of the aircraft, then stay in it all the way to the ground where he unbuckled and walked out. (Courtesy of Benjamin F. Guenther)

a tail wheel. No skids were used. The nose gear was located fairly far back on the fuselage (behind the cockpit) while the main gear retracted into compartments under the wing. The tail wheel was provided because of the relatively high approach attitude and was housed in the ventral stabilizer.[47]

"Flight out of the atmosphere is another new problem" that caused Douglas to provide a reaction control system equipped with 12 hydrogen peroxide thrusters, two in each direction about each axis. Two completely independent systems were provided (hence why two thrusters at each location), and either system was capable of maneuvering the airplane. The thrusters were powerful enough to rotate (and stop) the airplane through an angle of 90 degrees in 14 seconds when both systems were operational. Because of the large uncertainties involved, Douglas provided 640-percent of the amount of propellant they believed would be used on a single flight.[48]

A single liquid oxygen tank was located forward of the wing and there were two ammonia tanks; one in the upper fuselage over the wing carry-through and another that occupied the entire fuselage diameter behind the wing. All of the main propellant tanks were integral parts of the structure. Three hydrogen peroxide tanks were located under the wing carry-through between the main gear wells. It was noted that the compartment that contained these tanks "must be kept clean to prevent combustion in the event of fuel spillage and it is therefore sealed, vinyl coated and vented to an adjacent compartment through a filter that will prevent dirt contamination."[49]

The Model 684 was light enough that a B-50 could be used as a carrier aircraft with satisfactory results. This seemingly ignored the maintenance problems and low in-service rates being experienced at Edwards by the B-29 and B-50 carrier aircraft, and was a radical step backwards from the apparent use of a B-52 in the earlier D-558-III study. Surprisingly, very little modification to the X-2 carrier aircraft was required to accommodate the Model 684 – primarily making the front and rear bomb bay openings a little larger.[50]

The North American Proposal

North American seemed to be at a disadvantage, having never built an X-plane of any description. The company, however, did have a great deal of experience building early missile prototypes. The Missile Development Division conducted Project NATIV experiments during the late 1940s using captured German V-2 rockets, and then built major parts of similar vehicles themselves. The company had almost completed the design of the Mach 3 Navaho cruise missile and had developed what were arguably the three highest-performance fighters of their eras – the P-51 Mustang of World War II, the F-86 Sabre that came to fame in Korea, and the F-100 Super Sabre that was the first operational supersonic aircraft. The company was also involved in studies that would eventually lead to the fastest and most advanced bomber ever built (the XB-70A Valkyrie). They were on a roll, and the designers embraced the idea of building a hypersonic aircraft.[51]

Unlike the other competitors which largely went in their own directions, Hugh Elkin and the North American Advanced Design Group stayed fairly true to the configuration that John Becker and the team at Langley had proposed. Their goal was also similar, "the design objective must be to provide a minimum practical and reliable vehicle capable of exploring this regime of flight. Limiting factors are time, safety, state of the art, and cost."[52]

North American truly grasped what the government was trying to accomplish with the project. The other competitors – even Douglas, who otherwise came closest – worked at designing a airplane that met the performance requirements. North American, on the other hand, stated, "it has been determined that the specification performance can be obtained with very moderate structural temperatures; however, the airplane has been designed to tolerate much more severe heating in order to provide a practical temperature band within which exploration can be conducted..." Put another way, "This performance is attained without recourse to untested or complicated solutions to design problems. This should allow the major effort to be expended on obtaining the desired research information." This was, after all, the point of the whole exercise.[53]

An interesting passage from the proposal, especially considering the current trend towards trying to eliminate all risk from programs, came from the summary report: "Detailed definition and solution of all problems which will be encountered in this program are believed impossible for a proposal of this scope; indeed, if this were possible, there would be little need for a research airplane." Nevertheless, North American attempted to mitigate the inherent risk "by allowing for easy modification of critical areas if the need arises," again showing an understanding of the fundamental intent of the program. An example was that the forward nose section, the leading edges, and the wing tips were all designed to be easily replaceable "to allow panel structures and aerodynamic shapes to be tested economically."[54]

The North American design was structurally similar to the one developed at Langley. The basic wing was fabricated as a complete semi-span assembly to ensure its rigidity, and wing skin loads were directed to the fuselage ring frames for transfer across the fuselage. The wing structural box extended from the 25-percent chord line to the 75-percent chord line. A span-wise series of shear beams – made from corrugated 24S-T aluminum and titanium-manganese alloy attach points – provided the support for the taper-milled Inconel X skins. The skins panels varied from 0.060-inch thick at the tips to 0.125-inch thick at the fuselage fairing intersection.[55]

One controversial aspect of the North American design was the use of large fuselage side tunnels to carry propellant lines, control cables,

Unlike the Douglas entry, the North American ESO-7487 had the exhaust for the XLR30 engine centered in the aft fuselage. (Courtesy of Rob Goodwin)

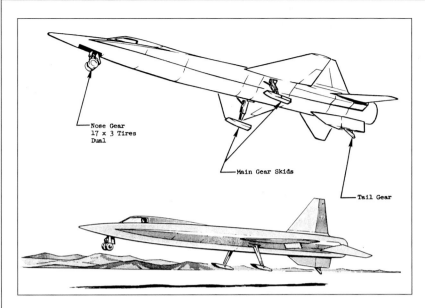

The original North American configuration for the landing gear had the main skids located under the leading edge of the wing, plus a small tail skid. The tail skid would make a return very late in the flight program as the "3rd skid" located inside the fixed portion of the ventral. (Courtesy of Benjamin F. Guenther)

etc. Douglas had placed a similar fairing on top of their fuselage with much less comment from the government. Insulation was required around the liquid oxygen tank to keep the cold temperatures out of the tunnels, and all along the outer skin to protect against the hot temperatures. The tunnels were made from Inconel X and were segmented every 20 inches to reduce thermal deflections and stresses.[56]

Unlike Bell, who did not believe that a hot-structure was compatible with integral propellant tanks, North American proposed such an arrangement from the beginning. The liquid oxygen and anhydrous ammonia tanks were each made from four sections (top, bottom, and beaded sides) welded together with intermediate Inconel X bulkheads and end domes. The sides were beaded because they were shielded from the temperature of the airstream by the fuselage side tunnels. A cylindrical tube ran coaxially through the liquid oxygen tank, serving two purposes: it stabilized the end dome bulkheads in the relatively long tank, and also housed the helium supply used to pressurize the propellant tanks.[57]

North American noted that "the lack of any convenient source of large quantities of either compressed air or ram air such as is associated with conventional jet aircraft, requires that a new and different approach be taken to the solution of pressurization and cooling." The selected approach was hardly unique, being similar to that taken by the other competitors – using compressed nitrogen gas. This led directly to one North American proposal that would occupy quite a bit of discussion after the contract was awarded. The company wanted to pressurize the pilot's full-pressure suit with nitrogen, providing breathing oxygen to the pilot through a separate breathing mask. This was done partly for simplicity, and partly to guard against the possibility of fire in the cockpit or suit – keeping oxygen exposure to the minimum seemed like the safest course of action.[58] As with the

choice of a face-mask oxygen system, North American's decision to provide a simple ejection seat and a full-pressure suit for the pilot would later prove controversial. This combination resulted in "minimum weight and complexity" and was believed to exceed the survival probabilities of "any capsule of acceptable weight that could be developed within the allowable time period." Many within the NACA and the Air Force disagreed with this approach, and discussions surrounding the full-pressure suits (and the use of a neck seal or a face seal) would come up many times during the first year of development, with Scott Crossfield leading the charge for North American.[59]

The wedge principle developed at Langley was evident in the vertical stabilizer proposed by North American. The dorsal stabilizer had a 10-degree wedge section; the ventral used a 15 degree wedge. Like the Douglas entry, the vertical was nominally a double-edge shape with the thickest part at 50 percent chord. A split trailing edge could open to form a "relatively obtuse blunt wedge" that greatly increased the tail lift curve slop at high Mach numbers and provided "sufficient directional stability without actual increase of tail area."[60]

Another innovative feature that was the subject of some debate after contract award was the use of all-moving "rolling" horizontal stabilizers instead of conventional ailerons and elevators.[61] These were operated symmetrically for pitch control and differentially for roll control. An all-moving dorsal stabilizer provided directional control, while the smaller ventral stabilizer was fixed. Split speed brakes were located on the sides of both the dorsal and ventral stabilizers.[62]

A "space control system" was provided using four thrusters in a cruciform arrangement at the nose and one thruster at each wingtip. The controls would be actuated by a separate lever located on the right console. The amount of propellant for the reaction controls seemed low by comparison with the other competitors: whereas Bell provided 54 gallons of hydrogen peroxide and Douglas provided nearly the same amount, North American only provided 3.15 gallons (36.2 pounds). The company expected this to be sufficient for "five gross attitude changes about each axis at approximately 6 degrees per second." This shows the amount of uncertainty that existed regarding the amount of use the reaction controls would receive – the first manned space flight was still six years away.[63]

The landing gear consisted of two strut-mounted skids that retracted against the outside of the fuselage beneath the wing leading edge. These were deployed via a manual cable release of the

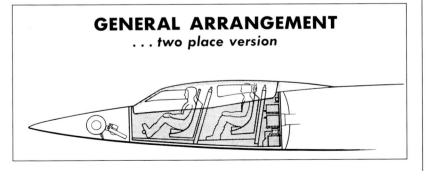

The North American response to carrying an observer was more sophisticated than Bell or Douglas, but less so than Republic. At least the observer sat in a fairly normal position and had a useful single-piece canopy with windows. (Courtesy of Benjamin F. Guenther)

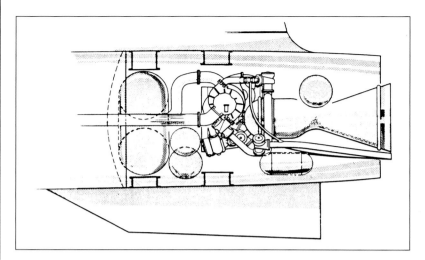

The proposed XLR30 installation did not differ significantly from the eventual XLR99 installation. Both were very compact engines burning liquid oxygen and anhydrous ammonia. (Courtesy of Benjamin F. Guenther)

THE REPUBLIC PROPOSAL

Republic also seemed at a disadvantage in the X-15 competition, for much the same reasons as North American. But the company was working on a Mach 3+ interceptor – the XF-103 – and had also developed the first supersonic combat-type aircraft, the experimental XF-91. With the XF-91 the company had gained experience integrating a liquid-fueled rocket engine into a manned aircraft. The XF-103 was providing a wealth of experience (most of it unhappy), including information concerning the effects of high-speed heating on aircraft structures. Perhaps most importantly, Republic had Alexander Kartveli, one of the most innovative aircraft designers in the world.[68]

The Republic AP-76 was the heavyweight of the competitors, but Republic nevertheless expected the design to very slightly exceed the speed specification at 6,619 fps, although it fell somewhat short of the altitude requirement at only 220,000 feet. Like Bell, Republic opted for XLR81-BA-1 engines, although the AP-76 needed four of them, providing a total of 58,000-lbf at 40,000 feet. Republic justified their choice as, "a sacrifice in weight … made in order to use these four units in place of a single thrust chamber engine. The increased safety of numbers as well as the increased reliability of starting one or more units influenced this choice."[69]

The engines were controlled from a switch panel at the normal throttle location on the left console. This was based on experience gained on the XF-91 prototype that had both switches and a conventional throttle quadrant, but the pilots preferred using the switches. A fixed hand grip was provided next to the switches to ensure that the pilot's hand would be near the switches at all times. There were nine 2-position switches on the panel; a "master arm" switch, four individual "arm" switches, and four "on" switches. Thrust was controlled by igniting varying numbers of the engines. Republic did not seem to incorporate the ability to use the "half thrust" feature of the XLR81.[70]

The pilot was submerged in the fuselage without a conventional canopy. Instead, three glass panels were provided on each side of the fuselage for side vision from the time of launch until the airplane had descended to approximately 25,000 feet. Once the AP-76 had descended to this altitude and slowed to Mach 0.7, a hatch on the upper surface of the cockpit raised up 13 degrees at its leading edge to expose a mirror system that provided forward vision during approach and landing. The system used two mirrors – one in the front of the hatch that reflected an image downward to a second mirror on top of the instrument panel. The pilot looked at the second image. This system was similar to the one developed for the XF-103 and had received favorable comments from pilots during simulations. Surprisingly, the system offered fairly good depth-perception and minimal loss of brightness.[71]

Given the amount of effort committed to developing an encapsulated escape system during the protracted XF-103 program, it is surprising that Republic opted for a simple ejection seat for the AP-76. "Consideration was given to the use of a pilot's escape capsule in the AP-76. It was found to be extremely difficult to design a capsule which would have the necessary stability characteristics in the low density air of the high altitudes attained by the AP-76." In its place, much like North American, was an escape seat with leg restraints; the pilot would rely on his partial-pressure suit for protection.[72]

Republic proposed a novel structure for the fuselage, using titanium as the main structural material for longitudinal "Z" stringers disposed with 10-degree separations. The structural skin was attached to the

uplock, with gravity and a bungee spring taking care of the rest. A two-wheel nose gear was provided far forward that was also released manually. A small "tail bumper" skid was installed in the aft edge of the ventral stabilizer that was also manually released and assisted by a spring bungee. All four gear were retracted by the simple expedient of having the ground crew manually move them into place after the aircraft was raised off of them.[64]

The skids had been chosen as much because they saved considerable space inside the relatively small airframe as any other reason: "the stowage of a wheel would not adapt itself to the configuration of the airplane without increasing the cross section area and wetted area." Braking was accomplished by the friction between the skid and the ground. The landing rollout was computed as 8,000 feet, well within the limits of the dry lakes at Edwards.[65]

As required by the government, North American performed an engineering study on a two-seat X-15 that would "provide an observer." The research instrumentation behind the cockpit was replaced by a second cockpit and ejection seat. An entirely new one-piece clamshell canopy was designed that covered both cockpits and faired into the upper fuselage further back than the normal canopy. Large flat-pane side windows were provided for the observer, along with "an abbreviated presentation of flight and research data." "Inasmuch as the launch and burn-out weights and airplane drag are identical to those of the single-place version, no change in performance will result."[66]

North American chose a B-36 as the carrier aircraft mostly because the only other available aircraft – the Boeing B-50 Superfortress – could not lift the proposed research airplane above 25,000 feet, and North American wanted a higher launch altitude. From a modification perspective, the B-36 appeared to be excellent; only one bulkhead had to be replaced and the basic engineering had already been accomplished for the FICON project. The flight profiles developed by North American assumed a launch at Mach 0.6 and 30,000 feet, but the proposal expected that the B-36 could actually achieve 38,000 feet with no difficulty.[67]

inner leg of the stringers and the outer leg held a series of 0.020-inch thick corrugated Inconel X shingles that formed a heat shield. In between the heat shield and inner skin were 0.5-inch-thick blocks of Marinite insulation. With the Inconel outer skin at its full 1,200°F, the interior titanium structure would never exceed 300°F.[73]

The trapezoidal wing used a slightly rounded leading edge with a flat airfoil between the 20 and 80-percent chord lines and a blunt trailing edge. Unlike the fuselage, no attempt was made to insulate the wing structure, and it was designed to carry the design loads and temperatures without developing thermal stresses. The leading edges were six kentanium (a titanium carbide alloy) castings segments per wing.[74]

The vertical and horizontal stabilizers were "of conventional size made possible by the use of double wedge type sections with rounded leading edges." The included angles were 10 and 12 degrees, respectively. The horizontal surfaces were all-moving, but the airplane used conventional ailerons instead of the differentially-moving horizontals found on the North American design. The vertical surfaces consisted of a dorsal stabilizer and a jettisonable ventral stabilizer. The rudder design was based upon wind tunnel data from the XF-103 project, although the overall shape was different. The rudder consisted of the upper 46 percent of the surface and the entire trailing edge aft of the 70 percent chord line. The trailing 30 and 35 percent of the vertical and horizontal stabilizers, respectively, were designed as split flaps that could be opened through a maximum included angle of 50 degrees to increase drag and reduce the speed of the aircraft during reentry.[75]

The landing gear consisted of two main and one tail skid. The 48x5-inch main skids were installed externally on the side of the fuselage bottom just ahead of the center of gravity. Just prior to landing, the skids would be extended 18.5 inches below the fairing using pneumatic shock absorbers. The tail skid was automatically exposed when the ventral stabilizer was jettisoned.[76]

The Republic approach to the required two-seat engineering study was a little different and decidedly more useful than the others. All of the other competitors had simply deleted all of the

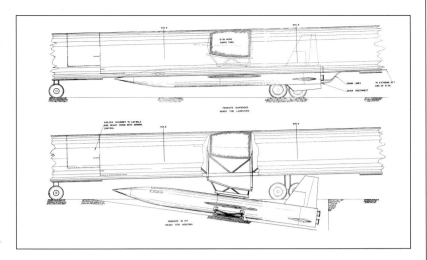

Republic had already built the RF-84K Thunderflash fighters that were carried operationally in the bomb bay of a GRB-36D, so all of the necessary information was at hand for the design team. Like the FICON fighters and early X-1s, the research airplane was loaded into the bomb bay by positioning the bomber over a pit in the ramp. (Courtesy of Benjamin F. Guenther)

research instrumentation and installed accommodations for an observer, although North American, at least, had provided a decent canopy arrangement. Republic, however, stretched the constant-section of the fuselage just ahead of the forward propellant tank by 29 inches. The research instrumentation on the single seat aircraft was split into two compartments; 550 pounds ahead of the pilot, and 250 pounds behind the pilot. The 250 pounds in the rear compartment were deleted, and combined with the 29-inch extension provided a full-size cockpit for the observer. The airplane could still

The Republic AP-76 model shows the wedge-shape created by the split trailing-edge elevators and rudder, as well as the four XLR81 engines in the tail. The basic shape seemed to borrow from Alexander Kartveli's XF-103 interceptor, also under development at Republic at the time. (Courtesy of Rob Goodwin)

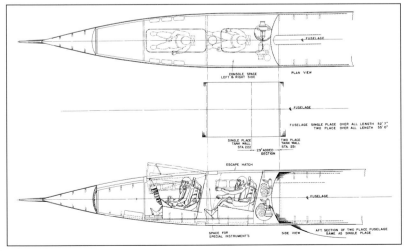

The two-seat design study by Republic was by far the most elegant of the competitors. A 29-inch fuselage extension allowed the addition of a true second cockpit, and the airplane could still carry more than half of its research instrumentation, the only design so capable. (Courtesy of Benjamin F. Guenther)

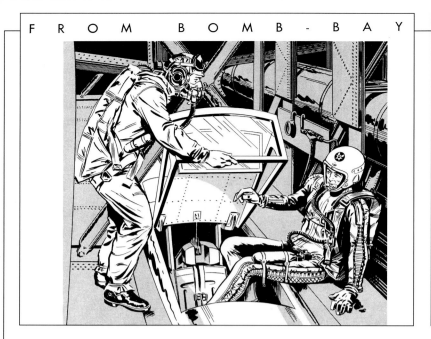

One of the major advantages to using a B-36 (or B-29/B-50) instead of the eventual B-52 was that the research pilot did not have to get into his airplane until nearly time to launch. (Courtesy of Benjamin F. Guenther)

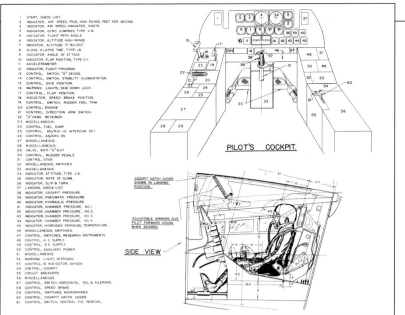

PILOT'S COCKPIT.

SIDE VIEW

The cockpit of the AP-76 was certainly unique. There was no canopy as such, and all forward vision was via a mirror system that was deployed as the airplane decelerated after the mission. (Courtesy of Benjamin F. Guenther)

carry the other 550 pounds of instrumentation, the only two-seater proposal that could carry any. The empty weight of the airplane increased 380 pounds and the launch weight increased 610 pounds resulting in a degradation of performance of 170 fps.[77]

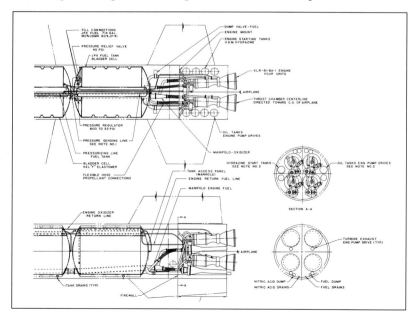

The Republic design was the heaviest of the competitors, and required four XLR81 engines to meet the performance requirements. This was a lot of hardware to pack into the aft fuselage, but Republic managed to pull it off neatly. (Courtesy of Benjamin F. Guenther)

Not surprisingly given the weight of the AP-76, Republic chose a B-36 as the carrier aircraft. Republic had experience using the B-36 since the company manufactured the RF-84K Thunderflash parasite fighter used in the FICON program. The AP-76 was sufficiently large that it took up the majority of all four B-36 bomb bays. Interestingly, the research airplane was actually launched by the bombardier.[78]

Unfortunately, Republic appears to have misread the intentions of NACA and the Air Force; the proposal stated that "the achievement of the speed [6,600 fps] is paramount whereas flight at very high altitudes has a secondary role." Because of this, Republic concentrated on designing an aircraft capable of meeting the velocity requirement, while ignoring the altitude requirement somewhat. Although the proposal listed 220,000 feet as the maximum altitude of the aircraft, other data submitted with the proposal indicated that the company believed the aircraft could achieve almost 300,000 feet if necessary.[79]

ENGINE PROPOSALS

The airframe manufactures had concentrated on two of the possible engines – Bell and Republic had opted for the Bell XLR81 while Douglas and North American used the Reaction Motors XLR30. Bell also included an alternate design that used the XLR30 engine. None of the bidders used the Aerojet XLR73.[80]

Bell was very conservative in their engine proposal and noted that "modifications have been limited to those necessary to permit the engine to be used in a piloted aircraft." The modified engine would be capable of multiple starts and could operate at 8,000-lbf thrust in addition to the normal 14,500-lbf full-thrust. Since the engine would be used in multiples (three in the Bell design; four in the Republic) there would be a variety of thrust levels available to the pilot (8,000-, 14,500-, 29,000-, 43,500- and for Republic 58,000-lbf), but the thrust

COMPARISON OF PROPOSED PHYSICAL CHARACTERISTICS

		Bell D171	Douglas Model 684	NAA ESO-7487	Republic AP-76
Fuselage:					
Length (feet):		44.42	46.75	49.33	52.58
Frontal Area (square feet):		25.00	21.00	?	?
Maximum Diameter (feet):		5.15	5.16	4.50	5.00
Fineness Ratio:		8.62	9.06	?	10.5
Wing:					
Airfoil:	biconvex (mod)	Clark Y (mod)	66005 (mod)	hexagonal
Span (feet):		25.67	19.50	22.36	27.66
Root Section (percent):		5.0	7.0	5.0	5.0
Tip Section (percent):		6.0	4.5	1.0	7.5
Root Chord (feet):		13.16	10.40	10.80	16.00
Tip Chord (feet):		3.86	2.75	3.00	2.25
Area (square feet):		220.0	150.3	200.0	254.0
Flap Area (square feet):		15.25	14.44	?	28.80
Aileron Area (square feet):		16.00	9.88	n/a	15.80
Angle of Incidence (degrees)		0	0	0	0
Dihedral (degrees):		0	0	0	0
Aspect Ratio:		3.00	2.53	2.50	3.00
Taper Ratio:		0.30	0.22	?	0.14
Aileron Deflection (degrees):		±15	±20	n/a	+17/-12
Flap Deflection (degrees):		-45	-45	-40	-38
Leading Edge Sweep (degrees):		37.0	40.0	25.0	38.4
MAC (inches):		112.50	105.26	123.23	130.87
Horizontal Stabilizer:					
Airfoil:	biconvex (mod)	5° wedge	66005 (mod)	10° wedge
Span (feet):		13.75	11.83	17.64	15.70
Root Chord (feet):		7.05	7.66	7.02	7.08
Tip Chord (feet):		2.11	1.66	2.10	1.83
Area (square feet):		63.00	55.20	51.76	69.70
Aspect Ratio:		3.00	2.54	2.81	3.48
Taper Ratio:		0.30	0.22	0.22	0.26
Leading Edge Sweep (degrees):		35.5	40.0	45.0	22.3
Deflection (degrees):		+1-/-20	+5/-20	+15/-45	+7/-20
Dorsal Stabilizer:					
Airfoil:	biconvex (mod)	diamond (mod)	10° wedge	12° wedge
Area (square feet):		45.30	39.25	38.14	47.60
Rudder Area (square feet):		13.5	7.85	?	32.0
Aspect Ratio:		0.8	1.277	1.25	1.6
Leading Edge Sweep (degrees):		45.0	40.0	52.0	27.9
Rudder Deflection (degrees):		±20	±30	±45	±20
Ventral Stabilizer:					
Airfoil:	10° diamond	7° edge	15° wedge	10° wedge
Area (square feet):		22.70	12.08	11.42	12.30
Leading Edge Sweep (degrees):		45.0	60.0	52.0	45.0
Weights:					
Launch (pounds):		34,140	25,300	27,722	39,099
Burnout (pounds):		12,942	10,600	10,433	15,300
Landing (pounds):		12,595	10,450	10,200	14,800
Empty (pounds):		11,964	9,208	9,959	14,388
Propellants (pounds):		21,600	14,700	16,410	23,660
Propulsion:					
Number of Engines:		3	1	1	4
Engine Type:		XLR81	XLR30	XLR30	XLR81
Total Thrust (lbf):		43,500	57,000	57,000	58,000
Fuel Type:		JP-X	ammonia	ammonia	JP-X
Fuel Quantity (gallons):		704	1,142	1,239	710
Oxidizer Type:		RFNA	LOX	LOX	RFNA
Oxidizer Quantity (gallons):		1,358	816	907	1,430
Performance (estimated):					
Maximum Speed (fps):		6,850	6,655	6,950	6,619
Maximum Altitude (feet):		400,000	375,000	800,000	220,000
Cost and Schedule:					
Three Aircraft (millions):		$36.3	$36.4	$56.1	$47.0
First Flight:		Jan. 59	Mar. 58	Nov. 57	Feb. 58

would not be continuously variable. Only one engine in each airplane would have the capability to provide the 8,000-lbf level. In an attempt to minimize the potential of mixed propellants accumulating and exploding, Bell wanted to replace the jet fuel normally used in the XLR81 with JP-X, which was a mixture of 40 percent unsymmetrical dimethylhydrazine (UDMH) and 60 percent jet fuel. This would make the two propellants hypergolic, eliminating the hazard. Bell also pointed out that these propellants would not need to be topped-off from the carrier aircraft since neither had an appreciable vaporization rate.[81]

Like that from Bell, the proposal from Reaction Motors was very brief (Bell had used 15 pages; Reaction Motors just 14). The XLR30 would be modified to: "1) emphasize safety and minimum development time, 2) start, operate and shutdown at all altitudes and attitudes, and 3) be capable of at least five successive starts without servicing or manual attention other than cockpit controls." Instead of the thrust stepping proposed by Bell, Reaction Motors offered an infinitely-variable thrust ranging from 13,500-lbf to 50,000-lbf at sea level. The company pointed out that "the highly developed state of the major engine components, i.e., turbopump, thrust chamber and control valves allows RMI to meet the schedule …." Unlike Bell that extensively discussed the modifications required to make their engine meet the X-15 requirements, Reaction Motors instead gave a technical overview of the XLR30 and it was impossible to determine what components were modified and which were not. Nevertheless, the overall impression was that the state of XLR30 development was very far along.[82]

There seemed to be some confusion within the government over the engine evaluation process, and on 27 June 1955 a meeting was held at NACA Headquarters to ensure everybody was on the same page. The meeting ended with an understanding that the engine evaluation was meant to determine if any of the engines was deemed unsuitable for use in the X-15, or if any of them was so clearly superior to the others that it should be selected regardless of the choice of the winning airframe contractor. If neither of these conditions existed, then whichever engine the airframe contractor selected would be the winner.[83]

This early wind tunnel model was made into a desk model, probably for one of the managers on the program. Note the skids against the fuselage under the wing leading edge and the side tunnels that extend all the way forward to the nose. Oddly, this model has a large pair of canted ventral stabilizers, a configuration that must have been unsuccessful during wind tunnel testing. (The Boeing Company Archives)

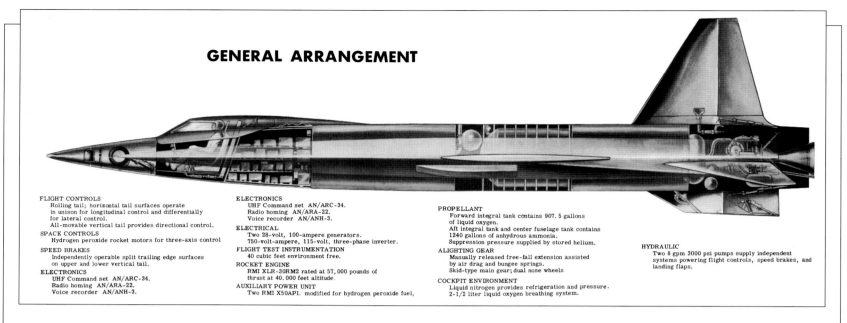

GENERAL ARRANGEMENT

FLIGHT CONTROLS
Rolling tail; horizontal tail surfaces operate
in unison for longitudinal control and differentially
for lateral control.
All-movable vertical tail provides directional control.

SPACE CONTROLS
Hydrogen peroxide rocket motors for three-axis control.

SPEED BRAKES
Independently operable split trailing edge surfaces
on upper and lower vertical tail.

ELECTRONICS
UHF Command set AN/ARC-34.
Radio homing AN/ARA-22.
Voice recorder AN/ANH-3.

ELECTRONICS
UHF Command set AN/ARC-34.
Radio homing AN/ARA-22.
Voice recorder AN/ANH-3.

ELECTRICAL
Two 28-volt, 100-ampere generators.
750-volt-ampere, 115-volt, three-phase inverter.

FLIGHT TEST INSTRUMENTATION
40 cubic feet environment free.

ROCKET ENGINE
RMI XLR-30RM2 rated at 57,000 pounds of
thrust at 40,000 feet altitude.

AUXILIARY POWER UNIT
Two RMI X50API. modified for hydrogen peroxide fuel,

PROPELLANT
Forward integral tank contains 907.5 gallons
of liquid oxygen.
Aft integral tank and center fuselage tank contains
1240 gallons of anhydrous ammonia.
Suppression pressure supplied by stored helium.

ALIGHTING GEAR
Manually released free-fall extension assisted
by air drag and bungee springs.
Skid-type main gear; dual nose wheels

COCKPIT ENVIRONMENT
Liquid nitrogen provides refrigeration and pressure.
2-1/2 liter liquid oxygen breathing system.

HYDRAULIC
Two 8 gpm 3000 psi pumps supply independent
systems powering flight controls, speed brakes, and
landing flaps.

The interior arrangement of the North American design during June 1956 is shown above. There was remarkably little change in the major internal components as the design progressed to production. The exterior was another matter, and the early vertical stabilizer concept shown here underwent major revisions before metal was cut for the three airplanes, as did the placement of the main landing skids (shown under the wing leading edge). A different drawing of the same design is shown below, but unfortunately the legend for the call-outs did not survive; most of them are obvious, however. (The Boeing Company Archives)

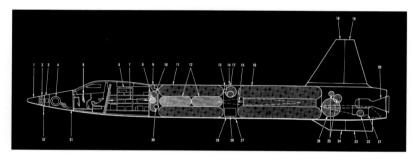

On 1 July the NACA submitted its engine evaluation but expressed concern "at the lack of development of all three of the proposed engines." Walter Williams again strongly recommended that an interim engine – the Reaction Motors LR8 was suggested based on previous HSFS experience – be used for the initial flights of the new research airplane. Since the early flights would be primarily concerned with proving the airworthiness of the airplane, they would not need the full power provided by the final engine.[84]

A meeting at Wright Field on 6-7 July attempted to sort out the engine selection, eventually reaching the conclusion that none of the engines was clearly superior or deficient, and therefore the selection should be left to the airframe contractor. Since none of the airframe proposals used the XLR73, it was dropped from consideration.[85]

AND THE WINNER IS ...

The airframe evaluation process lasted from mid-May until late July, with the Air Force, NACA, and Navy conducting independent evaluations based on a number of criteria. The results were completed by each organization in time for a meeting on 26-28 November, where the technical teams ranked the competitors. During the week of 1-5 August

1955, the results were evaluated in five areas: performance, technical design, research suitability, development capability, and costs.[86]

A meeting of the Air Force, NACA, and Navy was held at NACA Headquarters on 12 August for the final briefing on the evaluation, which had selected North American, and by default, Reaction Motors. Attendees included Hugh Dryden, Gus Crowley, Ira Abbott, Richard Rhode, and Hartley Soulé from NACA; Brigadier General Benjamin Kelsey, Colonel Donald H. Heaton, Lieutenant Colonels Gablecki and Maiersperger, and Major Heniesse from the Air Force; and Captain R. E. Dixon, Abraham Hyatt, and George Spangenberg from BuAer. Following this, the Research Airplane Committee met, accepted the findings of the evaluation groups, and agreed to present the recommendation to the Department of Defense.[87]

Because the estimated costs submitted by North American were far above the amount tentatively allocated for the project, the Research Airplane Committee recommended a funding increase that would need to be approved before the actual contract was signed. A further recommendation, one that would later take on greater importance, called for relaxing the schedule by 18 months.

CHANGE OF HEART

Events took an unexpected twist on the afternoon of 23 August 1955 when the North American representative in Dayton verbally informed the X-15 Project Office that his company wished to withdraw its proposal. This was followed on 30 August by a letter to the Air Force formally requesting that North American be allowed to withdraw because the company could not devote sufficient effort to complete the X-15 program within the required 30 months.[88]

On 1 September, Hugh Dryden informed Harley Soulé that he and General Kelsey had decided, pending receipt of a formal letter from

North American, to continue competition activities. In fact, even after the letter had been received, the competition process continued. By September 7 Soulé, now fully aware of the North American decision, contacted Dryden and recommended that the Research Airplane Committee give favorable consideration to the second-place bidder (Douglas). Dryden felt that the competition should be reopened instead.

On 20-21 September, the Department of Defense approved both the program and North American's selection. But there was a caveat – a reduction in annual budget outlays. As these instructions reached Wright Field, General Howell M. Estes, Jr., was conferring with the president of North American, John Leland "Lee" Atwood. Atwood told the general that his company would reconsider its decision if the program schedule was extended. The vice president and chief engineer for North American, Raymond H. Rice, explained on 23 September that the company had decided to withdraw from the competition because it had recently won new bomber (WS-110A) and long-range interceptor (WS-202A) studies, and also had increased activity on the YF-107 fighter program. He indicated that North American would be unable to accommodate the engineering manpower build-up that would be required to support the desired 30-month schedule.[89]

Rice went on that, "... due to the apparent interest that has subsequently been expressed in the North American design, the contractor wishes to extend two alternate courses which have been previously discussed with Air Force personnel: The engineering manpower work load schedule has been reviewed and the contractor wishes to point out that Project 1226 could be handled if it were permissible to extend the schedule ... over an additional eight month period; in the event the above time extension is not acceptable and in the best interest of the project, the contractor is willing to release the proposal data to the Air Force at no cost."[90]

As it turned out, extending the schedule had previously been approved by the Research Airplane Committee on 12 August 1955. Accordingly, on 30 September, Colonel Carl F. Damberg, Chief of the Aircraft Division at Wright Field, formally notified North American that its design had been selected as the winner. The letter of withdrawal was retracted, and the other bidders were subsequently notified that North American had been selected and thanked for their participation. In the competitive environment that exists in the early 21st Century, this course of events would undoubtedly lead to protests from the losing contractors and possibly Congressional investigations and court actions. However, as business was conducted in 1955 it was not considered cause for comment.[91]

Financing was another issue, and a meeting to discuss how to pay for the program was held on 5 October at Wright Field. The Defense Coordinating Committee for Piloted Aircraft had tentatively allocated $30,000,000 to the program; the problem was North American needed $56,100,000. The X-15 Project Office began attempting to reduce the expenditures by eliminating the static-test article, reducing the modifications to the B-36 carrier aircraft, and eliminating some previously-required studies and evaluations. The total cost was now estimated at $50,063,500 – $38,742,500 for the airframes, $9,961,000 for the engine, and $1,360,000 for the new radar range. It would quickly start to increase.[92]

A definitive contract for North American was signed on 11 June 1956, allowing the eventual expenditure of $40,263,709 plus a fee of $2,617,075. For this sum, the government was to receive three X-15 research airplanes, a high-speed and a low-speed wind tunnel model,

a free-spin model, a full-size mockup, propulsion system test stands, flight tests, modification of a B-36 carrier aircraft, a flight handbook, a maintenance handbook, technical data, periodic reports of several types, ground handling dollies, spare parts, and various ground support equipment. The contract costs did not include the engine, research instrumentation, fuel and oil, special test site facilities, or expenses to operate the B-36, all of which were considered government-furnished equipment. The delivery date for the first X-15 was 31 October 1958.[93]

A final contract for the engine, the prime unit of government furnished equipment, was signed on 7 September 1956 and covered the expenditure of $10,160,030 plus a fee of $614,000.[94] For this sum, Reaction Motors agreed to deliver one engine, a mockup, reports, drawings, and tools. The "propulsion subsystem" effort was known as Project 3116 and was carried on the books separately from the Project 1226 airframe.[95]

XLR30-RM-2 ROCKET ENGINE

Often talked about, but seldom seen – the Reaction Motors XLR30-RM-2 "Super Viking" engine that formed the basis of the XLR99 used in the X-15. The nozzle is shown at left with the turbopump assembly at right. A test firing on a stand at Lake Denmark is shown in the inset. (Reaction Motors, Inc.)

The Fastest Airplane in the World

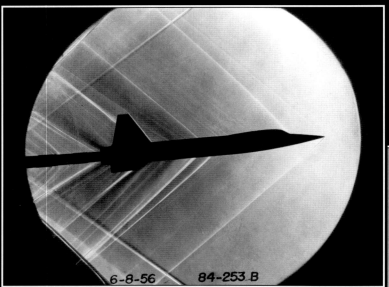

6-8-56   84-253 B

Left: *A high-tail X-15 model in an unidentified wind tunnel. Note the shock waves coming off the wing leading edge, and a separate shock wave just behind it coming off the front of the landing skid. Very soon the configuration would change substantially as the fuselage tunnels were made shorter, the vertical surfaces reconfigured, and the skids moved aft.* (NASA)

Right: *The escape system for the X-15 was the subject of much discussion and a great deal of testing. After it was agreed that an ejection seat-pressure suit combination was the best practical solution, a series of tests were conducted on the South Base sled track at Edwards AFB. This is run number 3 on 30 June 1958. This test reached 620 knots and a dynamic pressure of 1,130 psf, and was considered satisfactory.* (AFFTC History Office)

Harrison A. "Stormy" Storms, Jr., and Charles H. Feltz had a difficult job ahead of them. Although giving the appearance of having a rather simple configuration, the X-15 was perhaps the most technologically complex single-seat aircraft yet built. Project Engineer Feltz would lead the day-to-day activities of the design team; Storms was Chief Engineer for the entire division, and although greatly interested in the X-15, he had other responsibilities that precluded daily contact with the program. Directly assisting Storms and Feltz was test pilot A. Scott Crossfield, who had left the NACA and joined North American specifically to work on the X-15. Crossfield describes Storms as "... a man of wonderful imagination, technical depth, and courage ... with a love affair with the X-15. He was a tremendous ally and kept the objectivity of the program intact ...." According to Crossfield, Feltz was "... a remarkable 'can do and did' engineer who was very much a source of the X-15 success story."[1]

The other key members of the North American team were: assistant project engineers Roland L. "Bud" Benner, George Owl, and Raun Robinson; powerplant engineer Robert E. Field; regulators and relief valve expert John W. Gibb; chief of aerodynamics Lawrence P. Greene; project aerodynamicist Edwin W. "Bill" Johnston; and test pilot Alvin S. White. Storms remembers that "Al White went through all the required training to be the backup pilot to Crossfield and trained for several years – and was not even allowed one flight; that's dedication!" In addition, L. Robert Carman, who (along with Hubert Drake) had developed one of the earliest NACA ideas for a hypersonic airplane, had left the NACA and joined North American to work on the X-15.[2]

Years later Storms remembered his first verbal instructions from Hartley Soulé, "You have a little airplane and a big engine with a large thrust margin. We want to go to 250,000 feet altitude and Mach 6. We want to study aerodynamic heating. We do not want to worry about aerodynamic stability and control, or the airplane breaking up. So if you make any errors, make them on the strong side. You should have enough thrust to do the job." Added Storms: "And so we did."[3]

The day Scott Crossfield reported for work with Charlie Feltz, he defined his future role on the program. Said Crossfield in his autobiography, "I would be the X-15's chief son-of-a-bitch. Anyone who wanted Charlie Feltz or North American to capriciously change anything or add anything ... would first have to fight Crossfield and hence, I hoped, would at least think twice before proposing grand inventions." Crossfield played an essential role, for instance, in convincing the Air Force that an encapsulated ejection system was both impractical and unnecessary. His arguments in favor of an ejection seat saved significant money, weight, and development time.[4]

There has been considerable interest over whether Crossfield made the right decision in leaving the NACA since it effectively locked him out of the high-speed, high-altitude portion of the X-15 flight program. Crossfield has no regrets: "... I made the right decision to go to North American. I am an engineer, aerodynamicist, and designer by training ... While I would very much have liked to participate in the flight research program, I am pretty well convinced that I was needed to supply a lot of the impetus that allowed the program to succeed in timeliness, in resources, and in technical return. ... I was on the program for nine years from conception to closing the circle in flight test."[5]

When the contracts with North American had been signed, the X-15 was some three years away from its first flight. Although most of the basic research into materials and structural science had been completed, a great deal of work remained to be accomplished, including the development of fabrication and assembly techniques for Inconel X and the new hot-structure design. North American and its subcontractors eventually spent some 2,000,000 engineering man-hours on the X-15. More than 4,000 test hours were logged in 15 different wind tunnels and provided more than 2 million data points.[6]

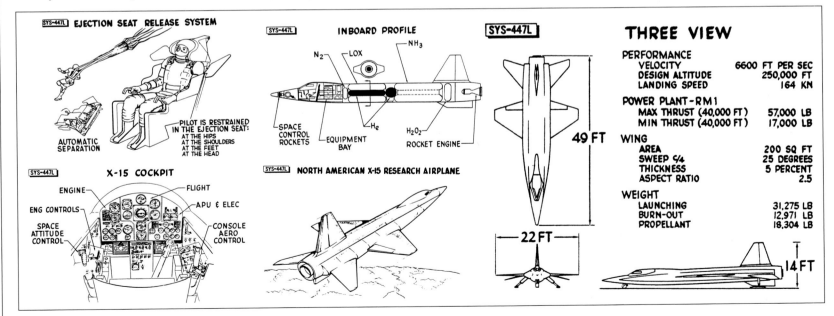

The 1956 Configuration 2 airplane was an interim design between the Configuration 1 described in the proposal and the final airplane. Note the long side tunnels and the high tail, inherited from the original design. Both would change as more wind tunnel tests were run, along with input from the fixed-base simulator. The instrument panel layout was getting close to the as-built design, as were many internal systems. (NASA)

It was never expected that the design proposed by North American would be the one actually built – it seldom works that way even for operational aircraft, let alone research vehicles. True to form, the design evolved substantially over the first year of the program, and a meeting was held on 14-15 November 1955 in Inglewood to resolve several issues. NACA indicated that the minimum design dynamic pressure should be 2,100 psf and that 2,500 psf would be desirable, while North American had proposed only 1,500 psf. A weight increase of slightly over 100 pounds would enable the design to withstand 2,500 psf and the change was approved.[7]

Neither the government nor North American engineers seemed to have any detailed information that would permit a final decision on the materials to be used in such critical structures as the wing leading edge and the speed brakes. Such diverse materials as plastic, fiberglass, titanium carbide, copper, and cermets (ceramic-metallic) were considered for the leading edges, but the only definite conclusion was that North American should investigate the relative advantages of each. Another weight increase of 13 pounds was approved to allow the substitution of an Inconel X sandwich in place of the stainless steel speed brakes proposed by North American, and to provide additional speed brake hinges. It was also agreed that 0.020-inch titanium alloy was a more desirable material for the internal structure of the wings and empennage than the 24S-T aluminum that had been proposed, although the titanium weighed an additional 7 pounds.[8]

One major difference between the Becker study and the design that North American proposed was the use of all-movable horizontal stabilizers that could be operated differentially to provide roll as well as pitch control (the "rolling tail"), resulting in the elimination of separate elevators and ailerons. This had been graded as a "potential risk" during the proposal evaluation, and several of the government evaluators believed that it represented an overly complicated approach. North American had gained considerable experience with the rolling-tail during the design of the YF-107A and, in this instance, the use of differentially-operated surfaces permitted a simpler wing structure and the elimination of the protuberances that would have been necessary if ailerons had been incorporated in the thin airfoil sections of the wings. Although the additional drag of the protuberances was of little concern, they also would have disturbed the airflow and created another heating problem.[9]

The original configuration with a large dorsal vertical stabilizer was shown to be unsatisfactory for the altitude mission when a random-direction 1-inch thrust misalignment was considered. In operational aircraft it was not terribly unusual for an installed engine to be up to a couple of degrees out of perfect alignment; normally this was easily corrected via aerodynamic trim. However, the extreme thrust and velocities of the X-15 made the issue a matter of some concern. This was one of several factors that led to changing the vertical stabilizer configuration. The government and North American also agreed that provisions would have to be made for correcting any potential thrust misalignment. This was the same issue that Douglas had worried about during their D-558-III study.[10]

The fact that the proposed design would probably be sensitive to roll-yaw coupling was also discussed and the acceptable limits were agreed upon. In the area of control systems, the government pointed out that a rate damping (stability augmentation) system in pitch and yaw – and possibly in roll – would most likely be necessary. North American estimated that the dampers would add approximately 125 pounds. The need to make the dampers redundant would be the subject of great debate throughout the development phase and early flight program, with the initial decision being not to. Conferees also decided that a damping system would not be needed in the ballistic control system, something that would change quickly during the flight program.[11]

It was tentatively agreed that the pilot's controls should consist of a conventional center stick, but that the aerodynamic controls should also be operable from a side-stick on the right console and that the ballistic controls would be operated by a second side-stick on the left console. This was one of the first – and the most successful – applications of a side-stick controller. It should be noted that these were mechanical devices, not the electrical side-sticks used in the much-later F-16.[12]

Per a recent service-wide directive, the Air Force had assumed that the X-15 would be equipped with some sort of encapsulated ejection system, but North American proposed an ejection seat instead. The company agreed to document the rationale for this and to provide a seat capable of meaningful ejection throughout most of the expected flight envelope, although all concerned realized that no method offered escape at all speeds and altitudes. After some discussions concerning the relative merits of using other gases, it was agreed that nitrogen would be used for cockpit pressurization.[13]

During the initial design phase, potential surface temperatures were calculated using the heat transfer theories in general use at the time. Most of these theories assumed full turbulent flow on the fuselage, but North American had designed their proposal using laminar flow for most of the flight profile. Extensive wind tunnel tests were conducted in the Unitary Plan tunnel at Langley and also at the Air Force Arnold Engineering Development Center (AEDC) at Tullahoma, Tennessee. These tests provided heat-transfer coefficients that were even higher than the theoretical values, particularly on the lower surface of the fuselage.

Because of these results, North American was directed to modify the design of the X-15 to withstand the higher temperatures. This proved particularly costly in terms of weight and performance; almost 2,000 pounds was added to the empty weight of the airplane by incorporating additional heat-sink material to the airframe. This is when the program changed their advertising; instead of using 6,600 fps as a design goal, the program began talking about Mach 6 – it was obvious to the engineers that the airplane would likely not attain 6,600 fps.

Interestingly, measurements from the flight program indicated that the skin temperatures of the primary structural areas of the fuselage, main wing box, and tail surfaces were actually several hundred degrees less than the values predicted by the modified theory; in fact, they were below predictions using the original theories. But resolving these types of uncertainties were part of the rationale for the X-15 program in the first place.[14]

On 11 June 1956, North American received a production go-ahead for the three X-15 airframes, although metal was not cut for the first aircraft until September. Four days later, on 15 June 1956, the Air Force assigned three serial numbers (56-6670, 56-6671, and 56-6672) to the X-15 program.[15]

The First Industry Conference (1956)

By the beginning of July the NACA felt that sufficient progress had been made on the development of the X-15 to make an industry conference on the project worthwhile and Hugh Dryden invited the Air Force and Navy to participate.[16]

The first Conference on the Progress of the X-15 Project was held at Langley on 25-26 October 1956. There were 313 attendees representing the Air Force, NACA, Navy, various universities and colleges, and most of the major aerospace contractors. Approximately ten percent of those attending were representatives of various Air Force activities, and over half of those were WADC personnel. However, in view of the part that the Air Force had played in evaluating the original design and in the financing and procurement activities, it was surprising that there was absolutely no Air Force participation in the presentations. The majority of the twenty-seven authors who contributed a total of 18 technical papers were from the NACA (16), while the remaining were from North American (9) and Reaction Motors (2). It was evident from the papers that a considerable amount of progress had already been made, but that a few significant problems still lay ahead.[17]

One of the papers summarized the aerodynamic characteristics that had been obtained by tests in eight different wind tunnels at Mach numbers ranging from less than 0.1 to about 6.9. These had investigated the effects of speed brake deflection on drag, the lift-drag relationship of the entire aircraft, of individual components such as the wings and fuselage tunnels, and of combinations of individual components. One of the interesting findings was that almost half of the total lift at high Mach numbers was derived from the fuselage tunnels. Another result was the confirmation of the NACA prediction that the original fuselage tunnels would cause longitudinal instability; for subsequent testing the tunnels had been shortened in the area ahead of the wing, greatly reducing the problem. Still other wind tunnel tests had established the effect of the vertical and horizontal stabilizers on longitudinal, directional, and lateral stability. The results of these tests were used to study the response characteristics of the airplane to determine if a stability augmentation system was needed. Although further studies were undertaken, the ultimate answer was that dampers would be required.[18]

It should be noted that wind tunnel testing was – and still is – an inexact science. For example, small (3- to 4-inch) models of the X-15 were "flown" in the hypervelocity free-flight facility at Ames. The models were made out of cast aluminum, cast bronze, or various plastics, and were actually fairly fragile. Despite this, the goal was to shoot the model out of a gun at tremendous speeds in order to observe shock wave patterns across the shape. As often as not, what researchers saw were pieces of X-15 models flying down the range sideways. Fortunately, enough of the models remained intact to acquire meaningful data.[19]

Other papers presented at the industry conference presented the results of exit and reentry profiles that had been flown using a fixed-base simulator at Langley and North American. Researchers reported that the pilots had found the early configurations nearly uncontrollable without stability augmentation, and that even with dampers the airplane was only marginally stable during some maneuvers. However, a free-flying model program had shown low-speed stability and control to be adequate. Since some aerodynamicists had questioned North American's use of the rolling tail instead of ailerons, the free-flying

In addition to the fixed-base simulators at North American and the FRC, this "Iron Cross" simulator was used to test concepts for the ballistic control system. This is NASA pilot Stanley P. Butchart trying to "fly" the beast. (NASA Dryden)

model had also been used to investigate that feature; the results indicated that the rolling tail would provide the necessary lateral control.[20]

Mockup Inspection

The previous year had resulted in some major changes to the configuration of the X-15. The wing size and shape was basically the same as proposed by North American, but the leading edge radius (along with the radius on the empennage and nose) was increased to satisfy aerodynamic heating concerns. The leading edge was also changed from replaceable fiberglass to a nearly-solid piece of Inconel X, eliminating the removable leading edge concept that was highly prized by

The free-flight facility at NACA Ames attempted to shoot small models of the X-15 out of what was essentially a gun against a rush of incoming air, giving a good approximation of high-speed flight. The odds were against the model surviving the experience, but high-speed cameras captured the shock wave patterns on film for later analysis. (NASA Ames photo A-25194)

These photos of the X-15 mockup were taken the day after the development engineering inspection and show essentially the airplane that was actually manufactured. The side tunnels have been shortened (they now ended just behind the canopy instead of just in front of it), the vertical surfaces have been revised (although the ventral rudder is missing here), and the main landing skids have been relocated to the aft fuselage where they could share the same support structure as the XLR99 engine. There would be some minor revisions, however, like the "bug eye" camera ports behind the cockpit changing shape. (The Boeing Company Archives)

Ames. The final configuration also increased the diameter of the fuselage by about six percent to allow a greater propellant capacity.[21]

The horizontal stabilizer was moved rearward 5.4 inches, the wing moved forward 3.6 inches, and the center of gravity was brought forward 10 inches to improve longitudinal stability. Perhaps the most visible change was increasing the area of the vertical stabilizers from 50 square feet to 75 square feet using full 10-degree wedge airfoils in place of the original double-wedge configuration. The area for the verticals was also redistributed; 55 percent for the dorsal stabilizer and 45 percent for the ventral instead of the original 73/27-percent configuration. In addition, both the dorsal and ventral now had rudders that were nearly symmetrical and operated together; originally only the dorsal had a rudder.[22]

A development engineering inspection of the full-scale mockup was held at the North American Inglewood facility on 12-13 December 1956, although the construction of various subassemblies had already begun. Thirty-four of the 49 individuals who participated in the inspection were representatives of the Air Force; 22 of them from WADC. The inspection committee considered 84 requests for alterations, rejecting 12, and deferring 22 for further study.[23]

The final configuration was tested in a variety of wind tunnels from landing speeds to almost Mach 7. These tests would continue throughout the flight program. (NASA)

Accepted changes included the addition of longitudinal trim indications, relocation of the battery switch, removal of landing gear warning lights, and improved marking for several instruments and controls. Other accepted recommendations concerned improved wiring for the fire detection system, better insulation of sensitive electrical equipment, inclusion of an overheat warning system for the hydrogen peroxide compartments, and the relocation of some of the electrical wiring in order to protect it from hydraulic fluids and to reduce the possibility of damage during the installation and removal of equipment.[24]

Some of the more interesting changes were rejected by the committee. For instance, suggestions were made that the aerodynamic and ballistic controller motions be made similar, that the ballistic controls be made operable by the same controller used for the aerodynamic controls, or that a third controller combining both functions be added to the right console. All were rejected on the grounds that actual flight experience was needed with the controllers already selected before a decision could be made on worthwhile improvements or combinations. The rejection was surprising since two of the three suggestions came from potential X-15 pilots (Iven Kincheloe and Joe Walker).[25]

Simplification of the hydraulic system was ruled out on the basis that there was nothing that could be spared. A request that the pilot be provided with continuous information on the nose-wheel door position (because loss of the door could produce severe structural damage) was rejected because the committee felt that a previously approved suggestion for gear-up inspection panels would make such information unnecessary. This decision would later be regretted when the nose gear door inadvertently opened at high speed, although there was nothing the pilot could have done in any case.[26]

An even more surprising rejection regarded the leading edges. The fact that the leading edges were no longer removable had been disclosed at the 1956 industry conference six week earlier. Nevertheless, Harry Goett from Ames did not agree with the change and asked that the lower flange of the front spar be widened and the ballistic control system roll thrusters moved to the rear of the same spar. He justified these requests on the grounds that the research goals for the X-15 included determining the best materials, shapes, and cooling methods for various leading edges, and that interchangeable leading edges had been a part of the original proposal. In spite of Goett's apparently logical arguments, the committee decided his request could not be approved because North American had already decided to use a solid plate for the lower wing surface and that the required changes would impose a three-pound weight penalty. It seemed to at least one participant that the negative decision on interchangeable leading edges marked the abandonment of a feature that would have considerably enhanced the research value of the X-15.[27]

That 22 change requests were deferred for further study indicated that a number of design features still were unsettled as late as the mockup inspection. Some of these concerned the B-36 carrier aircraft, which was eventually abandoned in favor of a Boeing B-52. Three deferred requests on the escape system required the results of further sled and tunnel tests. A request to move all controls and switches to locations where they could be easily reached from the pilot's normal seated position (even when the pilot was of small stature) received the "further study" classification, but in this case the group authorized such changes as appeared necessary.[28]

After the completion of the development engineering inspection, the X-15 airframe design changed in only relatively minor details.

This is the original XLR11-equipped instrument panel for the X-15-1. The layout reflected the typical analog instrumentation of the 1950s, and was divided into four primary groups: (left to right) propulsion, flight control, secondary propulsion/electrical, and environmental (cockpit). Note the two Mach meters, one going to 3.5 and the other to 4.0. (Boeing via the Gerald H. Balzer Collection)

Continued wind tunnel testing resulted in some external modifications, particularly of the vertical stabilizer, and some weight changes occurred as plans became more definite, but North American essentially built the X-15 described at the industry conference in October and inspected in mockup form during December 1956. The airplane that was being built was identified as "configuration 3" – "configuration 1" was the initial North American proposal, while "configuration 2" was that presented at the 1956 industry conference.

North American designed and built the X-15 ejection seat in-house, a fairly typical activity in the 1950s before the standardization of ejection seats by several dedicated manufacturers. (The Boeing Company Archives)

STRUCTURAL FABRICATION

The X-15 was breaking new ground when it came to structural materials since it had been obvious from the start that its surface would be subjected to very high temperatures. Exotic materials made from the rare elements had not advanced sufficiently to permit quantity production, so the list of candidate materials narrowed to corrosion resistant steels, titanium, and nickel-base alloys.[29]

Although 6A1-4V titanium and AM-350 CRES precipitation-hardened corrosion-resistant steel had good strength efficiencies over a wide temperature range, both alloys tended to fall off rapidly above 800°F. On the other hand, Inconel X had only a gradual drop in strength up to 1,200°F. Because of this stability, Inconel X was chosen for the outer skin for the entire airplane, although it could not be welded after its final heat treatment. Regular Inconel (as opposed to Inconel X) was not heat treatable but could be welded and was used in locations were high strength was not paramount or where final close-out welds were necessary following heat-treatment of the surrounding structures. To accomplish this, Inconel lands were incorporated into Inconel X structures prior to final heat treatment and access hole cover plates made from Inconel were welded to these lands.[30]

The internal structure was made from a variety of materials. High strength aluminum (2024-T4) was used to form the inner pressure shell of the cockpit and part of the instrument bay. Because of high thermal stresses, the internal structure of the wings and fuselage were constructed of titanium. Originally, two titanium alloys were used: 8-Mn, which was the highest strength alloy then available but not recommended for welding, and 5A1-2.5Sn which had acceptable strength and was weldable. Later, a high-strength weldable alloy – 6A1-4V – was introduced in some areas. Titanium framing was used almost exclusively in the aft fuselage structure where high concentrated loads were found. Fusion welding was used predominately, but a limited amount of resistance welding was also used. All critical welds were radiographically inspected to ensure quality.[31]

The material that presented the most problems was probably 5A1-2.5Sn titanium. This material proved to have inconsistent tensile prop-

The first integral propellant tank set in Inglewood. By this point it was beginning to look much like a fuselage, and in fact, the aft engine compartment has already been added. Note the large feed tube coming out of the side of the ammonia tank into the engine compartment. (Boeing via the Gerald H. Balzer Collection)

erties, making it difficult to work with and also exhibited low ductility, notch sensitivity, and had poor surface condition. These problems seemed to exist in both rolled and extruded forms of the metal. Surface condition was probably the most important factor governing the formability of titanium; a poor surface was characterized by oxygen contamination, inclusions, and grind marks. These had to be removed by machining, polishing, or chemical milling prior to final finishing. As a result, titanium extrusions for the X-15 were procured with sufficient material in all dimensions to allow North American to machine all surfaces prior to use. Approximately 0.625-inch of material was generally removed during this cleanup operation.[32]

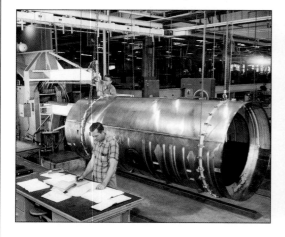

Finding the correct material for the main propellant tanks – especially the liquid oxygen tank – took some investigation. The originally-selected titanium alloy containing 5 percent aluminum and 2.5 percent tin handled the low temperatures well, but did not have the requisite strength at 1,200°F. It was finally decided to make the tanks out of Inconel X. (Boeing via the Gerald H. Balzer Collection)

The forward fuselage assembly of X-15-1 under construction on 8 July 1958. The nose wheel well and ballistic control system nozzles are visible on the nose. The actual nose cone would consist of either the NACA instrumentation boom, or the Northrop-developed ball nose. (Boeing via the Gerald H. Balzer Collection)

The aft fuselage of X-15-1. The side tunnel area is visible on either side of the circular fuselage, and the fixed portion of the dorsal stabilizer is on top. There will be a fuselage extension behind this section to shroud the XLR99 nozzle. The frames in this area absorbed the thrust from the engine as well as the landing loads from the main skids. The men give a good sense of the diameter of the fuselage. (Boeing via the Gerald H. Balzer Collection)

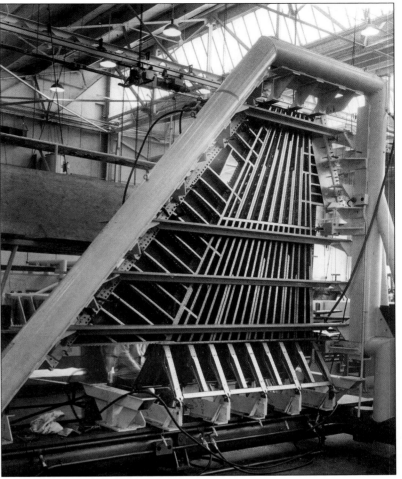

There was not much room inside the wing of the X-15; the hot structure necessary to absorb the heating loads required a great deal of Inconel and titanium. This is the wing destined for X-15-1. (Boeing via the Gerald H. Balzer Collection)

Finding the correct material for the main propellant tanks – especially the liquid oxygen tank – took some investigations. Most steel and common heavy structural alloys gain strength but lose ductility when operated at extremely low temperatures, although Inconel proved to be relatively insensitive to this. The martensitic alloys, such as heat-treated 4130 low alloy steel and AM-350 CRES, followed predictable curves that showed severe ductility loss as the temperature decreased below –100°F. Originally a titanium alloy containing 5 percent aluminum and 2.5 percent tin was selected. This handled the low temperatures well, but did not have the requisite strength at 1,200°F. It was finally decided to make the tanks out of Inconel X.[33]

Inconel X proved to be remarkably easy to work with considering its hardness, although severely-formed parts had to be shaped in multiple stages with annealing accomplished between each stage. Nevertheless, problems arose. One of the first concerned fabricating the large Inconel propellant tank bulkheads. The propellant tanks comprised a large portion of the fuselage, and were composed of an outer cylindrical shell and an inner cylinder. These were joined by Inconel X semi-torus bulkheads at each end of the tank. The bulkheads were formed in two segments with the split located midway between the inner and outer cylinders. The inner torus segment was welded to the inner cylinder, and the outer torus segments were welded to the outer tank; the two assemblies were then joined.[34]

The bulkheads were manufactured from cones that were built-up by welding smaller pieces together, with a complete X-ray inspection of each weld. After the cone was formed to the approximate size, they went through several stages of spinning, with a full anneal performed after each stage. The first spin blocks were made from hardwood; cast iron was used for the final sizing. A problem developed when transverse cracks began appearing while the bulkheads were being spun.[35]

Both North American and the International Nickel Company investigated the cracks, but determined that the initial welds had been nearly perfect and should not have contributed to the problem. Nevertheless, different types of welding wire were tried, and the speed, feed, and pressure of the spinning lathe were varied, but the welds continued to crack. It was finally determined that the welds were – ironically – too good; they needed to be softer. North American developed a new process that resulted in slightly softer, but still acceptable, welds, and the cracking stopped.[36]

Forming the ogive section of the forward fuselage also presented some problems. The engineers decided that the most expedient production method was to make a cone and bulge-form it into the final shape in one operation. The initial cone was made from four pieces of Inconel X welded together, carefully inspected to ensure the quality of the welds. It was placed in a bulge-form die and gas pressure was applied that forced the part to conform to the shape of the die. This process worked well, with one exception. For reasons that were never fully understood, one of the four pieces of Inconel X used for one cone had a tensile strength about 28,000 psi greater than the other parts used. During forming this piece resisted stretching and caused the welds to distort and created wrinkles. The cone was eventually discarded and another one made using four different sheets on Inconel.[37]

There had been a lot of concern about the effects of high temperatures upon the ultimate strength of its structure. A specimen of a fuselage frame at the wing attachment was tested under load at high temperatures in an attempt to better understand the problem. The temperature in the outer skin was 700°F, while the temperature in the inner flange of the frame was −25°F, simulating the cold liquid oxygen tank. The specimen was tested until it failed at a point slightly over the design load. The frame was then repaired and the opposite side tested at room temperature; failure occurred at a load three percent higher than for the temperature test. North American concluded that these tests showed negligible effects of thermal stresses on the failure of the specimen.[38]

Similarly, the wing box structure was tested under load and temperature; a failure at 800°F matched expectations. The box failed in wide flange buckling across the entire surface, but did not collapse and the load supported by the box after failure was nearly the same as at failure. Interestingly, the skin of this box was buckled at the load limit and temperature gradient, but the buckles caused no permanent set. To determine the effect of temperature on the failure, an identical box manufactured for a different test (which was successfully completed without compromising the structure) was tested at room temperature; the failure point was almost identical to the box tested at elevated temperature.[39]

The dorsal rudder for X-15-1; the ventral rudder was substantially similar. The blunt trailing edge of the 10-degree wedge is clearly visible. Unlike the wing, the rudder had a fair amount of internal volume and would host several follow-on experiments later in the program. (Boeing via the Gerald H. Balzer Collection)

The forward fuselage of X-15-3, with the upper instrument compartment cover being removed. Note the bug-eye camera fairings on the cover. The "North American Aviation, Inc." markings would be removed when the airplane was turned over to the government. (Boeing via the Gerald H. Balzer Collection)

Scott Crossfield testing a David Clark Company MC-2 full-pressure suit in an altitude chamber prior to the beginning of X-15 flight operations. This was the first truly workable full-pressure suit developed in the world, and was a tribute to David Clark and Crossfield. A multitude of heat lamps were used to provide a realistic test environment. (The Boeing Company Archives)

ESCAPE SYSTEM

The type of escape system to be used in the X-15 had been the subject of debate since the beginning of the program. The decision to use a stable-seat, full-pressure-suit combination had been a compromise based largely on the fact that the ejection seat was lighter and offered fewer complications than escape capsules. It has also been heavily lobbied for by Scott Crossfield.

Privately, Scott Crossfield had already decided he did not like capsule designs. Part of this came from past experience with the Douglas D-558-II program. According to Crossfield, "We had a capsule nose on the Skyrocket but knew from the wind-tunnel data that if you separated the nose from the fuselage, the g-force would be so great it could kill you. I made up my mind I would never use the Skyrocket capsule. I would ride the ship down and bail out." Later events with a very similar system on the X-2 would prove this fear correct.[40]

A North American analysis of potential accidents that would cause the pilot to abandon the X-15 produced some surprising results. Despite the extreme altitudes and speeds expected, North American determined that 98 percent of potential accidents were likely to occur at dynamic pressures below 1,500 psi, at Mach numbers below 4.0, and altitudes less than 120,000 feet. Using these as criteria, North American investigated four potential escape systems: fuselage-type capsules, cockpit capsules, encapsulated seats, and open ejection seats. The comparison took some 7,000 man-hours to complete. The results were not unexpected: the open ejection seat would impose the fewest performance penalties on the airplane and take the least time to develop. The estimates from North American showed that a capsule design would raise the weight of the airplane from 31,000 pounds to over 40,000 pounds. But just as importantly, North American – and Scott Crossfield, who would be making the first flights in the airplane – believed the ejection seat also offered the best alternative for the pilot in the event of an emergency due mainly to it relative mechanical simplicity.[41]

Despite the report, the Air Force was still not completely convinced. At a meeting held at Wright Field on 2-3 May 1956, the Air Force again pointed out the limitations of ejection seats. In the opinion of one NACA engineer who attended the meeting, the Air Force still strongly favored a capsule partly because of the perceived safety it would offer, but mostly because the use of such a system in the X-15 would provide information for future operational versions. Primarily due to the efforts of Scott Crossfield, the participants finally agreed that because of the "time factor, weight, ignorance about proper capsule design, and the safety features being built into the airplane structure itself, the X-15

A dramatically-posed photo of Scott Crossfield entering the altitude chamber The chamber could only simulate altitudes up to 85,000 feet with a rate of climb of 25,000 feet per minute; neither condition was truly representative of the performance expected of the X-15. (The Boeing Company Archives)

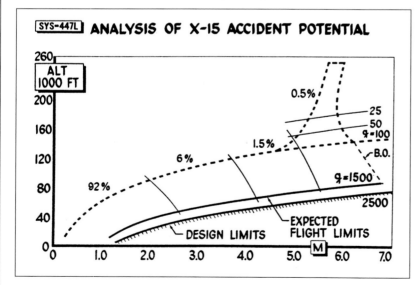

The X-15 escape system being tested on the rocket sled track at Edwards South Base. The sequence begins (top left) with the sled accelerating, the canopy being jettisoned, and the seat rocket engine firing. As soon as the seat clears the fuselage the stabilizing booms deploy. As the seat decelerated to an appropriate speed, the drogue chute deployed, followed by the main chute as the pilot separated from the seat. The seat was never used during the 199 flights. (AFFTC History Office)

was probably its own best capsule." About the only result of the reluctance of the Air Force to endorse an ejection seat was a request that North American yet again document the arguments for the seat.[42]

The first formal cockpit inspection was held during July 1956 in Inglewood and evaluated a fully equipped cockpit mockup, complete with instruments, control sticks, and an ejection seat. The seat was a custom design that featured a new type of pilot restraint harness and

ANALYSIS OF X-15 ACCIDENT POTENTIAL

SYS-447L

North American conducted several analyses of accident potentials, mainly to justify their selection of an ejection seat instead of a capsule design. The conclusion was that 92 percent of the likely accidents requiring escape would happen well below Mach 3 and 80,000 feet. Above those parameters, the pilot would just ride the stricken airplane down to acceptable speeds and altitudes. (NASA)

small stabilizers to "weather-vane" it into the wind blast and prevent tumbling or oscillation. A solid rocket motor provided about 3,000-lbf to ensure the seat cleared the X-15. Despite Air Force policy to the contrary, no objections were raised about the seat. By default, it had finally become part of the official design.[43]

The death of Milburn Apt in the crash of the X-2 on 27 September 1956 renewed apprehension as to the adequacy of the X-15 escape system. However, the accident also weakened the case for an escape capsule. The X-2 had used a semi-encapsulated system where the entire nose of the aircraft, including the cockpit, was blown free of the main fuselage in an emergency. Unfortunately, Bell engineers had expected the pilot to be able to unbuckle his seat straps and manually bail out of the capsule after it separated, something Apt was unable to do. It demonstrated that an encapsulated system was not necessarily the best solution, but then, neither was an ejection seat. Almost by definition, piloting X-planes was – and would remain – a dangerous profession.[44]

THE SECOND INDUSTRY CONFERENCE (1958)

As the first airframe was being completed, the Research Airplane Committee held the second X-15 industry conference at the IAS Building in Los Angeles on 28-29 July 1958. A total of 28 papers were presented by 43 authors: 15 authors came from North American, 14 from Langley, 6 from the High Speed Flight Station, 3 from the WADC, 2 from Ames, and 1 each from the AFFTC, Reaction Motors, and the Naval Aviation Medical Acceleration Laboratory at NADC Johnsville. There were 443 registered participants representing all of the military services and most of the major (and many minor) aerospace contractors. Interestingly, there was no university participation this time.[45]

The 1958 conference began, appropriately, where the 1956 conference had ended. Lawrence P. Greene from North American – who had presented the closing paper at the last conference – gave the technical introduction. Summing up the progress, "it can be positively said that through the efforts of all concerned, the development of the X-15 research system has been successfully completed."[46]

There had been a debate throughout the development program over the load limits of the airplane. North American had originally proposed +5.25/-2-g at 25-percent propellants remaining; the final load limits were set at +4.0/-2.0-g at full gross weight and +7.33/-3.0-g at 30-percent propellants remaining. But the increase came with restrictions. In order not to seriously increase weight, pull-outs at 7.33-g at maximum dynamic pressure could only be made once per reentry. During the maneuver the aircraft slowed appreciable, but heated up rapidly. If another pull-up was required, it had to be accomplished at a lower acceleration (g) or lower dynamic pressure (q) to avoid overheating the airframe.[47]

During mid-1957 the NACA had asked the Air Force to modify the X-15 specification to double the amount of research instrumentation carried by the airplanes. This became a major design driver, and in order to keep the airplane weight (and, hence, performance) from being too seriously degraded, numerous details were redesigned to save weight. The two areas that received the most rework were the propellant system plumbing and the nose gear. This is when Charlie Feltz came up with the idea of keeping the nose-gear strut compressed when it was stowed, allowing a much more compact – and lightweight – installation.[48]

Perhaps the most notable items to come out of the second conference were that the XLR99 was significantly behind schedule and that initial flight testing of the airplane would be undertaken using two interim XLR11-RM-5 engines. Some within the NACA had predicted this event three years earlier.[49]

SIMULATIONS

Simulation in the X-15 program meant much more than pilot training. It was perhaps the first program where the simulators played a major role in the development of the aircraft and its flight profiles. The simulators were used by the engineers and flight planners to determine heating loads, the effects of proposed technical changes, abort scenarios, and a host of other things. In this regard the term "flight planner" at the AFFTC and FRC encompassed a great deal more than somebody who determined launch and landing lakes; it is very possible that the flight planners – such as Robert G. Hoey and Johnny G. Armstrong at the AFFTC, and Elmore J. Adkins, Paul L. Chenoweth, Richard E. Day, Jack L. Kolf, John A. Manke, and Warren S. Wilson at the FRC – knew as much or more about the airplanes as the pilots and flight test engineers.[50]

In late 1956 a fixed-base X-15 simulator was installed at the North American Inglewood facility. This simulator had an X-15 cockpit and control system (called an "iron bird") that included production components such as cables, push rods, bellcranks, hydraulics, and a complete stability augmentation system. The device was controlled via three Electronics Associates PACE 231R analog computers, chosen because no existing digital system was capable of performing the computations in real time. The simulator could also output a real-time solution for temperature at any one of numerous points on the fuselage and wing.[51]

The simulator covered Mach numbers from 0.2 to 7.0 at altitudes from sea level to 1,056,000 feet (200 miles), although it was not capable of providing truly meaningful landing simulations. The initial round of simulations at Inglewood and in the centrifuge at NADC

Hardly a glamorous setting. This was the fixed-base simulator at the Flight Research Center on 10 July 1959. The bank of analog computers necessary to operate the device are along the back wall. (NASA Dryden)

Johnsville showed that the X-15 could reenter from altitudes as high as 550,000 feet as long as everything went well. If done exactly right, a reentry from this altitude would almost simultaneously touch the maximum acceleration limit, the maximum dynamic pressure limit, and the maximum temperature limit – the slightest error in piloting technique would cause one of these to be exceeded, prob-

The simulator at North American was more sophisticated, mainly because it had the "iron bird" rig behind it. This was a complete set of flight-rated hydraulics and electronics that operated identically to the real airplane. The iron bird would be transferred to the Flight Research Center in 1961 and hooked up to the NASA fixed-base simulator. (The Boeing Company Archives)

Bill Dana in the X-15 simulator on 17 August 1966. By this time the computers were on the second floor in what is now the Center Director's office. The iron bird rig still stretches behind the cockpit; the large empty space is where the propellants tanks were on the airplane. Note the lack of a canopy. (NASA Dryden)

ably resulting in the airplane and pilot being lost. An angle of attack of 30 degrees would be required with the speed brakes closed; this could be reduced to 18 degrees with the speed brakes open. The normal load factor reentering from 550,000 feet would reach 7-g,

Joe Walker in the simulator on 10 July 1963. The instrument panels used in the simulator were identical to the airplanes. There were some minor concessions, however, such as the hand grips on top of the instrument panel that made it easier to swap it out for a different configuration when needed. A video camera photographed a paper map on a horizontal plotter and presented the display to the pilot on the large CRT above the instrument panel. (NASA Dryden)

and a longitudinal deceleration of 4-g would last as long as 25 seconds. Simulations in the centrifuge showed that pilots could maintain adequate control during these periods and that the flight envelope was not limited by physiological considerations.[52]

Initially, the North American fixed-base simulator was computation limited, and researchers could only study one flight condition at a time. Later, complete freedom was provided over a limited portion of a mission, and by mid-1957 unlimited freedom was allowed over the complete flight regime. These first simulations indicated the need for a more symmetrical tail to reduce aerodynamic coupling tendencies at low angles of attack and potential thrust misalignment at high velocities and altitudes. This resulted in the change from the vertical stabilizer configuration proposed by North American to the one actually built. Reentry studies indicated that the original rate-feedback-damper configuration was not adequate for the new symmetrical tail, and an additional feedback of yaw rate to roll control (called "yar") was required for stability in the high angle-of-attack range.[53]

As crude as it may seem today, the fixed-base simulator nevertheless provided the program with an excellent tool. It was not unusual for 15-20 hours of simulation to precede each 8-10 minute mission. During the initial envelope expansion program, the simulator operated on predicted X-15 characteristics obtained from wind tunnel tests and theoretical studies. Simulator and actual flight results were then carefully compared, and the simulator modified to reflect the actual performance of the airplane. By July 1958, the fixed-base simulator at North American had already contributed more than 3,500 hours of experience under various flight conditions, including over 2,000 simulated flights.[54]

The Flight Research Center also had an X-15 simulator, but it was not as complete as the one at North American, at least initially. Computation-wise, it was nearly identical and used the same mechanization (programming) as the one in Inglewood. But the FRC did not have an iron-bird, and the original cockpit was decidedly simplistic. This was done as a cost-saving measure since North American was contractually-bound to deliver their simulator (except the computers) before the first airplane was turned over to the government. Because the FRC simulator was not fully operational, the flight planning for the first 20 missions was done in Inglewood. Dick Day and Bob Hoey spent a considerable amount of time during 1959 and 1960 in Inglewood for flight planning and training with the initial cadre of pilots.[55]

The X-15 simulator was the largest analog simulation ever mechanized in the Flight Simulation Facility. Since the FRC simulator did not initially have an iron-bird behind it, many vehicle functions had to be simulated. This ended when North American relocated the iron-bird to the FRC in May 1961 and a full set of flight hardware were connected to the simulator. The control surfaces on the iron-bird were emulated using weighted beams that bore little resemblance to anything on the X-15, but the hydraulics and other components were the real thing.[56]

The simulator was later modified to include a "malfunction generator" that could simulate the failure of 11 different cockpit instruments and 23 different aircraft systems The instruments included pressure airspeed, pressure altimeter, all three axis attitude indicators, dynamic pressure, angle of attack, angle of sideslip, inertial altitude, inertial velocity, and inertial rate of climb. Other systems that could be failed included the engine, ballistic control system, both generators, and any axis in the damper system. Later, the failure of almost any function of the MH-96 adaptive control system could also be simulated.[57]

Contrary to many depictions of flight simulators in movies, the fixed-base simulator for the X-15 was not glamorous. Essentially it consisted of a wall of analog computers and other electronics, a hydraulic source, and cockpit mockup. The iron bird system rig stretched behind the cockpit, but other than in size, did not resemble an X-15 at all. The cockpit was open; the sides of the "fuselage" extended only high enough to provide coverage for the side consoles and other controls inside of it. A canopy was subsequently added over the cockpit since some instruments (particularly for the experiments) were installed there for later flights.

However, unlike most of the previous simulators at the FRC, the X-15 cockpit did have an accurate instrument panel. In fact, experience gained during the program emphasized the need to maintain an accurate representation of the cockpit. On one occasion, the on/off switches for the ballistic control system and the APUs were interchanged between the simulator and the airplane. It was normal procedure for the pilot to turn off the ballistic controls after reentry; as with all flight events, this was practiced in the simulator. When it came time for the actual flight, the pilot found himself reaching for the APU switch instead of the switch he thought was there. Fortunately, he caught himself and avoided an emergency.[58]

When the X-15-3 came on line with a completely different instrument panel arrangement, it presented some problems for the simulator. Since the pilots had to train on the correct instrument panel layout, the simulator support personnel had to swap out instrument panels to accommodate which airplane was being simulated. A crank and pulley lift was installed in the ceiling to assist in making the change, along with cannon plugs for the electrical connections.[59]

Despite the apparent success of the fixed-base simulator, researchers realized its limitations. The fact that it was fixed-base and not motion-base was the primary concern. Because of the unavailability of a high-quality visual presentation, the fixed-base simulator could not be used for landing training, necessitating the need for the F-104 trainers. In addition, the precision needed to calculate data such as altitude and rate of climb for the landing phase was not readily possible with the parameter scaling used for the rest of the flight.[60]

JOHNSVILLE

A notable contribution to flight simulation was also made by the Navy, an otherwise rather silent partner in the X-15 program. A unique ground simulation of the dynamic environment was provided by the Aviation Medical Acceleration Laboratory (AMAL) at the Naval Air Development Center (NADC), Johnsville, Pennsylvania.[61]

The centerpiece of what became AMAL was a $2,381,000 high-performance human centrifuge. Work began in June 1947. The centrifuge carried a pilot in a simulated cockpit contained in a gondola, which could be rotated in two axes, mounted at the end of a 50-foot arm. Continuous control of the two axes in combination with rotation of the arm produced somewhat realistic high-g accelerations for the pilot. On 2 November 1951, Captain J. R. Poppin, the director of AMAL, became the first human tested in the centrifuge during facility validation.[62]

When the facility opened on 17 June 1952 it was the most sophisticated in the world, capable of producing accelerations up to 40-g. The centrifuge arm was driven by a 4,000-horsepower vertical electric motor in the center of the room. A gondola, suspended by a double gimbal system, was at the end of the arm, although many early experiments were conducted with the gondola mounted in intermediate positions along the arm. The outer gimbal permitted rotation of the gondola about an axis tangential to the motion of the centrifuge; the inner gimbal allowed rotation about the axis at right angles to the tangential motion. These two angular motions

The first X-15 in a posed photo during final assembly. The fuselage is substantially complete, but the wings and their associated support structure have not been installed yet. The nose has a NACA instrumentation boom installed. It appears the cockpit is mostly empty at this point. (The Boeing Company Archives)

The Human Centrifuge at NADC Johnsville. A test subject may be seen entering the gondola at the left side of the photo. This remarkable device could easily simulate 40-g accelerations along the main axis. Note the control station in the ceiling at the top right of the photo. (U.S. Navy)

were controlled by separate 75-horsepower motors connected through hydraulic actuators. The centrifuge could produce a radial acceleration of 40-g within 7 seconds.[63]

Initially the centrifuge was electro-mechanically controlled since general-purpose computers did not, for all intents, yet exist. In the centrifuge, the accelerations along the three axes were programmed by use of large masonite discs called cams. A series of cam followers were used to drive potentiometers that generated voltages to control the various hydraulic actuators and electric motors. The cams had a distinct advantage over manual control since they allowed fairly complex motions to be precisely reproduced. However, cutting the masonite discs proved to be somewhat of a problem. Many times cutting the discs amounted to little more than trial and error, and a great many discs had to be produced for each test.[64]

The X-15 represented the most elaborate and extensive use of the cams for centrifuge control. North American defined the acceleration parameters, which were then cut onto the cams at Johnsville. Initially, the tests concentrated on routine flights, measuring the pilot's reactions to the accelerations. Before long, emergency conditions were being programmed into the centrifuge. For instance, one condition was an X-15 returning from a high altitude mission with a failed pitch damper. The concern was whether the pilot could tolerate the accelerations expected under these conditions, which included oscillations between 0-g and 8-g on a cycle of 0.7 seconds. It was found that these conditions represented something near the physiological tolerance of the pilots – even with the best support the engineers could provide, petechiae formed on the hands, feet, and back; in one experiment Scott Crossfield blacked out due to a malfunction in his anti-g suit.[65]

The centrifuge was subsequently modified to incorporate responses to pilot input into the preprogrammed acceleration curves. In an early series of tests, researchers mounted an oscilloscope in front of the pilot and asked him to move the gondola to match a trace on the scope. For the first runs, the pilot used the conventional center stick; later tests used a side-stick controller. The results of these experiments indicated that under extreme conditions

A few frames of a pilot under acceleration in the centrifuge. (U.S. Navy)

the side-stick controller allowed the pilot to maintain better control of the aircraft since his arm was braced against the cockpit side console. Eventually the complexity of the acceleration patterns moved beyond the capabilities of the cam discs, and control was transferred to punched paper tape – something that found widespread use on early computers. During 1957 the centrifuge was connected to the newly-dedicated NADC computer facility, greatly expanding its capabilities.[66]

Eventually a complete X-15 instrument panel was installed in the gondola, with the instruments receiving data from the computer facility to emulate the flight profile being "flown" by the centrifuge. These simulations led to a recommendation to rearrange some of the X-15 cockpit instruments to reduce eye movement. As acceleration increased, the pilot's field of view became narrower; under greyout conditions the pilot could not adequately scan instruments normally in his field of view. Moving a few instruments so that they were closer together allowed the pilot to concentrate on one area of the instrument panel without having to move his head, an often difficult and occasionally impossible task under heavy g-loading.[67]

Certain inadequacies in the X-15 simulation were noted during these initial tests, particularly concerning the computation of aircraft responses at high frequencies, pilot restraints, the lack of simulated speed brakes, and certain control mechanisms. In May 1958 the centrifuge was modified in an attempt to cure these problems, and three additional weeks of X-15 tests were completed on 12 July 1958. During this time the pilots – Neil Armstrong, Scott Crossfield, Iven Kincheloe, Jack McKay, Joe Walker, Al White, and Bob White – and various other personnel, such as Dick Day and Bob Hoey, flew 755 static simulations using the cockpit installed in the gondola but with the centrifuge turned off. The pilots also completed 287 dynamic simulations with the centrifuge in motion. The primary objective was to assess the pilot's ability to make emergency reentries under high dynamic conditions following a damper failure. The results were generally encouraging, and the accelerations on most of these simulated reentries were more severe than those experienced later during actual flights.[68]

A typical centrifuge run for a high altitude mission commenced after the pilot had attained the exit flight path and a speed of Mach 2, and terminated after the pilot had brought the aircraft back to level flight after reentry. During powered flight, the thrust acceleration gradually built up to 4.5-g and the pilot was forced against the seat back. He could keep his feet on the rudder pedals with some effort, and could still reach the instrument panel to operate switches if required. The consequences of thrust misalignment were simulated, so that during powered flight the pilot had to apply aerodynamic control corrections with the right-hand side-stick and the rudder pedals. The pilot attempted to hold zero angle of attack as shown on the instrument panel.[69]

At burnout the acceleration component dropped to zero and the pilot's head came off the back rest. The pilot attempted to hold the aircraft attitude by using the ballistic control system. In the design mission the aircraft would experience less than 0.1-g for about 150 seconds; the centrifuge remained at rest (and 1-g) during this period since there was no way to simulate less than normal gravity.[70]

As the aircraft descended, the pilot actuated the pitch trim knob and the aerodynamic control stick at about 200,000 feet to establish the desired angle of attack. He continued to use the ballistic control system until the aerodynamic controls became effective. As the dynamic pressure built, the pullout acceleration commenced and the centrifuge began to turn. If the speed brakes were closed, the drag deceleration reached about 1-g; with the speed brakes open, this would increase to 2.8-g for the design mission and about 4-g for a reentry from 550,000 feet. The pilot gradually reduced the angle of attack to maintain the designed g-value until the aircraft was level at which time the simulation was stopped. During this period the pilot was also experiencing 5 to 7-g of normal acceleration, so the total g-vector was 6 to 8-g "eyeballs down and forward" – a very undesirable physiological condition. Nevertheless, the centrifuge established that, with proper restraints and anti-g suits the pilot of the X-15 could tolerate the expected accelerations. Pilot tolerance to the oscillating accelerations was unknown prior to this centrifuge program, and this contributed not only to the X-15 but also to Mercury and later space programs.[71]

The X-15 closed-loop program was the forerunner of centrifuges that NASA built at the Ames Research Center and the Manned Spacecraft Center (later the Johnson Space Center). Despite the contributions of the X-15 program, perhaps the most celebrated use of AMAL was the flight simulation training for Project Mercury astronauts, based largely on the experience gained during the X-15 simulations. Beginning in June 1959 the seven Mercury astronauts participated in centrifuge simulations of Atlas booster launches, reentries, and abort conditions ranging up to 18-g (transverse) at NADC Johnsville.[72]

Cost Overruns

It should not have been a surprise, but the original cost estimates for the X-15 and the XLR99 had been hopelessly optimistic. Initial "planning" figures – for everything – totaled $12,200,000. By the time the letter contracts were issued, the airframe was estimated at $38,742,500, with another $9,961,000 for the engine and $1,360,000 for the High Range also being required.

When the final contract was signed with North American, the total cost had already risen to $40,263,709 plus $2,617,075 in fee. By the beginning of 1959, the estimate for three airframes was $64,021,146. During the first six months of 1959 the estimates continued to rise, first to $67,540,178, and then to $68,657,644. By 1 June 1959, North American's informal cost estimate for the airframe had risen to nearly $74,500,000 – almost double what had been in the letter contract. The three airframes ended up costing $23.5 million; the rest represented research and development expenses.[73]

The XLR99 engine program involved even greater relative increases. In 1955, the WADC had been estimated that the engine costs would ultimately be about $6,000,000. The letter contract was for $9,961,000; by the time the final engine contract had been signed, the estimate had already risen to $10,160,030, plus an additional $614,000 for fee. At the end of FY58, engine costs had risen to over $38,000,000 and expenditures during FY59 brought the cost to $59,323,000. Estimated engine costs for FY60 were $9,050,000 – almost as much as the total program estimate of 1955. As of June 1959, the engine costs were $68,373,000 – over five times the original estimate for the entire X-15 program and almost a seven-fold increase over the costs contemplated when the engine contract was signed. Each of the ten "production" engines cost just over $1 million.[74]

While not nearly as bad as the engine, the cost of the stable platform ran over significantly as well. The original contract price was $1,213,518 plus an $85,000 fee. By May 1958 the cost had increased to $2,498,518 and a year later was at $3,234,188 plus $119,888 in fee. The auxiliary power units cost $2.7 million, the ball nose another $600,000, the MH-96 adaptive control system $2.3 million, and over $150,000 for the David Clark full-pressure suits.[75]

During the first five years of development a total of $121.5 million was spent on the X-15 program, not including laboratory and wind tunnel testing at Wright Field, the Arnold Engineering Development Center, NADC Johnsville, and the various NACA/NASA facilities. Together with approximately $11,500,000 for the High Range, it was obvious that the total cost of the X-15 program was going to exceed $150,000,000 before the flight program got underway. When the original development and manufacturing contracts were closed out in FY63 (replaced by sustaining engineering and support contracts), the total came to $162.8 million. By the time it was all over in 1968, this cost would almost double when all operational costs and modifications were included.[76]

One of the early experiments was asking the pilot to "fly" following a trace on the oscilloscope. Later, an X-15 instrument panel and controllers were installed (see photo at right) and the pilots flew representative X-15 missions. (U.S. Navy)

This is how the gondola looked with the X-15 cockpit installed. Note the ballistic side-stick controller on the pilot's left. Most runs were made wearing a David Clark Company full-pressure suit. (U.S. Navy via the Gerald H. Balzer Collection)

The High Range and Dry Lakes

Above: *The X-15 program had wanted to use Groom Lake, Nevada, as both a launch and intermediate lake, but security restrictions surrounding first the U-2, then the A-12 program, prevented that from officially happening. However, some flight plans did have a "blank" emergency lake for the portion of the mission between Delamar and Hidden Hills where it was understood the X-15 pilot could abort to Groom Lake if absolutely necessary. This photo of Groom Lake and its surroundings is from the mid-1980s.* (Tony Landis Collection)

Left: *High Range operations during Flight 1-A-3 on 10 April 1959. The plot boards shown here were state-of-the-art in the late 1950s, long before modern electronic displays were invented. The pens plotted the X-15 radar track on a pre-printed map that had been installed in the plotter before the mission.* (NASA Dryden)

The Mojave Desert – called the high desert because of its altitude – is approximately 100 miles northeast of Los Angeles. One of its most recognizable features is Rogers Dry Lake, a playa – or pluvial lake – that spreads out over 44 square miles, making it the largest such geological formation in the world. Its parched clay and silt surface undergoes a cycle of renewal each year as water from winter rains is swept back and forth by desert winds, smoothing the lakebed out to an almost glass-like flatness.[1]

In September 1933 the Army Air Corps established the Muroc Bombing and Gunnery Range as a training site for squadrons based at nearby March Field. It continued to serve in that capacity until 23 July 1942 when it became the independent Muroc Army Air Field. During World War II the primary mission at Muroc was to provide final combat training for aircrews prior to their deployment overseas, often using a wooden facsimile of a Japanese heavy cruiser – called the *Muroc Maru* – constructed on the lakebed for target practice.[2]

Until the beginning of World War II the Army Air Corps conducted all of its flight testing at Wright Field, but the immense volume created by the war led to a search for a new area to off-load some of the work. After examining a number of locations around the country, the Army Air Forces selected a site along the north shore of Rogers Dry Lake about six miles away from the training base at Muroc.[3]

On 2 October 1942 Bell test pilot Robert Stanley took the XP-59A Airacomet on its maiden flight, the first aircraft to be tested at Muroc. Despite its overall mediocrity, the Airacomet did have its moments – on 15 December 1943 Bell test pilot Jack Woolams established an unofficial U.S. altitude record of 47,600 feet in a YP-59A, the first of many records that would be set in the high desert. In early 1944 the Lockheed XP-80 Shooting Star began flight tests at Muroc, and the area would forever become synonymous with the cutting edge of flight research in the United States. Chuck Yeager's first supersonic flight in the Bell XS-1 would further cement that standing. In December 1949 Muroc was renamed in honor of Captain Glen W. Edwards, who was killed in the crash of a Northrop YB-49 flying wing on 4 June 1948.[4]

The Air Force Flight Test Center (AFFTC) was activated at Edwards on 25 June 1951 and a $120 million master plan included relocating the entire base two miles west of the original South Base location and the construction of a 15,000-foot concrete runway. With the increased number of flight test programs being conducted, the natural surfaces of

The Muroc Maru *was used for bombing practice during World War II; note the* North American B-25 Mitchell *making a low pass over the wooden facsimile on 4 October 1944.* (AFFTC History Office)

Rogers and Rosamond dry lakebeds took on even greater importance as routine and emergency landing sites. The first AFFTC commander, General Albert Boyd would later comment that the lakes were nothing less than "God's gift to the U.S. Air Force."[5]

THE FLIGHT RESEARCH CENTER

On 30 September 1946 Walter C. Williams and four others from Langley arrived at the Muroc to prepare for the NACA role in the XS-1 program. At the time, the assignment was considered temporary, and the group called itself the NACA Muroc Flight Test Unit. The conditions were, to say the least, primitive with no proper office space or quarters. Nevertheless, this was the beginning of the joint research airplane programs in which the X-15 would eventually play such an important part.[6]

The same day that Iven Kincheloe first flew the X-2 above 100,000 feet – 7 September 1947 – the NACA Muroc Flight Test Unit received permanent status from Hugh Dryden. Unsurprisingly, Walt

Three photos from the Flight Research Center's past. At left is the entire staff in front of the original building on South Base in 1950. In the center is the ground breaking ceremony for the facility on the new Main Base on a windy 27 January 1953. Left to right: Gerald Truszynski (Head of Instrumentation Division), Joseph Vensel (Head of the Operations Branch), Walter Williams (Chief of the Station) scooping the first shovel full of dirt, Marion Kent (Head of Personnel), and California state official Arthur Samet. Truszynski, Vensel, and Williams would all play crucial roles in the X-15. At the right is the entire staff of the HSFS in front of the new Building 4800 in 1954. This building would also house the X-15 control room, and still serves as the headquarters for NASA Dryden. (NASA Dryden)

Aerial view of Flight Research Center on 9 October 1962. The NB-52B is parked at the left, and an X-15 and JF-104 on the main ramp area at the right; another F-104 is at the bottom of the photograph. Building 4800 is between the two hangars with the NASA-1 control room located in the highest part of the building. The main Air Force ramp is located a couple of miles along the taxi way at the bottom left. (NASA Dryden)

Williams was named as head of the unit that now numbered 27 people. By the time the unit was redesignated the High-Speed Flight Research Station (HSFRS) on 14 November 1949, roughly 100 people worked for the NACA at Edwards, and Williams was named Chief of the Station. In February 1953 the Air Force formally leased 175 acres to NASA for a permanent installation.[7]

On 26 June 1954 the now-200-strong NACA contingent moved from their primitive quarters on South Base to a new headquarters, located in Building 4800 on the north side of the new Edwards flight line. This building still serves as the core of the Dryden Flight Research Center (DFRC). The new facility was built at a cost of $3.8 million – its first major modifications would come to support the X-15 program. In contrast to the tiny NACA station, the Air Force contingent at Edwards numbered over 8,000 personnel.[8]

The first of the aircraft that would fell all subsequent records – Mach numbers 4, 5, and 6 – arrived at the HSFS on 15 October 1958. Originated and nurtured by the NACA, it is ironic that two weeks before it arrived Doll Matay and John Hedgepeth put a ladder up in front of Building 4800 and took down the winged NACA emblem from over the entrance door. On 1 October 1958, the National Aeronautics and Space Administration (NASA) came into existence so that the United States could better compete in the "space race." Acknowledging the new role the HSFS would play with the X-15, on 27 September 1959 NASA Headquarters redesignated the facility the Flight Research Center (FRC).[9]

By this time Williams was gone. At the behest of Hugh Dryden, on 14 September 1959 he had joined Project Mercury as its operations director. In his place came Paul F. Bikle, a Pennsylvanian with long experience in flight test at Wright Field and the nearby AFFTC. Bikle replaced Williams on 15 September 1959, oversaw the transition to the Flight Research Center, and remained for the next 12 years. Bikle believed in doing things quietly and with a minimum of fuss and outside attention. "Under Paul Bikle," one engineer recalled, "we were well aware that headquarters was 3,000 miles away."[10]

THE HIGH RANGE

As early as 7 April 1955 Brigadier General Benjamin Kelsey wrote to Hugh Dryden – both were members of the Research Airplane Committee – requesting that an understanding be reached on the construction and operation of a new range to support the X-15 program. At a meeting of the Research Airplane Committee on 17 May 1955, the NACA agreed to cooperate with WADC and the AFFTC in planning the range – the Air Force was to be given the task of building and equipping it, and the NACA would operate the range after its completion. It was much the same agreement that governed the X-15 itself.[11]

The requirements were largely determined by the HSFS instrumentation staff under Gerald M. Truszynski. In November 1955 Truszynski informed the Research Airplane Committee that the range should be at least 400 miles long, with three radar and telemetry stations along a "reasonably straight course" back to Edwards. Besides the technical issues, many other factors determined where the range and its associated ground facilities would be located. Obviously, it would not be feasible to have the X-15 fly over any major metropolitan areas, at least not routinely. Avoiding commercial airline corridors would make flight planning easier; avoiding mountains would make the pilots happier. Ground stations needed proper "look angles" so that at least one of them could "see" the X-15 at all times. Emergency landing sites had to be spaced so that the X-15 was always within gliding distance of one of them. The parameters seemed endless.[12]

Truszynski and his staff concluded that the best course lay on a line from Wendover, Utah, to Edwards, with tracking stations near Ely and Beatty, Nevada, and at Edwards. The range would take the X-15 over some of the most beautiful, rugged, and desolate terrain in the Western Hemisphere. This led to construction of the High Altitude Continuous Tracking Range – generally known simply as the High Range. Officially, the effort was Project 1876 and the design and construction was accomplished by the Electronic Engineering Company (EECo) of Los Angeles under a contract awarded on 9 March 1956.[13]

Despite the hopelessly optimistic original budget of $1,500,000, the three tracking stations did not come cheap – the more-sophisticated Edwards station cost $4,244,000; the other two together cost about the same. The Air Force spent another $3.3 million on initial High Range construction; the NACA would spend a similar amount for improvements over the first few years of operations.[14]

Although the basic configuration of the High Range had been developed by Truszynski and his staff at the HSFS, it was still up to the Electronic Engineering Company – with the advice and consent of the government – to select the actual sites for the tracking stations. Since the HSFS staff had already made rough site selections, the next step was developing a radar coverage map. The range that a target can be "seen" by a radar at a specified altitude is limited by considerations

The NASA Gooney Bird was a workhorse on the range, transporting men and supplies to the uprange stations as well as conducting lake surveys. Here the R4D is shown at Yelland Field in Ely on 30 December 1961. (NASA Dryden)

such as obstructions on the horizon, the curvature of the Earth, and the maximum range of the radar. Tracking at low level is more difficult than at high altitudes because of the look angles, obstructions, and ground clutter. This map narrowed down the area that EECo needed to investigate in detail. Next came a lot of field work.[15]

Preliminary investigations by AFFTC, NACA, and EECo personnel indicated a possible site called VABM 8002 located 1.5 miles northwest of Ely, Nevada. The number referred to the site's elevation – 8,002 feet above sea level. Measurements and photographs from this site taken by EECo personnel showed that it would not provide the required radar sight lines because of an extremely wide and high blockage angle almost directly down-range. In addition, constructing an access road would have required a "considerable amount" of rock blasting. The site was ruled out.[16]

An alternate site in Ely was found on Rib Hill. This 8,062-foot high location was a considerable improvement over VABM 8002 in regard

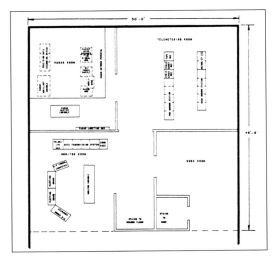

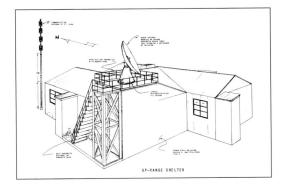

The preliminary plans for the High Range facilities. At left is the Edwards Station (NASA-1) control room. The center shows a generic plan for each of the uprange stations, although neither would actually adhere exactly to this layout due to site-unique tailoring. At the right is an artist concept of the uprange stations showing the Mod II radar antenna on top of the shelter. (EECo)

The High Range station at Ely, Nevada, on 30 December 1961, with snow on the ground. The main building is at the top and housed the radar and telemetry equipment, as well as basic accommodations for the staff. The building at the bottom of the photo housed the electrical generators. (NASA Dryden)

No snow at Beatty, Nevada, also on 30 December 1961. A large microwave antenna sits on the ground facing the photographer, and a water tank is at the extreme left. Both uprange stations generated their own power and used water trucked in from the neighboring community. (NASA Dryden)

to radar sight lines and the ability to build a road and construct the site itself. The downside was that the site was adjacent to the Ruth Copper Pit, and the Kennecott Copper Corporation was already planning to extend the operation into the side of Rib Hill. Even if the hill went untouched, the mining operation would have created too much earth movement for a precision radar installation.[17]

Fortunately, while investigating the Rib Hill site, EECo personnel ventured to the South Ridge of the Rib Hill Range. This site was very promising since the radar sight lines were excellent. A detailed land survey was conducted by the civil engineering firm of F. W. Millard and Son, mapping out the best location of the buildings and the access road. The site was ten miles southeast of Ely and only seven miles from U.S. Highway 50. The Ely Airport, which was a scheduled stop of several commercial airlines, was 5 miles east of the town. There were some drawbacks, however. Power could be purchased from the Kennecott Copper Company, but an evaluation of the mining company's generators showed that the current could fluctuate ±10 percent, which was considered unacceptable for the site. Voltage regulators and power lines were estimated to cost more than procuring primary and backup generators. Also, there was no water available at the site, so water would be hauled by tank trailer from Ely and stored in a tank at the site.[18]

The site at Beatty was somewhat easier to locate. Preliminary investigations by the AFFTC and NACA resulted in the selection of a location approximately 6 miles northwest of Springdale, Nevada. Further investigation by EECo personnel substantiated this selection. The site was at an elevation of 4,900 feet, approximately 3 miles west of U.S. Highway 95 and radar sight lines were excellent. No commercial power or water was available so diesel generators were again select-

ed. Water (at no cost, initially) from the Beatty City Water Supply would be trucked to the site and stored.[19]

The third site was the easiest – an extension would be added to the back of the third floor of Building 4800 at the High Speed Flight Station. The construction would extend the building towards the airfield ramp from the existing flight control room. The addition was dived into four roughly equal sized rooms: a monitor room with plotting boards, a radar room, a telemetry and communications room, and a utility/work area. No plumbing was required since the existing building housed adequate restroom facilities and dark rooms.[20]

The radar equipment ultimately selected for the High Range was a modification of equipment already used by the Air Force on the Atlantic Missile Range. The radars were World War II vintage S-band SCR-584 units modified to improve their azimuth, elevation, and range accuracy. The three Model II radars (generally called Mod II) had two selectable range settings – 768,000 yards (436 miles) and 384,000 yards (218 miles). Through the use of a unique (for the period) range-phasing system, two or more Mod II radars could simultaneously track the same target without mutual interference.[21]

Each of the three tracking sites had a "local" plotting board that showed the position of the X-15 as reported by its local radar; the station at Edwards also had a "master" board that correlated all of the results and plotted the vehicle along the entire trajectory. The local boards at each site could alternately display parallax-corrected data from another station. It is interesting to note that the technology of the day did not allow the parallax from the Ely station to be corrected digitally at Edwards since the results would cause the data receiver register to overflow (i.e., the resulting number would be too large for the available space). Since the parallax had to be corrected before the data was displayed on the master plotting board, engineers devised a method to alter the analog voltage signals at the input to the polar-to-Cartesian coordinate converter; it was an innovative solution to a technological limitation.[22]

The X-15 made extensive (for the time) use of telemetry data from the vehicle to the ground. As originally installed, the telemetry was a standard pulse duration modulation (PDM) system capable of receiving up to 90 channels of information in the FM band. A servo-driven helical antenna was located at each range station to receive the data. The antenna was slaved to the radar to track the vehicle, although it could also be positioned manually with a hand crank. The information was recorded onto magnetic tape, and immediately after each flight the receiving station processed the recorded information onto strip chart recorders. Alternately, the data could be processed by the Project Datum system at Edwards. At the very end of the flight program, the X-15-3 received a modern PCM telemetry system, and Ely and the FRC were modified to process the data.[23]

Each of the range stations contained two AN/GRC-27 UHF transmitters and receivers (one of each was a spare) and a special communication amplifier and switching unit. When a transmitter was keyed at any location, all three stations transmitted the same information simultaneously. The receivers at all three stations fed their outputs onto a telephone line and, regardless of which station received the information, it could be heard at all stations. Dedicated station-to-station communications links were also installed.[24]

The development of the UHF communications system presented something of a challenge. The problem was that the airborne receiver would most likely experience some sort of "audible beat or tone" interference since all three stations transmitted the same data simultaneously. The solution to this heterodyne interference problem was to offset each transmitter frequency by a small amount, but not enough to drift outside the frequency bandwidth of the receiver. It was also determined that each transmitter should be offset by an unequal amount to avoid creating a noticeable "beat" in the audio.[25]

Since all three transmitters were modulated simultaneously by a microphone at any one of the stations, the signal arrived at the aircraft at slightly different times because of differing distances from the station to the aircraft. In addition, signals originating on the aircraft would take slightly differing times to reach each of the ground stations. Given that the signals travel at the speed of light (186,000 miles per second), the time differences for actual transmissions were small (a maximum of approximately 4 milliseconds). There was a slightly longer delay encountered in sending the keying signals between stations, resulting in a total delay of about 12 milliseconds between the two outermost sites (Edwards and Ely).[26]

In the course of determining solutions to the various communications challenges, EECo engineers discovered that they were not the first to confront the issues. Commercial airlines had been using similar systems (except operating in VHF instead of UHF) for approximately five years. The airlines had installed communications networks under their frequently traveled routes to allow aircraft to be in constant touch with their home offices. Each of these networks was composed of several transmitter-receiver sets that contained between two and six stations tied together by a transmission link. The transmitters in a particular group were keyed simultaneously and were set up to operate with a slight offset in carrier frequency. Several groups made up a complete network.[27]

In order to evaluate a working communications system of this type before building the High Range, EECo arranged for a demonstration using one of the airline VHF networks. The particular group chosen ran in a line between Oceanside near San Diego, to San Francisco, California. Six transmitters were spread along the route. The NACA

A calm NASA-1 control room during Flight 2-29-50 on 28 September 1962. Radar data was processed by analog systems and displayed on the large plot board in the center of the photograph. (NASA Dryden)

This was the Mod II radar control console on the same flight. No large flat-panel displays, just a couple of small CRTs to monitor the progress of the world's fastest airplane. Graphical data was displayed on the plotting boards. (NASA Dryden)

The plot boards actually worked quite well, as long as everything went according to plan. The paper map was preprinted and pens traced the course and altitude shown by radar and telemetry data directly onto the map. This was Flight 2-A-32 on 20 June 1961. (NASA Dryden)

The staff does not look too happy during the aborted flight (2-A-32) on 20 June 1961. Most of the telemetry data was displayed on either strip charts (not shown here) or analog instruments on the various consoles. Although crude by today's standards, this was the ultimate 1960s hi-tech. (NASA Dryden)

flew a Boeing B-47 Stratojet from Los Angeles to San Francisco at an altitude of 15,000 feet, returning to Los Angeles at 40,000 feet. The pilot made contact with the ground at ten minute intervals. Air Force, NACA, and EECo representatives were located at the Los Angeles

The NASA-1 control room during Flight 3-55-82 on 31 September 1966. The facility was getting a little more hi-tech, with a radar repeater located in the center along the back wall. Still, the large plot boards may still be seen, along with the rotary-dial telephones. (NASA Dryden)

International Airport to monitor the two-way communications, which were also recorded on the ground and in the B-47.[28]

The ground network being evaluated was conceptually similar to the one planned for the High Range. The network spanned a distance of 400 miles, but used six stations (instead of the three planned for the High Range) in order to provide communications down to 1,000-feet altitude. Coverage for the High Range was primarily above 7,000 feet, and one of the goals of the evaluation was to determine how the concept worked at high altitudes. On the return flight at 40,000 feet, it was likely that the B-47 received signals from all six ground stations, and that all six ground stations received signals from the aircraft. Thus, potential interference was even greater than with the three-station network planned for the High Range. The only effect noted during the evaluation was a flutter or warble at certain positions in the flight path. The recorded tapes were played at Edwards for numerous pilots and ground personnel, and nobody noted any serious objections. This validated the concept and EECo began procurement activities for the radios, switching units, etc.[29]

The High Range underwent a series of modifications over the years. For instance, the Mod II radar at Ely was replaced with an improved Reeves Instrument Corporation MPS-19C unit that became operational on 2 May 1967. The MPS-19 had been built as an S-band unit, but was modified it to operate in C-band and also updated with a one megawatt transmitter to improve its skin tracking capabilities. A similar radar was subsequently installed at the Flight Research Center. Also in early 1967 the microwave relay system from Ely to Edwards was upgraded to handle the higher bandwidth PCM data that would be transmitted from X-15-3. The first successful test (at 144 Kbs) was on 29 March, and the system successfully supported Flight 3-58-87 on 26 April 1967.[30]

Dry Lakes

Despite having one of the most ideal test locations in the world, the Air Force and NACA could not simply go out and begin conducting X-15 operations. A number of hurdles had to be overcome before the airplane could ever do more than conduct low-speed flights over the Edwards reservation.

It had been recognized early during planning for the X-15 flights that suitable contingency landing locations would be needed in the event of an abort after separation from the B-52 carrier aircraft, or if problems forced the pilot to terminate the mission before reaching Edwards. Since the X-15 was designed to land on dry lake beds, the logical course of action was to identify suitable lake beds along the flight path – in fact, these lake beds had been one of the factors used to determine the route followed by the High Range.

Lakes had to be identified such that the X-15 was always within gliding range of a landing site. The launch point was selected to allow the pilot to glide to a position where a turn could be made to a downwind pattern for the landing. Normally this was about 19 miles from the lakebed runway with the track passing the runway 14 miles abeam. To establish this, a study was performed on the fixed-base simulator to determine the range of the X-15 during both forward glides and making a 180-degree turn and returning along its flight path. The gliding range varied somewhat if the airplane was powered by XLR11s because range potential increased much more slowly, and the altitude versus speed profiles made some difference also.[31]

The first hurdle for the Air Force was to secure the permission from the individuals and several government agencies that owned or controlled the lakebeds. Once this was accomplished, permission had to be given by the Federal Aviation Agency (FAA – it became an Administration later) to conduct flight operations over public land.

Although responsibilities concerning the lakebeds continued throughout the flight program, there were two major and one minor spurts of activities concerning them. The first was, logically enough, just prior to the beginning of the flight program when efforts began to secure the rights to the lakebeds needed for the initial flight tests. The second major undertaking was securing the lakes needed for the higher-speed and higher-altitude flights made possible by the introduction of the XLR99 engine. One final push was made to tailor the set of lakes for the introduction of the X-15A-2 and its external tanks.

Eventually, 10 different launch locations would be used, including eight dry lakes – Cuddeback would support a single launch, Delamar would be used most with 62 launches, Hidden Hills would see 50 launches, Mud hosted 34, Railroad only 2, Rosamond was used for 17,

There was never any doubt that the X-15 would make most of its landings on Rogers Dry Lake, the centerpiece of Edwards AFB. The lake is shown here on 5 June 1967. The Main Base complex is at top center, with the NASA facility at the end of the right side of the L-shaped taxiway near the compass rose. The original South Base is to the left, and North Base is at the far right. The main lakebed runway runs almost horizontally just below the upper edge of the lake. (AFFTC History Office)

Silver for 14, and Smith Ranch for 10. In addition, 8 flights were flown from the Palmdale VOR (OMNI) and a single flight was launched over the outskirts of Lancaster. The abortive 200th flight was usually scheduled for Hidden Hills. The vast majority of these flights – 188 – would land on Rogers Dry Lake. Two would land at Cuddeback, one at Delamar, four at Mud, one at Rosamond, one at Silver, and one at Smith Ranch; the X-15-3 broke up in flight and did not land on its last flight.[32]

Beginning in early 1957, AFFTC, NACA, and North American personnel conducted numerous evaluations of various dry lakes along the High Range route to determine which were suitable for X-15 contingency landings. Ten dry lakes, spaced 30 to 50 miles apart, were needed for initial X-15 use; five as emergency landing sites near launch locations and five as contingency landing sites.[33]

Rosamond Dry Lake, several miles southwest of Rogers, offered 21 square miles of smooth flat surface that was also used for routine flight test operations and for emergency landings. This dry lakebed had served as the launch point for many of the early rocket planes at Edwards. It is also the lakebed that most visitors to Edwards see first since the road from Rosamond (and Highway 14) to Edwards crosses the northern tip of the lakebed on its way to the Edwards main base area. The X-15 glide flight would be made over Rosamond Dry Lake, as would the first two dozen powered flights (plus several later ones). No particular permission was necessary to use Rosamond since the lakebed was completely within the restricted airspace that made up the Edwards AFB complex. Unfortunately, the lake did not allow much opportunity for high-speed work.

The processes to obtain permission to use the various lakebeds outside the Edwards complex were as diverse as the locations themselves. For instance, permission to use approximately 2,560 acres of land at Cuddeback Dry Lake as an emergency landing location was sought beginning in early-1957. The lake was within the land area reserved for use by George AFB, California – however, the lake itself was controlled by the Department of the Interior. Since the Air Force could not acquire land directly, officials at the AFFTC contacted the Los Angeles District of the Army Corps of Engineers, only to find out that George AFB had recently requested that the land be withdrawn from the public domain for use as an emergency landing site for their operations. The district had written a letter on 17 May 1957 to the Bureau of Land Management on behalf of the Secretary of the Air Force requesting a special land-use permit be granted for Air Force operations at the lake.[34]

By the end of July 1959, the Bureau of Land Management had approved the special-use permit that gave George AFB landing rights for several years, and also permitted the lakebed to be marked as needed to support flight operations. The Corps of Engineers – very intelligently – decided that any joint-use agreement between the AFFTC and George was an internal Air Force affair and bowed out of the process. Although there seemed to be no particular disagreement, the joint-use agreement had a fairly long gestation period. The final arrangement with George AFB essentially stated that the AFFTC was responsible for any unique preparations and marking of the lakebed required to support X-15 operations, although George offered to supply some emergency equipment and personnel as-needed.[35]

At the same time the request for Cuddeback was issued, a similar request for Jakes Lake and Mud Lake, both in Nevada, was also generated. The AFFTC was requesting approximately 2,500 acres of land in the public domain at Jakes Lake and 3,088 acres at Mud Lake. The requested indefinite-term special-use permits included the right to install fencing to keep cattle from grazing in certain areas; this would require modifying agreements with various ranchers that had already been granted grazing rights to the public domain land, plus compen-

Ballarat Lake, California on 14 June 1968 taken from 22,000 feet altitude. The marked runway had a heading of 15/33, was 2.4 miles long, and was at an altitude of 1,000 feet. (AFFTC History Office)

Cuddeback Lake, California on 14 June 1968 taken from an altitude of 22,600 feet. The marked runway had a heading of 01/19, was 3.0 miles long, and was at an altitude of 2,600 feet. (AFFTC History Office)

sating them using Air Force funds. This was proposed instead of trying to remove the land from the public domain because it appeared easier and less disruptive. In addition, the AFFTC wanted to use approximately 9,262 acres of land at Mud Lake that had already been withdrawn from the public domain for use as part of the Las Vegas Bombing and Gunnery Range.[36]

These two areas were under the purview of the Army Corps of Engineers Sacramento District. The district began the process by preparing Real Estate Requirements Estimates for the two lakes detailing the anticipated costs and these were forwarded to the ARDC Headquarters on 15 October 1957 for funding. By the end of January 1958, however, Lieutenant Colonel Donald J. Iddins at the AFFTC began to worry that the process was taking too long – the lakes were expected to be needed in July 1959, and no final action had been initiated. Part of the problem was that land actions involving over 5,000 acres (which the two requests together did) required the approval of the Armed Services Committees of Congress. The AFFTC reminded the Chief of Engineers that they did not want to remove the land from the public domain, which seemingly eliminated the need for Congressional approval. The result was a renewed effort to ensure all three lakes (Cuddeback, Jakes, and Mud) were available for X-15 use on schedule, including the right to build roads to the lakes, marking approach and landing areas, and fencing certain areas if necessary to ensure the safety of the X-15.[37]

On 14 February 1958 the Chief of Engineers responded that he had initiated the process to grant special-use permits, but had terminated the effort when he noted that the AFFTC wanted to fence off the land. The law did not permit fencing to be erected on special-use permitted land, meaning that the land would need to be withdrawn from the public domain after all, else go unfenced. It appears that the answer

to the problem was obtained by the AFFTC agreeing to a reduction in the Mud Lake acquisition to just under 2,500 acres (versus the original 3,088), bringing the total under 5,000 and circumventing Congressional approval. The lands were subsequently withdrawn from the public domain, and some of it was fenced as needed to keep stray cattle from wondering onto the marked runway.[38]

Simply getting access to the lakebeds was not always sufficient. For instance, at Mud Lake, approval had to be obtained from Nellis AFB (which controlled the Las Vegas Bombing and Gunnery Range) and also from the Sandia Corporation, which controlled Restricted Area R-271 as part of the Nevada Test Site nuclear area; Mud Lake was in the extreme northwest corner of R-271. A "Memorandum of Understanding Between the Air Force Flight Test Center and Sandia Corporation" was signed that allowed AFFTC support aircraft to operate in the immediate vicinity of Mud Lake during X-15 flights. Flight schedules needed to be furnished to Sandia one week prior to each anticipated mission and Sandia made a point that it had no radar search capability and could not guarantee that the area was clear of traffic. Sandia also agreed not to schedule any tests within the restricted area that might conflict with X-15 flights.[39]

Originally, the program had wanted to use Groom Lake as a launch site, but the security restrictions in place at "The Ranch" to protect the CIA-Lockheed reconnaissance programs led the AFFTC and NASA to abandon plans to use this location – officials at Nellis suggested Mud Lake as a compromise between the needs of the X-15 and the highly-classified CIA programs.[40]

On 3 November 1958 a team from the AFFTC made a trip to Tonopah, Nevada, to visit Mud Lake for a preliminary study of lakebed conditions and to determine what action would be required to clear areas of the lakebed for use as a landing strip. When the group arrived

Delamar Lake, Nevada, on 14 June 1968 taken from 24,000 feet altitude. The marked runway had a heading of 00/18, was 2.9 miles long, and was at an altitude of 4,000 feet. (AFFTC History Office)

Grapevine Lake, Nevada, on 14 June 1968 taken from an altitude of 24,000 feet. The marked runway had a heading of 01/19, was 2.2 miles long, and was at an altitude of 4,000 feet. (AFFTC History Office)

over the lake, the pilot made several low passes in order to obtain a general knowledge of the various obstructions that might conflict with landing on the lakebed. What the group saw was a general pattern of obstructions running east to west in a straight line across the center of the lakebed. The team landed at the Tonopah airport and proceeded by car the 16 miles to the lake for a closer inspection.[41]

They found that the obstructions down the center of the lake were a series of gunnery-bombing targets that had been used during World War II. Certain areas were littered with practice bombs, wooden stakes, and good-sized rocks that had formed bulls-eyes and "X"s for bombing practice. The targets were in a fairly narrow straight band down the center of the lake from west to east, but the debris was spread over a considerably wider area.

As would be come standard practice on all the lakes, the group dropped an 18-pound steel ball from a height of six feet and measured the diameter of the resulting impression. This gave a good indication of the relative hardness of the surface and its ability to support the weight of the X-15 and other vehicles and aircraft. At the edges of the lake, the ball left impressions of 3.25 inches or so, while towards the center of the lake the impressions were only 2.25 to 3.0 inches in diameter. At the time it was felt that impressions of 3.125 inches or smaller were acceptable. The group did not attempt any systematic approach to conducting the test, assuming that complete checks would be made later. The general surface condition of the lakebed varied from relatively smooth and hard to cracked and soft – although not ideal, the group thought the lakebed would be useable with minor effort.[42]

More lakebed evaluations followed on 13-14 July 1959. A Helio L-28 Super Courier was used by X-15 pilot Bob White and AFFTC Chief of Flight Test Operations Colonel Clarence E. "Bud" Anderson to visit 12 dry lakes along the High Range route. Again, the "imperial ball" was dropped from six feet and the diameter of the resulting impression was measured. By this time the criteria had been changed slightly – a diameter of 3.25 inches was considered acceptable, and anything above 3.5 inches was unacceptable. The survey included an evaluation of the surface hardness, surface smoothness, approximate elevation, the length and direction of possible runways, and obstacles. Anderson remembers that there was "… only one lake where we had to make a full power go-around as we watched the tires sink as we landed." This was one of the first of many surveys that would take AFFTC, NASA, and North American personnel to almost all of the larger dry lakes along the High Range route.[43]

Also on 13 July 1959, a meeting was held at the FAA 4th Region Headquarters in Los Angeles to discuss the use of Silver Lake, California, as a launch site to the X-15, and to seek FAA permission to do so. The FAA claimed jurisdiction under Civil Aeronautics Regulation 60.24, but was anxious to assist the Air Force within the limits of the law. The proposed 100-mile flight path was Silver Lake, Bicycle Lake, Cuddeback and/or Harpers Lake, then on to landing at Rogers. The FAA had no particular problem with the concept, but since their charter was to protect the safety of all users of public airspace, they felt that certain restrictions needed to be in place before approving the flights. Most of the meeting was spent discussing possible operational problems and concerns, then developing limitations or restrictions that mitigated the concerns.[44]

It should be noted that for Silver Lake launches, both the launch and the landing were to be accomplished in restricted airspace called a "test area." Silver Lake was inside Flight Test Area Four, while Edwards was at the center of Flight Test Area One. But the test areas surrounding Edwards were not restricted 24-hours per day, or seven days per week. Most of the time they were open to civilian traffic, and

Hidden Hills Lake, California, on 14 June 1968 taken from 22,000 feet altitude. The marked runway had a heading of 14/32, was 3.0 miles long, and was at an altitude of 2,000 feet. (AFFTC History Office)

Mud Lake, Nevada, on 14 June 1968 taken from an altitude of 35,000 feet. The marked runways had headings of 08/26 and 18/36, were 5.5 miles and 4.6 miles long, respectively, and was at an altitude of 5,000 feet. (AFFTC History Office)

their closure would need to be coordinated with the FAA (the airspace over Edwards was always closed to civilian traffic for obvious reasons). In addition, the flight path from Silver Lake to Edwards would take the X-15 into civilian airspace for brief periods. Future flights using the northern portion of the High Range would also be outside normal test areas. Plans and procedures for the use of that airspace needed to be coordinated with and approved by the FAA.[45]

On 1 September 1959 L. N. Lightbody, the Acting Chief of the General Operations Branch of the Los Angeles office (4th Region) of the FAA wrote to Colonel Roger B. Phelan, Deputy Chief of Staff for Operations at the AFFTC. The letter contained a "certificate of waiver covering the release of the X-15 research vehicle over Silver Lake" subject to some limitations. These were stipulated to ensure "maximum safety not only to your AFFTC personnel and equipment, but also to other users of the immediate airspace." The actual certificate of waiver (form ACA-400) was approved on 1 September 1959 and listed the period of waiver as 1 October 1959 to March 1961. This was subsequently extended to 1 July 1963, and later still through 1969.[46]

The second round of lake acquisitions began when the XLR99 engine came on line. The plan showed that the XLR99 research buildup flights would use Silver Lake and Hidden Hills Lake in California, Mud Lake, Nevada, and Wah Wah Lake in Utah as launch sites. First up was securing the rights to use Hidden Hills Lake, slightly west of the Hidden Hills Ranch airstrip. Simulator studies had confirmed that Hidden Hills would be ideal as an emergency-landing site during the launches for the initial XLR99 flights. The lakebed would serve as a contingency site as the program continued to launch further uprange into Utah.[47]

By early 1961 the X-15 Operations Subcommittee reported that security restrictions concerning Groom Lake seemed to be easing, and everybody agreed that Groom Lake was a preferable landing site to Delamar Lake. As it ended up, although one black project (the U-2) was ending at Groom, another (the A-12) was getting set to begin, and the X-15 program never would obtain permission to use the lakebed on a routine basis, although it was carried as a contingency site and at least some of the X-15 pilots flew approaches in F-104s over the lake.[48]

The X-15A-2 would use drop tanks on the very high-speed flights – something that had not been anticipated when the original X-15 flight program was initiated – and necessitated that additional property rights be acquired. All of this land was in Nevada, most of it owned by the federal government and a great deal of it already out of the public domain.[49]

The tanks were jettisoned at approximately Mach 2.1 and 65,000 feet. After some free-fall, recovery parachutes opened at 15,000 feet and lowered the empty tanks to the ground where they were recovered for further use. Obviously, the tanks could not be allowed to fall onto civilians or their property. The possible impact areas for the tanks were quite large due to possible dispersions in the X-15 flight conditions at the time of tank jettison, and because of unknowns in wind conditions after the parachutes were deployed. The tanks would be recovered by helicopter, then placed on flatbed trucks for the trips back to Edwards.[50]

Despite its increased performance potential, the initial of the acceleration of the X-15A-2 with full external tanks was considerably less than that of the basic X-15. This caused a reevaluation of the emergency lake coverage for flights with external tanks. A parametric simulator study showed that, of the originally-selected launch points, only Mud Lake was suitable for flights using the external tanks. However, since Mud Lake was just 215 miles from Edwards, it was not suitable for the high-speed flights that required more distance. The use of Smith Ranch as a launch point was desirable but, unfortunately, the distance

Rosamond Dry Lake, California, on 14 June 1968 taken from 23,000 feet altitude. This lake at 3,000 feet altitude had a variety of marked runways on it. The main road to Edwards travels across the upper left corner. (AFFTC History Office)

Silver Lake, California, on 14 June 1968 taken from an altitude of 21,000 feet. The marked runway had a heading of 15/33, was 3.2 miles long, and was at an altitude of 1,000 feet. (AFFTC History Office)

between Smith Ranch and Mud Lake was too great for the glide capability of the airplane, which would leave the X-15A-2 without a suitable landing site for a portion of its flight. It was hoped that a usable lake could be found between Smith Ranch and Mud Lake to fill the gap. A survey conducted in May 1965 focused on Edwards Creek Valley Dry Lake, 23 miles northwest of Smith Ranch, as a launch lake.[51]

The use of Edwards Creek Valley as a launch lake allowed the pilot to attempt a straight-in approach at either Smith Ranch or Mud Lake if the engine shut down at a critical time. There was even a small period of time where the pilot could elect to abort to either lake. As it turned out, there never were any launches from Edwards Creek Valley since the X-15A-2 program was terminated at Mach 6.7 instead of proceeding to Mach 8.[52]

Rogers Dry Lake was the designated landing site for all flights. Initially the runways on Rogers were marked in fairly typical fashion, showing left and right extremes, and thresholds on each end. A meeting of the original X-15 pilots was held on 19 October 1960 to establish a standard operational procedure for releasing the ventral stabilizer before landing. North American stated that it should be jettisoned no higher than 800 feet altitude and a speed of 300 knots to ensure it could be recovered in a reusable condition. It was established that if the touchdown point on Runway 18 (the most frequently used) was two miles from the north end, then the ideal jettison queue was when the pilot passed over the railroad tracks located one mile from the end of the runway. The pilots asked Paul Bikle to request that the AFFTC mark all Rogers runways with chevron patterns one mile from each end (to indicate the ventral jettison point), and also two miles down each runway (to indicate the touchdown point). These markings were subsequently adopted for most of the lakebed runways.[53]

The markings on the lakebed were not paint, but a tar-like compound that was laid on top of the soil. The runways were standardized at 300 feet wide, and generally at least 2 miles – and often 3 miles – long. The tar strips outlining the edges of the runways were 8 feet wide. The width of the strips was critical since they provided a major visual reference for the pilot to judge his height; many of the lakebeds were completely smooth and provided no other reference. The chevron patterns were marked at the appropriate places on each lakebed using the same compound. The Air Force was responsible for keeping each of the active lakebeds marked, and new tar was generally laid at least once per year after the rainy season. If the pilots complained the markings were not visible enough during the approaches practiced in the F-104s, the Air Force would remark the runway. Milt Thompson remembered that "over the years, the thickness of the tar strips increased with each new marking until they exceeded 3 or 4 inches in height …"[54]

The FRC was primarily responsible for checking the lakebeds during the course of the flight program. As often as not this involved taking the NASA Gooney Bird and landing on the lakebed where a visual inspection was accomplished – usually by Walter Whiteside riding a motorcycle. If the lakebed appeared damp the R4D would make a low pass and roll its wheels on the surface, making sure not to slow down enough to become stuck. It would then fly a slow pass and observe how far the wheels had sunk in the mud. If the R4D was not available the pilots used a T-33 or whatever other airplane they could get, although obviously the motorcycle could not be carried in these instances. On at least one occasion the pilots (Chuck Yeager and Neil Armstrong) got stuck in the mud when the lakebed turned out to be softer than they had anticipated.[55]

Smith Ranch Lake, Nevada, on 14 June 1968 taken from 35,700 feet altitude. The marked runway had a heading of 03/21, was 4.0 miles long, and was at an altitude of 5,700 feet. (AFFTC History Office)

Three Sisters (West), California, on 14 June 1968 taken from an altitude of 24,000 feet. The marked runway had a heading of 02/20, was 2.5 miles long, and was at an altitude of 3,000 feet. (AFFTC History Office)

Right: *A map of the High Range. At the lower left is the Pacific Ocean and Los Angeles, California; at the upper right is the Bonneville Salt Flats and Wendover, Utah. The three sets of concentric circles show the radar coverage from each of the High Range Mod II radars. The shaded areas around Edwards and Nellis are restricted airspace.* (Artwork by Dennis R. Jenkins)

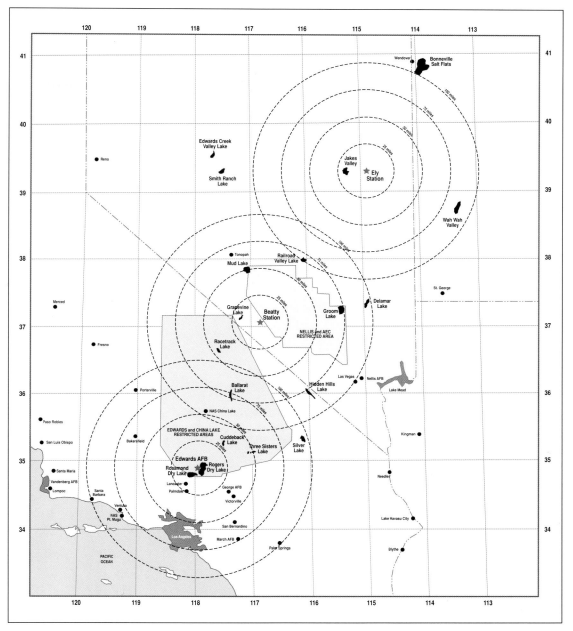

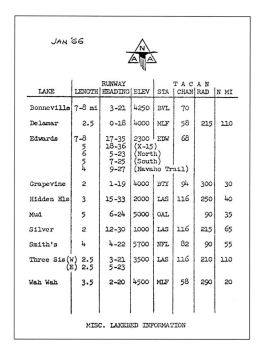

JAN '66

MISC. LAKEBED INFORMATION

LAKE	RUNWAY LENGTH	RUNWAY HEADING	ELEV	STA	TACAN CHAN	RAD	N MI
Bonneville	7-8 mi	3-21	4250	BVL	70		
Delamar	2.5	0-18	4000	MLF	58	215	110
Edwards	7-8	17-35	2300	EDW	68		
	5	18-36	(X-15)				
	6	5-23	(North)				
	5	7-25	(South)				
	4	9-27	(Navaho Trail)				
Grapevine	2	1-19	4000	BTY	94	300	30
Hidden Hls	3	15-33	2000	LAS	116	250	40
Mud	5	6-24	5000	OAL		90	35
Silver	2	12-30	1000	LAS	116	215	65
Smith's	4	4-22	5700	NFL	82	90	55
Three Sis (W)	2.5	3-21	3500	LAS	116	210	110
(E)	2.5	5-23					
Wah Wah	3.5	2-20	4500	MLF	58	290	20

Above: *A typed summary of lakebed information was issued to the pilots. Other sheets in the package showed hand-drawn sketches of the lakes along with their marked runways and some basic information (altitude, headings, etc.)* (The Boeing Company Archives)

The lakebeds and High Range were only part of the story, since none of them would be of much use without people and equipment. The agreement between NASA and the AFFTC provided that the Air Force was responsible for many of the support functions, both at Edwards and the uprange sites. For instance, the Air Force provided fire trucks at the primary emergency lakes for each X-15 flight. These trucks would be ferried to the lakebed aboard Lockheed C-130 Hercules transports before a flight, and back after the X-15 landed. Helicopters – normally H-21s – were also provided at the emergency lakes. Since the High Range radars were not continually manned, the Air Force also had to ferry operators to Ely and Beatty the morning of a flight. Of course, all of these types of services were also provided at Edwards.

Despite the time and effort of locating, acquiring, and marking the launch and intermediate lakes, none of the X-15 pilots had any real desire to land on any of them, although several did. A landing at the launch lake or an intermediate lake was considered to be an emergency, while a landing on Rogers Dry Lake was considered to be normal. Both were deadstick landings, so what was the difference? Milt Thompson summed it up well in his book; Rogers "was where God intended man to land rocket airplanes. It was big. It had many different runways. It was hard. It had no obstructions on any of the many approach paths. It had all of the essential emergency equipment. It was territory that we were intimately familiar with and it had a lot of friendly people waiting there." In other words, it was home.[56]

Carrier and Support Aircraft

Left: *The NT-33A variable-stability trainer was used to train the initial cadre of pilots, and also to demonstrate the innovative – and counter-intuitive – beta-dot technique in flight.* (NASA Dryden)

Below: *The two NB-52s, Balls Eight in the foreground and Balls Three in the back. The NB-52B was preferred for heavy carries or during the summer months because it had water injection on its engines.* (NASA Dryden)

During the ten years of operations at Edwards AFB, five major aircraft were involved in the X-15 flight program. The three North American X-15s were designated X-15-1 (Air Force serial number 56-6670), X-15-2 (56-6671), and X-15-3 (56-6672). The second airplane became the X-15A-2 after it was extensively modified following an accident mid-way through the flight program. The two Boeing carrier aircraft were an NB-52A (52-003 – called Balls Three – and an NB-52B (52-008, Balls Eight); although not identical, they were essentially interchangeable. However, during the proposal effort and early in the program the intent had been to use a Convair B-36 as a carrier aircraft. The B-52 would come later.[1]

CONVAIR B-36

Three of the four competitors had sized their X-15 concepts around using a Convair B-36 as the carrier aircraft. The B-36 would have carried the X-15 partially enclosed in its bomb bays, much like the X-1 and X-2 had been in earlier projects. This arrangement had some advantages; the pilot could move freely between the X-15 and B-36 during climb-out, and the cruise to the launch location. This was extremely advantageous if problems developed that required jettisoning the X-15 prior to launch. The B-36 was also a very large aircraft with more than adequate room for a propellant top-off system (liquid oxygen and ammonia), power sources, communications equipment,

breathing oxygen, and monitoring instruments and controls. Launch would have been at approximately Mach 0.6 at altitudes between 30,000 and 50,000 feet. At the time of the first industry conference in 1956, it was anticipated that a B-36 would be modified beginning in the middle of 1957 and ready for flight tests in October 1958.[2]

During their proposal effort, North American evaluated four different schemes for loading the research airplane into the bomber, generally similar to the other bidders. Using a pit (as had been done on the X-1, and was also done operationally for the FICON program) was quickly dismissed because of a potential "fire hazard and accumulation of fumes." Jacking the carrier aircraft nose gear was eliminated because of "the jockeying necessary to position the research aircraft plus the precarious position of the B-36." The most complicated scheme involved physically removing the vertical stabilizer from the research airplane, sliding the X-15 under the bomber, then reattaching the vertical once the airplane was hoisted into the bomb bay. The potential loss of structural integrity from frequently removing the vertical eventually eliminated this option.[3]

The final solution was called ramp loading, similar to another method used in the FICON program.[4] Loading the X-15 into the carrier began with "running the B-36 main landing gear bogies up on permanent concrete ramps by use of commercially available electric cable hoists attached to the gear struts." The research airplane was then towed under the bomber and hoisted into the bomb bays. The

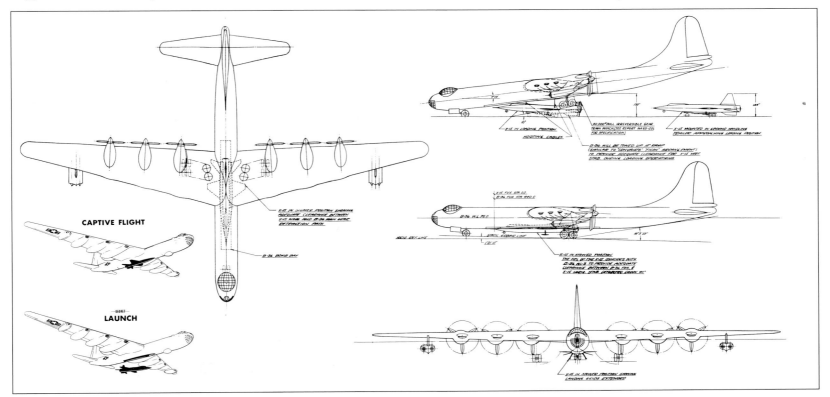

This was how North American showed the B-36 carrier aircraft in their Project 1226 proposal. The basic concept was generally similar to previous X-planes, and also to the FICON program used operationally by the Strategic Air Command. The use of a B-36 would have allowed the X-15 pilot to cruise to the launch lake in the relative comfort of the bomber instead of the confines of the research airplane. On the other hand, the bomber was being phased out of service and would have become a maintenance problem; it was also comparatively slow. (Courtesy of Benjamin F. Guenther)

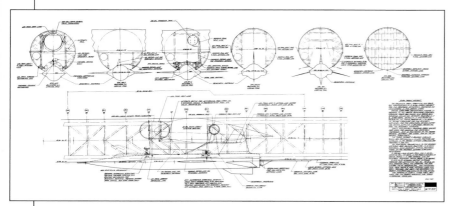

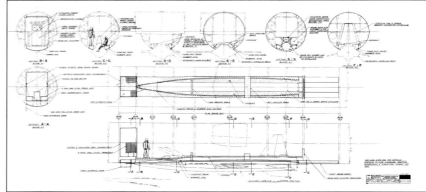

North American put a fair amount of engineering into the B-36 conversion before the effort was cancelled in favor of the B-52 carriers. The liquid oxygen top-off tank was located in front of the wing carry-through structure, with the ammonia top-off tank behind the structure. Both propellants could be vented overboard. A heated compartment was located at the front of the bomb bay, equipped with three seats for the X-15 pilot and his handlers. (Courtesy of Benjamin F. Guenther)

X-15 was suspended from three points: one on either side of the aft fuselage attached to the rear wing spar, and a third on the centerline behind the canopy firmly supported by the structure of the liquid oxygen tank forward bulkhead. The shackles were explosively separated during launch using the same type cartridges used to jettison external fuel tanks on fighter aircraft.[5]

The only major structural modification to the B-36 would be the removal of bulkhead No. 7 which separated bomb bays Nos. 2 and 3, although some minor structural stiffening would be required to compensate.[6] The X-15 would occupy most of the three forward bomb bays and a 9-foot diameter, 6.5-foot long heated compartment was installed in the front of bomb bay No. 1, and equipped with its own entrance hatch on the bottom of the fuselage. The compartment could seat three crewmen and included oxygen and intercomm connections. A 36-inch hatch opened onto catwalks on both sides of the bomb bay that allowed access to the X-15 in flight.[7]

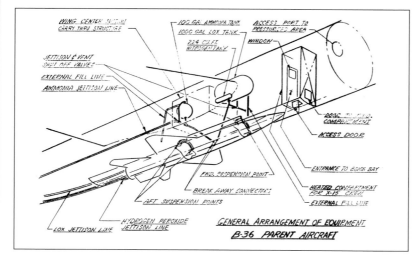

A slightly different perspective shows the location of the major support equipment in the B-36 carrier. (Courtesy of Benjamin F. Guenther)

One of the more interesting suggestions concerning the carrier aircraft was that "a bank of powerful lights be turned on several minutes prior to launching so that the pilot [of the research airplane] will not be blinded by the sudden glare of daylight during launching."[8]

North American initially expected the B-36 to be equipped with a 1,000-gallon liquid oxygen tank and a 100 gallon ammonia tank to allow the research airplane propellants to be topped off. This was surprising since both Bell and Douglas – as well as Reaction Motors – felt that the rate of ammonia boil-off was so slow that no topping-off would be required. Both tanks were suspended above the X-15 in the bomb bay to allow the propellants to be gravity-fed into the airplane. Lines running outside the fuselage to the former tail turret allowed the propellants to be jettisoned and vented as needed.[9]

A REPLACEMENT

In early 1957 – just as North American was preparing to begin modifications on the B-36 – the program began considering replacements for the B-36 for various reasons. There were some concerns that the research airplane would not be as stable as desired during launch because of the relatively slow speed of the B-36. Another reason was that as the weight of the X-15 and its subsystems grew, the Air Force and NACA began to look for ways to recover some of the lost performance; if a faster carrier could be found, it would compensate somewhat for the increase in X-15 weight. Perhaps most vocally, the personnel at Edwards believed that the ten-engine B-36 would be difficult to maintain since it was already being phased out of the Air Force inventory. The experience from the X-1 and X-2 programs showed both programs being delayed by a lack of spare parts and depot maintenance capabilities for the B-29 and B-50 carrier aircraft.[10]

The initial survey of possible B-36 replacements centered on the Convair B-58 Hustler, Boeing KC-135 Stratotanker, and the Boeing B-52 Stratofortress. It is interesting to note that Douglas had apparently chosen the B-52 for their D-558-III study four years earlier.[11]

The supersonic B-58 was considered very attractive from a performance perspective, but looked less attractive from the maintenance and availability standpoint. On 22 January 1957, Neil Armstrong traveled to the Convair plant in Fort Worth to discuss the possibility of using a B-58 to launch the X-15. The first problem was that the 22-foot wingspan and 18-foot tail-span of the X-15 both intersected the plane of the rearward-retracting main gear on the B-58. This would have necessitated moving the entire X-15 forward of the desired location. Convair engineers believed that this might be possible, but it would require designing a new nose gear for the B-58 since the X-15 would block the B-58 nose gear. Another possibility was to beef-up the X-15 nose gear and use it while the pair were mated on the ground. The inboard engine nacelles on the B-58 would likely need to be "toed" outward, or simply moved further out on the wing; either would have necessitated major structural changes. The vertical stabilizer on the X-15 would need to be folded since there was no room for it within the B-58 fuselage without severing a main wing spar. The B-58 was designed to carry a weapons/fuel pod that weighed 30,000 pounds, only slightly less than the X-15. However, the fuel in the pod was supposed to be used prior to the pod being dropped, and the maximum drop weight was only 16,000 pounds; this would necessitate a new series of tests to validate that a heavier object would cleanly separate. However unfortunately, the B-58 was obviously not going to work.[12]

The landing gear configuration on the KC-135 and B-52 precluded the ability to carry the X-15 under the fuselage, as had been the practice on all earlier research programs. Although the performance and availability of the KC-135 made it attractive, nobody could figure out where to carry the research airplane since the Stratotanker had a low-mounted wing and relatively short landing gear. It was quickly dropped from consideration.[13]

The B-52 also offered an excellent performance increment over the B-36, and since the Boeing bomber was still in production, the availability of spare parts and support was assured for the foreseeable future (or, as it turned out, for the next 50 years). The size and location of the bomb bay made it impossible to carry the X-15 there, so other alternatives were investigated. There was a large space on the wing between the fuselage and inboard engine nacelle that could be adapted to carry a pylon – investigations were already under way to install similar pylons on later B-52s to carry air-to-surface missiles. In May 1957 North American was directed to perform an initial feasibility study to determine if the B-52 could be used as an X-15 carrier; the study lasted several weeks, and the results were favorable. At a meet-

This is the standard photo of the wind tunnel tests on the B-52/X-15 combination; note that the X-15 is on the left side of the bomber. Some reports indicate this was done to make the tunnel testing easier, but other sources indicate it was originally planned to hang the X-15 on the left; moving it to the right made servicing of unidentified components easier. Since the mated pair were largely symmetrical, it probably did not matter much one way or the other. (NASA Langley photo GPN-2000-001882)

ing on 18-19 June 1957 the program officially adopted the B-52 as a carrier aircraft. The maintenance and availability issues were also discussed and it was decided to procure two carrier aircraft to ensure the flight program proceeded smoothly. North American was subsequently authorized to modify two B-52s in lieu of the single B-36.[14]

The North American investigations showed that the X-15, as designed, would fit under the wing between the fuselage and inboard engine pylon at an 18-percent semi-span location. The wing structure in this location was capable of supporting up to 50,000 pounds, so the 31,275-pound research airplane did not represent a problem. Nevertheless, this was not the ideal solution – the X-15 pilot would have to be

Many published reports over the years have indicated that the two B-52s were never equipped with armament or other operational systems prior to being used as carrier aircraft. These photos of 52-003 during her time as a defensive systems testbed at Boeing Seattle graphically dispute that. Both aircraft were equipped with defensive systems – including a turret with guns – but do not appear to have been equipped with offensive systems before they were turned over to the X-15 program. (The Boeing Company Archives)

Perhaps one of the most noticeable modification to the B-52s was the "wing notch" that provided clearance for the upper vertical stabilizer of the X-15. The flaps that normally occupied this space were permanently bolted closed and their actuators removed. This is Balls Three on 13 May 1959. (AFFTC History Office)

This is Balls Eight on 8 June 1960. There was only two feet of clearance on each side of the X-15 vertical, and the research airplane pilot had to make sure he did not exceed 20 degrees of bank before dropping at least 2.5 feet to clear the notch. Even this was reduced somewhat with the sharp leading edge rudder carried by X-15-3. (NASA Dryden)

Captain Charles C. Bock, Jr. and Captain John E. "Jack" Allavie prior to the first X-15 glide flight. These pilots would conduct all of the initial evaluations with the NB-52A; there was very little data for no-flaps take-offs and landings of a B-52, so Bock and Allavie would have to make it up as they went along. (AFFTC History Office)

locked in the research airplane prior to takeoff, and the large weight transition when the X-15 was released would provide some interesting control challenges for the B-52.[15]

Lawrence P. Greene the North American chief aerodynamicist wrote, "One item which caused considerable concern in the early evaluation was the fact that in this installation, the pilot could not enter the airplane in flight as had been possible in the B-36. This limitation was of concern from both the fatigue and safety aspects; however, the time from take-off of the B-52 to launching the X-15 is about 1.5 hours, and considerable effort has been expended in plans for making the pilot comfortable during this time. In the event of an emergency, the configuration permits the pilot to eject safely while the X-15 and B-52 are still connected."[16]

Interestingly, initially the X-15 was to be carried under the left wing of the B-52; it was moved to the right wing to "permit easier servicing of the X-15 when installed on the B-52" although exactly what was easier to service was not described. Most of the wind tunnel testing had been conducted with models of the X-15 under the left wing; since both aircraft were largely symmetrical, it was decided that the test results were still valid for the right wing configuration. The initial design also had an anti-buffet fairing that partially shielded the pylon from the airflow, but wind tunnel testing showed that the fairing did not significantly help anything so it was deleted.[17]

The change from a B-36 to a B-52 did not come cheaply – although the basic aircraft was provided at no charge to the program, North American submitted a bill for an additional $2,130,929.06 for the modification of the first B-52; the second airplane cost somewhat less since no wind tunnel testing needed to be accomplished and the engineering was already done.

Of course, the other major external change was the addition of the wing pylon, shown here on 13 May 1959. The pylon supported the X-15, contained the release mechanisms, liquid and gas plumbing, and later in the program a separate liquid nitrogen supply for stable platform cooling. (AFFTC History Office)

BALLS THREE AND BALLS EIGHT

Originally, the Air Force indicated that the two prototype B-52s – the XB-52 and YB-52 – could be made available to the X-15 program. Personnel at Edwards feared that the use of these two non-standard aircraft would result in the same maintenance and parts availability problems they were attempting to avoid. By August 1957 the Strategic Air Command had agreed that an early-production B-52A could be made available, and serial number 52-003 was assigned to the program in October 1957. In May 1958 an early RB-52B (52-008) was also made available. Both aircraft had been involved in isolating problems with the B-52 defensive fire control system and were delivered to North American after completing their test programs.[18]

On 29 November 1957, the B-52A arrived at Air Force Plant 42 in Palmdale, California, after a flight from the Boeing plant in Seattle; it was placed in storage pending modifications. On 4 February 1958, the aircraft was moved into the North American hangar at Plant 42 and modified to support the X-15 program. The aircraft, now designated NB-52A, was flown to Edwards on 14 November 1958 and was subsequently named *The High and Mighty* (the *One* was added later).

The RB-52B arrived in Palmdale for similar modifications on 5 January 1959, and was flown, as an NB-52B, to Edwards on 8 June 1959; the airplane would briefly wear the name *The Challenger*.[19]

Major modifications to the two B-52s consisted of:[20]

- Removal of the No. 3 right wing fuel cell to allow the installation of pylon tie fittings and supports in the front and rear wing spars.
- The inboard flap mechanism on both wings was disconnected, and the flaps were bolted to the flap tracks,. A cutout through the right inboard flap provided clearance for the X-15 vertical stabilizer.
- A pylon was installed between the right inboard engine nacelle and the fuselage. The pylon contained a primary hydraulic and a secondary pneumatic release mechanism.
- Changes to the B-52 avionics included adding an AN/APN-81 Doppler radar system to provide ground speed and drift angle information to the stable platform in the X-15, an auxiliary UHF communications system to provide additional communications channels, and a change in the AN/AIC-10 interphone system to provide an AUX UHF position.
- The fuselage static ports were removed from the right side of the B-52 to allow installation of the forward television camera. The airspeed system was recalibrated to use only the left static ports. This worked surprisingly well, even during sideslip maneuvers, with "no measurable difference" noted.
- Two television cameras were installed in streamline fairings on the right side of the B-52. The rear camera pointed generally forward and was equipped with the zoom lens to allow the launch operator to focus on areas of interest on the rear of the X-15. The forward camera used a fixed-length lens pointed outward and slightly rearward to allow a view of the X-15 forward fuselage. Two monitors were located at the launch operator position, and either could show the view from either camera. Four floodlights and three 16mm motion picture cameras were also installed. Two of these were Millikan DBM-5 high-speed units located in a window on the right side of the fuselage at station 374 and in an astrodome at station 1217. The third was an Urban GSAP gun camera mounted in the pylon pointed downward to show X-15 separation.

- The B-52 forward-body fuel cell was removed to provide space for inspecting and maintaining various fluid and gas lines installed in the wing. The mid-body fuel cell was removed and the fuselage area above the bomb bay reworked to provide space for 15 nitrogen and 9 helium storage cylinders. Early during the flight program a separate liquid nitrogen supply was added to the pylon to cool the stable platform on the X-15.
- Two stainless steel liquid oxygen tanks – a 1,000-gallon "climb" tank and 500-gallon "cruise" tank – were installed in the bomb bay. The tanks were not jettisonable although the contents could be vented through a streamlined jettison line protruding from the forward left side of the bomb bay. Liquid oxygen would be sucked into the right rear landing gear well if the doors were opened while liquids were being jettisoned; this was procedurally restricted.
- A launch operator station replaced the normal ECM compartment located on the upper rear flight deck. After the first flew flights with the X-15-1, an astrodome-type viewing window was added above the forward television camera in case the video system failed; a duplicate set of controls for the liquid oxygen top-off system were located above the window that allowed the launch operator to top off the X-15 while looking out the window. A defrosting system was provided for the window, and two steel straps across the window provided safety for the launch operator in case the window blew out.
- Changes to the B-52 flight deck included the addition of a master launch panel on the lower left side of the main instrument panel, launch indicating lights in the pilot's direct field of vision, a normal launch switch on the left console, and an emergency launch handle below and left of the master launch panel. Changes were also made to the B-52 fuel control panel in both aircraft to reflect the removal of the fuel cells and eliminate the external tank position on the NB-52B.
- Breathing oxygen was made available to the B-52 crew members at all times. Also, oxygen was tapped from the B-52 oxygen system to supply the research pilot with breathing oxygen until flight release.
- A high speed wheel, tire, and braking system was installed since the original landing gear was only rated to 174 knots. The new system incorporated an adequate margin for no-flap take-offs and landings at heavy weights, and was rated to 218 knots.
- Removal of all military systems including the tail turret and defensive fire control system. The ability to carry the reconnaissance pod on the RB-52B was also deleted.
- Later in the flight program, additional instrumentation was added to the launch operator position to allow monitoring the MH-96 adaptive flight control system and X-20 inertial flight data system. A "stable platform control and monitoring unit" was added to the NB-52B that allowed the launch operator to monitor and control the stable platform during captive-carries of the pod-mounted system used for post-maintenance validation.

These changes differed somewhat from those initially proposed for the NB-52. For instance the liquid oxygen top-off tank was going to be located in the upper fuselage, but was moved to the bomb bay when an observer's compartment scheduled to go there was deleted. The launch operator's position was moved from the left side of the aircraft to the right side to permit "continuous observation of the research vehicle" after the X-15 itself was moved to the right side. This also allowed the launch operator to remain in his ejection

Cockpit of Balls Three shortly after being modified on 13 May 1959. Note the X-15 arming switches on left and the emergency drop handle in the center of the photo. The remainder of the panel is standard B-52. (AFFTC History Office)

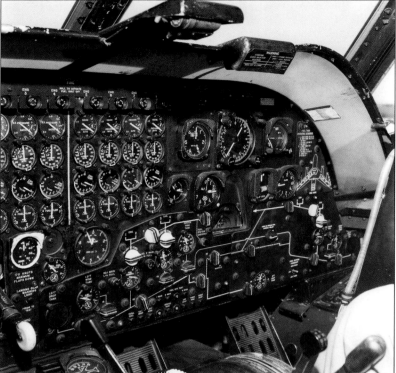

About the only changes to this side of the instrument panel was the removal of the No. 3 fuel level gage, and the blanking-off of the two external fuel tank gages (which were blanked in most, if not, all B-52As). (AFFTC History Office)

seat for the entire launch process; previously he had to stand up occasionally to visually check the X-15.[21]

After the modifications to the NB-52A, a ground vibration test was conducted on the pylon, first with an X-15 boilerplate mockup, then with the X-15-1 attached. The tests built on the data already accumulated by Boeing-Wichita when integrating the B-52F with the North American GAM-77 Hound Dog air-to-surface missile.[22] A structural steel frame was constructed to make the NB-52 wing as rigid as possible and the research airplane was excited by electro-magnetic shakers. The vibrations at various frequencies were determined measuring equipment mounted on the X-15 fuselage, wing, horizontal stabilizer, and vertical stabilizers. This information was used to verify data obtained from a series of flutter model tests of the B-52/X-15 combination conducted by Boeing in a low-speed wind tunnel. The results demonstrated that the flutter speed of the NB-52 when carrying the X-15 was above the expected launch conditions.[23]

There was concern about the jet exhaust from the Nos. 5 and 6 engines impinging on the X-15 empennage. Specifically, engineers were worried that the engine acoustic loads would be detrimental to the X-15 structural fatigue life. In order to mitigate the concern – at least initially – it was decided to restrict the Nos. 5 and 6 engines to 50-percent thrust while the X-15 was mated. This was thought to be an acceptable compromise between protecting the X-15 and providing adequate power and control for the NB-52 during takeoff.[24]

Although it appeared feasible to operate the carrier aircraft engines at reduced power, it was not desirable, so North American began redesigning some parts of the X-15 to increase their fatigue life. The modifications to the vertical stabilizers consisted of increasing the rivet diameter, using dimpled-skin construction rather than countersunk rivets, and increasing the gage of the corrugated ribs along the edge where they flanged over to attach to the cap strip. The horizontal stabilizer was changed to use larger rivets and dimpled construction. Static ground tests showed that the modifications were effective, and it was decided to retrofit all three X-15s with the new structure, but this would take a few months.[25]

Captain Charles C. Bock, Jr., and Captain John E. "Jack" Allavie, along with launch panel operator William "Bill" Berkowitz from North American, then began a series of flights tests on Balls Three. The initial flights were dedicated to developing techniques to be used for no-flap operations and to measure various performance parameters. During a normal B-52 takeoff with the flaps down, all four main gear leave the ground simultaneously. Very little no-flap takeoff and landing experience with the B-52 was available to draw on, so the initial tests were conducted using predicted information and recommendations from Boeing personnel.[26]

These tests involved a fair amount of trial and error. For instance, on the first test at a gross weight of 315,000 pounds (the maximum predicted weight for an actual X-15 flight), Bock set the stabilizer trim

0.5 degrees more than the normal recommended trim of zero degrees. Engines Nos. 5 and 6 were run at 50-percent power, and fuel simulated the weight (but not the drag) of the X-15 on the right wing. The predicted take-off distance was 10,500 feet at a speed of 176 knots. However, the B-52 would not rotate, even with the control columns pulled full-back. After the 10,000-foot marker on the runway was passed, the pilots went to full power on the Nos. 5 and 6 engines and the aircraft broke ground at 12,650 feet at 195 knots. Subsequent take-off tests established that a trim setting of 2 degrees nose up was the optimum – this represented one-half of the available trim.[27]

Landings also proved interesting. Unlike the traditional B-52 landing, which is on all four main gear at once, the NB-52s landed on their two aft main gears. The problem was that the B-52 was not meant to do this, and very little control was possible as the aircraft rotated to a level attitude – the forward main gear usually hit with a very noticeable impact. Accelerometers installed in the pylon after the initial landing tests measured impact loads of 1.5-1.8g. These were deemed annoying but acceptable.[28]

After the front main gear touched-down, the B-52 air brakes were fully extended and the drag chute deployed at 140 knots. Moderate braking was used when landing at heavier weights. Using these techniques with a 300,000-pound airplane, touch down speed was 172 knots and 10,800 feet were used during the landing roll. At 250,000 pounds, touchdown occurred at 154 knots and only 9,300 feet of runway were used with light braking. The importance of the drag chute was telling – one landing at 267,000 pounds with a failed drag chute required over 12,000 feet to stop even with heavy braking. The landing resulted in one brake being severely warped, necessitating its replacement.[29]

Despite the concerns over exhaust impingement from the Nos. 5 and 6 engines, the X-15 program had not taken a firm stand on power levels to be used, so Bock and Allavie decided to use full power on all eight engines for the first captive flight on 10 March 1959. The gross take-off weight was 258,000 pounds and the take-off distance was 6,085 feet at 172 knots. No attempt was made to achieve maximum performance – Bock just wanted to demonstrate the mated pair would actually fly as predicted, which it did for 1 hour and 8 minutes. On 1 April 1959 the second flight – which was supposed to result in an X-15 glide flight but didn't due to a radio failure – produced largely similar results. On the third flight, another unsuccessful attempt at the glide flight, the Nos. 5 and 6 engines were set to 50-percent thrust until an indicated airspeed of 130 knots was reached, then they were advanced to full power. This procedure extended the take-off distance to 7,100 feet at the same gross weight and similar atmospheric conditions.[30]

On all these flights, the Nos. 5 and 6 engines were set to 50-percent thrust at an altitude of approximately 5,000 feet and the mated pair continued to climb using a circular pattern around Rogers Dry Lake. This kept Scott Crossfield within gliding distance of a suitable lake in case the X-15 had to be jettisoned during an emergency. These early tests were flown to an altitude of 45,000 feet and Mach 0.85, which was pretty much the maximum performance of the pair. Simulated launch patterns were flown, emergency and aborted launch procedures were practiced, and X-15 propellant jettison tests were accomplished using a water-alcohol mixture that had been dyed red. The underside of the right horizontal stabilizer of the B-52 had been covered with a powdery substance so that impingement could be readily seen.[31]

The launch panel operator's station in Balls Eight on 10 May 1961. The liquid oxygen top-off valve controls are the levers at the right. Just to the left of the levers are the controls for setting up the stable platform on the X-15 using data from the carrier aircraft navigation instruments. (NASA Dryden)

The NB-52A launch panel operator's station on 13 May 1959. Note that the liquid oxygen control levers have not been installed yet. The two TV monitors could be switched to either the front or back cameras as needed. (AFFTC History Office)

The X-15 launch panel in Balls Eight (shown on 13 July 1962) was generally similar to the one in the NB-52A except the emergency launch handle says "X-15 ALTERNATE LAUNCH" instead of "X-15 EMERG LAUNCH." (NASA Dryden)

Since the X-15 horizontal and vertical stabilizers used for these initial carry flights were of the original design, it was decided to inspect them after the third flight. Several structural failures were found in the upper vertical stabilizer – the corrugated ribs had failed where they flanged over to attach to the cap strip. The most extensive failure was a complete separation of the rib from the flange for approximately 18 inches on the side away from the NB-52 engines. Subsequent investigation showed that the failures were largely a result of a previously unsuspected source – the turbulent airflow created by the X-15 pylon and the B-52 wing cutout. Pressure measurements were made to determine the exact environment around the wing cutout; estimates indicated an acceptable fatigue life for the modified structures in this environment, even if it had not been considered during design.[32]

It was recognized that heavyweight take-offs (315,000 pounds) with no flaps was going to require a considerable amount of runway during the summer heat, but most flight operations at Edwards during the summer were conducted in the early morning in any case. And if the take-off roll was computed to be too long, one of the lakebeds could always be used (although this only happened once actual flight operations). This particular deficiency was alleviated when the NB-52B joined the program. Unlike the A-model, Balls Eight was equipped with water injection for its engines. Allavie and Bock tested the NB-52B using water injection on just the outer four engines, and also on all engines except nos. 5 and 6, with promising results. The use of water injection "appreciably increases take-off performance and is considered mandatory for take-off from the

Fitz Fulton beside the NB-52B on 17 July 1963. Note that the "nose art" consists of an empty solid blue circle just to the left of Fulton. It appears that Balls Eight carried this art from May 1963 through August 1964. (NASA Dryden)

The liquid oxygen tanks in the bomb bay of the NB-52A on 13 May 1959. Although it looks like a single tank, there were separate 500-gallon and 1,000-gallon tanks inside. Note the straps suspending the tank. (AFFTC History Office)

The nose area of Balls Three after it was delivered to Edwards on 13 May 1959. Note the details on the underside of the pylon and that the astrodome above the forward television camera has not been added yet. (AFFTC History Office)

paved runway at a weight of 300,000 pounds when the ambient temperature exceeds 90°F."[33]

The lateral and directional control systems of the carrier aircraft were found to be capable of trimming out the unbalance of the B-52/X-15 combination. It was noted that lateral control became very sensitive above Mach 0.8, but the pilots felt that launches could be made up to Mach 0.85 with no problems. No buffeting in level flight was experienced during the evaluations. It was possible to induce a minor airframe buffet in maneuvering flight at 1.6-g (80-percent of the pylon load limit), but only at speeds well below the normal operating range. It was determined that the specific range deterioration of the NB-52 was about 7 percent with an empty pylon and about 16 percent with the X-15 attached. Given that the X-15 was never launched from more than 500 miles distance, and the B-52 had been intended as an intercontinental bomber, this decrease in range was not considered significant. As an aside, in May 1962 it was demonstrated that the pair could fly 1,625 miles nonstop from Edwards to Eglin AFB, Florida.[34]

Unsurprisingly, it was predicted that launching the X-15 would result in an instantaneous rearward shift of the B-52 center of gravity, coupled with a tendency to roll to the left. The X-15 glide flight (no fuel) was expected to result in a 4.5-percent shift in the center of gravity, while full-fuel flights would result in a 9-percent shift; it rose to about 12 percent on the later X-15A-2 flights. Both the rolling tendency and the pitch-up were calculated to be within the capabilities of the B-52 to counter, and in fact, no problems were experienced during actual operations. Under "normal" conditions, the center of gravity actually shifted approximately 7 percent and required a 40-pound push force on the control column to compensate. The resulting pulse was usually dampened in one cycle.[35]

There were some other minor problems discovered during the NB-52 flight tests. For instance, pre-launch operation of the X-15 nose ballistic control system produced some hydrogen peroxide residue that was sucked into the alternator cooling duct on the right wing leading edge and into the air ducts on the right side of the B-52 fuselage adjacent to the X-15. The residue was not considered to be hazardous since it was primarily water at that point. Interestingly, the operation of the ballistic control system while the X-15 was attached to the NB-52 had no noticeable affect on the bomber. Operation of the X-15 aerodynamic flight control also had no appreciable effect on the NB-52; however, a slight airframe buffet was noted when the X-15 speed brakes were extended. X-15 flap extension caused a small nose-down trim change; extension of the X-15 main landing skids was not even apparent in the bomber. Initially, the extension of the X-15 nose gear resulted in a "thump" felt and heard in the NB-52, but later changes in the X-15 nose gear extension mechanism eliminated the event.[36]

On the other side of the equation, the NB-52 did have some effects on the X-15. For instance, the B-52 fuselage and wing created noticeable upwash and sidewash on the X-15. Because of the NB-52 wing sweep, the right wing of the X-15 was nearer to the leading edge of the B-52 wing and, consequently, flow over the X-15 right wing was deflected downward more than over the X-15 left wing. This difference in effective angle of attack of the right and left wing resulted in a right rolling moment. There were also some concerns about the X-15 potentially striking the carrier aircraft during separation. Because there was only 2 feet of clearance between the X-15 dorsal stabilizer and the cutout in the NB-52 wing, the X-15 could potentially strike the cutout if

A good perspective of the position of the X-15 in relation to the carrier aircraft. The white patch on the X-15 is frost around the oxygen tank. Note the clearance between the X-15 wing and the B-52 fuselage. (Gerald H. Balzer Collection)

the X-15 bank angle exceeded 20 degrees before the airplane dropped below the NB-52 fuselage level (about a 2.5-foot vertical drop). It was decided that all X-15 controls should be in the neutral position when the airplane was dropped, allowing the automatic dampers to take care of correcting the attitude. The first few X-15 launches experimented

The NB-52A and X-15-1 during the ground vibration tests on 11 December 1958. Note the vertical stabilizer has been removed from the B-52 for the tests. (AFFTC History Office)

Above: *Balls Three mission markings on 19 June 1964.* (NASA Dryden)

Right and Below: *NB-52A profiles and markings legend.* (Artwork by Tony Landis)

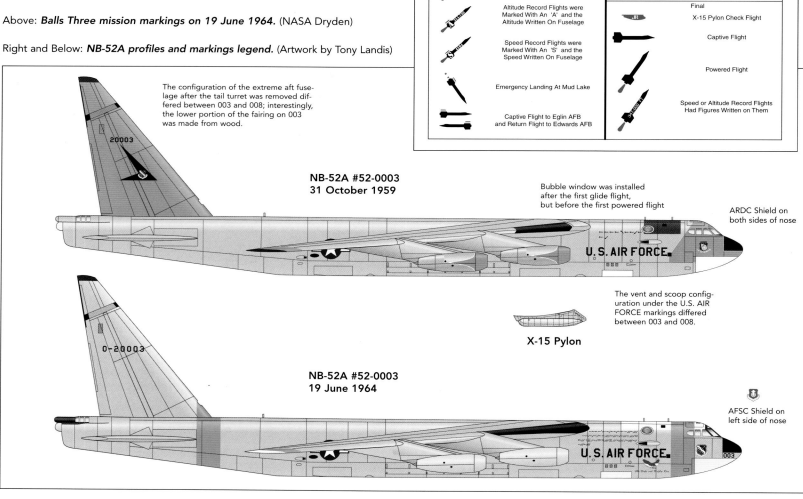

NB-52 Mission Markings Legend

NB-52A #52-0003
Original Markings

Captive Flight

Powered Flight

Glide Flight

First and Second Revisions

Captive Flight-Contractor

Glide Flight-Contractor

Powered Flight-Contractor

Third Powered Flight
Fuselage Broke on Landing

Powered Flight-NASA/A.F.

First Three XLR-99 Flights

Altitude Record Flights were
Marked With An 'A' and the
Altitude Written On Fuselage

Speed Record Flights were
Marked With An 'S' and the
Speed Written On Fuselage

Emergency Landing At Mud Lake

Captive Flight to Eglin AFB
and Return Flight to Edwards AFB

NB-52B #52-0008
Original Markings

Captive Flight-Contractor

Captive Flight-NASA/A.F.

Powered Flight-NASA/A.F.

First Revision

Glide Flight

XLR-11 Powered Flight

XLR-99 Powered Flight

Speed or Altitude Record Flights
Had Figures Written on Them

Emergency Landing At Mud Lake
Skid Collapse and A/C Rolled Over

Final

X-15 Pylon Check Flight

Captive Flight

Powered Flight

Speed or Altitude Record Flights
Had Figures Written on Them

The configuration of the extreme aft fuselage after the tail turret was removed differed between 003 and 008; interestingly,
the lower portion of the fairing on 003
was made from wood.

NB-52A #52-0003
31 October 1959

Bubble window was installed
after the first glide flight,
but before the first powered flight

ARDC Shield on
both sides of nose

The vent and scoop configuration under the U.S. AIR
FORCE markings differed
between 003 and 008.

X-15 Pylon

NB-52A #52-0003
19 June 1964

AFSC Shield on
left side of nose

The High And Mighty

Original nose art applied to
NB-52A 52-0003
July 1960 – December 1960
(no nose art was carried prior to this)

The High and Mighty One

Revised nose art on NB-52A 52-0003 from January 1961 until present

Original nose art applied to
NB-52B 52-0008
December 1960 – April 1962

Revised nose art applied to
NB-52B 52-0008
April 1962 – May 1963

May 1963 – August 1964
Just an empty blue circle
was used as nose art

Later nose art applied to
NB-52B 52-0008
August 1964 until present

Above: **Balls Three nose art.** (Artwork by Tony Landis)

Below: **NB-52B profiles.** (Artwork by Tony Landis)

Few people remember that Balls Eight was originally named The Challenger *and featured an eagle carrying an X-15. The circle was not complete because it butted up against the hi-visibility orange paint.* (Artwork by Tony Landis)

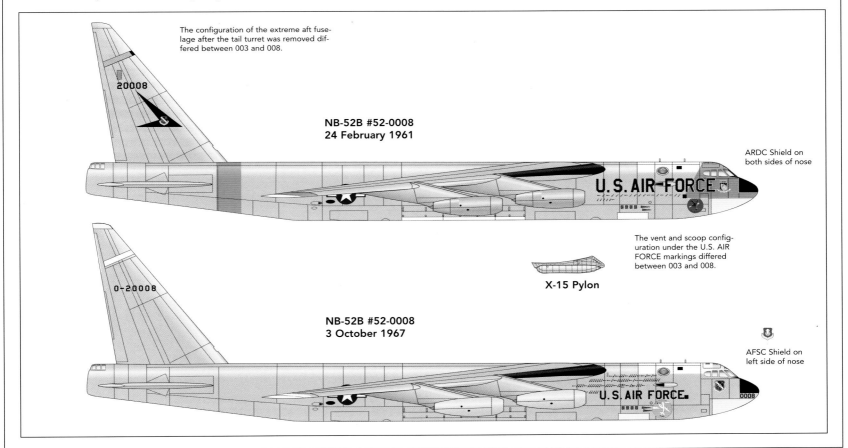

The configuration of the extreme aft fuse-lage after the tail turret was removed differed between 003 and 008.

**NB-52B #52-0008
24 February 1961**

ARDC Shield on
both sides of nose

The vent and scoop config-uration under the U.S. AIR FORCE markings differed between 003 and 008.

X-15 Pylon

**NB-52B #52-0008
3 October 1967**

AFSC Shield on
left side of nose

with the settings needed for the dampers to do this, but a consistent set of settings was soon developed by Scott Crossfield.[37]

In June 1965 the FRC estimated that the full-up weight of the X-15A-2 with a real ramjet and fuel had grown to 56,000 pounds. This was more than 1,000 pounds greater than the most recent analysis showed the NB-52 wing/pylon could safely tolerate. During 1966 the NB-52s were modified to increase the allowable pylon weight to 65,000 pounds, allowing for the heaviest expected X-15A-2 flight with some contingency reserve. The modifications were primarily the use of doublers and additional fasteners on various parts of the wing wing and pylon structure. Although the modifications allowed the X-15A-2 to be carried safely, performance suffered; the maximum launch altitude was 1,500 feet lower and the launch speed was restricted to about Mach 0.8 when the external tanks and ramjet were installed.[38]

NORTH AMERICAN XB-70

Various drawings and artist concepts were released during the X-15 program that showed the research airplane – particularly the proposed delta-wing version – being carried by a North American XB-70 Valkyrie. Needless to say, the use of this Mach 3+ capable aircraft would have greatly extended the performance envelope of the X-15. However, given the theoretical uncertainties of launching a large object from the

XB-70 / X-15 DELTA WING
TOP LAUNCH

(The Boeing Company Archives)

The XB-70 was proposed as a carrier aircraft for the still-born delta-wing X-15, but it was an unlikely proposition. (Terry Panopalis Collection)

HYDROGEN PEROXIDE
(H_2O_2)

LIQUID OXYGEN
(LO_2)

INERT GAS

LIQUID AMMONIA
($LN H_3$)

B-52-7-73-9A

The locations of the various ground support equipment and servicing vehicles around the mated pair before flight. (U.S. Air Force)

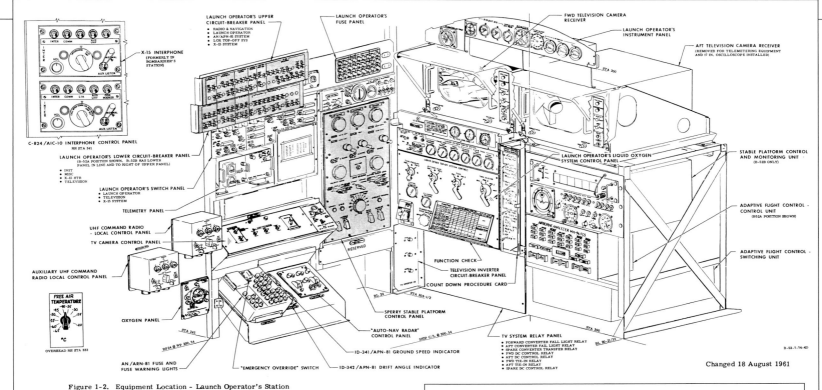

Figure 1-2. Equipment Location – Launch Operator's Station

Changed 18 August 1961

Above and right: *Illustrations from the "Operating and Maintenance Instructions" for the two carrier aircraft. The launch operator's panel is above, and the pilot's panel to the right. Note that there were subtle differences between the two aircraft.* (U.S. Air Force)

back of a larger aircraft traveling at Mach 3, it is unlikely this concept was ever seriously considered. After the fatal crash on 30 July 1966 of a Lockheed M-21 Blackbird while launching a D-21 drone from a similar configuration, it became even more unlikely. Nevertheless, sometime during 1966 North American conducted a study (logically titled "XB-70/X-15"), but unfortunately, a copy could not be found in any of the archives so its contents and conclusions are unknown.[39]

Chase and Support Aircraft

In addition to the B-52s and X-15s, there were numerous chase and support aircraft, mostly provided by the Air Force. The number of chase aircraft differed depending on what flight profile was being flown. Three chase were used on the early low-speed X-15 flights, four were used on most research flights, and five were used for the very long-range flights. Of course, all things were variable and it was not unusual to see additional chase aircraft, particularly during the middle years of the program.

Chase-1 was the prelaunch chase, and was usually a North American F-100F Super Sabre during the early years and a Northrop T-38A Talon later, although a Douglas F5D Skyray was used on a couple of occasions. During the North American flights, this chase was frequently flown by Al White, but once the government took over the airplane was generally flown by an Air Force

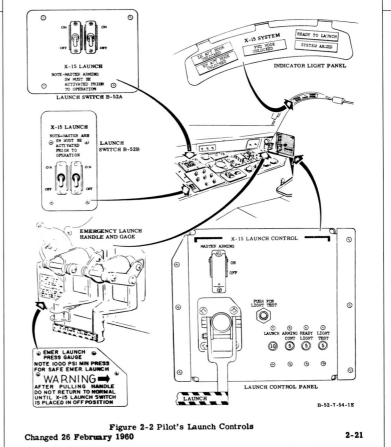

Figure 2-2 Pilot's Launch Controls

Changed 26 February 1960

2-21

The NB-52A takes-off on the first captive flight of the X-15 program. Scott Crossfield was in the research airplane, and Charlie Bock, Jack Allavie, and Bill Berkowitz were in the carrier. Note that the forward bogies and wing gear are beginning to retract. (The Boeing Company Archives)

This was the original nose art and markings on Balls Eight during July 1961. Note the ARDC badge on the nose and the APN-81 radar altimeter antenna on the bottom of the fuselage. (AFFTC History Office)

pilot. Chase-1 took off with the NB-52 and flew formation during the climbout and cruise to the launch lake. The chase pilot visually verified various parts of the X-15 checklist such as control surface movements, propellant jettison, ballistic system checks, APU start, and engine priming. The use of the F-100 presented some problems at the beginning of the program since the aircraft could not maintain a low enough speed to fly formation with the NB-52 during a right-hand turn; the T-38 proved to be more satisfactory.

Chase-2 was the launch chase, and provided assistance for the X-15 pilot in the event he had to make an emergency landing at the launch lake. Chase-2 was usually an Lockheed F-104 Starfighter flown by either another X-15 pilot or a NASA research pilot. The use of an F-104 was largely dictated by the fact that it was the only aircraft that could reasonably fly the X-15 profile during landing; the F-100 and T-38 could not produce enough drag to fly the steep final approach. Conversely, the F-104 could not cruise at 45,000 feet due to its high wing loading, making it unsuitable as Chase-1. Chase-2 normally stayed below 35,000 feet until 3 minutes before launch, then went into afterburner and climbed to 45,000 feet just before the X-15 was dropped. The pilot trailed the NB-52 during launch, then tried to keep up with the X-15 as it left the launch lake area; it was a futile gesture, but proved useful on the few occasions that the X-15 engine failed soon after ignition.

Chase-3 covered landings at the intermediate lakebeds and was usually an F-104 flown by either another X-15 pilot or an Air Force test pilot. Unlike Chases 1 and 2 that had taken off with the NB-52, Chase-3 waited until 30 minutes before X-15 launch to take off in order to have enough fuel to loiter for a while. On flight profiles that had multiple intermediate lakes, Chase-3 would orbit between them. In the event the X-15 had to make an emergency landing, the F-104 would attempt to join up to provide support for the X-15 pilot during final approach and touchdown. For flights out of Smith Ranch there were two intermediate chase, usually called 3 and 4 (the Edwards chase became Chase-5 in these cases).

Chase-4 covered the Edwards landing area, usually with an Air Force pilot. Again, an F-104 was used because it could keep up with the

JF-100C painting. (©1987 Mike Machat Illustration, reproduced with permission)

The three NASA Lockheed F-104Ns were used extensively by the X-15 program as chase aircraft and landing simulators. They were also among the most colorful F-104s in the inventory. Various Air Force F-104s from the nearby AFFTC and Test Pilot School were also used during the program. (NASA Dryden)

X-15 in the landing pattern. This chase took-off at the same time as Chase-3 and orbited 30-40 miles uprange along the flight path. The pilot began accelerating on cue from NASA-1 and the Edwards radar sites in an attempt to intercept the X-15 at the maximum possible speed and altitude as the X-15 descended into the Edwards area. Usually the intercept was made by chasing the vapor trail left as the X-15 pilot jettisoned his residual propellants since the research airplane was too small and too dark to acquire visually until the chase pilot was right on top of it. Chase-4 would make a visual inspection of the X-15 as it descended, and provided airspeed and altitude callouts to the X-15 pilot during the final approach as well as verifying the ventral had successfully jettisoned and the landing gear was down.[40]

At times there were other chase aircraft, with a photo-chase or a "rover" being the most frequent. The photo-chase was used to film

The JF-100C (53-1709), shown here on 15 August 1962, was used by the X-15 program between 1 November 1960 and 11 March 1964 as a variable stability trainer, giving higher performance than the NT-33A. (NASA Dryden)

The JF-104A (55-2961) was modified with a reaction control system in the nose and wingtip pods, and was used to train pilots in operating the system. This ground test was in the early morning of 15 December 1960. (NASA Dryden)

the X-15, although Chase-1 was frequently a two-seater and carried a photographer in the back seat as well. Rover was usually another X-15 pilot who just felt like tagging along. All of the X-15 pilots flew chase aircraft, as did many AFFTC test pilots, and students and instructors from the test pilot schools at Edwards. It was not unusual for the chase pilots (particularly other X-15 pilots) to use first names for themselves and the X-15 pilot during radio chatter; alternately, the callsign "chase" (without a number) was used since there was seldom more than one chase aircraft in the vicinity.

A number of other aircraft were used for various support functions. The NASA Gooney Bird (R4D) was used to ferry men and supplies to the uprange stations and to inspect the lakebeds as necessary. Several Lockheed C-130 Hercules transports were used to ferry fire engines and other material to the lakebeds and High Range stations for each flight. These aircraft often made several trips per day ferrying men and equipment; during the actual flight one of them orbited mid-way down the flight corridor, usually with a flight surgeon and emergency response team in case the X-15 had to make an emergency landing. Safety was taken very seriously.

Piasecki H-21 Shawnee helicopters were also ferried to the primary emergency landing lake in case of an emergency. Additional H-21s were located at Edwards. These provided a quick method of moving emergency personnel to an accident scene, surveying the runways, and evacuating the X-15 pilot if necessary. The H-21 pilots were also briefed on how to disperse fumes from a damaged X-15 by hovering near the crashed airplane; on at least one occasion this technique was actually used, probably saving the life of the X-15 pilot.

SIMULATED AIRCRAFT

In addition to the ground simulators and the centrifuge, various aircraft were also used to simulate the X-15 during early preparations and to familiarize pilots with some aspects of X-15 operations. Pilots used a Lockheed F-104A Starfighter to establish geographic checkpoints and

The NT-33A was a variable stability trainer operated by the Cornell Aeronautical Laboratory under Air Force contract, and was a frequent visitor to Edwards up through the 1980s. This aircraft provided a somewhat realistic reentry simulation to the original group of X-15 pilots. Unfortunately, the analog computer in the airplane could not handle the hot weather at Edwards during the middle of the summer; in the air it worked well enough, but on the ground the components just cooked and needed constant recalibration and maintenance. (NASA Dryden)

key altitudes around the landing pattern. The F-104A closely approximately the wing loading of an X-15 during landing, and with the right combination of extended landing gear, flaps, and speed brakes, the F-104A at idle-thrust did an excellent job simulating the X-15. For the first 50 or so flights of the program, each X-15 flight was preceded by the pilot dedicating an entire F-104 mission to practicing landing procedures. As new pilots entered the program they also practiced.[41]

Similar work was conducted by Scott Crossfield and Al White very early in the program using the North American YF-100A equipped with an eight-foot drag chute that could be opened in flight. Combined with extended gear and speed brake, the F-100 at idle-thrust also did an adequate job simulating the X-15 during landing, although not quite as well as the F-104A, and it was a bit trickier since it required the in-flight deployment of the drag chute.[42]

Al White later remembered "With gear down, speed brake extended, at idle power, and that drag chute deployed, the airplane was comparable to the X-15 on approach. I would start at about 25,000 feet, pick a spot on the lake bed, and see how close I could come to touching down on that spot. With all the room on the lake bed, it wasn't necessary to hit a spot, but it's always nice to have that much margin for error. I flew this trainer as much as I could, in preparation for that day that never came."[43]

Since no one had ever left the atmosphere and returned in a winged vehicle (or anything else) there had been concern that the very rapidly changing stability and control characteristics in the X-15 as it reentered the atmosphere might pose an unusually demanding piloting task. To address this question, engineers in the Flight Research Department of the Cornell Aeronautical Laboratory conceived the idea of simulating this brief (about 60 seconds duration) but unfamiliar X-15 piloting task in an NT-33A that was operated by Cornell as a variable stability trainer.[44]

The NT-33A already had been equipped with a larger internal volume F-94 nose section that contained a three-axis (pitch, roll and yaw) variable stability and control system for in-flight simulation purposes. To support the X-15 program, the front cockpit was modified to superficially resemble the X-15. The front instrument panel arrangement was like the X-15 panel, there was a side-stick controller on the right-hand console for atmospheric flight control and another side-stick on the left-hand console simulating the ballistic controls. An "instructor" pilot sat in the back cockpit with a more normal set of T-33 controls.[45]

The flight plan had the NT-33A entering a shallow dive at about 17,000 feet altitude and then pulling-up to a ballistic trajectory that produced about 60 seconds of zero-g – about the same as the initial part of the X-15 reentry. At the same time the variable stability system on the NT-33A changed the flight control sensitivities to simulate going from the vacuum of outer space to the rapidly increasing dynamic pressure of the atmosphere. Since the normal aerodynamic controls of the X-15 would be ineffective outside the atmosphere, the ballistic controller was used to establish the correct reentry pitch-attitude.[46]

In the NT-33A simulation the "ballistic controller" produced no physical response whatsoever but only changed the displayed pitch-attitude on the instrument panel. (At this point in the simulation the NT-33A was at zero-g.) In order to maintain the fidelity of the simulation, the NT-33A front cockpit was hooded and the X-15 pilot had no view of the outside world. (There would be little view of the real world in the X-15 at the simulated altitudes.) This deception was necessary for the high angle-of-attack deceleration at the end of the

The C-130s provided much-needed airlift capability for the program. Here an AFFTC C-130B (57-0525) supports Bob Rushworth's emergency landing at Mud Lake on 1 July 1966. (NASA Dryden)

The F-107s did not directly support the X-15 program, but contributed in many ways nevertheless. The airplane gave North American a great deal of experience during the design of the "rolling tail" and later, provided several pilots with their first experience using a side-stick controller. This is the third YF-107A (55-0120) on the lakebed and showing its side-stick controller on the right console in the cockpit. (NASA Dryden)

simulated reentry since, although the front cockpit instrumentation indicated to the pilot that he was flying an unbanked steep descent (in the X-15), he was actually flying a steep 5-g turn in the NT-33A. This was accomplished by gradually biasing the attitude indicator to a bank-angle of 75 degrees while the front cockpit pilot used the ballistic controller to maintain wing level flight at proper airspeed, angle of attack, and descent-rate on his cockpit instruments. It was a carefully choreographed ballet between the X-15 "student" and the pilot in the back seat who was trying to keep the NT-33 from becoming a crater in the high desert.[47]

Accordingly, a Cornell team headed by engineering test pilots Bob Harper and Nello Infanti arrived at Edwards in May 1960 to begin a series of flights in the NT-33A in order to provide training for six X-15 pilots – Armstrong, McKay, Petersen, Rushworth, Walker, and White – in the upcoming atmospheric reentry task. Each X-15 pilot was to receive six flights in the NT-33A that included a matrix of simulated Mach numbers, altitudes, and various control malfunctions – principally failed dampers. Nello Infanti was to be the "instructor pilot" for each of the 36 X-15 simulation flights in the NT-33A. The balance of the Cornell team for this ambitious project consisted of Howard Stevens as crew chief, Bud Stahl as electronics technician, and Jack Beilman as systems engineer. Jack Beilman remembers:[48]

"During one of the flights, with Neil Armstrong in the front seat, we were simulating failed dampers at something like Mach 3.2 and 100,000 feet altitude. Neil had great difficulty with this simulated undamped X-15 configuration and lost control of the airplane repeatedly. Nello had to recover the from each one of these 'lost-control' events using the controls in the back cockpit. [Infanti later recalled that some of these recoveries were 'pretty sporty.'] The ground crew was monitoring the test radio frequency as usual and followed these simulated flight control problems with great interest.

"After landing, the NT-33A taxied to the ramp and Howard Stevens attached the ladder to the cockpits and climbed up to talk to Infanti about the airplane status. I climbed up the ladder front side to talk to Neil Armstrong. He handed me his helmet and knee-pad, got down from the cockpit and we talked about the flight and walked toward the operations building. As we arrived at the door Armstrong extended his

right hand to grasp the door handle – but his hand still held the side-stick which he had broken during his last battle with the X-15 dampers-off simulation. I was unaware of any report of this incident during the flight and had not noticed the stick in Armstrong's hand when he exited the cockpit. Addressing the matter for the first time, Armstrong said – without additional comment – 'Here's your stick!'

(It developed that Infanti had been aware of the broken side-stick after it happened because Armstrong had held it up over his head in the front cockpit for Nello to see.)

"After the debriefing, we took the broken side-stick to the NASA workshop where Neil found the necessary metal tubing and repaired the stick while I mostly watched him work. The side-stick was reinstalled and ready for the first flight the next morning. Really good test pilots fix what they break!"

In general the pilots considered the NT-33 flights worthwhile, but initially there were some "obvious discrepancies or malfunctions" that limited the data obtained from the flights. Rushworth and White repeated the same flight profiles on the North American fixed-base simulator, allowing comparisons of the stability derivatives between the two devices.[49]

A few hundred miles away, Bill Dana made a check flight in a specially modified JF-100C (53-1709) at Ames on 1 November 1960, and delivered the aircraft to the FRC the following day. The aircraft had been modified as a variable-stability trainer that could simulate the X-15 flight profile somewhat more convincingly than the NT-33. This made it possible to investigate new piloting techniques and control-law modifications without using an X-15. Another 104 flights were made for pilot checkout, variable stability research, and X-15 support before the aircraft was returned to Ames on 11 March 1964.[50]

One of the tasks assigned to the JF-100C was to investigate the effects of damper failure on the controllability of the X-15. The early wind tunnel data with regard to sideslip effects had been obtained with the horizontal stabilizer at zero deflection. This data was used in the 1958 centrifuge program at Johnsville. Based on this data, reentries (static or with the wheel turning) could be completed using an angle of attack of 15 degrees, even with the roll damper off. On the other hand, reentries at angles of attack greater than 15

Northrop T-38A Talons took over as Chase-1 as soon as they were available in the AFFTC inventory. Here Captain Albert Crews is in formation on Balls Eight for Flight 3-21-32 on 19 July 1963. (AFFTC History Office)

degrees (which were required for altitudes above 250,000 feet) with the roll damper off showed a distinct tendency to become uncontrollable because of a pilot-induced oscillation (PIO).[51]

If the pilot released the stick, the oscillations damped themselves. Nevertheless, researchers suspected that a large portion of the X-15 flight envelope was uncontrollable with the roll dampers off or failed. Investigations were begun to find a way of alleviating the problem. The first method tried, probably because if would have been the easiest to implement, was pilot-display quickening. Sideslip and bank angle presentations in the cockpit were quickened (i.e., presented with less delay) by including yaw rate and roll rate, respectively. Various quickening gains were used in the investigation on the fixed-base simulator, but no combination that significantly improved the pilot's ability to handle the instability was found.[52]

Shortly after the centrifuge program a wind tunnel test was conducted to gather sideslip data with the horizontal stabilizer closer to

the normal trim position (which was a fairly large leading-edge-down deflection of –15 to –20 degrees). When the results of these tests were programmed into the fixed-base simulator at North American it showed that the PIO boundary for reentry with the roll damper off had dropped from 15 degrees to only 8 degrees.[53]

To obtain X-15 flight verification of the problem, several pilots were asked to explore the fringes of the expected uncontrollable region. This was generally done by setting the airplane up at the appropriate angle of attack and turning the roll and yaw dampers off. In each case lateral motions began immediately. Various combinations of angle of attack and control inputs were experimented with in both the X-15 and the JF-100C to further define the problem.[54]

Arthur F. Tweedie from North American along with Lawrence W. Taylor and Richard E. Day from the FRC independently investigated the use of the rolling tail to control sideslip angle for certain types of instability. An unconventional control technique – called beta-dot – that evolved from these investigations showed considerable promise on the fixed-base simulator. This technique consisted of sharp lateral control inputs to the left as the nose swung left through zero sideslip (or vice versa to the right). The pilot kept his hands off the stick except when making the sharp lateral inputs; this eliminated the instability induced by inadvertent inputs associated with merely holding onto the center stick. When the technique was attempted in the JF-100C airplane, however, it did not seem to work as well. Further investigations showed that it worked somewhat better in the X-15 when the pilot used the side-stick controller instead of the center stick.[55]

It appeared that the beta-dot technique might allow reentries from high altitudes with the dampers failed, if anybody could figure how to successfully perform the maneuver. Bob Hoey, one of the AFFTC flight planners who later discovered the ventral-off stability fix for the same problem recalls that "the beta-dot technique is one of those things that is really difficult to explain. You could watch someone make 20 simulated reentries and still not understand what they were doing. The basic method was based on making a very sharp aileron pulse, timed exactly right, and totally foreign to normal, intuitive piloting technique. Properly timed, this pulse would completely stop the rolling motion, although not necessarily at wings level. With a little finesse you could herd the thing back to wings level flight, but, if at any time you reverted back to a normal piloting technique, even for a second, you were in big trouble. Art Tweedie [who discovered this method] and Norm Coop-

Piasecki H-21 Shawnee helicopters played an important role in the X-15 program, mainly providing a fast method of moving emergency response personnel to the site of an accident. H-21s were deployed to the launch and intermediate lakes, as well as being stationed at Edwards. (Left: NASA Dryden; Center: AFFTC History Office; Right: NASA via the Terry Panopalis Collection)

An F-100F (56-3963) flies as Chase-1 for Flight 2-A-8 on 31 October 1958. The F-104 could not easily fly formation with the B-52 at altitude, making the F-100 the chase of choice until the T-38s became available. (AFFTC History Office)

Mud Lake after the emergency landing of the X-15A-2 on Flight 2-45-81. The NASA Gooney Bird and an AFFTC C-130 ferried in men and supplies to retrieve the X-15 for the trip back – via truck – to Edwards. (AFFTC History Office)

er [a North American flight controls expert] could make successful simulator reentries with the dampers off while drinking a cup of coffee! This obviously became a big challenge for the rest of us."[56]

All of the X-15 pilots were trained in the use of this technique, but its actual usefulness was questionable. Furthermore, a lateral input in the wrong direction, which was a conceivable mistake considering other potential problems clamoring for the pilot's attention, could be disastrous. One of the reasons that the technique was so foreign was that the aileron pulse had to be made in the same direction as the roll – hardly intuitive to most pilots – then immediately taken out. The pulse was made just as the beta needle on the attitude indicator hit the null mark. Hoey remembers that "about half the pilots were dead-set against it and essentially refused to consider it as an option. Others conquered the technique and actually became fairly proficient in its use on the fixed-base and in-flight simulations." The in-flight simulations were conducted using the NT-33 and JF-100C variable stability airplanes.[57]

There were two other answers to the PIO problem at high angles of attack. The first was to make the stability augmentation system truly redundant, at least in the roll axis. This was subsequently done with the alternate stability augmentation system (ASAS), but it took almost a year to accomplish. Another answer – discovered by the flight planners using the simulator – proved to be remarkably easy, and unexpected; remove the ventral rudder. With the lower rudder on, a considerable portion of the reentry from an altitude mission was within the uncontrollable region should a damper fail. However, a similar reentry with the lower rudder removed did not enter the predicted uncontrollable region at all. The down side was that the flying qualities at low angles of attack without the rudder were significantly reduced. It was ultimately decided that the lower rudder would be removed for almost all of the high altitude missions; only a few missions in the X-15A-2 were flown with the ventral, in this case providing an adequate stand-in for the eventual dummy ramjet.[58]

F-104s flew the landing pattern very much like the X-15 so they were most always used as the final chase, providing the X-15 pilot with altitude callouts and other information to ease his workload during landing. This is Pete Knight in an AFFTC F-104A (56-0768) with Flight 3-35-57. (AFFTC History Office)

F-104s did more than operate as chase aircraft. Here a JF-104A (55-2961) has an X-15 ventral rudder on its centerline station in preparation for a test of the parachute recovery system The photo was taken on 20 April 1964 on Rogers Dry Lake. (NASA Dryden)

Faster Than a Speeding Bullet

Right: *Design goal attained. Bob White drops away from Balls Eight on 9 November 1961 to what would be the first Mach 6 flight by any aircraft. White attained Mach 6.04 (4,093 mph/6,003 fps) and a maximum altitude of 101,600 feet on Flight 2-21-37. Note the thermal-sensitive paint covering the canopy and the liquid oxygen frost on top of the fuselage. As White decelerated through Mach 2.7 the right outer windscreen shattered (insert photo).* (AFFTC History Office)

Below: *On a couple of occasions, the program tried to fly two missions in a single day, but never succeeded. The attempt on 4 November 1960 ended with Bob Rushworth launching Flight 1-16-29, but a faulty APU forced Scott Crossfield to scrub (2-A-20) the first XLR99 flight.* (NASA Dryden)

By January 1958 everything had moved into high gear and the three Model NA-240 airplanes were in the assembly jigs at the North American facility in Inglewood, adjacent to the Los Angeles International Airport. Over 6,000 engineering drawings – including one that was 50 feet long – had been released by the end of 1957, although minor changes continued to be made. North American subcontracted about 200 items to various vendors, but the majority of the airplanes were manufactured on the premises. The construction of the three X-15s eventually consumed just over two years.[1]

Rollout

On 15 October 1958 the first X-15 (56-6670) was rolled-out in Inglewood to great pomp and circumstance. It was ironic, in a way. The NACA had given birth to a concept and had nurtured the X-15 for over four years; but two weeks before the airplane was rolled out, the committee itself had ceased to exist. In its place, the National Aeronautics and Space Administration (NASA) was created effective 1 October 1958. The X-15 had been the largest development program at the NACA; it would soon be one of the smallest at NASA.

The master of ceremonies at the rollout was Raymond H. Rice, vice president and general manager of the Los Angeles Division of North American Aviation. Keynote speakers included Major General Victor R. Haugen, assistant deputy commander of the ARDC; Brigadier General Marcus F. Cooper, commander of the AFFTC; Walt Williams, chief of the HSFS; and Harrison Storms, at that time chief engineer for the Los Angeles Division. Congressmen and senators sat in the grandstands and Vice President Richard M. Nixon was on hand to proclaim that the X-15 had "recaptured the U.S. lead in space." There were special exhibits featuring David Clark full-pressure suits and the Reaction Motors XLR99 engine mockup. Also in attendance were six future X-15 pilots: Neil Armstrong, Scott Crossfield, Jack McKay, Captain Bob Rushworth, Joe Walker, and Captain Bob White.[2]

In an era before elaborate multimedia rollout ceremonies became the norm, the X-15 represented the hopes and dreams of a nation. The space race had already begun, and the United States was desperate to show any progress that could be compared to the Soviet accomplishments. Considering that only four years earlier many believed that the "space leap" should be removed from the X-15 concept, this small black airplane was now portrayed as the American response to the threat. It may have been small, but it had not come cheaply. Despite the original $12,200,000 estimate prepared by the WADC in 1954, at the time of the rollout Major General Haugen estimated that nearly $120 million had been spent – and the airplane had not yet flown.[3]

Haugen also pointed out that the rollout was actually two weeks ahead of the schedule established in June 1956 when the contract was

Desktop computers had not been invented yet, but the X-15 program still managed to generate its share of paperwork. At the time the industry used real drafting tables and pens, not CAD/CAM systems, and reports were still prepared using typewriters and "onion skin" paper. Surprisingly, much of it was more informative than most current paperwork. (The Boeing Company Archives)

Top: *Guests and employees gather around the X-15-1 at the rollout ceremony.* Above: *Vice President Richard M. Nixon proclaims that the X-15 has recaptured the United States' lead in the "space race."* (The Boeing Company Archives)

signed. He called this "a tribute to all of the government and industry team ..." The general summed up the spirit of the program: "It has been said that there are two extremes to research or exploratory flying – the approach that for example would strap a man on an ICBM and see what happens, and the super safe approach that would have us take tiny steps into the unknown and be absolutely sure of each step. We believe the solution is neither of these but rather a bold step into the future within the known technical capabilities of our engineers. We believe that the X-15 represents such a bold step ... that will help us build better air and space vehicles in the future."[4]

Stormy Storms was even more direct: "The rollout of the X-15 marks the beginning of man's most advanced assault on space. This will be one of the most dramatic, as in the X-15 we have all the elements and most of the problems of a true space vehicle." Describing the potential performance of the airplane, Storms said: "The performance of the X-15 is hard to comprehend. It can out fly the fastest fighters by a factor of 3, a high-speed rifle bullet by a factor of 2, and easily exceed the world altitude record by many times."[5]

Following the conclusion of the official ceremonies, the X-15-1 was moved back inside the hangar and prepared for delivery. On the night of 16 October, covered completely in protective heavy-duty wrapping paper, it was shipped by truck overland through the Los Angeles foothills to Edwards for initial ground test work.

As rolled-out, the X-15 was not in her ultimate configuration, but the airplane was still the fastest research vehicle ever built. Two Reaction Motors XLR11 engines were in the aft fuselage as substitutes for the planned XLR99, and an instrumentation boom was installed instead of the ball nose. Still, in this configuration the airplane would ultimately reach Mach 3.31, significantly faster than the earlier X-planes. (The Boeing Company Archives)

In spite of the various problems that resulted in a heavier-than-expected airframe, an overweight and long-delayed rocket engine, and derated auxiliary power units, the performance expected from the new research airplane was truly phenomenal. Officially both the government and North American were certain the X-15 would achieve its design velocity of 6,600 fps and altitude of 250,000 feet. However, North American stated that "altitudes up to 650,000 feet … and Mach numbers up to approximately 7.0 can be achieved with this research airplane."[6]

Now it was time to prove it.

FLIGHT NUMBERS

The program used a three-part designation for each flight. The first number represented the specific X-15; "1" was for X-15-1, etc. No differentiation was made between the original X-15-2 and the modified X-15A-2. The second position was the flight number for that specific X-15. This included free flights only, not captive-carries or aborts; the first flight was 1, the second was 2, etc. If the flight was a scheduled captive-carry, the second position in the designation was replaced with a C; if it was an aborted free-flight attempt, it was replaced with an A. The third position was the total number of times that particular X-15 had been carried aloft by either NB-52. This number incremented for each captive-carry, abort, and actual release. A letter from Paul Bikle established this system on 24 May 1960; the 30 flights already accomplished were retroactively redesignated.[7]

FLIGHT DESCRIPTION

X-15 flights did not begin with the pilot waking up and deciding he wanted to go flying. Weeks or months before, a researcher would develop requirements for a set of data that had to be gathered under specific conditions. One of the flight planners – Johnny Armstrong, Richard Day, Bob Hoey, Jack Kolf, John Manke, to name a few – would take these requirements and lay out a flight plan that defined the entire mission. "Flight planner" does not begin to describe the expertise of the engineers that performed this function; they lived in the simulator and were experts on the airplane. In addition to planning specific flights, the flight planners performed a great many parametric studies not related to a particular flight or pilot training. Some of these included glide performance, peak altitude versus pitch angle, speed optimization techniques, and reentry trades involving dynamic pressure, load factors,

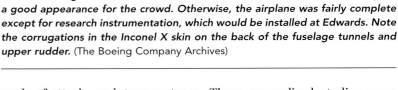

The XLR11 engines installed for the rollout were not functional units, but gave a good appearance for the crowd. Otherwise, the airplane was fairly complete except for research instrumentation, which would be installed at Edwards. Note the corrugations in the Inconel X skin on the back of the fuselage tunnels and upper rudder. (The Boeing Company Archives)

angle-of-attack, and temperatures. These generalized studies were then used in conjunction with specific mission requirements to quickly determine the critical features of a flight plan.[8]

Then they presented their plan to the pilot selected for the flight. Every second of each flight was scheduled, and the flight planner and pilot would spend the next week or month – depending on the complexity of the mission – in the simulator. By the time the flight planner was finished, the pilot knew exactly where the airplane should be at

Nixon looked around the airplane and chatted with various people. In the right photo Nixon is shaking hands with the President of North American Aviation, James H. "Dutch" Kindelberger, and test pilot Scott Crossfield. Note the North American name written on the airplane. (The Boeing Company Archives)

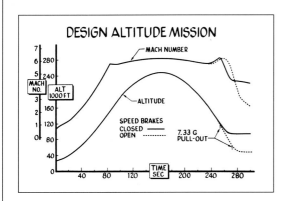

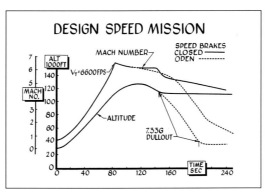

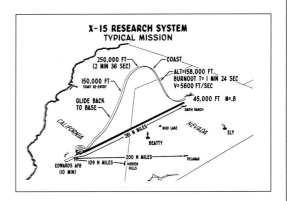

A trio of 1963-vintage charts showing the design flight profiles. At left is the altitude profile showing the variations possible with speed brakes deployed or retracted; a similar chart for the speed mission is in the center. Note that the speed chart shows the original 6,600 fps maximum speed, something that was never attained by the basic airplane configuration. A generic mission ground track and trajectory is shown at right; there were many variations to this profile. (NASA)

any given moment during the mission. After extensive practice with the nominal mission, off-design missions were flown to acquaint the pilot with the overall effect of changes in critical parameters. Variations in engine thrust or engine shutdown times were also simulated. For example, an error in total impulse of 120,000-lbm-sec – which could result from either a 1-second error in burn time or a 1,500-lbf (3 percent) error in average thrust – could result in a 7,500-foot difference in peak altitude. A one-degree error in pitch angle or a 100 fps difference in velocity during the exit phase could also result in a peak altitude difference of 7,500 feet. At this point the primary ground controller (called NASA-1) was brought in and the flight planner, pilot, and NASA-1 ran additional simulations. This familiarized all of them with the general timing of the flight.[9]

After the off-design missions were practiced, various anomalies were simulated. These normally included failures of the engine, stable platform, ball nose, radar and/or radio, dampers, and variations of the stability derivatives. Premature engine shutdowns were inserted at critical points to acquaint the pilot with the optimum techniques for returning to the lake behind him or flying to an alternate lake ahead of him. Failures of the stable platform allowed practicing alternate techniques to complete the mission or, at least, for landing safely. Normally the failure of the velocity or altitude instrument would not affect a flight; however, in the event of an attitude presentation failure during the exit phase of an altitude mission, the pilot had to initiate an immediate pushover from about 30 degrees pitch attitude to 18 degrees so that he could visually acquire the horizon. Failures

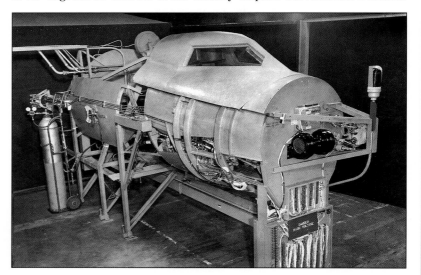

A simplified diagram showing the interrelationship between a typical mission profile and the High Range stations. This is an early drawing showing the original 240-knot landing pattern; later flights were closer to 300 knots. The launch altitude (38,000 feet shown) also increased, usually to about 40,000 feet. (Boeing via the Gerald H. Balzer Collection)

The original fixed-base simulator at the North American facility in Inglewood during February 1959. At this point the iron bird rig does not stretch out behind the cockpit, and somewhat surprisingly, a canopy is installed. All of the original X-15 pilots and flight planners trained in this simulator. (Boeing via the Gerald H. Balzer Collection)

of the ball nose were usually not terminal since the mission could still be flown using normal-acceleration, attitudes, and stabilizer position indications, but the results were not as precise. For flights into stability-critical areas, simulated missions were flown with the stability derivatives of the simulator altered to reflect the most pessimistic combination of errors that might exist.[10]

A simple flight would encompass 15-20 hours of simulator time; a complex mission could more than double that. Given that each flight was only 8-10 minutes long, this represented a lot of training. These were easily the most extensive mission simulations that had ever been attempted during the X-plane program, and would point the way to how the manned space program would proceed. Although the drill at times seemed tedious and time-consuming to all involved, it undoubtedly played a major role in the overall safety and success of what was unquestionably a potentially dangerous undertaking. All of the pilots praised the flight planners and the simulators; nobody believes the program would have succeeded nearly as well otherwise. It is one of the enduring legacies of the X-15 program.[11]

The X-15 flew for 8-10 minutes per flight; approximately 80-90 seconds of this was powered flight, the rest was spent as the world's fastest glider. Needless to say, energy management was an important part of the flight program. Energy management is the science (or perhaps black art) of figuring out where the airplane is going to land based on its current speed, altitude, and flight characteristics. For most of the X-15 program this determination was made based on nominal and off-nominal mission profiles that were computed before the flight since there was simply not sufficient computer power at the time to calculate it in real-time. Later in the program real-time energy management displays were added to the control room, and toward the end of the flight program a rudimentary display was added to the cockpit of X-15-3. This is also an enduring legacy since the concepts and experience were directly applicable to the Space Shuttle, which took over as the world's fastest – and heaviest – glider.

X-15 flights generally began early in the morning; actually, most flight testing at Edwards began early in the morning when the temperatures and winds were lower. The X-15 had been mated to the NB-52 the day before and the ground crews stayed all night or arrived early to prepare the airplane for the flight. Floodlights lit the scene as propellants and gases were loaded onto both the carrier aircraft and research airplane; liquid oxygen vapor drifted around the area, lending an surreal fog. When the X-15 pilot arrived, he generally went straight to the physiological support van to get into the David Clark full-pressure suit. Getting the suit on and hooking up the biomedical instrumentation took about 15 minutes once the program had switched to the A/P22S-2 suits; the MC-2 suits had taken considerably longer.[12]

When the ground crew was ready for the pilot to enter the cockpit, he was escorted by two technicians who carried a portable cooling system and other equipment; a scene vaguely similar to the astronauts at Cape Canaveral. A large ladder and platform were located alongside the X-15 to allow the pilot and his handlers easy access to the cockpit. The cockpit itself was fairly large for a single-seat airplane, but the bulk of the pressure suit made it seem somewhat smaller. Nevertheless, most pilots found it had more than adequate room, and some of the smaller pilots had difficulty reaching all of the controls mounted far forward since the seat was not adjustable. Once the pilot was in the cockpit the ground crew hooked up a myriad of lines, hoses, and straps that provided life support and monitored the pilot's biomedical data.

Neil Armstrong exiting the physiological support van for Flight 1-18-31 on 30 November 1960 wearing a David Clark Company MC-2 full-pressure suit. Note the mission marks on the back door of the van, each with a pilot's first name; the first flight has no engine exhaust since it was a glide, and the fourth flight has limited exhaust (and a broken airplane) since an engine exploded shortly after ignition. Another angle on the van (below) shows it to be a semi-trailer with more mission marks and an interesting piece of artwork on the side. (NASA Dryden)

Over the years Hank Caruso has used the X-15 as the subject of several pieces of his unique art. Above is "The Right Stuff," a scene at launch. Below, "A Spaceship Landed on Earth … in 1959" shows a landing. (above: ©1993 by Hank Caruso; below: ©2000 Forefeather Enterprises. Both reproduced with permission)

While this was happening the pilot began going through the preflight checklist to verify the status of all the aircraft systems. Once this was completed – usually a 30-minute process – the X-15 canopy was closed; the cockpit suddenly seemed smaller since the canopy fit snuggly around the pressure suit helmet.

While the pilot was being strapped into the cockpit, the ground crew was disconnecting the servicing carts that had been used to prepare the NB-52 and X-15 for flight. At this point the NB-52 started its engines and the carrier aircraft pilots went through their preflight checklist, taking about ten minutes to complete the activity. The ground crew then closed up the NB-52 hatches and the mated pair taxied towards the runway accompanied by a convoy of a dozen or so vehicles. Edwards is a large base, and depending which runway was in use, the taxi took

either 2 or 5 miles. One of the H-21 helicopters took-off and performed a visual check of the runway to make sure no debris was present, then took up a position beside and slightly behind the bomber, preparing to follow it down the runway for as long as possible.

At the end of the runway, the ground crew removed the safety pins from the X-15 release hooks. When everybody signaled they were ready, the NB-52 took-off and climbed to 25,000 feet while circling over Edwards to make sure the X-15 could make an emergency landing in the event it had to be jettisoned unexpectedly. Once above 25,000 feet the NB-52 turned toward the launch lake and began climbing to 45,000 feet. The X-15 liquid oxygen tank was being topped-off from the NB-52 supply and the inertial platform was receiving alignment data, but otherwise things were fairly quiet. Chase-1 was tucked in formation with the B-52, observing the X-15 for leaks or other anomalies that might signal a potential problem.

While the mated pair were on the way to the launch lake, the mission rules dictated that if there were a serious problem on the NB-52, the research airplane would be jettisoned; the extra 30,000 pounds of dead weight under the right wing would undoubtedly be detrimental to saving the carrier aircraft. Similarly, if something happened on the X-15 that looked like it would endanger the carrier aircraft, the X-15 would be jettisoned. As Scott Crossfield later observed, "It was not heroics; it was simple mathematics. Better to lose one man than four." In realty, the X-15 stood a chance of surviving if it was jettisoned, especially if the X-15 pilot had some advanced notice. The major problem was that the X-15 was carried with both of its APUs turned off – there was not enough propellant to last more than about 30 minutes. During the climbout all of the X-15 electrical needs were supplied by the NB-52, as was breathing oxygen, pressurization gas, etc. If the X-15 was jettisoned, the pilot would have his hands full trying to get the APUs started using a small emergency battery since without the APUs the pilot had no flight controls, no radio, no nothing. If the APUs started, the pilot could try to fly (with or without the engine) to a lakebed. Of course, the ejection seat was always an option. Fortunately, the program never had to find out what would happen in this scenario.[13]

At 12 minutes before the scheduled launch time, things began to happen. The APUs were started and the X-15 pilot began running through the prelaunch checklists. All of the X-15 systems were checked, the flight controls were exercised, the ballistic control system was tested, and all switch positions were set. Chase-1 observed the results of these tests and reported them back to the X-15 pilot. During this time the carrier aircraft was being guided into position near the launch lake by radar and radio communication with NASA-1. Eight minutes before launch the NB-52 began a long sweeping turn back towards Edwards, coming onto the final heading about 4 minutes later. At the same time the X-15 pilot began activating the propulsion system. At 2 minutes prior to launch the data recorders were started, the ball nose was checked one last time, and the cameras were turned on. One minute prior to launch the XLR99 was set to precool and the igniter to idle. More checks to make sure the engine looked ready to fire. The pilot took a deep breath.[14]

Three, two, one; launch. The X-15 separated from the NB-52 and began to fall. The launch was harder than most pilots initially expected because the X-15 was trimmed for 0-g at launch to ensure a clean separation from the NB-52. This meant that the pilot went from normal 1-g flight while attached to the carrier aircraft to 0-g flight instant-

Iven C. Kincheloe, Jr., was the original Air Force project pilot for the X-15, shown here with Neil Armstrong at the South Base sled track looking at the X-15 ejection seat test sled. Kinch was popularly called "The first of the spacemen" since he made the first flight above 100,000 feet in the Bell X-2. Unfortunately, on 26 July 1958 Kincheloe took off on a chase mission in an F-104. At 2,000 feet altitude the engine failed; although Kincheloe was able to roll the airplane inverted so the downward-firing ejection seat could work, he was too low for his parachute to open. (AFFTC History Office)

Edwards. But part of why the program had an excellent safety record was that the pilots and flight planners always developed contingency plans. Even for the contingency plans.

Most X-15 flights were conducted essentially in the vertical plane, and it was important to establish the proper heading back toward Edwards during the first 20 seconds after launch. Once the engine was shut down, the ballistics were pretty well established for the next few minutes of flight. If there was a wind at the launch altitude (and usually there was) the NB-52 would crab as necessary to maintain the proper ground track during the final 10 minute turn. At one minute to launch, the NB-52 pilot would turn to the desired launch heading and allow the carrier aircraft to drift. Since the X-15 trajectory would not be affected by the winds at launch, this minimized the workload on the X-15 pilot to obtain, and hold, the desired heading. After launch, any necessary heading corrections were done by the X-15 pilot using small bank angles while performing a 2-g rotation and accelerating from Mach 1 to 2 in about 20 seconds. Once the X-15 had reached the desired pitch attitude, the g-level was less than 1 and no further turning corrections were possible until after completion of the reentry.[16]

The pitch angle, in conjunction with the shutdown velocity, would establish both the range and maximum altitude of the ballistic arc that would follow. Total velocity continued to increase during the powered climb, but the dynamic pressure (q) decreased dramatically. At shutdown the dynamic pressure was 50 psf or less, so

The first four X-15 pilots during early 1960 (left to right): Scott Crossfield, Bob White, Joe Walker, and Forrest Petersen. Note the revised nose art on Balls Eight does not have the cut-off upper edge on the outer circle, and the international orange on the NB-52 does not extend obliquely aft. The forward television camera on the NB-52B may be seen above Walker's head. Petersen was in his Naval Aviator's brown shoes. (NASA Dryden)

ly. The X-15 also wanted to roll to the right because of downwash from the NB-52 wing and interference from the fuselage; X-15 pilots usually had left roll input applied at the moment of launch, although the airplane still rolled – sometimes more than others. As the X-15 was falling the pilot continued the engine start procedure. There were about ten seconds available to light the engine before the pilot had to abort to the launch lake; that was time for two ignition attempts.[15]

If the XLR99 did not light in two attempts, the pilot would be forced to make an emergency landing at the launch lake. If the engine died within the first 30 to 40 seconds of flight, the pilot would turn around and make an emergency landing at the launch lake. After about 40 seconds of burn the airplane was too far away to make it back to the launch lake; but if the engine burned less than 70 seconds it was unlikely the pilot could make it to Rogers Dry Lake. The 30 seconds in-between was why the program had a large assortment of intermediate lakebeds.

The intermediate lakes were more important for the high-speed flights than for the altitude flights. Given enough altitude, the X-15 could glide for over 400 miles, more than enough distance to make it back to Edwards from any point on the High Range. All flights were planned to have excess energy as the airplane arrived over

no aerodynamic maneuvering was possible during the final phase of powered flight. After shutdown, the pilot would immediately switch to the ballistic control system for attitude control.[17]

Thrust could be terminated two routine ways at the nominal end-of-burn. The most frequently used was called shutdown; when a specific set of flight conditions had been reached, the pilot would manually shut down the engine. Normally this was done after a pre-calculated amount of time based on a stopwatch in the cockpit that had been started when the main propellant valves opened. After the X-20 inertial flight data systems were installed later in the program the engine could also be shut down based on inertial velocity, and several of the high-altitude flights were based on the altitude predictor that was installed in X-15-3. The other type of thrust termination was called burn-out; the pilot just let the engine burn until the propellants were exhausted and the engine quit.[18]

The high-speed flights were generally conducted at fairly low altitudes – this is a relative term since these altitudes would have been considered extraordinary before the X-15 program had begun. For these flights, the X-15 was essentially an airplane; its wings generated lift, maneuvering was via a set of aerodynamic control surfaces, and the air created a great deal of drag and friction on the airframe. The pilot would begin a 2-g rotation to the desired pitch angle immediately after the engine lit; during this rotation the primary piloting task was to adjust bank angle to attain and hold the desired heading back to Edwards. As the airplane approached 70,000 feet the pilot initiated a gentle pushover to come level at something between 100,000 and 110,000 feet. As the airplane came level the pilot would either stabilize his speed at some present value to conduct various research maneuvers, or he would continue to accelerate to attain more speed. The research maneuvers would continue after engine burnout until the airplane decelerated to the point that no more useful data was forthcoming. These were the essential heating flights.[19]

Altitude flights began much the same way except the pilot continued a steep climb out of the atmosphere. The engine would be shut down on the way up and the airplane would coast over the top on a ballistic trajectory. As the airplane continued on the ballistic trajectory it was committed to a steep descent back into the atmosphere. The pilot set up the angle of attack for reentry, performed a pullout to level flight after reentry, and then began a shallow descent during the glide back to Rogers Dry Lake. The reentry was limited by a combination of dynamic pressure, load factor (g), and structural temperature; a relaxation of one resulted in an excess of one of the others. These flights spent between 2 and 5 minutes outside the atmosphere, much of that time in a weightless (i.e., no accelerations) environment. The ballistic control system allowed the pilot to maintain attitude control, but could not actually change the

A 1958-era map of the Edwards AFB ramp area. Several areas were used extensively by the X-15 program, with the primary two being marked "A" (hydraulic hoist area) and "B" (rocket aircraft servicing facility). Just right of "B" is #22, the Rocket Engine Test Facility (called the "rocket test facility – X-15" in the legend). The Flight Research Center (#31) is at the left end of the ramp and the Air Force Test Pilot School is at the lower right. (Tony Landis Collection)

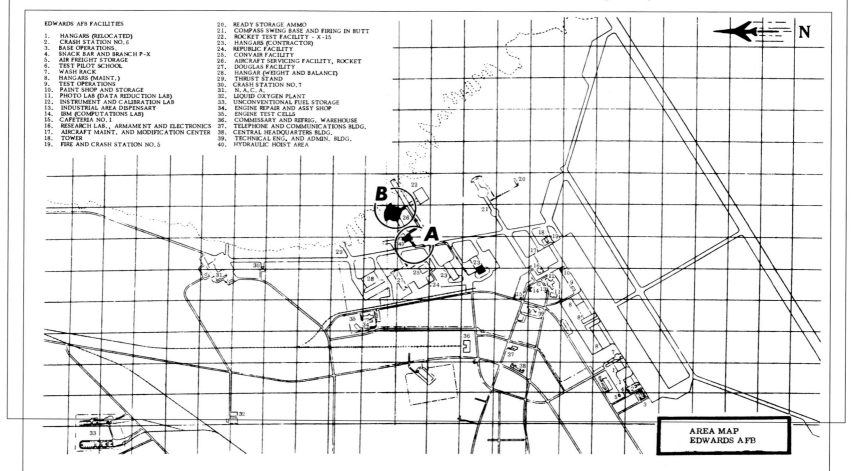

EDWARDS AFB FACILITIES

1. HANGARS (RELOCATED)
2. CRASH STATION NO. 6
3. BASE OPERATIONS.
4. SNACK BAR AND BRANCH P-X
5. AIR FREIGHT STORAGE
6. TEST PILOT SCHOOL
7. WASH RACK
8. HANGARS (MAINT.)
9. TEST OPERATIONS
10. PAINT SHOP AND STORAGE
11. PHOTO LAB (DATA REDUCTION LAB)
12. INSTRUMENT AND CALIBRATION LAB
13. INDUSTRIAL AREA DISPENSARY
14. IBM (COMPUTATIONS LAB)
15. CAFETERIA NO. 1
16. RESEARCH LAB., ARMAMENT AND ELECTRONICS
17. AIRCRAFT MAINT. AND MODIFICATION CENTER
18. TOWER
19. FIRE AND CRASH STATION NO. 5
20. READY STORAGE AMMO
21. COMPASS SWING BASE AND FIRING IN BUTT
22. ROCKET TEST FACILITY – X-15
23. HANGARS (CONTRACTOR)
24. REPUBLIC FACILITY
25. CONVAIR FACILITY
26. AIRCRAFT SERVICING FACILITY, ROCKET
27. DOUGLAS FACILITY
28. HANGAR (WEIGHT AND BALANCE)
29. THRUST STAND
30. CRASH STATION NO. 7
31. N.A.C.A.
32. LIQUID OXYGEN PLANT
33. UNCONVENTIONAL FUEL STORAGE
34. ENGINE REPAIR AND ASSY SHOP
35. ENGINE TEST CELLS
36. COMMISSARY AND REFRIG. WAREHOUSE
37. TELEPHONE AND COMMUNICATIONS BLDG.
38. CENTRAL HEADQUARTERS BLDG.
39. TECHNICAL ENG. AND ADMIN. BLDG.
40. HYDRAULIC HOIST AREA

N

AREA MAP
EDWARDS AFB

Support vehicles on Rogers Dry Lake for Flight 1-6-11 on 5 May 1960. Note the physiological support van on the left, and the fire truck and ambulance on the right. This was representative of the support the Air Force provided for the early flights; later flights got more complicated. (NASA Dryden)

flight path of the airplane. As fast as it was, the X-15 never flew anywhere near fast enough to attain orbital velocities.[20]

For the next few minutes the calls from NASA-1 were primarily comparisons between the planned profile (on the plot boards) and the actual radar track of the airplane. These calls alerted the X-15 pilot to how well he had flown the boost phase, but more importantly, what kind of maneuvering might be required following the reentry. If he was "high and long" then he would expect an immediate turn and speed brakes during the latter part of the reentry. If he was "low and short" then he would expect a straight-ahead glide with brakes closed. A "right of course" call would alert him to expect a left turn to a new heading after reentry. Comprehending some of these energy management subtleties, while simultaneously controlling aircraft attitude, subsystems, and accomplishing test maneuvers was one of the goals of the X-15 simulator training.[21]

Perhaps surprisingly, the altitude flights required a longer ground track than the high-speed flights. This was primarily because the airplane covered a lot of miles while it was outside the atmosphere. Just looking at the two maximum performance flights. Joe Walker's 354,200-foot flight required a ground track of 305 miles to climb out of the atmosphere, coast to peak altitude, reenter, make the pullout, and then slow down to land. On the other hand, Pete Knight's 4,520-mph speed flight only took 225 miles, mainly because the airplane slowed down very quickly after engine burnout since the speed flights were conducted in relatively dense atmosphere.[22]

During the envelope expansion flights, the pilots were given specific maneuvers – rudder pulses, angle-of-attack changes, rolls, etc. – that needed to be performed in order to determine the stability and control of the airplane in various flight regimes. Many times these maneuvers were very near the limits of controllability for the airplane, always with well-practiced contingency plans at the ready. Other tests provided information on control effectiveness, aerodynamic performance, lift-to-drag ratio, aero-thermo loads, etc. All of these maneuvers required that the pilot fly at a specific speed, attitude, and altitude while gathering the data. Often the exact profile needed to be repeated on subsequent flights in order to eliminate variables from the data being evaluated.[23]

As Milt Thompson later observed, 'This is the kind of thing a research pilot is required to do to earn his money – accomplishing good maneuvers for data purposes. Flying the airplane is just something the pilot does to get the desired test maneuver. He can be the greatest stick and rudder pilot in the world, but if he cannot do the required data maneuvers, he is worthless as a research pilot." Most of the X-15 pilots were very good research pilots.[24]

Assuming all went well, the X-15 arrived back at Edwards and set up a High Key at approximately 35,000 feet and 290 to 350 mph. As he approached Edwards, the X-15 pilot began dumping any residual propellants to lower the landing weight and to get rid of potentially explosive substances. It also made a convenient way for the chase planes to find the small X-15 in the vast skies over the high desert. The X-15 then entered a 35-degree banking turn while maintaining 250 to 300 knots; the turn was normally made to the left, although each pilot seemed to develop a preference and it really did not matter much. At the completion of the turn the X-15 was approximately 4 miles abeam of the intended touchdown point at 18,000 feet altitude headed in the opposite direction of the landing runway; this was called Low Key. The pilot then continued turning 180-degrees, turned onto final at about 8,000 feet and 300 knots, and flared at around 1,000 feet. The landing flaps were lowered as the airplane came level at about 100 feet, and the landing gear came down at 215 to 225 knots. Touchdown was generally around 190 to 200 knots. The pilot judged what possible crosswinds that might be encountered during landing and slideout by the simple expedient of looking at the smoke from flares that had been lit beside the runway.[25]

Not surprisingly, not all flights arrived at High Key exactly as planned. At least one flight arrived at High Key at 70,000 feet and over Mach 3; another made High Key at only 25,000 feet, and one made a straight-in approach because it was too low on energy upon arrival at Edwards. Despite these variances, the majority of X-15 touchdowns were within 2,000 feet of the intended spot, although a couple of flights missed by over 4,000 feet. Neil Armstrong managed to miss by 12 miles – fortunately, Rogers is a large dry lake. The X-15 generally slid for 8,000 to 10,000 feet before coming to a stop, being chased by a convoy of rescue and support vehicles.[26]

The general concept was very similar to that ultimately adopted as the terminal area energy management maneuver used by the Space Shuttle. The proven ability of the X-15 (and later the heavy-weight lifting-bodies) to make unpowered approaches was one reason the Space Shuttle program decided it could eliminate the complexity of landing engines and make the Orbiter a glider. It is another enduring legacy of the X-15 program.[27]

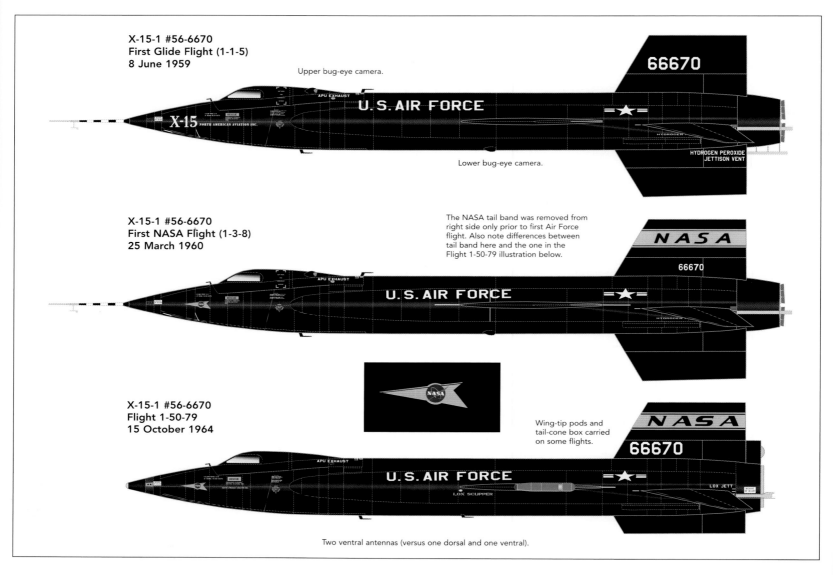

X-15-1 #56-6670
First Glide Flight (1-1-5)
8 June 1959

Upper bug-eye camera.

66670

U.S. AIR FORCE

HYDROGEN PEROXIDE
JETTISON VENT

Lower bug-eye camera.

X-15-1 #56-6670
First NASA Flight (1-3-8)
25 March 1960

The NASA tail band was removed from right side only prior to first Air Force flight. Also note differences between tail band here and the one in the Flight 1-50-79 illustration below.

NASA

66670

U.S. AIR FORCE

X-15-1 #56-6670
Flight 1-50-79
15 October 1964

Wing-tip pods and tail-cone box carried on some flights.

NASA

66670

U.S. AIR FORCE

LOX SCUPPER

LOX JETT

Two ventral antennas (versus one dorsal and one ventral).

Above and facing page: *X-15 profiles showing the appearance of the airplanes on various flights. Note the configuration of the antennas (top and bottom) and how much longer the engine exhaust nozzle fairing is on the XLR11-powered flights.* (Artwork by Tony Landis)

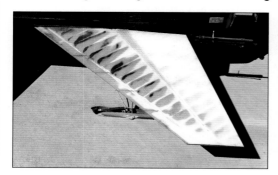

Temperature-sensitive paint after the return of Flight 2-19-35 shows the internal structure. (NASA Dryden)

Note that the BCS pitch thrusters are offset from the centerline. (NASA Dryden)

The X-15-3 on 9 August 1963. Note the pressure-sensing impact rake ahead of the art. (NASA Dryden)

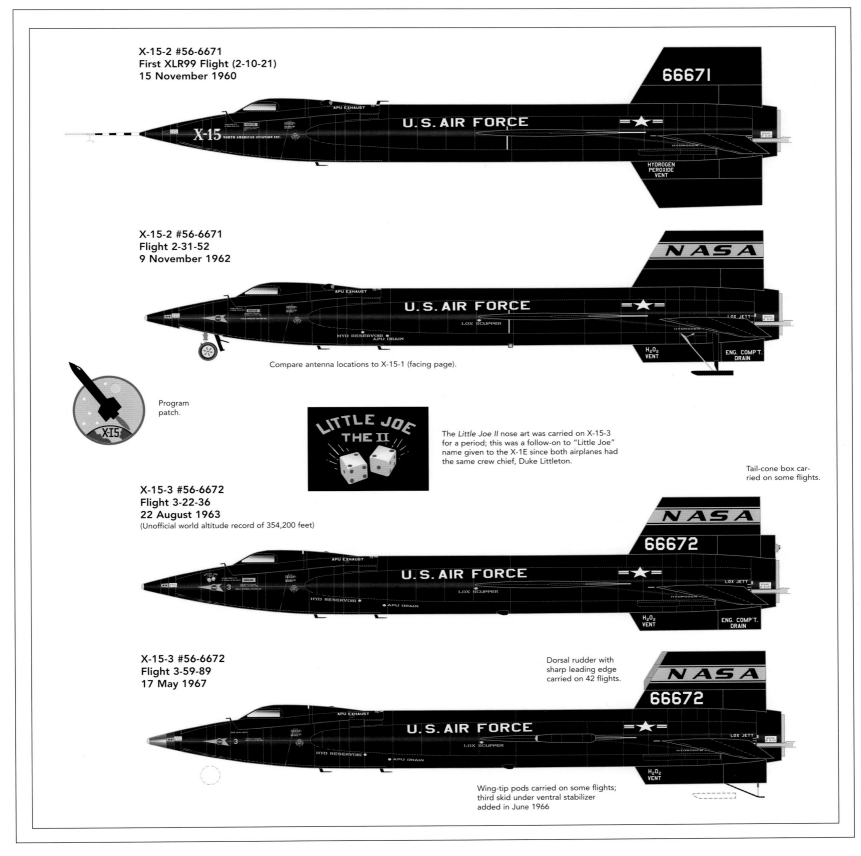

X-15-2 #56-6671
First XLR99 Flight (2-10-21)
15 November 1960

66671

APU EXHAUST

X-15 NORTH AMERICAN AVIATION INC.

U.S. AIR FORCE

HYDROGEN

HYDROGEN
PEROXIDE
VENT

X-15-2 #56-6671
Flight 2-31-52
9 November 1962

NASA

APU EXHAUST

U.S. AIR FORCE

LOX JETT

HYD RESERVOIR
APU DRAIN

LOX SCUPPER

HYDROGEN

H₂O₂
VENT

ENG. COMP'T.
DRAIN

Compare antenna locations to X-15-1 (facing page).

Program
patch.

X-15

LITTLE JOE
THE II

The *Little Joe II* nose art was carried on X-15-3
for a period; this was a follow-on to "Little Joe"
name given to the X-1E since both airplanes had
the same crew chief, Duke Littleton.

Tail-cone box car-
ried on some flights.

X-15-3 #56-6672
Flight 3-22-36
22 August 1963
(Unofficial world altitude record of 354,200 feet)

NASA

APU EXHAUST

66672

3

RESCUE

U.S. AIR FORCE

LOX JETT

HYD RESERVOIR

APU DRAIN

LOX SCUPPER

HYDROGEN

H₂O₂
VENT

ENG. COMP'T.
DRAIN

Dorsal rudder with
sharp leading edge
carried on 42 flights.

X-15-3 #56-6672
Flight 3-59-89
17 May 1967

NASA

66672

APU EXHAUST

3

U.S. AIR FORCE

LOX JETT

HYD RESERVOIR

APU DRAIN

LOX SCUPPER

HYDROGEN

H₂O₂
VENT

Wing-tip pods carried on some flights;
third skid under ventral stabilizer
added in June 1966

CAN IT FLY?

The X-15-1 arrived at Edwards on 17 October 1958, trucked over the hills from the North American plant in Inglewood. It was joined by the second airplane in April 1959; the third would arrive later. In contrast to the relative secrecy that had attended flight tests with the XS-1 a decade before, the X-15 program would offer the spectacle of pure theater.[28]

The task of flying the X-15 during the contractor program rested in the capable hands of Scott Crossfield – the person who arguably knew more about the airplane than any other individual. After various ground checks, the X-15-1 was mated to 003, then more ground tests were conducted. When the day for the first flight – 10 March 1959 – arrived, Scott Crossfield later described it as "a carnival at dawn." Things were different during the 1950s. Crossfield and Charlie Feltz had shared a room in the bachelor officer quarters at Edwards; no fancy hotel in town. They each dressed in a shirt and tie before driving to the flight line; nothing casual, even though Crossfield would soon be locked inside a David Clark MC-2 full-pressure suit. When they got to the parking lot next to the NB-52 mating area, more than 50 cars were already waiting. The flight had been scheduled for 07:00; based on his previous rocket-plane experience, Cross-

field predicted they would take off no earlier than Noon, and maybe as late as 14:00. Crossfield was pleasantly surprised – at 10:00 the mated pair took off on their scheduled captive-carry flight (retroactively called program flight number 1-C-1).[29]

During the captive flight the X-15 flight controls were exercised and airspeed data from the flight test boom on the nose was obtained in order to calibrate instrumentation. Crossfield lowered the X-15 landing gear just to make sure it worked, even if it looked a little odd while still mated to the NB-52. Part of the test sequence was to make sure the David Clark full-pressure suit worked as advertised, although Crossfield had no doubts it would. This was a decidedly straightforward test. The suit was designed to inflate as soon as the altitude in the cockpit went above 35,000 feet. As the mated pair passed 30,000 feet, Crossfield turned off the cabin pressurization system and opened the ram air door to equalize the internal pressure with the outside air. Once the airplanes climbed above 35,000 feet, Crossfield felt the suit begin to inflate, "from that point on my movements were slightly constrained and slightly awkward." Still Crossfield could reach all of the controls, including the hardest control in the cockpit to reach – the ram air door lever. Crossfield closed the door, and as the cockpit repressurized the suit relaxed its grip. This test would be repeated on every X-15 flight until the end of the program.[30]

X-15-1 was delivered to Edwards on 17 October 1958, being trucked overland from the North American Inglewood plant. The airplane was wrapped in heavy brown paper for the trip, which was promptly stripped off after arriving at Edwards so the airplane could be removed from the truck. All three X-15s would be transported to Edwards in this manner, although the wrapping paper was deleted for later trips. (AFFTC History Office)

X-15-1 is unloaded after delivery to Edwards. Note the empty holes for the XLR11s and lack of a ball nose. (AFFTC History Office via the Gerald H. Balzer Collection)

The next step was to release the X-15 from the NB-52 in order to ascertain its gliding and landing characteristics. The first glide flight was scheduled for 1 April 1959, but was aborted when the X-15 radio failed. The NB-52A and X-15 spent 1 hour and 45 minutes airborne conducting further tests in the mated configuration. A second attempt was aborted on 10 April 1959 by a combination of radio failure and APU problems. Yet a third attempt was aborted on 21 May 1959 when the X-15 stability augmentation system failed and a bearing in the No. 1 APU overheated after approximately 29 minutes of operation.[31]

The problems with the APU were the most disturbing. Various valve malfunctions, leaks, and several APU speed-control problems were encountered during these flights, all of which would have been unacceptable during research flights. Tests conducted on the APU revealed that extremely high surge pressures were occurring at the pressure relief valve (actually a blow-out plug) during initial peroxide tank pressurization. The installation of an orifice in the helium pressurization line immediately downstream of the shut-off valve reduced the surges to acceptable levels. Other problems were found to be unique to the captive-carry flights and the long-run times being imposed on the APUs; they were deemed to be of little consequence to the flight program since the operating scenario would be different. Still, reliability was marginal, at best. The APUs underwent a constant set of minor improvements during the flight program, but continued to be a source of irritation until the end.[32]

The crew at an X-15 pre-flight briefing. At left is Crossfield's backup pilot, Al White, who would fly Chase-1. Next to him is the North American Supervisor at Edwards, Q.C. Harvey, chase pilot Joe Jordan, and launch panel operator Bill Berkowitz. (Photo courtesy of Alvin S. White)

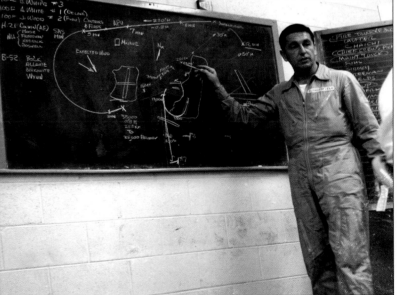

Scott Crossfield discusses the plan for the first glide flight. Note the names of the chase pilots and carrier aircraft crew at the upper left of the chalk board. The first glide flight was a North American operation, explaining Al White as Chase-1 and Bill Berkowitz as the launch panel operator. (AFFTC History Office)

The X-15-1 and Balls Three preparing to land after the first captive flight on 10 March 1959. Crossfield had extended the X-15 landing gear just to make sure it would work after being cold-soaked during the flight. At this point the NB-52's rear landing gear has already touched down, but the nose gear are still a bit off the runway; its an unusual way for a B-52 to land and required some practice by the carrier aircraft pilots. (The Boeing Company Archives)

Scenes from the first glide flight. Al White is flying chase in the F-100F, about as close as he would get to actually flying the X-15. (AFFTC History Office)

On 22 May the first ground run of the interim XLR11 engine was accomplished using the X-15-2 at the Rocket Engine Test Facility. Scott Crossfield was in the cockpit, and the test was considered successful, clearing the way for the eventual first powered flight – if the X-15-1 could ever make its unpowered flight. Another attempt at the glide flight was made on 5 June 1959 but was aborted even before the NB-52 left the ground when Crossfield reported smoke in the X-15-1 cockpit. Investigation showed that a cockpit ventilation fan motor had overheated. The continuing problems with the first glide flight were beginning to take their toll, both physically and mentally.[33]

Finally, at 08:38 on 8 June 1959, Scott Crossfield and the X-15-1 dropped from Balls Three at Mach 0.79 and 37,550 feet. Just prior to launch the SAS pitch damper failed but Crossfield elected to proceed with the flight, and switched the pitch channel to standby. At launch, the X-15 separated cleanly and Crossfield rolled to the right with a bank angle of about 30 degrees. Usually the obedient test pilot, on this flight Crossfield allowed himself to deviate slightly from the flight plan; one unauthorized aileron roll. But all was not well. On the final approach to landing, the X-15 began a series of increasingly wild pitching motions. Crossfield: "the nose of the X-15 pitched up sharply. It was a maneuver that had not been predicted by the simulator ... I was frankly caught off guard. Quickly I applied corrective elevator control. The nose came down sharply. But instead of leveling out, it tucked down. I applied reverse control. The nose came up but much too far. Now the nose was rising and falling like the bow of a skiff in a heavy sea ... I could not subdue the motions." The X-15 was porpoising wildly, sinking toward the desert at 175 knots.[34]

The airplane touched down safely at 150 knots, and slid 3,900 feet while turning very slightly to the right. After he landed, Crossfield believed that the airplane exhibited a classic case of static instability; Harrison Storms, on the other hand, was sure that a simple adjustment was all that was needed. In the end, Storms was right. As he would on all of his flights, Crossfield was using the side-stick controller during the flare instead of the center stick, and this subsequently proved to be the

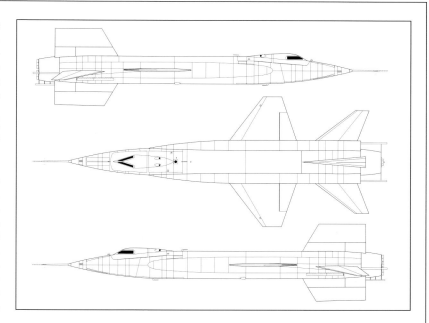

Three view drawing of the X-15-1 as-built with two XLR11s, the NACA nose boom, and four bug-eye camera ports. (Artwork by Tony Landis)

contributing cause of the oscillations. The side-stick controller used small hydraulic boost actuators to assist the pilot since it would have been impossible (or at least impractical) to move the side stick through the same range of motion required for the center stick. But a decision had been made to restrict the authority of these hydraulic cylinders somewhat, based on a best guess of the range of movement required. The guess had been wrong; because of this, a cable in the control system was stretching and retracting unexpectedly. What appeared to be

North American built at least two Propulsion System Test Stands; one was used at the Reaction Motors Lake Denmark test site, the other at the Rocket Engine Test Facility at Edwards. These were essentially an X-15 mid- and aft fuselage, including the propellant tanks and thrust structure, and were used to test both the XLR11 and XLR99 engines. The XLR11-equipped unit is shown during a test on 9 January 1959. (left: Gerald H. Balzer Collection; right: AFFTC History Office)

Scott Crossfield prepares to climb into the cockpit of X-15-1 for an attempt at the glide flight on 5 June 1959. It was a short ride; smoke in the cockpit forced an abort while the carrier aircraft was still taxiing to the runway; a ventilation fan motor had overheated. A more successful attempt would be made three days later. (AFFTC History Office)

pilot-induced oscillations during landing were really caused by the mechanics of the control system. The fix was to provide more authority to the hydraulic cylinder by changing an orifice. Simple.[35]

While the X-15-1 was being carried as expensive wing cargo on the NB-52, the XLR11s continued to be tested in the Rocket Engine Test Facility using the X-15-2. Despite the successful 22 May test, things were not going particularly well. Perhaps the engines had been out of service for too long between programs, or maybe too much knowledge had been lost during the comings and goings of the various engineers and technicians over the years, but the initial runs were hardly trouble-free. Various valves and regulators in the propellant system also proved to be surprisingly troublesome. And sometimes things just went to hell. After one engine run the ground crew began purging the hydrogen peroxide lines of all residual liquid by connecting a hose from a ground nitrogen supply to a fitting on the X-15-2. On this day it was a new hose. Despite careful procedures and great caution, the hose had a slight residue of oil. When the technician applied gas pressure to the hose, the film of oil was forced into the hydrogen peroxide lines. The only thing truly compatible with peroxide is more peroxide; not oil. The result was an explosion and fire that raced through the X-15 engine compartment. The Edwards fire crew had been standing by and quickly extinguished the fire, but not before the engine bay was gutted. One X-15 crewman was badly burned; if he had been standing two feet closer, he likely would have been killed. It took weeks to repair the airplane.[36]

Forty-six days after the first glide flight, and after being repaired from its explosion, the X-15-2 was taken for a captive-carry flight with full propellant tanks on 24 July 1959. One of the major purposes of this flight was to evaluate the liquid oxygen top-off system between the NB-52 and X-15; it proved to be erratic. Another test was to measure the time it took to jettison the propellants at altitude. While still safely attached to the wing of the NB-52, Crossfield jettisoned the hydrogen peroxide; it took 140 seconds. He then jettisoned the liquid oxygen and alcohol simultaneously; they took 110 seconds. The times matched the predictions. The APUs and pressure

The first glide flight was finally accomplished on 8 June 1959 and lasted just over 4 minutes and 56 seconds. Not surprisingly, it would end up being the slowest flight of the program. The flight itself was uneventful, but the landing had a bit more drama than anybody had intended; a very small design oversight led to severe porpoising just before touchdown. Fortunately, the fix was relatively simple and was installed in the airplane before the next flight attempt. Crossfield is doing last-minute paperwork in the photo at left, and he inspects the airplane in the post-landing photo at right. (The Boeing Company Archives)

suit performed flawlessly. Despite the failure of the top-off system, the flight was considered a success. The original contract had promised the first airplane would be turned over to the government in August 1959, and for a while it looked like North American might deliver the first X-15 on schedule. But it was not to be.[37]

During August and early September, several attempts to make the first powered flight were cancelled before leaving the ground due to leaks in the APU propellant system and hydraulic problems. There were also several failures of propellant tank pressure regulators; on one occasion liquid oxygen streamed out of the safety vent while the X-15 was still attached to the NB-52. No flight on that day. Charlie Feltz, Bud Benner, and John Gibb, along with a variety of North American engineers and technicians worked to eliminate these problems, all of which were irritating, but none were considered critical. Other than to moral, which was beginning to suffer from the constant delays.[38]

At last, the first powered flight was made by X-15-2 on 17 September 1959. The airplane was released from the NB-52A at 08:08 while flying Mach 0.80 at 37,600 feet, and reached Mach 2.11 and 52,341 feet during 224.3 seconds of powered flight using the two XLR11 engines. Crossfield surprised everybody, including most probably himself; another aileron roll, this time all the way around. Crossfield remembers that "Storms was tickled." On a more serious note, "With the rolling tail, one would expect very clean 'aileron' rolls without the classical adverse yaw from ailerons, and that is the way it rolled. No big deal at all."[39]

Crossfield landed on Rogers Dry Lake 9 minutes and 11 seconds after launch, despite some concerns about a crosswind across the lake. Following the landing, a fire was noticed in the area around the ventral stabilizer, and was quickly extinguished by ground crews. A subsequent investigation revealed that the upper XLR11 fuel pump diffuser case had cracked after engine shutdown and had sprayed fuel throughout the engine compartment. Alcohol collected in the ventral stabilizer and was ignited by unknown causes during landing. Crossfield said "the fire had burned through a large area, melting aluminum tubing, fuel lines, valves, and other machinery." For the second time in less than six months, the X-15-2 went back to Inglewood; it took about three weeks to repair the damage.[40]

The third flight (2-3-9) of X-15-2 took place on 5 November 1959 when the X-15 was dropped from Balls Three at Mach 0.82 and 44,000 feet. The flight got off to a bad start – during the engine start sequence, one chamber in the lower engine exploded. Chase planes reported external damage around the engine and base plate and the resulting fire convinced Crossfield to make an emergency landing at Rosamond Dry Lake. Crossfield shut down both engines, but the 13.9 seconds of powered flight had been sufficient to accelerate the X-15 to Mach 1. Unfortunately, the flight path needed to descend to the lakebed made dumping most of the remaining propellants impossible. The landing flare was initiated at about 950 feet altitude at a speed of 253 knots, and Crossfield jettisoned the ventral rudder on the final approach. The aircraft touched down near the center of the lake at approximately 161 knots and an 10.8-degree angle of attack with a 9.5 foot per second descent rate. Crossfield: "The skids dug in gently. The nose slammed down hard and the ship plowed across the desert floor, slowing down much faster than usual. Then she came to a complete stop within 1,500 feet instead of the usual 5,000 feet." When the nose gear had bottomed out, the fuselage literally broke in half at station 226.8, with about 70 percent of the bolts at the manufacturing joint being sheared out. The broken fuselage dug into the lakebed, creating a very effective brake.[41]

This is how it was done before computers. Engineers inspect recording film from the X-15 glide flight. Everything was recorded onboard the airplane on film, and film and stripcharts recorded the data acquired on the ground. Clockwise from left front: Glen Robinson, Bob Tremant, Tom Finch, Joe Weil, Jack Fischel, John McTigue, Dan Riegert, Tom Cooney, Roxanah Yancey, Chet Wolowicz, Tom Baker, Chris Pembo, and Roy Bryant. (NASA Dryden)

A contributing factor to the hard landing was the 15,138-pound touchdown weight. A limiting rate of sink of 9 fps had been established during development, based on a design weight of 11,500 pounds. However, the as-built airplane had increased to 13,230 pounds. In addition, some of the propellants could not be jettisoned because of the steep descending attitude necessary to reach the landing site, further increasing landing weight.[42]

The post-accident investigation revealed that, besides the known overweight issue, the principal problem existed in the nose gear. In order to conserve space when the nose gear was retracted, Charlie Feltz had devised a way to stow the strut in a nearly compressed position. Upon nose gear extension, the nitrogen gas that had been trapped by the oil under high pressure was released and produced a gas-oil foam within the cylinder. Approximately the first one-third of the cylinder stroke was rendered ineffective by this foam; consequently, the loads built up to excessive values during the remainder of the stroke. The permanent solution was to redesign the internal mechanism of the strut to incorporate a floating piston that kept the gas and oil separated at all times. Yet again, the X-15-2 was sent to Inglewood plant for repairs, and was subsequently returned to Edwards in time for its fourth flight on 11 February 1960. The damaged fuselage area was repaired and strengthened by doubling the number of fasteners and by adding top and bottom splice plates at the fuselage joint. Modifications were made to the other two airplanes to prevent similar problems.[43]

The X-15-1 made its first powered flight on 23 January 1960 again with Crossfield in the cockpit. The performance of the airplane was beginning to show – Crossfield reached 1,669 mph (Mach 2.53) and 66,844 feet during 267.2 seconds of powered flight. The stable platform was installed for the first time, and the performance of the system was considered encouraging. This was also the first X-15 flight that used Balls Eight as a carrier aircraft.

X-15-2 during the first powered flight on 17 September 1959. Note that only three chambers had lit on the upper engine when this photo was taken. Frost on the liquid oxygen tank can be seen in both photos; almost solid at launch, and little at landing. (AFFTC History Office via the Gerald H. Balzer Collection)

Under the terms of the contract, North American had to demonstrate the basic airworthiness and operation of the airplane before turning it over to the government. Everybody believed that this flight adequately passed these criteria although the X-15-1 had only made two flights. A pre-delivery inspection was accomplished a few days after the flight, and on 3 February 1960 the X-15-1 was formally accepted by the Air Force and subsequently turned over to NASA on long-term loan.[44]

The first X-15 flight (1-3-8) with a government pilot was launched on 25 March 1960 with Joe Walker at the controls. The X-15-1 was dropped at Mach 0.82 and 45,500 feet, although the stable platform had malfunctioned just prior to release. Two restarts were required on the top engine before all eight chambers were firing, and the flight lasted just over 9 minutes, reaching Mach 2.0 and 48,630 feet. Overall, Walker was impressed with the flight.

For the next six months, Joe Walker and Bob White alternated flying the X-15-1. The first flight (1-7-12) from a remote lake (instead of Rosamond) was made from Silver Lake on 12 May 1960 with Joe

Walker at the controls. The X-15-1 dropped away from the NB-52 at Mach 0.83 and 44,800 feet, and Walker ignited all eight chambers on the two XLR11s and set an 8-degree angle-of-attack to a maximum altitude of 77,882 feet. After the push-over to peak altitude and the entry into a slight dive, the aircraft accelerated more than expected; Walker turned off three chambers of the XLR11. Unfortunately, this resulted in an abrupt deceleration that caused the engine propellant pumps to cavitate, resulting in the other five chambers shutting down seconds later. A maximum speed of Mach 3.19 had been reached, marking the first Mach 3 flight for the X-15 program.[45]

Eventually, 30 flights would be flown with the interim XLR11 engines; X-15-1 would make 21 of these while the other 9 would be flown by X-15-2. In general the XLR11 flights stayed below 100,000 feet, although several were barely above that altitude and Bob White took the X-15-1 to 136,500 feet on 12 August 1960 (Flight 1-10-19), establishing a new altitude record for piloted aircraft. The maximum speed recorded with the XLR11 engines was Mach 3.50 (2,275 mph) on Flight 1-21-36, again with Bob White at the controls.[46]

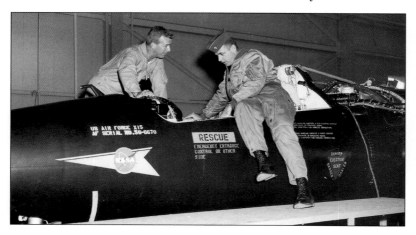

Joe Walker (on the left) from NASA and Major Bob White are shown on 25 February 1960 with X-15-1. These were the two government pilots that shared the XLR11 envelope expansion flights. (NASA Dryden)

A small alcohol fire broke out in the engine compartment on the first powered flight because an XLR11 fuel pump diffuser case had broken after engine shutdown. Otherwise, the flight had gone well. (AFFTC History Office)

The X-15-1 is launched on one of the later XLR11-powered flights (note the mission marks on the NB-52). The photo at left shows the research airplane just after release, and liquid oxygen from the top-off system may be seen streaming out of the pylon. The research airplane wanted to roll immediately after launch since the downwash from the swept wing on the bomber was not symmetrical. (The Boeing Company Archives)

An attempt for the fourth program flight ended on 31 October 1959 in an abort (2-A-8) for weather, although the sky here shows no reason for concern. Crossfield was in X-15-2 hanging under Balls Three with Bob Baker and John DeLong in the F-100F as Chase-1. (AFFTC History Office)

A good photo of the XLR11 installation on X-15-1 in December 1960. Note the mission markings on the ventral rudder, showing that this particular unit had been reused ten times. Also notice the additional vent tube on upper part of the aft fuselage – no explanation could be found, although it was likely an alternate hydrogen peroxide vent. (Tony Landis Collection)

Photos taken on 18 December 1959 show the loading and unloading procedure. The X-15 was towed into position on top of its hydraulic lifts, and the carrier aircraft towed into position over it (actually, it did not matter which airplane arrived first). The platforms would then be raised until the X-15 was just below the pylon. Various connections and verifications would be made, and the X-15 raised further and secured to the pylon at its three attach points. The hydraulic lifts were retracted and the ground crew installed the ventral rudder and raised the X-15 landing gear. At this point the ground crew began servicing the X-15 and NB-52 for the upcoming mission. (NASA Dryden)

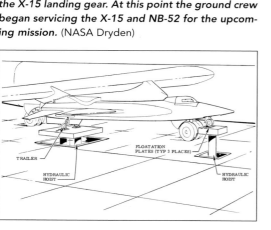

THE MILLION-HORSEPOWER ENGINE

The first ground test XLR99 (s/n 101) had arrived at Edwards on 7 June 1959, and the first hot test was accomplished without an actual X-15 at the Rocket Engine Test Facility on 26 August 1959. The X-15-3 arrived at Edwards on 29 June 1959 and was, for all intents and purposes, identical to the other two airplanes; it was equipped with a standard Westinghouse stability augmentation system, stable platform, and a normal cockpit instrument panel. What made it different – at this point – was that it had the XLR99 engine; the third X-15 was never equipped with the XLR11 engines.[47]

The first ground run with the XLR99 in the X-15-3 was made on 2 June 1960 at the Rocket Engine Test Facility. For all of the ground runs during the program, a pilot had to be in the cockpit since the engine could not be operated by remote control from the nearby blockhouse. For the early tests, it was Scott Crossfield, although all of the pilots would participate in ground runs during the course of the flight program. The MC-2 full-pressure suit was an order of magnitude more comfortable than earlier pressure suits, but Crossfield still had little desire to wear it more than necessary. Since there was no need for altitude protection during the engine runs on the ground, Crossfield generally wore street clothes in the cockpit. All other personnel required for the tests were in the blockhouse, with the exception of the Air Force fire crews a relatively safe distance away.[48]

The third ground run was conducted on 8 June at approximately 19:30 hours to demonstrate the restart capability and throttling characteristics of the XLR99. The pre-test operations, servicing, and APU starts were accomplished successfully and all systems were operating normally. The engine was primed, set to idle, then ignited at the 50-percent thrust level. After the chamber pressure stabilized for 7 seconds, the throttle was advanced to 100 percent for 5 seconds. The throttle was then moved to idle for 5 seconds and the engine was shut down. Nothing abnormal was noted during these events. After 15 seconds, the

The Propulsion System Test Stand at Edwards was modified for the XLR99 and used for the initial ground runs. As near as can be determined, the test article was built from flight-qualified hardware. (San Diego Aerospace Museum Collection)

throttle was moved to the 50-percent position. The turbopump started normally, first and second stage ignition occurred, and main chamber start appeared normal. After the main chamber pressure stabilized, it rapidly fell off and the engine shut down automatically. At this time a valve malfunction light came on in the cockpit; Crossfield moved the

Crossfield got to do everything first, including the first emergency landing when the lower XLR11 engine suffered a minor explosion during Flight 2-3-9 on 5 November 1959. Crossfield landed on Rosamond, breaking the back of the airplane at Station 226.5, but escaping uninjured. (AFFTC History Office)

The Rocket Engine Test Facility on 25 May 1960 with X-15-1 (foreground, with frost around the liquid oxygen tank) and X-15-2 in position. The blockhouse that monitored the tests is in the center. Note Scott Crossfield's Bonanza in background. Below are a few details of the test area, including the engine clamping mechanism and the special slide that supported the front of the X-15 during the tests. At below right, the X-15-3 during a ground run on 13 September 1966. (Above: Terry Panopalis Collection; Others: NASA Dryden)

The remains of X-15-3 after the XLR99 exploded during a ground run on 8 June 1960. Scott Crossfield and the cockpit were thrown approximately 30 feet forward. Subsequent investigation showed there was nothing wrong with either the engine or airframe design; the explosion had been caused by a component failure and the unique configuration required for ground testing. (two at above left: AFFTC History Office; below left: NASA; others: Gerald H. Balzer Collection)

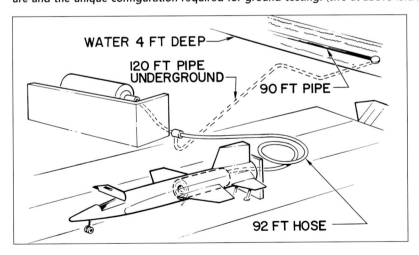

throttle to the off position and the light went out. In order to restart the XLR99 after a malfunction shutdown, the pilot had to push a switch that reset the automatic safety devices. As Crossfield wrote in his accident statement, "the reset button was depressed at which time the airplane blew up." It was approximately 19:45 hours.[49]

According to Crossfield, "During this entire sequence except for the malfunction shut down, there was no evidence in the cockpit of difficulty." The explosion appeared to be centered forward of the engine

compartment, and caused the aircraft to separate around fuselage station 483.5 – just forward of the liquid oxygen tank. Don Richter, in the main blockhouse, indicated that he observed the explosion originating 5 feet forward from the aft end of the airplane, with the fire ball quickly expanding to about 30 feet in diameter.[50]

The entire forward fuselage was thrown about 30 feet forward. Crossfield: "In the explosion, which is not describable, the cockpit translated abruptly forward and to the right with an acceleration

The X-15 program generated a lot of publicity and the mockup and various pilots were used extensively for goodwill tours. Here is the X-15 mockup at the CBS studios in Hollywood on 15 May 1959. (The Boeing Company Archives)

All of the pilots were kept busy either training or on tour. Here, Al White signs autographs in front of the X-15 mockup at the World Congress of Flight in Las Vegas in 1959. (Photo courtesy of Alvin S. White)

beyond the experience of this pilot." The basic X-15 airframe had been designed – largely at Crossfield's urging – to protect the pilot in the event of an emergency; it appeared to work well. Ever the competent test pilot, Crossfield turned off the engine switches and pulled all the circuit breakers. He attempted to contact personnel inside the blockhouse, but communications with the ground had been severed by the explosion.[51]

The fire truck that had been standing-by was on the scene within 30 seconds, water pouring from its overhead nozzle; a second fire truck arrived a minute or two later to help extinguish the fires. Art Simone and a suited fireman rushed to the cockpit and Crossfield was rescued uninjured – Simone inhaled some ammonia fumes and received minor burns to his hands, but suffered no lasting effects. The fires were largely out within a few minutes of the explosion and Crossfield was safe; it was time to figure out what had happened.[52]

The XLR99 was removed from the wreckage on 13 June and the remains of X-15-3 were transported to Inglewood by truck on 15 June. The Rocket Engine Test Facility required major repairs, but was brought back on line by the end of June. By 4 August the damage had been assessed. Essentially, the airframe would need to be replaced from fuselage station 331.9 aft. The dorsal and ventral stabilizers and all four speed brakes needed replaced, as did both horizontal stabilizers. The main landing skids and both propellant tanks would be replaced. The wings were considered repairable as were the APUs and stable platform. All of the miscellaneous equipment in the rear and center fuselage, along with most of the research instrumentation in the aft fuselage, also required replacement. The XLR99 was not considered repairable, although some parts were salvaged for future use.[53]

Subsequent investigation revealed that the initiating cause of the explosion was an overpressurization of the ammonia tank. Because of the toxic nature of ammonia fumes, a vapor disposal system had been incorporated into the Rocket Engine Test Facility that allowed the ammonia fumes from the airplane to be safely vented. Essentially the disposal system consisted of a 90-foot pipe connected to the airplane ammonia vent that ran to a water pond where the ammonia was diluted. At the time of the explosion, the ammonia tank pressurizing gas regulator froze or stuck in the open position while the vent valve was operating erratically or modulating only partially open. This condition had been considered as a potential failure on the airplane itself, and had been addressed. However, when combined with the back-pressure created by the vapor disposal system, the tank pressure surged high enough to rupture the tank. The center core of the ammonia tank shot backwards and damaged the hydrogen peroxide tank; the mixing of peroxide and ammonia caused an explosion.[54]

Post-accident analysis indicated that there were no serious design flaws with either the XLR99 or the X-15. The accident had been caused by a simple failure of the pressure regulator, exacerbated by the unique configuration required for the ground test. Nevertheless, several modifications were incorporated to preclude similar failures in the future.[55]

GETTING SERIOUS

In its own way, the X-15 program was "politically correct" even if the term had not been invented yet. Paul Bikle had decided that a NASA pilot should make the first government X-15 flight, but he would later give the honor of the first government XLR99 flight to an Air Force pilot. The initial piloting duties were split evenly between them. It seemed only fitting, therefore, that the third government pilot to qualify in the X-15 should be from the Navy.

Forrest Petersen was checked-out in the airplane while Joe Walker and Bob White conducted the envelope expansion phase with the XLR11 engine. Like all of the early pilot familiarization flights, Petersen's was scheduled to be low and slow; an easy flight. The flight was to launch over Palmdale heading toward Boron, then turn left and fly back towards Mojave, then another left turn towards Edwards. Mach 2 and 50,000 feet was the plan. The launch went well, but as the airplane approached Boron the upper engine began to fail; soon it stopped altogether. Petersen attempted to relight the engine but it steadfastly refused. Petersen reported that he "believed erroneously that the lower engine was still running but the inability to hold altitude, and airspeed variations from values expected for single engine operation, forced the pilot to the inevitable conclusion that both engines were shut down." Milt Thompson, who was NASA-1 for the flight, advised Petersen to head directly for Rogers Dry Lake. Petersen arrived at High Key with only 25,000 feet altitude, much lower than was desired, and Joe Walker tucked a chase plane into formation and coached Petersen through a tight turn onto final. The landing was almost perfect, Petersen handling the entire incident with his usual aplomb. Petersen's final report was understated: "Nothing during the flight surprised the pilot with the exception of early engine shutdown." The only Navy pilot was an excellent addition to the team.[56]

It was time for Crossfield to go back to work with the ultimate engine. The first flight attempt of X-15-2 with the XLR99 was on 13 October 1960, but was terminated prior to launch because of a peroxide leak in the No. 2 APU. Just to show how many things can go wrong on a single flight, there was also liquid oxygen impingement on the aft fuselage during the prime cycle, manifold pressure fluctuations during engine turbopump operation, and fuel tank pressure fluctuations during the jettison cycle. Two weeks later, Crossfield again entered the cockpit with the goal of making the first XLR99 flight. This time problems with the No. 2 APU forced an abort.

On 15 November 1960, everything went right and Crossfield made the first flight (2-10-21) of X-15-2 powered by the XLR99. The pri-

Some of the initial cadre of government X-15 pilots play around for the camera on 5 October 1960. Left to right: Bob Rushworth, Jack McKay, Forrest Petersen, Joe Walker, Neil Armstrong, and Bob White. (NASA Dryden)

mary flight objective was to demonstrate engine operation at 50-percent thrust. The launch was at Mach 0.83 and 46,000 feet, and the X-15 managed to climb to 81,200 feet and Mach 2.97 using somewhat less than half the available power. The second XLR99 flight (2-11-22) tested the engine's restart and throttling capability; Crossfield made the flight on 22 November, again using the second X-15. During the post-flight inspection of the aircraft and its engine, it was found that – like most of the ground test engines – the XLR99 was beginning to shed some of the Rokide coating on the exhaust nozzle.[57]

On 23 September 1960 Forrest Petersen's first Flight (1-13-25) provided a bit more excitement than planned when the XLR11s acted up. The pilot brought the airplane back to Rogers Dry Lake and made an uneventful landing. Petersen was the third government pilot to check out in the X-15. (NASA Dryden)

Flight 2-14-28 on 30 March 1961 marked the first use of the new A/P22S-2 full-pressure suit. Note how straight the X-15 tracked during landing. (NASA Dryden)

Despite being fast-paced, the X-15 program was never reckless. As the X-15-2 was being prepared for its next flight during December 1960, General Marcus Cooper, the commander of the AFFTC, heard rumors about the Rokide coating, and called a meeting in his conference room to discuss the matter. Representatives from Reaction Motors, North American, NASA, and the Air Force were present. Everybody gave their opinions, which were that it appeared safe to continue. Cooper dismissed the meeting, but asked Scott Crossfield and Harrison Storms to stay. During this session he questioned Crossfield on his feelings towards making the flight given the condition of the engine; Scott did not show any concern and indicated he was very willing to go ahead with the flight. Cooper excused Crossfield but asked Storms to stay.[58]

Storms continues the story: "When we were alone, General Cooper asked my opinion. I told him that earlier this day on my arrival at Edwards that I had inspected the thrust chamber in question and did not have any great concerns. Yes, some of the insulation was gone, but not to any great extent and the individual areas were small. It had not all been lost in one area, but the loss was fairly evenly well distributed over the entire area. Further, it certainly had not caused any negative comments from the manufacturer or their test engineers. The General's comment was, 'Very well, we will make it a joint decision to proceed with the flight.' ... Seriously, there is a point to be made here. That is, there is a very fine line between stopping progress and being reckless. That the necessary ingredient in this situation of solving a sticky problem is attitude and approach. The answer, in my opinion, is what I refer to as 'thoughtful courage.' If you don't have that, you will very easily fall into the habit of 'fearful safety' and end up with a very long and tedious-type solution at the hands of some committee. This can very well end up giving a test program a disease commonly referred to as 'cancelitis,' which results in little or no progress." It was an excellent observation.[59]

With Cooper's and Storms' blessing, the third and final XLR99 demonstration flight (2-12-23) was accomplished using X-15-2 on 6 December 1960. The engine throttling, shutdown, and restart objectives were successfully accomplished. This marked North American

Aviation's – and Scott Crossfield's – last X-15 flight. The job of flying the X-15 was now totally in the hands of the government test pilots. Crossfield was transferred to testing the Hound Dog cruise missile and then to North American's manned space flight programs.[60]

The X-15-2 was formally delivered to the Air Force and turned over to NASA on 7 February 1961. On the same day, X-15-1 was returned to the North American plant for conversion to the XLR99, having completed the last XLR11 flight (1-21-36) of the program the day before with Bob White at the controls.[61]

The first government flight (2-13-26) with the XLR99 took place on 7 March 1961 with Bob White at the controls. This was the first time any aircraft had flown faster than Mach 4, reaching Mach 4.43 and 77,450 feet. The objectives of the flight were to obtain aerodynamic and structural heating data, as well as information on stability and control of the aircraft at high speeds. The flight was generally satisfactory. Post-flight examination showed a limited amount of buckling to the side-fuselage tunnels, attributed to thermal expansion – the temperature difference between the tunnel panels and the primary fuselage structure was close to 500°F. The damage was not considered significant since the panels were not primary structure, but were only necessary to carry air loads. However, the buckling continued to become more severe as Mach numbers increased in later flights, and eventually NASA elected to install additional expansion joints in the tunnels to minimize the buckling.[62]

This flight had exceeded the intended velocity by almost half a Mach number. White had shut-down the XLR99 when directed to by NASA-1 based on radar data. Further analysis showed that the radar velocity display in the control room incorporated considerable smoothing of the data to provide a readable output. This introduced a lag of 4 seconds between the actual speed and the displayed speed, accounting for the overshoot. For the next few flights a stopwatch in the control room was used, started at the indication of chamber pressure on the telemetry, and a call to the pilot at shutdown. This appeared to be the simplest, and yet most accurate method of controlling energy, so a stopwatch was installed in the cockpit of all three airplanes. It was started – and stopped – by a signal from the main propellant valves so the total burn time was displayed on the watch even after shutdown. The pilot could then assess whether he had more or less energy than planned, and could also evaluate his energy condition and best emergency lake in the event of a premature shutdown.

Joe Walker's flight (2-14-28) on 30 March 1961 marked the first Hidden Hills launch and the first use of the new David Clark A/P22S-2 full-pressure suit instead of the earlier MC-2. Walker reported the suit was much more comfortable and afforded better vision. The flight began rather inauspiciously with an engine failure immediately after the X-15 was released from the NB-52, but Walker successfully restarted the XLR99. During the "coast" portion of the flight between 100,000 feet and 169,000 feet, Walker experienced about two minutes of weightlessness – a new record for piloted aircraft. But the flight pointed out a potential problem with the stability augmentation system; as Walker descended through 100,000 feet, a heavy vibration occurred and continued for about 45 seconds until recovery was affected at 55,000 feet. Incremental acceleration of approximately 1-g was noted in the vertical and transverse axes at a frequency of 13 cps, corresponding to the first bending mode of the horizontal stabilator. Subsequent analysis showed the vibration was sustained by the SAS at the natural frequency of the horizontal surfaces. Essentially, the oscillations began because of the increased activity of the controls on reentry, which excited the oscillation and stopped after the pilot reduced the pitch-damper gain.[63]

Two solutions to the vibration problem were discussed between the FRC, North American, the Air Force, and the manufacturer of the SAS – Westinghouse; a pressure-derivative feedback valve for the main stabilator hydraulic actuator and a notch filter for the SAS. The feedback valve damped the stabilator bending mode and the notch filter eliminated SAS control surface input at 13 cps. In essence, the valve corrected the source of the problem, while the notch filter avoided the problem. It was felt that either solution would likely effect a cure, but the final decision was to use both.[64]

This was the first acknowledged, in-flight occurrence of "structural resonance,"a phenomena associated with high gain flight control systems. It was a problem that would plague many subsequent aircraft, although as a result of the X-15 experience, ground tests were devised to reveal problems before flight.

VENTRAL-OFF

Although the X-15 was extensively tested in wind tunnels, and researchers at Langley and elsewhere performed years of theoretical analysis on the airplane configuration and missions, sometimes the best results came from the people in the trenches. The flight planners and pilots learned early-on that the best way to reenter from the high-altitude missions was to establish a constant angle-of-attack at the top and then allow the acceleration forces to build as the dynamic pressure increased. As the desired g-loading was reached, the angle-of-attack was gradually decreased and the maximum dynamic pressure was usually reached just prior to level flight. As the maximum altitude

The first two airplanes posed together, along with (left to right) Scott Crossfield, Bob White, and Neil Armstrong. X-15-2 still has the North American Aviation markings on the nose. (Boeing via the Gerald H. Balzer Collection)

increased, so did the initial angle-of-attack needed to avoid exceeding the airplane structural limits. This was practiced many times in the fixed-base simulator at North American and the FRC.[65]

The early simulations had showed that reentries with the SAS turned off were possible at initial angles-of attack-up to 15 degrees, adequate to achieve the goals of the X-15 program. Above 15 degrees, a serious instability developed and the airplane was uncontrollable without the dampers. The simulator was programmed with the results of all of the wind tunnel data accumulated so far in the program; the problem was, these early wind tunnel tests had been conducted with the horizontal stabilizer at zero deflection – but the airplane was usually flown with a substantial deflection. As the wind tunnel researchers expanded their tests to include runs at non-zero deflections, some serious concerns began to develop. When the new data was plugged into the simulator, flight planners and pilots discovered that the maximum angle-of-attack that was possible with the dampers failed (or turned off) was only about 8 degrees instead of 15 – this limited the maximum altitude to about 200,000 feet. The roll damper was required for control at higher angles-of-attack. This limitation was obviously unsatisfactory and a solution would have to be found.[66]

The original SAS was considered fail-safe since it consisted of dual channels, but they were not redundant; each axis had a working channel and a monitor channel. When a difference was detected between the working and monitor channels in any axis, the damper for that axis was shut down, eliminating any possibility it could do something untold. The system, therefore, was fail-safe but not fail-operational. Discussions – usually initiated by the pilots – on whether the SAS should be truly redundant (fail-operational) had taken place since the beginning of development contract, with the final conclusion being that the weight penalty was too severe. By 1961, however, the program had stopped worrying about saving a few pounds, concentrating instead on producing the most useful vehicle possible. If the simulations were right, a single failure in the roll channel would result in the loss of the airplane. Two flight planners, Bob Hoey from the AFFTC and Dick Day from the FRC, decided this needed further investigation since it potentially would keep the X-15 from achieving its design altitude.[67]

You can not take life too seriously. An unnamed somebody set up the X-15 egress trainer in this humorous scene on 11 June 1965. Note the "udder failure" (glove) hanging from the nose and the "moo" sign just above it. At left is the egress trainer as it appeared in mid-2002 at the AFFTC Museum. (above: NASA Dryden; left: Frederick A. Johnsen)

The obvious solution was the development of the alternate stability augmentation system (ASAS), which would add a redundant channel to the roll dampers, essentially eliminating the chances of a complete failure of the system. The ASAS was installed in X-15-1 and X-15-2 during April 1962; the X-15-3 did not require the ASAS because MH-96 was already largely redundant. But Hoey and Day were not convinced that the ASAS was the entire answer, although nobody questioned its potential usefulness. Hours in the simulator had convinced the flight planners that the airplane did not fly the high angle-of-attack reentry profile all that well even when all the dampers were functioning properly, and began exploring possible aerodynamic fixes.[68]

The wedge-shaped dorsal and ventral stabilizers actually prevented the airplane from being flown safely at high angles-of-attack because of a negative dihedral effect. The primary reason for the large, symmetrical vertical stabilizer configuration was to compensate for potential thrust misalignment at the end of the boost phase when dynamic pressure was low. This had been a major concern early-on, and the program had even evaluated using the ballistic control system as well as the rudder to handle thrust misalignments. As it turned out, Hoey remembers, "the engine guys figured out a clever way of aligning the engines in the airplanes which essentially eliminated thrust misalignment as a problem. We never experienced any significant thrust misalignment during flight test."[69]

Since it appeared that the problem was that the ventral stabilizer was too large, Hoey and Day decided to see what would happen if they made it smaller. This was easily accomplished – the lower rudder was jettisoned at the end of each flight anyway. There was a substantial base of wind tunnel and flight test data at low speeds with the ventral off since this was the standard landing configuration. However, the high-speed investigation of this configuration consisted of a single set of wind tunnel runs at Mach 3, hardly con-

clusive data. Nevertheless, Hoey and Day created a temporary modification to the simulator using this data and "some freehand guesses" to fill in the holes at other Mach numbers.[70]

As could easily be imagined, the directional stability was somewhat less throughout the envelope, but the dihedral effect was normal at all angles-of-attack and the Dutch Roll stability was about the same as the basic airplane. More importantly, the simulator was easily controllable with the dampers off from altitudes as high as 250,000 feet. Hoey and Day had sufficient confidence with the ventral-off scheme that they proposed to test it on an upcoming Mach 4 flight at 80,000 feet. When the two flight planners first presented their idea to the rest of the technical community, the results were treated with some skepticism, not least because of how they were obtained. The aerodynamicists wanted to run a complete set of wind tunnel tests to verify the concept, something that would take considerable time. But Paul Bikle and Bob Rushworth felt that the risks involved in testing the idea were minimal and worthwhile. The concept was approved.[71]

The technicians at the FRC began building a heat shield to bolt onto the bottom of the fixed portion of the ventral to protect the area from aerodynamic heating and also to clean up the drag in the area to ensure no local hot spots. As the proposed flight got closer, however, Hoey and Day became increasingly nervous since they knew their idea was based on "pretty thin evidence." What bothered them most was that the trend in high-speed flight had been to *increase* the vertical surface area; that was why the X-15 had such large surfaces to begin with. The vertical surfaces on most of the early supersonic combat aircraft had been increased 15 to 20 percent based on initial supersonic flight tests. Hoey and Day were proposing *decreasing* the surface area of the X-15 by 27 percent. But the planners had no idea what stability degradation might occur due to rocket plume effects, and no data on the effects of operating the speed brakes. The pair spent the last week before the flight run-

The 1964 pilot lineup (left to right): Jack McKay, Joe Walker, Milt Thompson, Bob Rushworth, and Joe Engle seen on 30 September. All that are ever published are the official portraits, such as above. But the pilots often clowned around during the photo shoots, evidenced at left; lets play "who can get into the cockpit first." (NASA Dryden)

ning off-nominal simulations and reassuring Rushworth. Observed Bob Hoey: "On the morning of the flight, I suspect that Bikle and Rushworth had more confidence in Hoey and Day than did Hoey and Day."[72]

Bob Rushworth flew the first ventral-off flight (1-23-39) on 4 October 1961, reaching Mach 4.3 and 78,000 feet. The flight went off without a hitch. The X-15 had sufficient directional stability during launch, and handling qualities were similar to the ventral-on configuration at low angles-of-attack, but better at 8 degrees. Rushworth performed several stability pulses that matched the trends seen in the simulator. This apparent success prompted the researchers at Langley to begin wind tunnel tests of the entire speed and altitude range, but it would be another year before the program began routinely flying without the ventral.[73]

The first flight to the (nearly) design altitude was flown (1-27-48) by Joe Walker, reaching 246,700 feet – with the ventral on and the ASAS installed. Five months later the researchers had completed the ventral-off wind tunnel tests and the results were mechanized on the simulator. The configuration was shown to allow reentries with the dampers off at angles-of-attack as high as 26 degrees. Wind tunnel data showed that there were some directional stability problems in the transonic region with the speed brakes deployed, but pilots were briefed on how to avoid this area. The second ventral-off flight (2-29-50) was flown on 28 September 1962 by Jack McKay, reaching 68,000 feet – the flight was completely nominal. In all, the program would make 73 flights with the ventral on and 126 with it off.[74]

It is interesting to note that things that sound potentially catastrophic, or at least important, in retrospect, were not necessarily so at the time. For instance during Flight 2-20-36 on 11 October 1961 the left outer windscreen glass cracked. The item did not figure at all in Bob White's post-flight report, and rated exactly three lines of radio chatter at the time. White to Forrest Petersen, who was NASA-1 that day: "OK, my ... outside windshield went ..." to which Petersen responded, "Understand, outside pane?" White confirmed "That's correct" and both men returned to their duties.[75]

White was not quite as calm on his next flight (2-21-37) when the right windshield shattered as he decelerated through Mach 2.7 after becoming the first person to pilot an aircraft above Mach 6. From his pilot report:[76]

"I would guess at about 2.7 Mach number at 70,000 feet, somewhere in that neighborhood, when I said, 'Good Lord, not again,' that's where the right windshield panel went. ... I could see out the left windshield panel fairly well, and the lake was just off to the left so it looked like it would be real handy for a left-hand circle landing pattern. As I got down lower I realized I couldn't see out the right side. For all intents and purposes, the visibility out of the right windshield was nonexistent. I asked the chase plane to stay in close, thinking right after it happened that it might also happen on the left side. In that event, I considered going to high face plate heat when I got subsonic, jettison the canopy and see what happened from there. The pattern was as per usual, but on the final approach I was quite surprised at what a compromise it offered being able to see out of only one windshield. ... There was no smoke in the cockpit during the flight and aside from the windshield there was really nothing at all that I didn't expect. Everything else continued to work fine."

It should be noted that on the first occasion the windshield cracked – a series of mostly longitudinal breaks, but generally spaced fairly far apart. The second time the windshield shattered completely, looking much like an automobile windshield after a major accident, and impeding all vision. On both of these occasions the heating and turbulent flow generated by the protruding cockpit enclosure had caused an outer panel of the windshield to fracture because heating loads in the

We gotta talk to David Clark about these helmets! The 1965 group had even more fun, but produced what is probably one of the most elegant of the X-15 group photos at above left (left to right): Pete Knight, Bob Rushworth, Joe Engle, Milt Thompson, Bill Dana, and Jack McKay on 2 December 1965. The other photos speak for themselves. (NASA Dryden)

A group photo to celebrate the 100th X-15 flight on 28 January 1964. Bob Rushworth would take the X-15-1 to Mach 5.34 and 107,400 feet on Flight 1-44-70. Up in back: LeRoy "Lee" Adelsback and Bruce Laub. Back group, left to right: Price Workman, Merle Curtis, Henry Maag IV, Ralph Haley, and Clyde Bailey. Standing, left to right: Paschal "Herm" Dorr, Darwin "Doc" Gray, John Gordon, Cyril Brennan, Chester Bergner, Edward Nice, Frank Brown, Homer Hall, unknown, Cecil Dome, Harold Bryan, Bryon Gibbs, James Wilson, David Stoddard, Donald Hall, Norman Gravatt, John "Jack" Russell, James Daniels, Edward Sabo, John (Bill) Lovett, and Lorenzo "Larry" Barnett. Kneeling, left to right: Ronald Waite, Billy Furr, unknown, unknown, William Bastow, Henry "Hank" Steiginga, Willard Glasscock, and Anthony Miksic. (NASA Dryden)

When Project Mercury began, it rapidly eclipsed the X-15 in the public's imagination. It also dominated some of the research areas that had first interested X-15 planners, such as zero-g studies. The use of reaction controls to maintain attitude in space proved academic after Mercury flew, but the X-15 would furnish valuable information on the blending of reaction controls with conventional aerodynamic surfaces during exit and reentry, a matter of concern to subsequent Space Shuttle development. The X-15 experience clearly demonstrated the ability of pilots to fly rocket-propelled aircraft out of the atmosphere and back to precision landings. Paul Bikle saw the X-15 and Mercury as a "... parallel, two-pronged approach to solving some of the problems of manned space flight. While Mercury was demonstrating man's capability to function effectively in space, the X-15 was demonstrating man's ability to control a high-performance vehicle in a near-space environment ... considerable new knowledge was obtained on the techniques and problems associated with lifting reentry."[78]

November 1961 saw the third industry conference convene; previous conferences had been held in 1956 and 1958. A total of 442 people were registered for the classified event at the Flight Research Center which featured 24 papers from 56 authors, including four X-15 pilots. Of the authors, 5 came from North American, 37 from various NASA centers, 13 from the Air Force, and 1 from the Navy. The attendees represented virtually every major aerospace contractor in the country, all of the NASA centers, several universities, the various military services, and, oddly enough, the British Embassy.[79]

The first year of the flight program had four broad objectives: verification of predicted hypersonic aerodynamic behavior and heating rates; study of the X-15's structural characteristics in an environment of high heating and high flight loads; investigation of hypersonic stability and control problems during atmospheric exit and reentry; and investigation of piloting tasks and pilot performance. Before the end of 1961, these four objectives had been generally satisfied and the X-15 had attained Mach 6 and flown well above 200,000 feet; by July 1962 it had flown above 300,000 feet. The revised design goals had effectively been satisfied.[80]

During this time, physiologists discovered the heart rates of X-15 pilots varied between 145 and 185 beats per minute in flight, as compared to a normal of 70 to 80 beats per minute for test missions in

expanding frame overstressed the glass. The difficulty was overcome by changing the glass frame from Inconel X to titanium, and eliminating the rear support (allowing the windscreen to expand slightly). This warned aerospace designers to proceed cautiously. During 1968 John Becker wrote: "The really important lesson here is that what are minor and unimportant features of a subsonic or supersonic aircraft must be dealt with as prime design problems in a hypersonic airplane. This lesson was applied effectively in the precise design of a host of important details on the manned space vehicles."[77]

Three of the men who made the X-15 possible: Paul Bikle, Hugh Dryden and Walt Williams in front of the X-15A-2 in April 1964. Williams, in particular, was instrumental to the entire "space race" that included the X-15. (NASA Dryden)

Joe Walker shows the Mercury Seven the X-15 on 14 September 1959. The performance of the X-15 and the Mercury-Redstone were generally similar; the Mercury-Atlas and later manned launch vehicles were in a completely different league. (NASA Dryden)

The X-15 program had well-known visitors from the scientific and entertainment communities on many occasions. Here Bill Dana talks with DeForrest Kelly, Dr. McCoy from the TV series Star Trek, on 13 April 1967, (NASA Dryden)

other aircraft. Researchers eventually concluded that pre-launch anticipatory stress, rather than actual post-launch physical stress, influenced the heart rate. They believed that these rates could be considered as probable baselines for predicting the physiological behavior of future astronauts; something confirmed on the Mercury flights. Interestingly, the pilots thought little about the weightlessness aspects of some of their mission profiles. Bob White commented that "zero-g, while apparently an interesting area to consider, has had no noticeable effect on the pilot control task for the approximate 2 minute period during which the weightless state was experienced."[81]

Researchers had already accomplished quite a bit of analysis on aerodynamic heating – one of the original research objectives of the X-15. Several theoretical models existed to predict heating rates, but little experimental data had been available to validate them since it was uncertain if wind tunnels were capable of realistically testing the conditions. The X-15 provided the first real-world experience at high Mach numbers in a well-instrumented recoverable vehicle. Data from the X-15 showed that none of the models were completely accurate, although all showed some correlation at differing Mach numbers. The data showed the wind tunnels were fairly accurate.[82]

THE BROWN SHOE LEAVES THE PROGRAM

Forrest Petersen's X-15 experience had begun with an engine failure on his first flight in 1960. It would end the same way on Flight 1-25-44 when the XLR99 refused to start – twice. Petersen had no choice but to land at Mud Lake, marking the program's first uprange landing. This was exactly why each flight was launched within gliding distance of a suitable emergency landing lake. Other than Crossfield's initial glide flight, this would be the only X-15 flight below Mach 1.[83]

Petersen's departure from the program had nothing to do with his flight experience; the record is quite complimentary about his contributions to the program. But Petersen was an up-and-coming Naval officer, and he needed to return to active service in order to continue advancing his career. His destination after leaving the program was to command VF-154 at NAS Miramar; subsequently he transferred to the "black shoe" navy and served as executive officer on the USS *Enterprise* (CVAN-65). He ultimately retired as a Vice Admiral.

Forrest Petersen ended his X-15 career much like it had begun: with an emergency landing. This time it was at Mud Lake on 10 January 1962 when the XLR99 in X-15-1 had two malfunction shutdowns during the first 3.3 seconds. As usual, the X-15 was trucked back to Edwards along the public highways through Death Valley. This time the photographer decided to take the scenic route home, leaving some interesting images of the world's fastest airplane. (NASA Dryden)

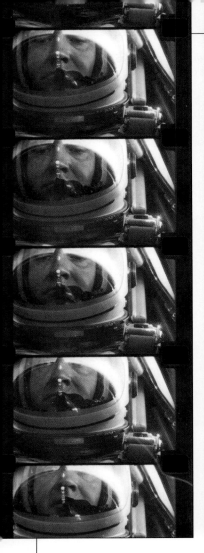
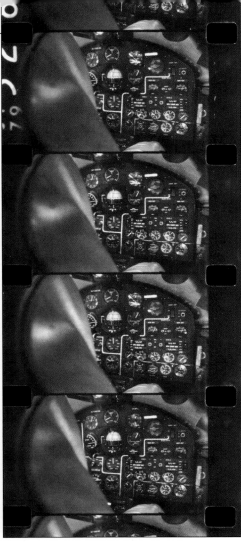

There were a variety of cockpit cameras carried during the X-15 flights, and almost always one was focused on the instrument panel and another on the pilot's faceplate. These strips are from Flight 2-29-50 on 28 September 1962 with Jack McKay at the controls. Interestingly, the film at right must have been taken on the ground since the altimeter reads nearly zero and the airplane is at 1-g acceleration. (NASA Dryden)

The X-15-1 was trucked back to Edwards on 13 January 1962 and the XLR99 was removed so that the engine mounts and main landing skids could be inspected; no damage was observed. After that the airplane was prepared for a 23 January flight and proceeded through a satisfactory ground run on 19 January. However, rain on 20 January closed Rogers (not-so) Dry Lake, so all flight activities ceased. The airplane was released to the maintenance shops for some minor modifications.[84]

The weather continued to get worse. It rained the following day, and then snowed the next day resulting in over half and inch of water on Rogers and over 12 inches of snow on Mud Lake. By this time only Silver, Hidden Hills, and Three Sisters were still dry and useable. A week of relative sunshine brightened the outlook, but things turned

for the worse when heavy rains pelted the area for five days beginning on 7 February. This essentially precluded any flights before 15 April so it was decided to take the opportunity to perform maintenance and modifications to all the airplanes.[85]

On 20 April 1962 Neil Armstrong's fourth MH-96 evaluation flight (3-4-8) would become the program's longest duration at 12 minutes and 28.7 seconds. The flight plan called for a peak altitude of 205,000 feet with Armstrong performing various maneuvers during exit and reentry to evaluate the MH-96. At the conclusion of the flight, Armstrong reported that "In general, aircraft control and damping during ballistic flight and entry were outstanding, and considerably more smooth than had been expected. Unfortunately, this may be at the expense of excessive reaction control fuel consumption." This was confirmed when the APU and BCS low-peroxide warning lights came on as the airplane descended through 160,000 feet. Armstrong initiated the transfer of unused turbopump propellant to the APU tanks and the light went out as he descended through 115,000 feet.[86]

Things began to get a bit strange at this point. As Armstrong initiated his pullout the airplane began a slight climb, unnoticed by Armstrong. As soon as Joe Walker (NASA-1) saw a slight positive rate of climb on the radar data he knew Armstrong was in trouble. When Walker told him to make a hard left turn, Armstrong rolled into a 60-degree left bank and pulled up to start the turn. When Walker called for the next hard left turn, Armstrong realized that he was above the atmosphere and was not turning. He sailed by Edwards at Mach 3 and 100,000 feet headed for Palmdale in a 90-degree bank with full nose-up stabilizer, but the airplane did not want to turn.[87]

Once a "skip" out of the atmosphere had been started, there was no choice but to wait until the vehicle peaked out in altitude and settled back into the atmosphere. By that time Armstrong was 45 miles south of Edwards, roughly over Pasadena. Ironically, whereas he had had way too much energy when he was over Edwards, now he might not have enough to make it back to Edwards.[88]

Palmdale was not really a viable option; the Air Force installation there had a concrete runway, not an ideal surface for the X-15 skids. Instead, Armstrong began setting up for a landing on runway 35 at the extreme south end of Rogers Dry Lake. This was about as far away as you could get from the normal runway 18 at the north end of the lake, and the recovery and emergency vehicles were racing at full speed to cover the 10 miles before Armstrong touched down. The landing itself was undramatic as Armstrong set the record for the longest miss distance during a non-emergency landing (12 miles). Milt Thompson later called this "Neil's cross-country flight."[89]

Astronaut Wings

As near as can be determined, the three X-15s spent their entire career in and around Edwards, with occasional trips back to Inglewood to be repaired or modified. There was one exception, part of Project Eglin 1-62. On 2 May 1962 Jack Allavie and Bob White, along with a pressure suit technician and the B-52 crew chief, took Balls Three and X-15-3 to Eglin AFB in Florida for the four-hour-long "Air Proving Ground Center Manned Weapons Fire Power Demonstration" being attended by President John F. Kennedy. According to Allavie, "we took off with an inert X-15 and flew all the way to Eglin AFB in Florida ... that's 1,625 miles and it was a simple flight. We landed there, put the X-15 on exhibit, and then flew it back to Edwards" on 5 May with a stop at Altus AFB, Oklahoma, for fuel. Although it was – by far – the longest captive flight of the program, it was not assigned a program flight number.[90]

Back at Edwards, during the summer of 1962, Bob White made three flights in X-15-3 that demonstrated the potential problems of matching the preflight profile. On the first flight (3-5-9) White became disoriented during the exit and decided that he needed to push the nose down slightly so that he could visually acquire the sky: "When we got up to 32 degrees, and at about 60 seconds in time, I guess it was just a small case of disorientation. I say a small case because I didn't lose complete orientation but when I was up at this climb angle, and this is the first time that I've had this feeling, I looked at the ball, I had 32 degrees in pitch, but I had the darndest feeling that I was continuing to rotate. I couldn't resist the urge just to push on back down until the light blue of the sky showed up. I never did get to the horizon, then I was satisfied that it wasn't happening." By the time he had satisfied himself and begun his climb again, his energy was such that he undershot his planned 206,000-foot peak by 21,400 feet. White's next flight (3-6-10) was only nine days later. This one was much better; White undershot by only 3,300 feet – about average for the program.[91]

If it seemed that White was getting better at hitting his planned altitude, the next flight would dispel any such thoughts. On 17 July 1962 White took the X-15-3 on a flight that was supposed to go to 282,000 feet, sufficient to qualify him for an Air Force Astronaut rating. The MH-96 failed just before launch, which probably should have meant scrubbing for the day. Instead, White reset the circuit breakers; the MH-96 appeared to function correctly, so White called for a launch. The climb angle was a bit steeper than called for, the engine produced a bit more thrust than usual, and it burned a bit longer than expected. The end result was a flight that was 32,750 feet higher than planned, setting a new FAI record for piloted aircraft of 314,750 feet and also becoming the first winged vehicle to exceed 300,000 feet, the first flight above 50 miles, and the first X-15 flight that qualified its pilot for an Air Force Astronaut rating. As the first astronaut from Edwards, White was suitably impressed with the view:[92]

> "You could just see as far as you looked. I turned my head in both directions and you see nothing but the Earth. It's just tremendous. You look off and the sky is real dark. … It amazed me. I looked up and was able to pick out San Francisco bay and it looked like it was down over there off the right wing and I could look out, way out. It was just tremendous, absolutely tremendous. You have seen pictures from high up in rockets, or these orbital pictures of what the guy sees out there. That's exactly what it looked like. The same thing."

The next day, on 18 July 1962, President John F. Kennedy presented the Robert J. Collier Trophy to four X-15 pilots – Scott Crossfield, Forrest Peterson, Joe Walker, and Bob White – "For invaluable technological contributions to the advancement of flight and for great skill and courage as test pilots of the X-15." By this point Crossfield had been gone for two years, and Petersen had already left to become the commanding officer at VF-154. Nevertheless, all four pilots journeyed to Washington to accept the trophy on the south lawn at the White House. The Collier Trophy is awarded annually by the National Aeronautic Association and is considered the most prestigious award for aerospace achievement in the United States. In the case of the X-15, the selection of the recipients was not arbitrary, but repre-

Bob White with his Model A on 23 May 1959. (AFFTC History Office)

sented the first pilot from each organization (North American, Navy, NASA, and Air Force) to fly the airplane. Later the same day White was presented his Astronaut Wings at the Pentagon, and that evening all four of the pilots were feted at a dinner in their honor and received the NASA Distinguished Service Medal from Vice President Lyndon B. Johnson. NASA Administrator James E. Webb commented at the dinner that the X-15 program was "a classic example of a most effective way to conduct research."[93]

President John F. Kennedy presents the Collier Trophy to (left to right) Bob White, Scott Crossfield, Joe Walker, and Forrest Petersen (mostly hidden by the trophy). (Gerald H. Balzer Collection)

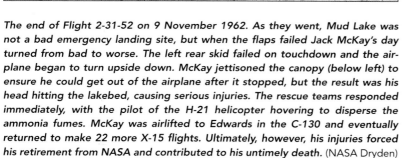

The end of Flight 2-31-52 on 9 November 1962. As they went, Mud Lake was not a bad emergency landing site, but when the flaps failed Jack McKay's day turned from bad to worse. The left rear skid failed on touchdown and the airplane began to turn upside down. McKay jettisoned the canopy (below left) to ensure he could get out of the airplane after it stopped, but the result was his head hitting the lakebed, causing serious injuries. The rescue teams responded immediately, with the pilot of the H-21 helicopter hovering to disperse the ammonia fumes. McKay was airlifted to Edwards in the C-130 and eventually returned to make 22 more X-15 flights. Ultimately, however, his injuries forced his retirement from NASA and contributed to his untimely death. (NASA Dryden)

A Really Bad Day

On 9 November 1962 Jack McKay launched the X-15-2 from Balls Eight on his way to what was supposed to be a routine heating flight (2-31-52) to Mach 5.55 and 125,000 feet. Just after the X-15 separated, Bob Rushworth (NASA-1) asked McKay to check his throttle position; McKay verified it was full open. Unfortunately, the engine was only putting out 35 percent thrust. In theory, the X-15 could have made a slow trip back to Rogers Dry Lake; but there was no way of knowing why the engine had decided to act up, or if it would continue to function. The mission rules dictated that the pilot shut down the engine and make an emergency landing; McKay would have to land at Mud Lake.[94]

As they went, Mud Lake was not a bad emergency landing site, being about 5 miles in diameter and very smooth. When Rushworth and McKay decided to land at Mud, the pilot immediately began preparing for the landing – the engine was shut down after 70.5 seconds, the airplane turned around, and as much propellant as possible was jettisoned. It was looking like a "routine" emergency until the X-15 wing flaps failed to operate. The resulting "hot" landing (257 knots) caused the left main landing skid to fail, and the left horizontal stabilizer and wing dug into the lakebed, resulting in the aircraft turning sideways and flipping upside down. Luckily, McKay realized he was going over and jettisoned the canopy just prior to rolling inverted. The unfortunate result was that the first thing to hit the lakebed was McKay's helmet.[95]

As was the case for all X-15 flights, a rescue crew and fire truck had been deployed to the launch lake. Normally it was a dull and boring assignment – on this day they earned their pay. The ground crew sped toward the X-15, but when they arrived less than a minute later, they found that their breathing masks were ineffective against the fumes from unjettisoned anhydrous ammonia escaping from the broken airplane. Fortunately, the pilot of the H-21 helicopter noted the vapors and maneuvered into a position where his rotor downwash dispersed the fumes. The ground crew was able to dig a hole in the lakebed and extract McKay. By this time the orbiting C-130 had landed with a paramedic and additional rescue personnel. McKay was loaded on the C-130 and rushed to the Edwards hospital; the ground crew tended to the damaged X-15.[96]

It had taken three years and 74 flights, but all of the emergency preparations had finally paid off. In this case, as for all flights, the rescue crew and fire truck had been flown to launch lake in a C-130 before dawn in preparation for the flight. The helicopter had flown up at daybreak. The C-130 had returned to Edwards to pick up another fire truck that was taken to an intermediate lake; they were possibly the most traveled fire trucks in the Air Force inventory. The C-130, loaded with a paramedic, then began a slow orbit mid-way between Mud Lake and Edwards, waiting. Outside the program, there had been those who had questioned the time and expense of keeping the lakebeds active and deploying the emergency crews for each mission. The flight program was beginning to seem so routine. But inside the program, nobody doubted the potential usefulness and the precautions had been taken for exactly this reason. Because of the time and expense, Jack McKay was resting in the base hospital, seemingly alive and well. Had the rescue crew not been there, the result might have been much different.[97]

Although the accident report stated that "pilot injuries were not serious," in reality Jack McKay had suffered several crushed vertebra that resulted in him being an inch shorter than when the flight had

A stable platform failure caused an abort (2-A-24) for Bob White on 21 February 1961. The dorsal rudder of the X-15-1 carried an infrared coating that was being considered for use on the B-70 program. Note the large spotlights on the fuselage of the NB-52B (two under the bomber's wing, one near the X-15 wing, and two just ahead of the X-15 horizontal stabilizer) to illuminate the X-15 as needed. (AFFTC History Office)

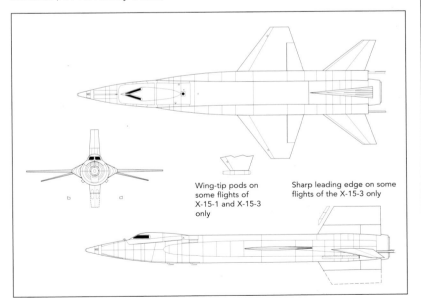

Wing-tip pods on some flights of X-15-1 and X-15-3 only

Sharp leading edge on some flights of the X-15-3 only

This was the configuration of the X-15 for most of the flight program: XLR99 engine and the ball nose. the ventral rudder was carried on most early missions, but deleted from the majority of later ones. (Artwork by Tony Landis)

The National Geographic Society photographed the X-15 on several occasions, and flew a camera onboard the aircraft numerous times. This 1961 image shows an X-15 pulling up into its climb. (National Geographic)

Joe Walker getting into the X-15-3 on 22 August 1963 in preparation for the maximum altitude flight. Note the Little Joe II nose art. This flight set an unofficial world altitude record for winged vehicles of 354,200 feet that would stand until the Space Shuttle Columbia went to orbit. (AFFTC History Office)

begun. Nevertheless, five weeks after his accident, McKay was in the control room as the NASA-1 for Bob White's last X-15 flight (3-12-22). McKay would go on to fly 22 more X-15 flights, but would ultimately retire from NASA because of lasting effects from this accident.[98]

The X-15-2 had not faired any better; the damage was major, but not total. On 15 November 1962 an Accident Board was officially designated with Donald R. Bellman as chairman. The findings of the board – which contained no surprises – were subsequently released in a detailed report that was distributed during December 1962. Six months after the Mud Lake accident North American was awarded a contract to modify the X-15-2 into an advanced configuration that was designed to investigate flight up to Mach 8.[99]

As it became obvious that the program was going to continue past its initial mandate to gather aero-thermo data the FRC began correcting some of the shortcomings of the original design. For instance, pilots had long complained that some aspects of the instrument panel were less than ideal. During the summer of 1963 modifications were made to the cockpit configuration to improve the scan pattern and to relieve certain overcrowded areas of the instrument panel. The resulting instrument panel bore little resemblance to the original; the original black color had given way to a medium gray that the pilots found contrasted better with the instruments.[100]

MAXIMUM ALTITUDE

Joe Walker would fly the maximum altitude flight (3-22-36) on 22 August 1963, his second excursion above 300,000 feet in just over a month. The simulator predicted that the X-15 could achieve altitudes well in excess of 400,000 feet, but there was considerable doubt if the airplane could successfully reenter from such heights. A very good pilot on a very good day could do it; if anything went wrong the results were usually less desirable. In order to provide a margin of safety, it was decided to limit the maximum altitude attempt to 360,000 feet, providing a 40,000-foot cushion for cumulative errors. This might sound like a lot, but the flight planners and pilots remembered that Bob White had overshot his altitude by 32,750 feet. The X-15 was climbing at over 4,000 fps, so every second that the pilot delayed shutting down the engine resulted in a 4,000-foot increment in altitude. The XLR99 also was not terribly precise – sometimes the engine developed 57,000-lbf; other times it developed 60,000-lbf. An extra 1,500-lbf for the entire burn translated into an additional 7,500 feet of altitude. A one-degree error in climb angle could also result in 7,500 feet more altitude. Add these all up and it is easy to understand why the program decided a 40,000-foot cushion was appropriate.[101]

Walker had made one build-up flight (3-21-32) prior to the maximum altitude attempt and had overshot his 315,000-foot target by 31,200 feet through a combination of all three variables; higher-than-expected engine thrust, longer-than-expected engine burn, and a 0.5-degree error in climb angle. Suddenly, the 40,000-foot cushion did not seem all that large.[102]

The record flight was surprisingly hard to launch, racking up three aborts over a two week period because of weather and APU problems. On the actual flight day things began badly when both the Edwards and Beatty radars lost track on the NB-52 during the trip to the launch lake, but both reacquired the target four minutes prior to the scheduled launch time. The launch itself was good and Walker began the climb to altitude. Although this was the first flight for a newly-installed altitude predictor, Walker flew the mission based on its results, changing his climb angle several times to stay within a predicted 360,000 feet. When the XLR99 depleted its propellants, the X-15-3 was traveling through 176,000 feet at 5,600 fps. It would take almost two minutes to get to the top of the climb, ultimately reaching 354,200 feet.[103]

Just to give a feeling for reentry. The airplane was heading down at a 45-degree angle, and as it descended through 170,000 feet it was traveling 5,500 fps – over a mile per second. The acceleration buildup was non-linear and happened rather abruptly, taking less than 15 seconds to go from essentially no dynamic pressure to 1,500 psf, then tapering off for the remainder of reentry, reaching a peak acceleration of 5-g at 95,000 feet. Walker maintained 5-g during the pullout until he came level at 70,000 feet. All the time the anti-g part of the David Clark full-pressure suit was squeezing his legs and stomach, forcing blood back to his heart and brain. Walker, "the comment of previous flights that this is one big squeeze in the pullout is still good." The glide back to Edwards was uneventful and Walker made a perfect landing. The flight lasted 11 minutes and 8 seconds, and had covered 305 ground miles from Smith Ranch to Rogers Dry Lake. Despite having traveled more than 67 miles high – well in excess of the 62-mile (100-kilometer) international standard supposedly recognized by NASA – no Astronaut rating awaited Joe Walker; those were apparently reserved for people that rode ballistic missiles at Cape Canaveral.[104]

Milt Thompson experienced a great deal more excitement than intended during Flight 3-29-48 on 21 May 1964 when the XLR99 shutdown after only 41 seconds into a planned 120-second burn as Thompson attempted to throttle back from 100-percent to 45-percent. There had been a pressure spike in the second-stage chamber pressure sensing line, a problem that had been present since the beginning. This engine had not shown a tendency to generate spikes during the three flights and four ground runs accomplished since its installation in X-15-3, but the intensity of the spike was sufficient in this case to deform the switch mechanically, holding the contacts closed and thus preventing an engine restart. Although the X-15-3 accelerated to Mach 2.90 at 64,200 feet, Thompson could not make Rogers Dry Lake and opted for an emergency landing on Cuddeback. This marked the program's first emergency landing at Cuddeback; the X-15 was not seriously damaged and Thompson was uninjured.[105]

THE FOURTH INDUSTRY CONFERENCE (1965)

The fourth conference on the progress of the X-15 program was held at the Flight Research Center on 7 October 1965. This conference was considerably smaller than the previous ones, with only 13 papers written by 25 authors. The FRC employed 18 of the authors, 4 came from other NASA centers, 1 from the AFFTC, and the remaining 2 from other Air Force organizations. Approximately 500 persons attended the event. At this point in the program, about 150 flights had been conducted over six years.[106]

Joe Engle ended up being the only X-15 pilot who would get to fly the next lifting-reentry vehicle – Space Shuttle. He also has the distinction of being the only person to fly back from orbit, on the second Space Shuttle flight (STS-2). Milt Thompson said that "Joe Engle seemed to have a charmed relationship with the X-15" because, for the most part, all of Engle's flights went according to plan. But everybody might not agree with that assessment of his fifteenth flight. On 10 August 1965 Engle took the X-15-3 to 271,000

feet – his second flight above 50 miles. But it was how he got there that was of interest. Mission rules stated that the X-15 pilot should fly an alternate low-altitude mission if the yaw damper channel on the MH-96 failed during the first 32 seconds of flight. This was because it was unlikely the airplane could make a successful reentry with a failed yaw damper. On this flight (3-46-70) the yaw channel failed 0.6 seconds after the X-15 dropped off the pylon. Engle reset the damper and continued, not feeling obligated to fly the alternate profile since the damper successfully reset. It was a temporary reprieve, however. The damper failed again 19 seconds later; the reset was successful, at least for ten seconds until it failed again. The damper failed three times in the first 32 seconds of flight. Engle successfully flew the mission, although he missed some of the profile for various reasons, including a preoccupation with resetting the failing yaw damper – it had failed 21 times during the flight.[107]

At the end of 1965, NASA could see that the end of the X-15 program was in sight. The basic flight research that had originally been envisioned had long-since been completed, and the aircraft were now primarily experiment carriers, although the X-15A-2 was still expected to extend the flight envelope somewhat. But plans to use the X-15A-2 as a hypersonic ramjet test bed were beginning to unravel. On 6 August

Jack McKay ended up at Delamar on Flight 1-63-104 when the XLR99 failed after 35.4 seconds. The airplane slid off the smooth lakebed and into the scrub, damaging one of the wingtip pod experiments, but was otherwise uneventful. Note the C-130 in the background. (NASA Dryden)

1965 Secretary of Defense Robert S. McNamara disapproved the funding necessary for the effort; the matter was referred to the Aeronautics and Astronautics Coordinating Board (AACB) for resolution, although it would be the middle of 1966 before any decisions were made.[108]

Under the best-case scenario, the FRC anticipated that the flight program using the basic X-15s would begin winding down at the end of 1967 when the X-15-3 would be taken out of service to be modified into the delta-wing configuration. By the end of 1969 the X-15-1 would be retired, leaving only the X-15A-2 and the newly-redelivered delta-wing X-15-3 in service. The X-15A-2 would finish its ramjet tests in mid-1970, transferring all flight activity to the delta-wing.[109]

Surprisingly, Paul Bikle had long believed that any extended operation of the X-15 program beyond its original objectives was unwise and hard to justify in view of the high cost and risk involved. As early as 1961 he had suggested the end of 1964 as a desirable termination date. When the X-15-2 had been seriously damaged during Jack McKay's emergency landing, Bikle had argued for minimal repairs rather than extensive modifications. As time went on, Bikle felt that continued extensions of the program were becoming increasingly hard to justify, and he personally had strong doubts that either the delta wing or the HRE would ever reach flight status on an X-15. In spite of these personal misgivings, Bikle continued to support the program in his public statements.[110]

RAIN IN THE HIGH DESERT

January 1966 was much like December 1965 in the high desert – wet. Between 12 November and 1 December 1965, more than 3 inches of rain had fallen in the area; 2 more inches fell during December. Rogers, Cuddeback, Three Sisters, Silver, Delamar, and Hidden Hills were all described as "wet;" Mud Lake was only "damp." In fact, over 95-percent of Cuddeback was under water and, on 29 December, visible snow was observed at Delamar. The X-15 program was grounded for lack of landing sites.[111]

This gave the program time to do maintenance on the airplanes and incorporate various modifications. For instance, the Honeywell IFDS was installed, finally, on X-15-3 along with a new Lear Siegler-developed vertical-scale instrument panel. The X-15-3 also received the changes necessary to carry the wing-tip experiment pods. The third skid under the ventral and the stick-kicker needed for higher landing weights were installed on X-15-3 during March and April 1966.[112]

The instrument panel that was being installed in X-15-3 was not met with overwhelming enthusiasm by the pilots. Paul Bikle noted that "there has been some evidence of reluctance to accept the vertical-scale, fixed-index [tape] instruments," although previously "no objective evaluation of the suitability of the panel for the X-15 mission had been made." A duplicate of the panel was installed in the fixed-base simulator and runs were made using "measurable flight control and pilot performance parameters in a comparison of the Lear panel with the traditional panel."[113]

Of all the performance measures taken, only two showed consistent and significant differences. These were the absolute error in velocity at power reduction and the burnout altitude; in both cases, the statistical results favored the Lear panel. An examination of the altitude and velocity indicators on both panels showed that the difference was the result of high scale resolution on the Lear instruments, which was almost twice that of the traditional panel instruments. The pilots were still not altogether happy with the new panel, but they no longer mistrusted it.[114]

As January passed with no relief from the wet lakebeds (another half-inch of rain fell at Edwards; snow on the upper areas of the High Range), more modifications were performed on the airplanes.

It may have been a Mach 6 airplane, but the State of California still had laws that could not be overlooked. After Mike Adams' first flight landed at Cuddeback on 6 October 1966, the airplane was trucked back to Edwards. Note the license plate tacked onto the back of the XLR99 nozzle. (NASA Dryden)

The instrument compartment behind the cockpit contained the majority of the recorders and signal processing equipment. North American had designed the compartment so that things were easily removable, saving the ground crew from working in the cramped confines of the compartment itself. (NASA Dryden)

Joe Engle aborted his first flight (1-A-62) on 4 October 1963 because of a communications failure. This is the preflight servicing. The side tunnels did not frost up as much as the fuselage since they stood-off some distance from the tank itself. Note the open bomb bay doors on Balls Eight. (NASA Dryden)

The time was also used to complete various analyses that had been in work for some time. Perhaps the most important was a complete simulation of reentry profiles at the increased weights currently being flown by the airplanes. The ground rules were that reentries would be limited to 1,600 psf using an angle of attack of 20 degrees. In order not to exceed the structural limitations of the airplanes, it was decided to restrict the X-15-1 to altitudes under 265,000 feet and the X-15A-2 to less than 250,000 feet. The X-15-3 continued to be allowed to operate up to 360,000 feet. This was not really a problem since the program had already reached the maximum altitude it was planning on, although the first two airplanes would bump into these restrictions on several future flights.[115]

By the beginning of April the weather had improved considerably. Rogers, Grapevine, and Mud were dry and in the process of being repaired and remarked; Cuddeback was dry but still too soft to remark. All of the other lakes were drying rapidly and were ready to use by the end of the month.[116]

Bob Rushworth left the program after Flight 2-45-81 on 1 July 1966, going on to a distinguished career that included a tour as the AFFTC commander some years later. Rushworth had flown 34 flights – more than any other pilot and more than double the statistical average. He had flown the X-15 for almost six years including most of the challenging heating flights.[117]

Rushworth was replaced in the flight lineup by Major Michael J. Adams, making his first flight (1-69-116) on 6 October 1966; he started

his career with a bang – literally. The X-15-1 was launched out of Hidden Hills on a scheduled low altitude (70,000 feet) and low-speed (Mach 4) pilot familiarization flight. The bang came when the XLR99 shut itself down 90 seconds into the planned 129-second burn after the forward bulkhead of the ammonia tank failed. Fortunately the airplane did not explode and Adams successfully landed at Cuddeback without major incident. It appears that Adams was just having a bad day. After he returned to Edwards, he took a T-38 on a scheduled proficiency flight. Shortly after takeoff, one of the J85 engines in the T-38 quit; fortunately, the Talon has two engines. Adams made his second emergency landing of the day, this time on the concrete runway at Edwards. Some days you should not bother getting out of bed.[118]

The program had experienced a few flights where the planned altitude had been overshot for various reasons, but Bill Dana would add one for the record books on 1 November 1966. This flight (3-56-83) was planned for 267,000 feet. Dana got the XLR99 lit on the first try and pulled into a 39-degree climb, or so he thought. In reality the climb angle was 42 degrees. Interestingly, Pete Knight in the NASA-1 control room did not notice the error either, and as the engine burned-out reported "We got a burnout, Bill, 82 seconds, it looks good. Track and profile are looking very good." As Dana climbed through 230,000 feet NASA-1 finally noticed and said "we got you going a little high on profile. Outside of that, it looks good." The flight eventually reached 306,900 feet – 39,900 feet higher than planned – maybe 40,000 feet was not enough cushion.[119]

Bill Dana in the X-15-1 prior to Flight 1-74-130 on 1 March 1968. Note the prop rod to keep the canopy open and the blue headrest. (NASA Dryden)

Bob Rushworth after Flight 3-10-19 on 4 October 1962. The gloves for the A/P22S-2 suit came in several colors including the more-usual silver, black, and white. The canopy on the X-15-3 is help up by two prop rods, in this case yellow instead of the red and white striped version shown at the top of the page. (NASA Dryden)

Pete Knight would eventually set the fastest flight of the program, but not before a very close call while flying X-15-1. As Knight told it in his pilot's report after the flight (1-73-126).[120]

"The launch and the flight was beautiful, up to a certain point. We had gotten on theta and I heard the 80,000-foot call. I checked that at about 3,100 fps. Things were looking real good and I was really enjoying the flight. All of a sudden the engine went 'blurp' and quit. There could not have been two seconds between the engine quit and everything else happening because it all went in order. The engine shut down. All three SAS lights came on. Both generator lights came on and then there was another light came on, and I think it was the fuel low line light. I am not sure. Then after all the lights got on; they all went out. Everything quit. By this time I was still heading up and the airplane was getting pretty sloppy. As far as I am concerned both APUs quit ... so the airplane was just wallowing up as it continued to climb. It never did really go, well, it was out of control, but it never got over on its back or anything else. ... I tried to control it with the BCS but I am not sure that the BCS was working or if it was, it was not giving me what I wanted. About this time I decided that I was going to have to leave it. I looked out on top to see where I was and I could see Mono Lake over to the right. It was clear and beautiful. When it rolled over to the left again I looked down and I was almost directly over Mud Lake. I thought, well, if we get anything running we will go back to Mud ... Coming down I got the emergency battery on and ... tried to start the right [APU] and it did not give me anything. I did the same thing on the left one. I heard the left one fire up, so I really do not understand why the generator would not engage, but I'd engage it and it would not engage at all. So I began to pick up control of the airplane and tried to pull it up to get some angle of attack on it for the reentry. ... Once I thought I was level enough I started a left turn back to Mud. Made a 6-g turn all the way around ... by the time I was leveled out and looking at Mud Lake I had at least 45,000 [feet] and I could see then that I could make Mud Lake so I headed right for the east shore. Once I was sure I could make the east shore of Mud Lake with sufficient altitude I used some speed brakes to get it down to about 20 to 25,000 and then varied the pattern to make the left turn into the runway landing to the west. ... I was getting pretty tired of that side stick so I began to use both hands. One on the center stick and one on the side stick taking the pressure off the stick with the left hand and flying it with the right. ... I did not have any qualms about landing it on the side stick that way because I really did not want to get both hands on that center stick. Came down and flared. ... I settled in and got it right down to the runway and it was a nice landing as far as the main skids were concerned, but the nose gear came down really hard. Once I got it on the ground I slid out to a stop. ... I could not open the canopy. I tried twice and could not move that handle, so I sat there and rested for a while reached up and grabbed it again. Finally it eased off and the canopy came open. Then I started to get out of the airplane and I could not get this connection off over here. I got the hat [helmet] off, to cool off a little bit, and tried it again. ... I pulled the emergency release and that headrest blew off and it went into the canopy and slammed back down and hit me in the head. I got out of the airplane and by that time the C-130 was there. Got into the 130 and came home."

It was one of the few times that an X-15 pilot extracted himself from the airplane without the assistance of ground crews. Normally there was a crew at each of the primary emergency lakes; but Mud

Mike Adams not too long after (there is still frost on the liquid oxygen tank) landing Flight 1-70-116 on 22 March 1967. Note that part of the "U.S. AIR FORCE" marking and NASA meatball burned off during the Mach 5.59 flight. The cockpit camera is visible near the aft edge of the canopy window. (NASA Dryden)

Pete Knight poses with the X-15A-2 on 2 December 1965. Note how much longer the nose gear appears compared with X-15-1 at left. All reports are that the nose strut itself was the same length, but the pivot point was moved down nine inches to help compensate for the longer struts on the skids. (NASA Dryden)

was not primary for this flight, and there was no equipment or personnel stationed there. Based on energy management, Knight should probably have landed at Grapevine, but when that decision had to be made the airplane had no power, and hence no flight controls, so it

was not really an option. It is likely that the personnel on the ground were more worried than Knight – when the APUs failed they took all electrical power, including to the radar transponder and radio. At the time, the radars were not skin tracking the X-15, so the ground lost

Joe Engle posed for his portrait on the same day as Knight and the resulting image looks much the same. Engle later became the first (and so far, only) person to manually fly the space shuttle orbiter during major portions of reentry and all the way to landing (on STS-2). (NASA Dryden)

Milt Thompson after Flight 3-34-55 on 3 September 1964. The pilots were always escorted by an Air Force flight surgeon carrying the air conditioning unit for the A/P22S-2 (or MC-2) full-pressure suit. Note the support vehicle and precautionary ambulance in the background. (NASA Dryden)

A couple of stills taken on 28 April 1961 during the filming of the motion picture "X-15" starring David Mclean, James Gregory, Richard Kirby, and Charles Bronson in his first motion picture. The X-15 replica built for the movie is now at the Pima Air Museum in Tucson, Arizona, modified as the X-15A-2. Note the inaccurate square bug-eye camera fairings on the X-15 and the way the simulated frost covers the side fairings. (NASA Dryden)

Yes, the chase planes came ALL the way down. On 15 November 1960 Scott Crossfield made the first flight (2-10-21) with the XLR99 engine. Note the F-104 (with either Bob White or Joe Walker) in the background, providing altitude and speed callouts to Crossfield. Barely visible behind the X-15 in the photo at above right is Al White and John DeLong in an F-100F, also almost on the desert floor. The photos were taken from another F-104 chase aircraft. (AFFTC History Office)

CHAPTER 7

The NASA hangar in September 1964 showing all three X-15s being prepared for flights. X-15-1 is in the foreground, followed by the modified X-15A-2, and the X-15-3 with its sharp leading edge dorsal rudder in the background. Note the cables going into the instrument compartment on the X-15-1. (NASA Headquarters)

track of the airplane; they had no telemetry and no radar lock. It was almost eight minutes later that Bill Dana flying Chase-2 caught sight of the X-15 just as it crossed the east edge of Mud Lake, "He's going into Mud … landing East to West … center of Mud and in good shape right now." Mike Adams was NASA-1 for the flight, "Roger, understand." Paul Bikle later commented that Knight's recovery of the airplane was one of the most impressive events of the program.[121]

The problem was most likely the result of arcing in the Western Test Range Launch Monitoring experiment. Unlike most experiments, this one was connected to the primary electrical bus. The arcing momentarily overloaded the associated APU, which subsequently stalled and performed an automatic safety shutdown. This transferred the entire load to the other APU which also stalled since the load was still present. After this flight the WTR and MIT experiments were moved to the secondary electrical bus, which was designed to

drop out if one generator shut down; this would preclude a complete power loss to the airplane.[122]

The flight planners had spent many hours devising methods for recovering the airplane with various malfunctions. These methods were often highly dependent upon the accuracy of the simulator for the worst-case, bare airframe aerodynamics. The simulator was constantly updated with the results from flights and wind tunnel tests to keep it as accurate as possible. The flight by Knight was the only complete reentry flown without any dampers, and Bob Hoey, an AFFTC flight planner, remembers that "we would have given a month's pay to be able to compare Pete's entry with those predicted on the sim, but all instrumentation ceased when he lost both APUs, so there was no data! Jack Kolf told Pete that we were planning to install a hand crank in the cockpit hooked to the oscillograph so he could get us some data next time this happened."[123]

The X-15A-2

Left: *Flight 2-C-93 on 7 August 1967 was a scheduled captive carry that allowed Pete Knight to evaluate the external tanks in flight while still attached to the NB-52B.* (AFFTC History Office)

Below: *The advanced X-15A-2 at its roll-out in Inglewood. The large external propellant tanks would be the key to the airplane's increased performance.* (The Boeing Company Archives)

During the 31st flight of the X-15-2, on 9 November 1962, the engine stuck at 35-percent thrust and Jack McKay made an emergency landing at Mud Lake. Unfortunately, the wing flaps failed to deploy, resulting in a very fast and somewhat heavy (due to unjettisoned propellants) landing. At touchdown the left main skid collapsed, causing the aircraft to veer sharply sideways and turn over onto its back. The aircraft suffered extensive damage during the rollover. At this point the aircraft had accumulated a total free flight time of 4 hours, 40 minutes, and 32.2 seconds.[1]

North American proposed modifying the X-15-2 to a configuration to test various advanced air-breathing propulsion concepts. NASA in general, and Paul Bikle in particular, were not particularly enthusiastic and felt the aircraft should simply be repaired to its original configuration. Many researchers believed that the X-15A[2] would be of limited value for propulsion research. Nevertheless, on 13 May 1963 the Air Force directed North American to repair and modify the aircraft at a cost of $4.75 million. The advanced aircraft was specifically intended to evaluate a hypersonic air-breathing research engine at a velocity of 8,000 fps and an altitude of 100,000 feet.[3]

The physical appearance of the X-15A-2 was not radically changed as a result of the modification. The wingspan was still 22.36 feet, but the airplane was 29 inches longer due to a plug being added to the center of gravity compartment between the propellant tanks. The access doors for this compartment were designed to accommodate optical windows looking up or down, and a liquid hydrogen tank, with a total capacity of 48 pounds, could be – but apparently never was – installed to fuel the ramjet mounted under the fixed portion of the ventral stabilizer.[4]

Perhaps the most obvious change was the ability to carry external propellant tanks on each side of the fuselage below the wings. These allowed approximately 70-percent more propellant to be carried, a necessary part of raising performance to 8,000 fps. The tanks provided an additional 60 seconds of engine burn time, for a total of 150 seconds at 100-percent power. Other modifications included adding hydrogen peroxide tanks within extended aft side fairings to supply the turbopump for the longer engine burn times, and additional pressurization gas in a spherical helium tank just behind the upper vertical stabilizer.[5]

In order to allow the X-15A-2 to land with the ramjet still attached to the ventral, a 6.75-inch longer main landing gear strut was developed that provided 33 inches of ground clearance to the bottom of the fixed ventral stabilizer; the expected ramjet was 30 inches in diameter. The new struts also provided a 1,000-pound increase in allowable landing weights, but there was some concern

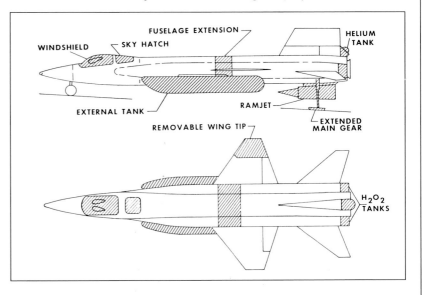

EXTENDED PERFORMANCE
EXTERNAL PROPELLANT TANKS

- LAUNCH WT .... 45,355 LB
- THRUST (VACUUM) ...... 58,900 LB
- PROPELLANT WT
  - X-15 .... 18,530 LB
  - TANKS .... 10,000 LB
- TOTAL IMPULSE 7,950,000 LB-SEC
- MAXIMUM VELOCITY ..... 8700 FPS
- MAXIMUM ALTITUDE ..... 520,000 FT

EJECTABLE / RECOVERABLE TANKS
EJECTED @ M 1.4/65,000 FT)

NH₃ — LOX

On 11 November 1960 North American released the "X-15 Research Capability" report on possible variants of the research airplane. The shape of the drop tanks differed from what was ultimately built, and the expected performance was much greater than actually achieved, but the concept was remarkably similar to what became the X-15A-2 a few years later. (The Boeing Company Archives)

WINDSHIELD — SKY HATCH — FUSELAGE EXTENSION — HELIUM TANK
EXTERNAL TANK — RAMJET — EXTENDED MAIN GEAR
REMOVABLE WING TIP — H₂O₂ TANKS

As ultimately built, the X-15A-2 included several external modifications, including a revised canopy, the skylight hatch on top of the instrument compartment, a 29-inch fuselage plug, extended fuselage tunnels, a helium sphere behind the dorsal stabilizer, and a removable right wing tip. The capability to carry two large external propellant tanks was also added. Less visible, unless you directly compare the airplanes, are the extended landing skids and the relocated pivot on the nose gear that made it appear to be much longer than usual. (U.S. Air Force)

At left, an early advanced X-15 concept showing two ramjets under the aft fuselage. By the time the drawing at right was published, the concept was essentially what was actually built. (San Diego Aerospace Museum Collection)

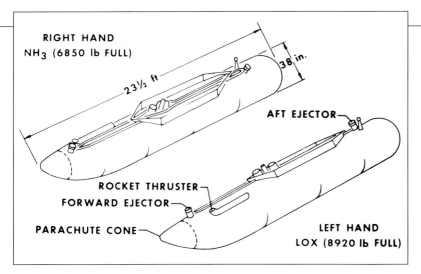

RIGHT HAND
NH₃ (6850 lb FULL)

23½ ft

38 in.

AFT EJECTOR

ROCKET THRUSTER
FORWARD EJECTOR

PARACHUTE CONE

LEFT HAND
LOX (8920 lb FULL)

The left and right drop tanks were the same size and shape, but differed considerably in their empty and full weights. This led to some interesting stability and control concerns, but caused no actual problems except for the loss of a good flight – 2-45-81 – due to bad instrumentation. The tanks were designed to be recovered and reused after each flight. (U.S. Air Force)

over the effects of the longer strut on nose-wheel and forward fuselage loads. In an attempt to provide an additional margin of safety, the nose gear trunnion was mounted nine inches lower (effectively lowering the nose gear by the same amount), allowing an attitude at nose-gear touchdown that was similar to the basic airplanes.[6]

The windshield of the X-15A-2 was revised to withstand the increased temperatures anticipated at Mach 8. Instead of the trapezoidal windows on the original airplanes, elliptical windows were installed that used three panes of glass. The outer pane was 0.65-inch thick fused silica, the middle pane was 0.375-inch alumino-silicate, and the inner pane was 0.29-inch laminated soda lime glass. The outside windshield retaining frame was mounted flush with the glass to prevent the reoccurrence of the flow-heating experienced early in the program.[7]

Since the temperatures at the expected Mach 8 velocities were well above what the X-15 airframe had been designed for, it was

decided to completely cover the airplane with an ablative heat shield. A real-time temperature simulation was developed using the former Dyna-Soar hybrid (part analog, part digital) simulator at the AFFTC. In conjunction with a fixed-base simulation of the X-15A-2, the hybrid had the capability of predicting the temperature at selected points for both protected and unprotected surfaces. A temperature-time history for a point aft of the nose gear door for a flight to Mach 7.6 at 100,000 feet was compared to the temperature at the same location for an actual Mach 6 flight. Both the effective heating rate (as evidenced by the change in temperature) and the maximum temperature were significantly more severe at the higher speed.[8]

During arc-tunnel tests of proposed ablative coatings it was observed that loosened material from the ablator tended to reattach to surfaces downstream. Flight tests were performed with a panel of windshield glass mounted on the vertical stabilizer aft of a sample patch of the ablator on X-15-1. The glass panel quickly became opaque, which would have seriously restricted the pilot's vision. Since the pilot obviously needed to see during landing, three different approaches were considered to restore the necessary vision: (1) explosive fragmentation of the outer windshield glass after the high-speed run was completed, (2) boundary layer blowing over the windshield during the entire flight, and (3) a hinged metal "eyelid" that could be opened after the high speed portion of flight.[9]

The explosive concept slightly worried everybody and was not pursued very far. The boundary layer idea was the only one that potentially provided a continuously-clear windshield, but the pilot actually had little reason to need completely clear vision at 100,000 feet; there was really nothing to run into at that altitude and the implementation was complex and expensive. Therefore, the eyelid was chosen as the easiest to accomplish. The right windshield was left unprotected and provided normal pilot vision during launch and initial climbout; during the high-speed run it would become opaque, allowing the pilot to see little more than light and dark patches of sky. The left windshield would have the eyelid installed; it would be closed before flight, then opened once the airplane slowed below Mach 3. The pilot would look out of the left side of the windshield for landing. This carried some risks – after one of his windshields shattered during a 1961 flight Bob White had reported that his vision was "compromised" during landing; the new configuration was very similar.

A set of external tanks on 27 June 1966. The outside was an aerodynamic shell, with the actual tanks located under a layer of insulation. The left tank contained 793 gallons of liquid oxygen and three helium bottles with a total capacity of 8.4 cubic feet. The right tank contained 1,080 gallons of ammonia. The tanks were attached to the X-15 at the center fluid and electrical connection under the leading edge of the wing, but had stand-offs fore and aft to stabilize the tank. (NASA Dryden)

When flight tests began, another phenomena was discovered – the eyelid created a small canard effect when opened, causing the airplane to pitch up, roll right, and yaw right. The effects were small but noticeable; fortunately the pilots found it fairly easy to correct.[10]

A new pitot-static system was also required because of the ablator. The static pickups had to be relocated since their normal locations on the sides of the forward fuselage were covered with MA-25S. A vented compartment behind the canopy was chosen as the static source and was found to be suitable during flight tests on X-15-1. The standard dog-leg pitot tube ahead of the canopy was replaced by an extendable pitot since the temperatures expected at Mach 8 exceeded the standard tube's limits. The retractable tube remained within the fuselage until the aircraft decelerated below Mach 2.[11]

The X-15A-2 modification also included a "skylight" hatch that had long been proposed. Two upward-opening 20-inch long by 8.5-inch wide doors were installed in the instrument compartment behind the cockpit The normal research instrumentation elevator was modified so that the upper shelf could extend upward through the open hatch during periods of very low dynamic pressure. This would allow experiments – such as star trackers – a clear view of the sky at high altitude.[12]

The outer portion of the right wing had been seriously damaged in the original accident. North American found that it could adequately repair the main wing box, but the outer 41-inches were a total loss. It was decided to modify the wing box to support a replaceable outer panel that would allow various materials and structures to be tested during hypersonic flight. The panel that was provided with the airplane (and the only one that apparently was ever flown) was similar in construction and materials to the standard X-15 wing except that it was equipped with an 26.7 by 23-inch access panel that allowed access to an extensive amount of research instrumentation.[13]

The expected performance of the X-15A-2 represented a significant improvement over the demonstrated 6,019 fps of the basic aircraft. When the external tanks were carried with the ventral rudder attached, the estimated velocity was between 7,600 and 7,700 fps at an altitude of 120,000 feet. Replacing the ventral with an assumed ramjet configuration would decrease that to about 7,200 fps at an altitude of 118,000 feet. This performance was appreciably less than the initial design goal of 8,000 fps at an altitude of 100,000 feet, but still a reasonable increment over the previous flights.[14]

Final assembly of the X-15A-2 was completed at the North American facility in Inglewood on 15 February 1964, and the airplane was accepted by the Air Force on 17 February, three weeks ahead of schedule and slightly below budget. The airplane was, however, 773 pounds overweight, explaining much of the performance loss. The design launch weight was 49,640 pounds, of which 32,250 pounds were propellants; 18,750 pounds internally and 13,500 pounds in the external tanks. Subsequent modifications would add another few hundred pounds in empty weight. The airplane was delivered to the Flight Research Center on 18 February and an "official" government acceptance ceremony was held on 24 February.[15]

After final systems checks were conducted, the modified aircraft made its first captive flight (2-C-53) on 15 June 1964. The first free flight (2-32-55) came on 25 June, mainly to check out the various systems, evaluate the handling qualities of the modified airplane, and to gain preliminary experience with the ultraviolet stellar photography experiment (#1). It was not bad for a maiden flight; using 77-percent thrust Bob Rushworth reached Mach 4.59 and 83,300 feet. In an iron-

A set of wind tunnel studies were run at the Jet Propulsion Laboratory to determine the effects of the external tanks on the X-15A-2. Note the model at left has only a single tank – tests were conducted with asymmetrical configurations, usually with undesirable results. Also of interest on the model at left are the "slipper" tanks above the rear of the fuselage tunnels. These were investigated several times during the program as a possible location for additional propellants for the ramjet. (Jet Propulsion Laboratory)

ic twist, Jack McKay – who had been injured on the flight that originally damaged the X-15-2 – was the NASA-1 controller. As expected, Bob Rushworth reported that the X-15A-2 handled much like a basic X-15. The static longitudinal stability remained about the same despite a 10-percent forward shift in the center of gravity. The already low directional stability of the basic airplane was somewhat lower in the X-15A-2, but was not deemed to pose a significant threat to safety. The longitudinal trim characteristics of the modified airplane were essentially unchanged up through Mach 3 at angles-to-attack up to 15 degrees. For reentry at higher Mach numbers and angles of attack, the trim capability of the modified airplane was reduced by approximately 3 to 5 degrees in angle-of-attack.[16]

Things got more exciting on the second flight (2-33-56). Shortly after obtaining a maximum Mach number of 5.23, the nose gear unexpectedly extended as the airplane decelerated through Mach 4.2. After the flight Rushworth wrote, "Everything was going along fine and just about the time I was ready to drop it over [lower the nose] I got a loud bang and … the resulting conditions … gave me quite a little bit of concern because the airplane began to oscillate wildly and I couldn't seem to catch up with it. I put the dampers back on and stuffed the nose down to about 5 degrees angle of attack and it seemed to be fairly normal then except I had a sideslip and I was then required to use left roll to hold the airplane level. A couple of seconds later I realized that this sound that I had heard was very much similar to the nose gear coming out in the landing pattern … I announced that and then a few seconds after that I began to get smoke in the cockpit, quite a bit more than I had ever seen before. This partially confirmed that the nose gear, at least the door, was open."[17]

For the time being, the chase planes were no help confirming the problem since they were some ten miles below the X-15. McKay also could not help much since no emergency procedures existed for this particular failure. NASA-1 did advise Rushworth that it would probably be best if the X-15 remained at high altitude until it had slowed down considerably, thereby easing the aero-thermo loads on the extended nose gear. At one point McKay advised Rushworth to use the brakes to slow down a bit; Rushworth had other ideas, "No, I don't want to get brakes out, I want to get the damn thing home."[18]

The X-15A-2 poses with its external tanks on 8 October 1965. Note the polished aluminum shine on the aft part of the tank. The pivot point for the nose landing gear was relocated to compensate for the longer rear skids; engineers wanted to keep the nose from slamming down too hard and breaking the airplane. The red stripe on top of the instrument compartment outlines the skylight hatch. (NASA Dryden)

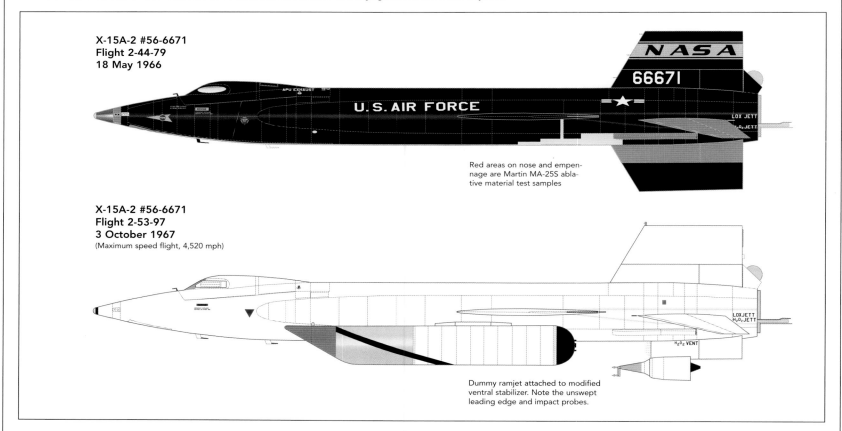

X-15A-2 #56-6671
Flight 2-44-79
18 May 1966

Red areas on nose and empennage are Martin MA-25S ablative material test samples

X-15A-2 #56-6671
Flight 2-53-97
3 October 1967
(Maximum speed flight, 4,520 mph)

Dummy ramjet attached to modified ventral stabilizer. Note the unswept leading edge and impact probes.

Ablators had been flown on many X-15 flights during the program, but things got serious with the X-15A-2. When MA-25S was selected as the primary thermal protection system, large samples of it were flown on the horizontal stabilizers, vertical stabilizers, and other locations on the airplane. When sufficient confidence was gained, the entire airplane was covered in the pink ablative material, then oversprayed with a white wear layer that protected the ablator against inadvertent liquid oxygen spillage (the ablator would explode with as little as 8 psi pressure when exposed to liquid oxygen) and the weather. (Artwork by Tony Landis)

The chase planes spotted the X-15 as it was descending 20 miles northeast of Edwards. Despite the degraded control and increased drag resulting from the extended nose gear, Rushworth was doing fine. Joe Engle in Chase-3 verified that the nose gear appeared to be in the locked-down position. As for the tires, Engle reported, "OK, Bob, your tires look pretty scorched, I imagine they will probably go on landing." There was a worry, however, that the oleo strut had also been damaged by the heat and dynamic pressure but there seemed to be little choice. As expected, the tires disintegrated shortly after the nose gear touched the lakebed, but Rushworth managed to stop the airplane without serious difficulty. Chase-3, "About 10 feet, 5, 3, 2, nice. OK, looks like the rubber is gone, nose wheel tires are gone but you're in good shape, Bob. Very nice show."[19]

An investigation revealed that aerodynamic heating was the cause of the problem. The expansion of the fuselage was greater than the amount of slack built into the landing gear release cable; this caused an effective pull on the cable that released the uplock hook. An additional load on the uplock hook was imposed by an outward bowing of the nose gear door. The load from both of these sources caused the uplock hook to bend, allowing the gear to extend. This was duplicated in the High-Temperature Loads Calibration Laboratory by simulating the fuselage expansion and by applying heat to the nose-gear door.[20]

The same stability and control data flight plan was duplicated for the next X-15A-2 flight (2-34-57) on 29 September 1964. Shortly after reaching a maximum Mach number of 5.20, Rushworth experienced a less intense noise and aircraft trim change at Mach 4.5 – the small nose gear scoop door had opened. Rushworth's post-flight report noted that, "Yes, I sensed it was the little door, because the magnitude of the bang when it came open wasn't as large as the other experience." During the normal gear extension sequence this door was used to impose air loads on the nose gear door to assist in the extension of the nose gear. The nose gear door was redesigned to provide positive retention of the scoop door regardless of the thermal stresses. Since the basic failure mode was common on the other two airplanes, they were also modified.[21]

A slower-speed flight (2-35-60) was flown next to a Mach number of 4.66 to check out the nose gear modifications. The flight planners decided to give Rushworth a break after the two previous missions, so Jack McKay made this flight, which went off without a problem. The nose gear performed normally and good stability data were obtained.[22]

Rushworth was in the cockpit again for the next fight (2-36-63) on 17 February 1965. In a run of bad luck that is difficult to fathom, this time the right main skid extended at Mach 4.3 and 85,000 feet. In his post-flight report Rushworth wrote, "Jack [McKay, NASA-1] was talking away and things were going along real nice and I couldn't seem to get a word in there to tell him that I had a little problem. It took several seconds to get the airplane righted and dampers back on, very much similar to the nose gear coming out. Once I got it righted, I realized that I had a tremendous sideslip, I guess 4 degrees and it took a lot of rudder deflection to get sideslip to zero. This persisted all the way down until I got subsonic. Once I had gone subsonic the airplane handled reasonably well." Again, Rushworth managed to make a normal landing, but after he finally got out of the airplane, he turned around and kicked it – enough was enough. Post-flight inspection revealed that the uplock hook had bent because of aerodynamic heating.[23]

Five more X-15A-2 flights (2-38-66 through 2-42-74) were flown before the envelope expansion program was begun. These flights

The X-15A-2 on Rogers Dry Lake after the nose gear extended at Mach 4.2 during Flight 2-33-56 on 14 August 1964. The airplane tracked remarkably straight during the slide-out, and concerns over the structural integrity of the nose gear strut proved unfounded – other than the tires, everything held together. In the photo below, note the four tracks caused by the rims of the dual nose wheels, and the skid track on either side from the main landing gear. (NASA Dryden)

Not particularly sophisticated, but effective. For the external tank separation tests, a large pit was dug beside the ramp and filled with sawdust covered by a plastic sheet. Steel beams simulated the drop tanks. The first of two tests was on 29 September 1965. Note that the canopy is missing. (NASA Dryden)

continued the stability and control evaluation, and included a new series of landing gear performance tests. Fortunately, the landing gear behaved throughout these flights.[24]

Engineers had always had some concerns about flying the X-15A-2 with the 23.5-foot long and 37.75-inch diameter external tanks. These were attached to the airplane structure within the side fairings at fuselage stations 200 and 411 and had propellant and gas interconnects through a tank pylon located between stations 317 and 397. A set of retractable doors covered the disconnects after the tanks were jettisoned. The left tank contained about 793 gallons of liquid oxygen and three helium bottles with a total capacity of 8.4 cubic feet. The right tank contained about 1,080 gallons of anhydrous ammonia. The empty left tank weighed 1,150 pounds and the empty right tank weighed only 648 pounds; when they were full of propellants they weighed 8,920 pounds and 6,850 pounds, respectively. Note that the left tank was over 2,000 pounds heavier than the right tank when they were full.[25]

Structural limitations of the aluminum tanks and degraded handling qualities dictated that the maximum allowable Mach number with the external tanks was 2.6 – the tanks had to be jettisoned before reaching that speed. In addition, it was not possible with the tanks with the tanks attached. Hence, considerable effort was expended to ensure the tanks could be jettisoned. Prior to the first flight using external tanks, two jettison tests were conducted with the X-15A-2 located over a 10-foot deep pit that had been dug in the ground beside the ramp. Steel beams with similar mass and inertia properties were constructed to simulate

Facing page: *The cockpit of the X-15A-2 on 7 September 1967. The external tank jettison buttons are on the left console just behind the speed brake handles. By this time indications for external tank propellant flow had been added to the cockpit, just under the angle-of-attack indicator near the 8-ball. The rotary switch on the center pedestal to the left of the stick was used to control the photo optical degradation experiment based on radar and altitude calls from NASA-1. The left side-stick controller has been removed in this photo, probably indicating that the ballistic control system had been removed from the airplane since it was not necessary on the high-speed flights. (NASA Dryden)*

empty tanks. Preloaded cables attached to the beams applied simulated aerodynamic drag and side loads. Both tests were successful and high-speed motion pictures showed good separation characteristics.[26]

The final ground-based external tank test took place on the Propulsion System Test Stand where the X-15A-2 completed a full-duration engine run with the external tanks installed on the aircraft. Several earlier tests had uncovered a couple of component deficiencies which were corrected prior to the final test.[27]

Although there were physical differences between the basic X-15 and the X-15A-2 without external tanks, the aerodynamic qualities were similar. With external tanks on the airplane, however, some rather dramatic differences existed with the general trend toward the unfavorable. The overall control task was further complicated by the offset center of gravity caused by the external tanks. At launch with full tanks the vertical center of gravity was approximately 9 inches below the aircraft waterline, moving upward as the propellants were consumed. This offset below the thrust vector resulted in a nose-down pitch at engine ignition that had to be counteracted by the pilot with additional nose-up stabilizer trim. The center of gravity was also displaced 2 inches to the left because of the heavier liquid oxygen tank on that side. This caused a left rolling moment that also had to be counteracted by the pilot.[28]

The nominal flight profile for the speed missions was to maintain a 12-degree angle-of-attack until a pitch attitude of 34 degrees was reached. This climb attitude was held until external-propellant depletion and the tanks were ejected at approximately Mach 2.1 and 67,000 feet. After tank ejection, an angle of attack of 2 degrees was maintained until the airplane reached 100,000 feet. The airplane then accelerated to maximum velocity.[29]

The first flight (2-43-75) with empty external tanks was on 3 November 1965, and was launched from Cuddeback about 60 miles north of Edwards, the only flight from this lake. The tanks were jettisoned at Mach 2.25 as the airplane passed through 70,300 feet. Bob Rushworth took the airplane to Mach 2.31 and 70,600 feet before landing at Rogers Dry Lake after a flight of only 5 minutes and 1 second (the shortest non-emergency powered-flight of the program).[30]

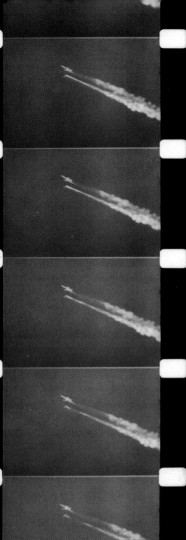

The tanks separated cleanly from the aircraft, However, it appeared that the tanks did not rotate nose down as much as expected, exhibited a tumbling action during flight with the drogue chutes attached, and tended to trim at an angle of attack of about −110 degrees. The drogue chutes occasionally collapsed during flight so the riser was lengthened for future flights. The nose cone containing the main descent chute did not separate on the liquid oxygen tank, which was destroyed on impact. The ammonia tank was recovered in a repairable condition.[31]

Post-flight analysis of this flight indicated that the handling qualities were essentially as predicted by the simulator. Rushworth – for a change flying without deploying part of the landing gear – commented that he thought that "roll stability was significantly less than I had expected" but that "longitudinal control wasn't quite as bad" as he had anticipated.[32]

Bob Rushworth's last flight (2-45-81), on 1 July 1966, was also the first flight with full external tanks. Johnny Armstrong later remembered that "with twenty-twenty hindsight, flight 45 was destined for failure." On the X-15A-2, propellants were supplied to the engine from the internal tanks in the normal fashion. The propellants from the external tanks were pressure-fed to the internal tanks. The fixed-base simulator had shown that the X-15 would quickly become uncontrollable if propellant from one external tank transferred but the other one did not – the moment about the roll axis was too large to be countered by the rolling tail. If this situation developed, the pilot would be advised to jettison the tanks, shut down the engine, and make an emergency landing.[33]

The problem was, for this first flight with full tanks, there was no direct method to determine if the tanks were feeding correctly. Instrumentation was being developed to provide propellant transfer sensors, but these were not available for this flight. Instead, a pressure transducer across an orifice in the helium pressurization line provided the only information. The pressure transducer had worked as expected during a planned captive carry flight (2-C-80) with propellants in the external tanks.[34]

During the flight to the launch lake, while still safely connected to the NB-52, Rushworth verified the pressure transducer was working by jettisoning a small amount of propellants from the internal tanks and NASA-1 watched the helium pressure come up as the external propellants flowed into the airplane – nobody had thought to provide the pilot with any indicators. But 18 seconds after the X-15 dropped away from the NB-52, Jack McKay (NASA-1) called to Rushworth: "We see no flow on ammonia Bob." Rushworth responded: "Roger, understand." McKay: "Shutdown. Tanks off, Bob." Rushworth got busy: "OK, tanks are away … I'm going into Mud." Any emergency landing is stressful, but this one ended well.[35]

A colorful combination: Balls Three and the X-15A-2 with orange-and-white drop tanks taxi out for Flight 2-43-75 on 3 November 1965. Bob Rushworth evaluated the handling characteristics of the X-15A-2 with the empty external tanks and engineers checked out the tank separation characteristics. This flight was flown from Cuddeback to allow the tanks to fall on the Precision Impact Range Area (PIRA), also known as the Edwards bombing range. (NASA Dryden)

The drogue chutes deployed immediately after separation and the dump valve in the tank allowed the propellants to flow out. Main chute deployment was satisfactory; however, the mechanism designed to cut the main chute risers failed and the tanks were dragged across the desert by high surface winds. Nevertheless, both tanks were recovered in repairable condition.[36]

The next X-15A-2 flight (2-49-86) was flown with the ventral on, primarily to familiarize Pete Knight with the handling qualities in this configuration since future flights would be flown with either the ventral or ramjet attached and external tanks installed. Flight 2-50-89 was the first flight where the external tanks operated (knowingly) successfully, including the improved instrumentation that let the ground and pilot know the propellants were transferring correctly.[37]

After this flight, the X-15A-2 received the final modifications needed to get ready for the maximum speed flight. Perhaps the most noticeable was the installation of the "eyelid" over the left-hand canopy window. The canopy was sent to Inglewood in January 1967 for the necessary modifications and returned to Edwards in early April. By the time the canopy was back on the airplane, three dummy ramjet shapes had been delivered to Edwards and wind tunnel tests in the JPL 21-inch hypersonic tunnel had verified the mated ramjet configuration.[38]

A final test was when Flight 2-51-92 evaluated the handling qualities with the dummy ramjet installed under the fixed portion of the ventral stabilizer. This flight was flown without the external tanks and reached Mach 4.8.

ABLATIVE COATINGS

It was obvious that the Mach 6.5 structural design of the basic X-15s was not adequate to handle the aerodynamic heating loads expected at Mach 8. For example, the total heat load for a location

Martin MA-25S ablative on the X-15A-2 during Flight 2-44-79 on 18 May 1966. This was the natural color of the ablative before the wear layer was added. A great deal of detail about the horizontal stabilizer attachment and the ground-towing wheels may also been seen here. (NASA Dryden)

on the underside of the nose was approximately 2,300 Btu per square foot at Mach 6, but over 13,000 Btu at Mach 8. Similarly, the wing leading edge absorbed 9,500 Btu per square foot at Mach 6,

A good shot of Flight 2-43-75 showing the external tanks connected to the X-15A-2. There was a set of doors that were spring loaded to close after the tanks were jettisoned, covering the fluid and electrical connections. On the last flight one of the doors failed to close, causing minor heat damage. (NASA Dryden)

Preparing for Flight 2-43-75. Note the impact rake on the side of the dorsal rudder, and the tubing running from it down the back of the rudder to the data recorders. The large hole beside the XLR99 nozzle is the turbopump exhaust. The back of the side tunnels were not corrugated on the X-15A-2. (NASA Dryden)

On 1 July 1966, during the first flight (2-45-81) with full external tanks, there was no direct way to determine if propellant was flowing from both tanks; if only one was flowing the airplane would quickly become uncontrollable. The indirect method being used did not function properly, and to be on the safe side, Bob Rushworth jettisoned the tanks and aborted to Mud Lake. Better instrumentation was available for the next flight to preclude a repeat of this incident. (AFFTC History Office)

but 27,500 Btu at Mach 8. Since the heat-sink capacity of the structure was essentially used up at just over Mach 6, some other method had to be found to protect the airplane.[39]

There had been some minor interest in ablators for the X-15 was early as 1961. For instance, on Flight 1-23-39 a sample of Avcoat No. 2 was tested on the leading edge of the right wing, directly over the semispan thermocouple. The coating (which was never called an ablator, but obviously was when looking at before and after photos of it) proved very effective in lowering the leading edge temperature. For example, the leading edge temperature at 144 seconds after launch was only 25°F underneath the test sample; the thermocouple on either side of it showed 350°F and 315°F.[40]

The ablator initially chosen by North American for the X-15A-2 was Emerson Electric Thermolag 500, and this is the product shown in most documentation as late as the end of 1964. This material had been extensively tested in the North American 2.5-inch 1-megawatt plasma tunnel for up to 317 seconds at a time; only 180 seconds were required for the actual flight conditions. The material was applied with a commercially-available paint spray gun and weighed only 303 pounds of the 400 allocated for the thermal protection system.[41]

Further evaluation, however, resulted in this ablator being considered unacceptable, primarily because of its cure cycle. The coating had to be subjected to 300°F for a prolonged period of time to cure properly; although this had not been a problem for small test areas, accomplishing it on the entire airplane would have been a challenge. Also, T-500 was found to be somewhat water soluble after it cured, not an ideal trait for something to be used outdoors.[42]

In late 1963 a joint Air Force and NASA committee was formed to select a more suitable ablative material, although T-500 continued to be carried as the baseline for another year. The committee set up an evaluation program and all major ablator manufacturers were requested to provide test samples. The primary factors used in evaluating the materials were shielding effectiveness, room-temperature cure cycle, bond integrity, operational compatibility with the X-15, and refurbishment

characteristics. Three facilities were used for this evaluation; the 2-inch arc jet tunnel at the University of Dayton Research Institute, the 2.5-megawatt arc tunnel at Langley, and the X-15 airplanes.[43]

Initial flight tests of various ablative coatings were made using X-15-1 and X-15-3 while the second airplane was being rebuilt. The coatings were applied to locations under the nose just behind the ball nose, canopy, fuselage centerline under the liquid oxygen tank, lower surface of the horizontal stabilizers, and on the ventral stabilizer, speed brakes, and rudder. The ventral stabilizer and speed brakes provided moderate heating rates in an easily accessible location, and the liquid oxygen tank provided a test area for checking the bond integrity at temperatures approaching –300°F during flight. The removable nose panels provided measured back-surface temperatures and allowed direct comparison of two materials under the same heating conditions. The canopy application was intended to show whether a windshield-contamination problem existed, however, no conclusive results were gained from the canopy tests. Flight testing began in late 1963 and concluded in October 1964.[44]

Eventually, 15 materials were flight tested and the more promising included General Electric ESM 1004B, Martin MA-32H and MA-45R, McDonnell B-44, and NASA E-2A-1 Purple Blend. The NASA product was developed at Langley as a backup in case the commercial products did not prove to be acceptable. Limited additional tests of alternate forms of the Martin and McDonnell materials were also performed.[45]

Flight testing proved to be an extremely valuable part of the overall evaluation. Many deficiencies in materials, bond systems, and spray techniques were discovered during the flights that probably would not have been found any other way – another example that there is no substitute for real-world experience. The heating conditions experienced at Mach 5 showed material problems that had not appeared in ground-facility tests, mainly a poor bond integrity and excessive erosion and blistering on some segments. Most of these problems, if they had occurred during a Mach 8 flight, would have likely resulted in the loss of the vehicle.[46]

In the end NASA and the Air Force determined that the General Electric, Martin, McDonnell, and NASA Purple Blend products were all potentially acceptable and sent requests for proposals to the manufacturers. In January 1966 NASA awarded a contract to Martin Marietta for one of the alternate materials tested late in the evaluation.[47]

The basic ablative material was designated MA-25S and had a virgin material density of 28 pounds per cubic foot. Martin had developed MA-25S "specifically for application over complex vehicle configurations such as the X-15," although it had existed well before the X-15 application had become known. Most significantly, the material could be sprayed and cured on the aircraft at room temperature (70 to 100°F). A special premolded fiber-reinforced elastomeric silicone material (ESA-3560-IIA) similar to that used on the Air Force X-23A PRIME reentry vehicles was selected to cover all the leading edges. A premolded flexible material (MA-25S-1) was developed to cover the seams around access panels, and smaller pieces of this material were used to cover fasteners and other items that required last minute access.[48]

A flight (2-44-79) of the X-15A-2 on 18 May 1966 provided the first relatively large-scale tests of MA-25S and ESA-3560-IIA leading edge material. The materials had been applied to three nose panels (F-3, F-4, and E-4), the UHF antenna, both main landing skids and struts, both sides of the ventral stabilizer, both lower speed brakes, and the left horizontal stabilizer. All of these panels were instrumented to determine the effects of the ablator. In general these tests were successful, although instrumentation failures did not allow any precise data to be gathered from the nose panels. There were lessons-learned from the various application techniques, all of which were factored into the plan for the full-scale application of the materials in preparation for the high-speed flights.[49]

ABLATOR APPLICATION

There had always been questions about exactly how easy it would be to apply an ablative coating over the surface of an entire airplane, even one as small as the X-15. There were even more questions on how easy it would be to work on the airplane after the coating had been applied, and how difficult it would be to refurbish the coating between flights. There appears to have been little actual concern about the effectiveness of the coating; if applied correctly, everyone was relatively sure the concept would work.

As part of their initial contract, Martin Marietta developed a comprehensive procedure for applying the coating, for maintaining it, and

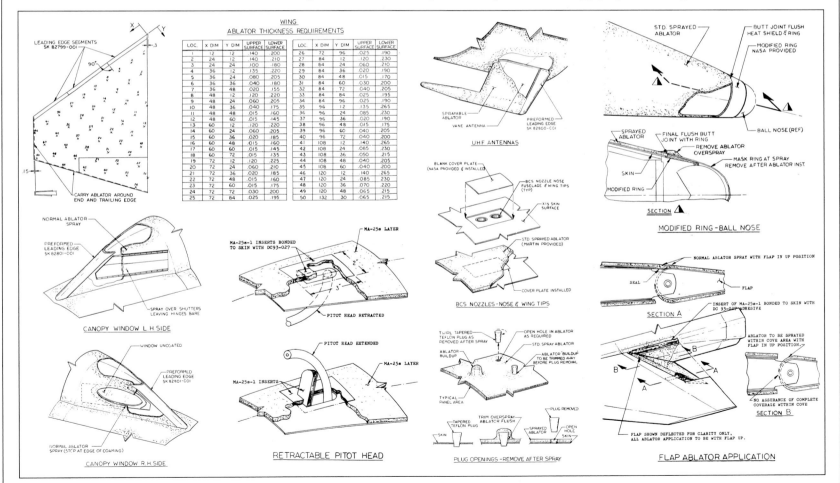

WING ABLATOR THICKNESS REQUIREMENTS

LOC.	X DIM	Y DIM	UPPER SURFACE	LOWER SURFACE	LOC.	X DIM	Y DIM	UPPER SURFACE	LOWER SURFACE
1	12	12	.140	.200	26	72	96	.025	.190
2	24	12	.140	.210	27	84	12	.120	.230
3	24	24	.100	.180	28	84	24	.060	.210
4	36	12	.135	.220	29	84	48	.020	.190
5	36	24	.080	.205	30	84	48	.015	.170
6	36	36	.040	.180	31	84	60	.030	.200
7	36	48	.020	.155	32	84	72	.040	.205
8	48	12	.120	.220	33	84	84	.025	.195
9	48	24	.060	.205	34	84	96	.025	.190
10	48	36	.040	.175	35	96	12	.135	.265
11	48	48	.015	.160	36	96	24	.085	.230
12	48	60	.015	.145	37	96	36	.020	.190
13	60	12	.120	.220	38	96	48	.015	.175
14	60	24	.060	.205	39	96	60	.040	.205
15	60	36	.020	.185	40	96	72	.040	.200
16	60	48	.015	.160	41	108	12	.140	.265
17	60	60	.015	.145	42	108	24	.085	.230
18	60	72	.015	.135	43	108	36	.050	.215
19	72	12	.120	.225	44	108	48	.040	.205
20	72	24	.060	.210	45	108	60	.040	.200
21	72	36	.020	.185	46	120	12	.140	.265
22	72	48	.015	.160	47	120	24	.085	.230
23	72	60	.015	.175	48	120	36	.070	.220
24	72	72	.030	.200	49	120	48	.065	.215
25	72	84	.025	.195	50	132	30	.065	.215

Martin produced a report that detailed the steps necessary to apply the ablative coating to the X-15A-2; these are some of the illustrations. (The Martin Company)

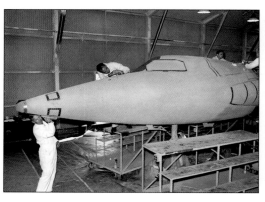

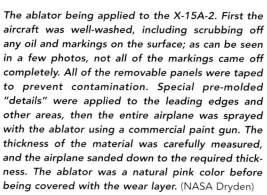

The ablator being applied to the X-15A-2. First the aircraft was well-washed, including scrubbing off any oil and markings on the surface; as can be seen in a few photos, not all of the markings came off completely. All of the removable panels were taped to prevent contamination. Special pre-molded "details" were applied to the leading edges and other areas, then the entire airplane was sprayed with the ablator using a commercial paint gun. The thickness of the material was carefully measured, and the airplane sanded down to the required thickness. The ablator was a natural pink color before being covered with the wear layer. (NASA Dryden)

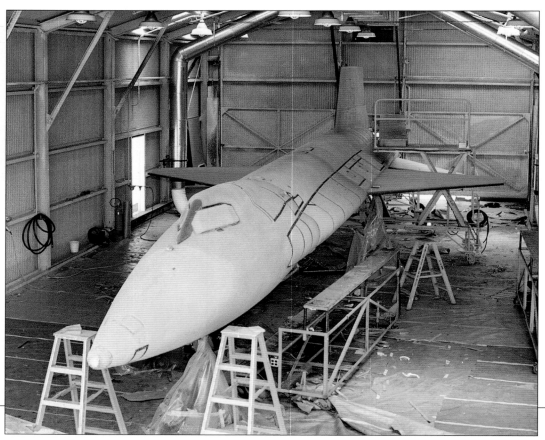

The X-15A-2 on 21 June 1967 after the MA-25S ablator had been applied, but before the wear layer was added. The black lines are areas that had been masked off to allow panels to be opened for servicing and inspecting the airplane. MA-25S has had a remarkably long career as an ablator, and is still being used on limited areas of the space shuttle external tank. (NASA Dryden)

The X-15A-2 emerges from the paint shop with its Dow Corning DC90-090 wear layer and a very limited number of caution and warning markings. (NASA via the Terry Panopalis Collection)

The dummy ramjet under the X-15A-2 on 3 October 1967. This is the 40-degree nose cone version used on the maximum speed flight; a 20-degree nose cone version had also been flown. (NASA Dryden)

The eyelid over the left window was designed to be opened below Mach 2 during deceleration to landing. Note the deployed pitot probe just ahead of the eyelid. (NASA Dryden)

Pete Knight with the X-15A-2 on 4 August 1967. Note the ablator has filled the BCS thruster holes since the system had been deleted from the airplane as unnecessary for the speed flights. (NASA Dryden)

The X-15A-2 on 4 August 1967, a couple of weeks before the first flight with the full ablative coating. Note that the modified ventral stabilizer and TAZ-8A ball nose are installed. Very few markings were applied over the ablator, just those absolutely necessary for the safety of the ground crew. (NASA Dryden)

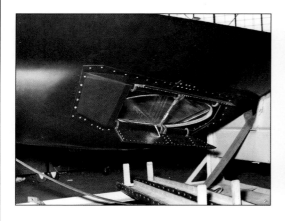

The eyelid open (left) and closed on 31 March 1967 after the canopy had returned from being modified in Inglewood. The unit is upside down in these photos. The X-15A-2 pilot would use the unprotected window during captive carry and launch, then switch to the eyelid-protected window for landing. (NASA Dryden)

Inside the canopy showing how the eyelid looked. Also note the retracted deceleration headrest at the top of the photo. (NASA Dryden)

for removing it if necessary. The first complete application of the ablative was accomplished in general agreement with the schedule and procedures that had been published earlier. Before the airplane had been turned over to Martin Marietta, NASA had made a few minor changes to accommodate the ablator installation. The retractable pitot tube was installed, for instance, as was a new ball nose that had a step at its aft end; when the ablator was built-up during the application, it would fill up to the top of the step, resulting in a smooth surface.[50]

The process began with cleaning the airplane, and Martin admitted that the preparatory cleaning was "somewhat overdone" for the first application. All joints, gaps, and openings were masked before the cleaning began to prevent the possibility of getting solvent into the airplane. The surface condition of the airplane, with its accumulation of contamination and overabundance of lacquer, necessitated the use of a great deal of solvent during the initial cleaning. The final cleaning was accomplished with powdered cleanser and water using a "water break free" test to ascertain when the surface was properly clean. "Excessive cleaning" was performed in the areas of external aircraft markings in an attempt to remove all trace of the markings. Repeated cleaning failed to eliminate visual evidence of the lettering, but the areas proved satisfactorily clean from a water-break free criterion.[51]

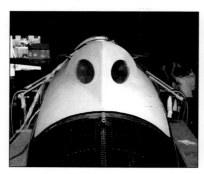

Before (left) and after photos of the X-15A-2 canopy covered with two different ablative coatings on Flight 2-49-86. The MA-25S ablator on the left side of the canopy (on the right in the photos) performed much better. (NASA Dryden)

Polyethylene tape was used to mask all of the seams between panels to keep the ablative material out of the aircraft compartments. The only problem encountered in the initial application was that nobody had anticipated masking the gap between the fixed portion of each vertical stabilizer and the rudders; the installation crew improvised a solution that was mostly successful. As a means of checking the adequacy of the masking during all phases of ablator operation, airborne contamination collectors were placed in nine aircraft compartments before beginning the application process. At the end of the process these collectors were removed and checked by both Martin Marietta and NASA quality inspectors. Very little contamination was found, indicating that the masking worked as expected.[52]

Next up was installing the molded ablator "details" on the aircraft. This included premolded leading edge covers made from ESA-3560-IIA for the wing and horizontal stabilizers, covers for various antennas, the canopy leading edge, and the vertical stabilizer leading edge. Although it had not been provided, the installation team fabricated a detail for the leading edge of the dummy ramjet nose instrumentation rake from a spare piece of the vertical stabilizer leading edge detail.[53]

After the details had been glued onto the surface of the leading edges, the majority of the airplane was covered with polyethylene sheeting to protect cleaned areas from overspray during the sequential ablator applications; the aircraft had been broken down into nine distinct areas that would be sprayed in sequence. Before the ablator was applied to each area, trim marker strips (a vinyl foam tape) were installed over the contamination masking and a layer of DC93-027 ablator was applied over fastener heads and peripheral gaps of the seldom removed panels. The MA-25S ablator was then sprayed over the area using a commercial paint spray gun. Thickness control during the early stages of the application was the most significant difficulty encountered by the installation team. However, experience prevailed and the team got better as they became more familiar with the characteristics of the material. Some areas – particularly the middle of the wing root and the crown centerline of the fuselage – proved to be too much of a stretch for the technicians standing on the ground. This resulted in a "somewhat cheezy" ablator application in those areas, but the layer was deemed adequate to protect the airframe.[54]

Once the entire surface had been covered, the next task was to remove the trim marker strips. This proved more difficult than had been expected because the tape was "too thick and possessed too high an adhesive tack." Nevertheless, the team eventually accomplished the task, but decided that a different tape would be used next time. As the marker strips were removed, it was important that the sealing tape under them not be disturbed since it would have to protect the compartments from the effect of the sanding operation still to come.[55]

The ablator was allowed to cure at room temperature for a few hours, then the entire surface was sanded to remove overspray and irregularities, and to bring the ablator layer down to its design thickness. A tolerance of ± 0.020-inch was allowed in thickness, although the team tended to leave a little too much instead of too little. This proved to be a very tedious operation. First grid lines had to be drawn on the airplane to establish precise monitor locations. A penetrating needle dial gage was used to determine the thickness at each point on the grid. Technicians then sanded the surface. Since this removed the grid lines, they would have to be redrawn and the thickness rechecked. The process continued until the desired thickness was reached. It was evident that some better way of establishing the grid on the airplane would need to be found.[56]

A layer of Dow Corning DC90-090 RTV was then brushed over the entire airplane to provide a wear coating and to seal the ablator. The MA-25S had a natural pinkish color and somehow this seemed inappropriate for the world's fastest airplane. However, the DC90-090 product was translucent white, so it did not completely hide the pink. At NASA's request Martin Marietta applied an extra coat (or two, in some areas) of the wear layer so that the airplane had a uniform white finish. This exhausted the available stock of DC90-090, and the additional coats were generally applied to the upper surfaces to enhance photographs of the aircraft on the ground. Unfortunately, DC90-090 had been discontinued by Dow Corning, replaced with a similar product called DC92-007. Martin requested samples of the new product to determine its suitability as a substitute.[57]

There was another reason for the wear layer and not contaminating the airplane with ablator dust. Tests had shown that MA-25S was very sensitive to liquid oxygen – in fact, exposing the ablator to liquid oxygen and applying as little as 8 psi pressure would cause an explosion. The white protective wear layer was one attempt to isolate the ablator from any minor liquid oxygen spillage. But the potential for contaminating the inside of the liquid oxygen lines, pumps, vents, etc. during the application (spraying and sanding) of the ablator was the most worrisome, explaining the great care to avoid contamination.[58]

At this point, a limited number of hazard and warning markings were applied to the exterior using standard high-temperature aircraft lacquer paint. The last step was to remove the polyethylene tape that had been used to seal the service panels. Strips of MA-25S-1 were installed around the periphery of all service panels to provide extra durability during panel removal and replacement.[59]

ABLATOR FLIGHTS

Late in the summer of 1967, the X-15A-2 was ready for flight with the ablative coating. The weight of the ablator – 125 pounds more than planned – together with expected increased drag reduced the theoretical maximum performance of the airplane to barely Mach 7, still a significant advance over the Mach 6.33 previously attained. The appearance was striking, an overall flat off-white finish, with the external tanks a mix of silver and orange-red with broad black striping.[60]

On 21 August 1967, Pete Knight completed the first flight (2-52-96) in the ablative-coated X-15A-2, reaching Mach 4.94 and familiarizing himself with its handling qualities. The first flight evaluation of the complete ablator system was made without the external tanks but did include the dummy ramjet. The post-flight inspection showed that, in general, the ablator had held up well. The leading edge details on the wings and horizontal stabilizers had uniform and minor charring along their lengths. A careful examination revealed only minor surface fissuring with all char intact, and good shape retention. The char layers were approximately 0.050-inch deep on the wing leading edge and 0.055-inch deep on the horizontal stabilizer.[61]

The ablator details for the canopy and dorsal vertical stabilizer showed almost no thermal degradation and local erosion and blistering of the wear layer was the only evidence of thermal exposure. The leading edge of the forward vane antenna suffered local erosion to a depth of 0.100 inch because of shock wave impingement set up by an excessively thick ablator insert over the ram air door just forward of the antenna. The remainder of the detail and leading edge detail on the aft vane antenna showed "minor, if not insignificant degradation."[62]

The most severe damage was to the molded ablator detail on the leading edge of the modified ventral; this part was heavily charred along its entire length. "The increased amount of thermal degradation was directly attributable to the shock wave interactions from the pressure probes and the dummy ramjet assembly." Additional shock waves originated from the leading edges of the skids. Very little char remained intact on the detail, and the lower portion had been completely eroded. It was difficult to ascertain how much of the erosion

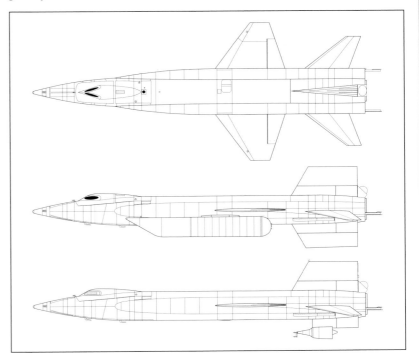

The X-15A-2. Note the ventral stabilizer leading edge configuration and ramjet installation in the lower side view. (Artwork by Tony Landis)

Flight 2-C-93 on 7 August 1967 was a scheduled captive-carry to evaluate the external tanks prior to their first flight with external propellants a few weeks later. (AFFTC History Office)

had taken place during the flight since sand impact at landing had caused similar, although much less significant, erosion during an earlier ablator test flight. Still, this should have been a warning to the program that something was wrong. Somehow, it was missed.[63]

The primary ablative layer over the airplane experienced very little thermal degradation. On the wings and horizontal stabilizers, only the areas immediately adjacent to the molded leading edges were degraded. Some superficial blistering of the ablative layer was evident on the outboard lower left wing surface; Martin Marietta believed the blistering was most probably the result of an excessively thick wear layer application. Not surprisingly, the speed brakes exhibited some wear, but there was no significant erosion or signs of delaminating. The only questionable area of ablator performance was the left side of the dorsal rudder where a number of circular pieces of ablator were lost during the flight. A close examination of the area revealed that all separation had occurred at the spray layer interface, and significant additional delamination had occurred. The heavy wear layer, however, had held most of the material in place. Similar delamination had been seen during some of the earlier test flights and had been traced to improper application of the material; procedures were changed in an attempt to prevent recurrence.[64]

After the inspection Martin Marietta set about repairing the ablator for the next flight. With the exception of the leading edge details for the ventral stabilizer and the forward vane antenna, the refurbishment effort was minimal. Only the wings and horizontal stabilizers had experienced any degree of charring and they were refurbished by merely sanding away the friable layer. No attempt was made to remove all of the thermally affected material, and sanding continued only until resilient material was encountered. The canopy leading edge detail required no refurbishment, but its surface was lightly sanded to remove the wear layer in an attempt to minimize deposition on the windshield during the next flight.[65]

The heavily charred material was removed from the forward antenna and the detail contour restored using an insert made from a trowelable version of the ESA-3560-IIA material. The lower portion of the ventral stabilizer detail was degraded beyond repair and was removed from the airplane. A replacement part was made using a spare piece of dorsal leading edge material that was bonded in place and faired into the adjacent detail.[66]

Local gouges in the main MA-25S ablator were repaired using a troweled mix; the patches were smoothed using kitchen spatulas, eliminating most of the sanding usually required for the patches. The speed brakes were sanded down to apparent virgin material and the areas resprayed to the original thickness. The left side of the dorsal rudder was completely stripped and the ablator reapplied from scratch.[67]

Although no significant thermal degradation had been experienced by the ablator around the nose of the airplane, a malfunction of the ball nose necessitated its replacement, tearing up the ablator in the process. Unfortunately, the supply of ablator had been depleted during the refurbishment process. A batch of MA-25S left over from a previous evaluation was tested and believed to be acceptable, so it was used. The entire surface of the airplane was then lightly sanded and a new coating of the replacement DC92-007 wear layer was brushed on.[68]

MAXIMUM SPEED

At 13:31 on the morning of 3 October 1967 Balls Eight took-off carrying the X-15A-2 and headed to Mud Lake. An hour later, some 43,750 feet over the Nevada desert near Mud Lake, Pete Knight dropped away from the NB-52B on his way to the fastest flight (2-53-97) of the program. At 14:30 Knight "reached up and hit the launch switch and immediately took my hand off to [go] back to the throttle and found that I had not gone anywhere. It did not launch." Not a good start, but a second attempt 2 minutes later resulted in a smooth launch.[69]

The flight plan showed that the X-15A-2 would weigh 52,117 pounds at separation, more than 50 percent heavier than originally conceived in 1954. As the X-15 fell away Knight lit the engine and set up a 12 degree angle-of-attack, resulting in about 1.5-g in longitudinal acceleration. As normal acceleration built to 2-g, Knight had to hold considerable right deflection on the side-stick to keep the X-15A-2 from rolling left due to the heavier liquid oxygen tank. When the aircraft reached the planned pitch angle of 35 degrees, Knight began to fly a precise climb angle. The maximum dynamic pressure experienced during the rotation was 560 psf, close to the 540 psf observed on the simulator. The planned pitch angle of 35 degrees was reached in 38 seconds and was maintained within ±1 degree.[70]

After 67.4 seconds, the airplane was going Mach 2.4 at 72,300 feet and Knight pushed over to a low angle-of-attack and jettisoned the tanks: "the tanks went awfully hard." The ammonia external tank door did not close after the tank was jettisoned, resulting in additional ablation of material around the door. Free of the extra weight and drag, the airplane began to accelerate quickly, and Knight came level at 102,100 feet. Knight: "We shut down at 6,500 [fps] and I took careful note to see what the final got to. It went to 6,600 maximum on the indicator."[71]

The XLR99 burned for 140.7 seconds and radar data showed the X-15A-2 attained Mach 6.70 (4,520 mph; 6,629 fps) at 102,700 feet, an unofficial record for winged-vehicles that would stand until the return of the Space Shuttle *Columbia* from its first orbital flight in 1981.[72]

After shutdown, Knight began his preplanned series of control pulses to obtain stability and control data. But as he decelerated through Mach 5.5, the HOT PEROXIDE light came on; unknown to anybody, the intense heat from shock waves impinging on the dummy ramjet were severely damaging the airplane. Unfortunately, the peroxide light distracted Knight from his planned maneuvers and his energy management. As worries mounted, NASA-1 directed Knight to jettison his peroxide and began vectoring him towards High Key. The X-15A-2 came across the north edge of Rogers at 55,000 feet and Mach 2.2. When Knight went to jettison the remaining propellants so the chase plane could find him, nothing came out; no help from the chase. Knight was high on energy, unable to jettison his propellants, and unsure about the condition of his airplane. He turned through High Key at 40,000 feet but was still supersonic. While on final approach, Knight tried to jettison the ramjet but later indicated that "I did not feel it go at all." The ground crew reported that they did not see anything drop; something was obviously wrong, but things were happening too quickly to worry about it. It was not a good day.[73]

Fortunately, things mellowed out after that and Knight made an uneventful landing. Once on the ground Knight realized something was not right when the ground crew rushed to the back of the airplane instead of helping him from the cockpit. After he finally egressed and walked toward the rear of the X-15 he understood: there were large holes in the side of the ventral with evidence of melting and skin rollback.[74]

Later analysis showed that the shock wave from the spike nose on the ramjet had intersected the ventral and caused severe heating. As Johnny Armstrong observed: "So now maybe we knew why the ramjet was not there." The telemetry indicated that the ramjet instrumentation ceased functioning 25 seconds after the XLR99 shutdown. Later that afternoon several people, including Armstrong, were reviewing the telemetry when they noted an abnormal decrease in the longitudinal acceleration trace, indicating a sudden decrease in drag. The conclusion was that this was when the ramjet had separated. Computing the flight profile, it was determined that this happened about the 180-degree point during the turn over the south area of Rogers Dry Lake at about Mach 1 and 32,000 feet. At this point the airplane was in a 57-degree left hand bank and pulling about 1.6-g. Armstrong began correlating the telemetry with recorded radar data, "I could say that I did a detailed calculation of the drag coefficient for a tumbling ramjet, then a 5th order curve fit of the potential trajectory, corrected for winds – but actually, I just made an engineering estimate." In other words, he guessed that it was somewhere on the Edwards bombing range.[75]

Not everybody believed Armstrong, but Bill Albrecht, the NASA operations engineer for X-15A-2, and Joe Rief, the AFFTC airfield manager, thought the theory had merit. Albrecht and Armstrong checked out a radio-equipped carryall van, cleared it with the tower, and headed out onto the range. Armstrong had previously marked up a map with some landmarks in the vicinity of where the telemetry and radar indicated the ramjet had separated. As they drove Armstrong indicated a place to stop, got out, and walked about 200 yards directly to the ramjet, which was laying in two major pieces. The pair gathered up the nose cone and pressure probes then headed back to the van; the main body of the ramjet was too large and heavy for only two men to lift. The next day Albrecht and Armstrong directed a helicopter to the location and the ramjet was retrieved. Subsequent inspection showed that three of the four explosive bolts that held the ramjet on had fired, probably due to the excessive temperatures that had melted large portions of the ramjet and ventral.[76]

DID IT WORK?

From the Martin Marietta post-flight report: "The actual flight environment in the area of the modified ventral fin proved to be much more severe than anticipated. The condition was directly attributable to interaction effects of the shock waves generated by the dummy ramjet, the ventral, and the pressure probes. The ablator applications in this area were inadequate to protect the structure under these flow conditions, and the vehicle suffered localized damage in the area."[77]

The ablator, including both the molded leading edge detail and the sprayed MA-25S layer, was completely eroded from the forward portion of the ventral following the flight. The exposed ventral had sustained major damage due to the excessively high heating in the shock impingement. The vehicle skin was burned through at the leading edge and on the sides of the ventral at the torque box assembly. The torque box was also damaged, and the wiring and pressure lines in the forward compartment were completely destroyed. The abnormally high temperatures caused the uncommanded jettison of the dummy ramjet.[78]

The dummy ramjet attached to the modified ventral. Note that the leading edge of the ventral is not swept and contains a variety of impact rakes. The white material on the leading edge is an ablative coating. This ramjet shape was non-functional, but was representative of possible operational ramjets. (NASA Dryden)

A ramjet after Flight 2-51-92 on 8 May 1967. This is the 20-degree cone version. The unit was designed to be jettisoned on final approach. (NASA Dryden)

A study of the thermocouple responses in the area of the ventral indicated that the ablator had provided at least some protection for the first 140 seconds of flight. Continual erosion of the ablator surfaces was occurring during this period, and by approximately 160 seconds, degradation was such that all protection broke down. Ablator materials that were predicted to have zero surface recession were, in fact, being continually eroded away. The particles from the forward sections of ablator, in turn, caused severe impact erosion of the downstream ablator layer. The lower speed brakes were bare of ablator, and the material on the inboard edges of the main landing skids and the undersides of the side fairings experienced considerable abrasion.[79]

Otherwise, the ablator had performed well enough. The details over the leading edges of the wings, horizontal stabilizers, canopy, and dorsal stabilizer were uniformly charred along their lengths. All the parts had maintained good shape retention and the char layers were tenaciously attached. There were some signs of localized surface melt in areas of shock impingement during peak heating, but because of a continually varying velocity during the flight, shock presence in any one

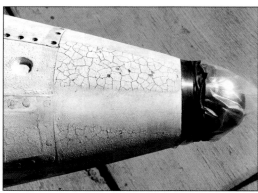

A walk-around of the X-15A-2 showing the damage sustained on the Mach 6.7 flight. The majority of the severe damage was confined to the ventral stabilizer where shock wave impingement effectively destroyed the ablator and melted the leading edge, also causing the explosive bolts to fire and the ramjet falling from the airplane. The ramjet itself (above center) was damaged by the shock wave heating, and also from its fall. The fissures around the nose were not as bad as they look, and were mostly caused by the use of an outdated batch of MA-25S. The rest of the airplane fared remarkably well. (NASA Dryden)

CHAPTER 8

area was limited and the degradation "was insignificant." The lower surface of the wing details were more heavily degraded than the upper surfaces; this condition was reversed for the horizontal stabilizers.[80]

The fixed portion of the dorsal stabilizer leading edge was somewhat more heavily charred than the upper, movable, rudder, and some evidence of unsymmetrical heating of the rudder was present with the left side sustaining a higher heat load. The ablator details for both of the vane antennas were heavily charred and had experienced local erosion or spallation of the char from their surface. They looked worse than they were; measurements showed more than half an inch of ablator remained on the antennas, which were undamaged in any case.[81]

The sprayed MA-25S layer over the fuselage and side fairings showed varying degrees of effects. Thermal degradation, with the resultant reticulation of the ablator surface, occurred only on the forward areas of the nose. Ablator fissuring extended along the fuselage belly to approximately the forward vane antenna. Along the sides, degradation was experienced back to the wing leading edge. The ablator on the crown of the fuselage and the belly aft of the vane antenna showed no evidence of thermal exposure.[82]

The varying amounts of charring experienced over the fuselage were easily correlated with their location or proximity to the various design features of the airplane. For instance, heavily charred areas were directly behind the pressure orifices in the ball nose. These openings were apparently sufficient to "trip" the flow, causing a rapid transition to turbulent boundary layer conditions. The non-flush reaction control thrusters greatly increased heating effects in their vicinity. Localized stagnation within the recesses apparently permitted burning of the ablator, evidenced by a surface discoloration. The thickness of the material behind the nose-gear door was seriously degraded.[83]

In the end, Martin believed that the ablator "performed satisfactorily except in the area of the modified ventral fin." Nevertheless, Martin went on to suggest a series of minor modifications that would solve some of the problems experienced on these two flights.[84]

Not everybody shared this view, although most agreed it was not the fault of the ablator itself, but rather a flawed concept. This was the closest any X-15 came to structural failure induced by heating. The ablator had actually prevented cooling of some hot spots by keeping the heat away from the hot-structure; on earlier flights without the ablator, some of those areas remained relatively cool because of heat transfer through the heavy Inconel X structure. To Jack Kolf, an X-15 project engineer at the FRC, the post-flight condition of the airplane "… was a surprise to all of us. If there had been any question that the airplane was going to come back in that shape, we never would have flown it."[85]

One interesting note. When photographs of the X-15 damage are shown, two areas are normally highlighted. The first is the ventral stabilizer and ramjet; these were unquestionably damaged by heating effects, although there had been indications on the previous flight that something was not right. The second area shown is usually the large fissures around the nose. When the ball nose was replaced between the two ablator flights, the ablator was replaced using an outdated batch of MA-25S because it was all that was available. Although its application characteristics, cure rate, and appearance were the same as the "fresh" ablator used elsewhere, thermal exposure resulted in a greater shrink rate than the newer material. This was evidenced by much more pronounced fissuring of the ablator. It appeared, however, that the ablator provided sufficient protection.[86]

The original contract with Martin Marietta indicated the company was responsible for "touching up" the ablator twice to allow a total of three flights with the initial application. The damage sustained by the ventral stabilizer precluded the aircraft flying again in the near future. Consequently, Martin was directed to perform a complete removal of the ablator so that the aircraft could be returned to North American for inspection and repair. The actual removal, however, was performed by NASA technicians under the direction of a Martin engineer. The initial operation required the removal of the MA-25S-1 strips from the service panel peripheries and local cleaning of the panel edges. This was followed by the application of polyethylene masking tape to protect the aircraft interior from contamination. The basic ablator layer was then stripped using plexiglass scrapers, followed by a scrubbing of the surface to remove all residual ablator material. Final cleaning was performed with aluminum wool and nylon pads with powdered cleanser; wooden toothpicks proved useful in dislodging the ablator material from skin gaps and the heads of permanent fasteners.[87]

NASA sent the X-15A-2 to North American for repair and general maintenance. The airplane returned to Edwards on 27 June 1968, and a series of non-destructive load and thermal tests on the instrumented right wing began on 15 July in the High Temperature Loads Calibration Laboratory. As it turned out, the airplane would never fly again.[88]

Some of the problems encountered with the ablator were non-representative of possible future uses. The X-15 had been designed as an uninsulated hot-structure. Any future vehicle would probably be designed with a more conventional airframe, eliminating some of the problems encountered on this flight. But other problems were very real. The amount of time it took to apply the ablator was unacceptable. Even considering that the learning curve was steep, and that after some experience the time could be cut in half or even further, the six weeks it took to coat the relatively small X-15 bode ill for larger vehicles. Nevertheless, ablators would continue to be proposed on various space shuttle concepts, in decreasing quantity, until 1970 when several forms of ceramic tiles and metal "shingles" would become the preferred concepts.[89]

The repaired X-15A-2 was returned from Inglewood on 27 June 1968 and it was stored in the FRC High Temperature Loads Calibration Facility. The airplane never flew again. (NASA Dryden)

Tragedy Before The End

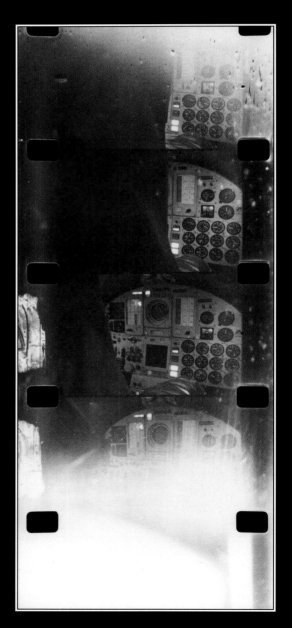

Above: *The Dryden Flight Research Center had this mockup of X-15-3 installed in front of the facility.* (NASA Dryden)

Left: *The last few frames from the cockpit camera aboard Flight 3-65-97 on 15 November 1967. At this point the airplane was in a 40° to 45° inverted dive and was nearing both the side-load and normal-load limits of the airframe. Note that the MASTER CAUTION, MH-96 COMP FAIL, 32° EM LIMIT, and LOW ENERGY warning lights are illuminated, along with the indication that the Ames Boost Guidance computer operating mode had been selected. (The EM LIMIT and LOW ENERGY were not pertinent to the accident.) The last frame shown here is number 829; number 830 was completely exposed to sunlight after the airplane broke up. In this frame the dive angle continues to increase, the bank angle has decreased somewhat, and the normal acceleration is nearly 3-g. The pilot has moved to the far left of the cockpit, suggesting that the lateral acceleration was also about 3-g.* (NASA Dryden)

At 10:30:07.4 on 15 November 1967, the X-15-3 dropped away from Balls Eight at 45,000 feet near Delamar Lake. At the controls was Major Michael J. Adams, making his seventh X-15 flight (3-67-95). Adams had spent slightly over 23 hours in the fixed-base simulator practicing this particular mission, which was intended to evaluate the Ames Boost Guidance display, and conduct several experiments, including measuring the ultraviolet plume of rocket exhausts at high altitude. About one minute after launch, as the X-15-3 passed through 85,000 feet, an electrical disturbance began that caused the MH-96 dampers to trip out. It was later determined the disturbance had most probably emanated from electrical arcing in the experiment in the nose of the right wing-tip pod that was being flown for the first time. Adams reset the dampers and continued.[1]

As planned, the pilot switched the cockpit attitude indicator to an alternate display mode. One of the more controversial aspects of the attitude indicator was a second use for the cross-pointers, developed later in the program to allow precise pointing of several experiments. In this mode the cross-pointers were used to display vernier attitude errors; pitch error was displayed on the alpha needle and bank error on the beta needle. A switch allowed the pilot to control which mode was displayed. During the climb the pilot switched the display to the vernier attitude error mode, and would normally have switched back to the alpha/beta mode prior to reentry.[2]

Unlike the other two airplanes, the X-15-3 automatically blended the ballistic thrusters with the aerodynamic controls as needed using the right side-stick, allowing the pilot to largely ignore the dedicated ballistic controller on the left. The electrical disturbances fooled the flight control system into believing that the dynamic pressure was higher than it actually was, resulting in the system failing to automatically engage the ballistic control system as would normally occur at high altitude. Adams felt the lack of response as the airplane approached maximum altitude and began using the left side-stick to operate the thrusters. Unfortunately, it appears that Adams then began suffering from vertigo as he continued to climb. At the same time, Adams reverted to flying the vertical needle on the attitude indicator as if it was still showing sideslip instead of its actual roll vernier attitude display.[3]

Pete Knight was NASA-1 and monitored the flight with a team of engineers on the ground. As the X-15 climbed after engine shutdown, Adams started a planned wing-rocking maneuver so that the ultraviolet plume experiment could sweep up and down across the horizon. Because Adams was interpreting the attitude indicator incorrectly, the wing rocking quickly became excessive, by a factor of two or three. At the conclusion of the wing-rocking portion of the climb, the X-15 began a slow drift; 40 seconds later, when the aircraft reached its maximum altitude, it was flying with a 15-degree sideslip to the right. Then the drift began again; within 30 seconds, Adams was descending at right angles to the flight path. At 130,000 feet, the X-15 entered a hypersonic spin as it encountered rapidly increasing dynamic pressure.[4]

In the control room there was no way to monitor heading, so nobody suspected the true situation that Adams faced. It was accepted that the ball nose did not accurately align with the relative wind at altitudes above 250,000 feet, so there was little concern when the angle of attack and angle of sideslip began to drift off nominal values near peak altitude. The controllers did not know that the airplane was yawing, eventually turning completely around. In fact, Knight advised Adams that he was "a little bit high," but in "real good shape." Just 15 seconds later, Adams radioed that the

Major Michael J. Adams in the cockpit of X-15-1 for his first flight (1-69-116) on 6 October 1966. (NASA Dryden)

This photo was taken on 9 November 1967 to document the Saturn launch vehicle insulation installed on the upper speed brakes of X-15-3. As it turned out, it was the last still photograph of the airplane taken by NASA before it was lost on 15 November. (NASA Dryden)

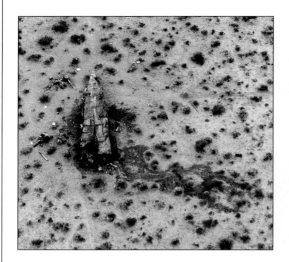

Left: *The forward fuselage wreckage from the airplane.* Center: *The wreckage of the X-15-3 aft fuselage.* Right: *A member of the accident team examines the canopy from the X-15-3.* (NASA Dryden)

airplane "seems squirrelly." At 10:34 came a shattering call: "I'm in a spin, Pete." Plagued by lack of heading information, the control room staff saw only large and very slow pitching and rolling motions. But Adams again called out, "I'm in a spin," followed by groans as the pilot was subjected to heavy accelerations. There was no recommended spin recovery technique for the X-15, and engineers knew nothing about the aircraft's supersonic spin tendencies.[5]

The landing chase pilots – Hugh M. Jackson and Bill Dana – realizing that the X-15 would never make Rogers Dry Lake, shoved their F-104s into afterburner and raced for the emergency lakes; Ballarat

and Cuddeback. Adams held the controls against the spin, using both the aerodynamic surfaces and the ballistic controls. Eventually, largely through a weathervane effect, the airplane recovered from the spin at 120,000 feet and a dynamic pressure of 140 psf. It then entered a Mach 4.7 dive at an angle between 40 and 45 degrees with the aircraft inverted. Adams was in a relatively high altitude dive and had a good chance of rolling upright, pulling out, and setting up a landing. But now came a technical problem: the MH-96 began a limit-cycle oscillation just as the airplane came out of the spin, preventing the gain changer from reducing pitch gain as dynamic pressure

Air Force personnel extinguish a small hydrogen peroxide fire after arriving on the scene of the X-15-3 wreckage in the desert outside Johannesburg, California. Mike Adams died in the crash. (NASA Headquarters)

At the accident scene, medical personnel examine the remains of Mike Adams, still in the cockpit of the X-15-3. Milt Thompson and Charlie Baker are in the center of photo, and Don Bellman is in white overalls at the left. (NASA Dryden)

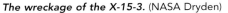
The wreckage of the X-15-3. (NASA Dryden)

increased. The X-15 began a rapid pitching motion of increasing severity, still descending at over 2,700 fps. Pilot inputs were effectively blocked by the severe oscillations in the flight control system. As the X-15 neared 65,000 feet, it was descending in an inverted dive at Mach 3.93 and approaching both the side-load and normal-load limits. At 10:34:57.5, the airplane broke up at approximately 62,000 feet at a velocity of about 3,800 fps and a dynamic pressure of 1,300 psf. A chase pilot spotted dust on Cuddeback, but it was not the X-15. Then an Air Force pilot, who had tagged along on the X-15 flight, spotted the main wreckage northwest of Cuddeback, near the town of Johannesburg. Mike Adams was dead; the X-15-3 destroyed.[6]

The Air Force and NASA convened an accident board chaired by Donald R. Bellman that took two months to prepare its report. Ground parties scoured the countryside looking for wreckage; critical to the investigation was the film from the cockpit camera. The weekend after the accident, an unofficial search party from the FRC found the camera; disappointingly, the film cartridge was nowhere in sight. Engineers theorized that the film cassette, being lighter than the camera, might be further away, blown north by winds at altitude. Victor Horton organized

a search and on 29 November, during the first pass over the area, Willard E. Dives found the cassette. The film was flown to the EG&G laboratory in Boston for processing by Dr. Harold Edgerton. Most puzzling was Adams' complete lack of awareness of major heading deviations in spite of accurately functioning cockpit instrumentation.

Johnny Armstrong and Jack Kolf began analyzing the cockpit film when it returned. Armstrong later recalled: "We had the time history from the flight recorded in the control room. We could see the vertical needle on the attitude indicator in the film and correlated the time of the film and the recorded time history. It became clear to us that the pilot was making manual ballistic inputs as if the vertical needle was sideslip rather than roll angle. His inputs were in the correct direction to make sideslip zero if it had been sideslip. However since it was roll angle his inputs drove the nose further from away from the flight path and eventually into … a spin."[7]

The accident board concluded that Adams had allowed the aircraft to deviate in heading as the result of a combination of distraction, misinterpretation of his instruments, and possible vertigo. The electrical disturbance early in the flight degraded the overall effectiveness of the

The X-15-3 wreckage was brought to the High-Temperature Loads Calibration Laboratory, Building 4820, at the Flight Research Center. These photos were taken on 22 November 1967. Engineers and accident investigators examined the wreckage of the various systems in an effort to determine what happened during the flight, eventually concluding that an electrical arc in one of the wing-tip pod experiments probably contributed to the accident. (NASA Dryden)

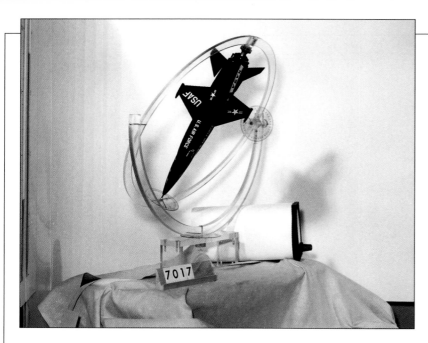

Using this model, engineers simulated the last minutes of Flight 3-65-97 prior to the airframe breaking up. This from the side of the flight path, which was approximately from left to right in the photo. Note that the model is configured with wing-tip pods and a tail box. This simulation figured heavily in the final accident report. The photo was taken on 19 December 1967. (NASA Dryden)

aircraft's control system and further added to pilot workload. The MH-96 adaptive control system then caused the airplane to break up during reentry. The board made two major recommendations: install a telemetered heading indicator in the control room, visible to the flight controller; and medically screen X-15 pilot candidates for

---

DEPARTMENT OF THE AIR FORCE
WASHINGTON

AERONAUTICAL ORDER   15 November 1967
130

MAJ MICHAEL J ADAMS, FR24934, AF Flight Test Center, AFSC,
Edwards AFB, Calif 93523, is awarded the aeronautical rating of
COMMAND PILOT ASTRONAUT per para 1-22, AFM 35-13.
Authority: Para 1-20, AFM 35-13.

BY ORDER OF THE SECRETARY OF THE AIR FORCE

                              J. P. McCONNELL, General, USAF
                              Chief of Staff

R. J. PUGH, Colonel, USAF
Director of Administrative Services

Flight 3-65-97 had reached 266,000 feet – 50.38 miles – altitude. Under Air Force regulations, this qualified Mike Adams for an Astronaut rating, which was posthumously awarded, although the orders were dated the day of the flight. (Dennis R. Jenkins Collection)

labyrinth (vertigo) sensitivity. As a result of the crash, the FRC added a ground-based "8-ball" attitude indicator in the control room to furnish mission controllers with real-time pitch, roll, heading, angle of attack, and sideslip information. Although not specifically called out in the accident report, many engineers came away with a more important lesson: do not use the same instrument to display multiple different indications in a high-workload or high-stress environment.[8]

Mike Adams was posthumously awarded Astronaut Wings for his last flight in the X-15-3, which had attained an altitude of 266,000 feet – 50.38 miles. This was the only fatality during the X-15 program's 199 flights.[9]

Happier days. Mike Adams on Rogers Dry Lake during a period that rain had delayed all flights at Edwards. In 1991 Adams' name was added to the Astronaut Memorial at the Kennedy Space Center in Florida; his family was in attendance for the belated tribute. (AFFTC History Office)

The End

The X-15 program would only fly another eight missions. During 1968 Bill Dana and Pete Knight took turns flying the X-15-1, amid sharp differences of opinion about whether the research results were worth the risk and expense – about $600,000 per flight.[10]

Nevertheless, during the first part of 1968 the AFFTC and FRC worked together to see if there was sufficient interest to extend the program. By October 1968 they had surveyed the current users of the airplane and potential future researchers. They found that some programs could likely benefit from the X-15 being available. Two of the Air Force experiments (20 and 24) might need more time, especially the WTR launch monitoring which would require extraordinary luck to get the X-15-1 and an ICBM in the air at the same moment. The groups investigating the impingement heating that had happened on X-15A-2 would also have been more than happy to keep that airplane flying since they had little other way of conducting experiments to fully understand the problem.[11]

Technically, the HRE flight program had already been cancelled, but it was acknowledged that the ramjet experiments could also benefit from flight testing, although everybody was a bit gun-shy after the bad experience on the X-15A-2 and the flight ramjet development was running well behind schedule. Several other programs within the defense community were studying advanced propulsion concepts – ramjets, turboramjets, or similar engines – and most of them could have potentially used the X-15 as a platform if it was still flying. There was even some talk about reviving the delta-wing concept that had been cancelled after the loss of the X-15-3.[12]

Despite this interest, in the end the AFFTC report concluded that "no known overpowering technological benefits will be lost if [the X-15] program ends on 31 December 1968." It noted that there was a firm requirement for the completion of the two Air Force experiments, and that "many USAF/USN technological activities [were] underway or planned for the Mach 4-6 regime" but the report failed to identify any specific requirements for the use of the small black airplanes. It noted that "the future value of the X-15 as a hypersonic test capability should be more evident by mid-late 1969" and that the "option to use X-15 resources after 1969 should be protected."[13]

On 24 October 1968, Bill Dana completed the 199th – and as it turned out the last – X-15 flight, reaching Mach 5.38 and 255,000 feet. Ten attempts were made to launch Pete Knight on the 200th flight, but a variety of maintenance and weather problems forced cancellation every time. The attempt on 12 December actually got airborne (1-A-142), but the X-15 inertial system failed and the launch was scrubbed. On 20 December 1968 things looked dismal, but everybody geared up for an attempt. Bill Dana began taxiing an F-104 for a weather flight, but John Manke noted that snow was falling – at Edwards! Dana was recalled before he took off and the attempt was cancelled. Later that afternoon the X-15-1 was demated from Balls Three for the last time. After nearly a decade of flight operations, the X-15 program ended.[14]

By the end of the program, the two remaining airplanes were tired. In absolute terms, they were still young airframes; just ten years old and with only about ten flight hours each. The total free-flight time for all three airplanes was only 30 hours, 14 minutes, and 57 seconds. Even if you count all the time spent under the wing of the two NB-52s, the total barely reached 400 hours. Despite early Air

Bill Dana in X-15-1 at the conclusion of Flight 1-81-141 on 24 October 1968; this ended up being the last flight of the program. (NASA Dryden)

Force estimates that the program might log 300-500 flights, that had not been the original idea. Bob Hoey remembers asking project aerodynamicist Edwin W. "Bill" Johnston how long the airplanes were meant to last. Johnston responded that North American had "expected that each airplane would only see 5 or 6 exposures to the design missions.(i.e., Mach 6 or 250,000 feet). They did much better.[15]

This was more flight time than any of the previous high-performance X-planes had ever been subjected to, and the environment was certainly extreme. They had frequently experienced dynamic pressures as high as 2,000 psf, and as low as (essentially) 0 psf. They were subjected to accelerations ranging from –2.5-g to +8.0-g. Temperatures varied from –245°F to over 1,200°F. It had been a rough life.

In addition, the airplanes were tested – a lot. After each flight almost every system was removed, disassembled, and thoroughly checked. Then it was reinstalled and tested. If any anomalies were noted during the test, it was fixed and tested again. Milt Thompson wrote: "my personal opinion is that we wore the airplanes out testing them in preparation for flight."[16]

It is interesting to note that although the X-15 is generally considered a Mach 6 aircraft, only two of the three airplanes ever exceeded

Bill Dana and his family on the lakebed after the last X-15 flight. (NASA Dryden)

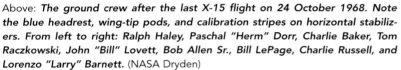

The X-15-1 was loaned to the Flight Research Center for their 25th anniversary, and sat outside in a storage yard for some time before it was returned to the Smithsonian for display. This is the airplane in 1975. (Mick Roth)

Above: *The ground crew after the last X-15 flight on 24 October 1968. Note the blue headrest, wing-tip pods, and calibration stripes on horizontal stabilizers. From left to right: Ralph Haley, Paschal "Herm" Dorr, Charlie Baker, Tom Raczkowski, John "Bill" Lovett, Bob Allen Sr., Bill LePage, Charlie Russell, and Lorenzo "Larry" Barnett.* (NASA Dryden)

Below: *The X-15-1 (foreground) and X-15A-2 in storage at the High-Temperature Loads Calibration Laboratory at the Flight Research Center. Note that the right wing on the X-15A-2 is off the airplane and sitting on the bench near the top center of the photo. The device at the center is a heating rig for the fuselage and one wing.* (NASA Dryden)

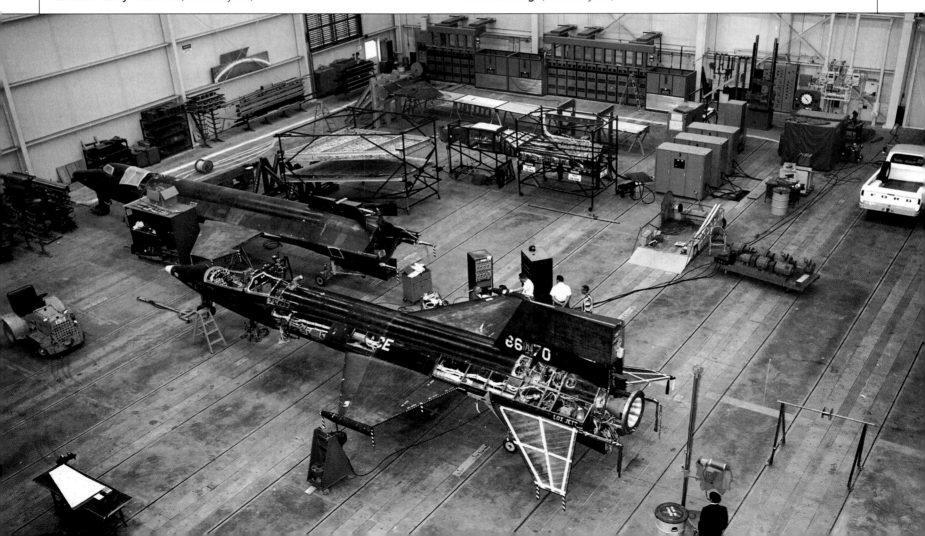

Mach 6, and then only four times. On the other hand, 108 flights exceeded Mach 5 (not including the four Mach 6 flights), accumulating 1 hour and 25 minutes of hypersonic flight. At the other end of the spectrum, two flights were not supersonic (one of those was the first glide flight), and only 14 others did not exceed Mach 2. It was a fast airplane. Similarly, there were only four flights above 300,000 feet (all by the X-15-3), but only the initial glide flight was below 40,000 feet.[17]

FINAL DISPOSITIONS

Officially, the X-15 program simply "expired" at the end of its authorized funding on 31 December 1968. After the New Year holiday, things began to happen quickly. Between the Apollo program and the increasing tempo of the air war in Southeast Asia, neither NASA nor the Air Force seemed particularly interested in the small black airplanes that were stored in the High-Temperature Loads Calibration Laboratory at the FRC.

On 4 January 1969 officials at Edwards formally requested reassignment instructions for the two remaining X-15s. A response came on 20 February directing that the "… number one X-15 be made available for display in the Smithsonian Museum. The Smithsonian is prepared to receive the X-15 and it may be transported to Andrews as soon as it is ready for shipment. In order to protect the option of any future flight test program, extreme care should be taken in handling the X-15 so that it will not be altered or damaged. The Air Force Museum should retain accountability for the aircraft and reassign it to the Smithsonian for display." A later message indicated that the X-15A-2 would be turned over to the Air Force Museum at Wright-Patterson AFB.[18]

The Smithsonian Institution's National Air and Space Museum (NASM) had begun its efforts to acquire an X-15 as early as 1962, but this was unlikely to happen as long as the flight program continued.

After the program funding expired the Air Force agreed to lend the X-15-1 to NASM for two years. The airplane was partially disassembled, loaded onto a flatbed trailer and flown to Andrews AFB inside an Air Force transport. On 13 May 1969 it was trucked from Andrews to the Silver Hill Facility (now the Paul E. Garber Facility) in Maryland. After some minor refurbishment, the X-15 was installed near the original 1903 Wright Flyer on the floor in the North Hall of the Arts and Industries Building that housed NASM at the time. On 7 July 1971 the Air Force officially transferred ownership of the X-15-1 to NASM, who subsequently loaned the airplane to the Federal Aviation Administration (FAA) for display at Transpo 72 during the Spring of 1972. It was then loaned to the Flight Research Center to help commemorate their 25th anniversary. The NASA loan was effective for one year beginning in August 1972 but was extended through the summer of 1975. The X-15 was returned to the Smithsonian in time to be displayed in the new NASM building when it opened to the public on 1 July 1976. The X-15-1 now hangs in the main gallery at the National Air and Space Museum in Washington D.C.[19]

The X-15A-2, completely refurbished after its unhappy experience with the ablative coatings, sits – in its black Inconel finish – in the modern aircraft hangar at the Air Force Museum at Wright-Patterson AFB, Ohio; a set of external tanks and a dummy ramjet are part of the display. The remains of the X-15-3 were buried at an undisclosed location on the Edwards reservation. In 1991, Mike Adams' name was added to the Astronaut Memorial at the Kennedy Space Center, Florida; a tacit reminder of an oft-forgotten manned space program.

The two NB-52s remained at Edwards to support the heavyweight lifting body program. Balls Three would be retired not too long afterwards, eventually being put on display at the Pima Air Museum outside Tucson, Arizona. Balls Eight is still serving as a carrier aircraft, launching the X-38 and X-43 vehicles; it is the oldest operational (and lowest flight time) B-52 in the Air Force.[20]

The X-15A-2 as it sat in the Air Force Museum during July 2001. For several years the airplane was left in its black natural metal finish with no markings; it was later painted in the representative markings shown here. (Tony Landis)

The X-15-1 in the Smithsonian Air and Space Museum in Washington D.C. in May 1990. The airplane hangs from the ceiling of the main gallery and still has its wing-tip pods, although the tail cone box has been removed. (Tony Landis)

The Follow-On Program

Left: *Cartoon showing an over-instrumented – and oddly enough, two-seat – X-15 from February 1961, just as planning for the follow-on research program and its plethora of experiments began.* (NASA Dryden)

Below: *Research instrumentation being removed from the instrument compartment of X-15-1 on 2 June 1960. Most of the signal processing and all of the early data recorders were located in this compartment.* (NASA Dryden)

The research program was the rationale for the X-15's existence, and flights to obtain basic aero-thermo data began as soon as North American and the government were sure the airplane was relatively safe for its intended purpose. Almost from the beginning, a few minor experiments were carried that had little to do with the basic aero-thermo research; the B-70 emission coating and a radiation detector were early examples. Still, the first couple of years of the flight program were primarily dedicated to expanding the flight envelope and obtaining the basic data needed by aerodynamicists to validate the wind tunnel predictions and theoretical models that had been used to build the X-15. As this goal was increasingly satisfied, more X-15 flights were allowed to carry unrelated experiments, such as tests of ablative materials and star trackers for the Apollo program. Usually these experiments required little support from the X-15 itself other than some power and recording capacity. Later in the program, flights began to be flown for the sole purpose of supporting the "follow-on" experiments, although even these usually gathered aero-thermo or stability and control data to support continued evaluation. In reality, the X-15 as an experiment ended sometime in 1963 (except for the advanced X-15A-2); after that the airplane was mostly a carrier for other experiments.

RESEARCH INSTRUMENTATION

At the beginning of the program, a group of researchers from the HSFS, Langley, and Lewis – with limited input from the WADC and AFFTC – decided that between 1,000 and 1,100 data points needed to be available on each airplane. Per the original specification, instrumentation was limited to 800 pounds and 40 cubic feet, and could use up to 2.25 kilowatts of power. The approved design included 1,050 instrumented points: 588 thermocouples, 64 strain gages, 28 control surface position indicators, 136 aerodynamic surface pressures, 22 basic flight parameters (angle-of-attack, etc.), and 212 airplane condition monitors. By contrast, the X-2 had used only 15 thermocouples and a few electrical pressure transducers.[1]

In mid-1957, the NACA asked the Air Force to modify the X-15 specification to essentially double the amount of research instrumentation carried by the airplanes. Given that the design had fairly well been frozen by that time, this came as something of a shock to North American. In order to keep the airplane weight (and, hence, performance) from being too seriously degraded, numerous structural and subsystem details were redesigned to save weight.[2]

When the X-15 finally emerged from North American, it could carry 1,300 pounds of research instrumentation, the majority installed in a removable elevator that fit into the instrumentation compartment just aft of the cockpit. Within the airframe itself, all of the wiring and tubing were routed through the fuselage side tunnels. Besides the instrumentation compartment, small amounts of equipment were also installed in the nose of the airplane, fuselage tunnels, a center of gravity compartment located between the oxidizer and fuel tanks, and in the rear fuselage. The main instrumentation compartment and nose compartment were pressurized and temperature controlled; the center-of-gravity compartment was temperature controlled but unpressurized, and the fuselage tunnels and rear fuselage area were insulated against high temperatures but otherwise uncontrolled.[3]

As manufactured, the first two airplanes each had 656 thermocouples, 112 strain gages, 140 pressure sensors, and 90 telemeter pickups.

The thermocouples were 30-gage chromel-alumel leads spot-welded to the inside surface of the skin. Since the thermocouples were inaccessible after the airplanes were constructed, the installation was designed to function for the life of the airplane and to need no maintenance.[4]

Most of the instrumentation was located on the right side of the airplane; however, there were some corresponding sensors on the left side of the forward fuselage and vertical stabilizer. Since the aircraft was largely symmetrical, it was assumed that the data was equally applicable to either side. No instrumentation was located near the integral propellant tanks because of the difficulty involved with installing such instrumentation. Similarly, no pressure instrumentation was initially installed in the horizontal stabilizers because of the difficulty in running tubing to this location; some strain gages were installed in the horizontal, with the wiring running through the pivot point. Late in the program instrumentation was contained in wing-tip pods on some flights and also in the ventral stabilizer. As part of a loads study late in the program, a new set of horizontal stabilizers were manufactured with electrical pressure transducers, loads sensors, and thermocouples.[5]

Initially, a pulse duration modulation (PDM) telemetry system was installed in the X-15; it represented the state of the art when it had been selected. However, the system was insufficient for many of the data types that researchers wanted to view on the ground, particularly the biomedical parameters. A separate FM-FM telemetry system was installed in late 1961 to support the biomedical instrumentation. A modern pulse-code modulation (PCM) system was later installed in X-15-3 and made its first flight (3-58-87) on 26 April 1967. By all accounts the new system worked remarkably well and provided a great deal more bandwidth than the old PDM and FM-FM telemetry systems. The other two aircraft were never updated to PCM.[6]

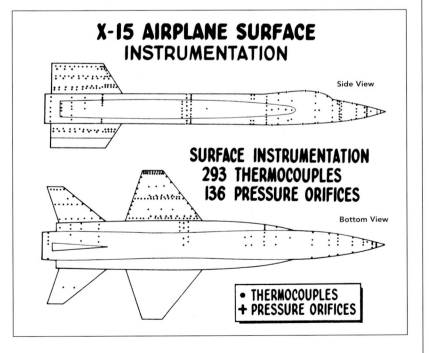

X-15 AIRPLANE SURFACE INSTRUMENTATION

Side View

SURFACE INSTRUMENTATION 293 THERMOCOUPLES 136 PRESSURE ORIFICES

Bottom View

- THERMOCOUPLES
+ PRESSURE ORIFICES

Of the 656 thermocouples initially installed on the airplane, 293 of them were in the skin; the others were embedded in the hot-structure. Note that the majority of the instrumentation was on the right side and bottom of the airplane. (NASA)

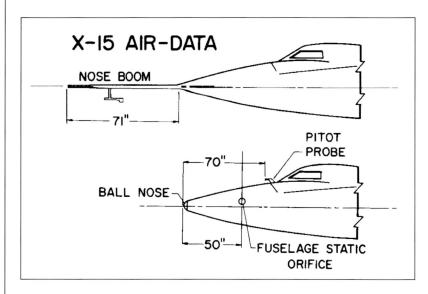

The NACA instrumentation boom was used for 30 flights; 27 with the XLR11 engines, and the first three XLR99 flights. The ball nose was used for the last three XLR11 flights and all subsequent XLR99 flights. (NASA)

Joe Pengilley and Allen Lowe calibrate the pitot-static system of a NACA instrumentation boom on 1 June 1960. The alpha and beta probes are protected by plastic covers to prevent damage. (NASA Dryden)

Early in the flight program, air data was acquired by a standard NACA pitot-static boom protruding from the nose of the X-15. This nose boom was a natural selection for the early X-15 flights based on extensive wind-tunnel studies and previous use on a variety of NACA research aircraft. The instrumentation boom contained static and total pressure pickups for velocity and altitude data, and flow-deflector vanes for angle of attack and angle of sideslip data. The nose boom had static pressure orifices that were 63 inches forward of the tip of the X-15 nose, putting them well ahead of the flow disturbance from the airplane.[7]

BIOMEDICAL RESEARCH

One of the few exclusively Air Force areas of research was into the physiological responses of the pilot to the demanding flight profiles required in high performance aircraft; although the NASA would monitor the results of the biomedical program, the effort was entirely conducted by the Air Force.[8]

The original biomedical instrumentation system was designed and fabricated by North American as part of the basic X-15 contract, and was considered very state of the art at the time. Eight separate measurements were made: ECG, oxygen flow rate, helmet-suit pressure differential, cabin-suit pressure differential, and pilot skin temperature from four locations. The helmet-suit differential pressure also served as a respirometer; since the breathing space in the helmet was relatively small, the pilot's respiration produced pressure fluctuations that the 0-0.5-psi transducer could follow, providing a real-time indication of respiratory rate. The ECG, oxygen flow rate, and skin temperatures were recorded using an onboard oscillograph recorder; the two pressure differentials were sent to the ground via telemetry and displayed in the control room, along with cabin pressure (obtained via vehicle, not biomedical, instrumentation) on a heated stylus stripchart recorder.[9]

In general, this instrumentation functioned well, but as experience was gained, minor deficiencies were corrected and the system simplified. For example, the original ECG used five electrodes that simulated the clinical I, II, III, and V4 leads. However, since the ST segment and T(minus) wave changes are essentially uninterpretable under dynamic conditions, a one-channel ECG gives just as much information as a multi-channel system; therefore the ECG was simplified to a three electrode configuration – two 0.75-inch diameter stainless steel

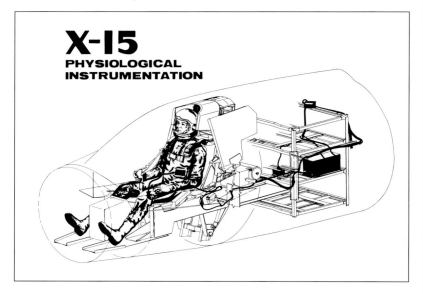

The X-15 gave the flight surgeons the first real exposure to high accelerations and weightlessness. The biomedical instrumentation system on the X-15 would change several times during the first part of the flight program. (U.S. Air Force)

screen mid-axillary leads with a similar reference electrode on the lower abdomen. The skin temperature sensors were also deleted after the first round of flights when it became obvious that the pilot was not exposed to any significant thermal stress during the mission.[10]

Researchers found the pilot's heart rate during flight usually increased from the normal 70 to 80 beats per minute to 140 to 150 per minute, but with no apparent effect on the pilot. One interesting finding, later confirmed on Mercury flights, was that the pilot's heart rate decreased during period of zero-g. The reduction, however, was not great – to about 130 beats per minute. The respiration rate followed similar trends, increasing to three or four times the resting rate, but was considered less meaningful because the respiratory system has a poor dynamic response rate and is also influenced by talking. On almost all flights there was a large peak in respiration rate during the powered portion of flight where the pilots tended to breathe rapidly and shallowly.[11]

After Paul Bikle approved installing an FM-FM telemetry system dedicated to the biomedical package, the Air Force awarded a $79,000 contract to the Hughes Aircraft Company to develop and manufacture the system.[12] The system could have a maximum volume of five cubic inches and would include an FM radio transmitter rather than using a hardwire link to the aircraft telemetry system. This feature was included to demonstrate the feasibility of the radio link in order to permit the mobility expected on future spacecraft such as the Dyna-Soar. The feasibility of the system was demonstrated during flights of the JTF-102A using MC-2 suits and, in an unusual test, a telemetered electrocardiogram was successfully obtained from a free-falling parachutist.[13]

The new FM-FM system was installed in all three X-15s during the summer of 1962. This installation permitted the ECG to be telemetered and displayed in the control room along with the helmet-suit and cabin-suit differential pressures, cabin pressure, and two axes of aircraft acceleration (vertical and longitudinal). These signals were multiplexed onto a single FM channel, then displayed on a 6-channel Sanborn stripchart recorder in the control room.[14]

During the summer of 1963 the biomedical instrumentation was again modified, this time by adding a blood-pressure monitoring system developed by the Air Force School of Aerospace Medicine at Brooks AFB, Texas. The system used an occlusive cuff crystal microphone to determine arterial pressure in the upper arm. The cuff was automatically inflated by an electro-pneumatic programmer that cycled once per minute. During the deflation of the cuff, the microphone detected the Korotkoff sounds and the output of the microphone was converted into an appropriate signal that was displayed simultaneously with the cuff pressure trace and the ECG. The system could be turned on or off by the pilot and had a fail-safe feature that dumped the pressure in the cuff in the event of a power failure; this prevented a tourniquet effect of the cuff. Surprisingly, the first few flights of the package did not yield meaningful blood pressure information – the pilot's pressures exceeded the maximum reading available on the instrumentation. The cuff inflation pressure was modified to allow up to 240 millimeters of mercury in order to obtain useful systolic pressure end-points.[15]

As the biomedical data was evaluated during the flight program, it became apparent that the initial objectives of obtaining data on the physiologic response to weightlessness were not feasible using the X-15. The duration of weightlessness (3 to 4 minutes) was too short and the pilot's responses were conditioned by too many uncontrollable variables that occurred simultaneously for any conclusions to be made concerning the physiologic response. In addition, the new manned space programs provided a much longer weightlessness duration without the attendant stresses of having to fly the airplane; this portion of the X-15 data was instantly obsolete. Nevertheless, the X-15 data provided a unique opportunity to observe basic physiological responses of pilots in manned vehicles flying exit and reentry profiles, something Mercury did not do since the astronaut was simply along for the ride during those periods.[16]

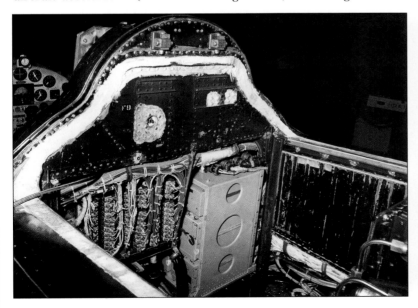

The empty instrumentation compartment of X-15-1 on 31 January 1969. The forward bulkhead is at left, the rear bulkhead at right. The instrumentation elevator has been removed. Note the wiring, fuses, and switches for various aircraft systems, most of which terminated in this compartment. (NASA Dryden)

THE FOLLOW-ON PROGRAM

During the early 1960s, the X-15 was the only platform that could routinely carry a useful payload above the Earth's atmosphere and return it for reuse. Researchers had been making use of various sounding rockets that provided relatively inexpensive access to the upper atmosphere and could be launched from a variety of locations around the world. However, in general they had very limited payload capabilities, could not provide much in the way of power or controlled flight, and were usually not recoverable. On the other hand, the X-15 was very limited in where it could fly (over Southern California and Nevada), but could provide a fair amount of power, was at least somewhat controllable for aiming purposes, and most importantly, was recoverable.

Experiment Accommodations

Although the X-15 provided some internal space for experiments, many researchers wanted specific views of the world outside the airplane, or to have their experiments located away from the "noise" of the airplane. This gave rise to several modifications that ultimately affected all three X-15s.

The X-15-1 with wing-tip pods on 1 December 1964. Note that each pod has been covered with a different color of temperature-sensitive paint. This was likely part of the investigation into whether the pods were in the X-15 flow field; as it turned out, they were, and this caused a few experiments not to operate as expected. (NASA Dryden)

Wing Tip Pods

Several experiments – particularly a proposed micrometeorite collection system – needed to be located outside the flow field of the X-15, and hopefully outside the contamination zone from the ballistic control system thrusters. The most obvious location was the wing tips.

Initially North American wanted to give the pods a rectangular cross-section since it would be easier to package the various experiments in them. However, after considering the effects of heating, drag, and turbulence it was decided to use circular-cross-section pods manufactured of Inconel X that were 8-inches in diameter and 58 inches long. Initially, each pod could weigh a maximum of 96.2 pounds, although this limit was apparently increased sometime during 1967 since the records indicate pod weights over 100 pounds.[17]

Initially, a single set of the pods was manufactured and permanently affixed to X-15-1. The attachment points, wing wiring conduit, and wiring harness were installed on X-15-1 during March 1964, and the first flight (1-50-79) with the pods was on 15 October 1964. The pods did not seem to have any major effect on the handling of the airplane. Subsequently, however, some pilots did complain that the pods seemed to introduce a buffet at load factors significantly below the previous buffet boundary. Accelerometers were installed in the pods to verify this, but failed to uncover any evidence of buffeting. However, the redistribution of mass due to the pod installation did result in a 17-cps vibration tied to the wing bending mode which was excited by some maneuvers and gusts, likely explaining what the pilots felt.[18]

It was subsequently determined that having only one set of pods put an unreasonable constraint on scheduling experiments and it was decided to manufacture a second set of pods, and to make them easily removable. The X-15-1 and X-15-3 was modified and the pods could be moved between the airplanes as needed to support the flight schedule. Frequently, the rear compartment on one or both pods contained cameras aimed at various parts of the airplane, usually the ablative panels on the vertical stabilizers, or one of the experiments in the tail-cone

A Schlieren photo of an X-15 model with wing-tip pods. The pods mostly escaped the shock waves generated by the nose of the airplane, but not those generated by the fuselage tunnels. Even worse, if the airplane yawed to one side slightly, the pods were in the nose field as well. Residue from the ballistic control system also impinged on the pods. (NASA)

Post-flight servicing on X-15-1 after Flight 1-74-130 on 1 March 1968. The tailcone box may be seen behind the upper speed brakes. On this flight it housed a star tracker that was part of the MIT-Apollo Horizon Photometer experiment (#17). This experiment was investigating various techniques for space navigation in support of the Apollo program. Note the third skid under the ventral stabilizer between the speed brakes. This skid was designed to absorb some of the landing loads as the airplane first touched down (it was in contact with the lakebed when the nose was high) to offset the ever-increasing landing weights. (NASA Dryden)

box. Despite the original intent – and the best efforts of all involved – the wing tip pods did not put the experiments outside the contamination zone of the ballistic control thrusters and hydrogen peroxide residue would render several experiments useless. The pods were also inside the nose shock wave interference zone at certain angles-of-attack, further hampering some experiments.[19]

Tail-Cone Box

Several experiments needed to view the sky behind the X-15 so it was decided to install a "tail-cone box" in back of the upper vertical stabilizer. In September 1961 North American was asked to investigate whether the installation would have an adverse effect on the aerodynamic stability of the airplane; after a brief analysis, none was expected. Detailed engineering was begun on 10 August 1962 and fabricating these "boat-tail" boxes took about two months.[20]

The box was immediately behind the upper speed brakes, was the same width as the vertical stabilizer, as high as the speed brakes, and protruded aft to the extreme rear of the fuselage. The box was closed on the sides and top, but open on the back to allow the instruments to view behind the airplane. The Inconel X structure provided no environmental control (temperature or pressurization) for the experiments it housed. Two different types of boxes were manufactured and they were installed on the airplane as needed to support the specific experiment manifested for a particular flight. The first style was equipped with a stabilized platform so that the experiment could be precisely aimed. This box could also be equipped with a removable panel that covered the back of the box during the boost

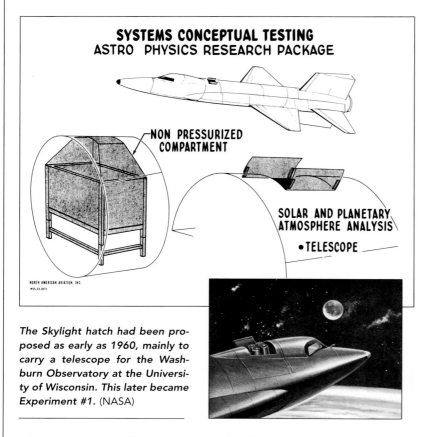

SYSTEMS CONCEPTUAL TESTING
ASTRO PHYSICS RESEARCH PACKAGE

NON PRESSURIZED COMPARTMENT

SOLAR AND PLANETARY ATMOSPHERE ANALYSIS
• TELESCOPE

NORTH AMERICAN AVIATION, INC.
WSS-33-3071

The Skylight hatch had been proposed as early as 1960, mainly to carry a telescope for the Washburn Observatory at the University of Wisconsin. This later became Experiment #1. (NASA)

bilized platform) could extend upward through the open hatch if needed. Pressurization bulkheads were added that isolated the data recorders on the lower shelf.[23]

During early 1966 the X-15-1 was modified with a skylight hatch that appears to have been the original 18 by 12-inch size. The Skylight hatch on the X-15-1 was used by the WTR and MIT experiments.[24]

Bug-Eye Camera Bays

As completed, each X-15 had four "bug-eye" structural camera bays. Two were located on top of the fuselage just behind the cockpit and two under the center of gravity compartment. Originally, each bay held a 16-mm motion picture camera that could be pointed through a limited field of view to observe the fuselage, wings, or stabilizers. Over the course of the program these bays were used to house a variety of other equipment. Sometimes the "bug-eye" fairings above the fuselage provided a viewing port for the experiments or simply extra volume, and other times flush plates were installed. The lower bays were usually faired-over later in the flight program with the internal space used by experiments or data recorders.

Although not truly an experiment, the upper bug-eye camera bays were occasionally used to carry cameras provided by the National Geographic Society. When you see photos looking back to the vertical stabilizer of the X-15 with the curve of the Earth in the background, more often than not the photo was taken by one of these cameras.[25]

phase to prevent efflux from contaminating the experiment. The second style was a "lightweight" box that could be used for experiments that did not require the stabilized platform. Initially the capability to carry the tail-cone box was added to the X-15-1, but a similar box was subsequently added to X-15-3. When it was rebuilt after its accident, a very similar protuberance was added to X-15A-2, but in this case the box housed a spherical helium tank that provided additional pressurization gas for the propellant system.[21]

Skylight Hatch

The Skylight modification consisted of a hatch that could be opened at high altitude to give a portion of the instrument compartment free access to the outside environment. This required the installation of pressure bulkheads to allow the lower portion of the instrument compartment that held the data recorders to remain pressurized. The proposed hatch was to be 18 by 12 inches, with the 18-inch dimension lengthwise of the aircraft and a pair of 6-inch wide doors split along the centerline. Several proposed experiments also required a stabilized platform inside the compartment. A change order was prepared for the modification and was awaiting approval when the X-15-2 was damaged in Jack McKay's landing accident.[22]

It was decided to press ahead with the Skylight modification during the rebuilding of X-15A-2, but for some reason the actual implementation changed. The hatch became slightly larger, using two upward-opening 20-inch long by 8.5-inch wide doors, and the instrumentation elevator was revised so that the upper shelf (with the sta-

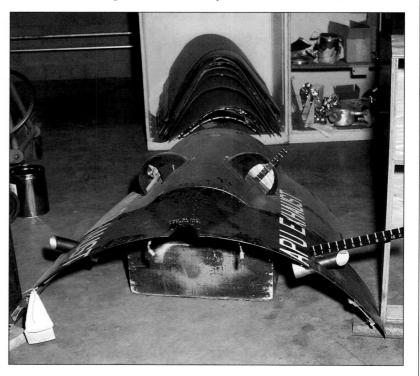

An interesting view of the hatch that covered the instrumentation compartment. This shows the upper bug-eye camera ports, and also the two APU exhaust stacks. Conveniently, somebody has placed rulers in each location so that their size may be determined. This was the hatch from X-15-1 on 29 January 1959. Note the pile of X-15 side tunnel panels just ahead of the hatch. (NASA Dryden)

During the early portion of the flight program, various small experiments were piggy-backed onto the airplanes as time and space permitted. These usually required little, if any, support from the airplane or pilot during the mission since the flight program was concentrating on acquiring aero-thermo and stability and control data.[26]

B-70 Signature Reduction: Perhaps the first true "follow-on" experiment came in 1961 when a coating material designed to reduce the infrared emissions of the proposed B-70 bomber was tested on X-15-2. During the very short YB-70 development period, North American developed a "finish system" (i.e., paint) that provided a low emittance at wavelengths used by Soviet infrared detecting devices, while radiating most of the excess heat from the surface in wavelengths not normally under surveillance. The finish system was somewhat difficult to apply to an aircraft as large as the B-70, but the engineers expected that further development would yield improvements in the process. The most difficult problem was that the underlying surface had to be highly polished prior to applying the basecoat, and the topcoat of the Type II finish had to be cured at 1,000°F (creating almost a ceramic finish).[27]

The coating was applied to one side of the dorsal rudder on Flight 2-13-26. No observable physical changes occurred during the Mach 4.43 flight which reached 525°F. No attempt was made to measure the infrared qualities of the coating during this single flight; it was simply to determine if the coating would survive the aero-thermo environment.[28]

Radiation Detection: Since the X-15 would routinely fly much higher than man had previously ventured, there was considerable concern over possible high-altitude radiation exposure for the pilots. On 3 August 1961 the Air Force Special Weapons Center at Kirtland AFB, New Mexico, delivered an ionizing radiation-detection device for use on the X-15. The package weighed about 10 pounds and was installed in the left side-console of the cockpit outboard of the ejection seat. The experiment was flown on several flights in late 1961, and the taped data from each flight were sent to Kirtland. The analysis of the density of ionizing radiation showed that the pilot received essentially a normal background dosage (0.5 millrads per hour) during the flight. Since there seemed to be no further cause for concern, the radiation detector was deleted from flights beginning in 1962.[29]

A different radiation detector was flown on X-15-2 from early 1961 until September 1963. The Earth Cosmic Ray Albedo experiment was used to investigate the cosmic-ray environment at altitudes over 50,000 feet. The experiment consisted of placing small photographic emulsion stacks in the upper and lower bug-eye camera bays to obtain information on the cosmic-ray albedo flux and spectrum as well as the flux and spectra of electrons and protons leaking out of the Van Allen belts. The stacks were carried to high altitudes on as many flights as practical and placed no restrictions on the flight path or trajectory. Similar packages were flown on the NB-52 during the same flights to provide lower-altitude references. The film stacks from these packages were developed and analyzed by the University of Miami, and the University of California at Los Angeles and Berkeley.[30]

In a very similar experiment, two nuclear-emulsion Cosmic-Radiation Measurement packages from the Goddard Space Flight Center were mounted on the aft ends of the side fairings on X-15-1 and X-15-2 to investigate the cosmic-radiation environment at

2 PLACE X-15 GENERAL ARRANGEMENT

- FULL SPACE TRAINING & BIOMEDICAL RESEARCH CAPABILITY

EXTENSION

2 PLACE X-15 BIOMEDICAL RESEARCH ADDITIONAL CAPABILITY

- APPROX 14 CU FT AVAILABLE

CONTROLLED ATMOSPHERE
- CONSTITUENTS
- TEMPERATURE
- PRESSURE
- ETC

- AERO-THERMO RESEARCH EQUIPMENT & PROVISIONS DELETED
- WEIGHT CHANGE -354 LB
- PERFORMANCE CHANGE +120 FPS

2 PLACE X-15 BIOMEDICAL RESEARCH ADDITIONAL CAPABILITY

- FULL PRESSURE SUIT AND NITROGEN ATMOSPHERE NOT REQUIRED
  ADDITIONAL PHYSIOLOGICAL SENSORS NUTRITIONAL STUDIES, ETC
  VEHICLE ESCAPE CAPSULE

Although a two-seat engineering study had been part of the original proposal, the government never approved any further action on the idea. Nevertheless, the concept came up again several times during the program. These illustrations are from a 1960 pitch from the flight surgeons. (NASA)

extreme altitudes. These emulsion stacks were considerably larger than those in the Earth Cosmic Ray Albedo experiment, and were carried on several flights to altitudes above 150,000 feet.[31]

APPROVED TEST-BED EXPERIMENTS

During the summer of 1961, a new initiative was proposed by the Air Force's Aeronautical Systems Division at Wright-Patterson AFB and NASA Headquarters: using the X-15 to carry a wide range of scientific experiments unforeseen when the aircraft was conceived in 1954. Of particular interest was the ability of the X-15 to carry experiments above the attenuating effect of the Earth's atmosphere.[32]

On 15 August 1961 the Research Airplane Committee signed a memorandum of understanding to form the X-15 Joint Program Coordinating Committee. The committee held its first meeting on 23-25 August 1961 and over 40 experiments were suggested by the scientific community. The committee met four more times – 9 May 1962, 7-8 January 1963, 18 September 1963, and 16 October 1963

– and forwarded proposals for 28 experiments to the Research Airplane Committee for approval. At least three others were subsequently approved for implementation, and it appears that several others were assigned experiment numbers, but the nature or purpose of many of them could not be ascertained.[33]

The final name used by the FRC for the follow-on research program was "test bed experiments," although the Research Airplane Committee and other sources continued to call it the Follow-On Program. The effort was formally announced in a news release on 13 April 1962: "The hypersonic X-15 will become a 'service' airplane to carry out new experiments in aeronautical and space sciences, in a program planned to make use of its capabilities for extremely high speeds and altitudes beyond Earth's atmosphere. The new program adds at least 35 flights … and may take two years to complete."[34]

Experiment #1 – Ultraviolet Stellar Photography

This experiment was sponsored by the NASA Office of Space Sciences to obtain measurements of the stellar brightness that could not be observed from the ground because of the ozone layer. Limited data had already been obtained via sounding rockets, but additional data was desired prior to the launch of the Orbiting Astronomical Observatory. Prior to the experiment, limited information had already been gathered on the ultraviolet intensity of the sky background; a photomultiplier had been installed in one of the upper bug-eye camera bays of X-15-1 during April 1962 and first flown on Flight 1-26-46.[35]

The stellar photography experiment consisted of an ultraviolet "star tracker" and an ultraviolet horizon scanner that were installed on a stabilized platform in the Skylight compartment on the X-15A-2 after its

This is the Washburn Observatory star tracker in the X-15A-2 skylight hatch on 30 October 1964. During Flight 2-47-84 the experiment photographed the stars Eta Aurigae, Alpha Aurigae, and Rho Aurigae from an altitude of 246,000 feet, becoming the first stellar ultraviolet images. (NASA Dryden)

modifications. The star tracker was first flown on Flight 2-33-56 and was aboard at least nine flights ending with 2-48-85. Researchers determined that the light from stars of moderate or larger magnitude was not absorbed by the atmosphere above 45 miles. During Flight 2-47-84 the experiment successfully photographed the stars Eta Aurigae, Alpha Aurigae, and Rho Aurigae at an altitude of 246,000 feet, some of the first stellar ultraviolet images. In late 1966 the experiment was removed from the X-15A-2 as it prepared for its Mach 8 envelope expansion program and moved to sounding rockets.[36]

Experiment #2 – Ultraviolet Earth Background

This experiment was sponsored by the Air Force Geophysics Research Directorate to measure the total Earth background radiation (albedo) in support of designing missile-warning surveillance satellites. As finally built the experiment consisted of a high-resolution Barnes ultraviolet scanning spectrometer and a solar-blind radiometer mounted on a stabilized platform in the tail-cone box on X-15-3. Mechanical problems with the experiment precluded any data collection through the end of 1963, and equipment and scheduling problems continued to conspire against the experiment which was finally cancelled in early 1965 without acquiring any useful data.[37]

Experiment #3 – Ultraviolet Exhaust-Plume Characteristics

This experiment was sponsored by the Aeronautical Systems Division to measure the exhaust radiation from a liquid oxygen-ammonia rocket engine and used the same basic equipment as experiment #2 without the stabilized platform. The first flight (3-41-64) was on 23 April 1965 and by the end of 1965 the high-resolution Barnes ultraviolet scanning spectrometer and solar-blind radiometer that had proved so troublesome on experiment #2 had successfully obtained good data. As a follow-up, a Millikan dual-channel radiometer was flown on Flight 3-55-82 but froze due to a failed heater; the equipment was returned to the experimenter for repair, but no record could be found of it ever flying again.[38]

Experiment #4 – Langley Horizon Definition

This experiment was sponsored by the Langley Research Center and consisted of a radiometer and 16mm motion-picture camera installed in the tail-cone box of the X-15-3. The camera provided wide-angle coverage to check for clouds or haze during the data-gathering period. The radiometer included a motor-driven scan mirror that swept the field of view through a 30-degree optical scan. The scan mirror reflected energy into a parabolic mirror that focused the energy on the detector.[39]

The experiment was first flown on Flight 3-16-26 and was carried five additional flights during 1963 to provide data for the MIT-Apollo Horizon Photometer experiment (#17). Three of these flights provided meaningful data. Another successful flight (3-30-50) was made on 8 July 1964 to investigate the near infrared region and two additional flights were flown during 1965 (3-42-65 and 3-44-67). This experiment provided the first infrared data gathered on the Earth's limb from above 30 miles. From this data, the horizon profile was modeled to an accuracy of 4 kilometers for use in attitude-referencing systems carried aboard early orbiting spacecraft.[40]

The Langley Horizon Definition experiment (#4) included this horizon scanner and 16mm camera installed on the X-15-3 on 22 June 1964. This experiment provided the first infrared data gathered on the Earth's limb from above 30 miles. Also note the impact rake on the side of the rudder. (NASA Dryden)

Experiment #5 – Photo Optical Degradation

This experiment was sponsored by the Aeronautical Systems Division to determine the degradation of optical imagery caused by high-speed flight using well-instrumented aerial cameras and multiple boundary-layer rakes. This program was very involved, and significantly funded under an Air Force contract to North American as part of Project 6220, Photographic Reconnaissance Technology.[41]

Phase I was sponsored jointly by the Army Corps of Engineers and the Aeronautical Systems Division. The initial requirement was for three separate flight profiles; high-speed, high-altitude, and one that mimicked the Mach 3 North American B-70 Valkyrie bomber. The B-70 profile placed another constraint on the program since it required that the XLR99 be operated at 40 percent thrust; early engines were incapable of doing this reliably.[42]

The targets would be located along the flight path from Delamar to Edwards with single 3-bar targets located near Pahrump and Indian Springs, and two sets of three targets straddling the flight path at Pilot Knob and Cuddeback. The single target at Pahrump determined the performance of the camera primarily at the extreme altitude point on the high-altitude missions; the single target at Indian Springs determined performance at the extreme speed point on the high-speed profile. The triple targets at Pilot Knob and Cuddeback allowed

for accumulated navigation errors and measured performance at high-supersonic speeds. Each target was a collection of differing width white stripes on a black background (a standard Mil-Std-150A photo-calibration target pattern) with an additional large contract patch and two sharp edges normal to each other to determine the atmospheric attenuation and edge-response. The entire setup was known as the Delamar Camera Range.[43]

The X-15 package for the cartographic program contained a KC-1 camera, an ART-15A stabilized mount, and photometric and environmental instrumentation. The KC-1 had been modified with a GEOCON I low-distortion mapping lens that had a focal length of 6 inches, a relative aperture of f/5.6, and could provide a resolution of 37 lines per millimeter on Super-XX film. The experiment support package, minus the camera, weighed approximately 156 pounds. The KC-1 camera and lens added another 85-90 pounds depending upon the film load and occupied a space about 16 inches long, 18 inches wide, and 21 inches high at the bottom of the instrument compartment. North American modified the X-15-1 with an 18-inch diameter window that was 1.5 inches thick in the bottom of the instrument compartment. The film was nominally 9 by 9 inches and 390 feet of it was stored in the magazine.[44]

The Phase I program involved six X-15-1 flights; the first (1-33-54) on 11 April 1963 and the last (1-38-81) on 18 July 1963. The majority of the detailed results are still classified.[45]

Phase II involved six data-gathering flights using X-15-1, beginning with Flight 1-42-67 and ending with Flight 1-49-77. There were also three checkout flights (1-39-62 through 1-41-65). The purpose of the experiment was to determine the effects of aero-thermo distortions associated with vehicles flying at high supersonic speeds and extreme altitudes. The results were directly applicable to the Lockheed A-12/SR-71 and North American B-70/RS-70 programs, and also to "future hypersonic reconnaissance systems."[46]

The experiment package was somewhat more sophisticated than Phase I, replacing the KC-1 camera with a more sensitive KS-25. In addition to the new camera on the same ART-15A stabilized mount,

The Photo Optical Degradation experiment (#5) was one of the more elaborate uses of the X-15. Phase I used this KC-1 camera installed in X-15-1, shown here on 27 June 1963. Six flights would carry this mapping camera. (NASA Dryden)

an analog computer was installed that collected signals from the X-15 stable platform to use for image motion compensation, and special instrumentation to measure photometric quantities. Seven downward-looking photometers were used to measure the spectral changes in light with respect to altitude and to provide a signal to the automatic exposure control system on the KS-25. Two additional upward-looking photometers monitored the amount of visible light remaining in the upper atmosphere. Instrumentation provided a continuous record of the temperature on the inner and outer surfaces of the photographic window, and a multiple-pickup boundary-layer rake was used to indicate whether the boundary layer was laminar or turbulent and to monitor its thickness for subsequent comparison with photographic quality.[47]

The KS-25 and its electronics weighed 325 pounds in addition to the 156-pound experiment support package. The KS-25 was much larger than the earlier KC-1, occupying a volume approximately 13 inches long, 10 inches wide, and 43 inches high; this camera took up the entire height of the instrument compartment. A special lens had a focal length of 24 inches, relative aperture of f/4, and provided a resolution of 70-90 lines per millimeter on Super-XX film. Each frame was 4.5 by 4.5 inches and 250 feet of film was stored in the magazine.[48]

On each flight a frame was exposed while the X-15 was still attached to the NB-52; this photo was used as a reference and most always had a resolution of over 80 lines per millimeter. On one flight, the X-15 photographed the Indian Springs target while at Mach 5.47 and 101,400 feet when the temperatures on the camera window were –4°F on the inner surface and +287°F on the outer surface. The resolution of the photograph was 60 lines per millimeter. A photograph of Indian Springs AFB taken at Mach 5.43 and 120,000 feet showed three readily identifiable three aircraft parked on the ramp. Researchers determined from these tests that the photographic quality was acceptable at high speeds and altitudes.[49]

The latter part of Phase II also tested several experimental near-infrared color films, the first time they had been successfully used in flight. It has been reported the X-15 flights directly led to the use of near-infrared color film during the conflict in Southeast Asia; the heat-sensitive colored emulsions showed enemy activity under the dense jungle canopy. Similar techniques were soon adopted for Earth-resource photography.[50]

Experiment #6 – Earth Atmospheric Degradation Effects

This experiment was functionally combined with experiment #5, which had been known as Environmental Effects on Optical Measurements. Originally, both experiments were covered under the name Induced Turbulence Experiments.[51]

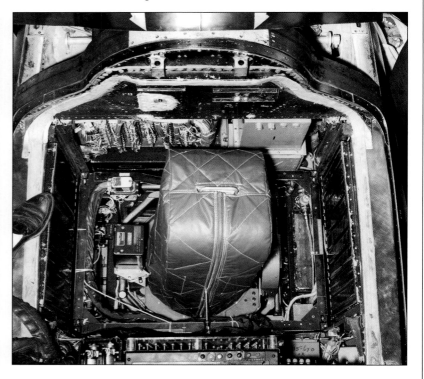

Phase II of experiment #5 was used a Fairchild KS-25 camera instead of the earlier KC-1 mapping camera. This is the installation in X-15-1 on 27 March 1964. The camera window on the bottom of the fuselage is shown at left. The KS-25 was a reconnaissance camera and this part of the experiment was directly applicable to the A-12/SR-71 and RS-70 (B-70) programs, as well as "future hypersonic reconnaissance systems." Researchers determined that high-speed flight did not seriously affect the quality of the photography. (NASA Dryden)

A briefing slide for the Electric Side-Stick Controller experiment (#7) that was cancelled at the same time as the Dyna-Soar program. (NASA)

The X-15-3 carried a sharp lead-edge on its dorsal rudder for 42 of its 65 flights. Note that the bottom of the leading edge is almost vertical (in photo at right). This was necessary to provide clearance when the X-15 was mated to the carrier aircraft; note how close the leading edge is to the wing cut-out. (NASA Dryden)

Experiment #7 – Electric Side-Stick Controller

This experiment was sponsored by the Aeronautical Systems Division and the Flight Research Center as an attempt to address various pilot complaints with the feel of the right-hand side-stick controller in the X-15 with possible applications to Dyna-Soar. The side-stick in the X-15 was criticized because of the adverse feel characteristics caused by connecting it mechanically to the center stick and to the power actuators that moved the control surfaces. The electric side-stick was not mechanically linked to the flight control system, but would have transmitted instructions to the MH-96 adaptive control system to fly the airplane. By the end of 1962 North American had begun flight testing a modified F-100C equipped with an electric side-stick but these were not completely successful. Plans to install the electric side-stick in the X-15 fixed-base simulator were put on hold, then cancelled at the end of 1963 when the Dyna-Soar program abruptly ended.[52]

Experiment #8 – Detachable High-Temperature Leading Edge

This experiment was sponsored by the Aeronautical Systems Division and the Flight Research Center to evaluate various leading edge concepts for use on future high-speed vehicles. The experiment modified a pair of ventral rudders to accommodate leading edges manufactured from different materials and configurations. The first two materials were René 41 and tantalum, and the modified rudders were ready for flight in mid-1966. However, it could not be ascertained if the rudders ever flew.[53]

The sharp leading edge studies were also part of this experiment. The standard X-15 rudder had a leading edge radius of 0.5-inch over the very forward 0.6-inch of chord. The modification extended the leading edge of the dorsal rudder 5.16 inches forward, resulting in an overall chord of 9.00 feet. This sharp 347-stainless-steel leading edge had a radius of only 0.015-inch at the tip, and was essentially a knife-edge shape.[54]

The sharp rudder first flew during Flight 3-23-39 on 7 November 1963 and was flown until Flight 3-33-54 when it was removed and replaced with a normal rudder borrowed from X-15-1 for Flight

3-34-55. Additional instrumentation was placed in the rudder and it was reinstalled in time for Flight 3-35-57. The airplane continued to fly with it until it was lost on Flight 3-65-97. A total of 42 flights were made with the sharp rudder.[55]

Experiment #9 – Landing Computer

This experiment was sponsored by the Aeronautical Systems Division to test a landing computer developed by Sperry in conjunction with the MH-96. The experiment was cancelled before being installed, but elements of the program were combined with experiment #14.[56]

Experiment #10 – Infrared Exhaust Signature

This experiment was sponsored by the Air Force Geophysics Research Directorate to determine the infrared characteristics of a liquid oxygen-ammonia rocket engine. This was conceptually similar to experiment #3 except in the infrared spectrum instead of the ultraviolet. The primary instrument was a Block Associates E-8 infrared radiometer that measured radiation in four spectral regions by focusing it through a calcium fluoride lens and four selective filters onto a lead sulfide detector.[57]

The 13-pound experiment was carried in the tail-cone box of the X-15-3 on seven flights during 1963 and early 1964, but mechanical problems resulted in data only being obtained on a single mission. Four additional flights were scheduled for late 1964, but none were actually conducted. The detailed results were classified.[58]

Experiment #11 – High-Temperature Windows

This experiment was sponsored by the Aeronautical Systems Division to investigate various transparent materials in the high-temperature environment. The rapid buildup of temperature and dynamic force as cold structures reentered the atmosphere at hypersonic velocities created severe problems for window designers. The X-15-2 canopy windows were instrumented to provide precise temperature data, as were the center-of-gravity compartment windows. Among others, the experiment tested the fused-silica windows used on the photo optical degradation experiment (#5). Useful data was obtained on several flights in late 1963.[59]

Experiment #12 – Atmospheric-Density Measurements

With increased operations of both manned vehicles and military missiles the Air Force considered it important to determine the atmospheric density at altitudes above 100,000 feet. The X-15 presented a unique opportunity to measure these characteristics using air data gathered by the normal X-15 ball nose and stable platform. Density-height profiles in the stratosphere and mesosphere were obtained from measurements of impact pressure, velocity, and altitude on two flights (2-14-28 and 2-20-36) in 1961 and four more (3-16-26, 3-20-31, 3-21-32, and 3-22-36) in 1963. The X-15 data generally indicated 5 to 7-percent greater densities than the standard predicted values at altitudes between 110,000 and 150,000 feet.[60]

A follow-on experiment was sponsored by the Air Force Geophysics Research Directorate to provide more precise data for the designers of future aerospace vehicles. A densatron ionization gage was installed in the nose of the right wing-tip pod on X-15-1, and two flights (1-50-79 and 1-51-81) were used to check out the installation and to measure temperatures in the instrument. A small amount of radioactive tritium was then installed in the gage in order to measure the atmospheric density above 90,000 feet. The third flight (1-52-85) was the first with the radioactive source installed and impact pressure data were recorded between 72,000 and 137,000 feet. However, the data were judged generally unreliable and the researchers set about modifying their experiment to correct the problem.[61]

The fourth flight (1-63-104) took place on 6 May 1966, but resulted in Jack McKay making an emergency landing on Delamar Lake. A modified instrument, using Americium as its radioactive element, was mounted in the right wing-tip pod on X-15-3 for the next flight (3-56-83) which collected good data. The intended goal of obtaining atmospheric density profiles on a regular basis was never realized; in fact,

the experiment only flew on three more flights. As the researchers later commented, "The research activity undertaken here was valuable if for no other reasons than to point out the numerous restrictions associated with a manned rocket vehicle."[62]

Experiment #13 – Micrometeorite Collection

This experiment was sponsored by the Air Force Geophysics Research Directorate to collect samples of micrometeorites and extraterrestrial dust at altitudes above 150,000 feet. This experiment was the impetus to manufacture the wing-tip pods and a collector was installed in the nose of the left wing-tip pod on X-15-1. At high altitude and low dynamic pressure the lid opened from the rear to a vertical position on top of the wing. As it lifted, rotating upward toward the front, it also swiveled so that the underside of the lid faced the aircraft fuselage and exposed the collector to the air stream. The collector then "broke seal" to expose a rotating six-surface collection unit behind an orifice in its side. The experiment flew on both the X-15-1 and X-15-3 and some particles were collected during six flights. Unfortunately, these were found to be so contaminated by residue from the ballistic control system thrusters that the experiment was cancelled.[63]

Experiment #14 – Advanced Energy Management Systems

This experiment was sponsored by the Aeronautical Systems Division and Flight Research Center. As finally defined for the X-15, this was an evaluation of vertical-tape displays, energy-management techniques, and command guidance for boost and trajectory control. The equipment consisted of a Honeywell inertial system, coupler, and computer; a Honeywell AN/AYK-5 Alert digital computer; a Lear Siegler instrument panel with vertical-tape displays; the Honeywell MH-96 adaptive flight control system; and the ball nose. The system was installed in the X-15-3 during the weather down period in early 1966.[64]

Another part of the experiment was a test of a boost-guidance technique and display developed by the Ames Research Center. This

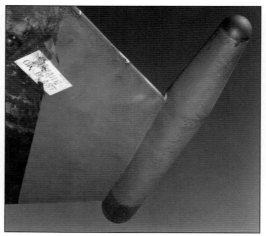
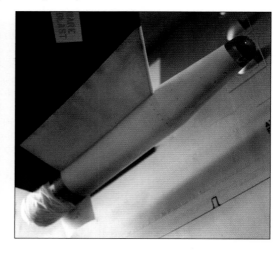

The Atmospheric Density Measurement experiment (#12) used a small amount of radioactive material to measure the air density above 100,000 feet. At left is the deployed sensor during testing on 13 April 1966; this flight would end with Jack McKay's emergency landing at Mud Lake. At right is the pod – covered in green thermopaint – on X-15-1 for Flight 1-51-81 on 10 December 1964. (NASA Dryden)

This wing-tip pod on X-15-1 contains the micrometeorite collection system (under the plastic wrap at the back), but no photos could be found of the collectors in the extended position. (NASA Dryden)

One of the more interesting concepts was the Rarefied Wake Flow experiment (#16) that intended to release a small Mylar balloon at 250,000 feet and photograph its wake flow. This is the tail-cone box installation on X-15-3 on 18 July 1963. The two attempts were both unsuccessful. (NASA Dryden)

Note the lack of clearance between the wing-tip pod (carrying a Pace flow transducer) and the NB-52 in this 13 September 1966 photo. (NASA Dryden)

was, logically enough, called the Ames Boost Guidance display evaluation. For the most part the experiment consisted of additional programming for the Alert computer. The boost guidance program was displayed on the horizontal pointer of the 3-axis attitude indicator, making it a "fly-to-null" display of altitude error plus altitude rate error. This program was intended to allow the pilot to fly a velocity-altitude window during boost, a bounded corridor during hypersonic cruise, and a precise corridor during reentry. It flew for the first time on Flight 3-58-87. Overall, the entire integrated flight data system appeared to work well enough during the next 15 flights.[65]

Experiment #15 – Heat-Exchanger / Vapor-Cycle Cooling

This experiment was sponsored by the Aeronautical Systems Division to verify performance estimates for evaporators and condensers at zero gravity. The experiment would be mounted in the instrument compartment of X-15-1 during four high-altitude flights with a large zero-g parabola at the top. The first of the new Garrett AiResearch heat-exchangers was delivered to North American in early November 1964, were tested aboard a KC-135 in early 1965, and were scheduled to be installed on X-15-1 in mid-1965.[66]

Difficulties bringing the experiment up to the safety standards demanded by the X-15 program delayed the installation of the hardware from 1965 to late 1966. As it ended up, the hardware was never installed on an X-15 and the experiment was moved to the Apollo Applications Program, which itself never got off the ground.[67]

Experiment #16 – Rarefied Wake Flow

This experiment was sponsored by the Flight Research Center with a rather fanciful concept. Initially the plan was to tow an inflatable plastic sphere behind the X-15; by measuring the tension on the tow rope, and from photographic observations, the researchers hoped to determine the atmospheric density above 200,000 feet, the drag characteristics of a towed sphere in free molecular flow regions, the effect of vehicle flow fields, and to study supersonic wakes. Nobody could figure out how to make it work.[68]

The experiment was modified so that a small Mylar balloon originally procured for Project Mercury would be released (instead of towed) from the tail-cone box on X-15-3 at altitudes above 250,000 feet to investigate the properties of supersonic wakes at low densities. Two unsuccessful release attempts (Flights 3-21-32 and 3-22-36) were made in mid-1963, marking the end of this idea.[69]

The experiment was reoriented, and in April 1966 the ballast nose cones for the wing-tip pods were modified to accept a Pace flow transducer, allowing some atmospheric measurements. The experiment flew several times on X-15-1 and X-15-3 during 1965 and 1966.[70]

Experiment #17 – MIT-Apollo Horizon Photometer

This experiment was sponsored by the Office of Manned Space Flight to measure the Earth's horizon-intensity profile at different wavelengths in the visible spectrum. This was officially called the Simultaneous Photographic Horizon Scanner experiment and was essentially a follow-on to the Langley Horizon Definition experiment (#4) using much more sophisticated equipment. The MIT project was large and wide ranging, using various aircraft, sounding rockets, as well as Mercury and Gemini spacecraft, to carry radiometers to measure the Earth's infrared horizon. Of these, the X-15 carried the largest and most sophisticated package as part of a project to define the Earth's limb for use as an artificial horizon for the space sextant carried aboard the Apollo spacecraft. The sextant was designed as a backup device for reinsertion into an Earth orbit in the event of a radar or communications failure.[71]

Phase I used a fixed platform in the tail-cone box supporting a photomultiplier photometer, a solid-state photometer, and a camera pointing aft. The fixed platform was checked-out on Flight 1-51-81, and four additional flights were flown to obtain photometer output levels.[72]

The Phase II experiment contained a spectral photometer, a camera, and a star tracker mounted on a three-axis stabilized platform in the tail-cone box on X-15-1. The star tracker was designed to acquire Polaris and the gimbaled system could control horizon scan rates to obtain data independent of aircraft maneuvering. The Phase II experiment was carried on nine flights beginning with 1-63-104[73]

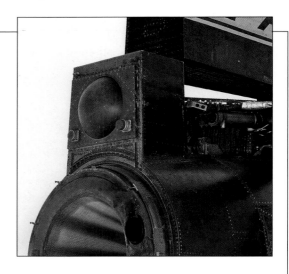

At left is the Phase I installation of the MIT-Apollo Horizon Photometer experiment (#17) that used a fixed platform in the tail-cone box on X-15-1. The photo was taken on 13 April 1966 and shows the two photometers and camera used by the experiment. The other two photos were taken after Flight 1-74-130 on 1 March 1968 and show the Phase II installation; in this case everything was behind protective covers that were transparent to the wavelengths of interest. (NASA Dryden)

Five later flights (part 2 of Phase II) added a Barnes infrared edge tracker designed for spacecraft attitude stabilization in the Apollo Applications Program. The Barnes instrument was essentially a telescope employing a 2.4-inch diameter silicon lens mounted on the elevator under the skylight hatch of X-15-1. This hardware was installed in early 1967 and was collocated with the WTR launch monitoring experiment (#20). The experiment was checked-out on Flight 1-76-134, and four data-gathering flights were made between June and September 1968.[74]

The experiment concluded that the concept was feasible for use as a space navigation technique, but because the most stable portions of the radiance were in the near-ultraviolet range, it was useable only during the daylight portions of an orbit. To verify that the idea worked from greater distances, the Apollo 8, 10, and 11 missions made visual sightings of the Earth's horizon using the onboard spacecraft sextant. This exercise was conducted several times enroute to and returning from the moon and the sextant was found to have relatively good accuracy compared against radar positioning.[75]

Experiment #18 – Supersonic Deceleration Devices

Initially, this experiment was proposed to test the concept of inflatable orbital structures, but was reoriented towards inflatable decelerator devices. In this incarnation, this experiment was sponsored by the Flight Research Center to evaluate the drag, stability, and deployment characteristics of various decelerator configurations at Mach 5 and 200,000 feet. The possibilities included inflatable spheres and cones, and various self-inflating parachutes. Some modifications to support the experiment were made to the X-15-3 during the weather down period in early 1966, but the experiment was apparently never installed.[76]

Experiment #19 – High-Altitude Sky Brightness

This experiment was sponsored by the Aeronautical Systems Division with the objective of determining the intensity, polarization, and spectral distribution of the daytime sky at high altitudes. The experiment had been initiated as the High Altitude Daytime Sky Background Radiation Measurement Program and Northrop Nortronics had been developing a spectrophotometer for use on a Lockheed U-2 that would be used to survey the sky at altitudes between 20,000 and 70,000 feet in 10,000-foot increments. The Air Force, however, desired data up to 200,000 feet; enter the X-15. The spectrophotometer was first flown in the rear portion of the left wing-tip pod during Flight 1-50-79 and flew on several subsequent X-15-1 and X-15-3 flights, acquiring useful data on at least two of them.[77]

Experiment #20 – Western Test Range Launch Monitoring

This experiment was originally funded by the Aeronautical Systems Division under the name Pacific Missile Range (PMR) Launch Monitoring to measure the signature of a ballistic missile from high altitude to determine the feasibility of using the ultraviolet spectrum for space-based detection and tracking systems. The experiment consisted of an optical tracking system, a vidicon camera, a four-spectral-band radiometer, and a servo-driven scanning mirror installed under the skylight hatch in X-15-1. The experiment first flew on Flight 1-72-125 and was subsequently carried on eight additional flights.[78]

The primary target for the experiment would be a Minuteman II ICBM launched from Vandenberg AFB, and one of the most pressing issues was how to make sure the target and the X-15 would both be in position at the right time. The X-15 was purposefully scheduled so that it arrived at its launch point either on time or slightly late – the Air Force could hold launching the target, but could not recall it once launched. Nevertheless, this experiment would have required extraordinary luck to have everything in place at exactly the right time.[79]

The Air Force apparently put a high priority on this experiment since it was one of the two reasons listed for continuing Air Force funding of the X-15 program. Unfortunately, on at least two occasions the equipment on the X-15 failed to operate as expected; another time Vandenberg could not launch the target because of a technical problem. Finally, the first coordinated launch of the X-15 and a Minuteman was accomplished on Flight 1-81-141. Bill Dana extended the experiment at approximately 235,000 feet as planned (roughly 137 seconds after X-15 launch), but 2.8 seconds later all power was lost to the system and the experiment automatically retracted.[80]

The last opportunity was have been on the 200th X-15 flight. The launch attempt on 21 November 1968 was coordinated with Vandenberg and a Minuteman II was launched at 10:28, but unfortunately the X-15 never left the ground because of a problem with *Balls Three*. A total of $700,000 had been spent by the Air Force on the experiment, not counting the normal flight costs of the X-15 or the cost of the Minuteman (which were being launched anyway).[81]

Experiment #21 – Structural Research

This experiment was sponsored by the Flight Research Center to investigate lightweight structures in the high-temperature environment by using the detachable outer wing panel on the X-15A-2. At least two configurations were proposed: one for sustained Mach 3 cruise, and one for hypersonic cruise. No evidence could be found that the panels were ever built or tested.[82]

Experiment #22 – Air-Breathing Propulsion

There had long been interest within the Air Force and NASA propulsion communities in developing air-breathing hypersonic engines to power future vehicles instead of the rocket engine used on the X-15. To many, including some researchers at the Flight Research Center, the X-15 seemed like an ideal test bed for such a propulsion system. As envisioned by the FRC during 1961, this idea was "an extensive air-breathing engine development program ... in which one

or more sub-scale modular experimental engines would be flown in a true flight environment aboard the X-15."[83]

Since the X-15s were fully committed to other research, the idea was not pursued further. However, when the X-15-2 was damaged during a landing accident on 9 November 1962, North American proposed modifying the aircraft in conjunction with its repairs. General support for the plan was found within the Air Force, which was willing to pay the estimated $4.75 million to rebuild and modify the aircraft.[84]

On the other hand, NASA was less enthusiastic, and felt the aircraft should simply be repaired to its original configuration. Researchers at Langley and Lewis believed that the X-15 would be of limited value for propulsion research. However, NASA did not press its views, and on 13 May 1963 the Air Force authorized North American to rebuild the aircraft as the X-15A-2 to test a hypersonic ramjet.[85]

Interestingly, although the X-15 was being modified to carry a ramjet, it appeared that nobody was actually designing such an engine. To rectify this, in early 1963 the FRC awarded a four-month study contract to the Marquardt Corporation to generate requirements applicable to possible engines. When the final report was issued in December 1963 the results bore little resemblance to the dummy ramjet that would ultimately fly on the X-15A-2. Marquardt determined that the X-15 was a viable platform for testing ramjets between Mach 4 and Mach 8, providing a useful complement to ground testing. The company proposed three different ramjets that could be tested with minimal modifications to the airplane. Surprisingly, the study investigated using one of the basic X-15s in addition to the advanced X-15A-2 as test beds.[86]

Instead of the round cross-section dummy ramjet that was ultimately hung from the ventral stabilizer on the X-15A-2, Marquardt proposed a rectangular shape that fit flush against the lower fuselage. The unit would be 188 inches long, 24 inches wide, and 21 inches

The most ambitious concept was the Western Test Range Launch Monitoring experiment installed in X-15-1, shown here on 2 August 1966. The experiment was intended to track an ICBM launched from Vandenberg AFB using equipment extended through the Skylight hatch (shown above). (NASA Dryden)

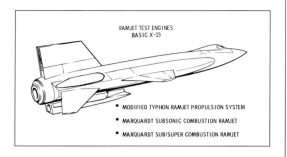

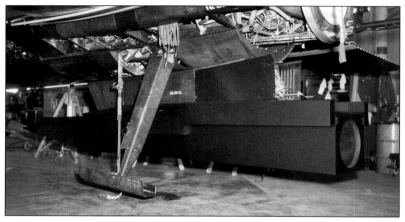

Various ramjets (above) and scramjets (left) were proposed to fly under the X-15, but none ever did. (NASA)

high, and weighed about 900 pounds. It was expected that the hydrogen-fueled ramjet could produce up to 1,000-lbf gross thrust, a figure that would likely not compensate for the additional drag of the installation. Still it would allow researchers a unique opportunity to observe an operable ramjet at hypersonic speeds.[87]

On the basic airplane, the entire ventral stabilizer and lower rudder actuator would be removed, a "roller support system" would be installed that actually supported the ramjet, a new frame would be added in the fuselage at station 483.5, and a pair of conformal liquid hydrogen slipper tanks would be installed over the aft portions of the side tunnels. Since the advanced X-15A-2 was being rebuilt with a liquid hydrogen fuel system included in the fuselage, the slipper tanks would be unnecessary, although some wind tunnel models investigated them in any case. The longer rear skid struts on the advanced airplane would also allow the ramjet to be mounted on the stub ventral stabilizer. This had a couple of desirable effects: the inlet was further from the flow disturbance caused by the X-15 fuselage, and at least a small ventral stabilizer remained if the ramjet had to be jettisoned at high speeds.[88]

Although the Marquardt proposal went nowhere, the basic concept had finally taken hold – especially at Langley – and the Hypersonic Ramjet Engine (HRE) experiment was formally approved by Hugh Dryden in September 1964. The project called for a two-phase effort to develop the engine and three parallel 9-month Phase I contracts were awarded to Garrett, General Electric, and Marquardt in June 1965.[89]

Phase I was supposed to develop a concept and preliminary design for the engine and research program. Whichever engine was selected as the best design would proceed to Phase II where actual engines would be fabricated and subjected to a battery of ground tests, including performance measurements and a flight safety eval-

uation. Once the engine was shown to work safely, it would be flight tested on the X-15A-2. From the initial competitors, Garrett was ultimately chosen to develop the engine.[90]

While this was happening at Langley, the FRC had three "dummy" ramjets constructed in order to gain basic aerodynamic data and to investigate the effects of carrying a generic ramjet shape on the X-15A-2. These were fabricated from a series of truncated cones and were about 7 feet long and 2 feet in diameter. Two different nose configurations were built; a 20-degree nose cone flown on Flights 2-51-92 and 2-52-96, and a 40-degree cone flown on Flight 2-53-97. The first flight with the 20-degree nose cone did not use any nose probes; the second flight with the 20-degree cone and the only flight with the 40-degree cone both used a rake with two probes protruding from the extreme nose in an "L" shape. The top cone probe was on the ramjet centerline and the lower cone was 8 inches below.[91]

In order to accommodate the dummy ramjet, the ventral stabilizer on the X-15A-2 was significantly modified. The root chord (next to the fuselage) was reduced by removing 2.8 feet from the front of the ventral and equipping it with a blunt, unswept leading edge. In addition, approximately 3 inches of the lower surface were removed for the first 3.3 feet of the ventral to allow the ramjet to be mounted in a semi-submerged location. Ten impact pressure probes were installed on the leading edge; most protruded approximately 5 inches in front of the ventral although the three closest to the ramjet were progressively shorter.[92]

However, the smooth cylindrical surface of the lower fuselage of the X-15A-2 was interrupted by a removable camera fairing installed over the center of gravity compartment. This camera window had been used for the Hycon/Mauer camera experiments and protruded 1.75 inches below the fuselage. This protrusion was located approximately 13 feet ahead of the leading edge of the pylon, or about 10.25 feet ahead of the tip of the 40-degree nose cone. A wind tunnel study conducted after the last X-15A-2 flight showed that shock waves generated by the wing leading edge, lower-fuselage camera window, and fuselage side fairing impinged on the dummy ramjet and pylon. This shock wave was found to be very sensitive to angle-of-attack, with a 1-percent increase in free-stream angle-of-attack resulting in a 10-percent increase in impact pressure at Mach 6.5.[93]

After the grounding of the X-15A-2, it was decided to reorient the HRE as a ground-based program. In early 1968 Garrett was ordered to stop work on the X-15 package and other items relating to flight testing; the dummy ramjet that had been tested on the X-15A-2 was built by the FRC and had little relation to the HRE being developed by Garrett. As John Becker later observed, "And thus was HRE adroitly decoupled from the X-15 which gave it birth and left to make its own way, apparently unchanged but actually now stripped of its glamour and its principal reason to exist." Nevertheless, the program continued – with dubious results – until 22 April 1974 when it was finally terminated.[94]

Experiment #23 – Infrared Scanning Radiometer

This was essentially a follow-on to the Infrared Exhaust Signature experiment (#10) sponsored by the Aeronautical Systems Division to determine the feasibility of an infrared imaging instrument operating at Mach 3-5 and altitudes between 90,000 and 120,000 feet. A Singer scanning radiometer was installed in the lower portion of the instrument compartment of the X-15-1 during mid-March 1965 and looked through a Iratran IV window that was installed in the lower fuselage. The instrument recorded the reflected solar radiation as well as radiation emitted by Earth on six flights between 26 March 1965 (Flight 1-53-86) and 30 September 1965 (1-60-99).[95]

Experiment #24 – High-Altitude Infrared Background

This experiment was sponsored by the Air Force Research Technology Division to obtain high-altitude infrared measurements of the Earth, horizon, and sky for use in various surveillance applications. The measuring device was a fairly simple dual-channel solid-state radiometer with a flat rotating mirror that provided a circular scan. The Autonetics Division of North American built the experiment hardware which was installed in the right wing-tip pod on X-15-1 during the weather down period in early 1966. Three flights to altitudes above 150,00 feet were requested, but the only verifiable attempt was on the aborted 200th flight.[96]

Experiment #25 – Optical Background Measurements

This experiment was sponsored by the Air Force Research Technology Division as an extension of the ultraviolet exhaust plume experiment (#3) to obtain narrow-band optical-background measurements. The Barnes high-resolution spectrometer and associated equipment from experiment #3 was modified to operate at visible wavelengths and the equipment was carried in the tail-cone box on X-15-3. The experiment had flown twice by the end of 1965 but had gathered little usable data because of system noise. Modifications were made during early 1966 and at least five flights were flown in mid-1966.[97]

Experiment #26 – SST Structural Demonstrations

This experiment began with grandiose plans to support the supersonic transport development effort, but could never find a sponsor or funding. As ultimately implemented, it was sponsored by the Flight Research Center and broken into two parts. Phase I used a normal set of horizontal stabilizers during several flights to gather baseline airplane data. The tests began on Flight 3-52-78 and concluded on Flight 3-61-91; data was not collected on every flight due to a variety of malfunctions, but sufficient data was gathered to be analyzed.[98]

Phase II included a new set of horizontal stabilizers that were manufactured by North American during May 1966 and the left-hand unit was instrumented with 128 strain gages and 125 thermocouples. The stabilizers were tested in the High Temperature Loads Calibration Laboratory and these were subsequently installed in time for Flight 3-62-92. Some unexpected buffeting was noted on this flight, so the original horizontal stabilizers were reinstalled for Flight 3-63-94 to investigate the phenomenon. No buffet was noted, leading researchers to suspect some minor manufacturing flaw in the new horizontal stabilizers. Unfortunately, no further work was accomplished on this experiment prior to the X-15-3 being lost.[99]

Another part of this experiment was to study the effect of various discontinuities on local surface heating between Mach 4 and Mach 6. To avoid having to make detailed local measurements, the experiment was designed to measure the ratio of the heating rates on two symmetrically-located panels under the center fuselage and on the wingtips; one panel in each location would have the discontinuity, the other would not. Discontinuities included forward and aft facing steps, wavy surfaces (sinusoidal distortions), streamwise corners, and antenna posts. The step panels were flown on at least two X-15-3 flights, with the wavy panels on at least three flights.[100]

Experiment #27 – Hycon Camera

This experiment was sponsored by the Air Force Research Technology Division and was, conceptually, an extension of experiment #5. The experiment used the X-15-2 and was approximately 80-percent complete at the time of Jack McKay's accident in the second airplane. The effort, however, continued after the X-15A-2 was returned to service.[101]

The first part of this experiment actually preceded experiment #5. A vertical camera with a 12-inch focal length and an oblique camera with a 6-inch focal length were installed in the center-of-gravity compartment in X-15-2. This provided data that permitted the investigation of contrast attenuation at high altitudes and showed the feasibility of obtaining aerial photography from supersonic vehicles. These tests began on Flight 2-30-51 when the 6-inch oblique camera was used to photograph the Las Vegas area from very high altitude using black & white film. A similar photo was taken on Flight 2-39-70 using color film. The 12-inch camera was also used on the latter flight, photographing Indian Springs AFB using color-infrared Ektachrome film.[102]

A new Maurer Model 500 camera was installed in the center of gravity compartment on X-15A-2 during early 1966 and was used on Flight 2-49-86 and two additional flights, all with satisfactory results. A Hycon KA-51A "Chicago Aerial" camera replaced the Maurer and flew on Flight 2-52-96; this was the only flight of the KA-51A, and no results could be ascertained. For the next flight of X-15A-2 the Hycon experiment was removed and replaced with an aft viewing Millikan 16-mm camera to photograph the dummy ramjet.[103]

Experiment #28 – X-Ray Air Density

The design and fabrication of this experiment began in late 1965 in anticipation of a flight in late 1966. The experiment consisted of an X-ray tube and detector located in the forward portion of the right wing-tip pod. X-rays would be transmitted through the wing-tip pod skin and were scattered; the back scatter was detected by solid-state cells and used to determine air density. The experiment was reportedly carried on several flights during 1967 and 1968, but no results could be ascertained.[104]

Experiment #29 – JPL Solar-Spectrum Measurements

This experiment was sponsored by the Jet Propulsion Laboratory and consisted of a spectrometer containing a block of 12 sensors and a servo-positioning system installed in the rear section of the left wing-tip pod of X-15-1. The data would be used to improve the methods of correcting for atmospheric absorption, and to determine the absolute energy of the Sun. The experiment was manufactured in early 1966 but a pop-up hatch used to expose the spectrometer failed qualification testing in April 1966. The experiment was subsequently redesigned to use a quartz window instead of a hatch. At the same time the experiment was modified to use the new PCM telemetry system in X-15-3.[105]

The experiment was finally installed for Flight 3-58-87. A preliminary review of the data showed excessive electrical noise on the data channel, but the experimenter considered the data to be acceptable. The experiment was flown on at least two additional flights with mostly the same results.[106]

Experiment #30 – Spectrophotometry

This experiment consisted of an objective spectrograph and two photometers to obtain spectra of the planets and observe day airflow at high altitude. As of April 1966 this experiment did not have a sponsor and had not been formally approved, although it was assigned an experiment number. By the end of 1966 the experiment had been cancelled, with no actual hardware development undertaken.[107]

Experiment #31 – Fixed Alpha Nose

Late in the program an FRC-developed experiment was carried on the nose of the left wing-tip pod that used a non-moving fixed ball nose to detect angle of attack. The sensor consisted of a ported sphere, 4.36-inches in diameter mounted on the nose of the pod. The total length of the sensor was 18.75 inches, but it looked like a simple extension of the pod. Five pressure ports were located on the pod; one port was 5 degrees below the zero angle-of-attack stagnation point and the remaining four ports were located symmetrically around this point in the vertical and horizontal planes. The vertical ports were used to measure angle-of-attack; it was planned (but never implemented) to use the horizontal ports for angle of sideslip. The sensor was flown on a single flight (1-53-86) and the data showed the same trends as the ball nose. Researchers concluded that the fixed ball nose was a feasible alternative to the ball nose.[108]

Confidence was high enough that a "fixed alpha nose" was manufactured and installed on X-15-1 wing-tip pod for six of its last seven flights. Again, the data did not precisely match the ball nose, but were repeatable enough that consistent correlation could be made. A conceptually similar system was used on the Apollo launch escape system to provide limited air data to the astronauts in the event of an abort that forced them to separate the capsule from the Saturn booster. A very similar system using ports in the nose cone was designed and installed on the Space Shuttle *Columbia* as the Shuttle Entry Air Data System (SEADS) experiment between 1986 and 1991.[109]

OTHER FLOWN EXPERIMENTS

In addition to the "numbered" experiments formally approved by the Research Airplane Committee, several other experiments were carried by the X-15.

<u>Saturn Insulation:</u> Usually heralded as a major contribution of the X-15, in reality this was a fairly low-key experiment that exposed various types of insulation material proposed for the Saturn launch vehicles to the hypersonic environment. Some documentation show this as experiment #41. At least five flights were made with pieces of Saturn insulation material installed on the speed brakes of X-15-1 and X-15-3. A camera was installed in the right wing-tip pod to look at the upper speed brakes, and a second camera was in the left pod pointed at the lower speed brakes. No detailed results could be ascertained.[110]

<u>Skid Materials:</u> This experiment was sponsored by the Aeronautical Systems Division and was essentially a product evaluation of materials selected for use on Dyna-Soar. Five flights were flown using X-15-3 in early 1964 to test cermet (ceramic-metallic composite) skids and two on X-15A-2 to evaluate Inconel X skids. This data was compared to five earlier flights that had used the standard 4130 steel skids but had car-

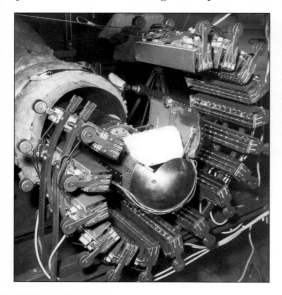

Two photos of the JPL Solar-Spectrum experiment (#29), with no explanation about how it was supposed to work. (NASA Dryden)

The Fixed Alpha Nose (#31) sensor installed on the nose of the left wing-tip pod of X-15-1 on 5 April 1968. (NASA Dryden)

 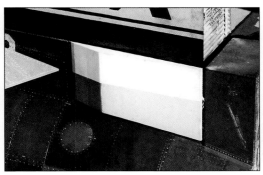 

The X-15 evaluated some of the insulation and ablatives used on the Saturn launch vehicle, but it did so after Saturn was already flying so it is difficult to ascertain its true contribution. The photo at left shows a camera in the rear of a wing-tip pod that was used to photograph the insulation on the speed brakes. (NASA Dryden)

ried additional instrumentation to measure landing loads. In addition, the X-15 landing gear simulator was used to test 1020-steel skids and a set of 3.0-inch wire brush skids at speeds up to 80 mph.[111]

Impact Rakes: Over the course of the flight program, the three airplanes were equipped with a variety of impact probes and pitot rakes. For instance a series of flights was made with a set of four pitots extending from the leading edge of the vertical stabilizers; three on the dorsal and one on the ventral. Another test used a single rake installed on the bottom of the fuselage just behind the wing leading edge; this rake was 2 inches wide and 5 inches high with 8 pitots protruding from its leading edge. Other tests were flown with two rakes at various locations on the right side of the dorsal rudder; these rakes were L-shaped about 6 inches at the base and 4.5 inches high with 7 pitots, including one set up to capture surface boundary-layer air. Another rake was flown at 63-percent semispan on the bottom of the wing; the rake was 2 inches wide and 4 inches high with 8 pitots. A flush static pressure port was always located near the rake or pitot. Later, during X-15A-2 flights with the dummy ramjet, ten pitots were installed on the leading edge of the fixed portion of the ventral stabilizer. Pressures were recorded on standard NACA aneroid-type manometers.[112]

Cold Wall: The X-15 offered a unique opportunity to measure heat transfer and skin friction under quasi-steady flight conditions at high Mach numbers. A considerable amount of heat-transfer data and some skin-friction data were obtained during the flight program and this indicated that the level and rate of change of turbulent skin friction and heat transfer were lower than predicted by the most widely used theories. However, comparisons of the X-15 data with the theory were not conclusive because of uncertainties of the boundary layer edge conditions as a result of non-uniform flow and conduction losses. In order to further evaluate the problem, researchers wanted to use a highly instrumented panel in a location with known flow characteristics. They also wanted the panel shielded from aerodynamic heating until the airplane was at a steady-state cruise condition.[113]

The X-15-3 with the sharp leading edge modification on the upper rudder was chosen to carry the experiment. The 0.0605-inch-thick Inconel X test panel was located just behind the right-side leading edge boundary-layer trips 15.1 inches below the top of the rudder. To obtain the desired wall-to-recovery temperature ratios and to ensure an isothermal test surface when the airplane reached the desired speed and altitude, it was necessary to insulate the test

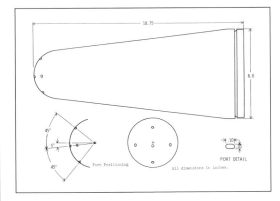 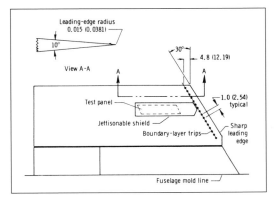 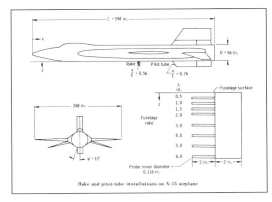

The fixed alpha nose was a much simpler solution than the ball nose, but required more computing power. A very similar experiment was carried on the nose of space shuttle Columbia during the 1980s. (NASA)

The cold wall measured heat transfer and skin friction during high-speed cruise. Thermocouples were shielded during boost by a panel located on the dorsal rudder of X-15-3 that was jettisoned over the Fort Irwin restricted area. (NASA)

The X-15 carried a variety of impact rakes on the rudders, fuselage, and wings over the course of the flight program. Frequently additional recorders would be located in the fuselage side tunnels to accommodate the rakes. (NASA)

Above: **No information could be found explaining this 14 November 1961 wind tunnel model carrying a Blue Scout with ASSET on the nose.** Below: **Various drawings from the Ford/North American proposal to carry Blue Scout on the X-15.** (above: The Boeing Company Archives; below: Ford Aeronutronic)

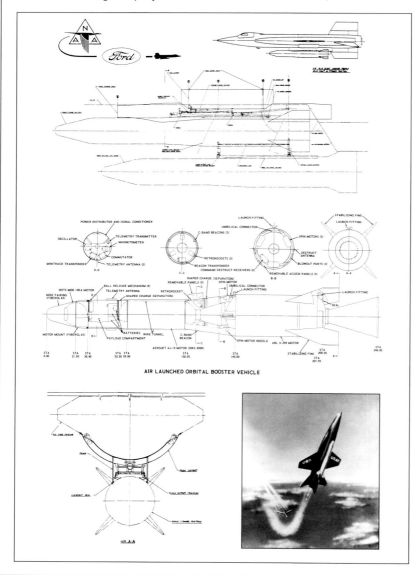

AIR LAUNCHED ORBITAL BOOSTER VEHICLE

panel during the initial phase of the flight. The insulating cover could be jettisoned from the test panel in approximately 50 milliseconds, resulting in an instantaneous heating of the test panel (the so-called "cold wall" effect). The test panel was instrumented with thermocouples, static-pressure orifices, and a skin friction gage with the data recorded on tape. A Millikan camera operating at 400 frames per second was installed in an upper bug-eye camera bay to record the panel being jettisoned. The measurements obtained were in general agreement with previous X-15 data.[114]

SONIC BOOMS

Just as the X-15 program was winding down, researchers noted that no sonic boom noise measurements had been made with an airplane flying faster than Mach 3 (the YF-12C/SR-71A and XB-70A). Some measurements had been made at Mach numbers up to 16 during the liftoff and reentry of Apollo spacecraft, but these were not considered representative of future aerospace vehicles such as the Space Shuttle. To correct this, measurements were taken on several X-15 flights at Mach numbers up to 5.5 and compared to theoretical methods of determining overpressures.[115]

During Flight 1-70-119 instruments were set up at Mud Lake to record the boom generated at Mach 5.3 and 92,000 feet. Satisfactory data was obtained even though the airplane was about 6 miles east of the monitoring site. The boom peak overpressure was about 0.34 psf.[116]

For another flight, microphone arrays were installed around Goldstone and Cuddeback. When the airplane arrived over Goldstone at Mach 4.8, the engine was operating at 50-percent thrust and the speed brakes were extended; at Cuddeback the engine had been shut down, the speed brakes were retracted, and the airplane was at Mach 3.5. Although the flight plan called for the airplane to fly directly over the microphone arrays, in reality it passed 1.7 miles south of the array at Goldstone and 7.9 miles south of the Cuddeback array – not an unusual amount of error.[117]

The data collected from Goldstone was scaled and corrected so that it could be compared to similar data obtained from an SR-71 flight. The two sets of data were in general agreement. The data from Cuddeback were not compared because of the X-15 miss distance. The results of the experiment also compared favorably to theoretical results, and no unusual phenomena related to the overpressure were encountered.[118]

RECOVERABLE BOOSTER SYSTEM

During 1961 North American and the Aeronutronic Division of the Ford Motor Company conducted a study to determine the feasibility of using the X-15 to launch modified RM-89 Blue Scout rockets. The intent was to provide a "recoverable booster system capable of accomplishing a wide variety of space probe and orbital experiment missions." The North American-Ford study defined a three-stage booster where the NB-52 was the first stage, the X-15 was the second stage, and a Blue Scout was the third stage. As usual, the X-15 would be launched at approximately 45,000 feet, climbing to altitudes between 130,000 and 200,000 feet to launch the Blue Scout. The X-15 engine shutdown and the ignition of the Blue Scout would occur simultaneously.[119]

The entire modification would add approximately 500 pounds to the empty weight of the X-15. With the missile pylon mounted on the bottom centerline of the fuselage, a slight reduction in directional stability was expected, however, it was anticipated that a level of directional stability comparable to the basic aircraft could be maintained (if necessary) by partial deflection of the speed brakes. Lateral stability would suffer from a slightly greater negative dihedral effect but this was not expected to be a cause for concern since it was within the capability of the SAS to counter. Reentry with the launcher pylon installed was not expected to present "any particular problems." The study estimated that the temperatures on and around the pylon would be less than 1,000°F, and any local hot spots could be tolerated through the use of ablative materials.[120]

The missile launch and jettison mechanism in the X-15 consisted of two arms that were pivoted at their upper ends, and guide rails on the lower ends that held the missile. The extension arms were lowered and retracted by a hydraulic actuator attached to the forward arm. Hydraulic power was obtained from two accumulators, one for the extension stroke and one for the retract stroke that were charged on the ground and completely independent from the X-15 hydraulic system. All of the mechanisms were housed in an Inconel X sheet metal pylon that was attached to the aircraft at the lower fuselage-wing attach fittings. The pylon was about the same height as the normal fixed portion of the ventral stabilizer, and without the missile attached, looked very much like the ventral had been extended forward to the leading edge of the wing.[121]

Before the launcher could be extended and the missile fired, the X-15 pilot had to arm the missile first-stage ignition circuit and the missile destruct system via switches in the cockpit. The launcher was extended and the missile fired by pressing a button on the center stick in the cockpit. Upon activation, the hydraulic actuator unlocked the uplock and extended the launch rail. Shortly before the bottom of the extension stroke, the actuator became a snubber and, when bottomed out, became a drag link. When the extension arms reached 60 degrees arc, the fire circuit for the first stage motor was energized and the missile left the launch rails. If the missile did not fire, it was automatically jettisoned at the bottom of the extension stroke along with the launch rails. During normal operation, the missile de-energized the jettison circuit as it left the launch rails; the rails were retained and automatically retracted into the pylon.[122]

Although the X-15 would be launched over Wendover AFB heading west, the missile would be tracked by the Pacific Missile Range at Pt. Mugu, and the expended stages would fall into the Pacific off of California. If the missile had to be destroyed during first stage boost, the remains would likely fall on government land along the High Range. It was expected that the X-15/Blue Scout configuration could launch 150 pounds into a 115-mile orbit, or 60 pounds into a 1,150-mile orbit.[123]

When Paul Bikle heard about the proposal, he raised several questions, primarily centering around range-safety aspects in the event of a Blue Scout failure, and the impacts on the X-15 research program of dedicating an airplane to this concept. It appears that the obstacles were too great for the expected return, and the concept quietly faded from the scene.[124]

OTHER IDEAS

Many other ideas were put forward for using the X-15 as a test vehicle. The Dyna-Soar program wanted to use the X-15 to test wire-brush main landing skids. These would increase the weight of the X-15 by 50 pounds, but would allow landing on a concrete runway with only a

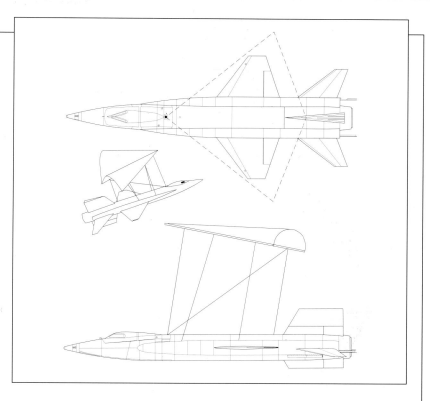

A paraglider on the X-15. During the early 1960s, this concept was being investigated for Project Gemini, and it was proposed to test the idea using an X-15 flying a high-speed reentry, then landing under the glider. (Artwork by Tony Landis)

3,800-foot slide. A variety of other Dyna-Soar systems were proposed for testing on the X-15 since the performance of each vehicle inside the atmosphere was similar. For instance, advanced control and autopilot systems could be evaluated, although the differing planforms of the aircraft would make the results hard to compare directly. An all-electrical fly-by-wire flight control system (as was planned for the X-20) would have used electric actuators for the horizontal and vertical stabilizers instead of the hydraulic system used on the X-15. An entirely new ventral stabilizer constructed from the unique truss structure developed for Dyna-Soar was also proposed to be flown on the X-15.[129]

Paragliders could be tested by releasing a simulated shape and glider at high altitude and speed; this was potentially important to the Gemini program. Alternately, a paraglider could be used by the X-15 itself for full-scale landing tests. Materials testing was frequently proposed, usually involving substituting new leading edges and vertical stabilizers. Alloys such as columbium, René 41, and Hastelloy X were proposed since these were expected to be used on the Dyna-Soar and any future reusable space vehicles (i.e., space shuttle concepts).[130]

By 1960 North American was already proposing "extended performance" variants of the X-15 that used external drop tanks to carry additional propellants. Unlike most of the ideas presented, this one actually came to fruition as the X-15A-2. At the same time North American proposed a version that would use two Castor solid rocket motors that produced 86,600-lbf in addition to the uprated XLR99's 58,900-lbf. The solids would be mounted under the wings in roughly the same position the X-15A-2 carried its external tanks. This configuration was expected to achieve 8,700 fps and 520,000 feet.[131]

Technical Description

Right: *A 1960 model of the gyro package from the original Sperry Gyroscope stable platform used in the X-15. Note each ring is marked with the axis it measures.* (NASA Dryden)

Below right: *A Reaction Motors XLR11-RM-5 rocket engine that was used in the first two airplanes until the ultimate XLR99 was available.* (Reaction Motors via the Terry Panopalis Collection)

Below: *Gilbert "Gil" Kincaid and David W. Stoddard attach a ground dolly to the X-15-1 on 30 January 1962. This also gives an excellent view of the landing skid, strut, and drag brace. The front of the airplane is to the right.* (NASA Dryden)

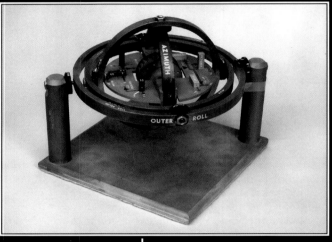

The X-15 was designed for a flight regime that had never been broached before, and required the development of new structures and systems. Many of the systems needed for space flight were developed for the X-15 since the airplane was designed to leave the sensible atmosphere, although it was not intended to (nor could) achieve orbit. In many ways the X-15 was as advanced – or perhaps slightly more so – as the Mercury spacecraft that would first take Americans into orbit.

STRUCTURE

The fuselage was a combination of monocoque and semimonocoque construction incorporating special frames and bulkheads at load distribution points. The Inconel X outer skin was stabilized between the special frames and bulkheads by light J-section frames, and in some locations by longitudinal stiffeners.[1]

The forward fuselage – nose wheel well, cockpit, and equipment compartments – was of conventional frame and longeron construction covered by Inconel X skin. The extreme nose section was removable and could consist of either the standard NACA flight test instrumentation boom or the ball nose. The section behind the nose and just forward of the nose wheel was a pressurized equipment compartment (officially known as Equipment Bay No. 1, but usually called the nose bay) provided with batt insulation and radiation blankets. The cockpit and main research instrumentation compartment (Bay No. 2) were of concentric shell construction that used riveted Inconel X fuselage skin and an inner shell made from 2024-T4 aluminum alloy to form the pressure barrier. The space between the two shells was filled with fiberglass batt insulation and a radiation shield. Immediately aft of the instrumentation compartment was an equipment compartment that contained the two APUs.[2]

The full monocoque center fuselage consisted of two integral circular cross-section main propellant tanks with a center-of-gravity equipment compartment (Bay No. 3) between them. The outer skin was welded Inconel X except for three mechanical joints used to facilitate assembly. The liquid oxygen tank consisted of an outer Inconel X shell and a series of torus frames. The torus frames at each end of the tank were constructed from welded Inconel; the intermediate frames were riveted aluminum alloy since they served mainly as slosh baffles. The end torus frames were welded directly to the outer shell while the aluminum baffles were riveted to Inconel ring segments that were welded to the outer shell. The center of the tank contained a cylindrical section for helium storage. The ammonia tank was located just aft of the liquid oxygen tank and was of similar construction. Using integral tanks meant that the flight control linkage, plumbing, electrical wiring, etc. had to routed outside the tank in the fuselage tunnels. The left tunnel housed the liquid oxygen transfer line that ran to the XLR99 turbopump, while the ammonia transfer tube was in the right tunnel. The side tunnels were constructed from Inconel X outer skins that initially suffered from panel flutter under some conditions. This was cured by reinforcing the panels with corrugated inner skins that were stitch-welded to the outer skin. The side tunnels were attached to the outer wall of the propellant tanks by a continuous longitudinal member.[3]

The use of monocoque tanks was somewhat controversial, but North American had sound engineering reasons for doing so. For a given heat input and material, there was a minimum skin thickness required to tolerate the heating environment expected for the X-15. For a semi-monocoque tank, this thickness was based exclusively on the heating loads; the underlying structure would be designed to withstand the dynamic loads, then the non-structural propellant tank would be designed to absorb the pressurization and sloshing loads of the propellants. North American found that by slightly increasing the thickness of

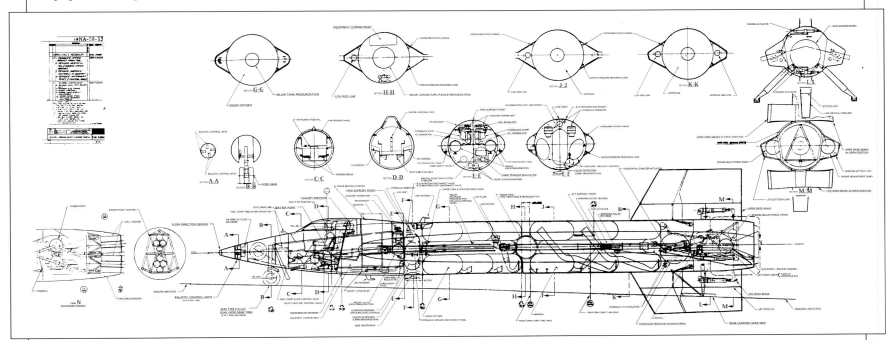

Internal arrangement of the X-15, including the XLR11 engine installation (at far left) and the XLR99 (in the airplane). (Courtesy of the AFFTC Museum)

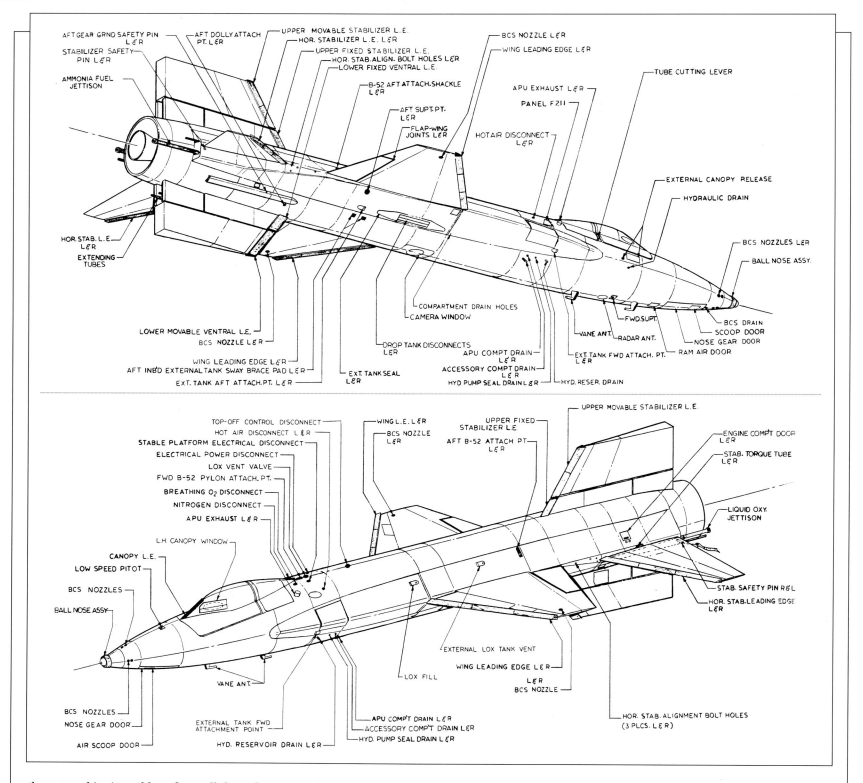

the outer skin, it could perform all three functions, eliminating the separate structure and propellant tank (i.e., becoming full monocoque). All of this had several advantages, but the primary one was minimizing thermal stresses. Since the structural material was on the surface, all of it had an equal opportunity to be heated and the temperature gradi-

This drawing was prepared by Martin as part of the X-15A-2 ablator application report, but interestingly it does not actually show the X-15A-2 – note the side tunnels do not extend all the way aft, although the external tank attachment fittings have been added. Nevertheless, the drawing gives a good indication of all the service points on the airplane. (The Martin Company)

ent quickly approached unity. The overall concept was also slightly lighter; although the skin itself was heavier, there was no underlying structure or tank, resulting in a small overall weight savings.[4]

The presence of the side tunnels complicated the thermal issue slightly since they shrouded the side of the tanks from the high aerodynamic heating. The resulting thermal strains in the upper and lower portions of the liquid oxygen tank would have buckled the side skin longitudinally at a temperature differential as low as 300°F. To eliminate this, the skins on the sides of both propellant tanks were beaded vertically in the vicinity of the tunnels.[5]

The aft fuselage was a semimonocoque structure that supported the empennage, main landing skids, and engine. Several heavy titanium frames were located in the aft fuselage to support the concentrated loads resulting from the engine thrust and landing gear. These frames were strengthened several times during the program as landing weights continued to increase. The engine compartment housed a tubular steel engine mount that held the engine and turbopump completely isolated from the remainder of the airframe by a firewall. A fire seal around the engine nozzle protected against the entry of engine exhaust gases or jettisoned propellants. The engine compartment could be purged using helium to extinguish a fire or relieve an overheat condition.[6]

The wing was a modified NACA 66005 airfoil having a tapered planform swept 25 degrees at the 25-percent chord line. The airfoil was modified forward of the 17-percent chord line and had a constant slope from the 67-percent chord line rearward to a 1-percent blunt trailing edge. It had an aspect ratio of 2.5 and no dihedral. Trailing edge flaps were located over the inboard 60 percent of the span. Since roll control was provided by the differentially-operated horizontal stabilizers, no ailerons were fitted. Interestingly, the wings only carried 55 percent of the total vehicle weight at moderate (0 to 10 degrees) angles of attack; the rest of the lift was generated by the fuselage. At a 20 degree angle-of-attack the fuselage was carrying 65 percent of the load.[7]

The wing was a multispar box with multirib leading and trailing edges. The exterior skin was Inconel X over an internal structure of A-110AT titanium alloy sheet and extrusions. The main wing box had three ribs located at the root, mid-span, and tip. The tip rib, which was also the exposed wing tip, was made of Inconel X. Between the root section and the mid-span rib there were 17 spars; outboard of the mid-span rib there were 9 spars. The leading-edge areas of the wing and vertical stabilizers were thick Inconel X heat sinks machined from bar stock. The leading edge of the horizontal stabilizer was formed from sheet stock and filled with weld material to serve as a heat sink. The Inconel X leading edge was originally divided into five segments to reduce the thermal stresses resulting from the extreme high temperature gradients. Following a very hot flight there was some evidence of local inter-rivet buckling adjacent to the slots and the number of segments was increased to nine. The gaps between the segments were approximately 0.050-inch wide.[8]

PROPELLANT SYSTEM

The vast majority of the X-15 fuselage was occupied by the propellant system, including the liquid oxygen and liquid anhydrous ammonia tanks. Both propellant tanks consisted of an annular tank and a core tank. In the liquid oxygen tank, the core tank contained helium that was used for pressurization. In the ammonia tank, the core tank contained

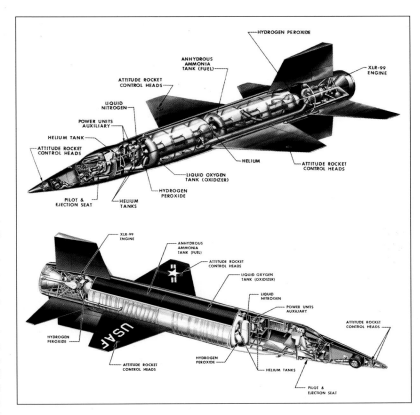

Two different views showing the general arrangement of components in the X-15. The entire center fuselage was taken up with propellants except for a small center-of-gravity compartments between the oxidizer and fuel tanks. Most of the nose was used for the landing gear. (NASA via the Gerald H. Balzer Collection)

additional ammonia. In both instances the use of the core tank allowed a more structurally rigid installation than was possible otherwise.[9]

The total volume of the liquid oxygen tank was 1,038 gallons. Of this, 14 gallons were considered residual at a liquid surface angle of 38 degrees, and 19 gallons was vent and expansion (ullage) space., leaving 1,005 gallons useable. The tank was filled on the ground through the carrier aircraft supply system, and a fluid sensing system automatically topped off the tank during captive flight. For ground operations, the tank could be serviced through a filler located on the top of the wing fairing tunnel on the left wing root leading edge. The total volume of the ammonia tank was 1,445 gallons. The tank was ground serviced through a filler receptacle on the underside of the right side tunnel near the wing trailing edge.[10]

The hydrogen peroxide monopropellant used to drive the XLR99 turbopump was contained in a 10-cubic-foot (854 pounds; 77.5 gallons) spherical tank located behind the ammonia tank. This was separate from the peroxide provided for the APUs and ballistic control system although a transfer system was later installed. There was a 7 cubic foot 3,600-psi helium tank that ran through the center of the liquid oxygen tank; the helium was used to pressurize the liquid oxygen system to approximately 48 psi. An additional 6.5 cubic feet of helium was contained in four spherical tanks. One tank was located between the liquid

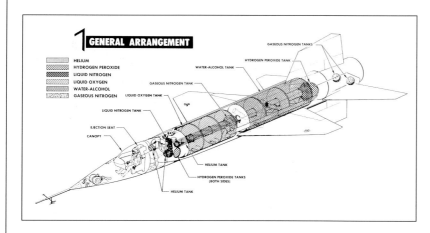

An early internal arrangement drawing showing water-alcohol fuel for the interim XLR11 engines and the NACA instrumentation boom on the nose. (NASA)

oxygen and ammonia tanks and two tanks were in the left and right wing root fairing tunnels outboard of the engine. These three tanks were interconnected and supplied 3,600-psi to pressurize the turbopump hydrogen peroxide tank and supply pneumatic pressure for the engine and propellant control valves. The fourth tank was located just to the right of the turbopump hydrogen peroxide tank and supplied 3,600-psi helium for emergency pneumatic control of the propellant jettison valves. The emergency tank was interconnected to the other three tanks for filling purposes only. The two wing root fairing tanks also supplied helium for engine compartment purging and fire extinguishing.[11]

The modified X-15A-2 included two additional hydrogen peroxide tanks within extended aft side fairings to supply the turbopump for the longer engine burn times, and additional pressurization gas in a spherical helium tank just behind the upper speed brakes.[12]

The two liquid oxygen "top off" tanks in the NB-52 were also considered part of the X-15 propellant system and were filled at the same time as the X-15. The 1,000-gallon "climb" tank was pressurized on the ground and used to replenish the X-15 during climb and initial cruise. During this time the 500-gallon "cruise" tank was allowed to free vent to the atmosphere; this evaporation kept the temperature lower than if it had been pressurized. About 30 minutes prior to launch, the system was switched over to the "cruise" tank so that the X-15 could be replenished with the colder – and thus denser – liquid oxygen. The X-15 contained a level-sensing device that was used to control valves in the NB-52 to maintain the proper liquid level in the X-15.[13]

The X-15 ammonia, helium, and hydrogen peroxide tanks were filled on the ground with no subsequent top-off provisions. The ammonia was pre-chilled to –35°F prior to filling, and the tank was sealed after it was full to stabilize at the evaporative pressure of ammonia. The hydrogen peroxide tanks were allowed to free-vent until they were pressurized using helium.[14]

XLR11 ENGINE

For the first 30 flights, thrust was provided by two Reaction Motors XLR11-RM-5 four-chamber rocket engines mounted one over the other on a single tubular steel mounting frame attached to the airplane at three points. The upper engine was canted in a slightly nose-down attitude and the lower engine was mounted in a slightly nose-up attitude so that their thrust vector intersected at the airplane center-of-gravity. Each engine had a rated sea level static thrust of 5,900 lbf, providing a total of 11,800 lbf. The XLR11s were numbered "1" on top and "2" on bottom. The fuel pump was on the right side and the oxygen pump was

An excellent photo showing the XLR11 installation on 2 December 1960. The engines used on the X-15 program had been built up mostly from parts left over from previous research airplanes, although some components were procured as necessary. Each engine had four thrust chambers; the fifth hole (in the lower left corner of each engine) was the turbopump exhaust. The tubular frame that the engines were mounted in shows up well. The XLR11s protruded further aft than the XLR99 and required an extended aft fuselage to cover them (removed in this photo). Note the corrugations on the back of the fuselage tunnels and inside the upper and lower speed brakes. The lower speed brake shows the single actuator and its linkage to both side panels; the upper speed brake was identical. The ventral rudder is not installed here; it never was when the airplane was on the ground except for special tests. (NASA Dryden)

on the left. The thrust chambers were numbered 1 through 4 in a clockwise direction as viewed from the rear, beginning at the top.[15]

The basic XLR11 configuration consisted of four individual thrust chambers producing 1,475-lbf each with a turbopump unit, valves, regulators, and controls mounted forward of the chambers. Propellants were liquid oxygen and ethyl alcohol-water, supplied under pressure by a turbopump. Each thrust chamber contained an igniter, and the chambers could be ignited, shut down, or reignited individually in any sequence. Normally, it took about 2 seconds to ignite an individual chamber; therefore, approximately 8 seconds were required for a four-chamber engine start (all eight chambers could also be started in eight seconds since they were two separate engines). Ten seconds after a four chamber start, two chambers could be turned off and on again; however, if all four chambers were turned off, a minimum of 20 seconds had to be allowed to cool the engine prior to attempting a restart. Fuel was circulated through coolant passages in each exhaust nozzle and around each combustion chamber individually for cooling before being injected into the firing chambers.[16]

Each XLR11 weighed 345 pounds dry (including turbopump) and was approximately 60 inches long, 36 inches high, and 24 inches wide. The XLR11 turbopumps were powered by hydrogen peroxide monopropellant from the same 77.5-gallon tank that would later be used for the XLR99, but only 41 gallons (450 pounds) were required for XLR11 flights. The engine compartment, pressurization system, and fire detection system were the same as the XLR99 systems. On paper, each engine cost about $80,000 including the turbopump, although all of the engines used in the X-15 program had been assembled on-site at Edwards from components left-over from earlier programs.[17]

Installing the XLR11s in the X-15 was surprisingly easy considering that the aircraft had not been designed to accept them. Part of this was due to the mounting technique used for the XLR99 where the engine was installed on a frame structure that was then bolted into the engine compartment of the aircraft. A new frame was required to mount the two XLR11 engines, but the structural interface to the aircraft remained constant. However, the XLR11 used ethyl alcohol-water fuel instead of the anhydrous ammonia used in the XLR99. This necessitated some modifications to the propellant system, but none of them were major – fortunately, both liquids were of a similar consistency and temperature. No conclusive documentation could be found that described the changes, but Scott Crossfield remembers that, "since the XLR11 engines were installed as two units including their own turbopumps, the X-15 needed only to supply the tank pressures to meet the pump inlet pressure requirement and the engines didn't know what airplane they were in. There were, of course, structural changes i.e.; engine mounting and I believe some ballast, but nothing very complex. That is a relative statement. The difference in mixture would make the ideal fuel/lox load different but I don't remember that was a significant problem."[18]

Charles Feltz remembers that there were no modifications to the propellant tanks themselves – they had already been built and sealed. It was determined that both the metal and the sealant were compatible with alcohol so there was no need to reopen the tanks. There were some minor changes to the plumbing and electrical systems to accommodate the new engines, along with cockpit modifications to provide the appropriate instrumentation and controls. But considering that the airplane had been designed with no intention of installing anything but the XLR99, the changes were of little consequence.[19]

An XLR11 engine package on 6 March 1961. Note the turbopumps at the far left. All of the rocket engines were maintained by the rocket engine shop run by the Air Force Flight Test Center, although there was support from Reaction Motors available as needed. (NASA Dryden)

X-15-1 on 18 December 1959. The hatch in the back of the ventral rudder contains the recovery parachute. The deployed landing skids show why the ventral had to be jettisoned prior to landing. (NASA Dryden)

An XLR11 (left) and XLR99 engine at the Air Force Flight Test Center Museum in July 2000. Given that the XLR99 generated almost ten times as much thrust as the earlier Reaction Motors engine, it is not all that much larger. Although it would not find another application, the XLR99 was a remarkable achievement in rocket engine development. Compare the size of the turbopump inlet (at the back left) and the overall area of the nozzle of each engine. (Tony Landis)

Each side of the Museum's XLR99. In the photo at left, the turbopump exhaust manifold shows its routing to the edge of the nozzle. At right, the turbopump liquid oxygen inlet is at the back of the engine. Most of the other tubing running to the nozzle are bleeds from the various pneumatic engine valves. (Tony Landis)

CHAPTER 11

XLR99 Engine

It is interesting to note that early in the proposal stage, North American determined that aerodynamic drag of the X-15 was not particularly important, largely due to the amount of excess thrust available from the XLR99.[20] Weight was considered a larger driver in the overall airplane design – only about 10 percent of the total engine thrust was necessary to overcome drag, and another 20 percent to overcome weight. The remaining 70 percent of engine thrust was available to accelerate the X-15.[21]

At the time of its design, the XLR99 was the largest man-rated rocket engine yet developed. Of course, this would soon change as the manned space program accelerated into high gear. The basic XLR99 could produced 50,000-lbf at sea level, 57,000-lbf at 45,000 feet, and 57,850-lbf at 100,000 feet. The amount of thrust varied somewhat between the engines because of manufacturing tolerances, and some engines reportedly produced over 61,000-lbf at altitude. The engine had a nominal specific impulse of 230-lbf-sec/lbm at sea level and 276-lbf-sec/lbm at 100,000 feet. The oxidizer-to-fuel ratio was 1.25:1, and the engine had a nominal chamber pressure of 600 psi. Initially, the engine could be infinitely throttled between 50 and 100 percent. In early 1962 the engines were cleared for operation at 30-percent thrust, but this caused some problems and the lower limit was subsequently raised to 42-percent. The duration of any given run was limited only by the supply of propellants. When it was all said and done, the engine had a dry weight of 915 pounds, including the turbopump. Reaction Motors estimated the mean time between overhaul (service life) at 1 hour or 100 starts. It was a remarkable piece of work.[22]

The XLR99 operating sequence was:[23]

1. While the NB-52 and X-15 were climbing to launch altitude, the precool cycle was started, passing liquid oxygen through the pumps and then overboard to bring the metal parts of the turbopump, lines, and valves down to cryogenic conditions. The final priming consisted of approximately 75 seconds at relatively high flow rates.
2. Immediately before drop, an engine "idle" cycle was initiated for 5 to 30 seconds and consisted of a thrust chamber purge cycle followed by pump run-up to 6,000 rpm and turning on the igniter. The pilot was able to monitor these functions during idle running and had a short period to determine that all was well before committing to flight.
3. After the X-15 was dropped, the main chamber firing was initiated by opening the main propellant valves. The engine was now under the direct control of the pilot and could be throttled up and down, shut down, or restarted at will.
4. Manual engine shut-down was accomplished by closing the pilot's throttle or by turning off the master switch. The engine responded by closing the main propellant valves and automatically applying a helium gas purge.
5. Engine restart could be initiated by a single switch or by opening the throttle. Purge gas was available for five restarts.
6. If the propellants were run to exhaustion ("burn-out"), shut down was accomplished automatically by the onset of cavitation in the appropriate pump.

Mechanically, the XLR99 was an exceptionally complex and sophisticated powerplant for its time. The thrust chamber, which had caused a great many problems during development, had a throat diameter of 8.64 inches and a nozzle diameter of 39.3 inches; the nozzle area ratio was 9.8:1.[24] The thrust chamber was regeneratively cooled by ammonia using a "two pass" arrangement where the coolant was passed down one tube and returned in the adjacent tube. The stainless steel tubes were furnace brazed in the chamber bundle; each tube had an outside diameter of 0.375 inch and a wall thickness of 0.033 inches. The interior surface of the chamber was coated to provide insulation and protection for the tubes from the 5,000°F flame. The initial coating was made up of a 0.005-inch thick Nichrome flame-sprayed undercoat with 0.010-inch of Rokide Z flame-sprayed zirconia as an insulating top coating. This coating

The XLR99 nozzle presented its share of problems over the years, mainly with the protective Rokide Z coating used inside the nozzle flaking off at high temperatures. Eventually the Rokide Z was replaced with a graduated Nichrome zirconia coating with a molybdenum primer. (NASA)

The XLR99 nozzle was regeneratively cooled by running ammonia through a series of small tubes built into the walls. (Gerald H. Balzer Collection)

There was a great deal to learn about the advanced technology in the XLR99, so Air Force and NASA personnel attended classes, usually taught by the Reaction Motors field engineers. This class was on 13 February 1962. Note the number of ashtrays on the table. (NASA Dryden)

tended to erode quickly on operational engines and the chambers were later changed to a graduated Nichrome zirconia coating with a molybdenum primer.[25]

The igniter, which was essentially a small rocket thrust chamber, provided two stages of combustion to assure dependable ignition with maximum safety. Three surface-gap spark plugs in the first stage ignited a mixture of gaseous oxygen and liquid anhydrous ammonia. The products of combustion were discharged through a throat into the second stage combustion cavity where they ignited the second stage flow. In the second stage igniter, the propellants were introduced into the combustion cavity through an impinging jet injector with the fuel flow being used to regeneratively cool the second stage chamber.

The turbopump was directly-driven by a turbine powered by decomposed hydrogen peroxide that spun a single shaft at approximately 13,000 rpm with an oxidizer pump at the far end and a fuel pump in the middle. The liquid propellants were fed from low-pressure tanks, and each pump generated nearly 1,500 horsepower with had an output pressure of approximately 1,200 psi. The combined oxidizer/fuel flow rate at maximum thrust was 13,000 pounds per minute, exhausting the basic X-15's 18,000-pound propellant supply in about 85 seconds. The ammonia had in input temperature between –50 and –28°F; the liquid oxygen was much colder, at –316 to –275°F. The 90-percent hydrogen peroxide monopropellant was between 50 and 120°F.[26]

The thrust level of the engine was controlled by altering the speed of the turbopump, thereby affecting the flow of propellants to the thrust chamber. The speed of the turbopump was changed by opening or closing a valve upstream of the catalytic bed; hydrogen peroxide passed over this bed and was turned to 1,360°F steam to drive the turbopump. Since the fuel and oxidizer pumps were directly connected to the turbopump output shaft, they turned at a constant ratio to each other, ensuring that the thrust chamber always received the proper ratio of propellants. Chamber pressure changes lagged the throttle position changes by 0.2 to 0.6 seconds; since rapid throttle response was not required by the research mission this was considered acceptable.[27]

Some documentation indicates that the XLR99 was redesignated YLR99 on 29 December 1961, although nothing appears to have changed on the engines themselves. The original source documentation from the period is very inconsistent in its use of XLR99 or YLR99.[28]

AUXILIARY POWER UNITS (APU)

Although called "auxiliary," in reality the two General Electric APUs provided all hydraulic and electrical power for the X-15. Each of the 40-horsepower APUs was powered by decomposed hydrogen peroxide and drove a hydraulic pump and an electrical generator.

The APUs were located side-by-side in a compartment just ahead of the liquid oxygen tank in the forward fuselage. Propellant for each APU was provided by an independent feed system, using helium pressure to move the monopropellant. Each APU operated completely independently from the other, and generally furnished roughly half the power required by the airplane. If one unit failed, the other provided sufficient power to critical components for limited flight.[29]

Each APU was started and stopped via a switch in the cockpit. When an APU was turned on, a solenoid-type shutoff valve allowed hydrogen peroxide to flow into the unit after being routed through the gear case as a coolant. After leaving the gear case, the monopropellant moved through a flow control valve that was the throttle for the APU. The normal operating speed of the APU was 51,200 rpm; any turbine speed greater than 56,000 rpm was automatically detected and the APU shutdown. From the flow control valve the hydrogen peroxide passed over a series of silver and stainless steel screens that decomposed the hydrogen peroxide into superheated steam. The steam entered the turbine housing through five nozzles directed at the turbine wheel. The turbine, acting through a reduction gear, transmitted power to the generator and hydraulic pump.[30]

ELECTRICAL POWER SYSTEM

The airplane was equipped with alternating current (ac) and direct current (dc) power systems. Power for the ac system was supplied by a 200/115-volt, 400-cycle, three-phase generator attached to each APU. The 28-volt dc system was normally powered from the ac system via two transformer-rectifiers, but could also be powered by a 24-volt emergency battery. Originally, the battery was unique to the X-15, but late in the flight program it was discovered that the batteries used in F-104s were the same size, provided slightly more power, and were more readily available. During ground operations both ac and dc power could be supplied from the ground via a receptacle on the upper surface of the fuselage just aft of the canopy. During captive flight all power was supplied by the carrier aircraft since the APUs did not carry sufficient propellant for the trip to the launch lake.[31]

HYDRAULIC SYSTEM

The X-15 was equipped with two completely independent, airless, modified Type III, 3,000-psi systems operating in parallel plus an emergency system; there was no utility system. The No. 1 and No. 2 systems were independent but operated simultaneously to supply hydraulic pressure to all necessary systems. Fluid was supplied to each hydraulic system from a reservoir, and pressure was maintained by a variable high-displacement pump and a constant low-displacement pump attached to each APU. The hydraulic systems provided power for operating the aerodynamic flight controls (rudders and stabilators), speed brakes, wing flaps, and ball nose. Dual tandem actuators were used such that failure or shutdown of one hydraulic system would still permit the other hydraulic system to operate the controls. Each hydraulic actuator was capable of holding half the maximum design hinge moment during single-system operation; this was deemed adequate for controlling the airplane. The SAS pitch-roll servo cylinders were powered by the No. 2 hydraulic system while the SAS yaw servo (installed late in the flight program) was operated by the No. 1 system. In case of a failure of the No. 2 system, an emergency hydraulic system could provide power to the SAS pitch-roll servos. The emergency system consisted of a fixed-displacement 3,000-psi pump driven by a hydraulic motor powered by the No. 1 hydraulic system. In this way the hydraulic systems were completely separate, not sharing any fluid and avoiding the possibility of losing fluid from the No. 1 hydraulic system if there was a leak somewhere in the SAS.[32]

Total fluid per system was 1.3 gallons, and each reservoir held 0.8 gallon. The maximum flow rate of the system was 16 gallons per minute; however, 90-95 percent of the time the flow rate was less than 1.5 gallons per minute. This led to an innovative "piggyback" pump arrangement. An E-14101-A pump provided a fixed flow output of 1.6 gallons per minute to cover the normal usage. A special

3913-type variable-volume pump was provided to handle the surge requirement up to 16 gallons per minute. Check valves automatically unloaded the large pump according to system demands. This piggyback arrangement was found to require less power from the APU, and also introduced less heat into the hydraulic fluid during normal operation. The unit was developed and manufactured by the Vickers Division of Sperry Rand Corporation.[33]

The temperature profile for the hydraulic system had it being maintained at –20°F while on the ground, rising to 0°F during climb and cruise-out, and reaching 50 degrees at launch. A maximum of approximately 400°F would be attained during the 8 minutes of free flight on a high-speed mission. In addition, there would be 22 minutes of heat-soak after landing. For 15 flights the hydraulic fluid would spend about 7.5 hours at or near 400°F.[34]

Five hydraulic fluids considered most likely to meet the X-15 requirements were evaluated by North American: MIL-O-5606 (standard Air Force hydraulic fluid), General Electric F-50, Monsanto OS-45-1, Oronite 8200, and Oronite 8515. The viscosity at 400°F was considered very critical since if it became too low major leaks could develop in the valves and seals, and pump output pressure would drop. Other things such as the lubricant value, thermal stability, and compatibility with sealing materials were also considered. In the end, Oronite 8515 was chosen, although Oronite 8200 possessed most of the same properties. The 8200 fluid was finally eliminated because it was not as compatible with the Neoprene WRT seals being used in most of the X-15 components.[35]

FLIGHT CONTROL SYSTEMS

The X-15 was equipped with two separate flight control systems. The aerodynamic flight controls consisted of an upper and lower rudder and a "rolling tail" (differentially-operated all-moving horizontal stabilizers) that provided maneuvering within the atmosphere. The ballistic control system used hydrogen peroxide thrusters to provide attitude control during flight above the sensible atmosphere.

The aerodynamic controls were considered effective up to about 150,000 feet, although the X-15-3 automatically began blending in the ballistic control system thrusters above 90,000 feet. Many X-15 pilots manually used the ballistic control system in addition to the aerodynamic controls above 100,000 feet. Neil Armstrong commented that "a rule of thumb is that when dynamic pressure on control surfaces reduces to 50 psf, there should be a switchover from aerodynamic to reaction control."[36]

Aerodynamic Flight Control System

The aerodynamic flight control system consisted of hydraulically-actuated yaw and pitch-roll control surfaces. Yaw control was provided by movable dorsal and ventral rudders; left and right horizontal stabilizers provided pitch and roll control. The irreversible characteristics of the hydraulic system held the control surfaces against any forces that did not originate from pilot control movement and prevented these forces from being transmitted back to the pilot controls. Thus, aerodynamic loads of any kind could not reach the pilot through the controls. An artificial feel system was built into the control system to provide some feedback to the pilot. Assistance in aerodynamic damping in pitch, roll, and yaw was provided by a stability augmentation system.[37]

Templac temperature-sensitive paint has been applied to the rudder for Flight 1-11-21. The paint turned various colors depending upon the maximum temperature it experienced. The photo at left shows the virgin paint; at right is the paint after being exposed to Mach 3.13 during the flight. Note the outlines of the internal structure, which absorbed more heat than the skin. (NASA Dryden)

Damaged ventral rudder from Flight 2-13-26, complete with its attached parachute. No record could be found how many rudders were built, or how many survived the program. (NASA Dryden)

Remarkably few photos exist of the sharp leading-edge dorsal rudder that was flown on 42 of the 65 flights of X-15-3. Note that the leading edge is extended forward compared to the fixed portion of the stabilizer. This photo shows the results of the Detecto Temp paint applied for Flight 3-53-79. (NASA Dryden)

Horizontal Stabilizer (Roll-Pitch Control)

The horizontal stabilizer consisted of two all-moving, one-piece surfaces that could be moved simultaneously, differentially, or in compound. Aerodynamic control in pitch was obtained by simultaneous displacement of both stabilizers; roll control was by differential displacement of the surfaces. Combined pitch-roll control was through compound movement of the surfaces. A series of mixer bell cranks summed the pilot control and SAS inputs to the two stabilizer actuator valves to obtain the desired displacements.[38]

The stabilizers were constructed as left and right-hand units and were not interchangeable. Each consisted of a main bending member (the main spar), two torque boxes formed by the Inconel X skin and the three spars, ribs for torsional stability, a torque-collecting rib at the root, and a segmented leading edge. The main spar was made from Inconel X and was located at the 57-percent chord line. An A-286 front spar was located just aft of the leading edge and the trailing edge beam was constructed of titanium. The transverse ribs were made of 8Mn titanium alloy aft of the main spar and Inconel X ahead of it. The leading edge was divided into 16-inch spanwise segments to reduce thermal expansion effects from stagnation-point temperatures. Each leading edge segment had a welded-in heat-sink mass of Inconel X.[39]

Vertical Stabilizers (Yaw Control)

The vertical stabilizers extended above and below the fuselage and had a 10-degree wedge shape cross-section for increased hypersonic stability. Each portion consisted of a fixed structure next to the fuselage and a movable section that acted as a rudder. The fixed parts were a mixture of Inconel X and titanium structure with Inconel X skins. The all-moving rudders were made entirely of Inconel X with a spindle support using two bearings spaced 18-inches apart.[40]

The two rudders were linked together and actuated simultaneously. Pilot pedal displacement and SAS yaw input were transmitted by mechanical linkage and cables to the synchronized dorsal and ventral rudder control valves. During the flight program it was decided that the lower rudder actually contributed to instability at high angles of attack and it was decided to fly without it. In all, the program would make 73 flights with the ventral on and 126 with it off.[41]

When installed, the ventral rudder had to be jettisoned prior to landing since it was lower than the rear skids were long. Four explosive bolts and a piston containing an explosive charge were electronically fired when the pilot depressed the jettison button. If this was not accomplished, or if it failed, a mechanical system would jettison the ventral automatically when the main skids were lowered. For either method to work, however, the ventral arming switch had to be turned on. After release a parachute lowered the rudder to the ground where it was recovered, refurbished, and reused.[42]

Center Stick

The center stick was designed for use during periods of normal accelerations. Pilot pitch and roll inputs to the center stick were summed by the mixer bell cranks and applied to the horizontal stabilizer actuator valves. A microphone button and alternate pitch trim switch were located on the grip. In reality, pilots used the center stick and right side-stick interchangeably based on individual preference.[43]

Right Side-Stick Controller

The side-stick controller on the right console (also called the console stick) enabled the pilot to control the airplane during periods of high longitudinal and vertical accelerations. The stick had a full range of surface control in pitch and roll and was coupled to the center stick linkage through separate pitch and roll hydraulic boost actuators to reduce pilot control forces and to synchronize displacement of the two sticks. The console stick had a microphone button and a pitch trim knob that was graduated in degrees between +3 and −25 degree stabilizer leading edge travel.[44]

Rudder Pedals

Conventional adjustable rudder pedals were mechanically linked to the yaw system mixer bell cranks. Pedal movement and SAS inputs were summed by a mixer bell crank, which in turn transmitted the summed signal mechanically to the stabilizer actuator control valves. Since the X-15 did not have brakes, there were no toe brakes fitted to the rudder pedals.[45]

Stability Augmentation System (SAS)

The first two airplanes were equipped with a Westinghouse SAS that provided damping inputs to the aerodynamic flight control system about all three axes; the MH-96 performed a similar function in the X-15-3. The SAS had three semi-independent channels, each consisting of a working circuit, a monitor circuit, and a malfunction detector. Each working circuit received commands from the gyro assembly in its particular axis and commanded the associated servo cylinder. The monitor circuits received identical commands from the gyro and passed them to the malfunction detector, which compared the monitor circuit command with the actual displacement of the servo cylinder. If a predetermined error limit was exceeded, the malfunction detector disabled the circuit in question, effectively eliminating the ability of the SAS to use that control surface.[46]

The working circuit command to the servo cylinder was an electrical signal that drove an electrohydraulic transfer valve on each servo cylinder. The transfer valve controlled hydraulic pressure on each side of the servo cylinder piston. The pitch-roll servo cylinders, powered by the No. 2 hydraulic system, were mechanically linked to the horizontal stabilizer control linkages by mixer bell cranks. The loss of the No. 2 hydraulic system would automatically engage the emergency hydraulic system. Should an abrupt loss of the No. 2 system pressure occur, the pitch and roll damping channels could trip offline, and the pilot had to manually reset them.[47]

The yaw servo cylinder was powered by the No. 1 hydraulic system and was mechanically linked to the vertical stabilizer linkage through a mixer bell crank. An interaction of the yaw and roll damping working surfaces (called "yar") was provided whereby signals from the yaw axis of the gyro were fed to the roll circuit to augment roll damping.[48]

The pilot controls for the SAS changed over the years. Initially, each axis had a function switch with two positions: STDBY and ENGAGE. In the standby mode the channel was functioning, but the input signals to the servo cylinder control valves and hydraulic pressure to the servo cylinders were shut off. There was also a "yar" function switch that allowed the pilot to disengage the cross-coupling function. Each axis

had a gain selector rotary knob that controlled the ratio of the damping signal to the servo cylinder displacement. There were ten positions (0 through 10) on each rotary knob, although position 3 was considered LO and 9 was considered HI. While the rotary knobs were installed, the pilots referred to damper settings such as 4-4-4, describing the knob position for pitch, roll, and yaw, respectively.[49]

After the alternate stability augmentation system was installed during 1962, the controls changed. The rotary knobs were deleted, and the switches for each channel were modified to have STDBY, LO-GAIN and HI-GAIN positions. The latter two positions corresponded roughly to the old 3 and 9 positions, but could be tweaked on the ground before flight based on flight profile and pilot preferences.[50]

Early in the flight program it was determined from an analysis of landing gear loads data that the SAS was causing increased landing loads, contributing to several landing gear failures. A LAND SAS DISENGAGE switch was added to the left console that armed a relay that automatically disabled the SAS after the main skids touched down.[51]

Alternate Stability Augmentation System (ASAS)

The ASAS provided pitch-roll damping inputs in the event of a failure of the primary SAS roll channel in X-15-1 and X-15-2; the MH-96 essentially performed the function in X-15-3. When the ASAS was armed, a failure of the roll channel in the SAS would automatically energize the ASAS. The change-over to the ASAS did not affect the yaw channel of the SAS, which continued to function in the normal manner. The ASAS consisted of a working circuit only and did not have selectable gains.

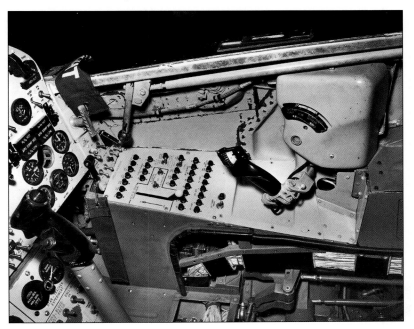

The X-15 was among the first aircraft to use a side-stick controller. Unlike the F-16 and the current generation of fighters, the controller was mechanically linked to the center stick, causing some grief for the pilots since this compromised its feel and operation somewhat. Still, it was an admirable first step. This is the X-15A-2 on 30 December 1964. (NASA Dryden)

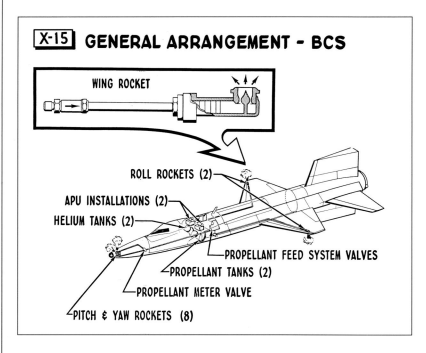

X-15 GENERAL ARRANGEMENT - BCS

WING ROCKET

ROLL ROCKETS (2)
APU INSTALLATIONS (2)
HELIUM TANKS (2)
PROPELLANT FEED SYSTEM VALVES
PROPELLANT TANKS (2)
PROPELLANT METER VALVE
PITCH & YAW ROCKETS (8)

The X-15 was the first aircraft that actually needed a ballistic control system. The BCS was not installed on many early flights because of development problems, and was deleted from the X-15A-2 for the later speed missions as unnecessary at the comparatively low altitudes flown. (Gerald H. Balzer Collection)

The ASAS was installed in X-15-1 and X-15-2 during April 1962. The ASAS in X-15A-2 was modified in early 1967 to include the yaw axis to provide an extra margin of safety at Mach numbers above 6; the same change was subsequently made to X-15-1 as a matter of commonality.[52]

Ballistic Control System (BCS)

The Bell Aircraft-developed BCS was used to control attitude at altitudes where the aerodynamic control surfaces were ineffective.[53] The BCS was always used whenever the dynamic pressure was below 25 psf (approximately 180,000 feet and above) although many pilots began using it as low as 100,000 feet (approximately 50 psf). At 25 psf the effectiveness of the ballistic controls approximated the effectiveness of the aerodynamic controls. It should be noted that the system could only control attitude, it did not have sufficient power to alter the course of the airplane. The BCS was operated by a side-stick controller located above the left console. This controller fired the thrusters to move the nose of the airplane in the same direction as the controller was being moved; moving the controller to the right moved the airplane nose to the right, etc. On the X-15-3 the system was blended automatically into the normal control stick by the MH-96, although the left side-stick remained for manual control.

Two independent systems normally operated simultaneously using a hydrogen peroxide monopropellant that was decomposed into superheated steam by passing over a silver screen. The steam was released through small thrusters in the nose and wingtips, causing the airplane to react in the opposite direction. The monopropellant was contained in the same storage tanks that supplied the APUs. The No. 1 ballistic system was supplied from the No. 1 APU tank; the No. 2 ballistic system was supplied from the No. 2 APU tank. During late 1961 it was decided that it should be possible to transfer residual turbopump monopropellant to the APU tanks after engine shutdown and a transfer system was subsequently installed in all three airplanes. The monopropellant transfer was initiated by the pilot via a switch on the upper right side of the instrument panel.[54]

There were eight 113-lbf thrusters located in the nose, two pointed in each of the major directions, plus two 40-lbf thrusters in each wingtip (one up and one down). The No. 1 system operated four thrusters in the nose (one in each direction) and the two left wing thrusters; the No. 2 system operated the other four nose thrusters and the two right wing thrusters. Each of the nozzles used a 1.40-inch diameter hole in the skin. The maximum propellant flow was 0.06-gallon per second for the pitch thrusters and 0.02-gallon per second for the roll thrusters. A typical high-altitude mission consumed about 2 gallons of hydrogen peroxide.[55]

With both systems operating, a nose-down command from the pilot caused the operation of the two thrusters in the top of the nose (one of which was controlled by each system). A nose-right command caused the operation of the two thrusters on the left side of the nose (again, one from each system). A right roll command caused the operation of the thruster in the bottom of the left wing (No. 1 system) and the top of the right wing (No. 2 system).[56]

The ballistic control system was removed from the X-15A-2 very late in the flight program since the airplane was no longer intended to go to altitudes that required reaction controls.

Left Side-Stick Controller

The ballistic side-stick controller was located above the left console. Yaw was obtained by direct left or right movement of the stick; roll was obtained by rotating the stick, and pitch was obtained by moving the stick up or down (airplane nose-up was obtained by raising the stick). As Isaac Newton said, any object in motion tends to remain in motion, and this was true of the X-15 above the atmosphere. Before the RAS was installed, once a pilot had commanded a change in attitude, he had to command an opposite change as he approached the desired condition, else the airplane would continue to rotate about its axis.[57]

Reaction Augmentation System (RAS)

There was debate during the development of the X-15 as to whether the ballistic control system needed dampers or not; as built, the airplane did not have them. However, it was quickly realized that such a system would be useful and the RAS was installed in the X-15-1 and X-15-2 during 1963; the MH-96 took care of the function in X-15-3.

The purpose of the RAS was to provide "rate damping to aid airplane control and minimize pilot over-control when the ballistic control system is used." The RAS used the No. 1 ballistic control system thrusters. Whenever the ballistic side-stick controller was in the neutral position, the RAS rate gyro sensed the angular rate about the three axes and at a preset angular rate automatically fired the proper No. 1 thruster to reduced the sensed angular acceleration. In simpler terms, after the pilot commanded the BCS to fire, the RAS began firing the opposite thrusters in a series of small bursts such that, if the pilot did not do anything further, would eventually stop the movement of the airplane. The pilot, however, normally had to provide a small input in order to stop the airplane exactly where he wanted it. The RAS automatically disengaged once a preset level of normal acceleration was sensed, indicating that the aerodynamic controls had become effective. Augmentation on any or all of the three axes could be selected by the pilot as desired.[58]

WING FLAPS

Simple two-position flaps were located on the inboard trailing edge of each wing. The flaps were of conventional titanium rib-type construction with Inconel X skins and front spar. To prevent panel flutter that had been detected during wind tunnel tests, the outer skin was reinforced with a corrugated Inconel X inner skin. Flap position was controlled by an electromechanical actuator containing two electric motors that were coupled together by a set of differential gears. The output of this actuator drove a push-pull cable system that opened the valves in the dual, tandem hydraulic flap actuators and positioned the flaps either full-up or full-down. Flap extension was possible even if one motor failed, although it took roughly twice as long. Normal extension from full-up to full-down required 8-10 seconds. No provisions were made for automatic pitch correction to compensate for flap deployment, and no capability existed for intermediate extension of the flaps. However, because of the use of hydraulic relief valves to limit the maximum air loads on the surfaces, the flaps could partially close at speeds above 250 knots. No flap position indicator was provided in the cockpit, the pilot relying primarily on feel and chase pilot callouts.[59]

Large speed brakes were installed on the aft portion of the fixed upper and lower vertical stabilizers. Each pair was actuated by a single hydraulic cylinder. This was Flight 1-23-39 on 4 October 1961. (NASA Dryden)

SPEED BRAKES

The airplane had two sets of speed brakes on the fixed portions of the upper and lower vertical stabilizers. Each set of brakes consisted of two symmetrical panels, hinged at the forward end and operated by a dual, tandem hydraulic actuator. One segment of each actuator was powered by the No. 1 hydraulic system, the other segment from the No. 2 system. Failure of a single hydraulic system still allowed the speed brakes to be used, albeit at a reduced rate under any particular air load. The speed brakes could be positioned at any position from full-open to full-closed. When fully deployed, the speed brakes formed an included angle of 35 degrees. The speed brakes used outer skins reinforced by a corrugated inner skin and ribs, all made of Inconel X.[60]

Two speed brake handles were provided in the cockpit on the left console. The inboard handle controlled the lower speed brake while the outboard handle controlled the upper speed brake. The handles were normally locked together by an interconnecting bolt to ensure symmetrical operation of the speed brakes, although at least one flight was flown with the bolt removed to test asymmetrical configurations. If the bolt was not installed, a spring-loaded lock lever on the inboard handle was designed to unlock the handles for independent speed brake operation and lock them for symmetrical operation. Speed brake position was indicated by a scale for each handle on the speed brake handle quadrant. The scales were calibrated in increments of 5 degrees.[61]

LAUNCH SYSTEM

The X-15 was attached to the NB-52 pylon by three hooks, one forward and two aft, equipped with primary hydraulic and secondary pneumatic release mechanisms. The primary hydraulic system consisted of a single hydraulic cylinder that caused a bell crank to rotate. The bell crank was connected to each of the three hooks and caused them to release simultaneously. The emergency pneumatic system actuated a secondary bell crank that was also connected to all three hooks. If the primary system failed to release the X-15, the NB-52 pilot could activate the pneumatic system.[62]

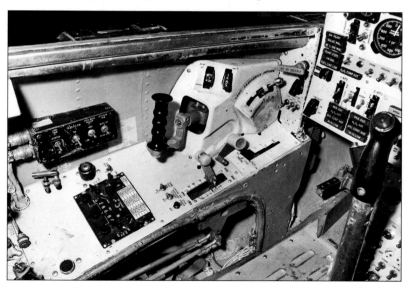

The final configuration of the X-15-1 left console, photographed on 31 January 1969, after the program ended. The black handle was the ballistic side-stick controller. Just below and to the right of it are the speed brake handles, with the XLR99 throttle ahead of them. The flaps were controlled by a toggle switch just ahead of the side-stick. Note the third skid switch just behind the speed brake handle, along with switches to disable the SAS after touchdown and to activate the stick pusher that was installed in late 1967. (NASA Dryden)

The main skids were a simple and effective landing gear, but ever-increasing landing weights led to a series of problems with them that eventually resulted in the installation of a third skin under the ventral stabilizer. (NASA Dryden)

A seldom seen modification that was installed on both X-15-1 and X-15-3 during early 1967 was the third skid under the ventral stabilizer. This is X-15-1 on 11 April 1967 showing the lower speed brakes open and the third skid deployed using two hydraulic cylinders. (NASA Dryden)

LANDING GEAR

The X-15 landing gear was somewhat unique, both in its approach and its simplicity. A dual nose wheel was used along with a pair of aft skids. The landing gear was designed for a 11,000-pound airplane with a sink rate of 9 fps touching down between 165 and 200 knots at an angle of attack of approximately 6 degrees. Unfortunately, the X-15 ended up weighing considerably more.

In order to save space, Charlie Feltz kept the nose gear strut almost fully compressed while stored in the wheel well; compressed nitrogen gas caused the strut to extend once it deployed. This caused some initial problems, however. Upon nose gear extension, the nitrogen gas that had been trapped by the oil under high pressure was released and produced a gas-oil foam within the cylinder. Approximately the first one-third of the cylinder stroke was rendered ineffective by this foam; consequently, the landing loads built up to excessive values during the remainder of the stroke. The internal mechanism of the strut was redesigned to incorporate a floating piston that kept the gas and oil separated at all times.[63]

Initially, cast magnesium wheels with aluminum rims were fitted with standard aircraft tires pressurized with 240-psi nitrogen. During 1966 the magnesium wheels were replaced on some flights by cast aluminum wheels that used new 12-ply 295-psi high-pressure tires. Both of these items were an attempt to increase the margin during touchdown at heavy landing weights. But the modification was not without problems. On 3 March 1967 while the X-15-1 was being prepared for flight the nose gear strut was found to be binding up when attempts were made to rotate or compress it during preflight checks. The gear was removed and sent to North American for inspection; it was found that the strut was bent, in a similar manner to an incident reported after Flight 1-64-107. No cause for that incident had been determined, and landing loads for both incidents were well within limits.[64]

Since X-15-3 had not experienced any nose gear deformation of this type a comparison of the two aircraft was made. The major difference was that the X-15-3 had been using up the remaining 10-ply tires while X-15-1 has been using the newer 12-ply high pressure tires. It was believed that the 12-ply tires, which had a slightly greater weight and inertia than the 10-ply, might be inducing excessively high drag loads during spin-up. Accordingly, the program decided that X-15-1 and X-15-3 would use only 10-ply tires, preferably mounted on the older (and lighter) magnesium wheels, instead of the 12 ply tires and high-pressure aluminum wheels. Because of its higher landing weights, the X-15A-2 would to use the stronger tires and aluminum wheels.[65]

The rear landing gear consisted of a 4130-steel skid and an Inconel X strut on each side of the aft fuselage. These were attached by trunnion fittings and bell cranks connected to shock struts inside the aft fuselage. The skids were free to move in pitch and roll, but were fixed in yaw for parallel alignment. Drag braces were attached to the fuselage ahead of the trunnion fittings and to the skids at the strut attachment pin and bungee springs were used to keep the skid in a nose-up position just before landing. The skids and struts were folded forward against the outside of the lower aft fuselage when retracted.[66]

An investigation was undertaken by North American during early 1965 to determine the modifications needed to increase the landing weight of the X-15-1 and X-15-3 to 16,000 pounds normal and 17,000 pounds emergency. The analysis included the use of the stick-kicker to rotate the horizontal stabilizer at landing to reduce main skid loads, although this would not eliminate the need to modify the skids for the higher weights. Preliminary studies showed that landing loads could be reduced appreciable by relocating the nose gear trunnion (as done on the X-15A-2) on the other two airplanes, even without the addition of a stick-kicker. An alternate study was conducted to determine the feasibility of incorporating a third main skid attached to the fixed portion of the ventral stabilizer.

This skid could redistribute the landing loads and relive the critically-stressed gear components, particularly if either the stick-kicker of the landing flaps failed to operate. The third skid was installed on the X-15-3 for Flight 3-52-78 on 18 June 1966 and the X-15-1 was modified in time for Flight 1-71-121 on 22 March 1967. The use of the third skid was also considered to provide an additional measure of safety for the ramjet project, but the skid was never installed on the X-15-A-2.

A T-type landing gear handle was located on the instrument panel left wing. The handle was linked via cables to the main gear uplocks and the nose gear and nose gear door uplocks. When the handle was pulled straight aft approximately 11 inches the uplocks were released, the spring-loaded scoop door in the nose gear door swung downward into the airstream, and the nose gear initiator fired. The initiator also actuated a piston that forced the nose gear door open under flight attitudes where air loads tended to hold the door closed. Gravity and air loads case the main gear to extend and lock. Air loads on the nose gear scoop door forced the nose gear down and locked. When the main gear was released, a switch on the left main gear activated an explosive charge, causing the ventral to jettison, provided the ventral arming switch was in the ARM position. None of the landing gear could be retracted by the pilot, and retraction was accomplished manually by ground personnel prior to launch. No gear-down indication was provided in the cockpit.[67]

Early in the program there were several instances where hot boundary-layer air seeped into the nose gear well, causing minor damage to tubing and structure. After Flight 1-23-39 a seal was added around the nose gear door to prevent reoccurrence of the problem.[68]

BALL NOSE

Traditional vane-type sensors to measure angle of attack (α) and sideslip (β) were considered inappropriate for the X-15 since they could not survive the temperatures during the high speed flights, and were mostly ineffective at the low pressures encountered on the altitude flights. Instead, a new type of attitude sensing device was developed. A contract was awarded to the Nortronics Division of Northrop Aircraft Corporation for the detailed deign and construction of a prototype and five production ball nose units based on a conceptual design developed by the NACA.[69]

The high-temperature flow-direction sensor was about 16.75 inches long and a base diameter of 13.75 inches. The total weight of the ball nose was 78 pounds, of which half was made up by the thick Inconel X outer skins (lip, cone, and sphere). Thirteen chromel-alumel thermocouples were located within the sphere to measure skin temperature, and 5 other thermocouples measured selected internal temperatures. Expanded nitrogen from the aircraft supply was used to cool the sensor. The ball nose was physically interchangeable with the standard NACA boom nose and all connections to the sensor were made through couplings that automatically engaged when the ball nose (or boom) was mounted to the airplane.[70]

If you need to test something at extreme temperatures, and have access to a jet engine ... this is the first ball nose being tested in the exhaust of a North American F-100 Super Sabre on 20 January 1959. (NASA Dryden)

The core of the ball nose consisted of a 6.5 inch diameter Inconel X sphere with two pairs of 0.188-inch diameter orifices, each 42 degrees from the stagnation point; one pair in the vertical plane (α orifices) and the other pair in the horizontal plane (β orifices). A 0.5-inch diameter orifice located at the sphere stagnation point provided a total pressure source for the aircraft. Two functionally identical hydraulic servo systems were used to rotate the sphere about the α and β axes; the hydraulics were powered by the normal X-15 systems. The servos drove the sphere to a position such that the impact pressures seen by all sensing orifices were equal. When this condition existed the sphere was oriented directly into the relative wind. Two synchro transducers were used to detect the position of the sphere with respect to the airframe, and this signal was fed to the various instruments in the cockpit and also to the recorders and telemetry system. Since the dynamic pressure during flight could vary between 1 psf and 2,500 psf, some

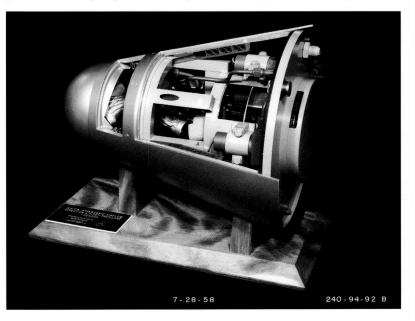

A Nortronics model of the NACA Hypersonic Airflow Direction & Pitot-Pressure Sensor, better known as the ball nose. An ingenious solution to the problem of high temperatures and extreme dynamic pressures, the ball nose worked remarkably well given the technology of the era. (The Boeing Company Archives)

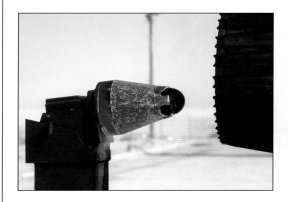

The X-15A-2 was going to go faster, and the ball nose was going to get hotter, so NASA had Rohr Industries manufacture a ball nose using a TAZ-8A cermet sphere. How to test it; get a hotter jet engine. On 22 May 1964 the new sensor was tested using a General Electric J79 from an F-104. (NASA Dryden)

The retractable (left) and fixed pitot tubes on the X-15A-2 in the Air Force Museum. When the ablator was applied, the fixed pitot was removed (Jay Miller)

serious gain adjustment was required in the servo loop to maintain stability and accuracy, The ball nose could sense angles of attack from –10 degrees to +40 degrees; the angle of sideslip range was ±20 degrees. The unit was capable of continuous operation at a skin temperature of 1,200°F. The angular accuracy of the sensor was established to be within ±0.25 degree for dynamic pressures above 10 psf.[71]

In early 1960 the FRC developed a simple technique for thermal testing the newly-delivered ball noses; expose them to the afterburner exhaust from a North American F-100 Super Sabre. This seemed to work well until one of the noses suffered a warped forward lip during testing. It was subsequently discovered that the engine was "operated longer than necessary" and had resulted in temperatures in excess of 2,400°F instead of the expected 1,900°F.[72]

A modified ball nose was manufactured for the X-15A-2 to handle the additional heat generated at Mach 8. A new sphere, manufactured from a TAZ-8A cermet developed at Lewis, was man-

ufactured by the Rohr Corporation and was delivered in mid-1966, but did not initially pass its qualification test due to a faulty weld around one of the pressure ports. The sphere was returned to the vendor where it was repaired. Interestingly, the FRC tested this new ball (and the forward lip of the cone, which was also manufactured from TAZ-8A) in much the same way as the original ball noses were qualified – this time in the afterburner exhaust of a General Electric J79 engine. The new ball nose was installed on the X-15A-2 to support Flight 2-52-96 on 21 August 1967.[73]

PITOT-STATIC SYSTEM

A total-head tube (also called the alternate probe) was installed ahead of the canopy to provide total pressure during subsonic flight. Static pressure ports were located on each side of the forward fuselage one inch above the aircraft waterline at station 50.[74]

A different pitot-static system was required for the X-15A-2 since the normal static locations were covered with MA-25S. A vented compartment behind the canopy was chosen as the static source and was found to be suitable during flight tests on X-15-1. The standard dog-leg pitot tube ahead of the canopy was replaced by an extendable pitot since the temperatures expected at Mach 8 exceeded the standard tube's limits. The retractable tube remained within the fuselage until the aircraft decelerated below Mach 2 when the pilot actuated a release mechanism and the tube extended into the airstream. This was very similar in concept to the system eventually installed on the Space Shuttle orbiters.[75]

STABLE PLATFORM

Early on, it was realized that the performance of the X-15 would necessitate a new means of determining altitude, speed, and aircraft attitude. The NACA had proposed a "stable platform" as a means of meeting these needs, something echoed in each of the original airframe proposals. This was a forerunner of much-later inertial navigation systems, and was amongst the first of its type to be designed and produced. Miscommunication between the Air Force and the NACA meant the project got off to a slow start, and

NASA FLOW DIRECTION SENSOR

HYDRAULIC FLOW
POWER IN
INFORMATION OUT
"Q" COMPENSATOR PRESSURE TRANSDUCER
α Δ P PRESSURE TRANSDUCER
β Δ P PRESSURE TRANSDUCER
"Q" COMPENSATOR SERVO UNIT
DIFFERENTIAL PRESSURE PORTS
RELATIVE WIND "Q"
BETA SERVO
PORTED SPHERE ASSEMBLY
ALPHA SERVO
PORTED POWER
RADIATION SHIELD
LN₂ VALVE
COLD WALL
CONE INSULATION
LN₂ FLOW
TOTAL PRESSURE
LN₂ FLOW TO RECORDER

ZONE ONE SPHERE | ZONE TWO COLLAR | ZONE THREE AFTER CONE

The ball nose required cooling nitrogen and hydraulic power from the X-15 in order to operate. (NASA Dryden)

problems finding a suitable vendor and getting a contract approved delayed things even more. Fortunately, the stable platform was not necessary for the initial low-speed flights.[76]

The Sperry Gyroscope Company stable platform was basically an Earth-slaved, Schuler-tuned system aligned in azimuth to a guidance vector that was coincident with centerline of the X-15. Attitudes, velocities, and height were provided to the pilot with reference to this coordinate system. The stable platform weighed approximately 165 pounds, occupied about 3 cubic feet of volume, and required a peak electrical load of 600 Watts. An analog computer was used for computing velocity and position data and applying the necessary acceleration corrections. The stable platform was cooled using nitrogen gas to counteract both the heat generated by the units, and also heat input from external temperatures. The system was "designed to operate over a limited portion of the Earth's surface" and could accept a launch point anywhere within a 275-mile wide corridor extending 620 miles uprange and 205 miles downrange from Edwards AFB.[77]

Several compromises were made during the development of the X-15 stable platform. Designers knew that within 300 seconds after launch (i.e., as the airplane decelerated to land), air data instruments would be adequate for vehicle height and velocity information. It was decided that providing a system capable of operation from carrier aircraft takeoff to X-15 landing would be too heavy and bulky so the stable platform was aligned just before launch and provided 300 seconds of velocity and height data and 20 minutes of attitude data.[78]

As delivered, the stable platform could provide pitch angle (degrees), roll angle (degrees), yaw angle (degrees), altitude (feet), total velocity (fps), down-range velocity (fps), cross-range velocity (fps), and vertical velocity (fps). The initial operational experience with the stable platform showed that it had a fairly large error potential that grew as time passed from the initial alignment due to drift and integration noise. In retrospect, the performance specifications established in 1956 were well beyond the state of the art with respect to available gyros, accelerometers, transistors, and circuit techniques. Compared to modern laser-ring-gyro and GPS-augmented systems, the X-15 stable platform seems woefully inaccurate. Nevertheless, late in the program it routinely bettered its 70 fps error specification for velocities, but was sub-standard at reporting altitude, averaging about 2,200 feet (rms) uncertainty; the requirement was 2,000 feet. Reliability was also very poor when the system was first delivered, but by mid-1961 the overall reliability was approaching the high 90-percentile. Unfortunately, this reliability proved to be short-lived.[79]

Beginning in late 1963 the FRC began redesigning critical components of the stable platform in an attempt to improve both accuracy and reliability. Eventually, some 60 percent of the subassemblies were redesigned. The weight and volume of the accelerometers, accelerometer electronics, and power supplies were reduced over 50 percent with an accompanying reduction in power and cooling requirements. Although the initial performance was a little erratic, the overall improvement was substantial. For instance, 400 seconds into flight the original system would have a +8,000-foot error in altitude; the revised system generally had a –1,000-foot error. (In both cases, the specification required less than a –5,000-foot error; nothing on the positive side was considered truly satisfactory.) Eventually the erratic performance was tuned out of the system. By May 1966 essentially the entire Sperry system had been replaced by components designed at the FRC, and the system was redesigned the "FRC-66 Analog Inertial System."[80]

Although the Honeywell IFDS was considered an improvement over the modified Sperry stable platform, it was decided the FRC-66 offered the best chance of success for the Mach 8 flights in the X-15A-2. By the end of 1965 one of the Sperry computers was modified with Mach 8 scaling coefficients and this unit supported all X-15A-2 flights.[81]

INERTIAL FLIGHT DATA SYSTEM

After the cancellation of the Dyna-Soar program, it was decided to replace the X-15 stable platform with surplus Honeywell digital inertial guidance systems originally procured for the X-20. This inertial flight data system (IFDS) was even smaller and required less power and cooling than the redesigned FRC-66 analog system, and had been built to more stringent requirements based on the X-120 once-around (one orbit) reference mission. The X-20 IFDS could automatically erect itself and perform an alignment cycle on the ground while the NB-52 was taxiing, completely eliminating the need for information from the N-1 compass and APN-81 Doppler radar onboard the NB-52. To improve accuracy, however, the altitude loop was synched to the NB-52 pressure altimeter until 1 minute before launch.[82]

The inertial measurement unit was a gyrostabilized, four-gimbaled platform that maintained local vertical orientation throughout the flight. All computations were performed by the digital computer which was actually a dual-function unit consisting of a digital differential analyzer and a general-purpose computer. The digital system was first checked out in X-15-1 on 15 October 1964 (1-50-79) with satisfactory results. The installation in the X-15-3 was not as straightforward as it had been in X-15-1, primarily because of the interface to the MH-96 adaptive control system and Lear Siegler energy management systems. The integration with the energy management displays turned out to the hardest to resolve. The Honeywell IFDS was finally installed in X-15-3 during the weather down-period at the end of 1965.[83]

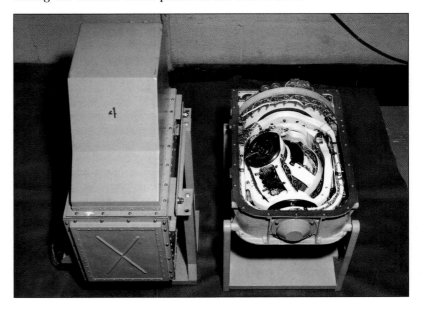

The X-15 stable platform was among the first inertial guidance systems ever developed for an airplane, and proved to be quite troublesome in service. Eventually NASA modified it into the improved FRC-66. (NASA Dryden)

Cockpit Instruments

Two separate cockpit instrument panels were supplied with each of the first two airplanes. These were tailored for either initial low-speed flights using the XLR11 engines and the nose-mounted flight test boom, or for hypersonic flights using the XLR99 engine and the ball nose. The instrument panels in the first two airplanes was significantly revised early in the flight program based on pilot comments that the original panel was difficult to scan under all flight conditions, especially in the MC-2 full-pressure suit.

As initially completed, the X-15-3 had an instrument panel essentially identical to the XLR99 panels manufactured for the first two airplanes. However, when the airplane was rebuilt following its XLR99 ground explosion, a decision was made to incorporate the Minneapolis-Honeywell MH-96 adaptive flight control system, and this necessitated a unique instrument panel. This panel was subsequently replaced late in the flight program with a set of high-tech displays developed by Lear-Siegler.

All of the instrument panels were in a constant state of flux as various switches and indicators were added to almost any available location in the cockpit to support the various experiments and data requirements for any given flight. Every attempt was made to keep the critical displays and switches in constant locations between the three airplanes (as much as possible given the radical difference in X-15-3), and at least twice the program created a "standard X-15" cockpit arrangement and brought the airplanes into compliance. This greatly eased the problems associated with keeping the simulator accurate and made life much easier for the pilots and flight planners.[84]

Attitude Indicator

The "8-ball" was, perhaps, the most critical instrument in the X-15 and occupied the center of the instrument panel. The attitude indicator derived its data from the stable platform (or IFDS). This was a pictorial-type instrument that combined displays of attitude and azimuth on a universally-mounted sphere displayed as the background for a miniature reference airplane that remained fixed relative to the cockpit. The sphere was remotely controlled by the stable platform and was free to rotate 360 degrees in pitch, roll, and azimuth. The miniature reference airplane was always in proper physical relationship to the simulated Earth, horizon, and sky areas of the background sphere.[85]

The horizon on the sphere was presented as a solid white line with an azimuth scale graduated in 5-degree markings from 0 through 360 degrees. Above the horizon line, the sky was indicated by a light-grey area; below the horizon line the Earth was indicated by a dull-black area. The sphere was marked by meridian lines spaced every 30 degrees. Pitch angle was referenced to the center dot on the fixed miniature airplane by horizontal marks spaced every 10 degrees on the meridians. A pitch adjustment knob on the lower right side of the instrument was used during the prelaunch checklist to set the proper pitch angle for the flight profile. Bank angles were read from a semi-circular bank scale on the lower quarter of the instrument.[86]

Two long horizontal pointers projected across the sphere. Movement of these pointers showed airplane displacement with respect to the air in which it was flying (small angles of attack and sideslip). The horizontal long pointer was a vernier indication of the angle-of-attack and moved upward when the angle of attack decreased and

This was the instrument panel in X-15-2 on 14 March 1961 for the initial flights with the XLR99. Note the "radio call" plate with the serial number at the upper left. By this time the stopwatch had been installed at the top-center of the panel, telling the pilot when to shutdown the engine. The "8-ball" attitude indicator is in the exact center of the panel, and the white lines differentiate the various functional areas (engines, flight control, etc.) of the panel. (NASA Dryden)

The first major revision to the panel included painting it a light grey instead of black (the side consoles also changed color). This is X-15-1 on 26 October 1963. The ASAS has been installed, and the SAS controls have been changed to toggle switches (just behind the center stick) instead of the rotary knobs used initially. The inertial velocity indicator goes to 7,000 fps, and the altimeter could display 999,999 feet, although the airplane could not achieve either. (NASA Dryden)

The original XLR11 instrument panel in X-15-1 on 8 February 1960. The original SAS controls are just behind the center stick, with a toggle switch and rotary knob for each axis. The XLR11 instruments are in the lower left corner, and the XLR11 "throttle" on the left console nearby. Note that the Mach meter only goes to 3.5 and the stopwatch has not been installed yet. It was not until the beginning of XLR99 flights that precise engine shutdowns became critical. (NASA Dryden)

downward when it increased. The vertical long pointer moved to the right to indicate a left sideslip and left to indicate a right sideslip. The range of either pointer movement was adjustable (on the ground) to operate within ±5 to ±10 degrees, depending on the flight profile and pilot preference.

One of the more controversial aspects of the attitude indicator was a second use for the cross-pointers, developed later in the program to assist in precise pointing of some experiments. In this mode the cross-pointers were used to display vernier attitude errors; pitch error was displayed on the alpha needle and bank error on the beta needle. A switch allowed the pilot to select which mode was displayed. Unfortunately this would directly contribute to the loss of the X-15-3; Adams had switched the instrument to the vernier mode, but when things started going wrong he resorted to flying the airplane as though the instrument was displaying the normal alpha/beta information.[87]

A turn-and-slip indication was on the lower portion of the instrument below the bank angle scale. Sideslip information could be displayed from either the ball nose or the stable platform; a selector switch on the instrument panel allowed the pilot to select DELTA PSI (or C BETA in X-15-1) for stable platform data or STANDBY (BETA in X-15-1) for ball nose data. This provided a backup mode in case of a failure of the ball nose, or for use during high altitude flights (above 250,000 feet) when the ball nose became erratic and responded to firings of the ballistic control system. In reality the ball nose mode was seldom used.[88]

A short horizontal pointer on the left side of the instrument was a vernier indication for the pitch axis of the sphere and moved in the same direction as the sphere. The pointer indicated displacement in a range of ±5 degrees of the value selected on the pitch angle set control. Immediately after launch, the pilot performed a 2-g rotation until the pitch angle reached the value that was preset on the pitch angle set control. Initially the sphere was used to approximate the angle, but as the airplane approached within 5 degrees of the preselected pitch angle, the small pitch pointer moved toward the center index (0). The pilot then switched his attention from the sphere to the pointer for fine adjustments. The pointer would remain at the zero position as long as the preset pitch angle was maintained.[89]

This was the "interim" instrument panel in X-15-3 on 15 March 1963; "interim" because it was an improvement from the original black panel, but was not the definitive Lear-Siegler vertical-tape panel. Note the MH-96 controls in the center, and that the engraved markings that are not painted. (NASA Dryden)

The pitch-angle set control was located next to the attitude indicator and set the pitch angle used by the pilot during climb or reentry. The instrument consisted of four counters and a pitch angle set controller knob and lever. Rotating the knob clockwise set up the desired pitch angle on three of the counters. The number on the far right counter was preceded by a "dot" to indicate the reading was in tenths of a degree. The counter range was from 0 to 90 degrees. Rotating the knob counterclockwise returned the three counters to zero. The lever, adjacent to the knob, could be rotated upward or downward to change the sign (positive or negative) of the selected pitch angle. When the lever was moved upward, a minus (-) sign showed on the left counter; downward movement produced a plus (+) sign. This was normally set before the NB-52 took-off based on the X-15 climb angle desired for that particular flight.[90]

The attitude indicator was a "fly to" instrument – the pilot flew the airplane to the attitude (pitch, yaw, and roll) on the 8-ball and to the relative air represented by the intersection of the two cross-pointers. The primary use of the cross-pointers was during the high altitude phase where the task was to keep the airplane pointed into the relative wind as indicated by the ball nose. Positive angle of attack (air coming from below the airplane) deflected the needle down; right sideslip (air coming into the right ear) deflected the needle to the right. The BCS side-controller moved the nose in the direction that the pilot translated the stick. If the beta needle was to the right and the alpha needle was low, the pilot moved the BCS stick to the right and down to move the nose into the relative wind. As the nose approached the correct attitude, the pilot would need to use the BCS to stop the airplane motion.[91]

This convention caused a great deal of discussion among non-X-15 pilots when they flew the simulator. For instance, the alpha pointer on the attitude indicator moved in the opposite direction of the needle on the angle of attack indicator. But once the pilots understood the differ-

The final X-15-1 cockpit, shown on 22 January 1968. The peroxide transfer switch (from turbopump tanks to the APU/BCS tank) is at left. The master "data" recorders "on" switch is at the left of the center pedestal. (NASA Dryden)

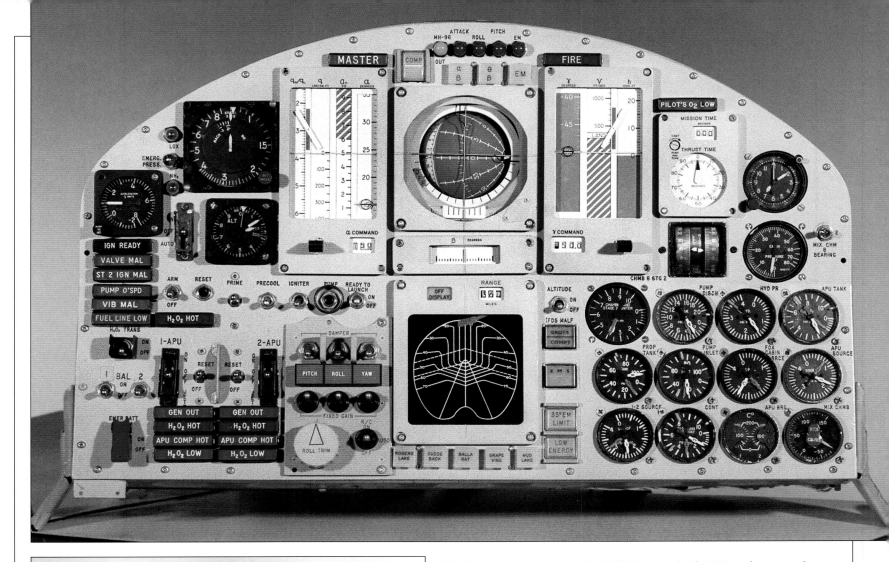

The final instrument panel for X-15-3 on 5 April 1966; only minor changes would be made after this. The black square in the lower center was the Ames boost guidance display. Note the five lake names under the Ames display; the pilot used these to select an abort lake for the system to guide him to. The back of the panel is shown at left. (NASA Dryden)

ent tasks associated with each instrument, the complaints usually went away. The pointer on the attitude indicator was merely a zero-reader to null out while flying at very low dynamic pressures; the angle of attack indicator was used to fly a particular angle of attack, such as setting up for reentry.[92]

THROTTLE

The XLR11 engine was not equipped with a throttle *per se.* Instead a series of eight switches were located on the left console, located in two groups of four. Each switch was in the same relative position as the thrust chamber it controlled and had two positions; forward was ON, and aft was OFF. Any combination of switches could be turned on or off as needed.[93]

The XLR99 throttle quadrant was a "backwards L" shaped slot located on the left console; the bottom corner of the L corresponded to minimum throttle and the most forward position was 100-percent power. Moving the throttle inboard started the engine. The throttle quadrant had various markings over the years. Initially there were four marked positions; OFF (outboard), START (inboard and aft), 50%, and 100% (forward). As the first modified XLR99s capable of operating at 30-percent power were installed, the 50% marking was changed to 30% and the linkage adjusted to compensate for the extra throttling range. When the decision was made to limit the lower setting to 42-percent the marking was changed to depict this and the linkage again adjusted.[94]

MH-96 Adaptive Flight Control System

When the X-15-3 was damaged during a ground test of the XLR99 and required major rebuilding, the Air Force seized the opportunity to modify the airplane to accommodate the prototype MH-96 being designed for the X-20 Dyna-Soar. The installation of the system into the X-15-3 began in December 1960 and presented something of a challenge. Although it allowed the original Westinghouse stability augmentation system to be removed, the MH-96 still required an even greater volume. Most of the system electronics were installed on the lower instrument-elevator shelf, but this required a "rather extensive revision of the original instrument-recording configuration" since the data recorders normally occupied this area.[95]

As installed in the X-15-3 the MH-96 provided stability augmentation in the pitch, roll, and yaw axes. In addition, autopilot modes provided control stick steering, pitch and roll attitude hold, heading hold, and angle of attack hold. Pilot commands to the system were electrical signals proportional to the displacement of the right side-controller or the center stick, and the rudder pedals. Provisions were also incorporated for electrically trimming the pitch and roll axes. Trimming presented some problems of its own, mainly because the MH-96 was adapted to use existing X-15 hardware instead of the newly-developed hardware it had been designed for. In order to keep the pitch servos centered, the "trim follow-up" system used a low rate trim motor to adjust the center point of the pilot's stick. This not only centered the servos, it also physically moved the stick. If the pilot was performing a precise task while the trim motor was moving the stick, it was easy to get out of phase with the trim motor and it would become saturated, oscillating at low amplitude, all by itself, at about 0.5 hz for several seconds. Needless to say, the pilots found this very disconcerting.[96]

Control of the airplane was accomplished using the normal hydraulic servos to position the horizontal and vertical stabilizers and the ballistic control system thrusters. Automatic blending of the aerodynamic and ballistic control systems was provided, with pilot control of both systems accomplished through the right side-stick controller or the center stick. Nevertheless, the left side-stick controller remained in the cockpit and could be used if desired to manually control the ballistic control thrusters.[97]

The basic system consisted of an adaptive controller that contained the various electronic modules and redundant rate gyro packages (each containing three rate gyros – one for each axis). The system also required an attitude reference (from the stable platform) and angle of attack and angle of sideslip information (from the ball nose). The electronics were programmed with an ideal response rate (the "model") for the aircraft; the MH-96 adjusted the damper gains automatically until the aircraft responded at this rate. Essentially, the gain changer operated by monitoring the limit-cycle amplitude and adjusting the

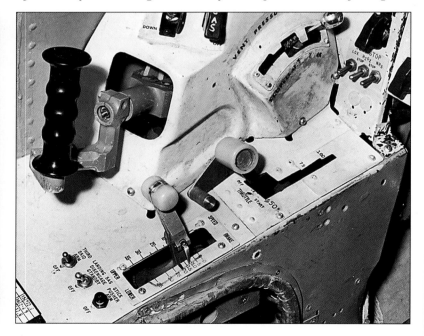

The XLR11 "throttle" in the X-15-1 on 1 June 1960. There were eight switches, one for each chamber, arranged in the same configuration as the engines. Just to the left of the throttle are the speed brake handles. (NASA Dryden)

The XLR99 throttle in the X-15-1 on 31 January 1969. At this point the minimum position was marked 50-percent, with other marks for 75- and 100-percent. Note the oxygen regulator has been moved. (NASA Dryden)

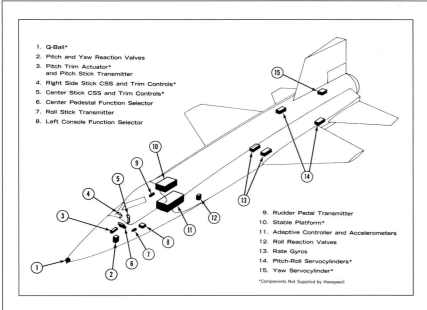

1. Q-Ball*
2. Pitch and Yaw Reaction Valves
3. Pitch Trim Actuator*
   and Pitch Stick Transmitter
4. Right Side Stick CSS and Trim Controls*
5. Center Stick CSS and Trim Controls*
6. Center Pedestal Function Selector
7. Roll Stick Transmitter
8. Left Console Function Selector

9. Rudder Pedal Transmitter*
10. Stable Platform*
11. Adaptive Controller and Accelerometers
12. Roll Reaction Valves
13. Rate Gyros
14. Pitch-Roll Servocylinders*
15. Yaw Servocylinder*

*Components Not Supplied by Honeywell

Locations for the MH-96 components. Installing the system required completely reworking the lower portion of the instrument compartment in order to accommodate the large electronics package. Because of this, the data recorder configuration in X-15-3 was always different than the other two airplanes. (Honeywell)

gain to maintain a constant amplitude. A tendency for the amplitude limit cycle to increase resulted in a gain reduction, whereas loss of the limit cycle initiated a gain increase. The limit-cycle frequency was largely determined by lead compensation and had to be higher than the aircraft natural frequency but lower than the aircraft structural frequency. On the X-15 that worked out to about 4 cycles per second.[98]

This model presented an early problem first seen in the X-15 simulator where a quick decrease in gain was required by the rapid buildup of control surface effectiveness during reentry. Delays in the gain reduction, partly caused by the lag in the mechanical control linkages, resulted in temporary oscillations as high as 3 degrees, peak-to-peak, at the servo. Modifications to the gain computer improved the situation but never eliminated it. A different issue proved easier to solve. A control problem existed whenever motions about one axis were coupled to another. To cure this, the MH-96 contained cross-control circuitry that commanded a roll input proportional to the yaw rate in order to combat the unfavorably high negative dihedral effect demonstrated by the X-15 during wind tunnel testing. This was, essentially, the MH-96 flying the beta-dot technique.[99]

One of the significant features of the MH-96 was its redundant design – something that would become a prototype of many future flight control systems. The system was one of the first to experience the conflicting objectives of reliability and fail safety. Extremely high reliability was a requirement

because of the low probability of a successful reentry from high altitude without damping. Fail safety was equally important since a large transient introduced in a high dynamic-pressure region would result in the destruction of the vehicle. The MH-96 provided completely redundant damper channels where either could control the vehicle. The adaptive feature of the circuitry permitted one channel to be lost with little or no loss in system performance since the remaining gain changer would increase in an attempt to match the limit cycle. The gain computers were interlocked, when operative, to prevent overcritical gain following a limit-cycle circuit failure and to provide the desired limiting effect for hard-over failures.[100]

In the case of a model or variable-gain amplifier failure, conventional monitor circuits would disengage either or both channels where required. Combined with the desire for increased system flexibility, this led to the addition of parallel fixed-gain channels with fail-safe passive circuitry. Since these channels operated simultaneously with the adaptive channels to avoid the time-lag penalties of switching, they effectively limited the minimum gain for adaptive operation. The fixed-gain circuits had to be sufficiently powerful for satisfactory emergency performance throughout the flight envelope, but had to be below the critical level in the high dynamic-pressure regions. A successful compromise was elusive and X-15-3 spent most of its career with some restrictions on its flight envelope. Fixed-gain operation could also be selected by the pilot through switches on the center pedestal.[101]

CANOPY

The one-piece pneumatically counterbalanced clamshell canopy was manually operated and mechanically locked in the down position. The canopy was hinged at the rear and opened about 45 degrees after moving slightly aft to unlock. The canopy could be manually locked from either inside or outside and a seal was incorporated into the rim to allow the cockpit to be pressurized. A retractable head support could be lowered from the top of the canopy to restrain the pilot's head during deceleration. A cartridge-type canopy remover was fired by an initiator when the ejection seat armrests were raised. This initiator also directed some of its expanding gases to extend a thruster at the forward end of the canopy. The canopy could also be ejected

The visibility out of the X-15 was surprisingly good, at least until the advent of the X-15A-2. Note the two spotlights illuminating the instrument panel in the photo at left. At right is Jack McKay locked into X-15-1 during his first flight on 28 October 1960. (left: Gerald H. Balzer Collection; right: NASA Dryden)

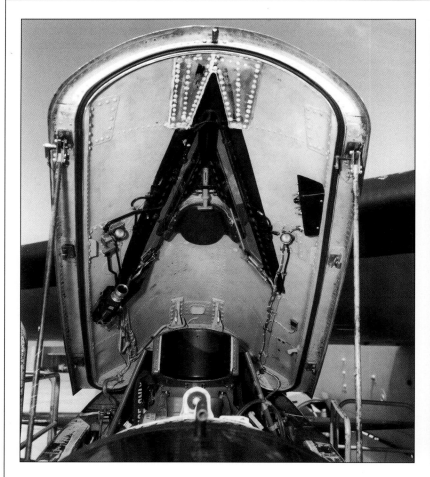

The inside of the X-15-1 canopy on 7 April 1964. The two spotlights and 16mm movie camera are visible, as is the swing-down headrest that supported the front of the pilot's helmet during deceleration. There were three latches on each side of the canopy, plus one in the front center. (NASA Dryden)

The rear bulkhead of the cockpit with the ejection seat removed. The photo was taken on 8 February 1960. Note the protective plywood installed on the floor. The slots on the sides of the ledge are for the latches on the underside of the canopy. (NASA Dryden)

with an internal T-handle that did not initiate ejection, and a similar T-handle was provided behind a door on the right side of the fuselage just below the canopy split line for ground use.[102]

The X-15 cockpit was illuminated by two floodlights attached to the canopy and located so that the light was directed forward and down. The lights were controlled by a switch on the right console. A movie camera was also installed on the canopy, filming the instrument panel in sufficient detail to allow post-mission analysis of instrument readings and switch settings. Various controls and indicators for the follow-on experiments were also installed on the inside of the canopy, often differing for each flight.[103]

WINDSHIELD

The windshield glass originally installed on the X-15 was soda-lime tempered plate glass with a single outer pane and double inner panes. This choice had been based on a predicted maximum temperature of 740°F. Data obtained on early flights indicated that outer-face temper-

atures near 1,000°F could be expected, with a differential temperature between panes of nearly 750°F. It was apparent that soda-lime glass would not withstand these temperatures, so a newly-developed alumino-silicate glass that had higher strength and better thermal properties was selected as a replacement.[104]

The new glass was subsequently installed in the 0.375-inch thick outer pane of all three X-15s; the inner panes continued to use soda-lime glass until the end. All of the glass was supplied by Corning. The thermal qualification test at Corning was interesting; an 8.4 by 28-inch panel of the glass was heated to 550°F in a salt bath for 3 minutes, then plunged into room-temperature tap water.[105]

A piece of soda-lime glass was inadvertently installed in the left panel of X-15-2 and it cracked during reentry from 217,000 feet on Flight 2-20-36. Ironically, an alumino-silicate panel in the right windshield shattered at Mach 2.7 while decelerating from Mach 6.04 on Flight 2-21-37. In both cases the glass fragments stayed in place during the remainder of the flight. Investigations revealed that the retainer frame buckled near the center of the upper edge of the glass and created a local hot spot, causing the glass to fail. The retainer was subsequently changed from its original 0.050-inch-thick Inconel X design to one using 0.10-inch thick 6A1-4V titanium alloy. The reduced coefficient of expansion of titanium compensated better for the differential expansion associated with the cooler Inconel X substructure. But as the flight envelope expanded and the environment became more severe, the glass deteriorated along the rear edge just forward of the aft windshield frame. This was cured by cutting away the aft retainer, eliminating the lip that was causing the hot spot on the glass.[106]

The windshield configuration of the X-15A-2 was revised to withstand the increased temperatures anticipated at Mach 8. An elliptical window using three panes of glass was installed on the right side of the canopy. The outer pane was 0.65-inch thick fused silica, the middle pane was 0.375-inch alumino-silicate, and the inner pane was 0.29-inch laminated soda lime glass. The outside windshield retaining frame was mounted flush with the glass to prevent the recurrence of the flow-heating experienced early in the program.[107]

EJECTION SEAT

The X-15 ejection seat was possibly the most elaborate ever designed for an X-plane. The ejection seat itself was not adjustable and each pilot was fitted for a personal seat pad, back pad, and armrest pad that positioned him properly in the cockpit. The seat pan included two oxygen cylinders to provide breathing oxygen and pressure-suit inflation. Foot rests included a set of ankle restraints that

were activated by the pilot bringing his feet back to strike a set of bars that locked the ankle shackles and, by mechanical linkage, raised a set of deflectors in front of his toes. Activating the ejection handles raised a set of thigh restraints and rotated the elbow restraints inward and also activated the emergency oxygen supply.[108]

As finally designed and qualified, the X-15 ejection seat permitted safe pilot ejection up to Mach 4, from any attitude, and at altitudes up to 120,000 feet. Ejection was initiated by the pilot jettisoning the canopy by raising either seat armrest to within 15 degrees of its full travel. As the canopy left the airplane it tripped a initiator that fired the two-stage catapult. The seat could not be ejected unless the canopy had left the airplane. At this point an emergency battery was activated to keep the pilot's visor clear and, later in the flight program, activate a rescue transponder. A ballistic-rocket type catapult ejected the seat and pilot from the airplane. During ejection, stabilizing fins and booms automatically extended to stabilize the seat. At 15,000 feet an aneroid device fired three initiators that ejected the headrest, freed the pilot from the restraints, and permitted him to separate from the seat. A handle was provided that allowed the pilot to manually release the restraints if necessary. If ejection was initiated below 15,000 feet altitude, a three-second delay was provided before the restraints were released.[109]

When the pilot separated from the seat, the parachute remained attached to the integrated harness that was an integral part of the David Clark full-pressure suit. A controller back pan was part of the integrated harness and contained an oxygen regulator, suit pressure regulator, anti-g valve, and an emergency oxygen supply for breath-

An X-15 ejection seat on 1 May 1967. Note the arm rest/support on each side, and the foot restraints in their closed position. The large stabilizing fins are folded alongside the head rest, and the tubes containing the stabilizing booms may be seen under the seat on each side. There was an ejection handle on each side The seat was not adjustable, and required custom-fitted seat pans, head rests, and arm rests be made for each pilot. (NASA Dryden)

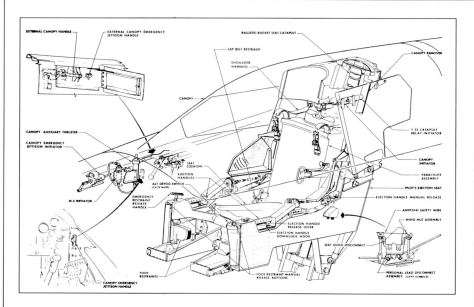

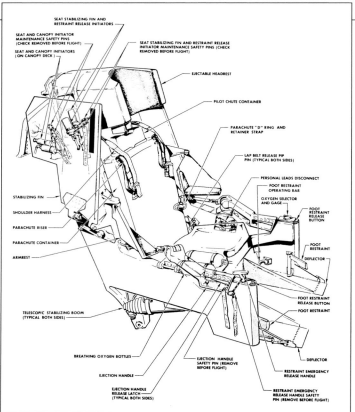

The X-15 ejection seat was probably the most sophisticated escape system yet developed for an aircraft. The seat was considered effective up to Mach 4 and 120,000 feet, well in excess of the performance of any aircraft except the X-15. The seat was extensively tested in wind tunnels and on the rocket sled track at Edwards, experiencing many initial failures but finally being perfected prior to the first X-15 flight. (NASA)

ing and suit pressurization. It should be noted that during ejection the full-pressure suit was filled with oxygen, not the normal nitrogen used when in the airplane. The emergency oxygen supply was sufficient for about 20 minutes after the pilot separated from the ejection seat and was actuated automatically when the seat ejection handles were raised, or could be manually activated by pulling a green ball on the right side of the suit.

The pilot was supplied with a backpack type parachute to use once he separated from the seat. Because of the design of the pressure suit, seat, and cockpit, the standard quarter-deployment bag and C-9 28-foot diameter parachute were not considered acceptable. North American produced a special 24-foot diameter chute and "skirt bag" specifically for the X-15. However, several flight surgeons had concerns that it would allow too high a descent rate for the pilot and urged a larger parachute be certified for use on the X-15. During October 1960 North American tested a redesigned 28-foot diameter parachute at the National Parachute Range. These tests were successful, and indicated no significant difference in opening time between the smaller and larger chutes. It became policy that each pilot could select whichever size parachute he wished to use; most continued to use the 24-foot chute because the reduced thickness of the backpack made it more comfortable to sit in the cockpit.[110]

In June 1965 the FRC authorized North American to purchase five new 28-foot parachutes to replace the 24-foot units that had reached their 7-year service limit. The new chutes had a disconnect device that allowed the pilots to release one-half of the shroud lines during descent. They were, however, still thicker than the original parachutes and therefore a bit less comfortable to wear. Nevertheless, they became standard as the smaller units were discarded.[111]

A rescue beacon transmitter, installed in the parachute container, was automatically energized into continuous operation when the pilot's parachute deployed. The transmitter antenna was attached to one of the parachute straps and the system transmitted on the X-15 telemetry frequency of 244.3Mhz. The transmitter allowed ground stations to obtain position fixes on the pilot after ejection.[112]

FULL-PRESSURE SUITS

The David Clark full-pressure suit would be one of the program's crowning achievements. When the X-15 program was initiated, the Aero Medical Laboratory at the WADC had met with only partial success in designing a full-pressure suit, leading to a certain amount of indecision as to the type of garment to be selected for the X-15. Several of the eventual bidders had specified only partial-pressure suits, but North American evidently had more confidence in the potential of full-pressure suits than the Air Force. Eventually a contract was issued to the David Clark Company of Worcester, Massachusetts, to develop what would become the standard U.S. full-pressure suit. It was a long and trying development effort that owed much of its success to Scott Crossfield and Dr. David M. Clark.

MC-2

The resulting MC-2 suits were individually tailored for each pilot and consisted of a ventilation suit, upper and lower rubber garments, and upper and lower restraint garments. The ventilation suit also included a porous wool insulation garment. The upper and lower rubber garments formed a seal at the waist by having their edges folded together three times. The lower half of the rubber garment incorporated an anti-g suit that was similar in design to the standard Air Force-issue suits and provided protection up to about 7-g. The portion of the suit below the rubber neck seal was ventilated and pressurized by gaseous nitrogen from the X-15 supply. The suit was designed to allow in-flight medical monitoring of the pilot.[113]

The restraint layer was the key factor that allowed the David Clark Company to manufacture a workable full-pressure suit. It was constructed of a unique distorted-angle "link-net" fabric that provided the lightweight non-rigid characteristic. The ballooning that had been associated with previous inflated pressure suits was controlled by this material. The "link-net material might best be described as a slipping torsion net which acts something like the old Chinese finger puzzle in that as it elongates, its circumference becomes smaller. As internal suit pressure increases, it tends to shorten the longitudinal dimension. Control over the suit's ballooning and elongation tendencies were achieved by a careful balance of the link-net material so that any tendency for the suit to elongate was offset and balanced by its tendency to increase in size circumferentially; thus the suit remained nearly the same size whether pressurized or not."[114]

The last garment to be donned was not actually required for altitude protection; an aluminized reflective outer garment contained the seat restraint, shoulder harness, and parachute attachments. This protected the pressure suit during routine use and served as a sacrificial garment during high-speed ejection. It also provided a small measure of additional insulation against extreme tempera-

ture. This was the first of the silver "space suits" that found an enthusiastic reception on television and at the movies.[115]

The modified MA-3 helmet consisted of a fiberglass shell with a molded full-head liner. The visor was a conductive-coated lens that provided defogging through electrical resistance heating. Communication provisions consisted of molded ear cups and miniature AN/AIC-10 earphones and microphone. All helmet services (oxygen and electrical) were contained internally within the helmet, presenting a "clean" profile to minimize blast effects during high-speed ejection. The helmet was joined to the suit by means of a lightweight, quickly detachable, positive-locking, sealed rotating bearing that allowed full head mobility at any pressure.[116]

The helmet was supplied with 100-percent oxygen for breathing, and the anti-g bladders within the suit were inflated during accelerated flight from the same oxygen source. The total oxygen supply was 192 cubic inches, supplied by two 1,800-psi bottles located beneath the ejection seat during free flight; for ground operations, taxi, and captive flight the oxygen was supplied from the NB-52 carrier aircraft. A rotary valve, located on the ejection seat, selected which oxygen source (NB-52 or X-15) to use. The suit-helmet regulator automatically delivered the correct oxygen pressure for the ambient altitude until absolute pressure fell below 3.5 psi (equivalent to 35,000 feet); the suit pressure was then held at 3.5 psi absolute. Expired air was vented into the lower nitrogen-filled garment through two one-way neck seal valves and then released into the aircraft cockpit through a suit pressure control valve. During ejection the nitrogen gas supply to the suit below the hel-

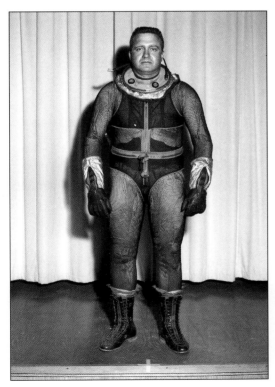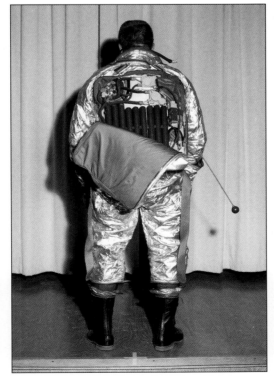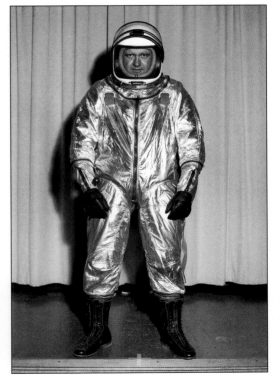

Jack McKay shows the various layers of David Clark MC-2 full-pressure suit on 15 April 1959. This suit was the first workable full-pressure suit developed in the United States (and likely the world) and worked as advertised. But it was difficult to put on, cumbersome to wear, and required a great deal of maintenance. Fortunately, the David Clark Company (and others) continued development, and only 16 X-15 flights would be flown using the MC-2. (NASA Dryden)

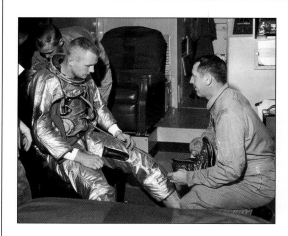

Various scenes of the MC-2 suits at Edwards. At left, Neil Armstrong gets suited up for Flight 1-18-31 on 30 November 1961. A modified JTF-102A was used to test the suits; at center is Scott Crossfield on 11 September 1958, with Joe Walker on 22 October 1958 at right. (left: NASA Dryden; others: AFFTC History Office)

met was stopped (since the nitrogen source was on the X-15), and the suit and helmet were automatically pressurized for the ambient altitude by an emergency oxygen supply located in the back pack.[117]

The X-15 was not the only program that required a pressure suit, although it was certainly the most visible in the public's eye. The basic MC-2 suit underwent a number of one-off "dash" modifications for use in various high-performance aircraft testing programs. Many of the movies and still photographs of the early 1960s show experimental test pilots dressed in the ubiquitous aluminized fabric covered David Clark MC-2 full-pressure suits.

Despite the fact that it worked reasonably well, the MC-2 was not particularly well liked by the pilots. It was cumbersome to wear, restricted movement somewhat, and had limited peripheral vision. It was also mechanically complex and required a considerable amount of maintenance. Despite this, there was only one serious deficiency noted in the suit: the oxygen line between the helmet and the helmet pressure regulator (mounted in the back kit) caused a delay in oxygen flow response time such that the pilot could reverse the helmet-suit

differential pressure by taking a quick, deep breath. Since the helmet pressure was supposed to be greater than the suit pressure to prevent nitrogen from leaking into the breathing space, this pressure reversal was less than ideal, but no easy solution was available.[118]

A/P22S-2

Fortunately pressure suits continued to evolve. The development by the David Clark Company of a new method of integrating a pressure-sealing zipper made it possible to incorporate all of the layers of the MC-2 suit into a one-piece garment on the new A/P22S-2 (David Clark Model S1023), significantly simplifying handling and maintenance. A separate aluminized-nylon outer garment was still used to protect the suit and provide mounting of the restraint and parachute harness. The neck seal, which had proven relatively delicate and subject to frequent damage, was replaced by a face seal that was more comfortable and more robust. The helmet was modified to permit the oxygen pressure regulator to be mounted within the helmet, eliminating the undesirable

The A/P22S-2 suit was a significant improvement. Bob White at left; Joe Engle after Flight 3-44-67 in center; and Bill Dana after Flight 3-56-83 at right. (right: NASA Dryden; others AFFTC History Office)

time delay in oxygen flow, and the suit pressure regulator was mounted in the suit in order to eliminate some of the plumbing.[119]

The consensus among X-15 pilots was that the A/P22S-2 represented a significant improvement over the earlier MC-2. The first attempt at using the A/P22S-2 in the X-15 was made by Joe Walker on 21 March 1961 in X-15-2; unfortunately, this flight was aborted (2-A-27) because of telemetry problems. Nine days later Walker made the first flight (2-14-28) in the A/P22S-2. Ultimately, the MC-2 would be used on only 36 X-15 flights.[120]

The A/P22S-2 was clearly superior to the earlier MC-2, particularly from the pilot's perspective. Some of the improvements included:[121]

- Increased visual area – The double curvature face plate in the A/P22S-2, together with the use of a face seal in place of the MC-2 neck seal, allowed the face to move forward in the helmet so that the pilot had a lateral vision field of approximately 200 degrees. This was an increase of approximately 40 degrees over the single contoured lens in the MC-2 helmet, with an additional increase of 20 percent in the vertical field of view.
- Ease of donning – The MC-2 was put on in two sections: the lower rubberized garment and its restraining coverall, and the upper rubberized garment and its restraining coverall. This was a rather tedious process and depended on folding the rubber top and bottom sections of the suit together to retain pressure. The A/P22S-2 was a one-piece garment with a pressure-sealing zipper that ran around the back portion of the suit and was zippered closed in one operation. It took approximately 30 minutes to properly don an MC-2; only 5 minutes for the newer suit.
- Removable gloves – In the original MC-2 the gloves were a fixed portion of the upper rubberized garment. The A/P22S-2 had removable gloves that contributed to general comfort and ease of donning. This also prevented excessive moisture from building up during suit checkout and X-15 preflight inspections, and also made it easier for the pilot to remove the pressure suit by himself if that should become necessary. Another advantage was that a punctured glove could be changed without having to change the entire suit.

The A/P22S-2 also featured a new system of biomedical electrical connectors installed through a pressure seal in the suit. This facilitated data acquisition and avoided the snap-pad arrangement used in the MC-2 suit. The snap pads had proven to be unsatisfactory for continued use; after several operations the snaps either separated or failed to make good contact because of metal fatigue, resulting in the loss of biomedical data during the flight. In the new suit, biomedical data was acquired through what was essentially a continuous electrical lead from the pilot's body to the seat interface. The new suit proved to be much better in terms of reliability and pilot acceptance.[122]

Like the MC-2 before them, the A/P22S-2 suits were custom tailored for each X-15 pilot, necessitating several trips to Worcester to be measured and fitted. It is interesting to note that although the X-15 pilots were still somewhat critical of the lack of mobility afforded by the full-pressure suits (particularly later pilots who had not experienced the MC-2), this was only true on the ground. When the suits occasionally inflated for brief periods during flight, the abundance of adrenaline present at the time allowed the pilot to easily overcome the resistance of the suit. At most it rated a slight mention in the post-flight report. The David Clark Company had produced an excellent product.

As good as it was, the A/P22S-2 was not perfect and the suit was modified somewhat based on initial X-15 flight experience. The principal modifications were: (1) rotating glove rings to provide greater mobility of the hands, (2) improved manufacturing, inspection, and assembly techniques for the helmet ring to lower the torque required to connect the helmet to the suit, (3) the installation of a redundant (pressure-sealing) restraint zipper to lower the leak rate of the suit, (4) the development and installation of a double face-seal to improve comfort and minimize leakage between the face-seal and suit, and (5) modifications to the tailoring of the link-net restraint garment around the shoulders to improve comfort and mobility. A weak point involving the stitching in the leather glove was solved by including a nylon liner that relived the strain on the stitched leather seams.[123]

The A/P22S-2 suit evolved into a series of variants designated A/P22S-4, A/P22S-6 and A/P22S-6A (David Clark designations S1024, S1024A, and S1024B, respectively). Today, the standard high altitude full-pressure suits used in almost all atmospheric flight operations (including U-2 missions), as well as those used during Space Shuttle ascent and reentry, are variations of the A/P22S-2 manufactured by the David Clark Company.[124]

Neil Armstrong took the X-15-3 to Mach 5.51 during Flight 3-2-3 on 17 January 1962. Note the gentle curve made by the skids during slide out. (NASA Dryden)

CHAPTER 12

Stillborn Concepts

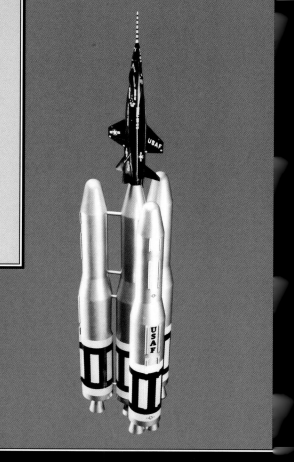

Above: *The evolution of the X-15 design. These 1/15-scale wind tunnel models show the basic X-15, advanced X-15A-2, and the X-15 thin delta-wing design. These models are currently displayed at the Air Force Flight Test Center Museum at Edwards AFB. Photographed on 5 August 2002.* (Tony Landis)

Right: *One of many orbital design studies, this time from 1957-58 showing an X-15 mounted on top a cluster of what appear to a cluster of Titan boosters. Note the X-15 has the NACA instrumentation boom on the nose, something that obviously would not survive the reentry.* (The Boeing Company Archives)

As the X-15 design was being finalized, the basic concept gave birth to a couple of interesting design studies, and many more "paper airplanes" created by the marketing departments of North American or other contractors. The paper airplanes are not worth serious discussion, but the design studies provide some insight into the early part of the manned space program.

PROJECT 7969

Project 7969, the Manned Ballistic Rocket Research System, was initiated by the Air Force in February 1956 with a stated goal of orbiting and recovering a manned space capsule. By the end of 1957 the Air Force had received at least 10 serious proposals that were evaluated by a joint Air Force-NACA team during a conference held at Wright Field on 29-31 January 1958. Avco, Convair, Goodyear, Lockheed, Martin and McDonnell proposed spherical reentry vehicles or blunt capsules while Bell, North American, Republic, and Northrop all proposed winged vehicles.[1]

The North American proposal included a "stripped" X-15 with an empty weight of 9,900 pounds. The vehicle would be launched from Cape Canaveral on a two-stage booster that allowed a single orbit with an apogee of 400,000 feet and a perigee of 250,000 feet. The launch vehicle consisted of four Navaho boosters; three were clustered together in the first stage and one acted as the second stage; the XLR99 in the X-15 was the third stage. The X-15 would be equipped with beryllium oxide leading edges and an René 41 alloy shingle heat shield, plus a thicker Inconel X hot structure. Due to the low perigee and aerodynamics of the X-15, no retrorocket was required for reentry, although the restartable XLR99 could be used if necessary. The pilot would eject and descend by parachute just before ditching the X-15 in the Gulf of Mexico, with the aircraft being lost. It was expected that a first manned orbital flight could be achieved 30 months after a go-ahead at a cost of $120 million.[2]

Given the early state of development of the X-15, there was almost no real engineering associated with this proposal. Nevertheless, it was further along than many of the others since the basic X-15 shape was known to be stable in most flight regimes and both it and the XLR99 were at least under active development.

After the launch of *Sputnik 1* on 4 October 1957, Project 7969 was reoriented into the Man In Space Soonest (MISS) project to ensure a U.S. Air Force pilot would be the first human in outer space. On 27 February 1958 General Curtiss E. LeMay, the Air Force Vice Chief of Staff, was briefed on three alternatives that included the X-15 derivative, speeding up the Dyna-Soar program, and building a simple non-lifting ballistic capsule that could be boosted into low orbit by an existing ICBM-derived booster. LeMay apparently expressed no preference and although it was a long and complicated evaluation, the end result was that a ballistic capsule appeared to offer the best hope of immediate success. This idea formed the basis for Project Mercury after the NASA was formed on 1 October 1958 and the first American manned space effort was transferred to the civilian agency.[3]

X-15B

Engineers at North American continued to refine their Project 7969 concept. A few days after the Soviet Union orbited *Sputnik 1* on 4 October 1957, North American packaged everything into a neat report, and Harrison Storms took the idea to Washington. This version used two Navaho boosters clustered together as the 830,000-lbf first stage, a single Navaho booster as a 415,000-lbf second stage, and an X-15B powered by a 75,000-lbf Rocketdyne XLR105 Atlas sustainer engine as the third stage. Unlike the 7969 proposal, this one had a great deal more engineering in it, although it was still very preliminary since no wind tunnel tests or detailed calculations on heating or aero loads had been conducted.[4]

The X-15B was larger than the basic X-15 and was capable of carrying two pilots. The Inconel X skin was thicker to withstand the increased reentry heating and the vehicle had larger propellant tanks to feed the Atlas sustainer engine that replaced the XLR99. But the shape and many of the internal systems were identical to that of the basic X-15 then under construction. The supersonic and subsonic stability of the X-15 had already been demonstrated in numerous wind tunnel tests and keeping the same shape eliminated the need to repeat many of them.

The flight plan was simple. The vehicle would be launched eastward from Cape Canaveral; after about 80 seconds, the first stage would drop away and the second stage would fire. At an altitude of about 400,000 feet the second stage would burn out and the X-15B would continue using its own power. The vehicle would eventually get up to 18,000 mph – enough for three orbits. The XLR105 would be used to deorbit at a point that would allow the X-15B to land at Edwards using the reentry profiles already developed for the basic X-15. It was a grand plan, and years ahead of its time. Unfortunately, when Storms got back from Washington he reported that "there were exactly 421" other people that had competing proposals. Eventually the X-15B just quietly faded from sight.[5]

There was one more orbital X-15 proposal. At the end of 1959 Storms presented a version of the X-15B that would be launched using

At the Marshall Space Flight Center, Dr. Wernher von Braun discusses a North American proposal to use the X-15 in space. Left to right: unknown, von Braun, Fred Payne (North American), Alvin S. White (North American), Howard Evans (North American Manager of Confidential Design), Raymond Rice (President of the North American Aviation Los Angeles Division), Harrison Storms (Vice President and Chief Engineer of the Los Angeles Division). (Courtesy of Alvin S. White)

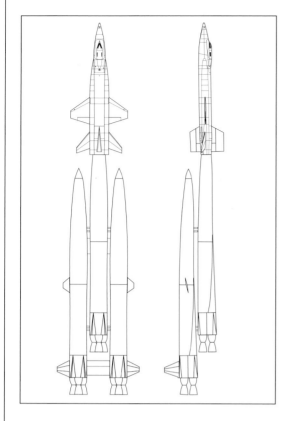

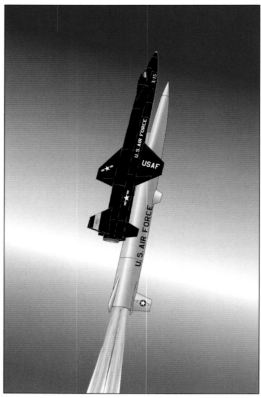

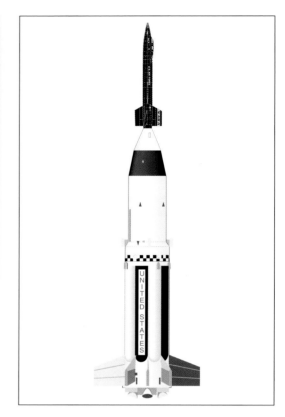

There were a variety of proposals to use Navaho boosters as a first stage for suborbital or orbital X-15s. In some cases the X-15 was a slightly modified version of the airplanes being used at Edwards; other times they were larger versions with much heavier hot-structures in an attempt to address reentry heating concerns. The XLR99 and XLR105 Atlas engines were most often proposed. (Artwork by Tony Landis)

There were proposals to use a Saturn I as a booster for a modified X-15, although the concept seems to ask more questions than it answered regarding the survivability of the X-15. (Artwork by Tony Landis)

a Saturn I first stage and an "ICBM-type" second stage. According to Storms, "We figure the X-15, carrying two pilots … could be put into orbit hundreds of miles above the earth. Or with a scientific or military payload of thousands of pounds … into a lower orbit." Storms estimated that it would take 3-4 years of development and the idea was presented to both the Air Force and NASA, but neither organization was interested. NASA was too busy with Mercury; the Air Force with Dyna-Soar and fighting off Robert McNamara.[6]

THIN DELTA WINGS

By 1965, a proposed delta-wing modification to the X-15-3 began to offer supporters the hope that the program might continue to 1972 or 1973. Unlike many proposals, such as the X-15B, the delta-wing was almost a real project and was the subject of a great deal of research and engineering.

The delta-wing X-15 had grown out of studies during the early 1960s on using the X-15 as a hypersonic cruise research vehicle. NASA proponents, particularly John Becker at Langley, found the idea very attractive since "the highly swept delta wing has emerged from studies of the past decade as the form most likely to be utilized on future hypersonic flight vehicles in which high lift/drag ratio is a prime requirement i.e., hypersonic transports and military hypersonic cruise vehicles, and certain recoverable boost vehicles as well."[7]

A meeting was held at the Flight Research Center on 9-10 December 1964 to determine exactly what a delta-wing hypersonic-cruise X-15 could be used for. Paul Bikle concluded that: "In general, a delta-wing X-15 program could establish a baseline of confidence and technology from which decisions regarding the feasibility and design of advanced air-breathing vehicles could be realistically made. The proposed time for the delta X-15 fits well with that for an overall hypersonic research vehicle program and the cost does not appear to be unreasonable."[8]

Things seemed to be progressing rapidly. In January 1965 the Flight Research Center drafted a statement of work to North American for a detailed study of the delta-wing concept. NASA directed that an existing "X-15 airplane would be modified to incorporate a representative slender hypersonic wing substituted for the present wing and horizontal tail. The wing structure would be designed for sustained hypersonic flight at a Mach number of 7, but would also be capable of flight to Mach number 8 for limited time periods. The basic X-15 fuselage structure, rocket engine, flight control and other systems would be retained with minimum modification, and the present NB-52 launch system and High Range facility would be utilized."[9]

The work statement went on to indicate that the airplane should have a design dynamic pressure of 2,000 psf and a load limit of 5-g. The baseline fuselage was the same length as the existing X-15-3, but the study would include an investigation of extending the fuselage by 8 feet to provide additional internal propellant capacity. Other potential "improvements" to be studied included the addition of a permanent thermal shield (in lieu of ablative coatings) over the fuselage to prevent contamination of the wing with ablative products, relocating the wing to be flush with the bottom of the fuselage, increasing the dynamic pressure limit to 2,500 psi and the load factor to 7.33-g, including external propellant tank(s), and relocating the nose landing gear.[10]

The delta-wing languished at Dryden for the remainder of the year while a project development plan was put together. By the end of the year the second draft of the plan had been released for internal review, providing more detail on how things might progress. The opening paragraph provided the justification for the program, "Three of the most probable uses for hypersonic airbreathing aircraft are transport over long ranges, military reconnaissance, and as maneuverable reusable first-stage boosters. There are currently no military or civilian requirements of over-riding importance for any one of these. Their potential, however, constitutes a clear justification to proceed with comprehensive programs to develop the required hypersonic technology." Unfortunately, the justification also included rationale why the program should not be supported given the budget crunch NASA was experiencing as it continued the Apollo program to the detriment of the aeronautics budget. Nevertheless, the FRC pressed on with fairly detailed plans.[11]

The FRC estimated the program would cost $29,750,000 spread between FY67 and FY73. Of this $24,600,000 would be paid to the contractor selected to build the flight vehicle, while the other $5,150,000 would be "in house" expenses. The planners warned, however, that "if the military withdraws their operational support from the general X-15 program, this project would be responsible for additional expenses over the 4-1/2 year operational period. These expenses could amount to as much as 17 million dollars." The preliminary schedule showed a request for proposals being released in August 1966, a contract award in March 1967, the X-15-3 being modified between December 1967 and October 1968, and a first flight in January 1969. The 37-flight research program would be completed in December 1972.[12]

Although it would seem logical that North American would do the modifications, several other contractors – Lockheed, Northrop, and Republic – expressed interest in the program, so the FRC decided to make it a competitive process. Despite negotiations between NASA and the Air Force at various levels, the X-15 Project Office declined to participate in the expected procurement of the delta-wing airplane, but agreed to formally transfer the X-15-3 airframe to NASA for the modification at the end of its flight program.[13]

After nearly two years of delay, on 13 March 1967 the FRC finally issued a request for proposal for the study. The objectives of the study were (1) development of a preliminary design for evaluating the modification of the X-15-3 to a delta-wing configuration, and (2) the formulation of an accurate estimate of performance, weight, cost, and schedule for such modification. A secondary objective was the analysis of alternate approaches such as unsegmented leading edges, the elimination of ablatives, the incorporation of a fly-by-wire control system, multiplane airfoils, symmetrical tip fins, and different propulsion systems.[14]

North American submitted a 2-volume, 500-page proposal containing detailed engineering concepts and cost data – and that was just the proposal to do the study! By this time North American had already been testing the delta-wing X-15 in wind tunnels for over a year. The North American low-speed and hypersonic tunnels and the Langley 20-inch hypersonic tunnel had tested 1/15-scale and 1/50-scale models at Mach numbers between 0.2 and 6.9. As far as can be determined, no other contractors submitted proposals, probably based on the large commitment North American had already demonstrated to the program.[15]

As proposed by North American, the delta-wing X-15-3 was not a simple conversion. The 603-square-foot delta-wing planform had a 76-degree leading edge sweep, but the wing span was the same as the original X-15 to ensure that there would be no clearance issues with the NB-52 carrier aircraft. Elevons (30.8 square feet each) at the trailing edge provided longitudinal and roll control by deflecting up to 4.5 degrees up or 5.0 degrees down. Directional stability was provided by the existing dorsal and ventral stabilizers with the addition of wing tip fins and directional control was provided by the existing dorsal rudder. The removable tip fins could be adjusted on the ground for cant and toe-in, allowing the relative levels of directional and lateral stability to be changed for investigating the handling qualities of the vehicle. The tip fins were provided to compensate for the normal centerline vertical stabilizers being blanked or shadowed by the fuselage at hypersonic speeds and large angles-of-attack. They could also be replaced with units of various configurations and construction as test beds.[16]

The "ideal" hot-structure for a high-speed cruise wing consisted of a monocoque shell fabricated from a single layer of skin stiffened internally for high efficiency biaxial loading, attached to a minimum number of restraining spars and ribs whose caps were exposed directly to aerodynamic heating to minimize the thermal gradient. Monocoque designs, although seldom applied to wings, were charac-

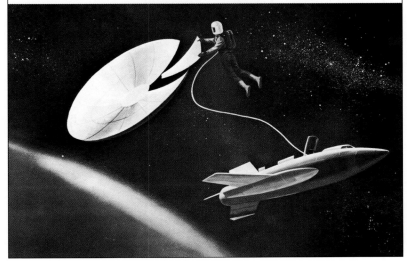

ADV X-15 MAINTENANCE & ASSEMBLY IN SPACE

An artist concept of an orbital X-15 with an astronaut performing an EVA. There was little chance the X-15 design could have been scaled into a truly orbital vehicle, but the beginning of the space race bred many fanciful concepts. (The Boeing Company Archives)

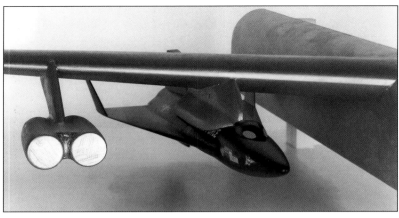

*Above and below: **This was the delta wing concept in August 1964. Notice the size of the upturned tips on the wings. The configuration of these auxiliary verticals changed several times during the delta wing program.** (NASA Dryden)*

One of the major constraints in the delta wing design was the that airplane still had to fit under the NB-52, meaning the wingspan could not increase substantially over the basic X-15 design. (NASA Dryden)

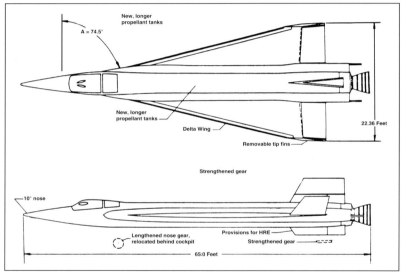

The early 1967 version of the thin delta wing X-15. The nose landing gear was moved rearward into the instrumentation compartment in order to lower the landing loads; half of the instrumentation was moved forward into the old nose landing gear area. Note the new profile on the nose. By the time the nose and propellant tanks (to gain additional capacity) were replaced, there was very little left of the original X-15 fuselage. (NASA)

terized by distributed loadings that eliminated the need for spars and ribs with heavy caps to carry large concentrated loads from spanwise and chordwise bending. Scalloped-type spar and rib designs could provide the necessary plate stability for the cover panels and the necessary shear strength. Eliminating the heavy caps would minimize local heating differentials by eliminating large heat-sinks.[17]

The position of the wing was the subject of a great deal of study since the hypersonic research engine was expected to be carried on the ventral stabilizer (like the dummy was on X-15A-2), but the air-

craft also had to be stable in flight without the 1,000-pound engine. It proved to be a difficult problem. Just before the program was terminated it was decided that the wing should be positioned in the best location to compensate for the HRE. On flights without the engine, as much research equipment or ballast as possible would be located in the aft 29-inch experiment compartment.[18]

Likewise, the shape of the wing leading edge was of some concern, but North American noted that "the effect of leading edge radius on the low-speed aerodynamic characteristics of highly swept delta wings is

Although the drawings were dated September 1967, this is actually a mid-term version of the proposed delta wing X-15. Note the location of the auxiliary vertical stabilizers inset slightly from the wing tips and the heavy corrugations on the wing surfaces themselves. The basic fuselage was from the X-15-3, but the XLR99 appears to have a nozzle extension on it. The dummy ramjet carried on the X-15A-2 is shown under the ventral stabilizer. (NASA Dryden)

not well understood." The effect on the leading edge shape at supersonic speeds was not thought to be significant, because most of the lift was produced by positive pressure on the wing lower surface. The leading edge shape significantly influenced the landing characteristics, so North American investigated various configurations in their low-speed wind tunnel. This issue was never satisfactorily solved and was awaiting further data from NASA wind tunnel tests.[19]

The material to be used on the leading edge was also somewhat uncertain, mainly because of the expected 2,200°F temperatures to be encountered on the design mission. North American built a segmented leading edge made from columbium alloy that was tested at 2,400°F and appeared satisfactory, at least for initial use. It was expected that no available material would prove satisfactory for the lower surface of the wing, and that some form of thermal protection system would need to be developed. Unsurprisingly, many of the ideas investigated by North American looked a lot like the concepts being looked at for the Space Shuttle that was being studied about the same time. One of the most promising ideas was using metallic heat shields supported by standoff clips with a layer of low-density insulation sandwiched between the shield and the wing skin. This protection would only need to be provided for an area about 2-feet wide just behind the leading edge; further back the airflow smoothed out sufficiently to keep temperatures within the ability of alloys such as TD nickel to survive unprotected.[20]

Originally North American had envisioned using upswept wingtips to replace the directional stability lost when the lower rudder was removed from the delta wing configuration. Although the lower rudder was seldom flown on the original X-15s later in the flight program, this was because most missions were flown at high angles of attack where the lower rudder was actually detrimental to stability. The delta-wing program, on the other hand, wanted to fly sustained high-speed cruise missions that would require little high angle of attack work. The initial round of tests in the North American hypersonic tunnel revealed that the upswept wingtips were inadequate above Mach 6. Various configurations were tested in both the North American hypersonic tunnel and the 20-inch Langley hypersonic tunnel until a set of tip fins extended both above and below the wing cen-

terline were discovered to be adequate. Nevertheless, part of the reason the fins were made removable was so that they could be easily replaced if the wind tunnel testing proved to be inaccurate.[21]

The airplane would be stretched 10 feet to 62.43 feet overall, involving manufacturing what was essentially a new fuselage from the cockpit rearward. The propellant tank section would be stretched 91 inches, and would be provided with new mounting provisions to accommodate the delta wing. North American manufactured test specimen from René 41 and Inconel 718 to determine which would be the best material for this area; the tests were in progress when the program was terminated. The space between the liquid oxygen and ammonia tanks would be used to accommodate the standard center of gravity instrumentation compartment, and a new 29-inch long compartment would be added behind the fuel tank but ahead of the engine. This compartment would normally hold the fuel and gases for the HRE, but could accommodate other research instrumentation as required. Designers also wanted to replace the existing ogive forward fuselage (in front of the canopy) with a new 20-degree included-angle cone section. This semi-monocoque

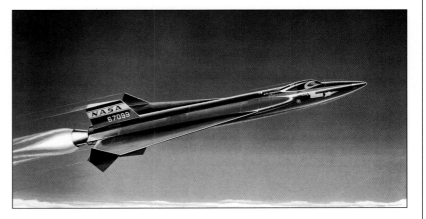

Pretty much the final delta wing configuration. Removable endplate verticals are on the wing tips, and the fuselage tunnels extend all the way to the back of the fuselage, much like the X-15A-2 design. (NASA Dryden)

structure would use René 41 outer skin and Inconel X (or Inconel 718) frames, with titanium used for the inner skin of the equipment compartment. The attachment frame at the very front would be sized and shaped to accept the ball nose used on the X-15, or a new non-movable Litton 7-port sensor system interchangeably.[22]

Several different powerplants were investigated for the airplane, with the leading candidate being the Aerojet YLR91-AJ-15 from the second stage of the Titan II. This engine used unsymmetrical dimethyl-hydrazine and nitrogen tetroxide as propellants and had already been man-rated for the NASA Gemini program. When equipped with a 25:1 nozzle, this engine would have permitted the reference mission to be completed without the use of an external propellant tank. In fact, at a launch weight of 52,485 pounds and a burnout weight of 18,985 pounds, the YLR91 would have allowed a maximum velocity of 8,745 fps, well in excess of the 7,600 fps required by NASA. The effect of carrying the 1,000-pound HRE would have reduced this about 400 fps.[23]

North American briefly investigated the idea of using a separate "sustainer" engine to provide thrust to overcome drag during hypersonic cruise. Although the integration issues surrounding how to incorporate a second engine and its propellants into the airframe eventually convinced all concerned that it would be too difficult, the particular engines investigated show how a program could come full-circle. One of the engines investigated was the Bell YLR81-BA-11, a variation of the one of the engines proposed to power the X-15 in 1954. Several variants of the Reaction Motors LR11 family – used for the initial X-15 flights – were also investigated, along with the Aerojet LR52 (AJ-10).[24]

The engine that was ultimately selected was a modified XLR99 that provided 83,000-lbf at 100,000 feet, and was throttleable down to 8,000-lbf for sustained cruise. The increased internal fuel would permit sustained flights at Mach 6.5 using the low-thrust "sustainer" capability of the modified XLR99 to overcome drag but not pro-

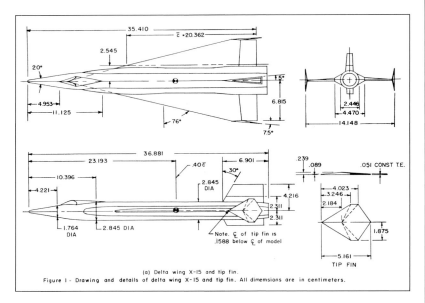

(a) Delta wing X-15 and tip fin.

Figure 1 - Drawing and details of delta wing X-15 and tip fin. All dimensions are in centimeters.

Three-view drawing of the final delta wing wind tunnel model. (NASA Dryden)

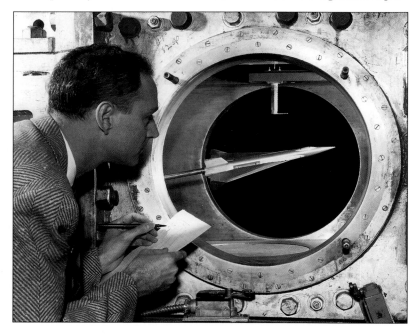

The final delta wing design being tested in the Langley 11-inch hypersonic wind tunnel. (NASA Langley via the Terry Panopalis Collection)

duce any acceleration. The addition of a single centerline propellant tank would allow Mach 8 flights.[25]

The main landing gear would be a version of the gear developed for the X-15A-2, appropriately strengthened for the almost 19,000-pound normal landing weight of the delta-wing design. The nose gear would be moved to the instrument compartment behind the pilot, with the recorders and other research instrumentation normally carried there moved to a new compartment in front of the pilot where the original nose gear well was.[26]

Although not part of the delta-wing baseline, North American was investigating the use of a fly-by-wire control system on the delta-wing X-15. Engineers believed that this would reduce overall system size, weight, and volume, and provide better overall performance. It should be noted that this system would have used an analog flight control system, not a digital one. The MH-96 adaptive control system was capable of accepting electrical inputs that were equivalent to flying in a fly-by-wire mode. In the X-15-3 these were paralleled with mechanical linkages; the delta-wing could eliminate these mechanical linkages altogether. Given the fact that a fly-by-wire system had never flown at this point in time, and that the delta-wing airplane was flying in a new performance envelope, NASA was not terribly supportive of this effort.[27]

Although generally described as a modification to the X-15-3, about the only structure that would remain from the original airplane would be the cockpit and the aft thrust structure. Most of the electronics – the inertial system and MH-96 – would also remain. But, at least by weight, the majority of the aircraft would be new. No data could be ascertained since the final North American study had not been completed when the X-15-3 was lost, but the cost would probably have been substantial.

Although no formal contracting arrangement existed, North American pressed on with a great deal of research into the delta wing configuration. By March 1967 wind tunnel models had accumulated over 300 hours of testing; a 1/50-scale model was used for high-speed tests and a 1/15-scale model for low speed tests. According to a North Amer-

One of the most radical proposals for a delta wing X-15 was this scramjet-powered concept. Very little remains of the basic X-15 design except the canopy area. Note the small retractable canards just ahead of the engine intakes. Nothing came of this concept. (The Boeing Company Archives)

ican news release, "the four year research program has also enabled North American to check out the integrity of components using new super alloys that will be required a hypersonic speeds. Tanks, wing sections, and other components have been fabricated of such materials and put through exhaustive thermal and structural tests."[28]

Despite endorsements from the FRC and John Becker at Langley, support remained lukewarm at best both within NASA and the Air Force. The proposal for the delta-wing study was still being evaluated on 15 November 1967 when the loss of Mike Adams and the X-15-3 effectively ended all thought of such a modification.[29]

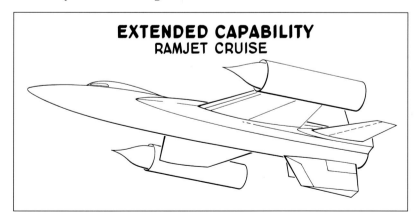

EXTENDED CAPABILITY
RAMJET CRUISE

One of the more fanciful ramjet ideas were this hypersonic cruise vehicle based on the X-15. North American included it in a November 1960 report on possible advanced derivatives, but no action was taken by NASA or the Air Force. (The Boeing Company Archives)

HIRES

Perhaps the most unusual concept proposed using X-15s was also the one the program should be most thankful never happened. During the late 1950s and early 1960s the Air Force investigated a single-stage-to-orbit concept called Aerospaceplane (not to be confused with the 1980's National Aero-Space Plane – NASP). The vehicles explored during this program included some very exotic propulsion concepts, including liquid air collection and enrichment systems (LACE) and air-collection engine systems (ACES) that extracted oxygen from the atmosphere during ascent and used it once the vehicle left the sensible atmosphere.[30]

Most of the contractors involved in the program did parametric evaluations of conventional concepts that carried all of the propellants from the ground – termed POBATO (propellants on-board at take-off) – in addition to the air collection schemes. However, an even more bizarre concept was called HIRES (hypersonic in-flight refueling system), and designers at Convair, Douglas, and North American each considered trying to refuel the Aerospaceplane in flight at Mach 6. This concept actually advanced far enough that preliminary discussions were held of using two X-15s flying in formation to validate the idea. The logistics of getting two X-15s in formation would have been formidable and the piloting task daunting. On two separate occasions the X-15 program had attempted to fly two flights in a single day (but not at the same time since the High Range could not support the concept) – each time one of the X-15s had a system problem that scrubbed its flight. Fortunately for the X-15 program, the refueling demonstration was never attempted.[31]

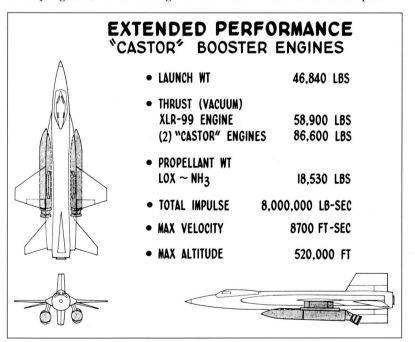

EXTENDED PERFORMANCE
"CASTOR" BOOSTER ENGINES

- LAUNCH WT   46,840 LBS

- THRUST (VACUUM)
  XLR-99 ENGINE   58,900 LBS
  (2) "CASTOR" ENGINES   86,600 LBS

- PROPELLANT WT
  LOX ~ NH₃   18,530 LBS

- TOTAL IMPULSE   8,000,000 LB-SEC

- MAX VELOCITY   8700 FT-SEC

- MAX ALTITUDE   520,000 FT

Another November 1960 proposal was this X-15 using Castor boosters. The extra thrust did not increase the speed of the aircraft, but would have allowed an increase in altitude, assuming controllability issues during reentry could have been solved. Nothing came of this concept. (The Boeing Company Archives)

Just the Facts ...

Left: *Fitz Fulton and Charlie Bock pilot Balls Eight on 26 March 1965 for Flight 1-52-85. After launch Jack McKay would take the X-15-1 to Mach 5.40 and 153,600 feet.* (NASA Dryden)

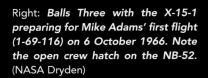

Right: *Balls Three with the X-15-1 preparing for Mike Adams' first flight (1-69-116) on 6 October 1966. Note the open crew hatch on the NB-52.* (NASA Dryden)

APPENDIX A

Selected Biographies

There were 14 pilots assigned to the X-15 program, although only 12 of them actually flew the airplane. Iven Kincheloe was the initial Air Force project pilot, but was killed before the airplanes were delivered. Al White was the backup pilot for Scott Crossfield and never needed to take over. In order of selection, the pilots were:[1]

Name	Pilot at Edwards	Assigned to X-15	Left the X-15
Scott Crossfield	1950-1960	September 1955	December 1960
Al White	1954-1966	September 1955	December 1960
Iven Kincheloe	1955-1958	April 1958	July 1958
Bob White	1955-1963	April 1958	December 1962
Bob Rushworth	1957-1967	April 1958	July 1966
Joe Walker	1951-1966	April 1958	August 1963
Jack McKay	1951-1971	April 1958	September 1966
Neil Armstrong	1955-1962	April 1958	August 1962
Forrest Petersen	1958-1962	August 1958	February 1962
Joe Engle	1962-1966	June 1963	April 1966
Milt Thompson	1956-1967	July 1963	August 1965
Bill Dana	1959-1991	May 1965	December 1968
Pete Knight	1958-1969/1979-1982	May 1965	December 1968
Mike Adams	1963-1967	July 1966	November 1967

There were also plans to allow four Dyna-Soar pilots to fly the X-15 before that program was cancelled, and some sources have indicated that Jacqueline Cochran had attempted to get permission to fly the X-15 to set the women's speed and altitude records.[2]

MICHAEL J. ADAMS, USAF

Mike Adams flew the X-15 for 13 months from 6 October 1966 until 15 November 1967, making seven flights. All of these were with the XLR99 engine and he reached Mach 5.59, a maximum speed of 3,822 mph, and an altitude of 266,000 feet. Adams was the twelfth (last) pilot assigned to the X-15 and the tenth pilot to leave the program; he was killed on Flight 3-65-97.

Michael James Adams was born on 5 May 1930 in Sacramento, California, and enlisted in the Air Force on 22 November 1950 after graduating from Sacramento Junior College. Adams earned his pilot wings and commission on 25 October 1952 at Webb AFB, Texas. He served as a fighter-bomber pilot in Korea, flying 49 missions during four months of combat service. This was followed by 30 months with the 613th Fighter-Bomber Squadron at England AFB, Louisiana, and six months rotational duty at Chaumont Air Base in France.[3]

In 1958 Adams received a Bachelor of Science degree in aeronautical engineering from Oklahoma University. After 18 months of astronautics study at the Massachusetts Institute of Technology he was

Michael J. Adams. (NASA Dryden)

selected in 1962 for the Experimental Test Pilot School at Edwards where he won the Honts Trophy as the best in his class. He subsequently attended the Aerospace Research Pilot School, graduating with honors on 20 December 1963, and was assigned to the Manned Spacecraft Operations Division at Edwards AFB on the Manned Orbiting Laboratory program. During this time he was one of four Edwards aerospace research pilots to participate in a five-month series of NASA moon landing practice tests at the Martin Company in Baltimore, Maryland. Four seven-day lunar landing simulations were scheduled, each with a five-week training period for the three-man crew.

In July 1966, Adams came to the X-15 program with a total of 3,940 hours total flight time, including 2,505 hours in single engine jets and an additional 477 hours in multiengine jets. Tragically, Adams was killed during Flight 3-65-97 on 15 November 1967. Mike Adams was posthumously awarded Astronaut Wings for his last flight in the X-15-3, which had attained an altitude of 266,000 feet – 50.38 miles. In 1991 Adams' name was added to the Astronaut Memorial at the Kennedy Space Center in Florida.

NEIL A. ARMSTRONG, NASA

Neil Armstrong flew the X-15 for 20 months from 30 November 1960 until 26 July 1962, making seven flights. These included two flights with the XLR11 and five with the XLR99. Armstrong reached Mach 5.74, a maximum speed of 3,989 mph, and an altitude of 207,500 feet. Accomplishments included making the first flight with the ball nose and the first flight with the MH-96 adaptive control system. Armstrong was the seventh pilot to fly the X-15 and the third pilot to leave the program.

Neil Alden Armstrong was born on 5 August 1930 in Wapakoneta, Ohio, and attended Purdue University, earning his Bachelor of Science degree in aeronautical engineering in 1955. During Korea, which interrupted his engineering studies, Armstrong flew 78 combat missions in F9F-2 fighters for which he earned the Air Medal and two Gold Stars. He later earned a Master of Science degree in aerospace engineering from the University of Southern California.

Armstrong joined the NACA Flight Propulsion Research Laboratory (now the Lewis Research Center) in 1955. Later that year, he transferred to the High-Speed Flight Station as an aeronautical research scientist and then as a pilot. Armstrong served as the project pilot on the F-100A, F-100C, F-101, and F-104A, and also flew the X-1B, X-5, F-105, F-106, B-47, KC-135, and Paresev. He left with a total of over 2,450 flying hours.

Armstrong was a member of the USAF-NASA Dyna-Soar Pilot Consultant Group before that program was cancelled, and studied X-20 Dyna-Soar approaches and abort maneuvers using F-102A and F5D aircraft. While flying the X-15, Armstrong was one of nine pilots selected for the second NASA astronaut class in 1962. In March 1966 he was commander of Gemini 8 with David Scott as pilot – this was the first successful docking of two vehicles in orbit. On 20 July 1969, Armstrong became the first human to set foot on the Moon during the Apollo 11 mission. Armstrong has a total of 8 days and 14 hours in space, including 2 hours and 48 minutes walking on the Moon.

After his lunar flight Armstrong became the Deputy Associate Administrator for Aeronautics at NASA Headquarters. He resigned from NASA in August 1971 to become Professor of Engineering at the University of Cincinnati, a post he held until 1979. Armstrong became Chairman of the Board of Cardwell International, Ltd. in 1980 and served in that capacity until 1982. During 1982-92 Armstrong was chairman of Computing Technologies for Aviation, and from 1981 to 1999 served on the board of directors for Eaton Corporation. He was also vice chairman of the Rogers Commission investigating the *Challenger* accident in 1986.

Armstrong has been the recipient of numerous awards, including the Presidential Medal for Freedom and the Robert J. Collier Trophy in 1969; the Robert H. Goddard Memorial Trophy in 1970; and the Congressional Space Medal of Honor in 1978.[4]

JOHN V. BECKER, NASA

John Becker is widely regarded as the father of the X-15, having served as the leader of the Langley researchers that defined the general concept of a hypersonic research airplane.

John Vernon Becker was born in 1913 in Albany, New York. He earned a Bachelor of Science degree in mechanical engineering and a Master of Science degree from New York State University in 1935 and 1956. He joined the NACA Langley Memorial Aeronautical Laboratory as a junior aeronautical engineer in 1936.[5]

He served as head of the 16-foot High-Speed Wind Tunnel Branch (1943), chief of the Compressibility Research Division (1947), and chief of the Aero-Physics Research Division (1955). In 1955 Becker was cited by New York University as one of its 100 outstanding graduates from the College of Engineering. Becker was associated not only with the X-15 program, but also with the X-1, Dyna-Soar, and hypersonic research engine programs.[6]

PAUL F. BIKLE, NASA

Paul F. Bikle was born on 5 June 1916 in Wilkensburg, Pennsylvania, and graduated from the University of Detroit with a Bachelor of Science degree in aeronautical engineering in 1939. His career with the Army Air Forces began in 1940 when he was appointed an aeronautical engineer at Wright Field, and in 1944 he was named Chief of the Aerodynamics Branch in the Flight Test Division. While working closely with other government agencies in establishing the first flying qualities specifications for aircraft he wrote AAF Technical Report 50693 "Flight Test Methods," which was used as a standard manual for conducting flight tests for more than five years. During World War II he was involved in more than 30 test projects and flew over 1,200 hours as an engineering observer.

In 1947, Bikle was appointed Chief of the Performance Engineering Branch and directed tests of the XB-43, XC-99, and F-86A. With the transfer of the flight test mission to the newly formed Air Force Flight Test Center at Edwards, Bikle came to the desert and advanced to Assistant Chief of the Flight Test Engineering Laboratory in 1951. From there, he advanced to the position of AFFTC Technical Director. He took Walt Williams place as

John V. Becker. (NASA Langley)

director of the NASA Flight Research Center in September 1959. Like Williams, Bikle had little use for unnecessary paperwork; often remarking that he would stay with NASA as long as the paperwork level remained below what he had experienced in the Air Force. He was also an avid soaring enthusiast and established two world soaring records during a flight near Lancaster in 1961; one of these, an altitude record of 46,620 feet, stood for almost 25 years. Bikle was awarded the 1963 FAI Lilienthal Medal, and in July 1962 was awarded the NASA Medal for Outstanding Leadership for directing the "successful X-15 Flight Operations and Research Activities." Bikle retired from the NASA in May 1971 and died in January 1991.[7]

A. SCOTT CROSSFIELD, NAA

Scott Crossfield flew the X-15 for 18 months, from 8 June 1959 until 6 December 1960, making 14 flights. These included one glide flight, ten flights with the XLR11, and three flights with the XLR99.

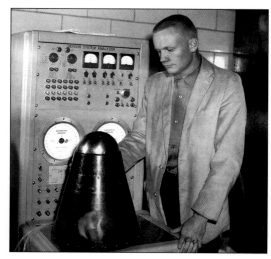

Neil A. Armstrong. (NASA Dryden)

Paul F. Bikle. (NASA Dryden)

Crossfield reached Mach 2.97, a speed of 1,960 mph, and an altitude of 88,116 feet. Accomplishments included the first X-15 glide flight, the first powered flight, the first flight with the XLR99, and the first emergency landing. Crossfield was the first to fly the X-15 and the first pilot to leave the program.

Albert Scott Crossfield was born on 2 October 1921 in Berkeley, California, and began his engineering training at the University of Washington in 1940. He interrupted his education to join the U.S. Navy in 1942 and was commissioned an ensign in 1943. Following flight training he served as a fighter and gunnery instructor and maintenance officer before spending six months in the South Pacific without seeing combat duty. After the war, Crossfield was the leader of a Navy acrobatic team flying FG-1D Corsairs at various exhibitions and airshows in the Pacific Northwest.[8]

He resumed his engineering studies in 1946 and graduated with a Bachelor of Science degree in aeronautical engineering from the University of Washington in 1949. He earned a Master of Science degree in aeronautical science the following year from the same university, and received an honorary Doctor of Science degree from the Florida Institute of Technology in 1982.

Crossfield joined the High-Speed Flight Station as a research pilot in June 1950. During the next five years he flew the X-1, X-4, X-5, XF-92A, D-558-I, and D-558-II aircraft, accumulating 87 rocket-powered flights in the X-1 and D-558-II aircraft, plus 12 D-558-II with jet power only. On 20 November 1953 Crossfield became the first pilot to exceed Mach 2, in the D-558-II Skyrocket. Crossfield left the NACA in 1955 to work for North American Aviation on the X-15 as both pilot and design consultant.[9]

In 1960, Crossfield published his autobiography (written with Clay Blair), *Always Another Dawn: The Story of a Rocket Test Pilot* (Cleveland and New York: The World Publishing Company, 1960; reprinted New York: Arno Press, 1971; reprinted North Stratford, NH: Ayer Company Publishers, 1999). There he covered his life through the completion of the early X-15 flights. It is a fascinating story for anybody interested in that period of flight test.

William H. Dana. (NASA Dryden)

A. Scott Crossfield. (Courtesy of Alvin S. White)

Crossfield also served for five years as the North American director responsible for systems test, reliability engineering, and quality assurance for the WS-131 Hound Dog missile, Paraglider, Apollo Command and Service Module, and the Saturn booster. From 1966 to 1967 he served as Technical Director, Research Engineering and Test at North American Aviation.

He served as an executive for Eastern Airlines from 1967 to 1973 and Senior Vice President for Hawker Siddeley Aviation during 1974-75. From 1977 until his retirement in 1993 he served as technical consultant to the House Committee on Science and Technology, advising committee members on matters relating to civil aviation. In 1993 he was awarded the NASA Distinguished Public Service Medal for his contributions to aeronautics and aviation over a period spanning half a century. Crossfield was a joint recipient of the 1961 Robert J. Collier Trophy that was presented by President John F. Kennedy at the White House in July 1962. Among his other awards were the International Clifford B. Harmon Trophy for 1960, the Lawrence Sperry Award, Octave Chanute Award, Iven C. Kincheloe Award, and the Harmon International Trophy. He has been inducted into the National Aviation Hall of Fame (1983), the International Space Hall of Fame (1988), and the Aerospace Walk of Honor (1990).[10]

WILLIAM H. DANA, NASA

Bill Dana flew the X-15 for 35 months from 4 November 1965 until 24 October 1968, making 16 flights. All of these were with the XLR99 engine. Dana reached Mach 5.53, a maximum speed of 3,897 mph, and an altitude of 306,900 feet. Dana was the eleventh pilot to fly the X-15 and made the last flight of the program.

William Harvey Dana was born on 3 November 1930 in Pasadena, California. He received his Bachelor of Science degree from the U.S. Military Academy in 1952 and served four years as a pilot in the Air Force. He joined NASA after receiving a Master of Science degree in Aeronautical Engineering from the University of Southern California in 1958.

During the late 1960s and in the 1970s Dana was a project pilot on the manned lifting body program, for which he was awarded the NASA Exceptional Service Medal. In 1976 he received the Haley Space Flight Award from the American Institute of Aeronautics and Astronautics for his research work on the M2-F3 lifting body control systems. In 1986 Dana became the Chief Pilot at the FRC, and later was an Assistant Chief of the Flight Operations Directorate. He was also a project pilot on the F-15 HIDEC (Highly Integrated Digital Electronic Control) research program, and a co-project pilot on the F-18 High Angle of Attack research program. In August 1993 Dana became Chief Engineer, a position he held until his retirement in 1998.[11]

In 1993 Dana was inducted into the Aerospace Walk of Honor and received the NASA Distinguished Service Medal in 1997. In 1998 he was honored by the Smithsonian Institution's National Air and Space Museum when he was selected to deliver the Charles A. Lindbergh Memorial Lecture.[12]

HUGH L. DRYDEN, NASA

Hugh Latimer Dryden was born July 2, 1898, in Pocomoke City, Maryland. He earned his way through Johns Hopkins University, completing the 4-year bachelor of arts course in 3 years, graduating with honors. Influenced by Dr. Joseph S. Ames, who for many years was chairman of the NACA, Dryden undertook a study of fluid dynamics at the Bureau of Standards while taking graduate courses at Johns Hopkins. His laboratory work was accepted by the university when it granted him a doctor of philosophy degree in 1919.[13]

Dryden was promoted in 1920 to head the Bureau's Aerodynamics Section. With A. M. Kuethe, in 1929 he published the first of a series of papers on the measurement of turbulence in wind tunnels and the mechanics of boundary layer flow. He was advanced to Chief of the Mechanics and Sound Division of the Bureau in 1934, and in January 1946 to Assistant Director. Six months later he was appointed Associate Director.

Hugh L. Dryden. (NASA Dryden)

In 1945 Dryden was made Deputy Scientific Director of the Army Air Forces Scientific Advisory Group. He was awarded the Nation's second highest civilian decoration, the Medal of Freedom, in 1946 for "an outstanding contribution to the fund of knowledge of the Army Air Forces with his research and analysis of the development and use of guided missiles by the enemy."

In 1947 he resigned from the Bureau of Standards to become Director of Aeronautical Research at the NACA. Two years later the agency gave him added responsibilities and the new title of Director. Dryden held this post until the creation of the National Aeronautics and Space Administration (NASA), and was named Deputy Administrator of the new agency when it was created. Dr. Dryden was honored by the National Civil Service League with the Career Service Award for 1958. He served as the NASA Deputy Administrator until his death on 2 December 1965.

JOE H. ENGLE, USAF

Joe Engle has the unique honor of having flown the X-15 and the space shuttle, bringing lifting-reentry vehicles full-circle. Engle flew the X-15 for 24 months from 7 October 1963 until 14 October 1965, making 16 flight with the XLR99 engine. Engle reached Mach 5.71, a maximum speed of 3,888 mph, and an altitude of 280,600 feet. He was the eighth pilot to fly the X-15 and the seventh pilot to leave the program.

Joe Henry Engle was born on 26 August 1932 in Abilene, Kansas, and graduated from the University of Kansas at Lawrence with a Bachelor of Science degree in aeronautical engineering in 1955. After graduation he worked at Cessna Aircraft as a flight test engineer before being commissioned through the Air Force ROTC program in 1956. Engle earned his pilot's wings in 1958 and was assigned to fly F-100s for the 474th Fighter Squadron (Day) and, later, the 309th Tactical Fighter Squadron at George AFB, California.

Engle graduated from the Test Pilot School in 1962 and was immediately selected to attend the

Joe H. Engle. (Gerald H. Balzer Collection)

Charles H. Feltz. (The Boeing Company Archives)

Aerospace Research Pilot School (ARPS) to train military astronauts. Engle graduated from ARPS in 1963 and was selected as a project pilot for the X-15 program. Milt Thompson remembers Engle as "an excellent pilot. He really took the job as a test pilot seriously except occasionally when his exuberance overcame him. That happened on his first X-15 flight. After he had completed the familiarization maneuvers, he slow-rolled the X-15. That maneuver really shocked the engineers in the control room. They did not immediately recognize it as a slow roll. They assumed the worse and thought Joe had a control problem. ... Joe was thoroughly chastised by Bob Rushworth [the chief pilot] after the flight." Engle went on to exceed the Air Force's 50-mile threshold for an astronaut rating on two X-15 flights. [14]

In 1966, at 32 years of age, Engle became the youngest person selected to become an astronaut. He served on the support crew for Apollo X and then as backup lunar module pilot for Apollo XIV. In 1977, he was commander of one of two crews that conducted the atmospheric approach and landing tests with the Space Shuttle *Enterprise*. In November 1981 he commanded the second orbital test flight (STS-2) of *Columbia* and manually flew significant portions of the reentry – performing 29 flight test maneuvers from Mach 25 through landing rollout. This was the first, and so far only, time that a winged aerospace vehicle has been manually flown from orbit through landing. He accumulated the last of his 224.5 hours in space when he commanded the *Discovery* during Mission 51-I (STS-27) in August 1985.

Brigadier General Engle has flown more than 180 different aircraft types and logged nearly 14,000 flight hours. Among his many honors, Engle has been awarded the Distinguished Flying Cross (1964), the AIAA Lawrence Sperry Award for Flight Research (1966), the NASA Distinguished Service Medal and Space Flight Medal, as well as the Harmon International, Robert J. Collier, Lawrence Sperry, Iven C. Kincheloe, Robert H. Goddard and Thomas D. White aviation and space trophies. In 1992, he was inducted into the Aerospace Walk of Honor. [15]

CHARLES H. FELTZ, NAA

Charles H. Feltz was born on 15 September 1916 on a small ranch near Dumas, Texas. He graduated from Texas Technological University in 1940 with a Bachelor of Science degree in mechanical engineering. He joined the Los Angeles Division of North American Aviation in 1940, becoming the design group engineer in charge of the design of the wing structure for the F-82 and F-86 series of aircraft. Between 1948 and 1956 Feltz was the assistant project engineer for the development of the FJ2 Fury and the F-86D Sabre, and in 1956 he became the project engineer and program manager for the X-15.

In 1962 Feltz became the chief engineer for the Apollo command and service module, advancing to assistant program manager in 1964. As the Apollo program ended, he became the assistant program manager for the Space Shuttle orbiter. Between 1974 and 1976, Feltz was the technical assistant to the president of the North American Rockwell Space Division. In 1976 he was appointed Vice President of the North American Aerospace Operations Division of Rockwell International, becoming president of the Space Transportation System Development Production Division of Rockwell International in 1980. Feltz retired from Rockwell International in 1981. [16]

IVEN C. KINCHELOE, JR., USAF

Iven Carl Kincheloe, Jr., was born on 2 July 1928 in Detroit, Michigan. In 1945 he entered Purdue University where he studied aeronautical engineering as a member of the Air Force ROTC unit. He graduated in 1949 with Bachelor of Science degree in aeronautical and mechanical engineering. [17]

Kincheloe received his wings at Williams AFB, Arizona in 1951. In early 1952, was promoted to Captain and entered the Korean War with the 5th Interceptor Wing, flying 131 missions and shooting down 5 MiG-15s to become the 10th jet ace. For his outstanding service he received the Silver Star and the Distinguished Flying Cross with two Oak Leaf

Iven C. Kincheloe, Jr. (Courtesy of Alvin S. White)

clusters. Returning to the United States, he was a gunnery instructor at Nellis AFB, Nevada, and in 1953 was accepted into the Empire Test School in Farnborough, England. While in England, he received a Master of Science degree in aeronautical engineering from Oxford in December 1954.[18]

Kincheloe flew the X-2 to an altitude of 126,200 feet, becoming famous as the "America's first spaceman." On 27 March Kincheloe was named chief of the Manned Spacecraft Section, Fighter Operations Branch of the Flight Test Operations Division that was responsible for the training of Air Force pilots who were to participate in the X-15 flight program. Kincheloe was also selected to be the Air Force project pilot for the X-15; unfortunately, he died before he had a chance to fly it. On 26 July 1958 Kincheloe took off on a chase mission in an F-104. At 2,000 feet altitude the engine failed; although Kincheloe was able to roll the airplane inverted so the downward-firing ejection seat could work, he was too low for his parachute to open. He is buried in Arlington National Cemetery.

A biography, *First of the Spacemen: Iven C. Kincheloe, Jr.* by James J. Haggerty, Jr., (New York: Duell, Sloan and Pearce) was published in 1960, and a CD-ROM biography was aboard the Space Shuttle *Discovery* on STS-70 during July 1995.

During the course of his career, Kincheloe accumulated 3,573 flying hours in 70 American and foreign aircraft. Numerous honors followed his death. One of the most meaningful came from his peers, when the Society of Experimental Test Pilots (SETP) renamed its prestigious Outstanding Pilot Award in his honor. His most public tribute, however, took place far away in his home state when Kinross AFB in Michigan's Upper Peninsula was renamed Kincheloe AFB in his memory.[19]

WILLIAM J. KNIGHT, USAF

Pete Knight flew the X-15 for 35 months from 30 September 1965 until 13 September 1968, making 16 flights with the XLR99 engine. Knight reached Mach 6.70, a maximum speed of 4,520 mph, and an altitude of 280,500 feet. Accomplish-

William J. "Pete" Knight. (NASA Dryden)

John B. "Jack" McKay. (NASA Dryden)

ments included the first flight with the dummy ramjet, the first flight with a full ablative coating, and the maximum speed flight. Knight was the tenth pilot to fly the X-15 and was the designated pilot for the aborted 200th flight.

William J. "Pete" Knight was born on 18 November 1929 in Noblesville, Indiana. He enlisted in the Air Force in 1951 and completed pilot training in 1953. Flying an F-89D for the 438th Fighter-Interceptor Squadron, Knight won the prestigious Allison Jet Trophy Race in September of 1954. He graduated with a Bachelor of Science degree in aeronautical engineering from the Air Force Institute of Technology in 1958 and from the Experimental Test Pilot School later that same year. In 1960, he was one of six test pilots selected to fly the Dyna-Soar; after the X-20 was cancelled in 1963 he completed the astronaut training curriculum at the new Aerospace Research Pilot School in 1964 and was selected to fly the X-15.

After nearly ten years of flying at Edwards, Knight went to Southeast Asia in 1969 where he completed a total of 253 combat missions in the F-100. Following this he served as test director for the F-15 System Program Office at Wright-Patterson AFB and became the tenth pilot to fly the F-15 Eagle. Knight returned to Edwards AFB as vice commander of the AFFTC in 1979 and remained an active test pilot in the F-16 Combined Test Force. After 32 years of service and more than 7,000 hours in more than 100 different aircraft, Colonel Knight retired from the Air Force in 1982. In 1984, he was elected to the Palmdale city council and became the city's first elected mayor in 1988. Knight was elected to the California State Assembly in 1992 and to the California State Senate in 1996.[20]

Among his many honors, Knight has been awarded the Legion of Merit with Oak Leaf Cluster, the Distinguished Flying Cross with two Oak Leaf Clusters, the Air Medal with ten Oak Leaf Clusters, the Harmon International Trophy, the Octave Chanute Award, and the Air Force Association Citation of Honor. He has been inducted into the National Aviation Hall of Fame (1988), the Aerospace Walk of Honor (1990), and the International Space Hall of Fame (1998).[21]

JOHN B. MCKAY, NASA

Jack McKay flew the X-15 for 70 months from 28 October 1960 until 8 September 1966, making 29 flights. These included 2 flights with the XLR11 and 27 with the XLR99. McKay reached Mach 5.65, a maximum speed of 3,938 mph, and an altitude of 295,600 feet. He made three emergency landings, and was seriously injured in one of them, although he returned to fly 22 more X-15 missions. He was the fifth pilot to fly the X-15 and the ninth pilot to leave the program.

John Barron "Jack" McKay was born on 8 December 1922 in Portsmouth, Virginia, and graduated from Virginia Polytechnic Institute in 1950 with a Bachelor of Science degree in aeronautical engineering. During World War II he served as a Navy pilot in the Pacific, earning the Air Medal with two Oak Leaf Clusters and a Presidential Unit Citation while flying F6F Hellcats.

He joined the NACA on 8 February 1951 and worked at Langley as an engineer for a brief period before transferring to the High-Speed Flight Station where he flew the F-100, YF-102, F-102A, F-104, YF-107A, D-558-I, D-558-II, X-1B, and X-1E. McKay accumulated more rocket flights than any other U.S. pilot except Crossfield, with a total of 46 before joining the X-15 program. Milt Thompson remembers that "Jack was an excellent stick and rudder pilot, possibly the best of the X-15 pilots." McKay retired from the NASA on 5 October 1971 and died on 27 April 1975, mostly from late complications resulting from his X-15 crash.[22]

FORREST S. PETERSON, USN

Forrest "Pete" Petersen flew the X-15 for 15 months from 23 September 1960 until 10 January 1962, making five flights. These included two flights with the XLR11 and three with the XLR99. He reached Mach 5.30, a maximum speed of 3,600 mph, and an altitude of 101,800 feet. Petersen was the fourth pilot to fly the X-15 and the second pilot to leave the program.

Forrest Silas Petersen was born on 16 May

Forrest S. Petersen. (NASA Dryden)

1922 in Holdrege, Nebraska. He was commissioned an Ensign upon graduation from the Naval Academy in June 1944 and reported to the destroyer USS *Caperton* (DD-650) where he participated in campaigns in the Philippines, Formosa and Okinawa. Switching from the "black shoe" Navy to "brown shoes," Petersen graduated from flight training in 1947 and was assigned to VF-20A.

Petersen completed two years of study at the Naval Post Graduate School and earned a Bachelors of Science degree in aerospace engineering. He continued his studies at Princeton University and received a Masters Degree in engineering in 1953. In 1956 he was selected to attend the Naval Test Pilot School and remained as an instructor following graduation. He was assigned to the X-15 program in August 1958 and served with NASA until January 1962. He was a joint recipient of the 1961 Robert J. Collier Trophy which was presented by President John F. Kennedy at the White House in July 1962 and the NASA Distinguished Service Medal, presented by Vice President Lyndon B. Johnson,

Petersen served as Commanding Officer of VF-154 prior to being assigned to the office of Director, Division of Naval Reactors, AEC for Nuclear Power Training. He reported to USS *Enterprise* in January 1964 and served as executive officer until April 1966; Petersen was awarded the Bronze Star during *Enterprise*'s first combat tour in Vietnam. He was then assigned duties as an Assistant to the Director of Naval Program Planning in the office of the Chief of Naval Operations. In November 1967 he assumed command of USS *Bexar* (APA-237) and was awarded the Navy Commendation Medal with Combat V. He later served as Deputy Chief of Naval Operations for Air Warfare and Commander of Naval Air Systems Command. Vice Admiral Petersen retired from active duty in May 1980, and died of cancer in Omaha, Nebraska on 8 December 1990.

ROBERT A. RUSHWORTH, USAF

Bob Rushworth flew the X-15 for 68 months from 4 November 1960 until 1 July 1966, making 34 flights. These included 2 flights with the XLR11 and 32 flights with the XLR99. Rushworth reached

Robert A. Rushworth. (NASA Dryden)

Hartley A. Soulé. (NASA Dryden)

Mach 6.06, a maximum speed of 4,018 mph, and an altitude of 285,000 feet. Accomplishments included the first ventral-off flight, the maximum dynamic pressure flight, the maximum temperature flight, the maximum Mach number (6.06) in the basic X-15, the first flight of the X-15A-2, and the first flight with external tanks. Rushworth was the sixth pilot to fly the X-15 and the eighth pilot to leave the program.

Robert Aitken Rushworth was born on 9 October 1924 in Madison, Maine. He joined the Army Air Forces, flying C-46 and C-47 transports in World War II as well as combat missions in Korea. He graduated from Hebron Academy, Maine, in 1943, and received Bachelor of Science degrees in mechanical engineering from the University of Maine in 1951 and in aeronautical engineering from the Air Force Institute of Technology in 1954. He graduated from the National War College at Fort Lesley J. McNair, Washington, D.C., in 1967.[23]

Rushworth began his flight-test career at Wright Field and transferred to Edwards in 1956. Following graduation from the Experimental Test Pilot School, Rushworth was assigned to the Fighter Operations Branch at Edwards and later as operations officer in the Manned Spacecraft Section while flying the X-15. Rushworth also served as a mentor to the Dyna-Soar pilots in his role as operations officer of the Manned Spacecraft Branch. He spent a lot of time in Seattle during the early development stages of Dyna-Soar. Prior to flying the X-15, Rushworth flew the F-101, TF-102, F-104, F-105, and F-106. He was awarded the Distinguished Flying Cross for an emergency recovery of the X-15 after premature extension of the nose gear at Mach 4.2, and the Legion of Merit for overall accomplishments in the national interest of initial space flights.[24]

He graduated from the National War College in August 1967 and attended F-4 Phantom II combat crew training at George AFB. In March 1968 Rushworth went to Cam Ranh Bay Air Base in Vietnam as the assistant deputy commander for operations with the 12th TFW and flew 189 combat missions. From April 1969 to January 1971, he was program director for the AGM-65 Maverick and in February 1971 became commander of the 4950th Test Wing at Wright-Patterson AFB. General Rushworth served as the inspector general for the Air Force Systems

Command from May 1973 to February 1974 and returned to the AFFTC as commander until November 1975 when he was selected to command the Air Force Test and Evaluation Center at Kirtland AFB, New Mexico. General Rushworth retired from the Air Force in 1981 as Vice Commander of the Aeronautical Systems Division at Wright-Patterson AFB. Bob Rushworth died of a heart attack on 18 March 1993 in Camarillo, California.[25]

HARTLEY A. SOULÉ, NASA

Hartley A. Soulé was born on 19 August 1904 in New York City. He received a Bachelor of Science degree in mechanical engineering from New York University in 1927 and joined the staff at Langley in October 1927 after working briefly for the Fairchild Airplane Company in Long Island. Soulé concentrated his research in stability and control and became Chief of the Stability Research Division in 1943. He was promoted to Assistant Chief of Research in 1947 and became the Assistant Director of Langley in August 1952.

Soulé was a co-inventor of the Stability Wind Tunnel and directed the construction of three other wind tunnels at Langley. He pioneered the use of computing machinery for analytical and data reduction. He was also instrumental in establishing the Pilotless Aircraft Research Division at Wallops Island. Soulé was appointed Chairman of the Interlaboratory Research Airplane Projects Panel where he directed research on the Bell X-1 program and was instrumental in managing the early years of the X-15 program. Later, he was project director for the Mercury world-wide tracking and ground instrumentation system. Soulé retired from NASA on 16 February 1962 and passed away in 1988.

HARRISON A. STORMS, JR, NAA

Harrison A. "Stormy" Storms, Jr., was born in 1915 in Chicago, Illinois. He attended Northwestern University graduating with a Master of Science degree in mechanical engineering in 1938. Storms then attended the California Institute of Technology, earning a Master of Science degree in aeronau-

Harrison A. Storms. (The Boeing Company Archives)

Milton O. Thompson. (NASA Dryden)

tical engineering. At CalTech he studied under Theodore von Kármán and worked in the wind tunnels at the Guggenheim Aeronautical Laboratory at CalTech (GALCIT). He went to work at North American Aviation in 1940 on the P-51 Mustang. Storms was chief engineer of the Los Angeles Division from 1957 until he became North American's vice president for program development, in charge of the development of the Apollo spacecraft. He was honored by the American Institute of Aeronautics and Astronautics (AIAA) 1970 Aircraft Design Award.[26]

MILTON O. THOMPSON, NASA

Milt Thompson flew the X-15 for 22 months from 29 October 1963 until 25 August 1965, making 14 flights with the XLR99 engine. Thompson reached Mach 5.48, a maximum speed of 3,723 mph, and an altitude of 214,100 feet. He was the ninth pilot to fly the X-15 and the sixth pilot to leave the program.

Milton Orville Thompson was born on 4 May 1926 in Crookston, Minnesota. Thompson began flying with the Navy and served in China and Japan during World War II. Following six years of active duty, Thompson entered the University of Washington and graduated with a Bachelor of Science degree in engineering in 1953. After graduation Thompson became a flight test engineer for the Boeing Aircraft Company testing, among other things, the B-52.

Thompson joined the High-Speed Flight Station on 19 March 1956 and became a research pilot in January 1958 – at the time, there were only five pilots: Joe Walker, Stan Butchart, Jack McKay, Neil Armstrong, and Thompson. In 1962 Thompson was selected by the Air Force to be the only civilian pilot on the X-20 Dyna-Soar, but that program was cancelled just over a year later. On 16 August 1963 Thompson became the first person to fly a lifting body, the lightweight M2-F1. He flew it a total of 47 times, and also made the first five flights of the all-metal M2-F2. Thompson concluded his active flying career in 1967, becoming Chief

of Research Projects two years later. In 1975 he was appointed Chief Engineer and retained the position until his death on 6 August 1993. Thompson also served on NASA's Space Transportation System Technology Steering Committee during the 1970s. In this role he was successful in leading the effort to design the Space Shuttle orbiters for power-off landings rather than increase weight with air-breathing engines. His committee work earned him the NASA Distinguished Service Medal.

He was a member of the Society of Experimental Test Pilots, and received the organization's Iven C. Kincheloe trophy as the Outstanding Experimental Test Pilot of 1966 for his research flights in the M2 lifting bodies. He also received the 1967 Octave Chanute award from the AIAA for his lifting-body research. In 1990, the National Aeronautics Association selected Thompson as a recipient of its Elder Statesman of Aviation award; the awards have been presented each year since 1955 to individuals for contributions "of significant value over a period of years" in the field of aeronautics.[27]

Thompson wrote about his experiences with the X-15 flight program in his *At the Edge of Space: The X-15 Flight Program* (Washington DC: Smithsonian Institution Press, 1992). Anybody interested in an inside look at the program should pick up a copy; it is a fascinating read.

JOSEPH A. WALKER, NASA

Joe Walker flew the X-15 for 41 months, from 25 March 1960 until 22 August 1963, making 25 flights. These included 5 flights with the XLR11 and 20 with the XLR99. Walker reached Mach 5.92, a maximum speed of 4,104 mph, and an altitude of 354,200 feet. His accomplishments include the first government flight, the maximum speed (4,104 mph) flight of a basic X-15, and the maximum altitude (354,200 feet) flight. Walker was the second pilot to fly the X-15 and the fifth pilot to leave the program.

Joseph Albert Walker was born on 20 February 1921 in Washington, Pennsylvania, and graduated from Washington & Jefferson College in 1942 with a Bachelor of Arts degree in physics.

Alvin S. White (Courtesy of Alvin S. White)

Joseph A. Walker. (Gerald H. Balzer Collection)

During World War II he flew P-38 fighters for the Army Air Forces in North Africa, earning the Distinguished Flying Cross and the Air Medal with seven Oak Leaf clusters.

He joined the NACA in March 1945 at the Aircraft Engine Research Laboratory (now the Lewis Research Center) where he was involved in icing research, spending many hours flying into the worse weather the Great Lakes region could dish out. He transferred to the High-Speed Flight Station in 1951 and became chief pilot in 1955. He served as project pilot on the D-558-I, D-558-II, X-1, X-3, X-4, X-5, and X-15, and also flew the F-100, F-101, F-102, F-104, and B-47. He was the first man to pilot the Lunar Landing Research Vehicle (LLRV) that was used to develop piloting and operational techniques for lunar landings.

Prior to joining the X-15 program, Walker did some pioneering work on the concept of reaction controls, flying an JF-104A to peak altitudes of 90,000 feet. The indicated airspeed going over the top of this maneuver was less than 30 knots, providing an ideal environment for evaluating the reaction control system.[28]

Walker was a joint recipient of the 1961 Robert J. Collier trophy that was presented by President John F. Kennedy at the White House in July 1962. Walker also received the 1961 Harmon International Trophy for Aviators, the 1961 Iven C. Kincheloe award, and the 1961 Octave Chanute award. He received an honorary Doctor of Aeronautical Sciences degree from his alma mater in June of 1962 and was named Pilot of the Year in 1963 by the National Pilots Association. He was a charter member of the Society of Experimental Test Pilots, and one of the first to be designated a Fellow. Tragically, Walker was killed on 8 June 1966 in a mid-air collision between his F-104 and the second XB-70A.[29]

ALVIN S. WHITE, NAA

Alvin S. White was born in December 1918 in Berkeley, California. In 1936 he enrolled in the University of California at Davis to study electrical engineering, transferring to the Berkeley campus two years later. In 1941 he enlisted as an Aviation Cadet in the Army Air Corps, graduating from flight school at Williams Field, Arizona in May 1942.[30]

After nearly two years as an advanced flight instructor at Williams Field, White joined the 355th Fighter Group in England on 4 June 1944. He flew two tours as a combat fighter pilot from D-Day until the end of the war in Europe. White returned to the University of California at the end of 1945, earning his degree in mechanical engineering with elective courses in aeronautical engineering in 1947.

In 1948 White reenlisted in the Air Force and spent nearly three years conducting parachute research at Wright-Patterson AFB and the National Parachute Range at El Centro. In 1952 White graduated from the Air Force Test Pilot School at Edwards and joined the fighter test section. In May 1954 he left the Air Force to join North American Aviation.

After four years of testing the F-86 series, the F-100 series, and the F-107 he was appointed as the back-up pilot to Scott Crossfield on the X-15. He participated in the centrifuge program, attended the training sessions, flew the fixed-base simulator, practiced the landing approach flights, and flew the photo chase airplane for many of the early X-15 flights. In his role as North American back-up pilot White was prepared, but never called upon, to fly the airplane.[31]

In 1957 White was appointed project pilot for the XB-70, and concentrated his work on that program after the completion of the North American X-15 flights.

Robert M. White, USAF

Bob White flew the X-15 for 32 months from 13 April 1960 until 14 December 1962, making 16 flights. These included 6 flights with the XLR11 and 10 with the XLR99. White reached Mach 6.04, a maximum speed of 4,093 mph, and an altitude of

Robert M. White. (Gerald H. Balzer Collection)

314,750 feet. Accomplishments include the maximum Mach number (3.50) and maximum altitude (136,000 feet) with the XLR11, the first Mach 4 flight (of any manned aircraft), the first Mach 5 flight, the first Mach 6 flight, the first flight over 200,000 feet (in any manned aircraft), the first flight over 300,000 feet, and an FAI record flight of 314,750 feet. White was the third pilot to fly the X-15 and the fourth pilot to leave the program.

Robert Michael White was born on 6 July 1924 in New York, New York. He entered the Army Air Forces in November 1942 and received his wings in February 1944. White subsequently joined the 354th Fighter Squadron in July 1944 flying the P-51 Mustang and was shot down in February 1945 during his 52nd combat mission. He was captured and remained a prisoner of war until being liberated two months later.

White returned to the United States and enrolled in New York University where he received a Bachelor's degree in electrical engineering in 1951. He was recalled to active duty in May 1951 as a pilot and engineering officer with the 514th Troop Carrier Wing at Mitchel AFB, New York. In February 1952 he was sent to Japan and assigned to the 40th Fighter Squadron as an F-80 pilot and flight commander until the summer of 1953.

White was then assigned as a system engineer at the Rome Air Development Center in New York. In January 1955 he graduated from the Experimental Test Pilot School and stayed at Edwards to test the F-86K, F-89H, F-102A, and the F-105B. He became the Deputy Chief of the Flight Test Operations Division, and somewhat later was named Assistant Chief of the Manned Spacecraft Branch. Following the death of Iven Kincheloe, backup pilot White was designated the primary Air Force pilot for the X-15 program in 1958.

In October 1963 White became the operations officer for the 36th Tactical Fighter Wing at Bitburg, Germany, then served as the commanding officer of the 53rd Tactical Fighter Squadron. He returned to the United States in August 1965 to attend the Industrial College of the Armed Forces in Washington, where he graduated in 1966. That same year, he received a Master of Science degree in business administration from George Washington University. White went to Southeast Asia in May 1967 as Deputy Commander for Operations of the 355th Tactical Fighter Wing and flew 70 combat missions.

In June 1968 he went back to Wright-Patterson as Director of the F-15 Systems Program Office. Brigadier General-selectee White assumed command of the AFFTC on 31 July 1970. White commanded the AFFTC until 17 October 1972 when he assumed the duties of Commandant, Air Force Reserve Officer's Training Corps. In February 1975 he received his second star and in March became Chief of Staff of the Fourth Allied Tactical Air Force. White retired from active duty as a Major General in February 1981.[32]

White was a joint recipient of the 1961 Robert J. Collier Trophy that was presented by President John F. Kennedy at the White House in July 1962. He also received the NASA Distinguished Service Medal, the Harmon International Trophy from the *Ligue Internationale des Aviateurs* for the most outstanding contribution to aviation for the year, and

the Iven C. Kincheloe award. Among his many military decorations are the Air Force Cross, the Distinguished Service Medal, the Silver Star with three Oak Leaf Clusters, the Legion of Merit, the Distinguished Flying Cross with five Oak Leaf Clusters, and the Knight Commander's Cross of the Order of Merit of the Federal Republic of Germany.[33]

Walter C. Williams, NASA

Walter Charles Williams was born on 30 July 1919 in New Orleans, Louisiana. He earned a Bachelor of Science degree in aerospace engineering from Louisiana State University in 1939 and went to work for the NACA in August 1940, serving as a project engineer to improve the handling, maneuverability, and flight characteristics of World War II fighters. Williams became the project engineer for the X-1 in 1946 and went to what became Edwards to set up flight tests for the X-1.[34]

He was the founding director of the organization that became Dryden Flight Research Facility. In September 1959 he became the associate director of the new NASA Space Task Group at Langley, created to carry out Project Mercury. He later became director of operations for the project, then associate director of the NASA Manned Spacecraft Center in Houston, subsequently renamed the Johnson Space Center.

In January 1963 Williams moved to NASA Headquarters as Deputy Associate Administrator of the Office of Manned Space Flight and was awarded an honorary doctorate of engineering degree from Louisiana State University. From April 1964 to 1975, he was vice president and general manager of The Aerospace Corporation. Williams returned to NASA Headquarters as Chief Engineer in 1975, retiring from that position in July 1982. Williams was twice awarded the NASA Distinguished Service Medal and received numerous awards from professional societies. He died at his home in Tarzana, California, on 7 October 1995.

Walter C. Williams. (NASA Dryden)

APPENDIX B

Flight Log

Program Flight #: Cumulative X-15 flight number. Includes all glide and powered free-flights.

Flight ID: X-15 flight identification.
First number is which X-15 (1, 2, or 3).
Second number is total number of free flights by that aircraft.
The second number is replaced by an "A" for unplanned aborts, and a "C" for planned captive flights.
Third number is total number of times that X-15 has been carried aloft by the B-52.

X-15 (s/n) The Air Force serial number (tail number) of the X-15.

Flight Date: The date the flight was actually flown.

Pilot (flight #): The pilot, and the number of flights he had made in an X-15.

Launch Lake: The dry lake the launch took place over (all launches took place near a dry lake to serve as an emergency abort landing site).

Launch Time: The time the launch took place. All X-15 times are given as hour:minute:second.tenths on a 24-hour clock.
All times are local to Edwards AFB, California.

Landing Lake: The dry lake the flight landed on.

Landing Time: The time the X-15 touched-down on the landing lake. Computed as the X-15 launch time plus the X-15 Flight Duration.

X-15 Configuration: Major configuration of the X-15 vehicle. Lists items such as the ball nose, MH-96, wing tip pods, etc.

Purpose of flight: The major purpose of this X-15 flight. In later flights this was frequently to exercise non-X-15 related experiments.

The following entries have two components.
The "Planned" column contains the preflight planning values.
The "Actual" column contains the values actually achieved on the flight.

Max Mach: The maximum Mach number attained by the X-15 on that flight.

Max Altitude: The maximum altitude (feet; mean sea level) attained by the X-15 on that flight.

Max Speed: The maximum speed attained by the X-15 on that flight. Listed in miles per hour, figured for a standard day.

Flight Time: The total flight time for the X-15 in hours:minutes:seconds.tenths. This information was obtained from flight records (recorded onboard for X-15-1 and X-15-2; telemetered to the ground for X-15-3).

Engine s/n: The serial numbers of the XLR11 engines used on that flight. The first number is the upper engine; then the lower.
The serial number of the XLR99 engine used on that flight.

Power Time: The total powered flight time. This disregards any momentary lapses in power due to restarts, etc.
For XLR11 flights, it includes any time at least one chamber on either engine was firing.
These entries may contain one of the following annotations
"B.O." indicates the engine burned-out (I.e. ran out of propellants).
"S.D." indicates the engine was shut down by the pilot.

Thrust: For XLR11 flights only. The total number of chambers that fired on that flight (of eight possible)

Thrust: For XLR99 flights only. The throttle setting for the flight. May have multiple entries if the flight required changing thrust levels.

Aborts: Any aborts leading up to this flight.
Includes the flight number (with an "A" as the middle component, signifying abort), date, and reason if the NB-52 took-off.
Includes date and reason if the NB-52 did not take off (no program flight number assigned).

NASA 1: The person who acted as the aircraft communicator in the NASA control room. Usually another X-15 pilot.

NB-52: The B-52 serial number.

NB-52 Pilots: The flight crew (pilot first, then copilot).

NB-52 LP Operator The X-15 launch panel operator in the B-52.

NB-52 Take-Off Time: The B-52 take off time. The majority of available data only lists this to hour:minute, so that is how it is presented here.
All times are local to Edwards AFB, California.

NB-52 Landing Time: The B-52 landing time.

NB-52 Flight Time: The total flight time for the B-52 in hours:minutes. This is computed as landing time minus take-off time.

Chase 1: The aircraft type and pilot(s) of the first chase aircraft.

Chase 2: The aircraft type and pilot(s) of the second chase aircraft.

Chase 3: The aircraft type and pilot(s) of the third chase aircraft.

Chase 4: The aircraft type and pilot(s) of the fourth chase aircraft, if any.

Chase 5: The aircraft type and pilot(s) of the fifth chase aircraft, if any.

Rover: The aircraft type and pilot(s) of the "rover" chase aircraft, if any.

Notes: Includes any anomalies encountered on the flight, additional chase aircraft, or other notes.

X-15 Serial Numbers

Designation	Serial Number	First Flight	X-15 Flights	Highest Mach	Highest Speed	Highest Altitude	Notes
X-15-1	56-6670	08 Jun 59	81	Mach 6.06	4,104 mph	266,500 feet	
X-15-2	56-6671	17 Sep 59	31	Mach 6.04	4,093 mph	217,000 feet	Airframe was rebuilt into X-15A-2.
X-15A-2	56-6671	25 Jun 64	22	Mach 6.70	4,520 mph	249,000 feet	
X-15-3	56-6672	20 Dec 61	65	Mach 5.73	3,897 mph	354,200 feet	Airplane was written-off on Flight 3-65-97.

X-15 Pilots

Log Entry Name	Name	X-15 Flights	Highest Mach	Highest Speed	Highest Altitude	Notes
Adams	Major Michael J. Adams, USAF	7	Mach 5.59	3,822 mph	266,000 feet	Killed on flight 3-65-97.
Armstrong	Neil A. Armstrong, NASA	7	Mach 5.74	3,989 mph	207,500 feet	Made first flight with ball nose and MH-96.
Crossfield	A. Scott Crossfield, NAA	14	Mach 2.97	1,960 mph	88,116 feet	Made first X-15 glide, first XLR11, and first XLR99 flights.
Dana	William H. Dana, NASA	16	Mach 5.53	3,897 mph	306,900 feet	Made last X-15 flight.
Engle	Captain Joe H. Engle, USAF	16	Mach 5.71	3,888 mph	280,600 feet	
Kincheloe	Captain Iven C. Kincheloe, Jr., USAF	0	—	—	—	Killed in an F-104 accident prior to his first X-15 flight.
Knight	Major William J. "Pete" Knight, USAF	16	Mach 6.70	4,520 mph	280,500 feet	Made maximum speed flight.
McKay	John B. "Jack" McKay, NASA	29	Mach 5.65	3,863 mph	295,600 feet	
Petersen	Lt. Cdr. Forrest S. Petersen, USN	5	Mach 5.30	3,600 mph	101,800 feet	Only Navy pilot.
Rushworth	Lt. Colonel Robert A. Rushworth, USAF	34	Mach 6.06	4,018 mph	285,000 feet	Made first flight of X-15A-2; made most X-15 flights.
Thompson	Milton O. Thompson, NASA	14	Mach 5.48	3,724 mph	214,100 feet	
Walker	Joseph A. Walker, NASA	25	Mach 5.92	4,104 mph	354,200 feet	Made maximum altitude flight.
White, Al	Alvin S. White, NAA	0	—	—	—	Scott Crossfield's backup; never flew the X-15.
White	Major Robert M. White, USAF	16	Mach 6.04	4,093 mph	314,750 feet	Made FAI record flight to 314,750 feet, first Mach 4, 5, and 6 flights.

Chase Aircraft Used by the X-15 Program

Designation	Serial No. (BuNo)	Notes
F-100A	52-5778	NASA support aircraft. Departed 10 Jun 60.
JF-100C	53-1717	NASA support aircraft. Used between 06 Nov 59 and 23 Feb 61.
F-100F	56-3726	AFFTC support aircraft.
F-100F	56-3963	North American support aircraft.
F-100F	56-3875	AFFTC support aircraft.
JF-104A	55-2961	NASA support aircraft.
JF-104A	56-0749	NASA support aircraft. Delivered 13 Apr 59; written-off 20 Dec 62.
F-104A	56-0740	AFFTC support aircraft.
F-104A	56-0743	AFFTC support aircraft.
F-104A	56-0744	AFFTC support aircraft.
F-104A	56-0746	AFFTC support aircraft.
F-104A	56-0748	AFFTC support aircraft.
F-104A	56-0749	AFFTC support aircraft.
F-104A	56-0755	AFFTC support aircraft.
F-104A	56-0757	AFFTC support aircraft.
F-104A	56-0763	AFFTC support aircraft.
F-104A	56-0764	AFFTC support aircraft.
F-104A	56-0766	AFFTC support aircraft.
F-104A	56-0768	AFFTC support aircraft.
F-104A	56-0790/N820NA	AFFTC support aircraft. To FRC on 27 Dec 66 as N820NA.
F-104A	56-0802	AFFTC support aircraft.
F-104A	56-0817	AFFTC support aircraft.
F-104B	56-3722	AFFTC support aircraft.
F-104B	57-1303	NASA support aircraft.
F-104D	57-1314	AFFTC support aircraft.
F-104D	57-1315	AFFTC support aircraft.
F-104D	57-1316	AFFTC support aircraft.
F-104D	57-1331	AFFTC support aircraft.
F-104D	57-1332	AFFTC support aircraft.
F-104N	NASA 011/N811NA *	NASA support aircraft. Delivered on 19 Aug 63.
F-104N	NASA 012/N812NA *	NASA support aircraft. Delivered on 6 Sep 63.
F-104N	NASA 013/N813NA *	NASA support aircraft. Delivered on 22 Oct 63; written-off 8 Jun 66.
F4H-1	145313	Navy support aircraft. Flown during Mar 61. (see next entry)
F-4A	145313	NASA support aircraft. Delivered on 3 Dec 65; departed on 14 Jun 66.
F-4C	63-7651	AFFTC support aircraft.
F5D-1	139208/NASA 212	NASA support aircraft. Delivered on 16 Jan 61; departed on 4 Mar 63.
F5D-1	142350/NASA 213	NASA support aircraft. Delivered on 15 Jun 61. Later NASA 802.
YT-38A	58-1197	AFFTC support aircraft.
T-38A	59-1596	AFFTC support aircraft.
T-38A	59-1598	AFFTC support aircraft.
T-38A	59-1599	AFFTC support aircraft.
T-38A	59-1600	AFFTC support aircraft.
T-38A	59-1601	AFFTC support aircraft.
T-38A	59-1604	AFFTC support aircraft.
T-38A	59-1606	AFFTC support aircraft.
T-38A	60-0563	AFFTC support aircraft.

Notes:
* The F-104Ns changed from 0xx to 8xx in March 1965.
Data supplied by Betty J. Love and Peter W. Merlin, DFRC History Office.

Chase Pilots Supporting the X-15 Program

Adams	Major Michael J. Adams, USAF
Armstrong	Neil A. Armstrong, NASA
Baker	Robert "Bob" Baker, NAA
Collins	Captain Michael Collins, USAF
Crews	Captain Albert H. Crews, Jr., USAF
Crossfield	A. Scott Crossfield, NAA
Curtis	Captain Lawrence C. Curtis, Jr., USAF
Cuthill	Major Fred J. Cuthill, USAF
Dana	William H. Dana, NASA
Daniel	Major Walter F. Daniel, USAF
Davey	Captain Thomas J. Davey, USAF
DeLong	John DeLong, NAA (cameraman)
Enevoldson	Einar Enevoldson, NASA
Engle	Captain Joe H. Engle, USAF
Evenson	Captain Mervin L. Evenson, USAF
Fulton	Lt. Colonel Fitzhugh L. Fulton, Jr., NASA
Gentry	Captain Jerauld A. Gentry, NASA
Gordon	Major Henry C. Gordon, USAF
Haise	Frederick W. Haise, Jr., NASA
Hoag	Captain Peter C. Hoag, USAF
Hover	Captain Robert C. Hover, USAF
Jackson	Hugh M. Jackson, NASA
Jordan	Captain Joe Jordan, USAF
Knight	Captain William J. "Pete" Knight, USAF
Krier	Gary E. Krier, NASA
Livingston	Captain David W. Livingston, USAF
Looney	Captain William R. Looney, USAF
Mallick	Donald L. Mallick, NASA
Manke	John A. Manke, NASA
Marrett	Captain George J. Marrett, USAF
McDivitt	Major James A. McDivitt, USAF
McKay	John B. McKay, NASA
Parsons	Major Robert K. Parsons, USAF
Petersen	Lt. Commander Forrest S. Petersen, USN
Peterson	Bruce A. Peterson, NASA
Powell	Captain Cecil Powell, USAF
Roberts	J. O. Roberts, NAA
J. Rogers	Major Joseph W. Rogers, USAF
R. Rogers	Major Russell L. Rogers, USAF
Rushworth	Major Robert A. Rushworth, USAF
Shawler	Captain Wendell H. "Wendy" Shawler, USAF
Smith	Captain Robert W. Smith, USAF
Smith	Captain Roger J. Smith, USAF
Sorlie	Major Donald M. Sorlie, USAF
Stroface	Captain Joseph F. Stroface, USAF
Thompson	Milton O. Thompson, NASA
Twinting	Major William T. "Ted" Twinting, USAF
Walker	Joseph A. Walker, NASA
Ward	Lt. Colonel Fred Ward, USAF
Whelan	Captain Robert E. Whelan, USAF
A. White	Alvin S. White, NAA
R. White	Major Robert M. White, USAF
Wood	Major James W. Wood, USAF

NB-52 Aircraft Used on the X-15 Program

NB-52A	52-003	*The High and the Mighty*
		The High and the Mighty One
NB-52B	52-008	*The Challenger*
		(none)

NB-52 Significant Dates

29 Nov 57	B-52A (52-0003) arrives at Air Force Plant 42 in Palmdale, California.
	The aircraft came from Boeing and was placed in storage pending modifications.
04 Feb 58	B-52A was moved into the North American hangar for start of modifications.
14 Nov 58	The modified NB-52A arrives at Edwards AFB.
14 Jan 61	NB-52A was flown to Wichita, Kansas, for major overhaul.
23 Mar 61	NB-52 returns to Edwards from Boeing-Wichita.
17 Apr 61	NB-52A returns to operational status.
06 Jan 59	RB-52B (52-008) is flown to North American facility in Palmdale for modification.
08 Jun 59	The modified NB-52B arrives at Edwards AFB.
	(Some source indicate this was originally designated NRB-52B.)

NB-52 Launch Panel Operators Supporting the X-15 Program

Berkowitz	William "Bill" Berkowitz, NAA
Butchart	Stanley P. Butchart, NASA
Dustin	Allen F. Dustin, NASA
Moise	John W. Moise, NASA
Peterson	Bruce A. Peterson, NASA
Russell	John "Jack" W. Russell, NASA

High Range Call Signs and Locations

NASA-1	Bldg. 4800 Control Room, Flight Research Center, Edwards, California
NASA-2	Beatty Radar Site, Beatty, Nevada
NASA-3	Ely Radar Site, Ely, Nevada

NB-52 Pilots Supporting the X-15 Program

Allavie	Captain John E. "Jack" Allavie, USAF
Anderson	Donald C. Anderson, USAF (one flight, 2-A-39)
Andonian	Colonel Harry Andonian, USAF
Archer	Squadron Leader Harry M. Archer, RAF
Bement	Captain Russell P. Bement, USAF
Bock	Captain Charles C. Bock Jr., USAF (later Major)
Bowline	Captain Jerry D. Bowline, USAF (later Major)
Branch	Brigadier General Irving "Twig" Branch, USAF (one flight, 1-44-70)
Campbell	Captain John K. Campbell, USAF
Cole	Major Frank E. Cole, USAF
Cotton	Lt. Colonel Joseph P. Cotton, USAF (later Colonel)
Cretney	Squadron leader David Cretney, RAF
Crews	Major Albert H. Crews Jr., USAF
Cross	Major Carl S. Cross, USAF
Doryland	Major Charles J. Doryland, USAF
Fulton	Major Fitzhugh "Fitz" Fulton, USAF (later Lt. Colonel)
Jones	Colonel Gay E. Jones, USAF
Kuyk	Captain Charles F. G. Kuyk Jr., USAF
Lewis	Colonel Kenneth K. Lewis, USAF
McDowell	Major Edward D. McDowell Jr., USAF
Miller	Squadron Leader John Miller, RAF
Mosley	Captain Robert L. Mosley, USAF
Reschke	Major William G. Reschke Jr., USAF (later Lt. Colonel)
Stroup	Captain Floyd B. Stroup, USAF
Sturmthal	Lt. Colonel Emil "Ted" Sturmthal, USAF
Townsend	Colonel Guy M. Townsend, USAF
Yeager	Colonel Charles E. "Chuck" Yeager, USAF (one flight, 2-A-38)

Personnel Who Served as NASA 1

Adams	Major Michael J. Adams, USAF
Armstrong	Neil A. Armstrong, NASA
Butchart	Stanley P. Butchart, NASA
Dana	William H. Dana, NASA
Engle	Captain Joe H. Engle, USAF
Harvey	Q.C. Harvey, NAA
Knight	Captain William J. "Pete" Knight, USAF
Manke	John A. Manke, NASA
McKay	John B. McKay, NASA
Petersen	Lt. Commander Forrest S. Petersen, USN
Rushworth	Major Robert A. Rushworth, USAF
Thompson	Milton O. Thompson, NASA
Walker	Joseph A. Walker, NASA
White	Major Robert M. White, USAF

Notes:
Names taken from flight logs. Only last names and ranks of Air Force personnel were given.

"First names supplied by Betty J. Love and Peter W. Merlin, DFRC/HO based on Test Pilot School and AFFTC History Office files, and personal interviews with Fitz Fulton, Wendell Shawler, and Johnny Armstrong.

On X-15 Flight 1-12-23, the NB-52 pilot is listed as "Kirk," but this appears to be a misspelling of Kuyk in the original record.

Miscellaneous Aircraft Supporting the X-15 Program

Designation	Serial No. (BuNo)	Notes
C-47H (R4D-5)	N817NA	NASA support aircraft used for lakebed surveys and recovery from remote sites. Originally R4D-5 (BuNo 17136).
C-130A	54-1624	AFFTC support aircraft. Used to ferry X-15 rescue and paramedic personnel to uprange lakebeds.
C-130A	54-1626	AFFTC support aircraft. Used to ferry X-15 rescue and paramedic personnel to uprange lakebeds.
C-130A	53-3132	Assigned to X-15 support.
C-130A	53-3134	Assigned to X-15 program after 20 March 1959.
C-130A	53-3135	Assigned to X-15 support. Used during Mud Lake emergency landing recovery operations on 10 January 1962.
C-130B	57-0525	Assigned to X-15 support. Used during Mud Lake emergency landing recovery operations on 1 July 1966.
C-130E	61-2358	Assigned to X-15 support. Used during the last flight of X-15-3.
UH-1F	63-13143	U.S. Army.
YUH-1H	60-6029	U.S. Army.
H-21B	51-15855	Originally bailed to Sperry Gyroscope. Became available to AFFTC around February 1959.
H-21B	53-4389	Originally bailed to Prewitt Aircraft Company. Became available to AFFTC around January 1959.
H-21B	(??)	Became available to AFFTC around September 1959.
JTF-102A	54-1354	Used from 1958 to early 1959 to test X-15 pressure suits and the biomedical package.
JF-100C	53-1709	NASA variable-stability aircraft.

Five Highest Mach X-15 Flights

Program Flight #	Flight ID	X-15 (s/n)	Flight Date	Pilot	Maximum Mach Number	Maximum Altitude	Maximum Speed (mph / fps)	Notes
188	2-53-97	56-6671	03 Oct 67	Knight	Mach 6.70	102,100 feet	4,520 mph / 6,629 fps	
175	2-50-89	56-6671	18 Nov 66	Knight	Mach 6.33	98,900 feet	4,250 mph / 6,233 fps	
97	1-42-67	56-6670	05 Dec 63	Rushworth	Mach 6.06	101,000 feet	4,018 mph / 5,893 fps	Highest Mach by basic airplane.
45	2-21-37	56-6671	09 Nov 61	White	Mach 6.04	101,600 feet	4,093 mph / 6,003 fps	
59	1-30-51	56-6670	27 Jun 62	Walker	Mach 5.92	123,700 feet	4,104 mph / 6,019 fps	

Five Highest Speed X-15 Flights

Program Flight #	Flight ID	X-15 (s/n)	Flight Date	Pilot	Maximum Mach Number	Maximum Altitude	Maximum Speed (mph / fps)	Notes
188	2-53-97	56-6671	03 Oct 67	Knight	Mach 6.70	102,100 feet	4,520 mph / 6,629 fps	
175	2-50-89	56-6671	18 Nov 66	Knight	Mach 6.33	98,900 feet	4,250 mph / 6,233 fps	
59	1-30-51	56-6671	27 Jun 62	Walker	Mach 5.92	123,700 feet	4,104 mph / 6,019 fps	Highest speed by basic airplane.
45	2-21-37	56-6671	09 Nov 61	White	Mach 6.04	101,600 feet	4,093 mph / 6,003 fps	
97	1-42-67	56-6670	05 Dec 63	Rushworth	Mach 6.06	101,000 feet	4,018 mph / 5,893 fps	

Five Highest Altitude X-15 Flights

Program Flight #	Flight ID	X-15 (s/n)	Flight Date	Pilot	Maximum Mach Number	Maximum Altitude	Maximum Speed (mph / fps)	Notes
91	3-22-36	56-6672	22 Aug 63	Walker	Mach 5.58	354,200 feet	3,794 mph / 5,565 fps	Unofficial world record for winged vehicles.
90	3-21-32	56-6672	19 Jul 63	Walker	Mach 5.50	347,800 feet	3,710 mph / 5,441 fps	
62	3-7-14	56-6672	17 Jul 62	White	Mach 5.45	314,750 feet	3,832 mph / 5,620 fps	FAI world altitude record (still stands).
174	3-56-83	56-6672	01 Nov 66	Dana	Mach 5.46	306,900 feet	3,750 mph / 5,500 fps	
150	3-49-73	56-6672	28 Sep 65	McKay	Mach 5.33	295,600 feet	3,732 mph / 5,474 fps	

Five Slowest Mach X-15 Flights

Program Flight #	Flight ID	X-15 (s/n)	Flight Date	Pilot	Maximum Mach Number	Maximum Altitude	Maximum Speed (mph / fps)	Notes
1	1-1-5	56-6670	08 Jun 59	Crossfield	Mach 0.79	37,550 feet	522 mph / 766 fps	Glide flight.
47	1-25-44	56-6670	10 Jan 62	Petersen	Mach 0.97	44,750 feet	645 mph / 946 fps	Two engine malfunction shutdown.
4	2-3-9	56-6671	05 Nov 59	Crossfield	Mach 1.00	45,462 feet	660 mph / 968 fps	Explosion and fire in lower XLR11.
74	2-31-52	56-6671	09 Nov 62	McKay	Mach 1.49	53,950 feet	1,019 mph / 1,495 fps	XLR99 stuck at 35-percent power.
7	2-5-12	56-6671	17 Feb 60	Crossfield	Mach 1.57	52,640 feet	1,036 mph / 1,519 fps	Restart on seven chambers.

Five Slowest Speed X-15 Flights

Program Flight #	Flight ID	X-15 (s/n)	Flight Date	Pilot	Maximum Mach Number	Maximum Altitude	Maximum Speed (mph / fps)	Notes
1	1-1-5	56-6670	08 Jun 59	Crossfield	Mach 0.79	37,550 feet	522 mph / 766 fps	Glide flight.
47	1-25-44	56-6670	10 Jan 62	Petersen	Mach 0.97	44,750 feet	645 mph / 946 fps	Two engine malfunction shutdown.
4	2-3-9	56-6671	05 Nov 59	Crossfield	Mach 1.00	45,462 feet	660 mph / 968 fps	Explosion and fire in lower XLR11.
74	2-31-52	56-6671	09 Nov 62	McKay	Mach 1.49	53,950 feet	1,019 mph / 1,495 fps	XLR99 stuck at 35-percent power.
7	2-5-12	56-6671	17 Feb 60	Crossfield	Mach 1.57	52,640 feet	1,036 mph / 1,519 fps	Restart on seven chambers.

Five Lowest Altitude X-15 Flights

Program Flight #	Flight ID	X-15 (s/n)	Flight Date	Pilot	Maximum Mach Number	Maximum Altitude	Maximum Speed (mph / fps)	Notes
1	1-1-5	56-6670	08 Jun 59	Crossfield	Mach 0.79	37,550 feet	522 mph / 766 fps	Glide flight.
47	1-25-44	56-6670	10 Jan 62	Petersen	Mach 0.97	44,750 feet	645 mph / 946 fps	Two engine malfunction shutdown.
159	2-45-81	56-6671	01 Jul 66	Rushworth	Mach 1.70	44,800 feet	1,061 mph / 1,556 fps	External tank feed indicator.
4	2-3-9	56-6671	05 Nov 59	Crossfield	Mach 1.00	45,462 feet	660 mph / 968 fps	Explosion and fire in lower XLR11.
12	1-4-9	56-6670	13 Apr 60	White	Mach 1.90	48,000 feet	1,254 mph / 1,839 fps	Pilot familiarization flight.

Speed Summary

The following represents to total time the three X-15s spent above the indicated Mach number. The total includes time spent below Mach 1. Includes glide flights. Does not include NB-52 carry time. Given as hours:minutes:seconds.

Aircraft	Mach 1	Mach 2	Mach 3	Mach 4	Mach 5	Mach 6	Total
X-15-1	07:35:24	04:40:59	03:17:31	02:12:34	00:27:55	00:00:08	12:40:43
X-15-2	04:31:41	02:48:16	01:56:07	01:11:02	00:12:57	00:01:10	07:51:37
X-15-3	06:09:23	04:41:29	03:37:55	02:35:16	00:44:41	00:00:00	09:42:37
Total	18:16:28	12:10:44	08:51:33	05:58:52	01:25:33	00:01:18	30:14:57

Flight # / ID; X-15 Pilot; Flight Date; Launch Lake; Launch Time; Landing Lake; Landing Time	X-15 Configuration; Purpose of Flight	NASA-1; NB-52; Pilots; LP Operator; Take-Off Time; Landing Time; Flight Time	Planned: Max Mach; Max Altitude; Max Speed; Flight Time; Engine s/n; Power Time; Thrust	Actual: Max Mach; Max Altitude; Max Speed; Flight Time; Engine s/n; Power Time; Thrust	Chase 1–5 Pilot(s)	Abort(s); Notes
1 / 1-1-5 Crossfield (1) 08 Jun 59 Rosamond 08:38:40.0 Rogers 08:43:36.6	XLR11s; Ventral on; Nose boom First (and only) X-15 glide flight Pilot familiarization – Crossfield's first X-15 flight	Harvey 52-003 Bock / Allavie Berkowitz 08:01 08:58 00:57	0.80 40,000 — — — 0 0	0.79 37,550 522 00:04:56.6 ?? 0 0	F-100F Al White / DeLong F-100F Wood F-100F White	1-C-1 10 Mar 59 Scheduled captive flight 1-A-2 01 Apr 59 Radio failure 1-A-3 10 Apr 59 Radio and APU failure 1-A-4 21 May 59 APU and SAS failure — 05 Jun 59 Smoke in cockpit during taxi All aborts used NB-52A 52-003; Crossfield was the X-15 pilot for all aborts Pitch damper failed pre-launch; Unauthorized aileron roll
2 / 2-1-3 Crossfield (2) 17 Sep 59 Rosamond 08:08:48.0 Rogers 08:17:59.0	XLR11s; Ventral on; Nose boom First X-15 powered flight; Aircraft checkout	Harvey 52-003 Bock / Allavie Berkowitz 07:31 08:46 01:15	2.00 50,000 — — — ?? 8 chambers	2.11 52,341 1,393 00:09:11.0 ?? 224.3 8 chambers	F-100F Al White / DeLong F-100F Walker F-104D White	2-C-1 24 Jul 59 Scheduled full-propellant captive flight 2-A-2 04 Sep 59 Vent malfunction All aborts used NB-52A 52-003; Crossfield was the X-15 pilot for all aborts Roll damper failed during flight; Unauthorized aileron roll; Flaps extended only 60 percent
3 / 2-2-6 Crossfield (3) 17 Oct 59 Rosamond 10:13:07.0 Rogers 10:22:44.7	XLR11s; Ventral on; Nose boom Aircraft checkout	?? 52-003 Bock / Allavie Moise 09:25 10:55 01:30	2.00 60,000 — — — ?? 8 chambers	2.15 61,781 1,419 00:09:37.7 ?? 254.5 8 chambers	F-100F Al White / DeLong F-104D Walker F-104 White	2-A-4 10 Oct 59 LOX topoff failure; Helium leak 2-A-5 14 Oct 59 LOX topoff failure; Cabin Pressure All aborts used NB-52A 52-003; Crossfield was the X-15 pilot for all aborts Roll damper off at launch - reengaged; Alcohol fire in engine bay after landing
4 / 2-3-9 Crossfield (4) 05 Nov 59 Rosamond 09:39:28.0 Rosamond 09:44:56.0	XLR11s; Ventral on; Nose boom Aircraft checkout	Harvey 52-003 Allavie / Fulton Moise 09:00 10:02 01:02	2.00 80,000 — — — 255 8 chambers	1.00 45,462 660 00:05:28.0 ?? 13.9 7 chambers	F-100F Baker / DeLong F-104 White F-104 Walker	2-A-7 22 Oct 59 Pilot's oxygen failure; torn gloves 2-A-8 31 Oct 59 Weather All aborts used NB-52A 52-003; Crossfield was the X-15 pilot for all aborts Roll damper dropped out at launch; Explosion and fire in lower engine; First X-15 emergency landing; First landing at other than Rogers Dry lake; Fuselage failed just forward of LOX tank (station 226.8) during landing
5 / 1-2-7 Crossfield (5) 23 Jan 60 Rosamond 16:17:05.0 Rogers 16:26:58.8	XLR11s; Ventral on; Nose boom Aircraft checkout; SAS evaluation; First powered flight by X-15-1	Harvey 52-008 Fulton / Kuyk Berkowitz 15:42 17:00 01:18	2.00 65,000 — — — ?? 8 chambers	2.53 66,844 1,669 00:09:53.8 3 and 10 267.2 (B.O.) 8 chambers	F-100F Baker / DeLong F-104 Walker F-104 White	1-A-6 16 Dec 59 Radio failure; LOX regulator Abort used NB-52B 52-008; Crossfield was the X-15 pilot on the abort First X-15 flight of the stable-platform; First launch from NB-52 52-008
6 / 2-4-11 Crossfield (6) 11 Feb 60 Rosamond 10:15:04.0 Rogers 10:25:19.5	XLR11s; Ventral on; Nose boom Aircraft checkout	Harvey 52-008 Allavie / Fulton Moise 09:07 10:34 01:27	2.00 80,000 — — — 260 8 chambers	2.22 88,116 1,466 00:10:15.5 ?? 251.2 8 chambers	F-100F Al White / DeLong F-104 Walker F-104 White	2-A-10 04 Feb 60 Loss of source pressure Abort used NB-52B 52-008; Crossfield was the X-15 pilot on the abort Good flight
7 / 2-5-12 Crossfield (7) 17 Feb 60 Rosamond 09:41:32.0 Rogers 09:52:07.9	XLR11s; Ventral on; Nose boom Aircraft checkout; SAS stability and control evaluation	Harvey 52-008 Fulton / Allavie Moise 08:54 10:02 01:08	2.00 50,000 — — — 260 8 chambers	1.57 52,640 1,036 00:10:35.9 ?? 309.4 7 chambers	F-100 White F-104 Walker F-104 ??	No aborts Upper engine problems - Restart on 7 chambers was successful
8 / 2-6-13 Crossfield (8) 17 Mar 60 Rosamond 08:31:25.0 Rogers 08:40:04.5	XLR11s; Ventral on; Nose boom Roll stability and control evaluation; Dampers on and off evaluation	Harvey 52-008 Allavie / Kuyk Moise 07:55 08:46 00:51	2.00 50,000 — — — ?? 8 chambers	2.15 52,640 1,419 00:08:39.5 ?? 233.5 8 chambers	F-100F Al White / DeLong F-104 White F-104 Walker	No aborts Good flight
9 / 1-3-8 Walker (1) 25 Mar 60 Rosamond 15:43:23.0 Rogers 15:52:31.0	XLR11s; Ventral on; Nose boom Pilot familiarization – Walker's first X-15 flight	?? 52-008 Fulton / Allavie Russell 14:44 16:12 01:28	2.00 50,000 — — — ?? 8 chambers	2.00 48,630 1,320 00:09:08.0 ?? 272.0 (B.O.) 8, 6 chambers	F-100 Crossfield F-104 White F-100 McKay	No aborts First government flight; Stable platform malfunctioned prelaunch; No roll damper at launch; Two restarts required on top engine;
10 / 2-7-15 Crossfield (9) 29 Mar 60 Rosamond 09:59:28.0 Rogers 10:08:38.5	XLR11s; Ventral on; Nose boom Launch characteristics evaluation; Minus 2-g pushover evaluation; Full throw rudder step evaluation	Harvey 52-008 Fulton / Allavie Moise 08:16 10:14 01:58	2.00 50,000 — — — 267 8 chambers	1.96 49,982 1,293 00:09:10.5 ?? 244.2 8 chambers	F-100F White F-104D Knight F-104C Rushworth	2-A-14 18 Mar 60 Fuel (alcohol) leak Abort used NB-52B 52-008; Crossfield was the X-15 pilot on the abort Good flight

Flight # / ID; X-15 Pilot; Flight Date; Launch Lake; Launch Time; Landing Lake; Landing Time	X-15 Configuration / Purpose of Flight	NASA-1; NB-52; Pilots; LP Operator; Take-Off Time; Landing Time; Flight Time	Planned: Max Mach; Max Altitude; Max Speed; Flight Time; Engine s/n; Power Time; Thrust	Actual: Max Mach; Max Altitude; Max Speed; Flight Time; Engine s/n; Power Time; Thrust	Chase 1–5 Pilot(s)	Abort(s) / Notes
11 / 2-8-16 Crossfield (10) 31 Mar 60 Rosamond 08:42:05.0 Rogers 08:51:01.5	XLR11s; Ventral on; Nose boom High-g maneuvers; SAS gains checkout	Harvey 52-008 Allavie / Fulton Moise 08:03 08:58 00:55	2.00 50,000 — — — ?? 8 chambers	2.03 51,356 1,340 00:08:56.5 ?? 254.5 8 chambers	F-100 White F-104 Rushworth F-104 Knight	No aborts Good flight; Landing was intentionally made with all dampers off
12 / 1-4-9 White (1) 13 Apr 60 Rosamond 09:15:11.0 Rogers 09:24:03.7	XLR11s; Ventral on; Nose boom Pilot familiarization – White's first X-15 flight	Walker 52-003 Allavie / Kuyk Russell 08:28 09:33 01:05	2.00 50,000 — — — ?? 8 chambers	1.90 48,000 1,254 00:08:52.7 ?? 253.7 (B.O.) 8 chambers	F-100 Al White / DeLong F-104 Walker F-104 Rushworth	No aborts First Air Force flight; First flight with stiffened side-tunnel panels; Flown on center stick; No research data until High Key (pilot forgot to activate); No landing data due to film drum failure
13 / 1-5-10 Walker (2) 19 Apr 60 Rosamond 08:51:44.0 Rogers 09:01:42.6	XLR11s; Ventral on; Nose boom Performance buildup; Stability and control buildup; Fuselage side fairing vibration and flutter data	?? 52-003 Fulton / Allavie Russell 08:00 09:10 01:10	2.35 60,000 — — — ?? 8 chambers	2.56 59,496 1,689 00:09:58.6 ?? 260.6 (B.O.) 8 chambers	F-100 Rushworth F-104D McKay F-104 Knight	No aborts Good flight; No landing gear data taken
14 / 1-6-11 White (2) 06 May 60 Rosamond 09:53:19.0 Rogers 10:02:42.2	XLR11s; Ventral on; Nose boom Performance buildup; Stability and control buildup	See Notes 52-003 Fulton / Allavie Russell 09:06 10:11 01:05	2.50 60,000 — — — ?? 8 chambers	2.20 60,938 1,452 00:09:23.2 ?? 246.5 (B.O.) 8 chambers	F-100F Knight F-104D McKay F-104A Rushworth	No aborts Roll damper failed at launch (reset); Normal ventral jettison failed; ventral came off when skids deployed; There was not a functional NASA 1 on this flight due to radio problems; Pete Knight served as a radio relay from a chase aircraft
15 / 1-7-12 Walker (3) 12 May 60 Silver 08:47:37.0 Rogers 08:57:47.3	XLR11s; Ventral on; Nose boom Performance buildup; Stability and control buildup	Armstrong 52-003 Bock / Allavie Russell 08:08 09:40 01:32	3.00 73,000 — — — ?? 8, 5 chambers	3.19 77,882 2,111 00:10:10.3 ?? 256.3 (B.O.) 8, 0 chambers	F-100F White F-104A Rushworth F-104 Knight F-104D McKay	No aborts First X-15 Mach 3 flight; Stable platform inoperative from launch; First launch (of any X-plane) from a remote lake; Three chambers intentionally shut down - remaining 5 shut down seconds later; Ventral chute failed, ventral extensively damaged
16 / 1-8-13 White (3) 19 May 60 Silver 0 08:46:47.0 Rogers 08:58:11.6	XLR11s; Ventral on; Nose boom Altitude buildup	Armstrong 52-003 Bock / Allavie Russell 08:05 09:20 01:15	2.20 110,000 — — — ?? 6, 8 chambers	2.31 108,997 1,590 00:11:24.6 ?? 274.7 6, 8 chambers	F-100F Knight F-104A Rushworth F-104D McKay	No aborts First X-15 flight above 100,000 feet
17 / 2-9-18 Crossfield (11) 26 May 60 Rosamond 09:08:36.0 Rogers 09:17:50.4	XLR11s; Ventral on; Nose boom High-g maneuvers; SAS gains checkout; High alpha stability and control; BCS checkout	Harvey 52-008 Bock / Allavie Moise 08:13 09:30 01:17	2.30 78,000 — — — 255 8 chambers	2.20 51,282 1,452 00:09:14.4 ?? 243.4 8 chambers	F-100F Al White / DeLong F-104 White F-104D Petersen	2-A-17 05 May 60 #1 APU failure Abort used NB-52A 52-003; Crossfield was the X-15 pilot on the abort Good flight; Last XLR11 flight of X-15-2
18 / 1-9-17 Walker (4) 04 Aug 60 Silver 08:59:13.0 Rogers 09:09:35.6	XLR11s; Ventral on; Nose boom Maximum speed flight with XLR11; Stability and control data; Aerodynamic heating data	Butchart 52-003 Fulton / Allavie Russell 08:15 09:40 01:25	3.30 75,000 — — — 260 8 chambers	3.31 78,112 2,196 00:10:22.6 ?? 264.2 (B.O.) 8 chambers	F-100F White F-104A Rushworth F-104A Petersen F-104D Knight	1-A-14 27 May 60 Loss of telemetry 1-A-15 03 Jun 60 #2 APU failure; Hydraulic pressure 1-A-16 08 Jun 60 Source pressure 1-A-14 and 1-A-16 used NB-52 52-003; 1-A-15 used NB-52B 52-008; Walker was the X-15 pilot for all the aborts
19 / 1-10-19 White (4) 12 Aug 60 Silver 08:48:43.0 Rogers 09:00:22.1	XLR11s; Ventral on; Nose boom Maximum altitude with XLR11; Stability and control data	?? 52-003 Fulton / Andoian Russell 08:06 09:15 01:09	2.50 133,000 — — — ?? 8 chambers	2.52 136,500 1,772 00:11:39.1 ?? 256.2 (B.O.) 8 chambers	F-100F Rushworth F-104A Petersen F-104D Looney	1-A-18 11 Aug 60 Loss of nitrogen source pressure Record altitude flight; Highest flight with XLR11 engines
20 / 1-11-21 Walker (5) 19 Aug 60 Silver 08:34:22.0 Rogers 08:44:04.4	XLR11s; Ventral on; Nose boom Aerodynamic heating data; Stability and control data; Performance data	?? 52-003 Allavie / Cole Butchart 07:51 09:20 01:29	3.00 70,000 — — — ?? 8 chambers	3.13 75,982 1,986 00:09:42.4 ?? 251.6 (B.O.) 8 chambers	F-100 White F-104 Rushworth F-104A Petersen F-104 Looney	1-A-20 18 Aug 60 APU #1 Failure Abort used NB-52A 52-003; Walker was the X-15 pilot on the abort Alpha cross-pointer hooked up backwards

Flight # / ID X-15 Pilot Flight Date Launch Lake Launch Time Landing Lake Landing Time	X-15 Configuration Purpose of Flight	NASA-1 NB-52 + Pilots + LP Operator + Take-Off Time + Landing Time + Flight Time	Planned + Max Mach + Max Altitude + Max Speed + Flight Time + Engine s/n + Power Time + Thrust	Actual + Max Mach + Max Altitude + Max Speed + Flight Time + Engine s/n + Power Time + Thrust	Chase 1 Pilot(s) Chase 2 Pilot(s) Chase 3 Pilot(s) Chase 4 Pilot(s) Chase 5 Pilot(s)	Abort(s) Notes
21 / 1-12-23 White (5) 10 Sep 60 Silver 11:45:10.0 Rogers 11:55:10.0	XLR11s; Ventral on; Nose boom Stability and control data; Performance data	Walker 52-008 Allavie / Kuyk Butchart 11:01 12:25 01:24	3.20 80,000 — — ?? 8 chambers	3.23 79,864 2,182 00:10:00.0 ?? 264.3 8 chambers	F-100F Looney F-104A Armstrong F-104A Rushworth F-104D Knight	— 01 Sep 60 Did not take off due to cloud cover 1-A-22 02 Sep 60 Telemetry failure Taxi used NB-52B 52-008; White was the X-15 pilot Abort used NB-52B 52-008; White was the X-15 pilot on the abort APU problem
22 / 1-13-25 Petersen (1) 23 Sep 60 Palmdale VOR 09:52:06.0 Rogers 09:59:15.6	XLR11s; Ventral on; Nose boom Pilot familiarization – Petersen's first X-15 flight	Thompson 52-008 Allavie / Fulton Russell 09:11 10:20 01:09	2.00 50,000 — — ?? 8 chambers	1.68 53,043 1,108 00:07:09.6 ?? 146.6 8, 4, 0 chambers	F-100F Looney F-104A Walker F-104D Rushworth	1-A-24 20 Sep 60 #2 APU would not stay on Abort used NB-52B 52-008; Petersen was the X-15 pilot on the abort First launch from Palmdale; Engines shut down early; Two unsuccessful restarts on upper engine
23 / 1-14-27 Petersen (2) 20 Oct 60 Palmdale VOR 09:30:27.0 Rogers 09:39:53.1	XLR11s; Ventral on; Nose boom Stability and control data; Performance data; Alternate airspeed calibration; Additional pilot familiarization	Thompson 52-008 Fulton / Kuyk Russell 08:59 09:47 00:48	2.00 50,000 — — ?? 8, 5 chambers	1.94 53,800 1,280 00:09:26.1 ?? 285.4 8, 5 chambers	F-100F White F-104A Rushworth F-104D Armstrong	— 05 Oct 60 X-15 failed preflight checks 1-A-26 11 Oct 60 Failed engine H2O2 tank regulator Abort used NB-52B 52-008; Petersen was the X-15 pilot on the abort Good flight
24 / 1-15-28 McKay (1) 28 Oct 60 Palmdale VOR 09:43:56.0 Rogers 09:53:01.3	XLR11s; Ventral on; Nose boom Pilot familiarization – McKay's first X-15 flight Stability and control data; Performance data; Alternate airspeed calibration	Thompson 52-008 Fulton / Cole Butchart 09:12 10:06 00:54	2.00 50,000 — — ?? 8 chambers	2.02 50,700 1,333 00:09:05.3 ?? 267.5 8 chambers	F-100 Looney F-104 White F-104 Petersen	No aborts Ventral chute did not open
25 / 1-16-29 Rushworth (1) 04 Nov 60 Palmdale VOR 12:43:33.0 Rogers 12:52:19.3	XLR11s; Ventral on; Nose boom Pilot familiarization – Rushworth's first X-15 flight Stability and control data; Performance data; Alternate airspeed calibration	McKay 52-008 Fulton / Cole Butchart 12:10 13:15 01:05	2.00 50,000 — — ?? 8 chambers	1.95 48,900 1,287 00:08:46.3 ?? 271 8 chambers	F-100 Looney F-104 White F-104 Armstrong F-100F Al White / DeLong	No aborts Good flight
26 / 2-10-21 Crossfield (12) 15 Nov 60 Rosamond 09:59:00.0 Rogers 10:07:28.4	XLR99; Ventral on; Nose boom XLR99 checkout; Stability and control evaluation	Harvey 52-003 Allavie / Kuyk Moise 08:59 10:16 01:17	2.70 60,000 — — 155 50 percent	2.97 81,200 1,960 00:08:28.4 103 137.3 (B.O.) 50 percent	F-100F Al White / DeLong F-104 Walker F-104 White	2-A-19 13 Oct 60 H2O2 leak in #2 APU 2-A-20 04 Nov 60 Failed #2 APU shutoff valve All aborts used NB-52A 52-003; Crossfield was the X-15 pilot for all aborts First XLR99 flight
27 / 1-17-30 Rushworth (2) 17 Nov 60 Palmdale VOR 12:43:07.0 Rogers 12:52:05.2	XLR11s; Ventral on; Nose boom Aerodynamic data	McKay 52-003 Fulton / Allavie Russell 12:10 13:00 00:50	2.20 55,000 — — ?? 8 chambers	1.90 54,750 1,254 00:08:58.2 ?? 261.9 8 chambers	F-100 Looney F-104 Walker F-104 Knight	No aborts Lower XLR11 engine shutdown and restarted; Upper XLR11 removed on 24 November 1960
28 / 2-11-22 Crossfield (13) 22 Nov 60 Rosamond 13:25:55.0 Rogers 13:33:26.7	XLR99; Ventral on; Nose boom XLR99 checkout - restart and throttle; Ballistic control system evaluation	Harvey 52-003 Allavie / Fulton Moise 12:46 13:40 00:54	2.30 54,000 — — 134 50, 75, 100	2.51 61,900 1,656 00:07:31.7 103 125.1 (B.O.) 50, 75, 100 percent	F-100F Al White / DeLong F-104 Walker F-104 White	No aborts First demonstration of XLR99 throttle capabilities; First XLR99 inflight restart First engine run was shutdown (S.D.); Second was a burnout (B.O.)
29 / 1-18-31 Armstrong (1) 30 Nov 60 Palmdale VOR 10:42:42.0 Rogers 10:52:35.8	XLR11s; Ventral on; Nose boom Pilot familiarization – Armstrong's first X-15 flight	McKay 52-008 Fulton / Cole Butchart 10:10 11:04 00:54	2.00 50,000 — — ?? 8 chambers	1.75 48,840 1,155 00:09:53.8 ?? 309.1 7 chambers	F-100F Looney F-104D Petersen F-104A Walker	No aborts Upper #3 chamber did not start; Inertial attitudes incorrect
30 / 2-12-23 Crossfield (14) 06 Dec 60 Lancaster 15:29:30.0 Rogers 15:37:37.2	XLR99; Ventral on; Nose boom XLR99 restart demonstration; BCS checks; High-g maneuvers	Harvey 52-003 Allavie / Cole Moise 14:50 16:00 01:10	2.30 54,000 — — 121 50, 70 percent	2.85 53,374 1,881 00:08:07.2 103 128.9 (B.O.) 50, 70 percent	F-100F Al White / DeLong F-104 Petersen F-104 White	No aborts Last North American Aviation flight of X-15; Only Lancaster launch Two engine inflight restarts; Last nose-boom flight; First engine run was shutdown (S.D.); Second was shutdown (S.D.); Third was a burn-out (B.O.)

Flight # / ID X-15 Pilot Flight Date Launch Lake Launch Time Landing Lake Landing Time	X-15 Configuration Purpose of Flight	NASA-1 NB-52 + Pilots + LP Operator + Take-Off Time + Landing Time + Flight Time	Planned + Max Mach + Max Altitude + Max Speed + Flight Time + Engine s/n + Power Time + Thrust	Actual + Max Mach + Max Altitude + Max Speed + Flight Time + Engine s/n + Power Time + Thrust	Chase 1 Pilot(s) Chase 2 Pilot(s) Chase 3 Pilot(s) Chase 4 Pilot(s) Chase 5 Pilot(s)	Abort(s) Notes
31 / 1-19-32 Armstrong (2) 09 Dec 60 Palmdale VOR 11:52:40.0 Rogers 12:03:29.0	XLR11s; Ventral on; Ball-nose Ball nose evaluation; Stability and control data; Alternate airspeed sources evaluation	McKay 52-008 Allavie / Cole Russell 11:21 12:17 00:56	1.90 50,000 — — ?? ?? 8 chambers	1.80 50,095 1,188 00:10:49.0 ?? 270.1 8 chambers	F-100F Daniel F-104D Petersen F-104A White	No Aborts First ball-nose flight
32 / 1-20-35 McKay (2) 01 Feb 61 Palmdale VOR 10:47:32.0 Rogers 10:57:19.7	XLR11s; Ventral on; Ball-nose Ball nose evaluation; Side-stick controller evaluation; Inertial velocity indicator checkout; Alternate airspeed sources evaluation	Thompson 52-008 Fulton / Lewis Russell 10:13 11:08 00:55	2.00 50,000 — — ?? ?? 8 chambers	1.88 49,780 1,211 00:09:47.7 ?? 263.7 8 chambers	F-100 White F-104 Petersen F-104 Wood	1-A-33 15 Dec 60 #2 hydraulic system failure 1-A-34 11 Jan 61 #2 hydraulic system failure 1-A-33 used NB-52A 52-003; White was the X-15 pilot 1-A-34 used NB-52A 52-003; McKay was the X-15 pilot Good flight
33 / 1-21-36 White (6) 07 Feb 61 Silver 12:56:10.0 Rogers 13:06:37.8	XLR11s; Ventral on; Ball-nose Stability and control data; Performance data; Flight systems evaluation	Armstrong 52-008 Fulton / Mosley Butchart 12:17 13:21 01:04	3.10 75,000 — — ?? ?? 8 chambers	3.50 78,150 2,275 00:10:27.8 ?? 276.1 8 chambers	F-100 Daniel F-104 Knight F-104 Petersen F-104 Rushworth	No Aborts Last X-15 XLR11 flight; Fastest flight with XLR11 engines
34 / 2-13-26 White (7) 07 Mar 61 Silver 10:28:33.0 Rogers 10:37:07.1	XLR99; Ventral on; Ball-nose Envelope expansion; Stability and control data; Temperature data; B-70 IR emission coating test	Butchart 52-008 Cole / Kuyk Russell 09:53 10:50 00:57	4.00 84,000 — — 108 116 50 percent	4.43 77,450 2,905 00:08:34.1 108 127.0 (S.D.) 50 percent	F-100 Rushworth F5D-1 Walker F4H-1 Petersen F-104 Looney	2-A-24 21 Feb 61 Inertial platform failure 2-A-25 24 Feb 61 Attitude gyro failure All aborts used NB-52B 52-008; White was the X-15 pilot for all aborts First X-15-2 ball-nose flight; First Mach 4 flight (for any aircraft); First government XLR99 flight
35 / 2-14-28 Walker (6) 30 Mar 61 Hidden Hills 10:05:00.0 Rogers 10:15:16.5	XLR99; Ventral on; Ball-nose Altitude buildup; Ballistic control system evaluation; Thermostructures data; Aerodynamic data	?? 52-008 Fulton / Kuyk Russell 09:20 10:35 01:15	3.70 150,000 — — 108 79 75 percent	3.95 169,600 2,760 00:10:16.5 108 81.9 (S.D.) 75 percent	F-100 White T-38A Knight F-104 Petersen F-104 Rushworth	2-A-27 21 Mar 61 NB-52 electrical problems Abort used NB-52B 52-008; Walker was the X-15 pilot for the abort in an A/P-22S First Hidden Hills launch; First use of new A/P22S-2 full-pressure suit; Telemetry failure; XLR99 lost fire signal, Restart required; SAS cycle limit; NB-52 brake chute failed on landing
36 / 2-15-29 White (8) 21 Apr 61 Hidden Hills 10:05:17.0 Rogers 10:15:20.4	XLR99; Ventral on; Ball-nose Velocity buildup; Aerodynamic heating data; Stability and control data; Performance data	Armstrong 52-003 Allavie / Mosley Russell 09:19 10:32 01:13	4.60 105,000 — — 108 67 100 percent	4.62 105,000 3,074 00:10:03.4 108 71.6 (S.D.) 100 percent	F-100F Looney F-104A Walker F-104A Rogers F-104D Wood	No aborts Restart required; Pitch damper dropout; Cabin pressure rose to 46,000 feet
37 / 2-16-31 Walker (7) 25 May 61 Mud 12:16:35.0 Rogers 12:28:43.1	XLR99; Ventral on; Ball-nose Velocity buildup; Aerodynamic heating data; Stability and control data; Performance data; SAS residual oscillation evaluation	?? 52-003 Allavie / Fulton Butchart 11:30 12:52 01:22	5.00 117,000 — — 103 73 100 percent	4.95 107,500 3,307 00:12:08.1 103 74.3 (S.D.) 100 percent	F-100 Looney F-104 Daniel F-104 Petersen F-104 Rushworth	2-A-30 19 May 61 Lost Beatty radar Abort used NB-52A 52-003; Walker was the X-15 pilot for the abort First launch from Mud Lake; SAS dropped out at launch; Cabin altitude went to 50,000 feet
38 / 2-17-33 White (9) 23 Jun 61 Mud 14:00:05.0 Rogers 14:10:10.7	XLR99; Ventral on; Ball-nose Velocity buildup; Performance data; Stability and control data; Aerodynamic heating data	?? 52-003 Allavie / Fulton Butchart 13:08 14:33 01:25	5.30 115,000 — — 103 75 100 percent	5.27 107,700 3,603 00:10:05.7 103 78.7 (S.D.) 100 percent	F-100 Looney F-104 Daniel F-104 Crews F-104 Walker	2-A-32 20 Jun 61 #1 APU failure Abort used NB-52A 52-003; White was the X-15 pilot for the abort First Mach 5 flight (for any aircraft); Cabin altitude rose to 56K feet; suit inflated
39 / 1-22-37 Petersen (3) 10 Aug 61 Silver 10:27:05.0 Rogers 10:36:29.4	XLR99; Ventral on; Ball-nose XLR99 systems checkout; Beta-dot control technique evaluation	Armstrong 52-003 Allavie / Archer Russell 09:43 10:44 01:01	3.70 75,000 — — 107 115 50 percent	4.11 78,200 2,735 00:09:24.4 107 117.7 (S.D.) 50 percent	F-100 White F-104 Rushworth F-104 Walker	No aborts First XLR99 flight for X-15-1; Delayed release from NB-52 due to drop switch problem
40 / 2-18-34 Walker (8) 12 Sep 61 Mud 14:40:17.0 Rogers 14:49:00.9	XLR99; Ventral on; Ball-nose Velocity buildup; Aerodynamic heating data; Stability and control data; Performance data; Baseline data for sharp-leading edge experiment on X-15-3	Butchart 52-008 Archer / Allavie Russell 13:44 15:10 01:26	5.60 120,000 — — 106 79 100, 50 75	5.21 114,300 3,618 00:08:43.9 106 115.0 (B.O.) 100, 50, 75 percent	F-100 White F-104 Petersen F-104 Daniel F-104 Rushworth 0 0	No aborts XLR99 fuel suction pressure switch failure; Fuel line low light at launch; Airplane very loose approaching 15 degrees angle of attack

Flight # / ID X-15 Pilot Flight Date Launch Lake Launch Time Landing Lake Landing Time	X-15 Configuration Purpose of Flight	NASA-1 NB-52 + Pilots + LP Operator + Take-Off Time + Landing Time + Flight Time	Planned + Max Mach + Max Altitude + Max Speed + Flight Time + Engine s/n + Power Time + Thrust	Actual + Max Mach + Max Altitude + Max Speed + Flight Time + Engine s/n + Power Time + Thrust	Chase 1 Pilot(s) Chase 2 Pilot(s) Chase 3 Pilot(s) Chase 4 Pilot(s) Chase 5 Pilot(s)	Abort(s) Notes
41 / 2-19-35 Petersen (4) 28 Sep 61 Hidden Hills 09:50:25.0 Rogers 09:59:06.6	XLR99; Ventral on; Ball-nose Heat transfer data; Thermostructural data; Stability and control data; Controllability at low dynamic pressure; Performance and stability data with speed brakes extended	Thompson 52-008 Allavie / Archer Russell 09:04 10:15 01:11	5.00 80,000 — — — 90 100, 50 percent	5.30 101,800 3,600 00:08:41.6 106 87.1 (B.O.) 100, 50 percent	F-100 Daniel F-104 McKay F-104 Rogers	No aborts Good flight
42 / 1-23-39 Rushworth (3) 04 Oct 61 Silver 10:40:50.0 Rogers 10:49:21.3	XLR99; Ventral off; Ball-nose Ventral-off handling quality evaluation; Ventral-off stability study	Knight 52-003 Allavie / Archer Russell 09:59 11:10 01:11	3.70 80,000 — — — 120 75, 50 percent	4.30 78,000 2,830 00:08:31.3 103 122.0 (S.D.) 75, 50 percent	F-100 Daniel F-104 McKay F-104 White	1-A-38 29 Sep 61 Stabilizer pulsing / feedback Abort used NB-52A 52-003; Rushworth was the X-15 pilot for the abort First ventral off flight; Leading-edge heating slot shields
43 / 2-20-36 White (10) 11 Oct 61 Mud 12:20:00.0 Rogers 12:30:14.7	XLR99; Ventral on; Ball-nose Altitude buildup; Aerodynamic heating during reentry data; Controllability at low dynamic pressure; Performance and stability data with speed brakes extended	Petersen 52-003 Allavie / Fulton Russell 11:22 12:52 01:30	5.00 200,000 — — — 79 100 percent	5.21 217,000 3,647 00:10:14.7 106 82.5 (S.D.) 100 percent	F-100 Daniel F5D McKay F-104 Wood F-104 Rushworth	No aborts Pete Knight was NASA 2; First aircraft flight above 200,000 feet; First X-15 flight that used ballistic control system for attitude control; Left outer windshield cracked on reentry; The highest Mach number was achieved during descent from max altitude
44 / 1-24-40 Walker (9) 17 Oct 61 Mud 10:57:33.0 Rogers 11:07:44.7	XLR99; Ventral on; Ball-nose Velocity buildup; Aerodynamic heating data; Stability and control data; Performance data	Petersen 52-003 Allavie / Archer Butchart 10:01 12:30 02:29	5.70 113,000 — — — 80 75, 100 percent	5.74 108,600 3,900 00:10:11.7 103 84.6 (S.D.) 75, 100 percent	F-100F White F-104D McKay F-104 Daniel F-104 Knight	No aborts Laterally out of trim to the right
45 / 2-21-37 White (11) 09 Nov 61 Mud 09:57:17.0 Rogers 10:06:48.2	XLR99; Ventral on; Ball-nose; Thermal paint over entire canopy Maximum velocity flight; Aerodynamic heating data; Stability and control data; Performance data	?? 52-008 Allavie / Archer Russell 09:00 10:26 01:26	6.00 110,000 — — — 83 100 percent	6.04 101,600 4,093 00:09:31.2 19-Apr 86.9 (B.O.) 100 percent	F-100 Rushworth F-104 Walker F-104 Gordon F-104 Daniel	No aborts Jack McKay was NASA 2; First Mach 6 flight (for any aircraft); Right outer window shattered decelerating thru Mach 2.7
46 / 3-1-2 Armstrong (3) 20 Dec 61 Silver 14:45:50.0 Rogers 14:56:15.4	XLR99; Ventral on; Ball-nose MH-96 evaluation; Checkout of X-15-3	McKay 52-003 Allavie / Bement Butchart 14:07 15:06 00:59	3.50 75,000 — — — 104 75, 50 percent	3.76 81,000 2,502 00:10:25.4 106 106.3 (S.D.) 75, 50 percent	F-100 Daniel F-104A Petersen F-104 Rushworth	3-A-1 19 Dec 61 XLR99 indication failure Abort used NB-52A 52-003; Armstrong was the X-15 pilot for the abort First X-15-3 flight; All three axes disengaged at launch - reset; Yaw limit cycle caused reversion to fixed gain
47 / 1-25-44 Petersen (5) 10 Jan 62 Mud 12:28:16.0 Mud 12:32:01.7	XLR99; Ventral on; Ball-nose High angle of attack stability and control data; Aerodynamic heating data	Thompson 52-003 Allavie / Bement Russell 11:29 13:20 01:51	5.70 117,000 — — — 95 100 percent	0.97 44,750 645 00:03:45.7 21-Apr 3.3 (S.D.) See notes	F-100 Daniel F-104 Walker F-104 McDivitt F-104 Rushworth	1-A-41 27 Oct 61 Weather in launch area 1-A-42 02 Nov 61 Cabin pressure 1-A-43 03 Nov 61 XLR99 purge pressure switch failure All aborts used NB-52A 52-003; White was the X-15 pilot for all aborts Two engine malfunction shutdowns;≈ 238 psia chamber pressure maximum Emergency landing at Mud Lake; First uprange landing Petersen's last flight
48 / 3-2-3 Armstrong (4) 17 Jan 62 Mud 12:00:34.0 Rogers 12:11:01.7	XLR99; Ventral on; Ball-nose MH-96 evaluation	Thompson 52-003 Allavie / Bement Butchart 11:05 12:34 01:29	5.00 100,000 — — — 100 75 percent	5.51 133,500 3,765 00:10:27.7 107 97.4 (S.D.) 75 percent	F-100 Gordon F-104 Petersen F-104 McDivitt F-104 Rushworth	No aborts Good flight
49 / 3-3-7 Armstrong (5) 05 Apr 62 Hidden Hills 10:04:25.0 Rogers 10:15:42.0	XLR99; Ventral on; Ball-nose MH-96 evaluation at high and low dynamic pressure	Walker 52-003 Fulton / Allavie Butchart 09:23 10:30 01:07	4.00 170,000 — — — 70 75, 100 percent	4.12 180,000 2,850 00:11:17.0 107 79.2 (S.D.) 75, 100 percent	F-100 Daniel F-104 McKay F-104 Rushworth	3-A-4 29 Mar 62 Inertial platform failure 3-A-5 30 Mar 62 Igniter idle malfunction 3-A-6 31 Mar 62 analyzer test #24 failed All aborts used NB-52A 52-003; Armstrong was the X-15 pilot for all aborts Engine failed to light on initial attempt; Restart required
50 / 1-26-46 Walker (10) 19 Apr 62 Mud 10:02:20.0 Rogers 10:11:18.9	XLR99; Ventral on; Ball-nose ASAS evaluation; 20-degree angle of attack evaluation; (#1) UV stellar photography experiment preliminary data gathering	White 52-003 Allavie / Archer Russell 08:58 10:37 01:39	5.90 153,000 — — — 83 100 percent	5.69 154,000 3,866 00:08:58.9 109 84.3 (B.O.) 100 percent	F-100 McKay (aborted) JF-104A Dana (new Chase 1) F-104 Rushworth F-104 Daniel F-104 Knight	1-A-45 18 Apr 62 Weather in launch area Abort used NB-52A 52-003; Walker was the X-15 pilot for the abort Beta cross-pointer wired backwards; First flight with ASAS installed (checkout only)

Flight # / ID; X-15 Pilot; Flight Date; Launch Lake; Launch Time; Landing Lake; Landing Time	X-15 Configuration; Purpose of Flight	NASA-1; NB-52; + Pilots; + LP Operator; + Take-Off Time; + Landing Time; + Flight Time	Planned: + Max Mach; + Max Altitude; + Max Speed; + Flight Time; + Engine s/n; + Power Time; + Thrust	Actual: + Max Mach; + Max Altitude; + Max Speed; + Flight Time; + Engine s/n; + Power Time; + Thrust	Chase 1–5 Pilot(s)	Abort(s) / Notes
51 / 3-4-8; Armstrong (6); 20 Apr 62; Mud; 11:26:58.0; Rogers; 11:39:26.7	XLR99; Ventral on; Ball-nose; Delta-h indicator on I-panel; MH-96 evaluation	Walker; 52-008; Allavie / Bement; Butchart; 10:35; 11:57; 01:22	5.35; 205,000; —; —; —; 81; 100 percent	5.31; 207,500; 3,789; 00:12:28.7; 110; 82.4 (S.D.); 100 percent	F-100 White; F-104 McKay; F-104 Gordon; F-104 Rushworth	No aborts. Overshot (bounced) during reentry - ended up 45 miles south of Edwards; Used max L/D glide to get back to Edwards; Longest flight in X-15 program
52 / 1-27-48; Walker (11); 30 Apr 62; Mud; 10:23:20.0; Rogers; 10:33:06.2	XLR99; Ventral on; Ball-nose; Altitude buildup; Aerodynamic heating during reentry data; Controllability at low dynamic pressure data; Performance and stability with speed brakes extended	Butchart; 52-008; Allavie / Bement; Russell; 09:34; 10:52; 01:18	5.35; 255,000; —; —; —; 81; 100 percent	4.94; 246,700; 3,489; 00:09:46.2; 109; 81.6 (S.D.); 100 percent	F-100 Daniel; F-104 White; F-104B Dana / Thompson; F-104 Rushworth	1-A-47 27 Apr 62 Weather. Abort used NB-52B 52-008; Walker was the X-15 pilot for the abort. FAI-certified altitude record; First flight of X-15-1 with operational ASAS
53 / 2-22-40; Rushworth (4); 08 May 62; Hidden Hills; 10:01:28.0; Rogers; 10:10:18.4	XLR99; Ventral on; Ball-nose; Heat transfer investigation; ASAS checkout; Stability at high-alpha with partial speed brakes	Armstrong; 52-008; Allavie / Bement; Russell; 09:07; 10:26; 01:19	5.00; 73,000; —; —; —; 103; 100, 30 percent	5.34; 70,400; 3,524; 00:08:50.4; 111; 97.9 (B.O); 100, 30 percent	F-100 Daniel; F-104 McKay; F-104 Rogers	2-A-38 25 Apr 62 Weather; 2-A-39 26 Apr 62 XLR99 pump idle too high. All aborts used NB-52A 52-003; White was the X-15 pilot for all aborts. First XLR99 operation at 30 percent; Vibrations noted; First X-15 flight above q=2,000 psf; First flight of X-15-2 with operational ASAS; Qbar overshoot due to lack of pilot presentation
54 / 1-28-49; Rushworth (5); 22 May 62; Hidden Hills; 10:04:46.0; Rogers; 10:14:02.2	XLR99; Ventral on; Ball-nose; Local flow investigation	Walker; 52-003; Allavie / Campbell; Russell; 09:24; 10:27; 01:03	5.20; 90,000; —; —; —; 77; 100 percent	5.03; 100,400; 3,450; 00:09:16.2; 109; 75.3 (S.D.); 100 percent	F-100 Daniel; F-104 Dana; F-104 Rogers	No aborts. Premature engine shutdown; Left roll out of trim
55 / 2-23-43; White (12); 01 Jun 62; Delamar; 10:51:15.0; Rogers; 11:01:16.9	XLR99; Ventral on; Ball-nose; ASAS checkout; Stability data at 23 degrees angle of attack	Walker; 52-008; Fulton / Bement; Russell; 10:00; 11:28; 001:28	5.80; 162,000; —; —; —; 93; 100, 30, 75	5.42; 132,600; 3,675; 00:10:01.9; 14-Apr; 86; 100, 30 percent	F-100 Daniel; F-104 Dana; F-104 Rogers; F-104 Collins	2-A-41 25 May 62 Inertial platform and telemetry failure; 2-A-42 29 May 62 Inertial platform cooling. All aborts used NB-52B 52-008; White was the X-15 pilot for all aborts. First launch from Delamar; Vibrations noted at 30% thrust
56 / 1-29-50; Walker (12); 07 Jun 62; Hidden Hills; 10:29:20.0; Rogers; 10:37:44.2	XLR99; Ventral on; Ball-nose; Local flow at high angles of attack	Rushworth; 52-003; Allavie / Bement; Peterson; 09:45; 10:53; 01:08	5.60; 100,000; —; —; —; 80; 100 percent	5.39; 103,600; 3,672; 00:08:24.2; 109; 81.5 (S.D); 100 percent	F-100 Daniel; F-104 McKay; F-104 White	No aborts. Ammonia check valve in fuel tank stuck; Rough engine operation
57 / 3-5-9; White (13); 12 Jun 62; Delamar; 12:04:00.0; Rogers; 12:13:33.9	XLR99; Ventral on; Ball-nose; Pilot checkout; Ballistic control system evaluation	Rushworth; 52-008; Fulton / Allavie; Russell; 10:56; 12:41; 01:45	5.15; 206,000; —; —; —; 77; 100 percent	5.02; 184,600; 3,517; 00:09:33.9; 106; 81.9 (S.D.); 100 percent	F-100 McDivitt; F-104 McKay; F-104 Collins; F-104 Gordon	No aborts. Overshot altitude by 21,400 feet
58 / 3-6-10; White (14); 21 Jun 62; Delamar; 09:47:05.0; Rogers; 09:56:38.6	XLR99; Ventral on; Ball-nose; Contractual demonstration of MH-96; (Good excuse for record altitude flight buildup)	Rushworth; 52-008; Allavie / Lewis; Butchart; 09:01; 10:23; 01:22	5.40; 250,000; —; —; —; 80; 100 percent	5.08; 246,700; 3,641; 00:09:33.6; 106; 82.3 (S.D.); 100 percent	F-100 Daniel; F-104 McKay; F-104 Armstrong; F-104 Collins	No aborts. Good flight
59 / 1-30-51; Walker (13); 27 Jun 62; Mud 0; 13:08:10.0; Rogers; 13:17:42.4	XLR99; Ventral on; Ball-nose; Trim on side-stick; High angle of attack stability	??; 52-003; Allavie / Townsend; Russell; 12:13; 13:38; 01:25	6.00; 107,000; —; —; —; 84; 100 percent	5.92; 123,700; 4,104; 00:09:32.4; 107; 88.6 (B.O.); 100 percent	F-100 Rushworth; F-104 McKay; F-104 Knight; F-104 Daniel	No aborts. Unofficial world absolute speed record; Ventral chute lost during flight; Pitch damper tripped out during pull-up maneuver
60 / 2-24-44; McKay (3); 29 Jun 62; Hidden Hills; 10:41:47.0; Rogers; 10:50:40.6	XLR99; Ventral on; Ball-nose; Q-meter on I-panel; Heating rates at low angle of attack and Mach; Notch filter evaluation	Walker; 52-008; Allavie / Archer; Peterson; 09:57; 11:05; 01:08	4.20; 84,000; —; —; —; 122; 85, 80, 50	4.95; 83,200; 3,280; 00:08:53.6; 110; 112.4 (B.O.); 85, 80, 50 percent	F-100 Rushworth; F-104 Armstrong; F-104 Daniel	No aborts. Speed brake handle seized temporarily; Two SAS tripouts (one pilot induced); Ballistic control system inoperative due to leaking valve

Flight # / ID; X-15 Pilot; Flight Date; Launch Lake; Launch Time; Landing Lake; Landing Time	X-15 Configuration; Purpose of Flight	NASA-1; NB-52; Pilots; LP Operator; Take-Off Time; Landing Time; Flight Time	Planned: Max Mach; Max Altitude; Max Speed; Flight Time; Engine s/n; Power Time; Thrust	Actual: Max Mach; Max Altitude; Max Speed; Flight Time; Engine s/n; Power Time; Thrust	Chase 1–5; Pilot(s)	Abort(s); Notes
61 / 1-31-52; Walker (14); 16 Jul 62; Mud; 14:09:25.0; Rogers; 14:19:02.8	XLR99; Ventral on; Ball-nose. — Notch filter evaluation at high dynamic pressure; Aerodynamic drag data; ASAS stability investigation	??; 52-008; Allavie / Archer; B. Peterson; 13:23; 14:40; 01:17	5.40; 105,000; —; —; —; 80; 100 percent	5.37; 107,200; 3,674; 00:09:37.8; 107; 83.9 (S.D.); 100 percent	F-100 Daniel; F-104 Dana; F-104 Engle; F-104 Rushworth	No aborts. — #2 generator tripped out during flight (not reset); Numerous pitch and roll tripouts; Ventral chute malfunctioned;
62 / 3-7-14; White (15); 17 Jul 62; Delamar; 09:31:10.0; Rogers; 09:41:30.7	XLR99; Ventral on; Ball-nose. — Contractual demonstration of MH-96. (0)	Walker; 52-003; Allavie / Archer; Butchart; 08:46; 10:03; 01:17	5.15; 282,000; —; —; —; 80; 100 percent	5.45; 314,750; 3,832; 00:10:20.7; 103; 82.0 (B.O.); 100 percent	F-100 McDivitt; F-104 McKay; F-104 Dana; F-104B Thompson / Petersen	3-A-11 10 Jul 62 NB-52 landing gear; 3-A-12 11 Jul 62 #1 APU pressure regulator; 3-A-13 16 Jul 62 Unplugged NB-52 umbilical; All aborts used NB-52A 52-003; White was the X-15 pilot for all aborts. — Originally scheduled for Smith Ranch (rain); Overshot altitude by 32,250 feet; FAI world altitude record for class; First Astronaut qualification flight; First aircraft flight above 300,000 feet; First flight above 50 miles;
63 / 2-25-45; McKay (4); 19 Jul 62; Hidden Hills; 09:53:45.0; Rogers; 10:02:08.8	XLR99; Ventral on; Ball-nose; Idle stop changed from 45 to 40 percent. — Aerodynamic heating rates at low angle of attack and low Mach; Aerodynamic drag data; Handling qualities data; Wing pressure distribution investigation	Armstrong; 52-008; Fulton / Bement; B. Peterson; 09:11; 10:20; 01:09	4.60; 73,000; —; —; —; 120; 80, 40 percent	5.18; 85,250; 3,474; 00:08:23.8; 110; 106.2 (B.O.); 80, 40 percent	F-100 Rogers; F-104D Dana; F-104A Rushworth	No aborts. — Alpha indicator had oscillations; Ventral chute failed
64 / 1-32-53; Armstrong (7); 26 Jul 62; Mud; 11:22:30.0; Rogers; 11:32:51.6	XLR99; Ventral on; Ball-nose; Side-stick with beep trim. — Aerodynamic stability and drag; Handling qualities	Walker; 52-003; Fulton / Bement; Russell; 10:34; 11:57; 01:23	5.70; 111,000; —; —; —; 83; 100 percent	5.74; 98,900; 3,989; 00:10:21.6; 106; 82.8 (B.O.); 100 percent	T-38A Rushworth; F-104 Collins; F-104 Daniel; F-104 White	No aborts. — Full back trim only gave 16 degrees of stabilizer; Smoke in cockpit; Armstrong's last flight
65 / 3-8-16; Walker (15); 02 Aug 62; Mud; 09:56:15.0; Rogers; 10:05:29.0	XLR99; Ventral on; Ball-nose; Q-meter on I-panel. — MH-96 fixed gain evaluation	White; 52-003; Fulton / Bement; Russell; 09:05; 10:31; 01:26	5.10; 160,000; —; —; —; 78; 100 percent	5.07; 144,500; 3,438; 00:09:14.0; 107; 80.0 (S.D.); 100 percent	T-38A Daniel; F-104 McKay; F-104 Collins; F-104 Rushworth	3-A-15 01 Aug 62 NH3 tank pressure unreadable; Abort used NB-52A 52-003; Walker was the X-15 pilot for the abort. — Theta vernier wired backwards
66 / 2-26-46; Rushworth (6); 08 Aug 62; Hidden Hills; 10:08:35.0; Rogers; 10:16:17.8	XLR99; Ventral on; Ball-nose. — Aerodynamic heating rates at high angle of attack and low Mach; RAS checkout; Aerodynamic drag data. (0)	Walker; 52-008; Fulton / Sturmthal; Russell; 09:15; 10:33; 01:18	4.00; 84,000; —; —; —; 98; 100, 75, 65, 40	4.40; 90,877; 2,943; 00:07:42.8; 111; 95.8 (B.O.); See note	T-38A McDivitt; F-104 McKay; F-104 Engle; F-104 Collins	No aborts. — ASAS engaged with pilot induced yaw damper; Actual engine thrust levels were 100, 75, 65, 52, and 39 percent
67 / 3-9-18; Walker (16); 14 Aug 62; Delamar; 10:41:35.0; Rogers; 10:50:39.9	XLR99; Ventral on; Ball-nose. — Constant theta reentry and stability at minimum yaw gain	White; 52-003; Fulton / Crews; Russell; 09:46; 11:16; 01:30	5.80; 220,000; —; —; —; 83; 100 percent	5.25; 193,600; 3,747; 00:09:04.9; 107; 84.2 (B.O.); 100 percent	T-38A Rushworth; F-104D Dana; F-104 Engle; F-104 White	3-A-17 10 Aug 62 #1 BCS valve failed to open; Abort used NB-52A 52-003; Walker was the X-15 pilot for the abort. — Roll damper dropped off during reentry; Last flight of X-15-3 with ventral on
68 / 2-27-47; Rushworth (7); 20 Aug 62; Hidden Hills; 10:08:40.0; Rogers; 10:17:18.2	XLR99; Ventral on; Ball-nose. — Heating rates at moderate angle of attack and high Mach; Aerodynamic drag data; ASAS evaluation; Stability and control data	??; 52-008; Fulton / Andonian; Russell; 09:20; 10:34; 01:14	4.90; 85,000; —; —; —; 92; 100, 75, 65, 40	5.24; 88,900; 3,534; 00:08:38.2; 111; 86.5 (B.O.); 100, 75, 60, 40	T-38A Gordon; F-104 McKay; F-104 Engle; F-104 Daniel	— 17 Aug 62 Weather prior to taxi. — Roll SAS failed at launch - would not reengage; XLR99 second stage igniter injector face damage
69 / 2-28-48; Rushworth (8); 29 Aug 62; Hidden Hills; 10:36:03.0; Rogers; 10:44:50.1	XLR99; Ventral on; Ball-nose; Cut-away windshield retainer. — Heating rates at high angle of attack and high Mach	Armstrong; 52-008; Fulton / Bement; Butchart; 09:50; 11:00; 01:10	4.80; 87,000; —; —; —; 91; 100, 80 percent	5.12; 97,200; 3,447; 00:08:47.1; 20-Apr; 92.0 (B.O.); 100, 80 percent	T-38A White; F-104 Walker; F-104 McDivitt; F-104 Knight	No aborts. — Intermittent roll SAS trip-outs; Speed brake vibrations
70 / 2-29-50; McKay (5); 28 Sep 62; Hidden Hills; 10:04:55.0; Rogers; 10:14:22.5	XLR99; Ventral off; Ball-nose. — Heating rates at low angle of attack and low Mach; Ventral-off stability data; Base data for sharp-leading edge experiment on X-15-3; (#1) UV stellar photography experiment preliminary data gathering	Armstrong; 52-008; Bement / Sturmthal; Butchart; 09:17; 10:34; 01:17	4.20; 87,000; —; —; —; 124; 87, 44, 35	4.22; 68,200; 2,765; 00:09:27.5; 108; 128.2 (B.O.); 87, 44, 35 percent	T-38A White; F-104 Walker; F-104 Engle; F-104 Rushworth	2-A-49 27 Sep 62 Left-hand ejection lever problems; Abort used NB-52B 52-008; McKay was the X-15 pilot for the abort. — XLR99 igniter malfunction before launch; First X-15-2 flight without ventral

Flight # / ID · X-15 Pilot · Flight Date · Launch Lake · Launch Time · Landing Lake · Landing Time	X-15 Configuration · Purpose of Flight	NASA-1 · NB-52 · Pilots · LP Operator · Take-Off Time · Landing Time · Flight Time	Planned (Max Mach · Max Altitude · Max Speed · Flight Time · Engine s/n · Power Time · Thrust)	Actual (Max Mach · Max Altitude · Max Speed · Flight Time · Engine s/n · Power Time · Thrust)	Chase 1–5 Pilot(s)	Abort(s)	Notes
71 / 3-10-19 Rushworth (9) 04 Oct 62 Delamar 10:10:11.0 Rogers 10:20:01.5	XLR99; Ventral off; Ball-nose Pilot checkout; Ventral-off stability data	White 52-008 Fulton / Lewis Butchart 09:26 10:53 01:27	5.00 103,000 — — 108 100, 50 percent	5.17 112,200 3,493 00:09:50.5 107 103.2 (B.O.) 100, 50 percent	T-38A Rogers / Daniel F-104 Walker F-104 Collins F-104 Gordon	No aborts	#1 APU failed 5 minutes after launch (first in-flight APU failure) (Ball-nose and yaw damper lost as a result)
72 / 2-30-51 McKay (6) 09 Oct 62 Delamar 10:58:32.0 Rogers 11:08:12.3	XLR99; Ventral off; Ball-nose; LH & RH windshield retainer Ventral-off stability data; (#27) Hycon camera experiment	Walker 52-003 Fulton / Lewis Russell 10:09 11:38 01:29	5.30 125,000 — — 81 100 percent	5.46 130,200 3,716 00:09:40.3 108 79.5 (S.D.) 100 percent	T-38A White F-104B F-104 Rushworth F-104 Rogers	No aborts	Roll failed to ASAS at launch - reengaged; XLR99 second stage igniter injector face damage
73 / 3-11-20 Rushworth (10) 23 Oct 62 Mud 11:30:40.0 Rogers 11:40:26.5	XLR99; Ventral off; Ball-nose; Aft windshield retainers removed Ventral-off stability data;	McKay 52-008 Bement / Cross Butchart 10:31 12:28 01:57	5.50 125,000 — — 79 100 percent	5.47 134,500 3,716 00:09:46.5 107 78.0 (S.D.) 100 percent	T-38A Rogers F-104D Dana F-104B Thompson F-104 Knight 100 percent	No aborts	B-52 launched X-15 (popped circuit breaker); Lateral out-of-trim with damper off throughout flight;
74 / 2-31-52 McKay (7) 09 Nov 62 Mud 10:23:07.0 Mud 10:29:38.1	XLR99; Ventral off; Ball-nose Ventral-off stability data; Aerodynamic boundary layer investigations	Rushworth 52-008 Bement / Lewis Russell 09:28 11:55 02:27	5.55 125,000 — — 79 100 percent	1.49 53,950 1,019 00:06:31.1 103 70.5 (S.D.) 35 percent	F-104 White F-104 Walker F-104 Evenson F-104 Daniel	— 07 Nov 62 Ammonia leak prior to taxi	Engine stuck at 35% power requiring abort; Flaps did not extend resulting in fast landing; Left skid failed; aircraft rolled over on ground damaging left wing and stabilizer; Pilot jettisoned canopy prior to roll-over; Pilot sustained crushed vertebrae but later returned to flight status
75 / 3-12-22 White (16) 14 Dec 62 Mud 10:44:07.0 Rogers 10:53:43.7	XLR99; Ventral off; Ball-nose; Delta-Psi indicator Ventral-off stability data; Heading vernier checkout; (#2) UV Earth background experiment	McKay 52-008 Bement / Cross Butchart 09:47 11:18 01:31	5.40 153,000 — — 79 100 percent	5.65 141,400 3,742 00:09:36.7 111 77.7 (S.D.) 100 percent	T-38A Rogers F-104 Dana F-104 Evenson F-104 Knight	3-A-21 13 Dec 62 Helium leak in cabin source Abort used NB-52B 52-008; White was the X-15 pilot for the abort	White's last flight
76 / 3-13-23 Walker (17) 20 Dec 62 Mud 11:25:04.0 Rogers 11:33:58.4	XLR99; Ventral off; Ball-nose Ventral-off stability data; MH-96 limit cycle investigation	McKay 52-008 Bement / Fulton Butchart 10:30 11:55 01:25	5.56 173,000 — — 90 100 percent	5.73 160,400 3,793 00:08:54.4 111 81.0 (S.D.) 100 percent	T-38A Rushworth F-104 White F-104 Daniel F-104 Gordon	No aborts	Good flight
77 / 3-14-24 Walker (18) 17 Jan 63 Delamar 10:59:16.0 Rogers 11:08:59.9	XLR99; Ventral off; Ball-nose Ventral-off altitude buildup; (#1) UV stellar photography experiment preliminary data gathering; (#10) IR exhaust signature experiment	Rushworth 52-008 Bement / Archer Butchart 10:07 12:08 02:01	5.22 250,000 — — 77 100 percent	5.47 271,700 3,677 00:09:43.9 109 81.2 (S.D.) 100 percent	T-38A White F-104 Dana F-104 Gordon F-104 Daniel	No aborts	#1 APU failed four minutes after launch; Ball-nose and rudder servo failed eight minutes after launch; Since Walker was a NASA pilot, he did not get astronaut wings for a flight above 50 miles (the NASA standard was 62 miles)
78 / 1-33-54 Rushworth (11) 11 Apr 63 Hidden Hills 10:03:20.0 Rogers 10:12:16.7	XLR99; Ventral off; Ball-nose; Squat switch (1st flight) Auxiliary power unit checkout; (#5) Optical degradation phase I (KC-1) experiment	52-008 Bement / Archer Russell 09:21 10:40 001:19	4.00 74,000 — — 121 50 percent	4.25 74,400 2,864 00:08:56.7 107 120.2 (B.O.) 50 percent	T-38A Rogers F-104 McKay F-104 Crews	0No aborts	Roll SAS disengaged at launch - reengaged
79 / 3-15-25 Walker (19) 18 Apr 63 Hidden Hills 12:16:26.0 Rogers 12:23:39.2	XLR99; Ventral off; Ball-nose Heat transfer at high Mach and low angle of attack; Local flow at high Mach and low angle of attack; (#10) IR exhaust signature experiment	McKay 52-008 Fulton / Archer Butchart 11:36 13:38 02:02	5.05 75,000 — — 86 100 percent	5.51 92,500 3,770 00:07:13.2 110 79.0 (B.O) 100 percent	T-38A White F-104 Dana F-104 Sorlie F-104 Rogers	No aborts	Nose gear scoop opened at 55,000 feet and Mach 3.4
80 / 1-34-55 McKay (8) 25 Apr 63 Delamar 14:04:19.0 Rogers 14:14:51.3	XLR99; Ventral off; Ball-nose (#5) Optical degradation phase I (KC-1) experiment	Rushworth 52-008 Bement / Fulton Russell 13:14 14:45 01:31	5.05 98,000 — — 80 100 percent	5.32 105,500 3,654 00:10:32.3 107 86.1 (B.O.) 100 percent	T-38A White F-104 Thompson F-104 Wood F-104 Knight	No aborts	Roll SAS trip-out at launch - reset

Flight # / ID X-15 Pilot Flight Date Launch Lake Launch Time Landing Lake Landing Time	X-15 Configuration Purpose of Flight	NASA-1 NB-52 + Pilots + LP Operator + Take-Off Time + Landing Time + Flight Time	Planned + Max Mach + Max Altitude + Max Speed + Flight Time + Engine s/n + Power Time + Thrust	Actual + Max Mach + Max Altitude + Max Speed + Flight Time + Engine s/n + Power Time + Thrust	Chase 1 Pilot(s) Chase 2 Pilot(s) Chase 3 Pilot(s) Chase 4 Pilot(s) Chase 5 Pilot(s)	Abort(s) Notes
81 / 3-16-26 Walker (20) 02 May 63 Mud 09:59:12.0 Rogers 10:08:29.2	XLR99; Ventral off; Ball-nose APU altitude checkout; High angle of attack aerodynamic flow data; (#2) UV Earth background experiment; (#10) IR exhaust signature experiment	Rushworth 52-008 Bement / Archer Russell 09:08 10:40 01:32	4.97 206,000 — — 78 100 percent	4.73 209,400 3,488 00:09:17.2 110 79.2 (S.D.) 100 percent	T-38A White F-104 Dana F-104 Rogers F-104 Knight	No aborts Good flight
82 / 3-17-28 Rushworth (12) 14 May 63 Hidden Hills 12:11:56.0 Rogers 12:19:29.0	XLR99; Ventral off; Ball-nose Aerodynamic heating rates at high Mach and high angle of attack; (#2) UV Earth background experiment; (#10) IR exhaust signature experiment	Walker 52-008 Bement / Archer Russell 11:30 12:39 01:09	4.80 90,000 — — 84 100, 80 percent	5.20 95,600 3,600 00:07:33.0 110 86.9 (S.D.) 100, 80 percent	T-38A Sorlie F-104 Dana F-104 Daniel F-104B McKay	3-A-27 10 May 63 Ruptured hydraulic line Abort used NB-52B 52-008; Rushworth was the X-15 pilot for the abort Engine restart required due to vibration shutdown
83 / 1-35-56 McKay (9) 15 May 63 Delamar 10:50:46.0 Rogers 11:01:06.5	XLR99; Ventral off; Ball-nose (#5) Optical degradation phase I (KC-1) experiment; Traversing probe development	Walker 52-003 Bement / Archer Butchart 09:57 11:28 01:31	5.53 98,000 — — 81 100 percent	5.57 124,200 3,856 00:10:20.5 17-Apr 84.1 (B.O.) 100 percent	T-38A Rushworth F-104 Dana F-104 Evenson F-104 Daniel	No aborts Nose gear scoop opened at Mach ≈5.2; Nose tires blew at touchdown
84 / 3-18-29 Walker (21) 29 May 63 Delamar 10:43:07.0 Rogers 10:54:55.0	XLR99; Ventral off; Ball-nose Ventral-off stability data; Aerodynamic heating rates at high Mach and low angle of attack	Rushworth 52-008 Bement / Fulton Butchart 09:53 11:22 01:29	5.60 90,000 — — 86 100, 40 percent	5.52 92,000 3,858 00:11:48.0 110 84.3 (B.O.) 100, 41 percent	T-38A White F-104D Dana F-104 Knight F-104 Rogers	— 28 May 63 Weather prior to taxi Left inner window cracked
85 / 3-19-30 Rushworth (13) 18 Jun 63 Delamar 10:34:21.0 Rogers 10:44:10.8	XLR99; Ventral off; Ball-nose Altitude buildup; Vertical stabilizer pressure distribution investigation; (#2) UV Earth background experiment	Walker 52-008 Archer / Bement Russell 09:43 11:40 01:57	5.20 220,000 — — 78 100 percent	4.97 223,700 3,539 00:09:49.8 110 79.3 (S.D.) 100 percent	T-38A Gordon F-104 Dana F-104 Ward F-104 Rogers	No aborts Inertial altitude and altitude rate failed
86 / 1-36-57 Walker (22) 25 Jun 63 Delamar 09:53:50.0 Rogers 10:03:49.3	XLR99; Ventral off; Ball-nose (#5) Optical degradation phase I (KC-1) experiment; Traversing probe development	Rushworth 52-003 Bement / Archer B. Peterson 09:03 10:30 01:27	5.50 102,000 — — 83 100, 55 percent	5.51 111,800 3,911 00:09:59.3 107 92.8 (B.O.) 100, 55 percent	T-38A Daniel F-104D McKay F-104 Wood F-104 Rogers	No aborts Good flight
87 / 3-20-31 Rushworth (14) 27 Jun 63 Delamar 09:56:03.0 Rogers 10:06:31.1	XLR99; Ventral off; Ball-nose Ventral-off stability data; Altitude buildup; (#2) UV Earth background experiment; (#10) IR exhaust signature experiment	Walker 52-008 Bement / Archer B. Peterson 09:07 10:33 01:26	5.10 278,000 — — 79 100 percent	4.89 285,000 3,425 00:10:28.1 110 80.1 (S.D.) 100 percent	T-38A Daniel F-104 McKay F-104 Wood F-104 R. Rogers	No aborts Rushworth's Astronaut qualification; The highest Mach number was achieved during descent from max altitude
88 / 1-37-59 Walker (23) 09 Jul 63 Delamar 12:12:12.0 Rogers 12:21:10.0	XLR99; Ventral off; Ball-nose (#5) Optical degradation phase I (KC-1) experiment; Traversing probe development; RAS checkout; Cork ablative evaluation on lower right speed brake	Rushworth 52-008 Archer / Lewis Russell 11:17 12:49 01:32	5.20 220,000 — — 81 100 percent	5.07 226,400 3,631 00:08:58.0 107 83.6 (S.D.) 100 percent	YT-38A Daniel F-104D McKay F-104D Rogers F-104A Wood	1-A-58 03 Jul 63 X-15 radio problem Abort used NB-52B 52-008; Walker was the X-15 pilot for the abort Good flight
89 / 1-38-61 Rushworth (15) 18 Jul 63 Mud 10:07:20.0 Rogers 10:16:44.1	XLR99; Ventral off; Ball-nose Ventral-off stability data; (#5) Optical degradation phase I (KC-1) experiment; Ablator evaluation on upper left speed brake; Ablator evaluation on fixed ventral leading edge	McKay 52-003 Fulton / Bock B. Peterson 09:17 10:42 01:25	5.60 112,000 — — 84 100 percent	5.63 104,800 3,925 00:09:24.1 17-Apr 84.1 (S.D.) 100 percent	T-38A Rogers F-104D Dana F-104D Evenson F-104D Gordon / Wood	1-A-60 17 Jul 63 Pilot O2 from NB-52 disconnected Abort used NB-52A 52-003; Rushworth was the X-15 pilot for the abort Good flight
90 / 3-21-32 Walker (24) 19 Jul 63 Smith Ranch 10:19:53.0 Rogers 10:31:17.9	XLR99; Ventral off; Ball-nose Expansion of ventral-off reentry; (#2) UV Earth background experiment; (#10) IR exhaust signature experiment; (#16) Rarefied gas experiment (balloon)	McKay 52-008 Fulton / Bement Butchart 09:20 11:04 01:44	5.40 315,000 — — 83 100 percent	5.50 347,800 3,710 00:11:24.9 111 84.6 (S.D.) 100 percent	T-38A Crews F-104A Rogers F-104 Daniel F-104D Wood / Gordon F-104 Dana	No aborts First Smith Ranch launch; Used left-hand side-stick (BCS) part of the flight; Instrumentation on balloon experiment failed; Overshot altitude by 31,200 feet; Technically, Walker qualified as an Astronaut under NASA's 62-mile rule

Flight # / ID X-15 Pilot Flight Date Launch Lake Launch Time Landing Lake Landing Time	X-15 Configuration Purpose of Flight	NASA-1 NB-52 + Pilots + LP Operator + Take-Off Time + Landing Time + Flight Time	Planned + Max Mach + Max Altitude + Max Speed + Flight Time + Engine s/n + Power Time + Thrust	Actual + Max Mach + Max Altitude + Max Speed + Flight Time + Engine s/n + Power Time + Thrust	Chase 1 Pilot(s) Chase 2 Pilot(s) Chase 3 Pilot(s) Chase 4 Pilot(s) Chase 5 Pilot(s)	Abort(s) Notes
91 / 3-22-36 Walker (25) 22 Aug 63 Smith Ranch 10:05:42.0 Rogers 10:16:50.6	XLR99; Ventral off; Ball-nose; Altitude predictor Expansion of vertical-off reentry; Altitude predictor checkout; (#3) UV exhaust plume experiment	McKay 52-003 Bement / Lewis Russell 09:09 10:53 01:44	5.38 360,000 — — — 84.5 100 percent	5.58 354,200 3,794 00:11:08.6 111 85.8 (B.O.) 100 percent	YT-38A Wood F-104D Dana F-104 Gordon F-104A Rogers	3-A-33 06 Aug 63 Weather during climbout 3-A-34 13 Aug 63 #1 APU would not keep running 3-A-35 15 Aug 63 Weather, #1 APU, Radio All aborts used NB-52 52-008; Walker was the X-15 pilot for all aborts #1 left roll BCS thruster froze; Unofficial world altitude record; Highest X-15 flight Walker's last flight Technically, Walker qualified as an Astronaut under NASA's 62-mile rule
92 / 1-39-63 Engle (1) 07 Oct 63 Hidden Hills 12:22:56.0 Rogers 12:30:33.0	XLR99; Ventral off; Ball-nose; Delta track indicator Pilot familiarization – Engle's first X-15 flight; (#5) Optical degradation phase II (KS-25) experiment checkout; Delta cross-range indicator checkout; Emerson T-500 ablator on fixed ventral and lower speed brakes	Rushworth 52-008 Bement / Jones Russell 11:22 13:00 01:38	4.00 74,000 — — — 122 50 percent	4.21 77,800 2,834 00:07:37.0 107 118.6 (S.D.) 50 percent	T-38A Sorlie F-104D Thompson F-104 Rogers	1-A-62 04 Oct 63 Communications failure Abort used NB-52B 52-008; Engle was the X-15 pilot for the abort Unauthorized 360-degree roll performed by pilot; Abort called for alpha indicator failure – launched after it began working again. Angle of attack indicator failed again at launch
93 / 1-40-64 Thompson (1) 29 Oct 63 Hidden Hills 12:42:34.0 Rogers 12:51:17.0	XLR99; Ventral off; Ball-nose Pilot familiarization – Thompson's first X-15 flight; (#5) Optical degradation phase II (KS-25) experiment; Delta cross-range indicator checkout; Emerson T-500 ablator on fixed ventral and lower speed brakes	McKay 52-008 Fulton / Jones Butchart 11:59 13:09 01:10	4.00 74,000 — — — 122 50 percent	4.10 74,400 2,712 00:08:43.0 107 126.1 (S.D.) 50 percent	T-38A Sorlie F-104 Walker F-104 Rushworth	No aborts
94 / 3-23-39 Rushworth (16) 07 Nov 63 Hidden Hills 10:11:45.0 Rogers 10:20:36.7	XLR99; Ventral off; Ball-nose; Sharp rudder Heat transfer with sharp upper rudder; Damper off controllability; Sharp leading edge data	McKay 52-008 Bement / Jones Butchart 09:27 10:41 01:14	4.05 79,000 — — — 115 100, 48 percent	4.40 82,300 2,925 00:08:51.7 108 108.2 (B.O.) 100, 48 percent	T-38A Gordon F-104A Thompson F-104 Sorlie	— 29 Aug 63 Damaged flap during preflight 3-A-37 14 Oct 63 Stable platform 3-A-38 25 Oct 63 Stable platform All aborts used NB-52B 52-008; Rushworth was the X-15 pilot for all aborts First flight with sharp leading edge on upper rudder
95 / 1-41-65 Engle (2) 14 Nov 63 Hidden Hills 11:19:21.0 Rogers 11:27:07.8	XLR99; Ventral off; Ball-nose (#5) Optical degradation phase II (KS-25) experiment; Delta cross-range indicator checkout	McKay 52-008 Bement / Jones Russell 10:36 11:55 01:19	4.50 92,000 — — — 82 100, 79 percent	4.75 90,800 3,286 00:07:46.8 104 83.1 (S.D.) 100, 79 percent	T-38A Rushworth F-104 Dana F-104 Rogers	No aborts Good flight
96 / 3-24-41 Thompson (2) 27 Nov 63 Hidden Hills 12:18:22.0 Rogers 12:25:26.3	XLR99; Ventral off; Ball-nose; Sharp rudder Pilot checkout	McKay 52-008 Fulton / Lewis Butchart 11:35 12:59 01:24	4.50 92,000 — — — 86 94, 78 percent	4.94 89,800 3,310 00:07:04.3 108 87.5 (S.D.) 94, 78 percent	T-38A Rushworth F-104D Dana F-104A Sorlie	3-A-40 19 Nov 63 Weather Abort used NB-52B 52-008; Thompson was the X-15 pilot for the abort Inertials failed at launch; Aircraft rolled left at launch (pilot induced)
97 / 1-42-67 Rushworth (17) 05 Dec 63 Delamar 11:04:36.0 Rogers 11:14:10.0	XLR99; Ventral off; Ball-nose (#5) Optical degradation phase II (KS-25) experiment; Delta cross-range indicator checkout; Emerson T-500 ablator on LN2 and LO2 tanks and side fairing	McKay 52-008 Bement / Jones Russell 10:11 11:39 01:28	5.70 104,000 — — — 78 100 percent	6.06 101,000 4,018 00:09:34.0 104 81.2 (B.O.) 100 percent	T-38A Wood F-104D Sorlie F-104N Dana F-104 Engle F-104N Petersen	1-A-66 03 Dec 63 X-15 radio failure — 04 Dec 63 X-15 radio failure Abort used NB-52B 52-008; Rushworth was the X-15 pilot for the abort Highest Mach number for unmodified X-15; Right inner windshield cracked in the pattern
98 / 1-43-69 Engle (3) 08 Jan 64 Mud 12:10:31.0 Rogers 12:19:21.7	XLR99; Ventral off; Ball-nose Pilot evaluation of damper-off stability	McKay 52-008 Fulton / Lewis Russell 11:15 12:44 01:29	5.20 130,000 — — — 74 100 percent	5.32 139,900 3,616 00:08:50.7 104 74.4 (S.D.) 100 percent	T-38A Rushworth F-104D Dana F-104D Wood F-104D Sorlie F-104N Petersen	1-A-68 18 Dec 63 Optical degradation experiment (#5) prior to launch Abort used NB-52B 52-008; Rushworth was the X-15 pilot for the abort Inertial malfunction at peak altitude KS-25 camera removed due to malfunction during abort
99 / 3-25-42 Thompson (3) 16 Jan 64 Hidden Hills 10:03:29.0 Rogers 10:11:46.0	XLR99; Ventral off; Ball-nose; Sharp rudder Heat transfer with sharp upper rudder; Damper off stability; Cermet skid evaluation; (#10) IR exhaust signature experiment	Rushworth 52-008 Fulton / Lewis Russell 09:20 10:30 01:10	4.65 72,000 — — — 104 100 percent	4.92 71,000 3,242 00:08:17.0 109 90.5 (S.D.) 100 percent	T-38A Gordon F-104D Peterson F-104 Crews F-104N Walker F-104N Dana	No aborts Speed brakes extremely hard to open during high heat phase of flight
100 / 1-44-70 Rushworth (18) 28 Jan 64 Delamar 12:11:36.0 Rogers 12:22:01.5	XLR99; Ventral off; Ball-nose; Speed brake link removed Stability evaluation using upper speed brake only	McKay 52-008 Bement / Branch Russell 11:15 12:55 01:40	5.50 102,000 — — — 76 100 percent	5.34 107,400 3,618 00:10:25.5 104 76.2 (S.D.) 100 percent	T-38A Engle F-104D Dana F-104 Crews F-104A Wood F-104N Petersen	No aborts SAS roll mode failed repeatedly

Flight # / ID X-15 Pilot Flight Date Launch Lake Launch Time Landing Lake Landing Time	X-15 Configuration Purpose of Flight	NASA-1 NB-52 Pilots LP Operator Take-Off Time Landing Time Flight Time	Planned Max Mach / Max Altitude / Max Speed / Flight Time / Engine s/n / Power Time / Thrust	Actual Max Mach / Max Altitude / Max Speed / Flight Time / Engine s/n / Power Time / Thrust	Chase 1–5 Pilot(s)	Abort(s) Notes
101 / 3-26-43 Thompson (4) 19 Feb 64 Hidden Hills 09:57:13.0 Rogers 10:04:16.1	XLR99; Ventral off; Ball-nose; Sharp rudder Heat transfer with sharp upper rudder; Boundary layer noise data; Cermet skid evaluation; Langley Purple Blend ablator evaluation	McKay 52-003 Fulton / Jones Russell 09:16 10:55 01:39	5.05 / 75,000 / — / — / — / 93 / 100, 40 percent	5.29 / 78,600 / 3,519 / 00:07:03.1 / 103 / 83.3 (B.O.) / 100, 40 percent	T-38A Rushworth F-104N Peterson F-104N Dana	No aborts Premature burn out - LOX line unported
102 / 3-27-44 McKay (10) 13 Mar 64 Hidden Hills 09:46:02.0 Rogers 09:53:31.0	XLR88; Ventral off; Ball-nose; Sharp rudder Heat transfer and skin friction with sharp upper rudder; Boundary layer noise data; Cermet skid evaluation	Rushworth 52-003 Bement / Lewis Butchart 09:01 10:13 01:12	4.20 / 71,000 / — / — / — / 107 / 100, 87, 43	5.11 / 76,000 / 3,392 / 00:07:29.0 / 103 / 105.0 (B.O.) / 100, 87, 43 percent	T-38A Rogers F-104D Peterson F-104 Engle	No aborts Good flight
103 / 1-45-72 Rushworth (19) 27 Mar 64 Delamar 10:10:18.0 Rogers 10:20:10.4	XLR99; Ventral off; Ball-nose (#5) Optical degradation phase II (KS-25) experiment;	Thompson 52-003 Bement / Lewis Butchart 09:16 11:30 02:14	5.70 / 103,000 / — / — / — / 81 / 100 percent	5.63 / 101,500 / 3,827 / 00:09:52.4 / 111 / 82.7 (S.D.) / 100 percent	T-38A Gordon F-104D Peterson F-104N Adams F-104A Engle	1-A-71 17 Mar 64 Optical degradation experiment (#5) prior to launch Abort used NB-52A 52-003; Rushworth was the X-15 pilot for the abort Inertial altitude about 10,000 feet off after shutdown
104 / 1-46-73 Engle (4) 08 Apr 64 Delamar 10:02:27.0 Rogers 10:12:12.7	XLR99; Ventral off; Ball-nose; Lines on window (#5) Optical degradation phase II (KS-25) experiment; Altitude buildup	Rushworth 52-003 Fulton / Bement Russell 09:10 10:38 01:28	5.20 / 180,000 / — / — / — / 78 / 100 percent	5.01 / 175,000 / 3,468 / 00:09:45.7 / 111 / 81.8 (S.D.) / 100 percent	T-38A Gordon F-104D Thompson F-104 Crews F-104 Rogers F-104N Peterson	No aborts Reference lines were added to the inside windshield to define a 30-degree airplane climb angle relative to the horizon Flight "missed" Pahrump and Pilot Knob targets, marginal image of Nellis target
105 / 1-47-74 Rushworth (20) 29 Apr 64 Delamar 10:00:27.0 Rogers 10:10:01.6	XLR99; Ventral off; Ball-nose; Lines on window (#5) Optical degradation phase II (KS-25) experiment; Optical attitude indicator checkout	Engle 52-003 Fulton / Bock Russell 09:09 10:40 01:31	5.70 / 102,000 / — / — / — / 84 / 100 percent	5.72 / 101,600 / 3,906 / 00:09:34.6 / 19-Apr / 81.3 (S.D.) / 100 percent	T-38A Sorlie F-104N Dana F-104 Crews F-104 Rogers	No aborts Right inner windshield cracked; Pilot reported smoke in cockpit; Split-vision mirror installed in cockpit to use Earth horizon as an attitude reference, This optical attitude indicator was deemed unsatisfactory Flight directly over Nellis, 0.5 mile right of Pahrump, and 1 mile left of Pilot Knob and Cuddeback (all within limits)
106 / 3-28-47 McKay 11 12 May 64 Hidden Hills 09:51:46.0 Rogers 09:59:57.3	XLR99; Ventral off; Ball-nose; Sharp rudder; Seat cutter Heat transfer and skin friction with sharp upper rudder; Boundary layer noise data; Cermet skid evaluation	Thompson 52-003 Bement / Jones Butchart 09:06 10:40 01:34	4.07 / 69,000 / — / — / — / 110 / 100, 43 percent	4.66 / 72,800 / 3,084 / 00:08:11.3 / 103 / 108.6 (B.O.) / 100, 43 percent	T-38A Sorlie F-104D Peterson F-104 Engle	3-A-45 31 Mar 64 Inertial system, cabin pressure 3-A-46 11 May 64 LOX tank regulator All aborts used NB-52 52-003; McKay was the X-15 pilot for all aborts Inertial velocities failed at launch; MH-96 pitch and roll disengaged twice during boost
107 / 1-48-75 Engle (5) 19 May 64 Delamar 10:26:28.0 Rogers 10:35:29.2	XLR99; Ventral off; Ball-nose; Optical horizon indicator in cockpit (#5) Optical degradation phase II (KS-25) experiment; Altitude buildup	Rushworth 52-003 Fulton / Jones Butchart 09:35 11:05 01:30	5.20 / 200,000 / — / — / — / 81 / 100 percent	5.02 / 195,800 / 3,494 / 00:09:01.2 / 109 / 78.3 (S.D.) / 100 percent	T-38A Sorlie F-104 Gordon F-104N Dana F-104 Daniel	No aborts Good flight
108 / 3-29-48 Thompson (5) 21 May 64 Silver 09:39:55.0 Cuddeback 09:47:51.5	XLR99; Ventral off; Ball-nose; Sharp rudder Heat transfer with sharp upper rudder; Boundary layer noise data; Cermet skid evaluation	McKay 52-003 Fulton / Jones Butchart 09:00 10:40 01:40	3.35 / 66,000 / — / — / — / 120 / 100, 45 percent	2.90 / 64,200 / 1,865 / 00:07:56.5 / 103 / 41.0 (S.D) / 100, 0 percent	T-38A Rushworth F-104 Dana F-104A Sorlie None — F-104N Petersen	No aborts Premature engine shut down at throttle back; Emergency landing; First Cuddeback landing
109 / 2-32-55 Rushworth (21) 25 Jun 64 Hidden Hills 09:34:47.0 Rogers 09:43:41.7	XLR99; Ventral off; Ball-nose Aircraft checkout and stability at low angle of attack	McKay 52-003 Fulton / Bement Russell 08:50 09:58 01:08	4.50 / 80,000 / — / — / — / 78 / 100 percent	4.59 / 83,300 / 3,104 / 00:08:54.7 / 106 / 77.0 (S.D.) / 100 percent	T-38A Engle JF-104N Peterson F-104 Rogers F-104N Sorlie	2-C-53 15 Jun 64 Scheduled captive flight to evaluate modified X-15A-2 2-A-54 23 Jun 64 #2 APU overspeed shutdown Captive used NB-52A 52-003; Rushworth was the X-15 pilot for the captive flight Abort used NB-52A 52-003; Rushworth was the X-15 pilot for the abort First flight of modified X-15A-2; Right roll out-of-trim
110 / 1-49-77 McKay (12) 30 Jun 64 Delamar 09:49:40.0 Rogers 10:01:07.0	XLR99; Ventral off; Ball-nose Pilot altitude buildup; (#5) Optical degradation phase II (KS-25) experiment	Rushworth 52-003 Fulton / Lewis Russell 08:59 10:27 01:28	5.20 / 182,000 / — / — / — / 80 / 100 percent	4.96 / 99,600 / 3,334 / 00:11:27.0 / 107 / 83.4 (S.D.) / 100 percent	T-38A Engle F-104D Peterson / Kennedy F-104D Sorlie F-104A Rogers F-104N Walker	1-A-76 11 Jun 64 Radio and SAS failure Abort used NB-52A 52-003; Thompson was the X-15 pilot for the abort McKay replaced Milt Thompson for this flight; Inertial malfunction at launch; Alternate profile flown; 250-foot film magazine for KS-25 (instead of 100-foot)

Flight # / ID X-15 Pilot Flight Date Launch Lake Launch Time Landing Lake Landing Time	X-15 Configuration Purpose of Flight	NASA-1 NB-52 + Pilots + LP Operator + Take-Off Time + Landing TIme + Flight Time	Planned + Max Mach + Max Altitude + Max Speed + Flight Time + Engine s/n + Power Time + Thrust	Actual + Max Mach + Max Altitude + Max Speed + Flight Time + Engine s/n + Power Time + Thrust	Chase 1 Chase 2 Chase 3 Chase 4 Chase 5	Pilot(s) Pilot(s) Pilot(s) Pilot(s) Pilot(s)	Abort(s) Notes
111 / 3-30-50 Engle (6) 08 Jul 64 Delamar 13:02:57.0 Rogers 13:12:52.9	XLR99; Ventral off; Ball-nose; Sharp rudder MH-96 pilot checkout; GE ablator on lower ventral and speed brakes; (#4) Langley horizon definition experiment;	Rushworth 52-003 Bement / Lewis Russell 11:59 13:45 01:46	5.20 180,000 — — — 77.5 100 percent	5.05 170,400 3,520 00:09:55.9 104 78.3 (S.D.) 100 percent	T-38A F-104D F-104 F-104 F-104N	Sorlie Dana Smith Rogers Mallick	3-A-49 02 Jul 64 XLR99 malfunction prior to launch Abort used NB-52A 52-003; Engle was the X-15 pilot for the abort Dampers disengaged ~10 seconds after launch; Had to shut off to reengage; Flew left hand BCS
112 / 3-31-52 Engle (7) 29 Jul 64 Hidden Hills 11:54:57.0 Rogers 12:02:46.1	XLR99; Ventral off; Ball-nose; Sharp rudder Heat transfer data with surface distortion panels; Local flow experiments; Thermopaint on F-3 and F-4 panels; GE ablator on lower ventral and speed brakes and LO2 tank	Rushworth 52-003 Fulton / Bement Russell 11:12 12:20 01:08	5.05 78,000 — — — 90 100, Tmin	5.38 78,000 3,623 00:07:49.1 104 93.6 (B.O.) 100, 45 percent	T-38A F-104 F-104 None F-104N	Sorlie McKay Rogers — Petersen	3-A-51 28 Jul 64 GN2 cooling gas depleted Abort used NB-52A 52-003; Engle was the X-15 pilot for the abort X-15-3 had been used to film "rescue movies" on 13-14 July Good flight;
113 / 3-32-53 Thompson (6) 12 Aug 64 Hidden Hills 10:12:27.0 Rogers 10:19:09.8	XLR99; Ventral off; Ball-nose; Sharp rudder Heat transfer data with surface distortion panels; Boundary layer noise data; Thermopaint on F-3 and F-4 panels; Local flow experiments	Engle 52-003 Fulton / Bement Russell 09:30 10:35 01:05	5.02 75,000 — — — 90 100, Tmin	5.24 81,200 3,535 00:06:42.8 104 82.1 (B.O.) 100, 47 percent	T-38A F-104N F-104	Rushworth McKay Sorlie	No aborts Premature engine burn out;
114 / 2-33-56 Rushworth (22) 14 Aug 64 Delamar 09:54:32.0 Rogers 10:06:38.3	XLR99; Ventral off; Ball-nose Stability and control evaluation; (#1) UV stellar photography experiment checkout	McKay 52-003 Fulton / Bement Russell 09:04 10:32 01:28	5.20 96,000 — — — 82 100 percent	5.23 103,300 3,590 00:12:06.3 106 80.3 (S.D.) 100 percent	T-38A F-104 F-104 F-104N F-104N	Knight Dana Engle Sorlie Thompson	No aborts First flight of redesigned FRC-66 stable platform Nose gear extended above Mach 4.2; Tires failed at landing;
115 / 3-33-54 McKay (13) 26 Aug 64 Hidden Hills 10:42:07.0 Rogers 10:49:26.6	XLR99; Ventral off; Ball-nose; Sharp rudder Heat transfer data with surface distortion panels; Boundary layer noise data; Local flow experiments; Three stripes of green thermopaint across nose wheel door	Thompson 52-003 Fulton / Bement Butchart 10:00 11:23 01:23	5.02 75,000 — — — 90 100, Tmin	5.65 91,000 3,863 00:07:19.6 104 94.4 (B.O.) 100, 47 percent	T-38A F-104B F-104	Sorlie Peterson Knight	No aborts Alpha indicator incorrect;
116 / 3-34-55 Thompson (4) 03 Sep 64 Hidden Hills 09:54:59.0 Rogers 10:01:17.1	XLR99; Ventral off; Ball-nose Blunt leading-edge rudder from X-15-1 installed for this flight Heat transfer data with surface distortion panels; Boundary layer noise data; Shear layer rakes data; Center stick evaluation	McKay 52-003 Bement / Jones Peterson 09:10 10:16 01:06	5.05 75,000 — — — 92 100, Tmin	5.35 78,600 3,615 00:06:18.1 104 91.0 (B.O.) 100, 47 percent	T-38A F-104N F-104	Knight Walker Rogers	No aborts U-2 took-off across the path of the X-15 during final approach
117 / 3-35-57 Engle (8) 28 Sep 64 Delamar 13:16:18.0 Rogers 13:25:52.3	XLR99; Ventral off; Ball-nose; Sharp rudder Martin MA-45R ablator on ventral and lower speed brakes; Langley Purple Blend ablator on F-3 panel; GE ESM-1004B ablator on F-4 panel; Boundary layer noise data; Skin-friction measurements	Thompson 52-003 Fulton / Lewis Butchart 12:24 13:54 01:30	5.65 98,000 — — — 82 100 percent	5.59 97,000 3,888 00:09:34.3 103 80.3 (B.O.) 100 percent	T-38A F-104N F-104 F-104	Rogers McKay Parsons Knight	3-A-56 23 Sep 64 Canopy Seal Problems Abort used NB-52A 52-003; Engle was the X-15 pilot for the abort Inertial velocity malfunctioned; Smoke in the cockpit after burnout
118 2-34-57 Rushworth (23) 29 Sep 64 Mud 13:00:05.0 Rogers 13:09:56.0	XLR99; Ventral off; Ball-nose Stability and control evaluation; Landing dynamics; (#1) UV stellar photography experiment checkout; (#27) Hycon camera experiment	McKay 52-008 Fulton / Townsend Butchart 12:10 13:30 01:20	5.20 96,000 — — — 81 100 percent	5.20 97,800 3,542 00:09:51.0 108 79.7 (S.D.) 100 percent	T-38A F-104 F-104 F-104 F-104N	Sorlie Thompson Parsons Engle Peterson	No aborts Nose gear scoop door came open above Mach 4.5; Theta vernier and 8-ball did not agree
119 / 1-50-79 McKay (14) 15 Oct 64 Hidden Hills 13:15:40.0 Rogers 13:24:20.9	XLR99; Ventral off; Ball-nose; X-20 IFDS; Tip pods Honeywell X-20 inertial system checkout; Tip-pod dynamic stability evaluation; (#12) Atmospheric density experiment checkout (#13) Micrometeorite collection experiment; (#19) High-altitude sky brightness experiment checkout	Engle 52-008 Fulton / Cotton Butchart 12:32 13:50 01:18	4.30 80,000 — — — 73 100 percent	4.56 84,900 3,048 00:08:40.9 17-Apr 72.9 (S.D.) 100 percent	T-38A F-104N F-104	Rogers Peterson Knight	1-A-78 02 Oct 64 SAS malfunction Abort used NB-52A 52-003; McKay was the X-15 pilot for the abort First flight with wing-tip pods installed; Micrometeorite collector opened while going transonic at high-key
120 / 3-36-59 Thompson (5) 30 Oct 64 Hidden Hills 09:51:52.0 Rogers 09:59:02.1	XLR99; Ventral off; Ball-nose; Sharp rudder Landing gear door mod checkout; Center stick evaluation; Boundary layer noise data; Skin-friction measurements; McDonnell B-44 ablator on ventral and lower speed brakes	McKay 52-008 Bement / Lewis Butchart 09:12 10:27 01:15	4.50 81,000 — — — 74 100 percent	4.66 84,600 3,113 00:07:10.1 103 74.4 (S.D.) 100 percent	T-38A F-104D F-104	Rushworth Peterson Engle	3-C-5829 Oct 64 Scheduled captive flight Captive used NB-52B 52-008; Thompson was the X-15 pilot for the captive flight Fire warning light 54 seconds after shutdown

Flight # / ID; X-15 Pilot; Flight Date; Launch Lake; Launch Time; Landing Lake; Landing Time	X-15 Configuration; Purpose of Flight	NASA-1; NB-52; + Pilots; + LP Operator; + Take-Off Time; + Landing Time; + Flight Time	Planned + Max Mach / Max Altitude / Max Speed / Flight Time / Engine s/n / Power Time / Thrust	Actual + Max Mach / Max Altitude / Max Speed / Flight Time / Engine s/n / Power Time / Thrust	Chase 1-5; Pilot(s)	Abort(s); Notes
121 / 2-35-60 McKay (15) 30 Nov 64 Hidden Hills 12:09:32.0 Rogers 12:18:06.8	XLR99; Ventral off; Ball-nose Landing gear door modification checkout; Stability and control data; (#1) UV stellar photography experiment checkout	Thompson 52-008 Bement / Bock Russell 11:29 12:42 01:13	4.50 80,000 — — — 80 100 percent	4.66 87,200 3,089 00:08:34.8 108 75.3 (S.D.) 100 percent	T-38A Sorlie F-104N Mallick F-104 Rogers F-104 Knight F-104 Twinting	2-C-58 06 Nov 64 Scheduled captive flight to evaluate landing gear mods 2-C-59 16 Nov 64 Scheduled captive flight to evaluate landing gear mods All captive flights used NB-52B 52-008; McKay was the X-15 pilot Blown fuse prevented UV experiment (#1) from acquiring data; Boost performance did not match simulator
122 / 3-37-60 Thompson (6) 09 Dec 64 Hidden Hills 10:36:17.0 Rogers 10:42:42.7	XLR99; Ventral off; Ball-nose; Sharp rudder Non-uniform 3-dimensional flow field measurements; Boundary layer noise data; Skin-friction measurements; McDonnell Y-7 and B-44 ablators on right lower speed brake	McKay 52-008 Fulton / Lewis Russell 09:53 11:05 01:12	5.20 85,000 — — — 104 100 percent	5.42 92,400 3,723 00:06:25.7 106 101.4 (S.D.) 100, 43 percent	T-38A Rushworth F-104N Peterson F-104A Sorlie F-104 Twinting	No aborts Purposely shutdown with negative g
123 / 1-51-81 Engle (9) 10 Dec 64 Delamar 11:10:26.0 Rogers 11:20:10.7	XLR99; Ventral off; Ball-nose; X-20 IFDS; Tip pods Dark green thermopaint on left wing-tip pod; Light green thermopaint on right wing-tip pod; Martin MA-25S ablator on nose BCS panels; X-20 IFDS checkout; Tip-pod dynamic stability evaluation; Center stick controller; (#12) Atmospheric density experiment; (#17) MIT horizon definition phase I checkout (fixed platform)	Rushworth 52-003 Bock / Fulton Russell 10:15 11:48 01:33	5.20 112,000 — — — 78 100 percent	5.35 113,200 3,675 00:09:44.7 107 80.5 (S.D.) 100 percent	T-38A Sorlie F-104N McKay F-104 Parsons F-104 Rogers	1-A-80 04 Dec 64 Fuel vent valve malfunction Abort used NB-52A 52-003; Engle was the X-15 pilot for the abort Originally scheduled for Mud Lake; Pitch SAS tripout after launch
124 / 3-38-61 Rushworth (24) 22 Dec 64 Hidden Hills 10:44:52.0 Rogers 10:52:42.0	XLR99; Ventral off; Ball-nose; Sharp rudder Langley Purple Blend ablator on F-3 panel; GE ESM-1004B ablator on F-4 panel; Boundary layer noise data; Skin-friction measurements; Non-uniform 3-dimensional flow field measurements;	McKay 52-003 Fulton / Bock Russell 09:55 11:08 01:13	5.18 81,000 — — — 101 100, 46 percent	5.55 81,200 3,593 00:07:50.0 103 88.0 (S.D.) 100, 46 percent	T-38A Twinting F-104N Mallick F-104A Knight	— 17 Dec 64 Lack of support aircraft High gear loads due to crosswind landing
125 / 3-39-62 Thompson (10) 13 Jan 65 Hidden Hills 10:50:50.0 Rogers 10:57:37.5	XLR99; Ventral off; Ball-nose; Sharp rudder Non-uniform 3-dimensional flow field measurements; Boundary layer noise data; Skin-friction measurements	Engle 52-003 Fulton / Bement Butchart 10:03 11:15 01:12	5.10 92,000 — — — 90 100, 46 percent	5.48 99,400 3,712 00:06:47.5 13-Apr 98.5 (B.O.) 100, 46 percent	T-38A Smith F-104A Dana F-104A Rushworth	— 12 Jan 65 Lack of C-130 support Rate limiting and loss of pitch and roll damping experienced during pull-up/roll maneuver after burnout
126 / 3-40-63 Engle (10) 02 Feb 65 Delamar 12:50:02.0 Rogers 13:00:00.3	XLR99; Ventral off; Ball-nose; Sharp rudder Martin MA-25S ablator on ventral, lower speed brakes, and F-4 panel Langley Purple Blend ablator on F-3 panel MH-96 fixed gain evaluation; Boundary layer noise data; Skin-friction measurements;	Thompson 52-008 Fulton / Bement Russell 12:00 13:15 01:15	5.64 94,000 — — — 82.5 100 percent	5.71 98,200 3,885 00:09:58.3 103 81.4 (B.O.) 100 percent	T-38A Sorlie F-104N Peterson F-104 Stroface F-104 Rushworth	No aborts Good flight
127 / 2-36-63 Rushworth (25) 17 Feb 65 Mud 10:44:27.0 Rogers 10:53:47.3	XLR99; Ventral off; Ball-nose; Precision Attitude Indicator Stability and control evaluation; Landing dynamics data; (#1) UV stellar photography experiment checkout	McKay 52-008 Bement / Fulton Butchart 09:54 11:16 01:22	5.20 96,000 — — — 81.5 100 percent	5.27 95,100 3,539 00:09:20.3 18-Apr 79.8 (S.D.) 100 percent	T-38A Sorlie JF-104A Dana F-104N Thompson F-104 Engle	2-C-61 15 Feb 65 Scheduled captive flight to evaluate X-15 gear loads 2-C-62 15 Feb 65 Scheduled captive flight to evaluate X-15 gear loads All captive flights used NB-52B 52-008; Rushworth was the X-15 pilot Right main skid extended at Mach 4.3 and 85,000 feet; Inertial altitude failed; Engine momentarily lost power
128 / 1-52-85 McKay (16) 26 Feb 65 Delamar 11:45:55.0 Rogers 11:55:19.7	XLR99; Ventral off; Ball-nose; X-20 IFDS; Tip pods "NO DROP" light in X-15 cockpit changed to "23 SECONDS"; Experiment #5 quartz window removed (replaced with steel plate) (#12) Atmospheric density experiment; (#17) MIT horizon definition phase I experiment; (#19) High-altitude sky brightness experiment	Rushworth 52-008 Fulton / Bock Russell 10:57 12:16 01:19	5.20 180,000 — — — 83 100, 52 percent	5.40 153,600 3,702 00:09:24.7 110 83.2 (S.D.) 100, 52 percent	T-38A Knight F-104N Peterson F-104 Stroface F-104 Engle	1-A-82 26 Jan 65 Inertial system failure 1-A-83 19 Feb 65 #2 APU failure 1-A-84 25 Feb 65 Edwards weather All aborts used NB-52B 52-008; McKay was the X-15 pilot for all aborts Modified RAS including 13-cycle notch filter; Computer malfunction at launch
129 / 1-53-86 Rushworth (26) 26 Mar 65 Delamar 11:02:30.0 Rogers 11:13:54.3	XLR99; Ventral off; Ball-nose; X-20 IFDS; Tip pods Honeywell X-20 inertial system checkout; (#23) Infrared scanning radiometer experiment; (#31) Fixed ball nose on tip pod evaluation	McKay 52-008 Fulton / Bock Russell 10:16 11:44 01:28	5.15 104,000 — — — 75.5 100 percent	5.17 101,900 3,580 00:11:24.3 18-Apr 79.6 (S.D.) 100 percent	T-38A Engle F-104N Dana F-104D Gentry F-104A Knight	— 25 Mar 65 Weather prior to taxi Alpha crosspointer did not work properly
130 / 3-41-64 Engle (11) 23 Apr 65 Hidden Hills 09:44:58.0 Rogers 09:52:40.1	XLR99; Ventral off; Ball-nose; Sharp rudder; Tmin changed from 40 percent to 50 percent; Martin MA-25S ablator on upper fixed vertical Heat transfer data with surface distortion panels; Boundary layer noise data; (#3) UV exhaust plume experiment	Thompson 52-008 Fulton / Cotton Butchart 09:05 10:13 01:08	5.20 78,000 — — — 93 100, 57 percent	5.48 79,700 3,657 00:07:42.1 111 91.4 (B.O.) 100, 57 percent	T-38A Rushworth F-104N McKay F-104 Knight F-104N Walker	No aborts

Table column headers:

Flight # / ID; X-15 Pilot; Flight Date; Launch Lake; Launch Time; Landing Lake; Landing Time	X-15 Configuration; Purpose of Flight	NASA-1; NB-52; +Pilots; +LP Operator; +Take-Off Time; +Landing Time; +Flight Time	Planned: +Max Mach; +Max Altitude; +Max Speed; +Flight Time; +Engine s/n; +Power Time; +Thrust	Actual: +Max Mach; +Max Altitude; +Max Speed; +Flight Time; +Engine s/n; +Power Time; +Thrust	Chase 1–5 Pilot(s)	Abort(s); Notes

---

131 / 2-37-64
McKay (17) — 28 Apr 65 — Hidden Hills — 12:26:32.0 — Rogers — 12:34:24.6

Configuration: XLR99; Ventral off; Ball-nose
Purpose: Stability and control evaluation; Landing gear loads data; Landing dynamics data; (#1) UV stellar photography experiment checkout

NASA-1: Rushworth; NB-52: 52-008; Pilots: Bock / Townsend; LP Operator: Russell; Take-Off: 11:41; Landing: 13:00; Flight Time: 01:19

Parameter	Planned	Actual
Max Mach	4.70	4.80
Max Altitude	84,000	92,600
Max Speed	—	3,260
Flight Time	—	00:07:52.6
Engine s/n		110
Power Time	83	78.9 (S.D.)
Thrust	100 percent	100 percent

Chase: YT-38A Sorlie; F-104N Thompson; F-104A Engle

Abort(s): No aborts
Notes: Highest 'q' for damper off flight during program (1200-1500 psf); Inertial altitude rate (H-dot) failed

---

132 / 2-38-66
McKay (18) — 18 May 65 — Mud — 09:56:56.0 — Rogers — 10:06:38.0

Configuration: XLR99; Ventral off; Ball-nose
Purpose: Stability and control evaluation; Landing gear loads data; Landing dynamics data; (#1) UV stellar photography experiment checkout

NASA-1: Rushworth; NB-52: 52-008; Pilots: Fulton / Jones; LP Operator: Russell; Take-Off: 09:07; Landing: 10:35; Flight Time: 01:28

Parameter	Planned	Actual
Max Mach	5.20	5.17
Max Altitude	96,000	102,100
Max Speed	—	3,541
Flight Time	—	00:09:42.0
Engine s/n		110
Power Time	81.5	78.9 (S.D.)
Thrust	100 percent	100 percent

Chase: T-38A Sorlie; F-104N Mallick; F-104 Gentry; F-104 Engle; F-104N Haise

Abort(s): 2-A-65 13 May 65 Cabin pressurization; Abort used NB-52B 52-008; McKay was the X-15 pilot for the abort
Notes: Engine shutdown during igniter idle - reset

---

133 / 1-54-88
Thompson (11) — 25 May 65 — Mud — 10:12:07.5 — Rogers — 10:21:10.0

Configuration: XLR99; Ventral off; Ball-nose; X-20 IFDS; Tip pods
Purpose: Honeywell X-20 inertial system checkout; Pilot altitude buildup; (#16) Pace transducer experiment; (#17) MIT horizon definition phase I experiment;

NASA-1: Engle; NB-52: 52-008; Pilots: Fulton / Jones; LP Operator: Butchart; Take-Off: 09:22; Landing: 10:35; Flight Time: 01:13

Parameter	Planned	Actual
Max Mach	4.90	4.87
Max Altitude	180,000	179,800
Max Speed	—	3,418
Flight Time	—	00:09:02.5
Engine s/n		108
Power Time	82	81.1 (S.D.)
Thrust	100 percent	100 percent

Chase: T-38A Rushworth; F-104D Peterson; F-104 Stroface; F-104 Knight; F-104N Walker

Abort(s): — 04 May 65 X-20 inertial failure prior to taxi; 1-A-87 11 May 65 SAS and APU malfunctions; Abort used NB-52B 52-008; Thompson was the X-15 pilot for the abort
Notes: Squat switch never armed

---

134 / 3-42-65
Engle (12) — 28 May 65 — Delamar — 09:43:47.0 — Rogers — 09:53:22.6

Configuration: XLR99; Ventral off; Ball-nose; Sharp rudder
Purpose: Pilot buildup; Boundary layer noise data; (#3) UV exhaust plume experiment; (#4) Langley horizon definition experiment;

NASA-1: Thompson; NB-52: 52-008; Pilots: Fulton / Jones; LP Operator: Butchart; Take-Off: 08:56; Landing: 10:24; Flight Time: 01:28

Parameter	Planned	Actual
Max Mach	5.40	5.17
Max Altitude	200,000	209,600
Max Speed	—	3,754
Flight Time	—	00:09:35.6
Engine s/n		107
Power Time	82	82.5 (S.D.)
Thrust	100 percent	100 percent

Chase: T-38A Sorlie; F-104N Haise; F-104 Parsons; F-104 Knight

Abort(s): No aborts
Notes: First flight for altitude predictor; Good flight

---

135 / 3-43-66
Engle (13) — 16 Jun 65 — Delamar — 10:26:14.0 — Rogers — 10:36:00.4

Configuration: XLR99; Ventral off; Ball-nose; Sharp rudder
Purpose: Pilot buildup; Boundary layer noise data; (#3) UV exhaust plume experiment;

NASA-1: McKay; NB-52: 52-003; Pilots: Fulton / Cretney; LP Operator: Russell; Take-Off: 09:38; Landing: 11:00; Flight Time: 01:22

Parameter	Planned	Actual
Max Mach	5.00	4.69
Max Altitude	240,000	244,700
Max Speed	—	3,404
Flight Time	—	00:09:46.4
Engine s/n		107
Power Time	79	77.8 (S.D.)
Thrust	100 percent	100 percent

Chase: T-38A Wood; F-104N Mallick; F-104D Sorlie; F-104A Twinting

Abort(s): No aborts
Notes: Good flight; The highest Mach number was achieved during descent from max altitude

---

136 / 1-55-89
Thompson (12) — 17 Jun 65 — Delamar — 09:40:53.0 — Rogers — 09:49:47.0

Configuration: XLR99; Ventral off; Ball-nose; X-20 IFDS; GE ablator on forward BCS panels
Purpose: Honeywell X-20 inertial system checkout; Cross-track vernier; (#23) Infrared scanning radiometer experiment;

NASA-1: Rushworth; NB-52: 52-008; Pilots: Fulton / Cotton; LP Operator: Russell; Take-Off: 08:56; Landing: 10:23; Flight Time: 01:27

Parameter	Planned	Actual
Max Mach	5.15	5.14
Max Altitude	104,000	108,500
Max Speed	—	3,541
Flight Time	—	00:08:54.0
Engine s/n		108
Power Time	81.5	82.2 (S.D.)
Thrust	100 percent	100 percent

Chase: T-38A Twinting; F-104N McKay; F-104 Stroface; F-104 Engle; F-104N Mallick

Abort(s): No aborts
Notes: Two pitch-out SAS tripouts (to ASAS) - reset once

---

137 / 2-39-70
McKay (19) — 22 Jun 65 — Delamar — 09:43:44.0 — Rogers — 09:53:31.7

Configuration: XLR99; Ventral off; Ball-nose; RAS installed
Purpose: Landing gear loads data; (#1) UV stellar photography experiment checkout; (#27) Hycon camera experiment

NASA-1: Engle; NB-52: 52-008; Pilots: Fulton / Bock; LP Operator: Butchart; Take-Off: 08:57; Landing: 10:15; Flight Time: 01:18

Parameter	Planned	Actual
Max Mach	5.40	5.64
Max Altitude	160,000	155,900
Max Speed	—	3,938
Flight Time	—	00:09:47.7
Engine s/n		103
Power Time	83	85.3 (B.O.)
Thrust	100 percent	100 percent

Chase: T-38A Rushworth; F-104N Peterson; F-104 Gentry; F-104 Knight; 0 — 0

Abort(s): 2-A-67 04 Jun 65 Cockpit pressure regulator; 2-A-68 08 Jun 65 Helium source pressure; 2-A-69 11 Jun 65 Helium source leak; All aborts used NB-52B 52-008; McKay was the X-15 pilot for all aborts
Notes: Good flight

---

138 / 3-44-67
Engle 14) — 29 Jun 65 — Delamar — 10:21:18.0 — Rogers — 10:31:50.3

Configuration: XLR99; Ventral off; Ball-nose; Sharp rudder
Purpose: Reentry maneuver techniques; Boundary layer noise data; (#3) UV exhaust plume experiment; (#4) Langley horizon definition experiment;

NASA-1: Thompson; NB-52: 52-008; Pilots: Fulton / Andonian; LP Operator: Russell; Take-Off: 09:38; Landing: 11:05; Flight Time: 01:27

Parameter	Planned	Actual
Max Mach	5.10	4.94
Max Altitude	283,000	280,600
Max Speed	—	3,432
Flight Time	—	00:10:32.3
Engine s/n		107
Power Time	82	81.0 (S.D.)
Thrust	100 percent	100 percent

Chase: T-38A Wood; F-104 McKay; F-104 Gentry; F-104 Parsons

Abort(s): No aborts
Notes: Engle's astronaut qualification flight; The highest Mach number was achieved during descent from max altitude

---

139 / 2-40-72
McKay (20) — 08 Jul 65 — Delamar — 09:16:50.0 — Rogers — 09:26:23.4

Configuration: XLR99; Ventral off; Ball-nose; ASAS manual engage switch added; MA-25S ablator test sections
Purpose: Altitude buildup; Landing dynamics data; (#1) UV stellar photography experiment;

NASA-1: Rushworth; NB-52: 52-003; Pilots: Fulton / Cotton; LP Operator: Russell; Take-Off: 08:28; Landing: 09:50; Flight Time: 01:21

Parameter	Planned	Actual
Max Mach	5.20	5.19
Max Altitude	200,000	212,600
Max Speed	—	3,659
Flight Time	—	00:09:33.4
Engine s/n		13-Apr
Power Time	82.5	82.9 (S.D.)
Thrust	100 percent	100 percent

Chase: T-38A Adams; F-104N Peterson; F-104 Gentry; F-104 Knight

Abort(s): 2-A-71 02 Jul 65 Inertial platform (loose umbilical); Abort used NB-52A 52-003; McKay was the X-15 pilot
Notes: RAS failed to operate

---

140 / 3-45-69
Rushworth (27) — 20 Jul 65 — Delamar — 09:59:28.0 — Rogers — 10:10:02.5

Configuration: XLR99; Ventral off; Ball-nose; Sharp rudder
Purpose: Boundary layer noise data

NASA-1: Thompson; NB-52: 52-008; Pilots: Jones / Andonian; LP Operator: Russell; Take-Off: 09:09; Landing: 10:38; Flight Time: 01:29

Parameter	Planned	Actual
Max Mach	5.50	5.40
Max Altitude	92,000	105,400
Max Speed	—	3,760
Flight Time	—	00:10:34.5
Engine s/n		107
Power Time	80	79.5 (S.D.)
Thrust	100 percent	100 percent

Chase: T-38A Knight; F-104D Dana; F-104 Whelan; F-104 Gentry

Abort(s): 3-A-68 13 Jul 65 Cabin pressurization; — 15 Jul 65 Weather prior to taxi; — 16 Jul 65 Weather prior to taxi; Abort used NB-52B 52-008; Rushworth was the X-15 pilot for the abort
Notes: Alpha exceeded 20 degrees after launch (subsonic)

Flight # / ID X-15 Pilot Flight Date Launch Lake Launch Time Landing Lake Landing Time	X-15 Configuration Purpose of Flight	NASA-1 NB-52 + Pilots + LP Operator + Take-Off Time + Landing Time + Flight Time	Planned + Max Mach + Max Altitude + Max Speed + Flight Time + Engine s/n + Power Time + Thrust	Actual + Max Mach + Max Altitude + Max Speed + Flight Time + Engine s/n + Power Time + Thrust	Chase 1 Pilot(s) Chase 2 Pilot(s) Chase 3 Pilot(s) Chase 4 Pilot(s) Chase 5 Pilot(s)	Abort(s) Notes
141 / 2-41-73 Rushworth (28) 03 Aug 65 Delamar 12:39:50.0 Rogers 12:49:22.0	XLR99; Ventral off; Ball-nose Altitude buildup; RAS checkout; Landing dynamics data; (#1) UV stellar photography experiment;	Engle 52-008 Bock / Andonian Butchart 11:51 13:05 01:14	5.15 200,000 — — — 82 100 percent	5.16 208,700 3,602 00:09:32.0 13-Apr 82.4 (S.D.) 100 percent	T-38A Sorlie F-104D Dana F-104D Whelan F-104A Stroface	No aborts Right roll out of trim; The highest Mach number was achieved during descent from max altitude
142 / 1-56-93 Thompson (13) 06 Aug 65 Delamar 09:41:40.0 Rogers 09:51:53.0	XLR99; Ventral off; Ball-nose; X-20 IFDS Stability and control data (#23) Infrared scanning radiometer experiment;	McKay 52-008 Fulton / Andonian Butchart 08:51 10:36 01:45	5.15 104,000 — — — 81 100 percent	5.15 103,200 3,534 00:10:13.0 108 83.0 (S.D.) 100 percent	T-38A Rushworth F-104D Haise F-104 Livingston F-104 Engle	— 22 Jul 65 Weather prior to taxi 1-A-90 23 Jul 65 Pressure Suit anomaly 1-A-91 27 Jul 65 X-15 radio antenna damage 1-A-92 28 Jul 65 Pilot error during preflight All aborts used NB-52A 52-003; Thompson was the X-15 pilot for all aborts Engine time did not start; No experiment #23 data due to broken wire
143 / 3-46-70 Engle (15) 10 Aug 65 Delamar 11:24:10.0 Rogers 11:34:01.8	XLR99; Ventral off; Ball-nose; Sharp rudder Boundary layer noise data; Reentry maneuver techniques; (#25) Optical background experiment	Rushworth 52-003 Jones / Andonian Butchart 10:28 12:00 01:32	5.20 266,000 — — — 81 100 percent	5.20 271,000 3,550 00:09:51.8 107 82.1 (S.D.) 100 percent	T-38A Sorlie F-104D Dana F-104D Gentry F-104A Stroface F-104N Haise	— 04 Aug 65 Pitch angle sensor failed prior to taxi — 05 Aug 65 Inertial system failure prior to taxi Engle's second flight above 50 miles; Yaw damper dropped off at launch, and 20 other times during the flight, but the alternate flight profile was not flown The highest Mach number was achieved during descent from max altitude
144 / 1-57-96 Thompson (14) 25 Aug 65 Delamar 09:54:46.8 Rogers 10:03:38.5	XLR99; Ventral off; Ball-nose; X-20 IFDS; Tip pods Stability and control data; (#17) MIT horizon definition phase I experiment; (#16) Pace transducer experiment	Engle 52-003 Fulton / Cotton Russell 09:05 10:38 01:33	5.20 222,000 — — — 81 100 percent	5.11 214,100 3,604 00:08:51.7 108 84.5 (S.D.) 100 percent	T-38A Rushworth F-104N McKay F-104D Marrett F-104A Parsons	— 12 Aug 65 Weather prior to taxi 1-A-94 20 Aug 65 Cabin pressure regulator 1-A-95 24 Aug 65 IFDS computer failure All aborts used NB-52A 52-003; Thompson was the X-15 pilot for all aborts Poor pitch control during landing due to aft center of gravity location; Thompson's last X-15 flight
145 / 3-47-71 Rushworth (29) 26 Aug 65 Delamar 09:51:47.0 Rogers 10:02:14.5	XLR99; Ventral off; Ball-nose; Sharp rudder Boundary layer noise data; (#3) UV exhaust plume experiment	Engle 52-008 Cotton / Bock Russell 09:01 10:30 01:29	5.00 240,000 — — — 79 100 percent	4.79 239,600 3,372 00:10:27.5 107 78.6 (S.D.) 100 percent	T-38A Sorlie F-104D Haise F-104A Livingston F-104A Parsons 0 0	No aborts The X-15A-2 structure was X-ray inspected at the AFFTC X-ray facility, no flaws were found Experienced limit cycle 4-5 times during flight
146 / 2-42-74 McKay (21) 02 Sep 65 Delamar 09:40:26.0 Rogers 09:49:38.8	XLR99; Ventral off; Ball-nose Altitude buildup; RAS checkout; Landing dynamics data; (#1) UV stellar photography experiment	Engle 52-008 Bock / Jones Russell 08:52 10:15 01:23	5.00 228,000 — — — 82 100 percent	5.16 239,800 3,570 00:09:12.8 104 84.0 (S.D.) 100 percent	T-38A Rushworth F-104D Peterson F-104 Stroface F-104 Knight F-104N Haise	No aborts Good flight; The highest Mach number was achieved during descent from max altitude
147 / 1-58-97 Rushworth (30) 09 Sep 65 Delamar 09:55:33.0 Rogers 10:06:43.2	XLR99; Ventral off; Ball-nose; X-20 IFDS; GE ablator on ventral and lower speed brakes (#23) Infrared scanning radiometer experiment	Knight / Thompson 52-008 Bock / Fulton Russell 09:09 10:40 01:31	5.15 104,000 — — — 80 100 percent	5.25 97,200 3,534 00:11:10.2 108 82.1 (S.D.) 100 percent	T-38A Wood F-104N Peterson F-104A Livingston F-104A Parsons F-104N Haise	No aborts Alpha indicator failed; Unexplained buffet during flight
148 / 3-48-72 McKay (22) 14 Sep 65 Delamar 10:01:42.0 Rogers 10:11:40.0	XLR99; Ventral off; Ball-nose; Sharp rudder Boundary layer noise data; (#25) Optical background experiment	Dana 52-008 Bock / Jones Russell 09:12 10:39 01:27	5.10 230,000 — — — 80 100 percent	5.03 239,000 3,519 00:09:58.0 107 80.9 (S.D.) 100 percent	T-38A Rushworth F-104N Haise F-104D Evenson F-104A Knight	No aborts Auto-BCS affect adversely by servo transients; The highest Mach number was achieved during descent from max altitude
149 / 1-59-98 Rushworth (31) 22 Sep 65 Delamar 10:59:05.0 Rogers 11:09:59.3	XLR99; Ventral off; Ball-nose; X-20 IFDS; Tip pods (#23) Infrared scanning radiometer experiment	Knight 52-003 Bock / Jones Russell 10:08 11:38 01:30	5.15 104,000 — — — 80 100 percent	5.18 100,300 3,550 00:10:54.3 18-Apr 82.0 (S.D.) 100 percent	T-38A Sorlie F-104D Dana F-104 Adams F-104 Engle F-104N McKay	— 17 Sep 65 Weather prior to taxi Infrared experiment (#23) failed during flight
150 / 3-49-73 McKay (23) 28 Sep 65 Delamar 10:08:06.0 Rogers 10:20:02.8	XLR99; Ventral off; Ball-nose; Sharp rudder; Martin MA-25S ablator on F-3 and F-4 panels Horizontal tail loads data; Boundary layer noise data; (#3) UV exhaust plume experiment;	Dana 52-003 Bock / Andonian Russell 09:24 10:42 01:18	5.15 260,000 — — — 79 100 percent	5.33 295,600 3,732 00:11:56.8 109 80.8 (S.D.) 100 percent	T-38A Rushworth F-104N Peterson F-104N Haise F-104 Engle	No aborts Roll-hold drop-out at launch; Overshot altitude by 35,600 feet; The highest Mach number was achieved during descent from max altitude; Since McKay was a NASA pilot, he did not get astronaut wings for a flight above 50 miles (the NASA standard was 62 miles)

Flight # / ID; X-15 Pilot; Flight Date; Launch Lake; Launch Time; Landing Lake; Landing Time	X-15 Configuration; Purpose of Flight	NASA-1; NB-52; + Pilots; + LP Operator; + Take-Off Time; + Landing Time; + Flight Time	Planned: + Max Mach; + Max Altitude; + Max Speed; + Flight Time; + Engine s/n; + Power Time; + Thrust	Actual: + Max Mach; + Max Altitude; + Max Speed; + Flight Time; + Engine s/n; + Power Time; + Thrust	Chase 1–5 Pilot(s)	Abort(s) / Notes
151 / 1-60-99 Knight (1) 30 Sep 65 Hidden Hills 09:43:55.0 Rogers 09:52:17.6	XLR99; Ventral off; Ball-nose; X-20 IFDS; Tip pods Pilot familiarization – Knight's first X-15 flight; (#23) Infrared scanning radiometer experiment	Rushworth 52-003 Bock / Fulton Russell 08:55 10:10 01:15	4.00 74,000 — — — 126 53 percent	4.06 76,600 2,718 00:08:22.6 108 127.4 (S.D.) 94, 53 percent	T-38A Sorlie F-104N Peterson F-104 Engle None —— F-104D Haise	— 21 Sep 65 Weather prior to taxi Good flight; Infrared experiment (#23) even though Flight 1-59-98 was supposed to be the last flight (but no data was acquired)
152 / 3-50-74 Knight (2) 12 Oct 65 Hidden Hills 09:43:14.0 Rogers 09:50:21.8	Ventral off; Ball-nose; Sharp rudder Pilot checkout	Rushworth 52-008 Jones / Fulton Russell 09:01 10:22 01:20	4.50 91,000 — — — 93 78 percent	4.62 94,400 3,108 00:07:07.8 109 86.2 (S.D.) 93, 78 percent	T-38A Sorlie F-104A Petersen F-104 Engle F-104N Haise	No aborts #2 APU shut down 1.5 seconds after launch; APU restarted 90 seconds later Pitch/roll SAS servos locked up for 5 seconds
153 / 1-61-101 Engle (16) 14 Oct 65 Delamar 12:45:57.0 Rogers 12:55:14.7	Ventral off; Ball-nose; X-20 IFDS; Tip pods (#16) Pace transducer experiment; (#17) MIT horizon definition phase I experiment	Rushworth 52-003 Bock / Jones Peterson 11:54 13:26 01:32	5.15 250,000 — — — 83 100 percent	5.08 266,500 3,554 00:09:17.7 18-Apr 84.8 (S.D.) 100 percent	T-38A Sorlie F-104N McKay F-104A Parsons F-104A Knight F-104N Haise	1-A-100 08 Oct 65 Leak in ballistic pitch thruster — 13 Oct 65 Weather prior to taxi Abort used NB-52A 52-003; Engle was the X-15 pilot for the abort Engle's third flight above 50 miles; Engle's last X-15 flight; Yaw damper tripped twice - reset; Internal NASA data timer problem The highest Mach number was achieved during descent from max altitude
154 / 3-51-75 McKay (24) 27 Oct 65 Delamar 10:49:29.0 Rogers 11:01:22.7	XLR99; Ventral off; Ball-nose; Sharp rudder Horizontal tail loads data; Boundary layer noise data; (#3) UV exhaust plume experiment	Rushworth 52-003 Fulton / Jones Russell 09:56 11:20 01:23	5.15 260,000 — — — 79 100 percent	5.06 236,900 3,519 00:11:53.7 109 75.6 (S.D.) 100 percent	T-38A Sorlie F-104N Peterson F-104A Stroface F-104A Engle	No aborts Roll-hold engaged 8 degrees off heading at launch
155 / 2-43-75 Rushworth (32) 03 Nov 65 Cuddeback 09:09:32.0 Rogers 09:14:33.6	XLR99; Ventral on; Ball-nose; External tanks (empty); TM antenna moved to forward fuselage Handling qualities with external tanks; Tank separation characteristics; Tank trajectory evaluation	McKay 52-003 Bock / Doryland Russell 08:26 09:33 01:07	2.20 70,000 — — — 80 58 percent	2.31 70,600 1,500 00:05:01.6 14-Apr 84.1 (S.D.) 58 percent	T-38A Knight F-104D Haise F-104A Engle JT-38A Sorlie	No aborts First, and only, launch from Cuddeback; First flight with external tanks (empty); Tanks dropped at Mach 2.25, 70,300 feet, q=343 psf, 5° alpha LOX chute did not deploy - tank not repairable; Ventral chute did not deploy
156 / 1-62-103 Dana (1) 04 Nov 65 Hidden Hills 09:11:13.0 Rogers 09:19:58.8	XLR99; Ventral off; Ball-nose; X-20 IFDS; Tip pods Pilot familiarization – Dana's first X-15 flight;	Rushworth 52-008 Bock / Doryland Russell 08:22 09:33 01:11	4.00 74,000 — — — 123 55 percent	4.22 80,200 2,765 00:08:45.8 110 124.2 (S.D.) 55 percent	T-38A Sorlie F-104A Peterson F-104 Knight None — F-104N Haise	1-A-102 02 Nov 65 Cockpit pressure regulator Abort used NB-52B 52-008; Dana was the X-15 pilot for the abort Two engine restarts required

157 / 1-63-104
McKay (25)
06 May 66
Delamar
13:29:03.0
Delamar
13:35:05.7
	XLR99; Ventral off; Ball-nose; X-20 IFDS; Tip pods;
	Window shade installed on left canopy window to eliminate sun glare
	  normally associated with afternoon flights
	(#12) Atmospheric density experiment;
	(#13) Micrometeorite collection experiment;
	(#17) MIT horizon definition phase I experiment;
	(#19) High-altitude sky brightness experiment
		Dana
		52-003
		Fulton / Doryland
		Butchart
		12:34
		14:22
		01:48
			5.30
			199,000
			—
			—
			—
			82
			100, 28 percent
				2.21
				68,400
				1,434
				00:06:02.7
				103
				35.4 (S.D.)
				100, 28 percent
					T-38A Knight
					F-104D Peterson
					F-104D Gentry / Hoag
					F-104 Stroface
					T-38A Curtis / Livingston
						— 22 Apr 66 No C-130 support
						
						Pump failure required premature shutdown;
						Landing at Delamar; aircraft slid off lakebed; no damage;
						  Canopy jettisoned prior to reaching end of lakebed;
						Micrometeorite experiment

158 / 2-44-79 Rushworth (33-11) 18 May 66 Mud 10:23:50.0 Rogers 10:32:46.8	XLR99; Ventral on; Ball-nose; Stabilizer torque tube enclosures; Large-scale test of MA-25S/ESA-3560 ablators Ventral-on stability and control; MA-25S ablator evaluation	McKay 52-003 Fulton / Doryland Russell 09:33 11:00 01:27	5.38 100,000 — — — 84 100 percent	5.43 99,000 3,689 00:08:56.8 106 81.9 (S.D.) 100 percent	T-38A Sorlie F-104D Dana / Manke F-104N Peterson F-104 Gentry	— 05 Ap 66 No C-130 support — 12 Apr 66 High winds at Edwards prior to taxi 2-A-76 13 Ap 66 Inertial system (cross-range) 2-A-77 20 Apr 66 Yaw SAS would not engage 2-A-78 05 May 66 Yaw SAS would not engage All aborts used NB-52A 52-003; Rushworth was the X-15 pilot for all abort Good flight

159 / 2-45-81
Rushworth (34)
01 Jul 66
Mud
11:01:55.0
Mud
11:06:23.6
	XLR99; Ventral on; Ball-nose; External tanks; Alternate pitot
	Full external tank checkout; MA-25S Ablator evaluation;
	Alternate pitot-static checkout;
	(#27) Maurer camera experiment checkout
		McKay
		52-008
		Fulton / Doryland
		Russell
		10:11
		11:55
		01:44
			6.00
			100,000
			—
			—
			—
			132
			100, 58 percent
				1.70
				44,800
				1,061
				00:04:28.6
				106
				33.2 (S.D.)
				100, 58 percent
					T-38A Knight
					F-104D Peterson
					F-104 Curtis
					T-38A Sorlie
					F-104N Dana
						2-C-80 27 Jun 66 Scheduled captive with full tanks
						Captive used NB-52B 52-008; Rushworth was the X-15 pilot
						
						Telemetry indicated no NH3 flow from external tanks caused pilot
						  to throttle back, jettison external tanks, and land
						  at Mud Lake - faulty TM signal;
						Rushworth's last X-15 flight

160 / 1-64-107 Knight (3) 12 Jul 66 Mud 11:32:13.0 Rogers 11:40:51.5	XLR99; Ventral off; Ball-nose; X-20 IFDS; Window shade Pilot checkout; Electrical loads survey; Window shade checkout Non-glare glass evaluation;	McKay 52-003 Fulton / Bowline Russell 10:44 12:25 01:41	5.30 130,000 — — — 80 100 percent	5.34 130,000 3,652 00:08:38.5 107 83.2 (S.D.) 100 percent	T-38A Curtis F-104B Dana F-104 Hoag F-104 Gentry	1-A-105 02 Jun 66 Inertial System Failure 1-A-106 10 Jun 66 Inertial System Computer failure All aborts used NB-52A 52-003; McKay was the X-15 pilot for all aborts Was originally scheduled as a 200,000-foot flight with Jack McKay as pilot

Flight # / ID; X-15 Pilot; Flight Date; Launch Lake; Launch Time; Landing Lake; Landing Time	X-15 Configuration; Purpose of Flight	NASA-1; NB-52; + Pilots; + LP Operator; + Take-Off Time; + Landing Time; + Flight Time	Planned: + Max Mach; + Max Altitude; + Max Speed; + Flight Time; + Engine s/n; + Power Time; + Thrust	Actual: + Max Mach; + Max Altitude; + Max Speed; + Flight Time; + Engine s/n; + Power Time; + Thrust	Chase 1–5 Pilot(s)	Abort(s); Notes
161 / 3-52-78; Dana (2); 18 Jul 66; Hidden Hills; 11:38:20.0; Rogers; 11:45:50.2	XLR99; Ventral off; Ball-nose; X-20 IFDS; Sharp rudder; 3rd skid; Lear cockpit display, Window shade. Pilot checkout; Honeywell X-20 inertial system checkout; Horizontal tail loads data	McKay; 52-003; Fulton / Doryland; Russell; 10:52; 12:15; 01:23	5.15; 104,000; —; —; —; 80; 100 percent	4.71; 96,100; 3,217; 00:07:30.2; 21-Apr; 95.5 (S.D.); 71 percent	T-38A Curtis; F-104A Manke; F-104A Gentry; None —; JF-104A Peterson	3-A-76 20 Jun 66 Inertial Computer overheat; 3-A-77 13 Jul 66 Computer light and TM failure; All aborts used NB-52A 52-003; Dana was the X-15 pilot for all aborts. Could not see through the sunshade during 90-degree left bank; First flight with Lear cockpit display
162 / 2-46-83; Knight (4); 21 Jul 66; Delamar; 12:01:16.0; Rogers; 12:10:07.0	XLR99; Ventral off; Ball-nose; Alternate pitot; PAI on I-panel. Pilot altitude buildup; Alternate pitot static system checkout; MA-25S ablator evaluation; Base drag study; (#1) UV stellar photography experiment;	Dana; 52-003; Doryland / Bowline; Russell; 11:08; 12:30; 01:21	5.10; 180,000; —; —; —; 81; 100 percent	5.12; 192,300; 3,568; 00:08:51.0; 106; 81.3 (S.D.); 100 percent	F-104D Manke; F-104A Sorlie; F-104A Gentry; None —; F5D-1 Peterson	2-A-82 20 Jul 66 Weather at launch lake; Abort used NB-52A 52-003; Knight was the X-15 pilot for the abort. Right roll out of trim
163 / 1-65-108; McKay (26); 28 Jul 66; Delamar; 10:01:03.0; Rogers; 10:10:46.0	XLR99; Ventral off; Ball-nose; X-20 IFDS; Tip pods. (#13) Micrometeorite collection experiment; (#16) Pace transducer experiment; (#17) MIT horizon definition phase I experiment; (#19) High-altitude sky brightness experiment	Dana; 52-008; Fulton / Bowline; Russell; 09:08; 11:05; 01:57	5.20; 220,000; —; —; —; 83; 100 percent	5.19; 241,800; 3,702; 00:09:43.0; 17-Apr; 85.4 (S.D.); 100 percent	T-38A Curtis; JF-104A Peterson; F-104D Sorlie / Adams; F-104A Gentry	— 25 Jul 66 IFDS failed preflight. H-dot failed pre-launch; Computer malfunction and pitch trip-out during boost; Inertials degraded after malfunction;
164 / 2-47-84; Knight (5); 03 Aug 66; Delamar; 08:43:26.0; Rogers; 08:52:36.7	Ventral off; Ball-nose; Alternate pitot. Pilot altitude buildup; Base drag study; Alternate pitot static system checkout; (#1) UV stellar photography experiment	Dana; 52-008; Doryland / Bowline; Russell; 07:52; 09:24; 01:31	5.02; 230,000; —; —; —; 82; 100 percent	5.03; 249,000; 3,440; 00:09:10.7; 106; 81.8 (S.D.); 100 percent	T-38A Curtis; F-104A Manke; F-104A Parsons; F-104A Sorlie; F-104N Petersen	— 03 Aug 66 Weather prior to taxi. Inertial altitude read wrong most of the flight; The highest Mach number was achieved during descent from max altitude
165 / 3-53-79; Dana (3); 04 Aug 66; Mud; 09:55:23.0; Rogers; 10:03:51.0	XLR99; Ventral off; Ball-nose; X-20 IFDS; Sharp rudder; 3rd skid. Pilot checkout; Boundary layer noise data; Lear Panel checkout; Horizontal tail loads data; (#25) Optical background experiment	McKay; 52-008; Doryland / Bowline; Russell; 09:06; 10:45; 01:39	5.50; 130,000; —; —; —; 80; 100 percent	5.34; 132,700; 3,693; 00:08:28.0; 21-Apr; 78.9 (S.D.); 100 percent	T-38A Curtis; JF-104A Manke; F-104D Parsons / Sorlie; F-104A Gentry	No aborts. Tape 'q' read 50 psf higher than the gauge
166 / 1-66-111; McKay (27); 11 Aug 66; Delamar; 09:44:26.0; Rogers; 09:53:48.2	XLR99; Ventral off; Ball-nose; X-20 IFDS; Tip pods. (#13) Micrometeorite collection experiment; (#16) Pace transducer experiment; (#17) MIT horizon definition phase II experiment; (#19) High-altitude sky brightness experiment	Dana; 52-003; Doryland / Bowline; Russell; 08:53; 10:19; 01:26	5.15; 250,000; —; —; —; 84; 100 percent	5.21; 251,000; 3,590; 00:09:22.2; 107; 84.8 (S.D); 100 percent	T-38A Sorlie; JF-104A Manke; F-104D Evenson / Smith; F-104A Gentry	1-A-109 09 Aug 66 Inertial system failure; 1-A-110 10 Aug 66 Launch lake helicopter lost engine; All aborts used NB-52A 52-003; McKay was the X-15 pilot for all aborts. Computer malfunction and pitch-roll trip-out during boost - reset; Highest dynamic pressure (2,202 psf) for any X-15; The highest Mach number was achieved during descent from max altitude
167 / 2-48-85; Knight (6); 12 Aug 66; Delamar; 10:25:05.0; Rogers; 10:33:41.6	XLR99; Ventral off; Ball-nose; Alternate pitot. Alternate pitot static system checkout; Base drag study; (#1) UV stellar photography experiment	McKay; 52-003; Doryland / Bowline; Russell; 09:38; 11:04; 01:26	5.02; 230,000; —; —; —; 82; 100 percent	5.02; 231,100; 3,472; 00:08:36.6; 16-Apr; 81.7 (S.D.); 100 percent	T-38A Sorlie; JF-104A Mallick; F-104D Smith; F-104A Adams; F-104A Gentry; F-104N Dana (Rover)	No aborts. Good flight; The highest Mach number was achieved during descent from max altitude
168 / 3-54-80; Dana (4); 19 Aug 66; Delamar; 10:03:03.0; Rogers; 10:12:36.1	XLR99; Ventral off; Ball-nose; X-20 IFDS; Sharp rudder; 3rd skid. Altitude buildup; Lear Panel checkout; Boundary layer noise data; Horizontal tail loads data; (#25) Optical background experiment	Knight; 52-003; Fulton / Bowline; Russell; 09:03; 10:45; 01:42	5.20; 180,000; —; —; —; 80; 100 percent	5.20; 178,000; 3,607; 00:09:33.1; 110; 75.8 (S.D.); 100 percent	T-38A Sorlie; JF-104A Manke; F-104D Smith / Evenson; F-104A Adams; F-104D Gentry	No aborts. Tape 'q' read 80 psf higher than gauge; Landed with center stick
169 / 1-67-112; McKay (28); 25 Aug 66; Delamar; 09:47:09.0; Rogers; 09:57:25.2	XLR99; Ventral off; Ball-nose; X-20 IFDS; Tip pods. (#13) Micrometeorite collection experiment; (#16) Pace transducer experiment; (#17) MIT horizon definition phase II experiment	Dana; 52-003; Doryland / Bowline; Russell; 08:56; 10:35; 01:39	5.15; 250,000; —; —; —; 84.5; 100 percent	5.11; 257,500; 3,543; 00:10:16.2; 107; 83.4 (S.D.); 100 percent	T-38A Adams; F-104N Manke; F-104D Smith; F-104A Knight	No aborts. Telemetry lost after launch; Inertial malfunction after launch; The highest Mach number was achieved during descent from max altitude
170 / 2-49-86; Knight (7); 30 Aug 66; Mud; 09:50:53.0; Rogers; 09:59:50.9	XLR99; Ventral on; Ball-nose; Alternate pitot. Ventral on stability and control data; Glass fog test; MA-25S ablator tests; Base drag study; (#27) Maurer camera experiment	Dana; 52-008; Doryland / Cotton; Peterson; 09:01; 10:30; 01:29	5.30; 102,000; —; —; —; 81.8; —	5.21; 100,200; 3,543; 00:08:57.9; 106; 80.5 (B.O.); 100	F-104A Curtis; F-104N Manke; F-104D Hover; F-104A Stroface; F-104N Thompson; 100	No aborts. First flight with Maurer camera on board; Pitch and roll SAS drop-out; Ventral chute deployed premature - ventral lost

Flight # / ID / X-15 Pilot / Flight Date / Launch Lake / Launch Time / Landing Lake / Landing Time	X-15 Configuration / Purpose of Flight	NASA-1 / NB-52 / + Pilots / + LP Operator / + Take-Off Time / + Landing Time / + Flight Time	Planned + Max Mach / + Max Altitude / + Max Speed / + Flight Time / + Engine s/n / + Power Time / + Thrust	Actual + Max Mach / + Max Altitude / + Max Speed / + Flight Time / + Engine s/n / + Power Time / + Thrust	Chase 1–5 Pilot(s)	Abort(s) / Notes
171 / 1-68-113 McKay (29) 08 Sep 66 Smith Ranch 10:37:24.0 Smith Ranch 10:43:50.5	XLR99; Ventral off; Ball-nose; X-20 IFDS Horizontal stabilizer angle of attack investigation; Electrical loads survey; (#17) MIT horizon definition phase II-1 experiment	Adams 52-008 Doryland / Cotton 09:40 11:40 02:00	5.42 243,000 — — — 85.5 100 percent	2.44 73,200 1,602 00:06:26.5 107 45.5 (S.D.) 100 percent	T-38A Curtis F-104N Manke F-104D Stroface F-104A Gentry JF-104A Peterson	No aborts McKay's last X-15 flight Fuel line low indication caused a throttleback, shutdown, and emergency landing at Smith Ranch Lake
172 / 3-55-82 Dana 5) 14 Sep 66 Delamar 12:00:14.0 Rogers 12:09:12.6	XLR99; Ventral off; Ball-nose; X-20 IFDS; Tip pods; Sharp rudder; 3rd skid Altitude buildup; Lear Panel checkout; (#3) UV exhaust plume experiment; (#16) Pace transducer experiment; (#29) Solar spectrum measurement experiment	Knight 52-003 Doryland / Cotton 11:11 13:10 01:59	5.10 250,000 — — — 77 100 percent	5.12 254,200 3,586 00:08:58.6 110 79.3 (S.D.) 100 percent	T-38A Curtis JF-104A Manke F-104D Hover F-104A Stroface F-104N Peterson	3-A-81 13 Sep 66 Blown fuse in new ARC-51 radio Abort used NB-52A 52-003; Dana was the X-15 pilot for the abort First wing-tip pod flight on X-15-3; Alert computer would not turn on (too cold); Third skid did not deploy; The highest Mach number was achieved during descent from max altitude
173 / 1-69-116 Adams (1) 06 Oct 66 Hidden Hills 12:16:09.0 Cuddeback 12:24:35.0	XLR99; Ventral off; Ball-nose; X-20 IFDS Pilot familiarization – Adam's first X-15 flight	Knight 52-003 Doryland / Cotton 11:30 13:10 01:40	4.00 74,000 — — — 129 90, 50 percent	3.00 75,400 1,977 00:08:26.0 107 89.9 (S.D.) 88, 52, 0 percent	T-38A Sorlie F-104D Dana F-104A Gentry	— 22 Sep 66 Wet lakes uprange 1-A-114 28 Sep 66 Weather in launch area — 29 Sep 66 Rain at Edwards 1-A-115 04 Oct 66 Cabin source pressure — 05 Oct 66 Weather in launch area All aborts used NB-52A 52-003; Adams was the X-15 pilot for all aborts Ruptured fuel tank caused premature shutdown and landing at Cuddeback
174 / 3-56-83 Dana (6) 01 Nov 66 Smith Ranch 13:24:47.0 Rogers 13:35:30.8	XLR99; Ventral off; Ball-nose; X-20 IFDS; Tip pods; Sharp rudder; 3rd skid Precision attitude checkout; (#13) Micrometeorite collection experiment; (#19) Sky brightness experiment; (#25) Optical background experiment	Knight 52-003 Doryland / Reschke 12:23 14:23 01:59	5.27 267,000 — — — 81 100 percent	5.46 306,900 3,750 00:10:43.8 110 82.8 (S.D.) 100 percent	T-38A Adams F-104N Peterson F-104D Stroface F-104A Gentry F-104N Manke	— 31 Oct 66 Malfunction of PAI Last X-15 flight above 300,000 feet; Overshot altitude by 39,900 feet Micrometeorite collector did not cycle; The highest Mach number was achieved during descent from max altitude; Since Dana was a NASA pilot, he did not get astronaut wings for a flight above 50 miles (the NASA standard was 62 miles)
175 / 2-50-89 Knight (8) 18 Nov 66 Mud 13:24:54.0 Rogers 13:33:20.8	XLR99; Ventral on; Ball-nose; Eyelid; External tanks; Alternate pitot Full tanks handling qualities; (#27) Maurer camera experiment	Dana 52-008 Fulton / Cotton Russell 12:29 14:10 01:40	6.00 100,000 — — — 132 100 percent	6.33 98,900 4,250 00:08:26.8 106 136.4 (S.D.) 100 percent	T-38A Adams F-104N Peterson F-104 Curtis F-104N McKay F-104 Gentry	2-A-87 07 Oct 66 Telemetry malfunction 2-A-88 19 Oct 66 MH3 low tank pressure — 20 Oct 66 Overcast skies at Edwards — 08 Nov 66 Weather at Edwards 2-A-87 used NB-52B 52-008; 2-A-88 used NB-52A 52-003; Knight in X-15 for both X-15-3 aborted a flight earlier in the day; World absolute speed record Tanks dropped at Mach 2.27, 69,700 feet, q=340 psf, 3.5° alpha; Recovered;
176 / 3-57-86 Adams (2) 29 Nov 66 Hidden Hills 11:38:49.0 Rogers 11:46:45.2	XLR99; Ventral off; Ball-nose; X-20 IFDS; Tip pods; Sharp rudder; 3rd skid Pilot checkout; Tip pod accelerometer data; (#16) Pace transducer experiment;	McKay 52-003 Fulton / Cotton Russell 10:55 12:25 01:30	4.50 95,000 — — — 98 75 percent	4.65 92,000 3,120 00:07:56.2 110 97.9 (S.D.) 75 percent	T-38A Knight F-104N Manke F-104A Gentry	3-A-84 18 Nov 66 Loss of Hadley transformer 3-A-85 23 Nov 66 APU bearing temperatures too high 3-A-84 used NB-52A 52-003; Dana was the X-15 pilot 3-A-85 used NB-52A 52-003; Adams was the X-15 pilot No radio from launch to Cuddeback
177 / 1-70-119 Adams (3) 22 Mar 67 Mud 09:52:56.0 Rogers 10:02:25.5	**XLR99**; Ventral off; Ball-nose; X-20 IFDS; 3rd skid; PAI Electrical loads evaluation; Third skid checkout; Sonic boom study at Mach 5.5,	McKay 52-003 Cotton / Reschke Russell 08:58 10:15 01:17	5.50 130,000 — — — 82.5 100 percent	5.59 133,100 3,822 00:09:29.5 18-Apr 79.7 (S.D.) 100 percent	T-38A Gentry JF-104A Peterson F-104A Evenson F-104A Knight F-4C Hoag F-104A Cuthill (Chase 6) F-104N Manke (Rover)	1-A-117 15 Mar 67 Weather 1-A-118 21 Mar 67 Inertial system failure All aborts used NB-52A 52-003; Adams was the X-15 pilot for all aborts Cockpit pressure lost during boost; Inertials failed after shutdown; Roll out of trim
178 / 3-58-87 Dana (7) 26 Apr 67 Silver 11:18:36.0 Silver 11:23:52.8	XLR99; Ventral off; Ball-nose; X-20 IFDS; Tip pods; Sharp rudder; 3rd skid; Cold wall panel; PCM telemetry system Boost guidance checkout; Cold wall heat transfer panel; Horizontal tail loads data; PCM system checkout; Sonic boom study	Adams 52-008 Cotton / Bowline Russell 10:17 12:09 01:52	1.65 71,000 — — — 103 100 percent	1.80 53,400 1,163 00:05:16.8 103 23.2 (S.D.) 100 percent	T-38A Gentry JF-104A Manke F-104A Knight None F-104N Petersen	No aborts First flight with PCM telemetry system; Frozen ball-nose required a 10 minute turn prior to launch; Premature shutdown due to fuel line low indication (frozen pressure sensing line);
179 / 1-71-121 Adams (4) 28 Apr 67 Delamar 09:23:41.0 Rogers 09:32:56.9	XLR99; Ventral off; Ball-nose; X-20 IFDS; 3rd skid; PAI Third skid checkout; IRIG timer checkout; (#17) MIT horizon definition phase II-1 experiment; (#20) WTR experiment checkout; Sonic boom study	McKay 52-003 Cotton / Bowline Russell 08:31 10:30 01:58	5.20 180,000 — — — 81 100 percent	5.44 167,200 3,720 00:09:15.9 14-Apr 82.0 (S.D.) 100 percent	T-38A Sorlie F-104N Manke F-104D Evenson F-104A Cuthill JF-104A Jackson F-104N Dana (Rover)	1-A-120 20 Apr 67 Weather in launch area Abort used NB-52A 52-003; Adams was the X-15 pilot for the abort Pitch attitude malfunction; Inertial velocity erratic
180 / 2-51-92 Knight (9) 08 May 67 Hidden Hills 12:27:28.0 Rogers 12:35:54.6	Ventral off; Ball-nose; Eyelid; Alternate pitot; Dummy ramjet with 20-degree nose cone Stability and control data with dummy ramjet; Canopy eyelid checkout; Ramjet separation characteristics; MA-25S ablator test	McKay 52-008 Cotton / Reschke Russell 11:43 12:59 01:15	4.50 90,000 — — — 74 100 percent	4.75 97,600 3,193 00:08:26.6 109 76.9 (S.D.) 100 percent	T-38A Sorlie F-104D Evenson F-104N Dana F-104A Adams	2-C-90 22 Dec 66 Scheduled captive with ramjet 2-A-91 05 May 67 Weather in launch area Captive flight used NB-52A 52-003; Knight was the X-15 pilot Abort used NB-52B 52-008; Knight was the X-15 pilot Three-axis transients when eyelid opened; Ramjet chute came off but ramjet was refurbishable; Left window fogged when eyelid opened in pattern

Flight # / ID; X-15 Pilot; Flight Date; Launch Lake; Launch Time; Landing Lake; Landing Time	X-15 Configuration / Purpose of Flight	NASA-1; NB-52; Pilots; LP Operator; Take-Off Time; Landing Time; Flight Time	Planned (Max Mach; Max Altitude; Max Speed; Flight Time; Engine s/n; Power Time; Thrust)	Actual (Max Mach; Max Altitude; Max Speed; Flight Time; Engine s/n; Power Time; Thrust)	Chase 1–5 Pilot(s)	Abort(s) / Notes
181 / 3-59-89 Dana (8) 17 May 67 Silver 10:43:45.0 Rogers 10:50:40.6	XLR99; Ventral off; Ball-nose; X-20 IFDS; Tip pods; Sharp rudder; 3rd skid; cold wall; PCM telemetry Boost guidance checkout; Horizontal tail loads data; Cold wall heat transfer panel; PCM system checkout; Sonic boom study	Adams 52-003 Reschke / Cotton Russell 09:55 11:22 01:27	4.65 71,000 — — — 103 100, 50 percent	4.80 71,100 3,177 00:06:55.6 103 96.1 (B.O.) 100, 50 percent	T-38A Sorlie F-104N Manke F-104D Evenson F-104A Cuthill F-104N McKay	3-A-88 12 May 67 Ball-nose failure Abort used NB-52A 52-003; Dana was the X-15 pilot for the abort Cold-wall panel ejected at q=1,500 psf - caused a severe oscillation in upper vertical tail
182 / 1-72-125 Adams (5) 15 Jun 67 Delamar 11:10:07.0 Rogers 11:19:18.0	XLR99; Ventral off; Ball-nose; X-20 IFDS 3rd skid; PAI IRIG timer checkout; (#17) MIT horizon definition phase II-1 experiment; (#20) WTR experiment	Knight 52-003 Cotton / Reschke Russell 10:10 12:00 01:50	5.15 220,000 — — — 81 100 percent	5.14 229,300 3,606 00:09:11.0 104 81.4 (S.D.) 100 percent	T-38A Gentry F-104N Manke F-104A Davey F-104A Hoag F-4A Jackson F-104N Dana (Rover)	1-A-122 25 May 67 Inertial system failure 1-A-123 01 Jun 67 Inertial system failure 1-A-124 14 Jun 67 X-15 radio failure All aborts used NB-52A 52-003; Adams was the X-15 pilot for all aborts Stick kicker inoperative; The highest Mach number was achieved during descent from max altitude
183 / 3-60-90 Dana (9) 22 Jun 67 Hidden Hills 14:55:40.0 Rogers 15:02:46.5	XLR99; Ventral off; Ball-nose; X-20 IFDS; Tip pods; Sharp rudder; 3rd skid; Window shade; Cold wall Cold wall heat transfer panel; Sonic boom study	McKay 52-008 Cotton / Sturmthal Russell 13:55 15:38 01:42	5.30 82,000 — — — 95 100, 50 percent	5.34 82,200 3,611 00:07:06.5 103 93.2 (B.O.) 100 percent	T-38A Knight F-104N Manke F-104B Krier F-104A Gentry	— 20 Jun 67 PCM failure prior to taxi Cold wall panel ejected at q=1,200 psf - severe oscillations; Window shade would not retract; Buffet at 10 degrees pull-up at Mach 3
184 / 1-73-126 Knight (10) 29 Jun 67 Smith Ranch 11:28:23.0 Mud 11:38:30.0	XLR99; Ventral off; Ball-nose; X-20 IFDS; 3rd skid Horizontal stabilizer angle of attack data; Yaw ASAS checkout; (#17) MIT horizon definition phase II-1 experiment; (#20) WTR experiment	Adams 52-008 Reschke / Sturmthal Russell 10:22 12:00 01:38	5.70 250,000 — — — 87 100 percent	4.17 173,000 2,870 00:10:07.0 108 67.6 (S.D.) 100 percent	T-38A Cuthill F-104N Dana F-104A Jackson F-104A Evenson F-104D Hoag / Davey	No aborts Total power failure going through 107,000 feet both APUs shut down (loss of all electrics and hydraulics); One APU restarted; Emergency landing at Mud Lake (should have landed at Grapevine per energy)
185 / 3-61-91 Dana (10) 20 Jul 67 Hidden Hills 10:10:26.0 Rogers 10:18:02.5	XLR99; Ventral off; Ball-nose; X-20 IFDS; Tip pods; Sharp rudder; 3rd skid; Cold wall; PCM telemetry Boost guidance checkout; Horizontal tail loads data; Cold wall heat transfer panel; PCM system checkout	Knight 52-008 Cotton / Fulton Russell 09:19 10:42 01:23	5.30 82,000 — — — 95 100, 50 percent	5.44 84,300 3,693 00:07:36.5 13-Apr 92.1 (B.O.) 100 percent	T-38A Adams F-104N Krier F-104 Davey None — F-104N Manke	No aborts Alert computer did not operate; Cold wall panel ejected at q=1,000 psf
186 / 2-52-96 Knight (11) 21 Aug 67 Hidden Hills 10:58:52.0 Rogers 11:06:31.3	XLR99; Ventral off; Ball-nose; Eyelid; Ablator; Dummy ramjet with 20-degree nose cone Stability and control data with dummy ramjet; MA-25S full ablator test; (#27) Hycon phase II camera experiment	Dana 52-008 Cotton / Reschke Russell 10:00 11:30 01:29	5.10 90,000 — — — 85 100 percent	4.94 91,000 3,368 00:07:39.3 110 82.2 (B.O.) 100 percent	T-38A Cuthill F-104D Gentry F-104A Manke F-104D Davey F-104A Adams	2-C-93 07 Aug 67 Scheduled captive flight (with external tanks) 2-A-94 11 Aug 67 LN2 leak in pylon 2-A-95 16 Aug 67 #2 APU source pressure loss Scheduled captive flight used NB-52B 52-008; Knight was X-15 pilot Both aborts used NB-52B 52-008; Knight was the X-15 pilot for both aborts First flight with full ablative; Ramjet ejected too close to ground - refurbished; No tanks; Forward quarter of window smeared due to ablative;
187 / 3-62-92 Adams (6) 25 Aug 67 Hidden Hills 13:29:35.0 Rogers 13:37:12.0	XLR99; Ventral off; Ball-nose; X-20 IFDS; Sharp rudder; 3rd skid; Cold Wall Cold wall heat transfer panel; Horizontal tail loads data; Boundary layer noise data	Dana 52-003 Bowline / Reschke Dustin 12:35 14:01 01:26	6.00 100,000 — — — 132 100 percent	4.63 84,400 3,115 00:07:37.0 13-Apr 71.3 (S.D.) 100 percent	T-38A Gentry F-104A Jackson F-104 Knight None — F-104N Krier	No aborts Engine relight required at 16 seconds; Inertials and Ball-nose failed 10 seconds prior to touchdown (circuit breaker)
188 / 2-53-97 Knight 12 03 Oct 67 Mud 14:32:11.0 Rogers 14:40:23.1	XLR99; Ventral off; Ball-nose; Eyelid; External tanks; Ablator; Dummy ramjet with 40-degree nose cone Ramjet local flow tests; Stability and control with ramjet; MA-25S full ablator tests; Fluidic temperature probe test	Dana 52-008 Cotton / Reschke Russell 13:31 15:20 01:48	6.50 100,000 — — — 141 100 percent	6.70 102,100 4,520 00:08:12.1 110 140.7 (S.D.) 100 percent	T-38A Cuthill F-104D Twinting F-104B Krier F-104A Adams F-104N Jackson	No aborts Fastest flight of X-15 program; Last flight of X-15A-2 aircraft; Extensive thermal damage to pylon and ramjet; Unofficial world's speed record for class Tanks dropped at Mach 2.4, 72,300 feet, q=287 psf, 4.4° alpha; Eyelid opened at Mach 1.6;
189 / 3-63-94 Dana (11) 04 Oct 67 Smith Ranch 10:16:35.0 Rogers 10:27:22.5	XLR99; Ventral off; Ball-nose; X-20 IFDS; Tip pods; Sharp rudder; 3rd skid (#3) UV exhaust plume experiment; (#13) Micrometeorite collection experiment; (#14) Ames boost guidance; (#29) Solar spectrum measurement experiment	Adams 52-003 Cotton / Reschke Dustin 09:12 11:03 01:51	5.50 130,000 — — — 82.5 100 percent	5.53 251,100 3,897 00:10:47.5 13-Apr 84.7 (B.O.) 100 percent	T-38A Cuthill F-104N Krier F-104 Gentry JF-104A Manke	3-A-93 22 Sep 67 Weather at launch lake Abort used NB-52B 52-008; Dana was the X-15 pilot for the abort Pilot's oxygen low light in pattern; Micrometeorite experiment did not retract; Inertials failed after shutdown; The highest Mach number was achieved during descent from max altitude
190 / 3-64-95 Knight (13) 17 Oct 67 Smith Ranch 09:38:36.0 Rogers 09:48:42.4	XLR99; Ventral off; Ball-nose; X-20 IFDS; Tip pods; Sharp rudder; 3rd skid (#3) UV exhaust plume experiment; (#13) Micrometeorite collection experiment; (#14) Ames boost guidance; (#29) Solar spectrum measurement experiment	Dana 52-008 Reschke / Miller Dustin 08:41 10:28 01:46	5.60 273,000 — — — 84.4 100 percent	5.53 280,500 3,869 00:10:06.4 103 84.2 (B.O.) 100 percent	T-38A Cuthill F-104 Twinting F-104 Gentry F-104 Adams F-104N Krier	No abort Third skid did not deploy; Knight's Astronaut qualification flight; The highest Mach number was achieved during descent from max altitude

Flight # / ID / X-15 Pilot / Flight Date / Launch Lake / Launch Time / Landing Lake / Landing Time	X-15 Configuration / Purpose of Flight	NASA-1 / NB-52 / Pilots / LP Operator / Take-Off Time / Landing Time / Flight Time	Planned + Max Mach + Max Altitude + Max Speed + Flight Time + Engine s/n + Power Time + Thrust	Actual + Max Mach + Max Altitude + Max Speed + Flight Time + Engine s/n + Power Time + Thrust	Chase 1–5 Pilot(s)	Abort(s) / Notes

191 / 3-65-97 — Adams (7) — 15 Nov 67 — Delamar — 10:30:07.4 — N/A — 10:34:57.5

- X-15 Configuration: XLR99; Ventral off; Ball-nose; X-20 IFDS; Tip pods; Sharp rudder; 3rd skid; Saturn insulation on upper speed brakes
- Purpose of Flight: (#3) UV exhaust plume experiment; (#13) Micrometeorite collection experiment; (#14) Ames boost guidance; (#29) Solar spectrum measurement experiment; Saturn insulation evaluation
- NASA-1: Knight; NB-52: 52-008; Pilots: Cotton / Miller; LP Operator: Russell; Take-Off Time: 09:13; Landing Time: 11:25; Flight Time: 02:12

	Planned	Actual
Max Mach	5.10	5.20
Max Altitude	250,000	266,000
Max Speed	—	3,570
Flight Time	—	00:04:50.1
Engine s/n	—	111
Power Time	79	82.3 (S.D.)
Thrust	100 percent	100 percent

- Chase: T-38A Cuthill; F-104N Jackson; F-104N Dana; F-104 Twinting
- Abort(s): 3-A-96 31 Oct 67 Engine would not go into igniter idle; Abort used NB-52B 52-008; Adams was the X-15 pilot for the abort
- Notes: Probable electrical short in experiment caused general systems disruption; Inertial malfunction, damper malfunction, lack of proper response to heading error caused uncontrolled gyrations, aircraft broke up and crashed; Adams posthumously awarded Astronaut Wings

---

192 / 1-74-130 — Dana (12) — 01 Mar 68 — Hidden Hills — 11:30:05.0 — Rogers — 11:37:39.7

- X-15 Configuration: XLR99; Ventral off; Ball-nose; X-20 IFDS; 3rd skid; Saturn ablatives on upper speed brakes
- Purpose of Flight: Aircraft systems and yaw ASAS checkout; Saturn ablative evaluation; (#17) MIT horizon definition phase II-1 experiment; (#20) WTR experiment
- NASA-1: Manke; NB-52: 52-008; Pilots: Cotton / Stroup; LP Operator: Dustin; Take-Off Time: 10:34; Landing Time: 11:55; Flight Time: 01:21

	Planned	Actual
Max Mach	4.10	4.36
Max Altitude	106,000	104,500
Max Speed	—	2,878
Flight Time	—	00:07:34.7
Engine s/n	—	109
Power Time	66	65.6 (S.D.)
Thrust	100 percent	100 percent

- Chase: T-38A Twinting; F-104N Krier; F-104D Knight; F-104A Hoag; F-104N Jackson
- Abort(s): 1-C-127 06 Feb 68 Scheduled captive; 1-C-128 07 Feb 68 Cabin pressurization and weather; 1-A-129 27 Feb 68 SAS failure; Captive flight used NB-52 52-008; Dana was the X-15 pilot; Both aborts used NB-52 52-008; Dana was the X-15 pilot for both aborts
- Notes: g-suit grabbed at 1.5-g during pattern;

---

193 / 1-75-133 — Dana (13) — 04 Apr 68 — Delamar — 10:03:46.0 — Rogers — 10:13:08.8

- X-15 Configuration: XLR99; Ventral off; Ball-nose; X-20 IFDS; Tip pods; 3rd skid; Tip pod camera; Saturn ablatives on upper speed brakes
- Purpose of Flight: Saturn ablative evaluation; (#20) WTR experiment; (#31) Fixed alpha nose experiment
- NASA-1: Manke; NB-52: 52-008; Pilots: Cotton / Sturmthal; LP Operator: Russell; Take-Off Time: 08:29; Landing Time: 10:43; Flight Time: 02:13

	Planned	Actual
Max Mach	5.00	5.27
Max Altitude	180,000	187,500
Max Speed	—	3,610
Flight Time	—	00:09:22.8
Engine s/n	—	109
Power Time	79	78.8 (S.D.)
Thrust	100 percent	100 percent

- Chase: T-38A Cuthill; F-104N Jackson; F-104A Smith; F-104A Hoag; F-104N Fulton
- Abort(s): 1-A-131 28 Mar 68 Radio and source pressure; 1-A-132 03 Apr 68 Weather at Delamar; All aborts used NB-52B 52-008; Dana was the X-15 pilot for all aborts
- Notes: First flight with second set of wing-tip pods installed; Emergency retract of WTR experiment

---

194 / 1-76-134 — Knight (14) — 26 Apr 68 — Delamar — 11:51:49.8 — Rogers — 12:01:06.9

- X-15 Configuration: XLR99; Ventral off; Ball-nose; X-20 IFDS; Tip pods; 3rd skid; Saturn (2nd stage) ablatives on upper speed brakes
- Purpose of Flight: (#17) MIT horizon definition phase II-2 experiment; (#31) Fixed alpha nose experiment
- NASA-1: Dana; NB-52: 52-008; Pilots: Sturmthal / Reschke; LP Operator: Dustin; Take-Off Time: 10:49; Landing Time: 12:45; Flight Time: 01:55

	Planned	Actual
Max Mach	5.10	5.05
Max Altitude	100,000	209,600
Max Speed	—	3,545
Flight Time	—	00:09:17.1
Engine s/n	—	108
Power Time	80	81.5 (S.D.)
Thrust	100 percent	100 percent

- Chase: F5D-1 Manke; F-104A Krier; F-104D Livingston; F-104D Gentry; F-104N Fulton
- Abort(s): No aborts
- Notes: Low alpha, high-q rotation performed with 10° speed brakes during boost for Saturn experiment

---

195 1-77-136 — Dana 14) — 12 Jun 68 — Smith Ranch — 08:31:01.0 — Rogers — 08:42:33.9

- X-15 Configuration: XLR99; Ventral off; Ball-nose; X-20 IFDS; Tip pods; 3rd skid; Saturn ablatives on lower speed brakes
- Purpose of Flight: (#17) MIT horizon definition phase II-2 experiment; (#20) WTR experiment; (#31) Fixed alpha nose experiment
- NASA-1: Knight; NB-52: 52-008; Pilots: Reschke / Cotton; LP Operator: Russell; Take-Off Time: 07:19; Landing Time: 09:24; Flight Time: 02:05

	Planned	Actual
Max Mach	5.40	5.15
Max Altitude	222,000	220,100
Max Speed	—	3,563
Flight Time	—	00:11:32.9
Engine s/n	—	108
Power Time	84.6	83.4 (S.D.)
Thrust	100 percent	100 percent

- Chase: T-38A Gentry; F5D-1 Manke; F-104N Jackson; F-104A Hoag; F-104N Fulton
- Abort(s): 1-A-135 23 May 68 Malfunction of second stage igniter; Abort used NB-52B 52-008; Dana was the X-15 pilot for the abort
- Notes: Emergency retract of WTR experiment

---

196 / 1-78-138 — Knight (15) — 16 Jul 68 — Railroad — 15:23:06.7 — Rogers — 15:32:49.3

- X-15 Configuration: XLR99; Ventral off; Ball-nose; X-20 IFDS; Tip pods; 3rd skid; Tip pod camera; Fluidic probe
- Purpose of Flight: (#19) High-altitude sky brightness experiment; (#20) WTR experiment; (#31) Fixed alpha nose experiment
- NASA-1: Dana; NB-52: 52-003; Pilots: Sturmthal / Reschke; LP Operator: Russell; Take-Off Time: 14:17; Landing Time: 16:24; Flight Time: 02:07

	Planned	Actual
Max Mach	4.95	4.79
Max Altitude	250,000	221,500
Max Speed	—	3,382
Flight Time	—	00:09:42.6
Engine s/n	—	104
Power Time	83	80.5 (S.D.)
Thrust	100 percent	100 percent

- Chase: F-104A Gentry; F5D-1 Manke; F-104A Cuthill; F-104A Davey; F-104N Krier
- Abort(s): 1-A-137 15 Jul 68 Roll RAS malfunction; Abort used NB-52A 52-003; Knight was the X-15 pilot for the abort
- Notes: First launch from Railroad Valley; Hydraulic gauge malfunction during boost; WTR experiment not extended due to vibrations; The highest Mach number was achieved during descent from max altitude

---

197 / 1-79-139 — Dana (15) — 21 Aug 68 — Railroad — 09:04:48.0 — Rogers — 09:14:11.3

- X-15 Configuration: XLR99; Ventral off; Ball-nose; X-20 IFDS; Tip pods; 3rd skid; Fluidic probe
- Purpose of Flight: (#17) MIT horizon definition phase II-2 experiment; (#20) WTR experiment; (#31) Fixed alpha nose experiment
- NASA-1: Manke; NB-52: 52-003; Pilots: Sturmthal / Fulton; LP Operator: Russell; Take-Off Time: 07:52; Landing Time: 10:30; Flight Time: 02:38

	Planned	Actual
Max Mach	4.95	5.01
Max Altitude	250,000	267,500
Max Speed	—	3,443
Flight Time	—	00:09:23.3
Engine s/n	—	104
Power Time	82.5	82.9 (S.D.)
Thrust	100 percent	100 percent

- Chase: T-38A Cuthill; F-104N Krier; F-104D Hoag; F-104A Gentry; F-104A Shawler
- Abort(s): No aborts
- Notes: WTR retracted on timer due to altitude overshoot; Last X-15 flight over 50 miles altitude; The highest Mach number was achieved during descent from max altitude; Since Dana was a NASA pilot, he did not get astronaut wings for a flight above 50 miles (the NASA standard was 62 miles)

---

198 / 1-80-140 — Knight (16) — 13 Sep 68 — Smith Ranch — 11:19:23.2 — Rogers — 11:30:18.7

- X-15 Configuration: XLR99; Ventral off; Ball-nose; X-20 IFDS; Tip pods w/braces; 3rd skid; Fluidic probe
- Purpose of Flight: (#17) MIT horizon definition phase II-2 experiment; (#20) WTR experiment; (#31) Fixed alpha nose experiment
- NASA-1: Dana; NB-52: 52-003; Pilots: Sturmthal / Miller; LP Operator: Dustin; Take-Off Time: 10:06; Landing Time: 12:15; Flight Time: 02:09

	Planned	Actual
Max Mach	5.47	5.37
Max Altitude	250,000	254,100
Max Speed	—	3,723
Flight Time	—	00:10:55.5
Engine s/n	—	103
Power Time	88	84.3 (B.O.)
Thrust	100 percent	100 percent

- Chase: T-38A Twinting; F-104N Manke; F-104A Shawler; F-104A Gentry; F-104A Krier; F-104A Powell (Rover)
- Abort(s): No aborts
- Notes: Knight's last flight in the X-15; Emergency retract of WTR experiment; The highest Mach number was achieved during descent from max altitude

---

199 / 1-81-141 — Dana (16) — 24 Oct 68 — Smith Ranch — 10:02:47.3 — Rogers — 10:14:15.3

- X-15 Configuration: Ventral off; Ball-nose; X-20 IFDS; Tip pods w/braces; 3rd skid; Fluidic probe
- Purpose of Flight: (#20) WTR experiment; (#31) Fixed alpha nose experiment
- NASA-1: Knight; NB-52: 52-003; Pilots: Sturmthal / Miller; LP Operator: Russell; Take-Off Time: 08:56; Landing Time: 11:05; Flight Time: 02:09

	Planned	Actual
Max Mach	5.45	5.38
Max Altitude	250,000	255,000
Max Speed	—	3,716
Flight Time	—	00:11:28.0
Engine s/n	—	103
Power Time	84	83.8 (S.D.)
Thrust	100 percent	100 percent

- Chase: T-38A Cuthill; F-104N Krier; F-104A Enevoldson; F-104A Evenson; F-104A Hoag; F-104B Manke (Rover)
- Abort(s): No aborts
- Notes: WTR experiment extended but lost power; No. 2 BCS never turned on; Last flight of the X-15 program

Program Flight #:	200

Flight ID:	Not Flown	Configuration:	Ventral off; Ball-nose; X-20 IFDS
X-15 (s/n):	56-6670 (82)		Tip pods w/braces; 3rd skid
Flight Date:	Not Flown		(#24) High-altitude IR background experiment
Pilot (flight #):	Knight (17)		(#19) High-altitude sky brightness experiment
			(#31) Fixed alpha nose experiment

Cancellation:	(1-82-142)	21 Nov 68	Flight cancelled due to 52-003 problems. Would have been a Smith Ranch launch. X-15 transferred to 52-008
		27 Nov 68	Flight cancelled due to a helium leak in APU #2
Cancellation:	(1-82-142)	27 Nov 68	Flight cancelled due to hydrogen peroxide leak and other problems. X-15 transferred back to 52-003 on 9 December. The launch lake would have been Railroad Valley.
Cancellation:	(1-82-142)	10 Dec 68	Cancelled due to weather.
Cancellation:	(1-82-142)	11 Dec 68	Cancelled due to weather.
Abort:	1-A-142	12 Dec 68	Last X-15 flight attempt. Aborted due to an inertial guidance system failure. The launch lake would have been Railroad Valley.
Cancellation:	(1-82-143)	13 Dec 68	Cancelled due to weather.
Cancellation:	(1-82-143)	17 Dec 68	Cancelled due to lack of C-130 support.
Cancellation:	(1-82-143)	18 Dec 68	Cancelled due to weather.
Cancellation:	(1-82-143)	19 Dec 68	No microwave available. Launch lake changed to Hidden Hills.
Cancellation:	(1-82-143)	20 Dec 68	Bill Dana taxied an F-104 for a weather flight, but was recalled by John Manke due to snow at Edwards. The launch lake would have been Hidden Hills.
The End.		20 Dec 68	X-15 demated from 52-003 and prepared for indefinite storage. The X-15 program ends.

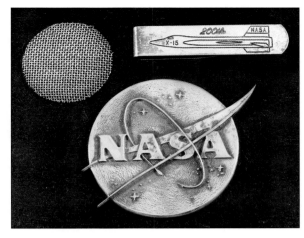

The silver catalyst screens used in the various hydrogen peroxide systems (upper left) were often recast into various mementos. Here are a NASA "meatball" and a 200th flight tie clip. (Artifacts courtesy of Betty J. Love; photo by Tony Landis)

Yes, that is snow at Edwards AFB. The gang gathers after the last attempt at the 200th flight is called-off on 20 December 1968. Standing, left to right: Donald L. Hall, Cyril G. Brennan, Gilbert W. Kincaid, Robert L. Schuck, Gaston A. Moore, Vincent N. Capasso, Jr., Paschal "Herm" Dorr (8mm camera), Allen F. Dustin, Harvey B. Price, Nicholas Kantartzis, Richard H. Simon, James B. Craft, George E. Perusich, Edward T. Ryan, Walter P. Redman, unknown, and Ira O. Cupp. On the stairs, left to right: Richard L. Blair and Marshall E. McCracken. Nobody seems to remembers who was in the cockpit at the time. (Dryden History Office Collection)

APPENDIX C

Notes and Citations

Preface – The Grand Experiment

1. The Armstrong quote is from his foreword in Milton O. Thompson, *At the Edge of Space: The X-15 Flight Program*, (Washington and London: Smithsonian Institution Press, 1992), p. xii.
2. The "basic" X-15 did not quite meet its original design speed, recording 6,019 feet per second versus the 6,600 fps goal. The modified X-15A-2, however, flew at 6,629 fps – slightly exceeding the original specification.
3. John V. Becker, "The X-15 Program in Retrospect," 3rd Eugen Sänger Memorial Lecture, Bonn, Germany, 5 December 1968), pp. 1-2
4. Officially Johnny Armstrong (Chief Engineer in the Access to Space Office) maintains the AFFTC Access to Space Office Project Files, and is – fortunately – something of a pack rat. But to everybody on Edwards and Dryden, this wonderful collection is simply the Armstrong Memorial Library.

Chapter 1 – The Antecedents

1. Telegram, Colonel Signa A. Gilkey to Colonel George F. Smith, 14 October 1947. ["PD" was shorthand for "period" or "stop"] In the files at the AFFTC History Office. The XS-1 managed Mach 1.06 (approximately 700 mph) at 42,000 feet on that flight. "XS" stood for "experimental, supersonic" – the designation would later be shortened simply to X-1.
2. The DH.108 was a single seat research aircraft built to specification E.18/45 and intended to provide data for the Comet airliner and DH.110 fighter. The airplane was based on a standard Vampire fuselage, with a Goblin 2 engine, but with a new 43-degree swept wing and single vertical stabilizer. The first proto-type flew on 15 May 1946 but crashed in May 1950, killing the pilot. The second aircraft was intended to assess the high speed characteristics of the design and the wing sweep was increased to 45 degrees. The first flight was in June 1946, but the aircraft broke up on 27 September while flying at a speed in excess of Mach 0.9, killing Geoffrey de Havilland. A third Swallow was first flown on 24 July 1947 and finally exceeded the speed of sound on 9 September 1948 flown by John Derry, the first supersonic flight in Great Britain.
3. *Webster's Ninth New Collegiate Dictionary*, (Springfield, MA: Merriam-Webster, 1986).
4. John D. Anderson, Jr., "Research in Supersonic Flight and the Breaking of the Sound Barrier," in *From Engineering Science to Big Science: The NACA and NASA Collier Trophy Research Project Winners*, edited by Pamela E. Mack, NASA SP-4219, (Washington, DC: NASA1998), p. 62. On an ISO standard day at sea level the speed of sound was subsequently defined by the NACA as 1,117 feet per second. (This number was chosen for engineering convenience. The actual speed of sound depends on what model you look at and varies from 1,116.4 fps in the 1959 ARDC Model Atmosphere to 1,116.9 fps in the 1954 ICAO Model Atmosphere.) For more see, Pierre Simon Marquis de Laplace, "Sur la vitesse do son dans l'aire et dan l'eau," *Annales de Chimie et de Physique*, 1816 and "Minutes of the Meeting of Committee on Aerodynamics, 12 October 1943," p. 9. In the archives at the Langley Research Center.
5. John V. Becker, *The High-Speed Frontier: Case Histories of Four NACA Programs, 1920-1950*, NASA SP-445, (Washington, DC: NASA, 1980), p. 3. The text is also located on the web at http://www.hq.nasa.gov/office/pao/History/SP-445/contents.htm. For more on Robins' work, see his *New Principles of Gunnery* published in 1742.
6. Anderson, *Modern Compressible Flow: With Historical Perspective*, pp. 92-95. An excellent example of a shock wave may be observed as the Prandtl-Glauert singularity when an aircraft goes supersonic, particularly at low altitude when the air has a high moisture content. See http://www.eng.vt.edu/fluids/msc/gallery/conden/pg_sing.htm for some excellent photographs illustrating this.
7. Anderson, "Research in Supersonic Flight and the Breaking of the Sound Barrier," pp. 62-63; http://otokar.troja.mff.cuni.cz/RELATGRP/Mach.htm, accessed 17 July 2002. This web site has copies of the original shadowgraphs taken in 1877.
8. Becker, *The High-Speed Frontier*, pp. 3-5. For more see John William Strutt (the Third Baron Rayleigh), *The Theory of Sound*, a landmark of acoustics originally published in 1877. An online version is available at http://www.measure.demon.co.uk/docs/Strutt.html.
9. On 18 October 1917 McCook Field was established outside Dayton as the military aviation research and development site, based largely on its proximity to the American aviation industry, i.e., the Wright Brothers. But within ten years the facility had become too small and offered no room for expansion. The citizens of Dayton, not wanting to lose the activity, collected donations and purchased 4,000 acres of land that was donated to the government. The new Wright Field was dedicated on 12 October 1927. On 1 July 1931, that portion of Wright Field east of Huffman Dam was redesignated Patterson Field in honor of Lieutenant Frank Stuart Patterson. Patterson Field was the home of Air Force logistics and concentrated in that role; Wright Field was the home of research and development. The adjacent Wright Field and Patterson Field were once again joined on 13 January 1948 to become Wright-Patterson AFB. However, most development activities were still conducted on the "Wright Field" part of the base, and in most contemporary literature (and official correspondence) it generally continued to be referred to as Wright Field until the late 1950s.
10. In an unusually far-sighted move, on 3 March 1915 Congress passed a Public Law establishing "an Advisory Committee for Aeronautics." As stipulated in the Act, the purpose of this committee was "… to supervise and direct the scientific study of the problems of flight with a view to their practical solution" and to "direct and conduct research and experiment in aeronautics."
The NACA received its direction via a committee system. The committees and their subcommittees were composed of representatives from industry, the military, and NACA scientists and engineers. A subcommittee, which had the most direct contact with the "real world" might recognize a new area of research and pass a resolution recommending further efforts. The overarching committee would then take up the resolution, and after discussion at a higher level in the food chain, either table or pass its own resolution. This would, in turn, pass to the Executive Committee which was composed of distinguished members of industry, high-ranking military officers, and government officials appointed by the President. If the Executive Committee endorsed the resolution, it would direct the NACA laboratories (Ames, Langley, and Lewis) and stations (Auxiliary Flight Research Station and, later, the High-Speed Flight Station) to conduct the research. Funding was a more interesting matter, and was often provided through the various military services, although the NACA also had a separately appropriated budget.
11. G. H. Bryan, "The Effect of Compressibility on Streamline Motions," R & M No. 555, Technical Report of the Advisory Committee for Aeronautics, December 1918; G. H. Bryan, "The Effect of Compressibility on Streamline Motions, Part II," R & M No. 640, Technical Report of the Advisory Committee for Aeronautics, April 1919; Becker, *The High-Speed Frontier*, pp. 3-5.
12. Becker, *The High-Speed Frontier*, pp. 6-7. Surprisingly, one 1924 French document envisioned aircraft flying at Mach 0.8 or more by 1930, including development of some wholly new but unspecified type of propulsion plus appropriate new high-speed wind tunnels to support these developments. See the English translation of *La Technique Aeronautica*, December 1924 by E. Huguenard, "High-Speed Wind Tunnels," NACA Technical Memorandum 318, 1925.
13. W.F. Hilton, "British Aeronautical Research Facilities," *Journal of the Royal Aeronautical Society*, volume 70, (Centenary Issue, 1966), pp. 103-104.
14. In July 1948 the "Memorial" was dropped, the facility becoming the Langley Aeronautical Laboratory. It would subsequently be renamed the Langley Research Center (Langley) when NASA came into existence on 1 October 1958.
15. Becker, *The High-Speed Frontier*, p. 88.
16. John Stack, "Effects of Compressibility on High Speed Flight," *Journal of the Aeronautical Sciences*. (January 1934), pp. 40-43; James R. Hansen, *Engineer in Charge: A History of the Langley Aeronautical Laboratory, 1917-1958*, NASA SP-4305, (Washington, DC: NASA,1987), p. 256.
17. Hansen, *Engineer in Charge: A History of the Langley Aeronautical Laboratory, 1917-1958*, p. 259.
18. Jay D. Pinson, ed., *Diamond Jubilee of Powered Flight: The Evolution of Aircraft Design*, (New York: American Institute of Aeronautics and Astronautics, 1978), pp. 51-64; Becker, *The High-Speed Frontier*, pp. 89-90.
19. Becker, *The High-Speed Frontier*, pp. 90-91.
20. Ibid., pp. 91-92.
21. Ibid., pp. 91-92. It should be noted that several rocket-powered combat types – such as the Republic XF-91 Thunderceptor – were proposed during the 1940s and 1950s, although none entered service.
22. Richard P. Hallion, *Supersonic Flight*, (New York: Macmillan, 1972), p. 34; Becker, *The High-Speed Frontier*, pp. 91-92. Woods had worked at Langley during 1928-1929 but had left the NACA and in 1935 teamed with Lawrence D. Bell to form the Bell Aircraft Corporation in Buffalo, New York.
23. Becker, *The High-Speed Frontier*, pp. 92-93. Ironically, it was the turbojet-powered D-558-1 that ultimately killed NACA pilot Howard C. Lilly due to engine failure. With further irony, it was the transonic and supersonic flight achievements of the rocket-powered X-1 that brought the NACA and John Stack a share of the Collier Trophy.
24. John Stack, "Methods for Investigation of Flows at Transonic Speeds" Aeroballistics Research Facilities Dedication Symposium, 27 June-1 July 1949. See also an updated version presented at the 3rd International Aero Conference, London, 7-11 September 1951. The XS-1 was powered by a Reaction Motors XLR11 rocket engine, which was a redesignated version of the LR8 developed by the Navy. The D-558-I was powered by an Air Force-funded Allison J35-A-11 turbojet. The United States Air Force superceded the Army Air Forces by virtue of the National Security Act of 1947 which became law on 26 July 1947.
25. Becker, *The High-Speed Frontier*, pp. 93-94; email, Robert G. Hoey to Dennis R. Jenkins, 11 December 2002.
26. Ibid., pp. 93-94.
27. For a look at all the X-planes, please see Jay Miller's excellent work: *The X-Planes: X-1 to X-45*, (Hinckley, England: Midland Publishing, 2001). Jay is currently working on a companion volume for the same publisher that will deal with experimental aircraft not directly in the "X" designation category (such as the Douglas D-558s).
28. http://www.dfrc.nasa.gov/History/x-planes.html, accessed on 18 July 2002.
29. http://www.dfrc.nasa.gov/PAO/PAIS/HTML/bd-2001-04-035.html, accessed 29 July 2002.
30. Becker, *The High-Speed Frontier*, pp. 93-94. Crossfield suggests – as do others – that the first Mach 1 dive by an F-86 occurred "within weeks" of Yeager's first supersonic flight (telephone conversation, Scott Crossfield to dennis R. Jenkins, 31 October 2002).
31. Miller, *The X-Planes*, pp. 20-35.
32. http://www.dfrc.nasa.gov/History/X-1/X-1.html, accessed on 18 July 2002.
33. Miller, *The X-Planes*, pp. 20-35.
34. Miller, *The X-Planes*, pp. 20-35; biography, Herbert Henry Hoover, 5 December 2001. In the files at the DFRC History Office.
35. Miller, *The X-Planes*, pp. 37-45.
36. Ibid., pp. 37-45.
37. Ibid., pp. 37-45.
38. Ibid., pp. 37-45.
39. Ibid., pp. 418-419. Scott Crossfield is one engineer who was intimately involved with the airplanes that tends toward the 400-series stainless steel theory (telephone conversation, Scott Crossfield to Dennis R. Jenkins, 31 October 2002).
40. Ibid., pp. 37-45. A similar set of reaction controls was soon installed on the Lockheed JF-104A Starfighter, providing a much better platform for further investigations.
41. Ibid., pp. 46-51.
42. Anderson, "Research in Supersonic Flight and the Breaking of the Sound Barrier," pp. 88-89. The three men represented, depending whom you talk to, either the NACA, Bell, and the Air Force; or the researcher, designer, and pilot.
43. http://www.dfrc.nasa.gov/History/x-planes.html, accessed on 18 July 2002.
44. Discussions concerning the Reaction Motors LR8 and XLR11 gets confusing. At the time, Navy rocket engines used even numbers in the designations; Air Force engines used odd numbers. They were essentially identical engines, both based on the Reaction Motors 6000C4. Within each family, early models relied on pressurized propellant tanks, later models used turbopumps. All of the engines had four thrust chambers that could be ignited and extinguished independently, providing some "thrust stepping." (Data verified with Bill Arnold, RMI engineer, 4 November 2002.)
45. The Muroc Flight Test Unit from Langley had been informally established by Walter C. Williams on 30 September 1946 in support of testing the XS-1, and achieved permanent status on 7 September 1947. It was redesignated the High-Speed Flight Research Station (HSFRS) on 14 November 1949, the High-Speed Flight Station (HSFS) on 1 July 1954, the Flight Research Center (FRC) on 27 September 1959, and the Hugh L. Dryden Flight Research Center (usually abbreviated DFRC) on 26 March 1976. On 1 October 1981 it was administratively absorbed into the Ames Research Center and changed its name to the Ames-Dryden Flight Research Facility (DFRF). It reverted to Center status on 1 March 1994 and again became DFRC. At some point between 1954 and 1959, the hyphen between "High" and "Speed" seems to have been dropped.
46. http://www.dfrc.nasa.gov/PAO/PAIS/HTML/FS-035-DFRC.html, accessed 18 July 2002.
47. http://www.dfrc.nasa.gov/History/x-planes.html, accessed on 18 July 2002.
48. Miller, *The X-Planes*, pp. 52-67.
49. Ibid., pp. 52-67. Although the XLR25 was a man-rated throttleable rocket engine, it was a fairly small powerplant and did not offer much in the way of help when it came time to develop the much-larger XLR99 engine for the X-15.
50. Ibid., pp. 52-67.
51. Ibid., pp. 52-67.
52. Telephone conversations with Scott Crossfield and John Becker, various dates, plus writings in a multitude of books, letters, and memos in archives around the country. The debate is probably never ending, and largely moot since what happened has already happened.
53. The XP-86 officially broke the sound barrier in a shallow dive on 26 April 1948. Some sources have maintained that this event actually took place slightly before Yeager's flight, and Scott Crossfield suggests – as do others – that the first Mach 1 dive by an F-86 occurred "within weeks" of Yeager's first supersonic flight (telephone conversation, Scott Crossfield to dennis R. Jenkins, 31 October 2002).
54. The XF-91 was hardly a successful attempt, although it did record the "first supersonic rocket-powered flight by a U.S. combat-type airplane" in December 1952. The aircraft was powered by a single General Electric J47-GE-9 jet engine and four Curtiss-Wright XLR27-CW-1 rocket engines. A modified XF-91A traded the Curtiss-Wright rockets for a Reaction Motors XLR11-RM-9, but was apparently never tested.
55. The first flight of an XF-104 powered by a Wright XJ65-W-6 engine was on 7 February 1956, but this aircraft was only capable of Mach 1.79; the General Electric J79-GE-3-powered YF-104A exceeded Mach 2 on 27 April 1956.
56. Interview with Gene Matranga, 3 December 1976, transcript in the files at the DFRC History Office; http://www.dfrc.nasa.gov/History/Publications/SP-4303/ch4-6.html, accessed on 18 July 2002.
57. John V. Becker, "The X-15 Project: Part 1 – Origins and Research Background," *Astronautics & Aeronautics*, February 1964, pp. 53.

Chapter 2 – A New Science

1. *Webster's Ninth New Collegiate Dictionary*, (Springfield, MA: Merriam-Webster, 1986).
2. Despite the apparent success of the A-4b, most engineers on the program believed that heat transfer problems would ultimately doom the A-4b – there were no provisions for cooling the airframe and little was understood about potential heating effects. For further information, see Michael Neufeld's interview of Karl Werner Dahm, 25 January 1990. In the files at the National Air and Space Museum.
3. John V. Becker, "The X-15 Program in Retrospect," 3rd Eugen Sänger Memorial Lecture, Bonn, Germany, 5 December 1968, p. 1.

4. Letter, John V. Becker to the Langley Chief of Research, subject: Proposal for new type of supersonic wind tunnel for Mach number 7.0, 3 August 1945. In the Becker Archives, Virginia Polytechnic Institute, Blacksburg, Virginia; letter, John V. Becker to Dennis R. Jenkins, 29 July 2002.
5. Letter, John V. Becker to Dennis R. Jenkins, 29 July 2002, containing comments to a draft copy of this manuscript. The original writeup was based largely on James R. Hansen, *Engineer in Charge: A History of the Langley Aeronautical Laboratory – 1917-1958*, NASA SP-4305 (Washington DC: NASA, 1987); Becker commented that "Hansen's account is generally very good. I agree with most of it. There are, however, some important omissions. Unfortunately, no one in our hypersonics group had an opportunity to review this part of it."
6. Arthur Kantrowitz and Coleman duP. Donaldson, "Preliminary Investigation of Supersonic Diffusers," NASA wartime report L713, May 1946 (originally published as L5D20, 1945). Becker was serving as the chairman of the technical editorial committee when he first read the paper.
7. Letter, John V. Becker to Dennis R. Jenkins, 29 July 2002.
8. Ibid.
9. Hunsaker was chairman of the NACA from 1941 to 1956. Among the notable achievements in a long and accomplished career, his work in aircraft stability was published as NACA Technical Report No. 1 in 1915.
10. John V. Becker, "Results of Recent Hypersonic and Unsteady Flow Research at the Langley Aeronautical Laboratory," *Journal of Applied Physics*, volume 21, number 7, July 1950, pp. 619-628; letter, John V. Becker to Dennis R. Jenkins, 29 July 2002.
11. In 1919 Lewis became the first Executive Officer of the NACA; in 1924, he was given the title Director of Aeronautical Research which he kept until 1947. Lewis died at his summer home, Lake Winola, Pennsylvania, on 12 July 1948
12. Letter, John V. Becker to Dennis R. Jenkins, 29 July 2002. Becker, "The $39,500 estimate contained in the 3 August 1945 memo seems ridiculous by today's standards. However, it did not include any NACA overhead costs and construction would take place in NACA shops using NACA personnel. The expenditure increased to over $200,000 when the cost of the heater that was subsequently added was included."
13. Letter, John V. Becker to Dennis R. Jenkins, 29 July 2002.
14. Becker, "Results of Recent Hypersonic and Unsteady Flow Research at the Langley Aeronautical Laboratory," pp. 619-628; letter, John V. Becker to Dennis R. Jenkins, 29 July 2002.
15. Letter, John V. Becker to Dennis R. Jenkins, 29 July 2002. For an example of the investigations made during this period, see Charles H. McLellan, "Exploratory Wind Tunnel Investigations of Wings and Bodies at M=6.9," *Journal of the Aeronautical Sciences*, volume 18, number 10, October 1951, pp. 641-648.
16. James R. Hansen, *Engineer in Charge: A History of the Langley Aeronautical Laboratory – 1917-1958*, NASA SP-4305 (Washington DC: NASA, 1987), p. 347.
17. The Ames Aeronautical Laboratory became the Ames Research Center when NASA came into being on 1 October 1958.
18. Hansen, *Engineer in Charge*, p. 560.
19. Letter, John V. Becker to Dennis R. Jenkins, 29 July 2002.
20. H. Julian Allen and Alfred J. Eggers, Jr., "A Study of the Motion and Aerodynamic Heating of Ballistic Missiles Entering the Earth's Atmosphere at High Supersonic Speeds," NACA confidential research memorandum A53D28, August 1953; Edwin P. Hartmann, *Adventures in Research: A History of the Ames Research Center, 1940-1965*, NASA SP-4302 (Washington DC: NASA, 1972), pp. 216-218. Allen had worked at Langley between 1936 and 1940 before joining the team on the west coast. As told by John Becker, Allen's given name was "Harry," but he disliked the name and always used "H. Julian" instead. Occasionally he used "Harvey" as a nickname, leading to the use of that name in many publications.
21. Allen and Eggers,"A Study of the Motion and Aerodynamic Heating of Ballistic Missiles Entering the Earth's Atmosphere at High Supersonic Speeds." The NACA published updated versions of the same report as TN4047 and TR1381 in 1958; Hartmann, *Adventures in Research*, pp. 218.
22. The accepted standard at the time was to report extreme altitudes in statue miles; this equated to 264,000 to 396,000 feet. It is ironic that this almost exactly foretold the performance ultimately obtained by the X-15.
23. According to *Websters'* – antipodal: of or relating to the antipodes; *specif*: situated at the opposite side of the Earth. Or, points on opposite sides of a sphere. The original Sänger concept was that the Silverbird would land on the opposite side of the Earth from where it took off, dropping its bombs mid-way through the mission.
24. Eugen Sänger, *Rocket Flight Engineering*, NASA TTF-223 (Washington DC: NASA, 1965). Sänger's concepts for skip-glide aircraft date back as far as his doctoral thesis of 1928, and formed the basis for several post-war American projects such as BoMi and RoBo. His "dynamic-soaring" terminology also inspired the name Dyna-Soar given to the Step III hypersonic research program, and later the X-20 vehicle.
25. Robert J. Woods to the NACA Committee on Aerodynamics, "Establishment of a Study Group on Space Flight and Associated Problems," 8 January 1952. A few weeks later, Dornberger would outline an even more ambitious version of the aircraft that would be launched from a B-47 and would be capable of 6,210 fps (4,250 mph) and altitudes of 564,000 feet. It was, for all intents, a version of the A-4b or A-9 that had been investigated by the Germans at Peenemünde during the war. See a letter from Walter R. Dornberger to Robert J. Woods of 18 January 1952. In the files at the NASA History Office.
26. Minutes of the Meeting, NACA Committee on Aerodynamics, 30 January 1952. In the files at the NASA History Office.
27. Minutes of the Meeting, NACA Committee on Aerodynamics, 24 June 1952. In the files at the NASA History Office.
28. Hubert M. Drake and L. Robert Carman, "A Suggestion of Means for Flight Research at Hypersonic Velocities and High Altitudes," unpublished, 21 May 1952. In the files at the Dryden History Office.
29. The PARD was established in June 1946 from the Auxiliary Flight Research Station (AFRS) on Wallops Island, off the eastern shore of Virginia. This group had been set up during World War II to launch "pilotless aircraft" – the military's name for all guided missiles of the time – to obtain research data on them. On 4 July 1945, the AFRS launched its first test vehicle, a small two-stage, solid-fuel rocket to check out the installation's instrumentation. At the end of the war the typical model weighed about 40 pounds and had a maximum speed of Mach 1.4 before it fell into the Atlantic Ocean. The models were instrumented and provided telemetry during their flights. Despite the fact that PARD launched 386 models from 1947-1949, the "real" researchers in the Langley wind tunnels never believed that the operation obtained much useful data. Nevertheless, the PARD continued and soon began launching large-scale models of aircraft on top of their rockets, obtaining data at speeds the wind tunnels could only dream of at the time. Tests were conducted on many types of aircraft – for instance, tests of the Convair F-102 Delta Dagger helped verify the effectiveness of Richard T. Whitcomb's area rule principle.
30. Letter, David G. Stone to Chief of Research, subject: Preliminary study of the proposal for the flight of manned vehicles into space, 21 May 1952. In the files at the Dryden History Office.
31. Becker, "The X-15 Program in Retrospect," p. 2.
32. Minutes of the Meeting, Interlaboratory Research Airplane Projects Panel, NACA Headquarters, 4-5 February 1954; letter, John W. Crowley to distribution, subject: Request for comments on possible new research airplane, 9 March 1954. In the Becker Archives at Virginia Polytechnic Institute, Blacksburg, Virginia. The Research Airplane Projects Panel was formed by NACA Associate Director of Aeronautical Research Gus Crowley in September 1948 to coordinate the efforts of Langley, Ames, Lewis, the Auxiliary Flight Research Station, and the High Speed Flight Station. Each laboratory reported quarterly to the panel detailing what research was being performed in support of each specific airplane, and the outcome of the research. The panel met in formal session annually. This was different than the Research Airplane Program Committee headed by Langley's John Stack that included representatives from the Army Air Forces and the Navy Bureau of Aeronautics.
33. John V. Becker, "Development of Winged Reentry Vehicles, 1953-1963" unpublished, 23 May 1983, p. 30. In the Becker Archives at Virginia Polytechnic Institute, Blacksburg, Virginia. The quotes are Becker's recollections of how other engineers felt at the time, not his personal feelings on the subjects. BoMi was an acronym for "Bomber-Missile;" RoBo stood for "Rocket-Bomber." Both would be consolidated into the HYWARDS program that later evolved into the Boeing X-20 Dyna-Soar.
34. The Aircraft Engine Research Laboratory was founded on 23 June 1941 in suburban Cleveland, Ohio. In April 1947 it was renamed the Flight Propulsion Research Laboratory; a year later it was renamed the Lewis Flight Propulsion Laboratory. When NASA was formed on 1 October 1958, the laboratory was renamed the Lewis Research Center (abbreviated LeRC to differential it from the Langley Research Center – Langley). On 1 March 1999 it was renamed the John H. Glenn Research Center at Lewis Field.
35. Letter, Floyd L. Thompson/Langley to NACA, 3 May 1954, enclosing a copy of a memo from John V. Becker entitled "Research Airplane Study;" letter, HSFS to NACA, 5 May 1954, enclosing an informal report entitled "Suggested Requirements for a New Research Airplane;" letter, Ames to NACA, no subject, 7 May 1954; memorandum from Lewis/Associate Director to NACA, 7 May 1954 (actually written 27 April 1954); Hansen, *Engineer in Charge*, p. 357. According to Hard D. Wallace, Jr., *Wallops Station and the Creation of an American Space Program*, NASA SP-4311, (Washington DC: NASA, 1997) p. 19, note 41: "Note that unlike the earlier X-series aircraft, no models of the X-15 appear to have been tested at Wallops." This statement appears to be incorrect since several references were uncovered to various X-15 tests at the PARD.
36. Becker, "Development of Winged Reentry Vehicles, 1953-1963," p. 30; letter, John V. Becker to Dennis R. Jenkins, 12 June 1999.
37. Becker, "Development of Winged Reentry Vehicles, 1953-1963," p. 30.
38. Although it had always been assumed that air-drop would be the preferred launch method, the original "Research Airplane Study" did not specifically mention any launch method.
39. Unpublished paper, "11-Inch Tunnel Contributions to the X-15," no author (probably Becker), no date; Becker, "Development of Winged Reentry Vehicles, 1953-1963" p. 10. Both in the Becker Archives at Virginia Polytechnic Institute, Blacksburg, Virginia.
40. Hansen, *Engineer in Charge*, p. 359.
41. John V. Becker, "The X-15 Project, Part I: Origins and Research Background," *Astronautics and Aeronautics*, February 1964, p. 56; letter, John V. Becker to Dennis R. Jenkins, 29 July 2002. The temperatures in the boundary layer at Mach 7 exceed 3,000°F. The 2,000°F "equilibrium" temperature is the surface temperature of the underside of the wing where the imposed heating would be balanced by the heat loss due to radiation away from the surface. It should be noted that the angle of attack was between 11 and 26 degrees, but the reentry flight path was generally around –32 degrees, meaning the airplane was actually flying between 21 and 6 degrees nose-down.
42. Wind tunnel tests of the X-1A had extended only to Mach 2.
43. Arthur Henderson, Jr., NACA research memorandum L55I23, "Wind tunnel Investigation of the Static Longitudinal and lateral Stability of the Bell X-1A at Supersonic Speeds," October 1955; and Hubert M. Drake and Wendell H. Stillman, NACA research memorandum H55G26, "Behaviors of the X-1A Research Airplane during Exploratory Flights at Mach Numbers near 2.0 and at Extreme Altitudes," October 1955; Herman O. Ankenbruck and Chester H. Wolowicz, NACA research memorandum H54I27, "Lateral Motions Encountered With the Douglas D-558-II All-Rocket Research Airplane During Exploratory Flights to a Mach Number of 2.0." December 1954.
44. Becker, "The X-15 Project, Part I," p. 56. Charles H. McLellan had outlined the findings of his original study in "Investigation of the Aerodynamic Characteristics of Wings and Bodies at a Mach Number of 6.9," a paper presented at a NACA conference on supersonic aerodynamics held at Ames in early 1950. A version of this paper appeared in the October 1950 edition of the *Journal of the Aeronautical Sciences*, volume 18, number 10, pp. 641-648. In 1963 McLellan received a $2,000 award for the development of "wedge tails for hypersonic aircraft" under Section 306 of the National Aeronautics and Space Act of 1958 (see Jane Van Nimmen and Leonard C. Bruno with Robert L. Rosholt, NASA SP-4012, *NASA Historical Data Book Volume I: NASA Resources 1958-1968*, Washington DC, 1988, p. 556).
45. Charles H. McLellan, NACA research memorandum L544F21, "A Method for Increasing the Effectiveness of Stabilizing Surfaces at High Supersonic Mach Numbers," August 1954.
46. Becker, "The X-15 Project, Part I," p. 56-57. These same trade studies would be repeated many times during the concept definition for Space Shuttle.
47. Ibid., p. 56-57. Possible insulators included water, several different liquid metals, air, and various fibrous batt materials. The liquids would require active pumps and large reservoirs, making them exceptionally heavy concepts.
48. Inconel X" is a temperature-resistant alloy whose name is a registered trademark of Huntington Alloy Products Division, International Nickel Company, Huntington, West Virginia. Inconel X is 72.5 percent nickel, 15 percent chromium, and 1 percent columbium, with iron making up most of the balance.
49. Letter, John V. Becker to Dennis R. Jenkins, 29 July 2002.
50. Becker, "The X-15 Project, Part I," p. 57-58.
51. Project Hermes was begun in 1944 as the Army effort to study the German V-2 rockets, and the first of five Hermes A-1s was launched at the White Sands Proving Grounds on 19 May 1950. This was, essentially, the beginning of the Redstone development process. A Hermes A-1 can be seen sitting on its launch pad at the White Sands museum.
52. Thrust-stepping was not a new idea. The XLR11 used on the X-1 and many other early X-planes had four "chambers" that could be started and extinguished individually. This allowed the thrust for any given flight to be tailored to one of four levels. Unfortunately, once a chamber was extinguished, it could not be started again in flight. The Curtiss-Wright XLR25 being developed for the X-2 was a truly throttleable engine, but its development was proving to be unexpectedly difficult and was running well behind schedule. The XLR25 was also no more powerful than the Hermes engines, and so offered little in the way of a solution for the new research airplane.
53. Becker, "The X-15 Program in Retrospect," p. 2.
54. Hugh L. Dryden, "Toward the New Horizons of Tomorrow," First von Kármán Lecture, *Astronautics*, January 1963; James R. Hansen, *Spaceflight Revolution: NASA Langley Research Center from Sputnik to Apollo*, NASA SP-4308, (Washington DC: NASA, 1995), p. 98; John V. Becker, "The X-15 Program in Retrospect," 3rd Eugen Sänger Memorial Lecture, Bonn, Germany, 5 December 1968, p. 2.
55. Becker, "The X-15 Program in Retrospect," p. 2; "Preliminary Outline Specification for High-Altitude, High-Speed Research Airplane," NACA Langley, 15 October 1954; "General Requirements for a New Research Airplane," NACA Langley, 11 October 1954.
56. Letter, Hugh L. Dryden to USAF Headquarters, no subject, 4 May 1954; letter, Lieutenant General Donald L. Putt to Dryden, no subject, 26 May 1954; letter, Hugh L. Dryden to USAF Headquarters (invitation), 11 June 1954; letter, Hugh L. Dryden to Navy Bureau of Aeronautics (invitation), 11 June 1954; memorandum for the files (NACA Headquarters), subject: Minutes of joint USAF-USN-NACA new research airplane briefing, 3 September 1954. In the files at the NASA History Office; Hugh L. Dryden, "General Background of the X-15 Research Airplane Project" (a paper presented at the NACA Conference on the Progress of the X-15 Project, Langley Aeronautical Laboratory, 25-26 October 1956), pp. xvii-xix.
57. Office of Naval Research contract Nonr-1266(00). The "D-558-III" designation was never used in any of the official reports describing the concept, although it was widely used in the more popular press and most historical works. For a slightly more in-depth look at the Douglas Model 671, see Dennis R. Jenkins, "Douglas D-558-III," *Aerospace Projects Review*, volume 3, number 6, November-December 2001, pp. 14-27.
58. There were several reports published on the Douglas study. See, for instance, Douglas report ES-17657, "High Altitude and High Speed Study," 28 May 1954; and Douglas report ES-17673, "Technical Report on High Altitude and High Speed Study," 28 May 1954; One of the few contemporary articles written on the concept was by Irwin Stambler in the May 1959 *Aircraft & Missile Engineering* journal, pp. 20-21 and 77-79. Copies supplied by Bob Bradley, San Diego Aerospace Museum.
59. Douglas report ES-17657, p. 7; Douglas report ES-17673, p. 7.
60. Douglas report ES-17673, p. 15.
61. Douglas report ES-17673, p. 7. The wedge principle that would play such an important role in the X-15 design was still languishing in the archives, and the Bell X-2 had not provided its own contribution to understanding "high speed instability."
62. Douglas report ES-17673, p. 40; Douglas report ES-17657, pp. 18-19. The eventual X-15 design took a somewhat similar approach, at least for the ventral stabilizer. By the 1970s, of course, augmentation systems were finally beginning to allow inherently unstable aircraft to fly – Space Shuttle being a prime example.
63. Douglas report ES-17657, pp. 1-14. The selection also foretold the X-15 since the XLR30 would provide the initial basis for the XLR99.
64. Douglas report ES-17673, pp. 54 and 58. In 1954 calculations of this nature normally had to be made by hand or on mechanical calculators since general-purpose electronic computers were not widely available, and were quite slow in any case.
65. Douglas report ES-17657, pp. 1-14 and 20-21; Douglas report ES-17673, pp. 55-57.
66. Over half the atmosphere lies below 40,000 feet. Douglas report ES-17673, pp. 7 and 15-16.
67. Douglas report ES-17673, pp. 18-19.
68. Ibid., pp. 42-43. In 1954 manned space flight was still seven years in the future and no airplane had yet flown above the sensible atmosphere; this made it impossible to accurately guess how much control a pilot would want – or need – at extremely high altitudes.
69. Douglas report ES-17657, pp. 15-17 and 23; quote is from Douglas report ES-17673, p. 37.
70. The same technique used by the V-2 and several other early rockets.
71. This involves injecting a small amount of gas along the wall on one side of the exhaust nozzle, causing a flow separation that results in slightly asymmetrical thrust. The technique was later used on the solid rocket motors for the Titan III/IV launch vehicle and other programs.
72. Douglas report ES-17673, pp. 37-39.
73. Ibid., p. 21.
74. Douglas report ES-17657, p. 26.

Chapter 3 – Project 1226

1. Memorandum, E. C. Phillips, Chief, Operations Office, Power Plant Laboratory, to Director of Laboratories, WADC, subject: NACA Conference on 9 July 1954 on Research Aircraft-Propulsion System, 5 August 1954. In the files at the ASD History Office; memorandum, J. W. Rogers, Liquid Propellant and Rocket Branch, Rocket Propulsion Division, Power Plant Laboratory, to Chief, Non-Rotating Engine Branch, Power Plant Laboratory, WADC, subject: Conferences on 9 and 10 August 1954 on NACA Research Aircraft-Propulsion System, 11 August 1954. In the files at the AFMC History Office.
2. Letter, Colonel Victor R. Haugen to Commander, ARDC, no subject, 13 August 1954; memorandum, R. L. Schulz, Technical Director of Aircraft, to Chief, Fighter Aircraft Division, WADC, no subject, not dated (presumed about 13 August 1954). Both in the files at the AFMC History Office. A published summary of the 9 July NACA presentations did not appear until 14 August.
3. "NACA Views Concerning a New Research Airplane," August 1954. In the files at the NASA History Office.
4. Letter, Major General Floyd B. Wood, Deputy Commander of Technical Operations, ARDC, to Director of R&D, USAF, subject: New Research Aircraft, 20 September 1954. In the files at the ASD History Office.
5. Letter, A. Scott Crossfield to Dennis R. Jenkins, 30 June 1999. Largely because he wanted to become more involved in the X-15 development, Crossfield would leave the NACA in 1955 to work for North American Aviation.
6. "Minutes of the Meeting, NACA Committee on Aerodynamics," 4-5 October 1954. In the files at the NASA History Office. Johnson is one of the modern legends in the aerospace community. Founder of what became known as the Lockheed "Skunk Works," Johnson was largely responsible for such landmark designs as the P-80, U-2, F-104, and SR-71.
7. Ibid.
8. Resolution, 5 October 1954. In the files at the NASA History Office; Hugh L. Dryden, "General Background of the X-15 Research Airplane Project" (a paper presented at the NACA Conference on the Progress of the X-15 Project, Langley Aeronautical Laboratory, 25-26 October 1956), pp. xvii-xix.
9. Letter, Clarence L. Johnson to Milton B. Ames, secretary, Committee on Aerodynamics, subject: Minority Opinion of Extremely High Altitude Research Airplane, 21 October 1954.
10. Walter C. Williams, "X-15 Concept Evolution" (a paper in the *Proceedings of the X-15 30th Anniversary Celebration*, Dryden Flight Research Facility, Edwards, California, 8 June 1989, NASA CP-3105), p. 11.

11. Memorandum of Understanding, signed by Hugh L. Dryden, Director of NACA, James H. Smith Jr., Assistant secretary of the Navy (Air), and Trevor Gardner, Special Assistant for R&D, USAF, 23 December 1954, subject: Principles for the Conduct by the NACA, Navy, and Air Force of a Joint Project for a New High-Speed Research Airplane. In the files at the NASA History Office. The Research Airplane Committee was separate from the Research Airplane Projects Panel or the Research Airplane Program Committee.
12. Teletype, AFDRD-AN-43671, C/S, USAF, to Commander, ARDC, 8 December 1954; letter, Colonel Paul F. Nay, Chief, Aeronautics and Propulsion Division, Deputy Commander of Technical Development, ARDC, to Commander, WADC, subject: Competition for New Research Aircraft, not dated (but approximately 30 November 1954); memorandum, A. L. Sea, Assistant Chief, Fighter Aircraft Division, to Director of Weapons Systems Office, WADC, subject: New Research Aircraft, 29 December 1954. All in the files at the ASD History Office.
13. Letter, Colonel Carl F. Damberg, Chief, Aircraft Division, AMC, to Bell, et al., subject: Project 1226 Competition, 2 February 1955; memorandum, J. W. Rogers to Chief, Power Plant Laboratory, 4 January 1955. In the files at the AFMC History Office; WADC report 54MCP-199342, confidential, no date. In the files at the AFFTC History Office.
14. WADC report 54MCP-199342.
15. Bell report 02-945-106, "Project 1226: X-15 Liquid Rocket Engine Proposal," secret, 25 February 1955. Courtesy of Benjamin F. Guenther; WADC report 54MCP-199342.
16. WADC report 54MCP-199342.
17. WADC report 54MCP-199342; Reaction Motors report TR-9405-C, "Rocket Engine for New Research Airplane," secret, 26 February 1955. Courtesy of Benjamin F. Guenther. This was the engine used by the Martin Viking sounding rocket, which eventually formed the first stage of the ill-fated Vanguard launch vehicle. Reaction Motors had begun developing the engine for this vehicle on 1 October 1946, and the first launch was on 3 May 1949. A total of 14 Vikings were launched at White Sands Missile Range in New Mexico.
18. Letter, Clotaire Wood to Ames, Lewis, Langley, HSFS, NACA Liaison Office, no subject, 2 February 1955; R&D Project Card, DD-EDB(A)48, Project 1226, 7 March 1955. In the files at the AMC History Office; a "rewritten" Project Card may be found in the AFFTC History Office dated 22 March 1956. The later card lists the requirements as "to provide exploratory data on the aerodynamic, structural, and physiological problems of manned flight at speeds up to 6,600 fps and at altitudes up to 250,000 feet." Interestingly, the designation was classified confidential until after the mockup was approved.
19. Letter, Hugh L. Dryden, Director of NACA, to Deputy Director of R&D DCS/D, USAF, no subject, 20 May 1955; letter, Rear Admiral Robert S. Hatcher, Assistant Chief of R&D, BuAer, USN, to Commander, WADC, subject: Agreements Reached by "Research Airplane Committee," on Evaluation Procedure for X-15 Research Airplane Proposals, 31 May 1955. In the files at the Navy History Center.
20. Hugh L. Dryden, "General Background of the X-15 Research Airplane Project" (a paper presented at the NACA Conference on the Progress of the X-15 Project, Langley Aeronautical Laboratory, 25-26 October 1956), pp. xvii-xix.
21. Author's note. Reading the Bell proposal and accompanying data, it is easy to see why the company was scored low in the evaluation that followed. Although it was readily apparent that Bell had a great deal of talent, the proposal never offered the reader a sense that they had their hands wrapped around the problem of building a hypersonic research aircraft. Almost every innovation they proposed was hedged in such a manner as to make the reader doubt that it would work. The proposal itself seemed rather poorly organized, and was internally inconsistent (i.e., weights and other figures frequently differed between sections). Coupled with the fact that the design appeared to be an attempt to build an operational aircraft instead of one intended to do research into the high-temperature structural environment, it is understandable that Bell placed lower than Douglas or North American.
22. Bell report D171-945-003, "X-15 Airplane Proposal Summary Report," 5 May 1955, p. 8; Bell report D171-945-004, "X-15 Research Airplane Proposal Aircraft Design Report," 6 May 1955, pp. 11-12.
23. Bell report D171-945-003, p. 8.
24. Ibid., pp. 9-10.
25. Bell report D171-945-004, pp. 15-16; Bell report D171-945-003, p. 14.
26. Bell report D171-945-003, p. 3 and 15.
27. Ibid., p. 16.
28. Ibid., pp. 17-18.
29. Ibid., p. 23.
30. Ibid., pp. 23-24.
31. Ibid., p. 23. Essentially, a "Pittsburgh" joint is made by folding a length of the edge of each of two pieces of sheet metal back upon itself (bending the sheet 180 degrees), and then with one sheet upside down relative to the other, sliding the folds together.
32. Ibid., pp. 27-29.
33. Ibid., pp. 29-30.
34. Ibid., p. 51.
35. Ibid., pp. 63-64.
36. Exactly why Bell thought this was an issue is not clear. The B-36 had a maximum bomb capacity of 84,000 pounds, not including several tons of 20mm cannon and ammunition, plus military electronics (radar, ECM, etc.), all of which would have been removed. The 34,000-pound research airplane – with or without a liquid oxygen top-off system – was hardly pushing the lifting ability of the bomber.
37. Bell report D171-945-003, pp. 65-66.
38. Ibid., pp. 57-58.
39. The information presented here came from the various Douglas proposal documents. See, for example: Douglas report ES-17926, "USAF Project 1226, Douglas Model 684 High Altitude Research Airplane," 20 May 1955; Douglas report ES-17918, "Strength Analysis and Criteria," 29 April 1955; Douglas report 19720, "Estimated Weight and Balance, Substantiation of Weights, and Moment of Inertia," 29 April 1955. All originally classified secret. All provided courtesy of Benjamin F. Guenther. For a slightly more in-depth look at the Douglas Model 684, see Dennis R. Jenkins, "The X-15 Research Airplane Competition: The Douglas Aircraft Proposal," *Aerospace Projects Review*, volume 4, number 2, March-April 2002, pp. 10-23.
40. Douglas report ES-17926, no page numbers.
41. Ibid.
42. Ibid.
43. The heat required to raise one unit of mass one degree of temperature.
44. Douglas report ES-17926.
45. Ibid.
46. Douglas report ES-17926. For additional information of the Bell X-2 see Jay Miller, *The X-Planes*, (Hinckley, England: Midland Publishing, 2001).
47. Ibid.
48. Ibid.
49. Ibid.
50. Ibid.
51. The information presented here came from the various North American proposal documents. See, for example: North American report NA-55-221, "X-15 Advanced Research Airplane Design Summary," 9 May 1955; North American report NA-55-223, "Preliminary Structural Data for a X-15 Research Aircraft, Project 1226 (NAA Designation ESO-7487), 13 May 1955; North American report NA-55-224, "Aerodynamic Characteristics Report for a X-15 Research Aircraft, Project 1226 (N.A.A. ESO-7487)," 9 May 1955; North American report NA-55-226, "Ground Handling Equipment and Procedures for a X-15 Research Aircraft, Project 1226 (NAA Designation ESO-7487)," 9 May 1955; North American report NA-55-227, "Carrier Modification Data for a X-15 Research Aircraft, Project 1226 (NAA Designation ESO-7487)," 9 May 1955; North American report NA-55-228, "Alighting Gear Data for a Research Airplane X-15 (NAA Designation ESO-7487)," 9 May 1955; North American report NA-55-229, "Space Control System Data for the X-15 Research Airplane (NAA Designation ESO-7487)," 9 May 1955; North American report NA-55-574, "Propulsion System Operation for a X-15 Research Aircraft, Project 1226 (NAA Designation ESO-7487)," 9 May 1955; North American report NA-55-577, "Structure Thermal Suitability Data for a X-15 Research Aircraft, Project 1226 (NAA Designation ESO-7487)," 9 May 1955. All originally classified secret. All provided courtesy of Benjamin F. Guenther.
52. North American report NA-55-221, pp. 1-2.
53. Ibid., pp. 1-2. Authors' note: As an engineer for several large aerospace companies working on NASA contracts, I both wrote and reviewed too many proposals over the years. Reading through the X-15 proposals, two things struck me. The Bell proposal (as mentioned in that section) was terrible – you walked away not entirely sure that Bell had committed themselves to the project. The exact opposite was true of the North American proposal. From the opening page you knew that North American understood what was trying to be accomplished with the X-15 program, and had attempted to design an airplane that would help accomplish the task – not just meet the performance specifications (which did not fully describe the intent of the program).
54. North American report NA-55-221, pp. 2 and 6.
55. Ibid., p. 9.
56. Ibid., pp. 10 and 12. It was later determined that this spacing was less than ideal to prevent hypersonic panel flutter, and additional stiffeners were added during the flight program. Initially the government was concerned over possible aero- and thermodynamic effects of the tunnels, but early wind tunnel studies helped North American reshape them slightly and they actually ended up providing beneficial lift.
57. North American report NA-55-577, pp. 30-31.
58. This caution should have been remembered during the design of the Apollo spacecraft.
59. North American report NA-55-577, p. 8; North American report NA-55-221, pp. 11 and 40.
60. Ibid., p. 14.
61. Other competitors bid all-moving horizontal stabilizers, but only North American proposed to operated them differentially ("rolling") for roll control instead of providing conventional ailerons.
62. North American report NA-55-229, pp. 1-5; North American report NA-55-221, pp. 2 and 19.
63. North American report NA-55-229, pp. 1-5; North American report NA-55-221, p. 19.
64. North American report NA-55-228, pp. 1-2; North American report NA-55-221, pp. 2 and 23.
65. Ibid.
66. North American report NA-55-221, pp. 44-45.
67. North American report NA-55-221, p. 39; North American report NA-55-227, pp. 1-2.
68. The information presented here came from the various Republic proposal documents. See, for example: Republic report ED-AP76-101, "Static and Dynamic Stability and Control for the Republic AP-76 Airplane," 6 May 1955; Republic report ED-AP76-200, "Estimated Weight and Balance and Mean Aerodynamic Chord for AP-76," 6 May 1955; Republic report ED-AP76-900, "Summary of Engineering Data for Republic AP-76 Research Airplane Under Project 1226 Competition," 6 May 1955; Republic report 55WCS-9231-A, "AP-76: Project 1226 Summary Brochure," 6 May 1955; Republic report 55WCS-9231-AA, "Preliminary Model Specification (ES-348): Republic Model AP-76 Research Airplane," 6 May 1955. All originally classified secret. All provided courtesy of Benjamin F. Guenther. For a slightly more in-depth look at the Republic AP-76, see Dennis R. Jenkins, "The X-15 Research Airplane Competition: The Republic Aviation Proposal," *Aerospace Projects Review*, volume 4, number 3, May-June 2002, pp. 3-19.
69. Republic report ED-AP76-900, pp. 10-11; Republic report 55WCS-9231-A, pp. 6-7, 20 and 40.
70. Republic report 55WCS-9231-AA, pp. 74-75; Republic report 55WCS-9231-A, p. 41.
71. Republic report ED-AP76-900, pp. 6-7 and 20.
72. Republic report 55WCS-9231-A, pp. 47-48.
73. Republic report ED-AP76-900, pp. 12-13; Republic report 55WCS-9231-A, pp. 20-21.
74. Republic report ED-AP76-900, p. 14; Republic report 55WCS-9231-A, pp. 6 and 23.
75. Republic report ED-AP76-900, p. 16; Republic report 55WCS-9231-A, p. 6.
76. Republic report ED-AP76-900, pp. 17 and 68; Republic report 55WCS-9231-AA, p. 23; for the landing data, see Wendell H. Stillwell, NACA Research Memorandum H54K24, "Results of Measurements Made During the Approach and Landing of Seven High-Speed Research Airplanes," 4 February 1955.
77. Ibid., pp. 52-53.
78. Ibid., pp. 50-53.
79. Ibid., pp. 10 and 14.
80. Letter, John L. Sloop/Lewis Evaluation Group to Hartley A. Soulé/Research Airplane Project Leader, no subject, 8 June 1955. See the various airframe proposals for descriptions of the engines selected. A copy of the Aerojet proposal could not be located.
81. Bell report 02-945-106, "Project 1226: X-15 Liquid Rocket Engine Proposal," secret, 25 February 1955. Courtesy of Benjamin F. Guenther.
82. Reaction Motors report TR-9405-C, "Rocket Engine for New Research Airplane," secret, 26 February 1955. Courtesy of Benjamin F. Guenther.
83. Letter, John L. Sloop/Lewis Evaluation Group to Hartley A. Soulé/Research Airplane Project Leader, no subject, 24 June 1955; letter, Clotaire Wood to William J. Underwood, no subject, 29 June 1955.
84. Letter, Walter C. Williams/HSFS Evaluation Group, to Hartley A. Soulé/Research Airplane Project Leader, no subject, 5 July 1955.
85. Letter, Clotaire Wood to Langley, no subject, 13 July 1955.
86. Air Force report RDZ-280, "Evaluation Report on X-15 Research Aircraft Design Competition," 5 August 1955. In the files at the Air Force Historical Research Agency.
87. Dryden, Kelsey, and Dixon were members of the Research Airplane Committee. Captain Dixon had replaced Rear Admiral Robert Hatcher when he retired.
88. Letter, North American to Commander/ARDC, no subject, 6 September 1955. In the files at the Boeing Archives.
89. Letter, Raymond H. Rice, Vice President and Chief Engineer/North American Aviation, to Commander/ARDC, no subject, 23 September 1955. In the files at the Boeing Archives. The WS-110A and WS-202A studies would eventually become the B-70 and F-108 programs, respectively. In addition, North American was in the midst of a major Navy competition that eventually resulted in the North American A3J (A-5) Vigilante. The YF-107A program was an indirect competitor to the Republic F-105 Thunderchief. The program had started as an improved F-100 Super Sabre in October 1953, and nine prototypes were ordered in August 1954. Only three were ever completed. The first YF-107A (55-5118) would not makes its maiden flight until 10 September 1956, at Edwards AFB with North American test pilot Bob Baker at the controls. The program was cancelled in February 1957.
90. Letter, Raymond H. Rice, Vice President and Chief Engineer/North American Aviation, to Commander/ARDC, subject: Project 1226, Research Airplane, 23 September 1955. In the files at the Boeing Archives.
91. X-15 WSPO Weekly Activity Report, 22 September 1955; letter, Colonel Carl F. Damberg, Chief, Aircraft Division, AMC, to North American Aviation, subject: X-15 Competition, 30 September 1955. In the files at the Air Force Historical Research Agency; letters, from Colonel Carl F. Damberg to Bell, Douglas, and Republic, no subject, 30 September 1955.
92. Memorandum, Arthur W. Vogeley to Hartley A. Soulé/Research Airplane Project Leader, no subject, 13 October 1955; letter, Major General Howell M. Estes, Jr., Assistant Deputy Commander for Weapons Systems/ARDC to Brigadier General J. Stanley Holtoner, Commander/AFFTC, no subject, 10 May 1957. In the files at the AFFTC History Office.
93. Air Force contract AF33(600)-31693.
94. As events later demonstrated, even this erred badly on the side of underestimation. The final fee paid to Reaction Motors was greater than the original estimate for the total engine development program; the definitive contract exceeded more than 20 times the original estimate, and more than twice the original total program approval estimate.
95. Air Force contract AF33(600)-32248; System Development Plan, X-15 Research Aircraft, Supporting Research System Number 447L, 22 March 1956. In the files at the AFFTC History Office.

Chapter 4 – The World's The Fastest Airplane

1. Letter, Scott Crossfield to Dennis R. Jenkins, 30 June 1999.
2. Harrison A. Storms, "X-15 Hardware Design Challenges" (a paper in the *Proceedings of the X-15 30th Anniversary Celebration*, Dryden Flight Research Facility, Edwards, California, 8 June 1989, NASA CP-3105), p. 33.
3. Ibid., p. 27.
4. The quote is from A. Scott Crossfield, *Always Another Dawn: The Story of a Rocket Test Pilot*, (New York: The World Publishing Company, 1960), p. 225. The book was republished, without change (North Stratford, NH: Ayer Company Publishers, 1999).
5. Letter, Scott Crossfield to Dennis R. Jenkins, 30 June 1999.
6. Harrison Storms, "The X-15 Rollout Symposium," 15 October 1958. Released statements. In the files at the AFFTC History Office.
7. Memorandum for the engineering files (HSFS), Walter C. Williams, 18 November 1955; memorandum, Hartley A. Soulé/Research Airplane Project Leader to the Members of the Project 1226 Evaluation Group, no subject, 7 December 1955; North American report NA-55-1237, "Supplementary Data X-15 Technical Evaluation Meeting," 22 November 1955, no page numbers.
8. Memorandum for the engineering files (HSFS), Walter C. Williams, 18 November 1955; memorandum, Hartley A. Soulé/Research Airplane Project Leader to the Members of the Project 1226 Evaluation Group, no subject, 7 December 1955; North American report NA-55-1237.
9. *Research Airplane Committee Report on the Conference on the Progress of the X-15 Project*, A Compilation of the Papers presented at the Langley Aeronautical Laboratory, 25-26 October 1956, pp. 23-31; letter, Colonel Carl F. Damberg to Bell, no subject, 30 Dec. 1954. In the files at the ASD History Office.
10. Lawrence P. Greene and Rolland L. Benner, "X-15 Experience from the Designer's Viewpoint," (a paper in the *Research Airplane Committee Report on the Conference on the Progress of the X-15 Project*, A Compilation of the Papers presented at the Flight Research Center, 20-21 November 1961), p. 321; memorandum for the engineering files (HSFS), Walter C. Williams, 18 November 1955; memorandum, Hartley A. Soulé/Research Airplane Project Leader to the Members of the Project 1226 Evaluation Group, 7 December 1955; North American report NA-55-1237.
11. North American report NA-55-1237.
12. Memorandum for the engineering files (HSFS), Walter C. Williams, 18 November 1955; memorandum, Hartley A. Soulé/Research Airplane Project Leader to the Members of the Project 1226 Evaluation Group, 7 December 1955; North American report NA-55-1237.
13. North American report NA-55-1237.
14. Joseph Weil, NASA technical note D-1278, "Review of the X-15 Program," June 1962, p. 7; telephone conversation, Charlie H. Feltz to Dennis R. Jenkins, 12 May 2002; telephone conversation, A. Scott Crossfield to Dennis R. Jenkins, 8 August 2002.
15. Memorandum, M. A. Todd, Acting Chief, Contractor Reporting and Bailment Branch, Support Division, to Chief, Fighter Branch, Aircraft Division, Director Procurement and Production, AMC, subject: Confirmation of Serial Numbers Assigned, 15 June 1956. In the files at the AFMC History Office.
16. Letter, Hugh L. Dryden, Director of NACA, to Chief, Fighter WSPO, ARDC, no subject, 6 July 1956. In the files at the NASA History Office.
17. *Research Airplane Committee Report on the Conference on the Progress of the X-15 Project*, A Compilation of the Papers presented at the Langley Aeronautical Laboratory, 25-26 October 1956, passim.
18. Herbert W. Riyard, Robert W. Dunning, and Edwin W. Johnston, "Aerodynamic Characteristics From Wind tunnel Studies of the X-15 Configuration," (a paper in the *Research Airplane Committee Report on the Conference on the Progress of the X-15 Project*, A Compilation of the Papers presented at the Langley Aeronautical Laboratory, 25-26 October 1956), pp. 39-56. The list of wind tunnels included the North American 8.75x11-foot tunnel, the Langley 8-foot transonic tunnel, the North American 16-inch tunnel, the Massachusetts Institute of Technology supersonic tunnel, the Langley 9x9-inch Mach 4 blowdown jet, the Ames 10x14-inch tunnel, and the Langley 11-inch hypersonic tunnel.
19. Dale L. Compton, "Welcome," (a paper in the *Proceedings of the X-15 30th Anniversary Celebration*, Dryden Flight Research Facility, Edwards, California, 8 June 1989, NASA CP-3105), p. 3. The free-flight tunnel at Ames had been conceived by H. Julian Allen and opened in 1949 at a cost of about $20,000. It had a test section 18 feet long, 1 foot wide, and 2 feet high. By forcing a flow through the tunnel at a speed of about Mach 3 and firing a model projectile upstream, velocities of up to Mach 18 could be simulated. Schlieren cameras were set up at seven locations long the test section, three on the side and four

on the top, to make shadowgraphs that showed the airflow over the models. The facility proved to be an important tool not only for the X-15 but also for Project Mercury.

20. Herbert W. Riyard, Robert W. Dunning, and Edwin W. Johnston, "Aerodynamic Characteristics From Wind tunnel Studies of the X-15 Configuration," (a paper in the *Research Airplane Committee Report on the Conference on the Progress of the X-15 Project*, A Compilation of the Papers presented at the Langley Aeronautical Laboratory, 25-26 October 1956), pp. 39-56.
21. Benjamin F. Guenther, "X-15 Research Airplane," an unpublished manuscript written in 1982. Supplied by Ben Guenther at Langley.
22. Ibid.
23. Report, "Development Engineering Inspection of the X-15 Research Aircraft – 13 December 1956," Director of Systems Management, ARDC. A "request for alteration" is the form used to request changes as the result of a mockup or engineering inspection within the Air Force.
24. Ibid.
25. Ibid.
26. Ibid.
27. Ibid.
28. Ibid.
29. Richard L. Schleicher, "Structural Design of the X-15," North American Aviation, 1963, pp. 13-14. In the files at the San Diego Aerospace Museum.
30. Ibid.
31. Ibid., p. 14.
32. I. J. Wilson, North American report NA58-973, "Forming and Fabrication Methods for the X-15 Airplane," 18 July 1958, no page numbers.
33. F. R. Kostoch, "X-15 Material and Process Development," (a paper in the *Research Airplane Committee Report on the Conference on the Progress of the X-15 Project*, A Compilation of the Papers presented in Los Angeles, California, 28-30 July 1958), p. 259.
34. I. J. Wilson, North American report NA58-973.
35. Ibid.
36. Ibid.
37. Ibid.
38. C. L. Davis, "X-15 Structure and Structural Development," (a paper in the *Research Airplane Committee Report on the Conference on the Progress of the X-15 Project*, A Compilation of the Papers presented in Los Angeles, California, 28-30 July 1958), p. 215.
39. Ibid., p. 216.
40. A. Scott Crossfield, *Always Another Dawn: The Story of a Rocket Test Pilot*, (New York: The World Publishing Company, 1960), p. 231.
41. J. F. Hegenwald, "Development of X-15 Escape System," (a paper in the *Research Airplane Committee Report on the Conference on the Progress of the X-15 Project*, A Compilation of the Papers presented in Los Angeles, California, 28-30 July 1958), p. 129; Crossfield, *Always Another Dawn*, p. 232.
42. Memorandum, Hartley A. Soulé/Research Airplane Project Leader to Members of the NACA Research Airplane Project Panel, 7 June 1956. In the files at the NASA History Office.
43. Crossfield, *Always Another Dawn*, pp. 232-233.
44. Jay Miller, *The X-Planes*, (Hinckley, England: Midland Publishing, 2001), pp. 62-67.
45. *Research Airplane Committee Report on the Conference on the Progress of the X-15 Project*, A Compilation of the Papers presented in Los Angeles, California, 28-30 July 1958. From the Table of Contents and List of Conferees.
46. Lawrence P. Greene, "X-15 Research Airplane Development Status," (a paper in the *Research Airplane Committee Report on the Conference on the Progress of the X-15 Project*, A Compilation of the Papers presented in Los Angeles, California, 28-30 July 1958), pp. 1-2.
47. Richard L. Schleicher, "Structural Design of the X-15," a paper presented to the Royal Aeronautical Society on 18 April 1963, and printed in the *Journal of the Royal Aeronautical Society*, Vol. 67, October 1963, pp. 618-636. In the files at the AFFTC Access to Space Office Project Files.
48. Crossfield, *Always Another Dawn*, pp. 263-264; telephone conversation, Charles H. Feltz to Dennis R. Jenkins, 12 May 2002.
49. De E. Beeler and Thomas A Toll, "Status of X-15 Research Program," (a paper in the *Research Airplane Committee Report on the Conference on the Progress of the X-15 Project*, A Compilation of the Papers presented at the Flight Research Center, 20-21 November 1961).
50. NASA has published several good looks into simulation during the X-15 period. See, for example, Gene L. Waltman, *Black Magic and Gremlins: Analog Flight Simulations at NASA's Flight Research Center*, NASA Monographs in Aerospace History No. 20, SP-2000-4520 (Washington D.C.: NASA, 2000) and John P. Smith, Lawrence J. Schilling and Charles A. Wagner, NASA technical memorandum 101695, "Simulation at Dryden Flight Research Facility from 1957 to 1982," February 1989; flight planner names remembered by Johnny G. Armstrong and William H. Dana, told to the author via email, April 2002.
51. Edward N. Videan, Richard D. Banner, and John P. Smith, "The Application of Analog and Digital Computer Techniques in the X-15 Flight Research Program," a paper presented at the International Symposium on Analog and Digital Techniques Applied to Aeronautics, 9-12 September 1963, pp. 2-3; Lieutenant Colonel Burt Rowen, "Human-Factors Support of the X-15 Program," *Air University Quarterly Review*, Air War College, Volume X, Number 4, Winter 1958-59, pp. 36-37; George B. Merrick and C. H. Woodling, "X-15 Flight Simulation Studies," (a paper in the *Research Airplane Committee Report on the Conference on the Progress of the X-15 Project*, A Compilation of the Papers presented in Los Angeles, California, 28-30 July 1958), pp. 94-96.
52. Rowen, "Human-Factors Support of the X-15 Program," pp. 36-37; Merrick and Woodling, "X-15 Flight Simulation Studies," pp. 94-98; letter, Robert G. Hoey/AFFTC Flight Planner to Dennis R. Jenkins, 20 May 2002, containing comments on a draft copy of this manuscript. The simulator was overly optimistic. In theory the X-15 could reach a maximum altitude of 700,000 feet; however, 550,000 feet represented the peak altitude from which a reentry could be made without exceeding the 7.33-g load factor or the 2,500 psf dynamic pressure limit. Thermal studies indicated that something around 550,000 feet would also be the limit from a thermodynamic perspective. See Johnson, "X-15 Structural Loads," p. 202.
53. Merrick and Woodling, "X-15 Flight Simulation Studies," p. 94.
54. Edward N. Videan, Richard D. Banner, and John P. Smith, "The Application of Analog and Digital Computer Techniques in the X-15 Flight Research Program," a paper presented at the International Symposium on Analog and Digital Techniques Applied to Aeronautics, 9-12 September 1963, pp. 3-4.
55. X-15 Status Report, Paul F. Bikle/FRC to H. Brown/NASA Headquarters, 13 January 1961, p. 2. In the files at the DFRC History Office; Jane Van Nimmen and Leonard C. Bruno, with Robert L. Rosholt, *NASA Historical Data Book, 1958-1968, Volume I: NASA Resources 1958-1968*, NASA SP-4012 (Washington DC: NASA, 1988) p. 300. Bob Hoey remembers that Day and Hoey generally traveled to Inglewood two or so days per week, accompanied by one of the initial pilots when the detailed flight planning was being finalized. The team often flew from the FRC to Inglewood in the NASA DC-3.
56. Gene L. Waltman, *Black Magic and Gremlins: Analog Flight Simulations at NASA's Flight Research Center*, NASA Monographs in Aerospace History No. 20, SP-2000-4520 (Washington D.C.: NASA, 2000), pp. 47-49.
57. Videan, Banner, and Smith, "The Application of Analog and Digital Computer Techniques in the X-15 Flight Research Program," pp. 2-3 and 14; Waltman, *Black Magic and Gremlins*, p. 52.
58. John P. Smith, Lawrence J. Schilling and Charles A. Wagner, NASA technical memorandum 101695, "Simulation at Dryden Flight Research Facility from 1957 to 1982," February 1989, p. 3.
59. Letter, Johnny G. Armstrong to Dennis R. Jenkins, 3 August 2002, containing comments to a draft copy of this manuscript.
60. Waltman, *Black Magic and Gremlins*, p. 56; Videan, Banner, and Smith, "The Application of Analog and Digital Computer Techniques in the X-15 Flight Research Program," p. 5.
61. The Naval Air Development Center (known as NADEVCEN at the time), Johnsville, Pennsylvania, was established after World War II to meet a growing need for research and development in naval aviation. In 1944, the Navy acquired the Brewster Aircraft plant located on approximately 370 acres of fairly level farmland in Bucks County, Pennsylvania, about midway between Philadelphia and Trenton, New Jersey. The Brewster facilities consisted of production shops and administration spaces covering over a million square feet plus the adjoining airfield and hangar spaces. The Navy designated the plant the Naval Air Modification Unit (NAMU), a branch of the Naval Air Materiel Center (NAMC) in Philadelphia. The NAMU converted and modified newly produced aircraft prior to delivery to the fleet for combat use. With the capitulation of the Axis powers, the need for NAMU vanished. But the growing need for a centralized research and development activity resulted in the redesignation of NAMU, effective 1 August 1947, as the Naval Air Development Station (NADS), an independent activity under the Bureau of Aeronautics. Activities from other parts of the country were transferred to NADS and expansion reached a significant juncture on 1 August 1949 when the Station was reorganized into a coordinated research and development activity known as the Naval Air Development Center. The mission of the NADEVCEN was expanded to include three laboratories: the Pilotless Aircraft Development Laboratory (PADL), the Aeronautical Electronic and Electrical Laboratory (AEEL), and the Aircraft Armament Laboratory (AAL). In July 1950, the Aeronautical Computer Laboratory (ACL) was added, first as a small engineering team, and later as a laboratory using the Typhoon Computer. At the time the Typhoon was the world's largest analog computer and was used for theoretical studies and analyses of missile flight and performance. The addition of an IBM Magnetic Drum Electronic Data Processing Machine (IBM 650) provided digital problem-solving techniques. Eventually the Typhoon was modernized by adding GALE A and B analog computers to provide a large, versatile hybrid facility. The Aviation Medical Acceleration Laboratory (AMAL) became a part of the Center on 17 June 1952. This laboratory was created to conduct research into aviation medicine. It soon began supporting space medicine and dynamic flight simulation studies involving the X-15. See http://www.resuba.com/wa3dsp/k3nal/nadchistory1.html for additional history of NADC Johnsville.
62. http://www.vnh.org/FSManual/AppendixA.html, accessed on 8 February 2002.
63. Carl C. Clark, "Centrifugal Simulation of the X-15," (a paper in the *Research Airplane Committee Report on the Conference on the Progress of the X-15 Project*, A Compilation of the Papers presented in Los Angeles, California, 28-30 July 1958), pp. 107-108.
64. James D. Hardy and Carl C. Clark, "The Development of Dynamic Flight Simulation," *Aero/Space Engineering*, Volume 18, Number 6, June 1959, pp. 48-52; James E. Love, "History and Development of the X-15 Research Aircraft," not dated. In the files at the DFRC History Office, p. 10.
65. Hardy and Clark, "The Development of Dynamic Flight Simulation," pp. 48-52. A petechiae is a small skin hemorrhage.
66. Ibid.
67. Clark, "Centrifugal Simulation of the X-15," p. 108.
68. Clark, "Centrifugal Simulation of the X-15," p. 108; James E. Love, "History and Development of the X-15 Research Aircraft," not dated. In the files at the DFRC History Office, p. 10; Robert G. Hoey, "Riding 'The Wheel'," in Fred Stoliker, Bob Hoey, and Johnny Armstrong, *Flight Testing at Edwards: Flight Test Stories – 1946-1975*, (Edwards, CA: Flight Test Historical Foundation, 2001), pp. 166-167; letter, Robert G. Hoey to Dennis R. Jenkins, 20 May 2002. There is some disagreement in the numbers. Wendell H. Stillwell, *X-15 Research Results*, NASA SP-60, (Washington DC: NASA, 1965) indicates that over 400 dynamic flights were conducted during this initial series of tests. Harrison Storms ("The X-15 Rollout Symposium," 15 October 1958) supplied the numbers used here, and these are also contained in the Clark paper. Bob Hoey would later talk his way into a ride on "The Wheel" during centrifuge simulations for the X-20 Dyna-Soar program.
69. Clark, "Centrifugal Simulation of the X-15," pp. 109-110.
70. Ibid.
71. Letter, Robert G. Hoey to Dennis R. Jenkins, 20 May 2002; Clark, "Centrifugal Simulation of the X-15," pp. 109-110.
72. Hardy and Clark, "The Development of Dynamic Flight Simulation," pp. 48-52; http://www.vnh.org/FSManual/AppendixA.html, accessed on 8 February 2002.
73. Cost projections, Contract AF33(600)-31693, prepared quarterly by North American Aviation Department of Pricing, 1955-59. In the files at the Boeing Archives; interview, Captain Chester E. McCollough, Jr., Assistant Chief, X-15 WSPO, Director of Systems Management, ARDC, 12 June 1959, by Robert S. Houston, History Branch, WADC. Written transcript in the files at the AFMC History Office; James E. Love and William R. Young, NASA technical note D-3732, 10 August 1966, p. 6.
74. Interview, Captain Chester E. McCollough, Jr., Assistant Chief, X-15 WSPO, Director of Systems Management, ARDC, 12 June 1959, by Robert S. Houston, History Branch, WADC. Written transcript in the files at the AFMC History Office; James E. Love and William R. Young, NASA technical note D-3732, 10 August 1966, p. 6.
75. James E. Love and William R. Young, "Operational Experience of the X-15 Airplane as a Reusable Vehicle System," a paper presented at the SAE Second Annual Space Technology Conference, Palo Alto, California, 9-11 may 1967, p. 3; Love and Young, "Survey of Operation and Cost Experience of the X-15 Airplane as a Reusable Space Vehicle," p. 6. The cost of the MH-96 was just that portion charged to the X-15 program; other parts were paid for by the Dyna-Soar program.
76. [signed W.T.G.] "X-15: The World's Fastest and Highest-Flying Aeroplane," *Flight*, 8 May 1959; James E. Love and William R. Young, "Operational Experience of the X-15 Airplane as a Reusable Vehicle System," a paper presented at the SAE Second Annual Space Technology Conference, Palo Alto, California, 9-11 may 1967, p. 3; Love and Young, "Survey of Operation and Cost Experience of the X-15 Airplane as a Reusable Space Vehicle," p. 6. The numbers vary widely, with some as high as $160 million between FY55 and FY60. The $121.5 million figure is the one that is most often used by sources that are considered reliable.

Chapter 5 – The High Range and Dry Lakes

1. http://www.edwards.af.mil/history/docs_html/center/pre-military_history.html, accessed 25 January 2002. For additional history of the area see Michael H. Gorn, *Expanding the Envelope: Flight Research at NACA and NASA*, (Lexington, Kentucky: The University Press of Kentucky, 2001).
2. http://www.edwards.af.mil/history/docs_html/center/pre-military_history.html, accessed 25 January 2002. Despite its usage, legal title for the land did not pass to the Army until 1939.
3. Ibid. The Army Air Forces superseded the Army Air Corps on 20 June 1941.
4. http://www.edwards.af.mil/history/docs_html/center/flight_evolution.html, accessed 25 January 2002.
5. http://www.edwards.af.mil/history/docs_html/center/lakebeds.html, accessed 25 January 2002; Gorn, *Expanding the Envelope*, p. 204.
6. http://www.dfrc.nasa.gov/Dryden/mistone.html accessed on 25 January 2002. Many sources say that 13 personnel arrived on 30 September, but DFRC Historian J.D. Hunley says only 5 (Williams, Cloyce E. Matheny, William S. Aiken, George P. Minalga, and Harold B. Youngblood) arrived on this date and the total of 13 was not reached until early December.
7. Jane Van Nimmen and Leonard C. Bruno, with Robert L. Rosholt, *NASA Historical Data Book, 1958-1968, Volume I: NASA Resources 1958-1968*, NASA SP-4012 (Washington DC: NASA, 1988), pp. 297-298; http://www.dfrc.nasa.gov/Dryden/mistone.html accessed on 25 January 2002.
8. http://www.dfrc.nasa.gov/Dryden/mistone.html accessed on 25 January 2002.
9. Richard P. Hallion, *On the Frontier: Flight Research at Dryden, 1946-1981*, NASA SP-4303, (Washington DC: NASA, 1984), p. 101. Within the NACA, the pecking order was headquarters, the research laboratories, and then the stations. NASA maintained a similar cast system, calling them centers and facilities instead. Robert L. Rosholt, *An Administrative History of NASA, 1958-1963*, NASA SP-4101 (Washington DC: NASA, 1966), p. 79.
10. Hallion, *On the Frontier*, p. 101.
11. Letter, Brigadier General Benjamin S. Kelsey, Director for Research and Development DCS/D, USAF, to Director of the NACA, no subject, 7 April 1955; letter, Dryden to Deputy Director for Research and Development, no subject, 20 May 1955. In the files at the NASA History Office.
12. Letter, Gerald M. Truszynski to Dennis R. Jenkins, 9 May 2002; memorandum, John L. Sloop/HSFS to Hartley A. Soulé/Research Airplane Project Leader, no subject, 7 November 1955; memorandum for the files (HSFS), unsigned, 10 November 1955. Gerry Truszynski had arrived at Muroc in 1947 and remained there until mid-1960 when he left to join the Office of Space Flight Operations in the Space Sciences Directorate at NASA Headquarters. This organization later became the Office of Tracking and Data Acquisition, with Truszynski as its chief; the group's primary legacy was the development of the Mercury tracking and communications network.
13. Letter, Hartley A. Soulé/Research Airplane Project Leader, to NACA Liaison Officer, WPAFB, subject: Air Force-North American-NACA conference on Project 1226 Range, 20 December 1955; System Development Plan, X-15 Research Aircraft, Supporting Research System Number 447L, 22 March 1956; Engineering Plan, Project High Range, Electronic Engineering Company of California, not dated (but probably late 1956). In the files at the AFFTC History Office; Walter C. Williams, "X-15 Concept Evolution" (a paper in the *Proceedings of the X-15 30th Anniversary Celebration*, Dryden Flight Research Facility, Edwards, California, 8 June 1989, NASA CP-3105), p. 14; R&D Project Card, Project 1876 (part of Project 1226), 27 March 1956. The EECo contract was AF04(611)-1703. The range appears to have had two official names. The NACA called it the High Altitude Continuous Tracking Range; the Air Force referred to it as the X-15 Radar Range. Fortunately, both agreed on the "short term" of High Range.
14. X-15 WSPO Weekly Activity Report, 21 June 1956; "Advanced development Plan for X-15 Research Aircraft, Advanced Technology Program 653A," 17 November 1961, pp. 19-20. In the files at the AFFTC History Office; Jane Van Nimmen and Leonard C. Bruno, with Robert L. Rosholt, *NASA Historical Data Book, 1958-1968, Volume I: NASA Resources 1958-1968*, NASA SP-4012 (Washington DC: NASA, 1988) p. 300. The Air Force paid for the construction of the physical facilities, radar equipment, roads, and the communication system; the NACA paid for procurement of the telemetry systems, consoles, recorders, strip charts, and other items of "instrumentation." Ely cost $2,688,000; Beatty cost $2,122,000 according to the Data Book.
15. "Engineering Plan, Project High Range," Electronic Engineering Company of California, not dated (but probably late 1956), pp. 2-1 through 2-7. In the files at the AFFTC History Office; "X-15 Range Facility," prepared by the NASA Flight Research Facility, November 1959. In the files at the DFRC History Office.
16. "Engineering Plan," p. 2-8. In the files at the AFFTC History Office. VABM (vertical angle bench mark) is a USGS accuracy code that provides a standardization of observed gravity precision, elevation control, and latitude and longitude control. It was also the nearest name on the map to the desired location.
17. "Engineering Plan," pp. 2-8 and 2-9.
18. "Engineering Plan," pp. 2-9 through 2-10, 3-4, and 3-10 to 3-11.
19. "Engineering Plan," pp. 2-10 through 2-11.
20. "Engineering Plan," pp. 2-12 and 3-8 to 3-9.
21. "Engineering Plan," p. 2-3; "X-15 Range Facility," prepared in November 1959. In the files at the DFRC History Office; email, Jack Kittrell to Dennis R. Jenkins, 16 August 2002. The Atlantic Missile Range became the Eastern Test Range, and is now known as the Eastern Range. It stretches from Cape Canaveral, Florida to Ascension Island in the South Atlantic and has been host to all U.S. manned space missions as well as thousands of unmanned launches.
22. "Engineering Plan," pp. 4-21 through 4-23; "X-15 Range Facility."
23. "X-15 Range Facility."
24. "Engineering Plan," p. 6-3; "X-15 Range Facility."
25. "Engineering Plan," pp. 6-5 through 6-6.
26. "Engineering Plan," pp. 6-8 through 6-11.
27. "Engineering Plan," pp. 6-12 through 6-14.
28. "Engineering Plan," pp. 6-12 through 6-14.
29. "Engineering Plan," pp. 6-14 through 6-17.
30. X-15 Status Reports, Paul F. Bikle/FRC to J. Martin/NASA Headquarters, 4 April 1967, p. 6 and 5 May 1967, p. 5. Both in the files at the DFRC History Office; telephone conversation, Jack Kittrell with Dennis R. Jenkins, 1 August 2002. The MPS-19 at Ely was replaced by an FPQ-5 in the early 1970s when the site was transferred to Air Force control.
31. Robert G. Hoey and Richard E. Day, "X-15 Mission Planning and Operational Procedures," (a paper in the *Research Airplane Committee Report on the Conference on the Progress of the X-15 Project*, A Compilation of the Papers presented at the Flight Research Center, 20-21 November 1961), pp. 155-157; letter, Johnny Armstrong to Dennis R. Jenkins, 5 July 2002, containing comments to a draft copy of this manuscript.
32. For those who care about such things, the longitude and latitude of the lakes are:

Cuddeback Lake, California	117.5 W	35.3 N
Delamar Dry Lake, Nevada	114.9 W	37.4 N
Hidden Hills, California	116.0 W	36.0 N

Lancaster (Fox Field), California	118.2 W	34.8 N
Mud Lake, California 117.1 W	37.9 N	
Palmdale OMNI, California	118.1 W	34.6 N
Railroad Valley Lake, Nevada	116.0 W	38.0 N
Rogers Dry Lake, California	117.8 W	34.9 N
Rosamond Dry Lake, California	118.1 W	34.8 N
Silver Lake, California 116.1 W	35.3 N	
Smith Ranch Lake, Nevada	117.5 W	39.3 N

33. Wendell H. Stillwell, *X-15 Research Results*, NASA SP-60, (Washington DC: NASA, 1965); http://www.edwards.af.mil/history/docs_html/center/lakebeds.html, accessed 25 January 2002. Rogers Dry Lake has been declared a National Historic Landmark by the National Park Service because of its role in the development of the nation's space program, and has also been used since 1977 as the landing site for many Space Shuttle test and operational flights.
34. The expected first-use date is contained in a letter, Colonel Carl A. Ousley, Chief of Project Control Office at AFFTC, to Richard J. Harer, AFFTC, 17 February 1958. In the AFFTC Access to Space Office Project Files; Various letters from John J. Shipley, Chief of the Real Estate Division, Los Angles District of the Army Corps of Engineers, to the Commander, George AFB, the Bureau of Land Management, and the AFFTC, dated 17 and 20 May 1957. In the AFFTC Access to Space Office Project Files.
The original public domain includes the land ceded to the Federal Government by the Thirteen Original States, supplemented with acquisitions from Native Indians and foreign powers. It encompasses major portions of the land area of 30 western States. All lands in the public domain are established and regulated by the Bureau of Land Management, although control may pass to other government agencies (the military, etc.) as stipulated in various laws (see U.S. Code Title 43 for example). At the time, the Army Corps of Engineers acted as the land management agent for the U.S. Air Force.
35. Letter, Colonel Carl A. Ousley, Chief of Project Controls/AFFTC to distribution (internal AFFTC codes), 17 February 1958. In the AFFTC Access to Space Office Project Files; Disposition Form (DD96), Colonel Carl A. Ousley, Chief of Project Controls/AFFTC to Phyllis R. Actis, also at AFFTC, requesting she make contact with George AFB, 26 September 1957; Reply to Colonel Carl A. Ousley from Major John W. Young, Jr., AFFTC, 16 October 1957. In the AFFTC Access to Space Office Project Files.
36. Disposition Form (DD96), Lieutenant Colonel Donald J. Iddins, Acting Deputy Chief of Staff, AFFTC, to Mrs. Phyllis R. Actis, also at AFFTC, 30 January 1958; letter, Colonel Carl A. Ousley, Chief of Project Controls/AFFTC to distribution (internal AFFTC codes), 17 February 1958; memorandum for the record, Phyllis R. Actis, Planning Specialist, 17 February 1958; memorandum for the Chief of Engineers, Department of the Army, not signed or dated (but received in the files on 19 February 1958). All in the AFFTC Access to Space Office Project Files.
37. Disposition Form (DD96), Lieutenant Colonel Donald J. Iddins, Acting Deputy Chief of Staff/ AFFTC, to Mrs. Phyllis R. Actis, also at AFFTC, 30 January 1958; letter from Colonel Carl A. Ousley, Chief of Project Controls at AFFTC to distribution (internal AFFTC codes), 17 February 1958; memorandum for the record, Phyllis R. Actis, Planning Specialist, 17 February 1958; memorandum for the Chief of Engineers, Department of the Army, not signed or dated (but received in the files on 19 February 1958). All in the AFFTC Access to Space Office Project Files. The Corps of Engineers was responsible for acquiring the land from the landowners, but the Air Force was still expected to pay for it since it was required for AFFTC use.
38. Disposition Form (DD96)/ Lieutenant Colonel Donald J. Iddins, Acting Deputy Chief of Staff/AFFTC, to Mrs. Phyllis R. Actis, also at AFFTC, 30 January 1958; letter from Colonel Carl A. Ousley, Chief of Project Controls/AFFTC to distribution (internal AFFTC codes), 17 February 1958; memorandum for the record, Phyllis R. Actis, Planning Specialist, 17 February 1958; memorandum for the Chief of Engineers, Department of the Army, not signed or dated (but received in the files on 19 February 1958). All in the AFFTC Access to Space Office Project Files.
39. Memorandum of Understanding Between the Air Force Flight Test Center and Sandia Corporation, undated. In the AFFTC Access to Space Office Project Files.
40. Memorandum for the Record, Captain Byron E. Hanes, First Lieutenant John T. Craddock, and Glendon Johnson, AFFTC, 10 November 1958. In the AFFTC Access to Space Office Project Files.
41. Memorandum for the Record, Captain Byron E. Hanes, First Lieutenant John T. Craddock, and Glendon Johnson, AFFTC, 10 November 1958. In the AFFTC Access to Space Office Project Files. Other documentation says that the ball weighed 17 pounds, 9 ounces and was 5 inches in diameter. Many of those involved referred to this as the "imperial ball."
42. Email, Clarence E. "Bud" Anderson to Dennis R. Jenkins, 28 January 2002; Trip Report, Colonel Clarence E. Anderson/Chief of the Flight Test Operations Division/AFFTC, 17 July 1959. In the AFFTC Access to Space Office Project Files. The Helio L-28 Super Courier was redesignated U-10A in 1962.
43. Letter, Colonel Roger B. Phelan/AFFTC to Administrator, 4th Region, FAA, 24 July 1959, subject: Proposed X-15 Operation Involving Controlled Airspace in the Vicinity of Silver Lake, California; letter, R. D. Freeland, Chief General Operations Brach, 4th Region, FAA, to Colonel Roger B. Phelan, AFFTC, 29 July 1959.
44. Letter, Colonel Roger B. Phelan/AFFTC to Administrator, 4th Region, FAA, 24 July 1959, subject: Proposed X-15 Operation Involving Controlled Airspace in the Vicinity of Silver Lake, California.
45. Letter, L. N. Lightbody/FAA to Colonel Roger B. Phelan/AFFTC, 1 September 1959. In the files at the AFFTC History Office.
46. Letter, Richard J. Harer AFFTC to Phyllis R. Actis, AFFTC, 3 May 1960, subject: Hidden Hills Dry Lake Right-To-Use Permit.
47. Memorandum for Record, Richard J. Harer, Chairman X-15 Operations Committee, 4 October 1960.
48. The CIA-Lockheed A-12 Blackbird would arrive at Groom Lake in early 1962.
49. Memorandum, Colonel Guy M. Townsend, AFFTC Deputy for Systems Test to Phyllis R. Actis, Planning Specialist, 10 May 1965, subject: Land Requirements for Flight Test of the Advanced X-15. In the AFFTC Access to Space Office Project Files.
50. Ibid.
51. Johnny G. Armstrong, AFFTC technology document FTC-TD-69-4, "Flight Planning and Conduct of the X-15A-2 Envelope Expansion Program, July 1969, pp. 13-15; Johnny G. Armstrong, AFFTC Flight Research Division office memorandum AV-64-4, "Geographical Impact Areas for the X-15A-2 Drop Tanks," 22 July 1964. In the AFFTC Access to Space Office Project Files
52. Memorandum, Colonel Guy M. Townsend/AFFTC Deputy for Systems Test to Phyllis R. Actis, Planning Specialist, 10 May 1965, Land Requirements for Flight Test of the Advanced X-15; Johnny G. Armstrong, AFFTC Flight Research Division memorandum AV-65-6, "Emergency Lake Coverage for Flights of the X-15A-2 with External Tanks," April 1965, p. 5. Both in the AFFTC Access to Space Office Project Files.
53. Letter, Paul F. Bikle/FRC to Commander/AFFTC, subject: Rogers Lake Runway Markings for X-15 Flights, 21 October 1960.
54. Milton O. Thompson, *At the Edge of Space: The X-15 Flight Program*, (Washington and London: Smithsonian Institution Press, 1992), pp. 51-52.
55. Ibid., p. 52. The NASA DC-3 was really a former Navy R4D, which was the Navy equivalent of the Army/Air Force C-47.
56. Thompson, *At the Edge of Space*, p. 152.

Chapter 6 – Carrier and Support Aircraft

1. Contrary to many sources, the basic X-15s did not carry an "A" suffix (i.e, they were "X-15" not "X-15A"), even after the 1962 DoD redesignation effort. During the 1950s it was not unusual for the first development model of an aircraft to not carry a suffix (e.g., YF-102, YF-105, etc.). The "A" was applied to the first major modification of the design, in this case the rebuilt X-15A-2. It should also be noted that according to the DoD designation system, the number after the designation was normally reserved for a "production block" number that was used to track minor changes on the production line. In the case of the X-15 that was not strictly true, and each airplane was simply numbered sequentially. The X-15 designation was also written without the manufacturer abbreviation normally used in Air Force designations, so it never appeared as X-15-NA-1, but always as X-15-1.
2. System Development Plan, X-15 Research Aircraft, Supporting Research System Number 447L, 22 March 1956, p. 19. In the files at the AFFTC History Office; Lawrence P. Greene, "Summary of Pertinent Problems and Current Status of the X-15 Airplane" (a paper presented at the NACA Conference on the Progress of the X-15 Project, Langley Aeronautical Laboratory, 25-26 October 1956), p. 250; Captain Charles C. Bock, Jr., "B-52/X-15 Flight Operations," undated (but probably late 1958). In the files at the AFFTC History Office.
3. North American report NA-55-221, "X-15 Advanced Research Airplane Design Summary," 9 May 1955, p. 35; North American report NA-55-227, "Carrier Modification Data for a X-15 Research Aircraft, Project 1226 (NAA Designation ESO-7487)," 9 May 1955, pp. 3-9. The fourth competitor – Douglas – used a Boeing B-50.
4. The operational FICONs at Fairchild AFB used a large pit where the RF-84K was parked, then the GRB-36D was towed over the pit and the fighter hoisted into position. All other sites – mainly Edwards AFB and the Convair plant in Fort Worth – used a large set of ramps. The B-36 was towed up the ramps and the fighter was then towed under the B-36 and raised into position. Interestingly, the Air Force also investigated removing the vertical from the F-84, but this was more in case the mated pair landed at a site not equipped with either normal method and it was imperative to remove the F-84 for some reason. For more information on FICON, see Dennis R. Jenkins, *Magnesium Overcast: The Story of the Convair B-36*, (North Branch, MN: Specialty Press, 2001).
5. North American report NA-55-221, p. 35; North American report NA-55-227, pp. 3-9.
6. The B-36 had four bomb bays, but there was no permanent structure separating Nos. 1 and 2, or Nos. 3 and 4. In each case a removable bulkhead separated the bays – this allowed large bombs to be carried without structural changes. There was a bulkhead between Nos. 2 and 3, but since the wing carry-through structure was immediately above this bulkhead, removing it did not seriously compromise the structural integrity of the airplane.
7. North American report NA-55-227, pp. 10-12.
8. North American report NA-55-221, p. 38.
9. North American report NA-55-227, pp. 15-19.
10. Harrison A. Storms, "X-15 Hardware Design Challenges" (a paper in the *Proceedings of the X-15 30th Anniversary Celebration*, Dryden Flight Research Facility, Edwards, California, 8 June 1989, NASA CP-3105), p. 27; Captain Charles C. Bock, Jr., "B-52/X-15 Flight Operations," undated (but probably late 1958). In the files at the AFFTC History Office.
11. Based upon the performance parameters specified in the Douglas study, the B-52 was the most likely platform.
12. Memorandum, Neil A. Armstrong to Walter C. Williams, subject: Visit to Convair, Fort Worth, on 22 January 1957, to discuss possible utilization of a B-58 aircraft as a research vehicle launcher, 31 January 1957.
13. Captain Charles C. Bock, Jr., "B-52/X-15 Flight Operations," undated (but probably late 1958). In the files at the AFFTC History Office.
14. Contract Change Notice No. 11, "Replacement of a B-52 Airplane in lieu of a B-36 for use as X-15 Carrier Airplane, 30 August 1957; Bock, Jr., "B-52/X-15 Flight Operations;" letter, Harrison A. Storms/North American Aviation, to Commander/Air Materiel Command, subject: Contract AF-31693, Modification of B-52A For Use as X-15 Carrier Airplane, 28 June 1957. In the files at the AFFTC History Office.
15. Letter, Harrison A. Storms/North American, to Commander/Air Materiel Command, subject: Contract AF-31693, Modification of B-52A For Use as X-15 Carrier Airplane, 28 June 1957. In the files at the AFFTC History Office; Gene J. Matranga, unpublished NASA technical report, "Launch Characteristics of the X-15 Research Airplane as Determined in Flight," undated but sometime in May 1960. In the AFFTC Access to Space Office Project Files; Lawrence P. Greene, "X-15 Research Airplane Development Status," (a paper in the *Research Airplane Committee Report on the Conference on the Progress of the X-15 Project*, A Compilation of the Papers presented in Los Angeles, California, 28-30 July 1958), p. 4; William J. Alford, Jr., and Robert T. Taylor, "Aerodynamic Characteristics of the X-15/B-52 Combination," (a paper in the *Research Airplane Committee Report on the Conference on the Progress of the X-15 Project*, A Compilation of the Papers presented in Los Angeles, California, 28-30 July 1958), p. 69.
16. Greene, "X-15 Research Airplane Development Status," p. 4. No other reference could be found that indicated ejection was possible in the mated configuration; the flight manual states that the X-15 will be dropped and then the pilot would eject, although this obviously would not help during an emergency on the take-off roll or shortly after rotation. The X-15 pilots, however, remember that ejection was possible while still attached to the NB-52.
17. Letter, Harrison A. Storms/North American, to Commander/Air Materiel Command, subject: Contract AF-31693, Modification of B-52A For Use as X-15 Carrier Airplane, 28 June 1957. In the files at the AFFTC History Office; Gene J. Matranga, unpublished NASA technical report, "Launch Characteristics of the X-15 Research Airplane as Determined in Flight," undated but sometime in May 1960. In the AFFTC Access to Space Office Project Files The change from the left wing to the right wing happened sometime between June 1957 and June 1958, but exactly when could not be determined. The wind tunnel models were eventually updated for continued testing, but the initial tests were not repeated.
18. Bock, Jr., "B-52/X-15 Flight Operations;" various B-52 history cards and reports in the files at the Boeing Archives.
19. The "N" designation indicated that the aircraft had undergone permanent modifications to a non-standard configuration. Some sources show this as an NRB-52B, which would have been correct. However, the RB-52 configuration did not actually change anything substantial on the aircraft other than adding a capability to carry a self-contained reconnaissance capsule in the bomb bay. The Strategic Air Command quickly decided that they had little use for the RB-52s and all were subsequently redesignated B-52. The reconnaissance capability was deleted from future procurements.
20. Procurement Specification Amendment No. 1 to specification NA57-802, "Procurement Specification, Carrier Airplane Modification Program, X-15 Research Aircraft, 19 September 1957; letter, Harrison A. Storms/North American, to Commander/ARDC, subject: Contract AF33(600)-31693, X-15 Research Airplane, Revision – Procurement and Model Specification, 7 November 1957; North American report NA-58-824D, "Operating and Maintenance Instructions for B-52A Carrier Airplane AF52003 and B-52B Carrier Airplane AF52008," 15 May 1959 (changed 18 August 1961), pp. 1-1 through 1-24C. Copy courtesy of Mick Roth; Bock, Jr., "B-52/X-15 Flight Operations;" Captain John E. Allavie, Captain Charles C. Bock, Jr., and First Lieutenant Charles E. Adolph, AFFTC report TR-60-33, "Flight Evaluation of the B-52 Carrier Aircraft for the X-15," September 1960. In the AFFTC Access to Space Office Project Files.; internal letter (North American Rockwell), Charles C. Bock, Jr., to G. Boswell, subject: B-52 and X-15 Launch Programs, 12 November 1973; letter, Charles C. Bock, Jr., to Dennis R. Jenkins, 20 May 2002, containing comments on a draft copy of this manuscript.
21. Procurement Specification Amendment No. 1 to specification NA57-802, "Procurement Specification, Carrier Airplane Modification Program, X-15 Research Aircraft, 19 September 1957; letter, Harrison A. Storms/North American, to Commander/ARDC, subject: Contract AF33(600)-31693, X-15 Research Airplane, Revision – Procurement and Model Specification, 7 November 1957; letter, Walter C. Williams, to Commander/ARDC, subject: Modification of B-52A airplane for use as X-15 carrier airplane, 6 August 1957. Both In the files at the DFRC History Office.
22. The GAM-77 was a large jet-powered cruise missile that was originally designated B-77; later redesignated AGM-28. Specially modified B-52s could carry a single Hound Dog on a pylon under each wing in a location very similar to where the X-15 pylon was mounted.
23. Bock, Jr., "B-52/X-15 Flight Operations;" Boeing report D3-2121, "B-52/X-15 Ground Vibration Test," 29 January 1959. In the files at the DFRC History Office.
24. Gareth H. Jordan, Normal J. McLeod, and Lawrence D. Guy, "Structural Dynamic Experiences of the X-15," (a paper in the *Research Airplane Committee Report on the Conference on the Progress of the X-15 Project*, A Compilation of the Papers presented at the Flight Research Center, 20-21 November 1961), pp. 48-49 (this was later republished as NASA technical note D-1158, March 1962); Bock, Jr., "B-52/X-15 Flight Operations."
25. Bock, Jr., "B-52/X-15 Flight Operations;" Harry L. Runyan an Harold R. Sweet, "Flutter, Noise, and Buffet Problems Related to the X-15," (a paper in the *Research Airplane Committee Report on the Conference on the Progress of the X-15 Project*, A Compilation of the Papers presented in Los Angeles, California, 28-30 July 1958), pp. 235-236; Jordan, McLeod, and Guy, "Structural Dynamic Experiences of the X-15," pp. 48-49.
26. Bock, Jr., "B-52/X-15 Flight Operations." Around Edwards the two NB-52s were known by the last three digits of their tail numbers. Sometimes they were referred to as "balls three" (or eight), "double-balls three," or simply "zero-zero-three."
27. Bock, Jr., "B-52/X-15 Flight Operations."
28. Ibid.
29. Ibid.
30. Ibid.
31. Ibid.
32. Jordan, McLeod, and Guy, "Structural Dynamic Experiences of the X-15," pp. 48-49.
33. Bock, "B-52/X-15 Flight Operations;" Allavie, Bock, and Adolph, "Flight Evaluation of the B-52 Carrier Aircraft for the X-15," p. 6.
34. Bock, "B-52/X-15 Flight Operations;" Allavie, Bock, and Adolph, "Flight Evaluation of the B-52 Carrier Aircraft for the X-15," p. 7; telephone conversations with John E. Allavie and Robert M. White to Dennis R. Jenkins, various dates in May and June 2002.
35. Bock, "B-52/X-15 Flight Operations;" Allavie, Bock, and Adolph, "Flight Evaluation of the B-52 Carrier Aircraft for the X-15," p. 9.
36. Ibid., p. 8.
37. Gene J. Matranga, unpublished NASA technical report, "Launch Characteristics of the X-15 Research Airplane as Determined in Flight," undated but sometime in May 1960. In the AFFTC Access to Space Office Project Files; North American report NA-67-344, "Technical Proposal for a Conceptual Design Study for the Modification of an X-15 Air Vehicle to a Hypersonic Delta-Wing Configuration," 17 May 1967, volume I, pp. 39-40. In the files at the JSC History Office.
38. X-15 Status Report, Paul F. Bikle/FRC to J. Martin/NASA Headquarters, 2 June 1965, p. 2; Major William J. "Pete" Knight, "Increased Piloting Tasks and Performance of X-15A-2 in Hypersonic Flight," *The Aeronautical Journal of the Royal Aeronautical Society*, Volume 72, September 1968, pp. 793-802 (derived from a lecture given to the Test Pilot's Group of the Society on 30 January 1968).
39. North American report TFD-66-208, "XB-70/X-15" (undated, but obviously 1966); various emails, Michael J. Lombardi/Boeing Historian to Dennis R. Jenkins, May and June 2002 confirming the report could not be located in the Boeing archives. It also could not be located in the Dryden archives, National Archives, Air Force Historical Research Agency, or any of the major aerospace museums. For more information on the crash of the M-21, see Dennis R. Jenkins, *Lockheed SR-71/YF-12 Blackbird*, (North Branch, MN: WarbirdTech Series Volume 10, Specialty Press, 1999), p. 50-52.
40. Letter, Johnny G. Armstrong to Dennis R. Jenkins, 5 July 2002, with comments to a draft version of this manuscript.
41. Major Robert M. White, Glenn H. Robinson, and Gene J. Matranga, "Résumé of X-15 Handling Qualities," (a paper in the *Research Airplane Committee Report on the Conference on the Progress of the X-15 Project*, A Compilation of the Papers presented at the Flight Research Center, 20-21 November 1961), p. 120; Gene J. Matranga, NASA Technical note D-1057, "Analysis of X-15 Landing Approach and Flare Characteristics Determined from the First 30 Flights," July 1961, pp. 18-19.
42. Letter, Alvin S. White to Dennis R. Jenkins, 8 June 2002, containing comments to a draft copy of this manuscript; Lieutenant Colonel Burt Rowen, "Human-Factors Support of the X-15 Program," *Air University Quarterly Review*, Air War College, Volume X, Number 4, Winter 1958-59, p. 37; Gene J. Matranga, NASA technical note D-1057, "Analysis of X-15 Landing Approach and Flare Characteristics Determined from the First 30 Flights," July 1961, pp.18-19.
43. Letter, Alvin S. White to Dennis R. Jenkins, 1 July 2002.
44. Jack Beilman, 5 September 1999, a short unpublished paper supplied to the author via email, 31 March 2002. Calspan was originally formed in 1946 as the Cornell Aeronautical Laboratory, Inc., as part of Cornell University located in Ithaca, New York. In 1972, the laboratory was reorganized as the publicly-held Calspan Corporation. In 1978 Calspan was acquired by Arvin Industries, and merged with Texas-based Space Industries, Inc. in 1995 to form Space Industries International. The company merged with Veda in 1997 to become Veridian Corporation.

45. Jack Beilman, 5 September 1999, a short unpublished paper supplied to Dennis R. Jenkins via email, 31 March 2002.
46. Ibid.
47. Ibid.
48. Ibid; X-15 Status Report, Paul F. Bikle/FRC to H. Brown/NASA Headquarters, 29 July 1960, p. 2. In the files at the DFRC History Office.
49. X-15 Status Reports, Paul F. Bikle/FRC to H. Brown/NASA Headquarters, 29 July 1960, p. 3, 31 August 1960, pp. 3-4, and 14 September 1960, p. 3. In the files at the DFRC History Office.
50. Email, Peter W. Merlin/DFRC History Office to Dennis R. Jenkins, 18 November 1999.
51. Letter, Robert G. Hoey to Dennis R. Jenkins, 20 May 2002.
52. Lieutenant Commander Forrest S. Petersen, Herman A. Rediess, and Joseph Weil, "Lateral Directional Control Characteristics," (a paper in the *Research Airplane Committee Report on the Conference on the Progress of the X-15 Project*, A Compilation of the Papers presented at the Flight Research Center, 20-21 November 1961), pp. 135-138. (This paper was later republished as NASA classified technical memorandum X-726, March 1962.)
53. Letter, Robert G. Hoey to Dennis R. Jenkins, 20 May 2002.
54. Petersen, Rediess, and Weil, "Lateral-Directional Control Characteristics of the X-15 Airplane," pp. 134-135.
55. Ibid., pp. 138-139.
56. Email, Robert G. Hoey to Dennis R. Jenkins, 6 June 2002.
57. Letter, Robert G. Hoey to Dennis R. Jenkins, 4 June 2002; telephone conversation, Robert G. Hoey to Dennis R. Jenkins, 8 June 2002.
58. Petersen, Rediess, and Weil, "Lateral-Directional Control Characteristics of the X-15 Airplane," pp. 139-140.

Chapter 7 – Faster Than a Speeding Bullet

1. A. Scott Crossfield, *Always Another Dawn: The Story of a Rocket Test Pilot*, (New York: The World Publishing Company, 1960), p. 289.
2. Raymond H. Rice, "The X-15 Rollout Symposium," 15 October 1958. Released statements in the files of the AFFTC History Office; Crossfield, *Always Another Dawn*, pp. 303-304. The Nixon quote is as Crossfield remembered it on page 303.
3. Cost estimate from Major General Victor R. Haugen, "The X-15 Rollout Symposium," 15 October 1958. Released statements in the files of the AFFTC History Office. Ironically, as a Colonel, Haugen had been the director of the WADC laboratories when the NACA proposal that eventually became the X-15 had been evaluated and had concurred with the original $12,200,000 estimate for the project.
4. Major General Victor R. Haugen, "The X-15 Rollout Symposium," 15 October 1958. Released statements in the files of the AFFTC History Office.
5. Harrison Storms, "The X-15 Rollout Symposium," 15 October 1958. Released statements in the files of the AFFTC History Office.
6. North American report NA58-190, "X-15 Research Airplane: NAA Model NA-240 Flight Test Program," 1 August 1958. In the AFFTC Access to Space Office Project Files. Despite the official posturing, most involved already knew the airplane would not meet its speed goal, and most documentation began calling "Mach 6" the design instead of 6,600 fps (about Mach 6.5). Almost all of the performance deficit was the result of the airplane being overweight. Nobody expected that the 10-percent reduction in speed would have any significantly adverse effect on the research goals.
7. Memorandum, Paul F. Bikle to NASA Headquarters (RSS/Mr. H. Brown), subject: X-15 Flight Designation, 24 May 1960. In the files at the DFRC History Office. The 30 flights included 13 carries of the X-15-1 that had resulted in 8 free flights, and 17 carries of the X-15-2 that had also resulted in 8 free flights.
8. Letter, Johnny G. Armstrong to Dennis R. Jenkins, 5 July 2002; letter, Robert G. Hoey to Dennis R. Jenkins, 12 August 2002.
9. Letter, Johnny G. Armstrong to Dennis R. Jenkins, 5 July 2002; Robert G. Hoey and Richard E. Day, "X-15 Mission Planning and Operational Procedures," (a paper in the *Research Airplane Committee Report on the Conference on the Progress of the X-15 Project*, A Compilation of the Papers presented at the Flight Research Center, 20-21 November 1961), pp. 158-159. (This paper was later published as NASA technical note D-1159, March 1962.) Various sources contain slightly different numbers for the possible performance deltas; the numbers used here were provided by Johnny Armstrong.
10. Hoey and Day, "X-15 Mission Planning and Operational Procedures," pp. 159-160; letter, Robert G. Hoey to Dennis R. Jenkins, 12 August 2002.
11. Milton O. Thompson, *At the Edge of Space: The X-15 Flight Program*, (Washington and London: Smithsonian Institution Press, 1992), p. 70.
12. Letter, Johnny G. Armstrong to Dennis R. Jenkins, 5 July 2002.
13. Thompson, *At the Edge of Space*, pp. 186-187; A. Scott Crossfield, during an interview in the NBC documentary film *The Rocket Pilots*, 1989.
14. Letter, Robert G. Hoey to Dennis R. Jenkins, 12 August 2002.
15. Ibid.
16. Email, Robert G. Hoey to Dennis R. Jenkins, 9 August 2002.
17. Ibid.
18. Letter, Johnny G. Armstrong to Dennis R. Jenkins, 5 July 2002; letter, Robert G. Hoey to Dennis R. Jenkins, 12 August 2002.
19. Email, Robert G. Hoey to Dennis R. Jenkins, 25 August 2002.
20. Letter, Johnny G. Armstrong to Dennis R. Jenkins, 5 July 2002; letter, Robert G. Hoey to Dennis R. Jenkins, 12 August 2002.
21. Email, Robert G. Hoey to Dennis R. Jenkins, 25 August 2002.
22. Joseph A. Walker, "Pilot Report for Flight 3-22-46," 22 August 1963; Major William J. Knight, "Pilot Report for Flight 2-53-97," 3 October 1967. Both in the files at the DFRC History Office; Thompson, *At the Edge of Space*, p. 53; letter, Johnny G. Armstrong to Dennis R. Jenkins, 5 July 2002. Despite the thicker atmosphere, the speed brakes were frequently used to decelerate into the Edwards area on speed flights.
23. Letter, Johnny G. Armstrong to Dennis R. Jenkins, 5 July 2002. A notable exception to this was flight 3-7-14 which was always intended as a record flight (that still stands today) although research data was also collected during the flight.
24. Thompson, *At the Edge of Space*, p. 53.
25. Letter, Johnny G. Armstrong to Dennis R. Jenkins, 5 July 2002. Even if the engine had been run to burnout, there were usually propellants left in the tanks since the sump system was not 100-percent effective, especially at some flight attitudes.
26. Letter, Johnny G. Armstrong to Dennis R. Jenkins, 5 July 2002.
27. Ibid. Similar unpowered approaches were later demonstrated in the lifting-body program, usually landing on the concrete runway instead of a lakebed. The lifting-body contributions have received a great deal more attention in the popular press than the X-15 landings, which were arguably closer in profile.
28. Richard P. Hallion, editor, *The Hypersonic Revolution: Case Studies in the History of Hypersonic Technology* (Aeronautical Systems Division, Wright-Patterson AFB, Ohio, 1987), Volume I, "Transiting from Air to Space: The North American X-15," p. 129.
29. James E. Love, "History and Development of the X-15 Research Aircraft," not dated, p. 12. In the files at the DFRC History Office; A. Scott Crossfield, *Always Another Dawn: The Story of a Rocket Test Pilot*, (New York: The World Publishing Company, 1960), pp. 322-323.
30. Love, "History and Development of the X-15 Research Aircraft," p. 12; Crossfield, *Always Another Dawn*, pp. 322-323.
31. Love, "History and Development of the X-15 Research Aircraft," p. 13; Crossfield, *Always Another Dawn*, pp. 323-324.
32. Ibid.
33. Because the NB-52 never left the ground, this attempt does not have a program flight number.
34. The aileron roll was confirmed in an email, A. Scott Crossfield to Dennis R. Jenkins, 14 May 2002; A. Scott Crossfield and Harrison Storms, during an interview in the NBC documentary film *The Rocket Pilots*, 1989; Crossfield, *Always Another Dawn*, pp. 342-343.
35. A. Scott Crossfield and Harrison Storms, during interviews in the NBC documentary film *The Rocket Pilots*, 1989; Crossfield *Always Another Dawn*, pp. 343-346; telephone conversation, A. Scott Crossfield to Dennis R. Jenkins, 8 August 2002. The side-stick and center stick were mechanically interconnected to the control system cables through bell-cranks; this was years before an electric side-stick would be flown. Crossfield had long believed the center stick should be "cut off and thrown away."
36. Crossfield, *Always Another Dawn*, pp. 348-350. This event is described in Crossfield's book and was confirmed by him during telephone conversations. However, no independent documentation could be found; much of the surviving North American record is incomplete.
37. Crossfield, *Always Another Dawn*, pp. 352-353.
38. Ibid., pp. 350-357.
39. Emails, A. Scott Crossfield to Dennis R. Jenkins, 13 and 14 May 2002; The roll was captured by the camera chase, and video can be seen in the NBC documentary film *The Rocket Pilots*, 1989. "Aileron" is in quotes because the X-15 did not have ailerons, using the rolling tail for control instead. Still, aerodynamicists continue to use the term aileron to describe motion.
40. Love, "History and Development of the X-15 Research Aircraft," p. 13; Crossfield, *Always Another Dawn*, pp. 365-366.
41. A. Scott Crossfield, during an interview in the NBC documentary film *The Rocket Pilots*, 1989; Gene J. Matranga, NASA technical note D-1057, "Analysis of X-15 Landing Approach and Flare Characteristics Determined from the First 30 Flights," July 1961, pp. 13-14. In the files at the DFRC History Office; Crossfield, *Always Another Dawn*, pp. 381-382.
42. Matranga, "Analysis of X-15 Landing Approach and Flare Characteristics Determined from the First 30 Flights," pp. 13-14.
43. Love, "History and Development of the X-15 Research Aircraft," p. 14; telephone conversation, Charles H. Feltz to Dennis R. Jenkins, 10 July 2002.
44. "Advanced Development Plan for X-15 Research Aircraft, Advanced Technology Program 653A," 17 November 1961, p. 1. In the files at the AFFTC History Office.
45. X-15 Status Report, Paul F. Bikle/FRC to H. Brown/NASA Headquarters, 1 June 1960, p. 2; Joseph A. Walker, "Pilot Report for Flight No. 15 (later redesignated 1-7-12)," 12 May 1960. In the files at the DFRC History Office. The use of Silver Lake by this flight represented not only the first X-15 launch from a remote lake, but the first launch of any powered rocket plane from a remote lake; all previous X-plane flights had been conducted over the Edwards reservation.
46. One of the 21 X-15-1 flights was unpowered, although the XLR11s were physically installed in the airplane.
47. Email, Bill Arnold (Reaction Motors) to Dennis R. Jenkins, various dates in September 2002. North American operated the PSTS until they turned over the last XLR99-equipped airplane to the government. At that time the AFFTC Rocket Engine Group under the Maintenance Division took over the operation and maintenance of the PSTS and all engine maintenance and overhaul. NASA performed all engine operations including minor engine maintenance while installed in the airplanes. The lack of the MH-96 in X-15-3 at this point can be derived from various documents, but it was confirmed by Scott Crossfield in an email to the author on 28 May 2002. The XLR99 was popularly considered to be a million horsepower engine. By the definition in Webster's, the horsepower of a rocket engine is determined by multiplying the thrust (in pounds) times the speed (in mph), divided by 375. Therefore, the XLR99 would be 57,000 lbf * 4,520 mph / 375 = 687,040 hp. Not quite a million, but still impressive for an 900 pound engine.
48. Crossfield, *Always Another Dawn*, p. 400; telephone conversation, A. Scott Crossfield to Dennis R. Jenkins, 8 August 2002.
49. Accident investigation report 60-RWRL-568, not dated, no page numbers. In the files at the AFFTC Access to Space Office Project Files.
50. Ibid.
51. Ibid.
52. Ibid.
53. Ibid; X-15 Status Report, Paul F. Bikle/FRC to H. Brown/NASA Headquarters, 1 July 1960, p. 5. In the files at the DFRC History Office.
54. Lawrence P. Greene and Rolland L. Benner, "X-15 Experience from the Designer's Viewpoint," (a paper in the *Research Airplane Committee Report on the Conference on the Progress of the X-15 Project*, A Compilation of the Papers presented at the Flight Research Center, 20-21 November 1961), pp. 315-316.
55. Greene and Benner, "X-15 Experience from the Designer's Viewpoint," pp. 315-316.
56. Lieutenant Commander Forrest S. Petersen, "Pilot Report for Flight 1-13-25," 23 September 1960. In the files at the DFRC History Office; Thompson, *At the Edge of Space*, pp. 93-94.
57. Love, "History and Development of the X-15 Research Aircraft," pp. 15-16.
58. Harrison A. Storms, "X-15 Hardware Design Challenges" (a paper in the *Proceedings of the X-15 30th Anniversary Celebration*, Dryden Flight Research Facility, Edwards, California, 8 June 1989, NASA CP-3105), pp. 32-33.
59. Storms, "X-15 Hardware Design Challenges" pp. 32-33.
60. Love, "History and Development of the X-15 Research Aircraft," pp. 15-16.
61. X-15 Status Report, Paul F. Bikle/FRC to H. Brown/NASA Headquarters, 30 December 1960, pp. 1. In the files at the DFRC History Office; North American report NA-65-1, "X-15 Research Airplane Flight Record," revised 15 May 1968; "Advanced Development Plan for X-15 Research Aircraft, Advanced Technology Program 653A," 17 November 1961, p. 1. In the files at the AFFTC History Office. The North American report says that the X-15-2 was delivered on 8 February 1961; the Air Force report says 7 February. Engine 103 was removed and replaced with engine 104; these were the only two flight engines available at the time (105 had been destroyed in the X-15-3 ground accident, 106 and 108 were in acceptance testing, and 107, 109, and 111 were in assembly).
62. Love, "History and Development of the X-15 Research Aircraft," p. 20; letter, Major General Robert M. White (USAF, Retired) to Dennis R. Jenkins, 13 June 2002.
63. Love, "History and Development of the X-15 Research Aircraft," p. 21; Clarence J. Geiger, Albert E. Misenko, and William D. Putnam, "History of the Wright Air Development Division: July 1960-March 1961," AFSC historical publication 61-50-2, August 1961, pp. I-51 to I-52. In the files at the Air Force Historical Research Agency (K234.011); block text from Joseph A. Walker, "Pilot Report for Flight 2-14-28," 3 April 1961. In the files at the DFRC History Office.
64. Love, "History and Development of the X-15 Research Aircraft," p. 21; Geiger, Misenko, and Putnam, "History of the Wright Air Development Division: July 1960-March 1961," pp. I-51 to I-52; X-15 Status Reports, Paul F. Bikle/FRC to H. Brown/NASA Headquarters, 15 May 1961, p. 4 and 1 June 1961, p. 4. In the files at the DFRC History Office.
65. Robert G. Hoey, "X-15: Ventral-Off," in Fred Stoliker, Bob Hoey, and Johnny Armstrong, *Flight Testing at Edwards: Flight Test Stories – 1946-1975*, (Edwards, CA: Flight Test Historical Foundation, 2001), pp. 155-158. Anybody interested in getting a better "feel" for how testing progressed at Edwards during this period should find a copy of this excellent collection of short stories written by some of the Flight Test Engineers and Flight Planners.
66. Hoey, "X-15: Ventral-Off," pp. 155-158.
67. Robert G. Hoey, AFFTC technology document FTC-TDR-62-7, "Envelope Expansion with Interim XLR11 Rocket Engines," 1962; Hoey, "X-15: Ventral-Off," pp. 155-158; Joseph A. Walker, "A Pilot's Impression of the X-15 Program," (a paper in the *Research Airplane Committee Report on the Conference on the Progress of the X-15 Project*, A Compilation of the Papers presented at the Flight Research Center, 20-21 November 1961), p. 305; Robert A. Tremant, NASA technical note D-1402, "Operational Experiences and Characteristics of the X-15 Flight Control System," December 1962, pp. 10-11.
68. X-15 Status Report, Paul F. Bikle/FRC to H. Brown/NASA Headquarters, 16 April 1962, pp. 3. In the files at the DFRC History Office; Hoey, "X-15: Ventral-Off," pp. 155-158.
69. Letter, Robert G. Hoey to Dennis R. Jenkins, 20 May 2002.
70. Wendell H. Stillwell, *X-15 Research Results*, NASA SP-60, (Washington DC: NASA, 1965), pp. 51-52; Gene J. Matranga, NASA technical note D-1057, "Analysis of X-15 Landing Approach and Flare Characteristics Determined from the First 30 Flights," July 1961, pp. 8-9. In the files at the DFRC History Office; Hoey, "X-15: Ventral-Off," pp. 155-158.
71. Hoey, "X-15: Ventral-Off," pp. 155-158.
72. Ibid., pp. 155-158.
73. Ibid.
74. Joseph A. Walker, "Pilot report for Flight 1-27-48," 30 April 1962; Jack B. McKay, "Pilot Report for Flight 2-29-50," 28 September 1962. Both in the files at the DFRC History Office; Hoey, "X-15: Ventral-Off," pp. 155-158; letter, Johnny G. Armstrong to Dennis R. Jenkins, 3 August 2002; letter, Robert G. Hoey to Dennis R. Jenkins, 13 August 2002.
75. Radio transcript, Flight 2-20-36. In the files at the DFRC History Office.
76. Robert M. White, "Pilot Report from Flight 2-21-37," 9 November 1961. In the files at the DFRC History Office.
77. John V. Becker, "The X-15 Program in Retrospect" (paper presented at 3rd Eugen Sänger Memorial Lecture, Bonn, Germany, 5 December 1968); and James E. Love, *X-15: Past and Future*, paper presented to the Fort Wayne Section, Society of Automotive Engineers, 9 December 1964. In the first case, an old soda-lime windscreen had inadvertently been installed in the airplane. The second incident, however, used the later alumino-silicate glass. In both cases later analysis indicated that a local hot spot at the rear edge of the frame had caused the glass to crack. The frame was subsequently modified and no further incidents were reported.
78. Stillwell, *X-15 Research Results*, p. v; see also Walter C. Williams, "The Role of the Pilot in the Mercury and X-15 Flights" (in the *Proceedings of the Fourteenth AGARD General Assembly*, 16-17 September 1965, Portugal)
79. Table of contents and registered guest list in the front of the *Research Airplane Committee Report on the Conference on the Progress of the X-15 Project*, A Compilation of the Papers presented at the Flight Research Center, 20-21 November 1961.
80. Crossfield, *Always Another Dawn*, pp. 307-366.
81. Stillwell, *X-15 Research Results*, pp. 65; quote from Robert M. White, Glenn H. Robinson, and Gene J. Matranga, NASA confidential technical memorandum X-715, "Résumé of X-15 Handling Qualities," March 1962, p. 5.
82. Richard D. Banner, Albert E. Kuhl, and Robert D. Quinn, "Preliminary Results of Aerodynamic Heating Studies on the X-15," (a paper in the *Research Airplane Committee Report on the Conference on the Progress of the X-15 Project*, A Compilation of the Papers presented at the Flight Research Center, 20-21 November 1961), pp.14-15. The theoretical models included ones from Ernst Eckert at Wright Field, Eva Winkler at the Naval Ordnance Laboratory, and E. R. Van Driest.
83. Informal Interview (no interviewer noted) with Lieutenant Commander Forrest S. Petersen, 11 January 1962. Written transcript in the files at the DFRC History Office.
84. X-15 Status Report, Paul F. Bikle/FRC to H. Brown/NASA Headquarters, 1 February 1962, p. 1. In the files at the DFRC History Office.
85. X-15 Status Reports, Paul F. Bikle/FRC to H. Brown/NASA Headquarters, 1 February 1962, p. 5 and 15 February 1962, p. 1. In the files at the DFRC History Office.
86. Neil A. Armstrong, "Pilot Report for Flight 3-4-8," 20 April 1962. In the files at the DFRC History Office.
87. Ibid.; letter, Robert G. Hoey to Dennis R. Jenkins, 12 August 2002.
88. Ibid.
89. Thompson, *At the Edge of Space*, p. 106; letter, Johnny G. Armstrong to Dennis R. Jenkins, 3 August 2002.
90. Telephone conversation, John E. Allavie to Dennis R. Jenkins, 22 May 2002; telephone conversation, Major General Robert M. White to Dennis R. Jenkins, 24 May 2002; email, Tony Landis/DFRC to Dennis R. Jenkins, 5 June 2002; email Peter W. Merlin/DFRC Archivist to Dennis R. Jenkins, 10 June 2002. The Kennedy Library checked the Appointment Books and determined that the President had been at Eglin on 4 May 1962. James B. Hill, the Audiovisual Archivist at the Library, reports that the library does not have any photographs showing Kennedy inspecting the X-15, although there are 16 photos of him at the event. As near as can be determined, this was the only time an X-15 was carried without a pilot in the cockpit.
91. Major Robert M. White, " Pilot Report for Flight 3-5-9," 12 June 1962; Major Robert M. White, " Pilot Report for Flight 3-6-10," 21 June 1962.
92. Major Robert M. White, " Pilot Report for Flight 3-7-14," 17 July 1962. The Air Force recognized 50 miles (264,000 feet) as the beginning of space, and Air Force pilots flying above this altitude qualified for an Astronaut rating. NASA recognized the international standard 100 kilometers (62.14 miles, 328,099 feet). As of 2 July 2002 the Fédération Aéronautique Internationale still regards Flight 3-7-14 as a record for the class "Class C-1 (landplanes), Group IV (rocket engine), Launched from an aircraft." Interestingly, neither the record, nor even the class, show at the FAI website (fai.org). The current status was obtained via an email, Anne-Laure Perret/FAI Executive Officer to Dennis R. Jenkins, 2 July 2002.
93. William MacDougall, "White, 3 Other X-15 Pilots Get Collier Trophy," *Los Angeles Times*, 19 July 1962; Pamela E. Mack, "Introduction," *From Engineering Science to Big Science: The NACA and NASA Collier Trophy Research Pro-*

ject Winners, edited by Pamela E. Mack, NASA SP-4219, 1998, p. xi. The caption for the photo on page 150 of the book incorrectly identifies the event as happening on 18 July 1961 (it was 1962). Mack had some interesting observations concerning the trophy, although none were particularly applicable to the X-15 award. One paragraph is particularly telling. "The United States has had and still has a number of aviation and aerospace organizations, ranging from booster groups to professional societies. The National Aeronautic Association fits somewhere in the middle of that range. In turn, its prize is shaped by the composition of the committee that awards it and by a series of rules, in particular that the prize be given for an achievement in the preceding year. While the Nobel Prize is usually given for an accomplishment whose significance has been proven by years of experience, the Collier Trophy represents an almost concurrent evaluation of an achievement (and like the Pulitzer Prize, it sometimes lacks the wisdom of hindsight)."

94. Johnny G. Armstrong, "Expanding the X-15 Envelope to Mach 6.7," in Fred Stoliker, Bob Hoey, and Johnny Armstrong, *Flight Testing at Edwards: Flight Test Stories – 1946-1975*, (Edwards, CA: Flight Test Historical Foundation, 2001), pp. 200-201. In his book, Johnny Armstrong says that Pete Knight was NASA-1 for this flight; however, all other documentation – including the radio transcripts – indicate that Bob Rushworth was the communicator. Additionally, most contemporary documentation (including the flight report) indicates the engine was at 30-percent power; subsequent analysis showed it was really at 35-percent.
95. William P. Albrecht/X-15 Project Engineer, "X-15 Operations Flight Report for Flight 2-31-52," 16 November 1962; William P. Albrecht/X-15 Project Engineer, "X-15 Operations Flight Report Supplement for Flight 2-31-52," 22 May 1964. Both in the files at the DFRC History Office; Armstrong, "Expanding the X-15 Envelope to Mach 6.7," pp. 200-201; Thompson, *At the Edge of Space*, p. 229. The 257 knot landing speed was almost 60 knots higher than normal.
96. William P. Albrecht/X-15 Project Engineer, "X-15 Operations Flight Report for Flight 2-31-52," 16 November 1962; William P. Albrecht/X-15 Project Engineer, "X-15 Operations Flight Report Supplement for Flight 2-31-52," 22 May 1964. Both in the files at the DFRC History Office; "Expanding the X-15 Envelope to Mach 6.7," pp. 200-201; Thompson, *At the Edge of Space*, p. 229.
97. William P. Albrecht/X-15 Project Engineer, "X-15 Operations Flight Report for Flight 2-31-52," 16 November 1962; William P. Albrecht/X-15 Project Engineer, "X-15 Operations Flight Report Supplement for Flight 2-31-52," 22 May 1964. Both in the files at the DFRC History Office; Armstrong, "Expanding the X-15 Envelope to Mach 6.7," pp. 200-201.
98. Ibid.
99. William P. Albrecht/X-15 Project Engineer, "X-15 Operations Flight Report Supplement for Flight 2-31-52," 22 May 1964; Armstrong, "Expanding the X-15 Envelope to Mach 6.7," p. 201.
100. "Semi-Annual Summary Status Report of X-15 Program," October 1963, p. 19.
101. Thompson, *At the Edge of Space*, p. 123; letter, Johnny G. Armstrong to Dennis R. Jenkins, 3 August 2002; letter, Robert G. Hoey to Dennis R. Jenkins, 12 August 2002.
102. Joseph A. Walker, "Pilot Report for Flight 3-21-32," 19 July 1963. In the files at the DFRC History Office.
103. Ibid.
104. Ibid; Thompson, *At the Edge of Space*, p. 53; letter, Robert G. Hoey to Dennis R. Jenkins, 12 August 2002.
105. Vincent N. Capasso/X-15 Project Engineer, "X-15 Operations Flight Report for Flight 3-29-48," 28 May 1964; "X-15 Semi-Annual Status Report No. 3," 1 December 1964, p. 1. Both in the files at the DFRC History Office.
106. *Progress of the X-15 Research Airplane Program*, A Compilation of the Papers presented at the Flight Research Center, 7 October 1965, NASA SP-90, (Washington, D.C.: NASA, 1965), p. iii; X-15 Status Report No. 65-10, Paul F. Bikle/FRC to J. Martin/NASA Headquarters, 14 October 1965, p. 2. The conference had been planned for two days (7-8 October), but was reduced to a single day a few months previously. Unfortunately, this proceedings report did not include a list of attendees. The other industry conferences had been in 1956, 1958, and 1961.
107. Joe H. Engle, "Pilot Report for Flight 3-46-70," 23 August 1965; memorandum, Joseph A. LaPierre/FRC to Chief, Research Division, X-15 Project Office, subject: Flight Research Report on Flight 3-46-70, 23 August 1965. In the files at the DFRC History Office.
108. John V. Becker, "A Hindsight Study of the NASA Hypersonic Research Engine Project," 1 July 1976, p. 22. Prepared under contract NAS1-14250, but never published. Copy in the author's collection. On 13 September 1960, the AACB had been formally established to coordinate various activities between the Department of Defense and the NASA. The Deputy Administrator of NASA and the Assistant Secretary of Defense were named as co-chairmen of the AACB; initially this meant Hugh Dryden and Herbert F. York. In an indirect way, the Research Airplane Committee that had been created in 1954 to manage the X-15 program fell under the auspices of the AACB. However, given that the X-15 program was well established by the time the AACB was created, it had little direct impact on the program and the Research Airplane Committee continued to function much as it always had. By 1965 this was beginning to change. See the interview, Dr. Robert C. Seamans, Jr., by Martin Collins, 15 December 1988, electronic transcript available at http://www.nasm.si.edu/nasm/dsh/trasncpt/seaman10.htm, accessed 25 April 2002. The AACB also oversaw the Manned Spacecraft Panel, Unmanned Spaceflight Panel, Launch Vehicle Panel, Spaceflight Ground Environment Panel, and the Supporting Space Research and Technology Panel.
109. Project Development Plan, "Delta Wing X-15," second draft, December 1965, pp. 36-37. In the files at the DFRC History Office.
110. Letter, Paul F. Bikle to USAF/ASD, no subject, 2 November 1961; Becker, "A Hindsight Study of the NASA Hypersonic Research Engine Project," p. 26.
111. X-15 Status Reports, Paul F. Bikle/FRC to J. Martin/NASA Headquarters, 1 December 1965, and 3 January 1966. In the files at the DFRC History Office.
112. X-15 Status Reports, Paul F. Bikle/FRC to J. Martin/NASA Headquarters, 3 January, 2 February, and 1 March 1966. In the files at the DFRC History Office.
113. X-15 Status Report, Paul F. Bikle/FRC to J. Martin/NASA Headquarters, 1 March 1966, p. 3. In the files at the DFRC History Office.
114. X-15 Status Report, Paul F. Bikle/FRC to J. Martin/NASA Headquarters, 1 March 1966, p. 3. In the files at the DFRC History Office. The introduction of tape-style instruments into operational aircraft underwent a similar mistrust initially. The scientific ("human factors") community was sure that the new displays were easier to read and provided better information; the pilots pointed to 50 years of using the older round instruments without problem. In the end the tape-style instruments had a relatively short life in most combat aircraft and were eventually replaced by the old-style round dials – at least until the advent of the "glass cockpit" in the 1980s.
115. X-15 Status Report, Paul F. Bikle/FRC to J. Martin/NASA Headquarters, 1 March 1966, p. 2. In the files at the DFRC History Office. The X-15-1 was restricted to lower altitudes than the X-15-3 since it was not equipped with the MH-96 adaptive flight control system; the X-15A-2 was never intended to fly much above 100,000 feet, so this restriction was not an impediment to the flight program.
116. X-15 Status Report, Paul F. Bikle/FRC to J. Martin/NASA Headquarters, 1 April 1966, pp. 7-8. In the files at the DFRC History Office.
117. Thompson, *At the Edge of Space*, p. 239.
118. Major Michael J. Adams, "Pilot report for Flight 1-69-116," 6 October 1966. In the files at the DFRC History Office; Thompson, *At the Edge of Space*, pp. 248-249. Note that the "low and slow" familiarization flights given to the original group of X-15 pilots had gone from Mach 2 and 50,000 feet to Adams' Mach 4 and 70,000 feet.
119. William H. Dana, "Pilot Report for Flight 3-56-83," 1 November 1966; Radio Transcript for Flight 3-56-83. Both in the files at the DFRC History Office.
120. Major William J. Knight, "Pilot Report for Flight 1-73-126," 29 June 1967. In the files at the DFRC History Office.
121. Ibid; memorandum, Perry V. Row to Paul F. Bikle, subject: Flight Suitability of the Number One X-15, 30 January 1968.
122. Letter, Robert G. Hoey to Dennis R. Jenkins, 12 August 2002.
123. Ibid.

Chapter 8 – The X-15A-2

1. Johnny G. Armstrong, AFFTC technology document FTC-TD-69-4, "Flight Planning and Conduct of the X-15A-2 Envelope Expansion Program," July 1969, p. 2.
2. The basic X-15s did not carry a model suffix; the modified airplane added an "A" to become the X-15A (usually written X-15A-2 or simply A-2).
3. Elmor J. Adkins and Johnny G. Armstrong, "Development and Status of the X-15A-2 Airplane," (a paper in the *Progress of the X-15 Research Airplane Program*, A Compilation of the Papers presented at the Flight Research Center, 7 October 1965, NASA SP-90, (Washington, D.C.: NASA, 1965), pp. 103-104; Edwin W. Johnston, "Current and Advanced X-15," a paper presented at the Military Aircraft Systems and Technology Meeting, Washington D.C., 21-23 September 1964, no page numbers; Armstrong, "Flight Planning and Conduct of the X-15A-2 Envelope Expansion Program," p. 2. The repair and modifications were accomplished under Air Force contract AF33(657)-11614.
4. Adkins and Armstrong, "Development and Status of the X-15A-2 Airplane," p. 105; Johnston, "Current and Advanced X-15."
5. Adkins and Armstrong, "Development and Status of the X-15A-2 Airplane," pp. 104-105.
6. Adkins and Armstrong, "Development and Status of the X-15A-2 Airplane," p. 105; Johnston, "Current and Advanced X-15;" Major William J. Knight, "Increased Piloting Tasks and Performance of X-15A-2 in Hypersonic Flight," *The Aeronautical Journal of the Royal Aeronautical Society*, Volume 72, September 1968, pp. 793-802 (derived from a lecture given to the Test Pilot's Group of the Society on 30 January 1968).
7. Armstrong, "Flight Planning and Conduct of the X-15A-2 Envelope Expansion Program, " p. 6; Adkins and Armstrong, "Development and Status of the X-15A-2 Airplane," p. 105.
8. Adkins and Armstrong, "Development and Status of the X-15A-2 Airplane," pp. 105-111.
9. Armstrong, "Flight Planning and Conduct of the X-15A-2 Envelope Expansion Program," pp. 25-26.
10. Knight, "Increased Piloting Tasks and Performance of X-15A-2 in Hypersonic Flight," pp. 793-802; Armstrong, "Flight Planning and Conduct of the X-15A-2 Envelope Expansion Program," p. 26; Lieutenant Colonel Robert M. White, "Pilot Report for Flight 2-21-37," 9 November 1961. In the files at the DFRC History Office.
11. Armstrong, "Flight Planning and Conduct of the X-15A-2 Envelope Expansion Program," p. 26; X-15 Status Report, Paul F. Bikle/FRC to J. Martin/NASA Headquarters, 12 July 1966, p. 9. In the files at the DFRC History Office.
12. Adkins and Armstrong, "Development and Status of the X-15A-2 Airplane," p. 105; Armstrong, "Flight Planning and Conduct of the X-15A-2 Envelope Expansion Program," p. 7. In a way it was rather odd to incorporate this modification in the X-15A-2, which was intended for high-speed work at 100,000 feet, not high altitude flights (which were the purview of the MH-96-equipped X-15-3).
13. Adkins and Armstrong, "Development and Status of the X-15A-2 Airplane," p. 105.
14. Ibid., p. 110.
15. Johnston, "Current and Advanced X-15;" Knight, "Increased Piloting Tasks and Performance of X-15A-2 in Hypersonic Flight," pp. 793-802.
16. "X-15 Semi-Annual Status Report No. 3," 1 December 1964, pp. 1, 5-6; Major Robert A. Rushworth, "Pilot Report for Flight 2-32-55," 25 June 1964; Armstrong, "Expanding the X-15 Envelope to Mach 6.7," p. 202.
17. Armstrong, "Flight Planning and Conduct of the X-15A-2 Envelope Expansion Program," p. 10; Radio Transcript, Flight 2-33-56, 14 August 1964. In the files at the DFRC History Office.
18. Radio Transcript, Flight 2-33-56, 14 August 1964. In the files at the DFRC History Office.
19. Major Robert A. Rushworth, "Pilot Report for Flight 2-33-56," 14 August 1964; Radio Transcript, Flight 2-33-56, 14 August 1964. In the files at the DFRC History Office.
20. Armstrong, "Flight Planning and Conduct of the X-15A-2 Envelope Expansion Program," p. 10.
21. Major Robert A. Rushworth, "Pilot Report for Flight 2-34-57," 29 September 1964. In the files at the DFRC History Office.
22. Armstrong, "Flight Planning and Conduct of the X-15A-2 Envelope Expansion Program," p. 10.
23. Major Robert A. Rushworth, "Pilot Report for Flight 2-36-63," 17 February 1965. In the files at the DFRC History Office; Armstrong, "Flight Planning and Conduct of the X-15A-2 Envelope Expansion Program," p. 10; Thompson, *At the Edge of Space*, p. 237; Adkins and Armstrong, "Development and Status of the X-15A-2 Airplane," p. 107; The Pilot's Panel, (a paper in the *Proceedings of the X-15 30th Anniversary Celebration*, Dryden Flight Research Facility, Edwards, California, 8 June 1989, NASA CP-3105), p. 149.
24. Armstrong, "Flight Planning and Conduct of the X-15A-2 Envelope Expansion Program," p. 12.
25. Armstrong, "Flight Planning and Conduct of the X-15A-2 Envelope Expansion Program," p. 5; Adkins and Armstrong, "Development and Status of the X-15A-2 Airplane," p. 107; North American report NA-67-344, "Technical Proposal for a Conceptual Design Study for the Modification of an X-15 Air Vehicle to a Hypersonic Delta-Wing Configuration," 17 May 1967, volume I, pp. 182-184. In the files at the JSC History Office.
26. Adkins and Armstrong, "Development and Status of the X-15A-2 Airplane," p. 108; Armstrong, "Flight Planning and Conduct of the X-15A-2 Envelope Expansion Program," p. 16.
27. Armstrong, "Flight Planning and Conduct of the X-15A-2 Envelope Expansion Program," p. 24.
28. Adkins and Armstrong, "Development and Status of the X-15A-2 Airplane," p. 108; Knight, "Increased Piloting Tasks and Performance of X-15A-2 in Hypersonic Flight," pp. 793-802; Armstrong, "Flight Planning and Conduct of the X-15A-2 Envelope Expansion Program," pp. 19-20.
29. Adkins and Armstrong, "Development and Status of the X-15A-2 Airplane," p. 108.
30. Armstrong, "Expanding the X-15 Envelope to Mach 6.7," p. 202.
31. Lieutenant Colonel Robert A. Rushworth, "Pilot Report for Flight 2-43-75," 3 November 1965; Armstrong, "Flight Planning and Conduct of the X-15A-2 Envelope Expansion Program," p. 29; X-15 Status Report 65-12, Paul F. Bikle/FRC to J. Martin/NASA Headquarters, 1 December 1965, p. 3. In the files at the DFRC History Office.
32. Lieutenant Colonel Robert A. Rushworth, "Pilot Report for Flight 2-43-75," 3 November 1965; Armstrong, "Flight Planning and Conduct of the X-15A-2 Envelope Expansion Program," p. 29. Local folklore has it that after Rushworth's February 1965 flight the ground crew installed a placard that read "do not deploy landing gear above Mach 4" and that this was the solution to the landing gear problems.
33. Armstrong, "Expanding the X-15 Envelope to Mach 6.7," pp. 202-203.
34. Ibid., pp. 202-203.
35. Radio Transcript for Flight 2-45-81; Armstrong, "Expanding the X-15 Envelope to Mach 6.7," pp. 202-203.
36. William P. Albrecht/X-15 Project Engineer, "X-15 Operations Flight Report for Flight 2-45-81," 5 July 1966; memorandum, Lieutenant Colonel Robert A. Rushworth to Chief, Research Projects Office, subject: Preliminary Report of X-15 Flight 2-45-81, 21 July 1966.
37. Major William J. Knight, "Pilot Report for Flight 2-49-86," 30 August 1966. Knight had made six previous X-15 flights, but all were without the ventral rudder.
38. X-15 Status Report, Paul F. Bikle/FRC to J. Martin/NASA Headquarters, 10 January 1967, p. 1 and 4 April 1967, pp. 2 and 5. Both in the files at the DFRC History Office.
39. Joe D. Watts, John P. Cary, and Marvin B. Dow, "Advanced X-15A-2 Thermal-Protection System," (a paper in the *Progress of the X-15 Research Airplane Program*, A Compilation of the Papers presented at the Flight Research Center, 7 October 1965, NASA SP-90, (Washington, D.C.: NASA, 1965), pp. 117 and 123.
40. X-15 Status Report, Paul F. Bikle/FRC to H. Brown/NASA Headquarters, 16 October 1961, p. 7 plus attached photos. In the files at the DFRC History Office.
41. Edwin W. Johnston, "Current and Advanced X-15," a paper presented at the Military Aircraft Systems and Technology Meeting, Washington D.C., 21-23 September 1964. The ablator was manufactured by the Electronics and Space Division of Emerson Electric, St. Louis, Missouri.
42. Armstrong, "Flight Planning and Conduct of the X-15A-2 Envelope Expansion Program," pp. 24-25.
43. Watts, Cary, and Dow, "Advanced X-15A-2 Thermal-Protection System," p. 118.
44. "X-15 Semi-Annual Status Report No. 2," April 1964, pp. 6-7; Watts, Cary, and Dow, "Advanced X-15A-2 Thermal-Protection System," p. 119.
45. "X-15 Semi-Annual Status Report No. 3," 1 December 1964, p. 2; "X-15 Semi-Annual Status Report No. 4," 1 April 1965, p. 3.
46. Watts, Cary, and Dow, "Advanced X-15A-2 Thermal-Protection System," pp. 118-119.
47. Armstrong, "Flight Planning and Conduct of the X-15A-2 Envelope Expansion Program, " p. 25; X-15 Status Report, Paul F. Bikle/FRC to J. Martin/NASA Headquarters, 2 February 1966, p. 6. In the files at the DFRC History Office. NASA contract NAS4-1009.
48. Martin Marietta design report ER-14535, "Thermal Protection System: X-15A-2," undated (but probably April 1967), pp. 59-60; Armstrong, "Flight Planning and Conduct of the X-15A-2 Envelope Expansion Program," p. 25. Originally, Martin Marietta apparently used a small "s" in the trade name of the ablator – MA-25s. However, it is generally known as MA-25S and seems more readable that way, so that is what will be used here. MA-25S and ESA-3560 have both had long lives, currently being used to insulate some portions of the space shuttle external tank.
49. Martin Marietta Monthly Letter Report No. 5, subject: X-15 Thermal Protection System, 10 June 1966. In the files at the DFRC History Office.
50. Martin Marietta design report ER-14535, "Thermal Protection System: X-15A-2," undated (but probably April 1967), passim. For the detailed instructions of how to apply, maintain, and remove the ablative coating, see Martin Marietta design report ER-14535, "Thermal Protection System: X-15A-2," undated (but probably April 1967). Copies are in the files at the AFFTC and DFRC History Offices.
51. Martin Marietta Monthly Progress Report No. 3, subject: X-15 Full Scale Ablator Application, 14 July 1967. In the files at the DFRC History Office; A. B. Price, Martin Marietta report MCR-68-15, "Full Scale Flight Test Report: X-15A-2 Ablative Thermal Protection System, December 1967, pp. 5-6. A clean surface is a "water break free" area on which the water sheets out over the surface, while the presence of oil or contaminants will cause water to bead up. This is a standard terminology and test used in many, particularly painting, industries.
52. Price, Martin Marietta report MCR-68-15, pp. 6-7. The collectors were essentially petri dishes with millipore filters in them that collected any dust that settled in the bottom of the compartments.
53. Ibid., pp. 8-9.
54. Ibid., pp. 9-10.
55. Ibid., p. 10.
56. Ibid., p. 11.
57. Martin Marietta Monthly Progress Report No. 3, subject: X-15 Full Scale Ablator Application, 14 July 1967. In the files at the DFRC History Office; Price, Martin Marietta report MCR-68-15, p. 13.
58. Martin Marietta Monthly Letter Report No. 3, subject: X-15 Thermal Protection System, 7 April 1966. In the files at the DFRC History Office; Armstrong, "Flight Planning and Conduct of the X-15A-2 Envelope Expansion Program," p. 25; letter, Robert G. Hoey to Dennis R. Jenkins, 13 August 2002.
59. Price, Martin Marietta report MCR-68-15, pp. 13-14.
60. Knight, "Increased Piloting Tasks and Performance of X-15A-2 in Hypersonic Flight."
61. Price, Martin Marietta report MCR-68-15, pp. 64-65.
62. Ibid., p. 65.
63. Ibid., p. 65.
64. Ibid., pp. 65-67.
65. Ibid., p. 15.
66. Ibid., pp. 16-17.
67. Ibid., pp. 16-17.
68. Martin Marietta Monthly Progress Report No. 6, subject: X-15 Full Scale Ablator Application, 6 October 1967. In the files at the DFRC History Office; Price, Martin Marietta report MCR-68-15, p. 19.
69. Knight, "Pilot Report for Flight 2-53-97," 3 October 1967; memorandum, Major William J. Knight to Chief, Research Projects Office, subject: Preliminary Report of X-15 Flight 2-53-97, 26 October 1967.
70. Flight Plan for Flight 2-53-97, 19 September 1967; Major William J. Knight, "Pilot Report for Flight 2-53-97," 3 October 1967; Memorandum, Major William J. Knight to Chief, Research Projects Office, subject: Preliminary Report of X-15 Flight 2-53-97, 26 October 1967; Armstrong, "Expanding the X-15 Envelope to Mach 6.7," pp. 204-205; X-15 Status Report, Paul F. Bikle/FRC to J. Martin/NASA Headquarters, 8 November 1967, p. 4. In the files at the DFRC History Office.

71. Memorandum, Major William J. Knight to Chief, Research Projects Office, subject: Preliminary Report of X-15 Flight 2-53-97, 26 October 1967; Armstrong, "Expanding the X-15 Envelope to Mach 6.7," pp. 204-205; X-15 Status Report, Paul F. Bikle/FRC to J. Martin/NASA Headquarters, 8 November 1967, p. 4. In the files at the DFRC History Office.
72. Memorandum, James R. Welsh (for Elmor J. Adkins/X-15 Research Planning Office) to Assistant Chief, Research Projects, subject: Preliminary Report on X-15 Flight 2-53-97, 26 October 1967; Major William J. Knight, "Pilot Report for Flight 2-53-97," 3 October 1967. Both in the files at the DFRC History Office. This is sometimes shown as 4,534 mph and Mach 4.72. The difference is what atmospheric corrections were applied to convert Mach and dynamic pressure to miles per hour. The official NASA records show 4,520 mph and Mach 6.70; the Air Force tends to use the higher figures. This was the only X-15 flight that actually exceeded the original design goal of 6,600 fps; the next closest was Flight 2-50-89 at 6,233 fps. The fastest "basic" X-15 flight was 1-30-51 at 6,019 fps.
73. Major William J. Knight, "Pilot Report for Flight 2-53-97," 3 October 1967; Radio Transcript for Flight 2-53-97. Both in the files at the DFRC History Office; Thompson, *At the Edge of Space*, pp. 243-245.
74. Armstrong, "Expanding the X-15 Envelope to Mach 6.7," pp. 204-205; memorandum, William J. Knight to Chief, Research Projects Office, subject: Preliminary Report of X-15 Flight 2-53-97, 26 October 1967.
75. Armstrong, "Expanding the X-15 Envelope to Mach 6.7," pp. 205-206.
76. Ibid., pp. 205-206. Armstrong still has the pressure probes in his desk and is happy to show them to visitors at his AFFTC office.
77. Price, Martin Marietta report MCR-68-15, pp. 70-71.
78. Ibid., pp. 78-79.
79. Ibid., pp. 78-79.
80. Ibid., p. 71.
81. Ibid., p. 72.
82. Ibid., pp. 72-73.
83. Ibid., pp. 72-73.
84. Ibid., p. 77.
85. John V. Becker, "The X-15 Program in Retrospect," 3rd Eugen Sänger Memorial Lecture, Bonn, Germany, 5 December 1968); interview with Jack Koll, 28 February 1977 (interviewer not noted). Transcript in the files at the DFRC History Office.
86. Price, Martin Marietta report MCR-68-15, pp. 74-75.
87. Ibid., pp. 20-21.
88. X-15 Status Report, Paul F. Bikle/FRC to J. Martin/NASA Headquarters, 17 July 1968, p. 1. In the files at the DFRC History Office.
89. Dennis R. Jenkins, *Space Shuttle: The History of the National Space Transportation System – The First 100 Flights*, (Cape Canaveral, FL: the author, 2001), pp. 160-162.

Chapter 9 – Tragedy Before The End

1. Donald R. Bellman, et al., NASA report (no number), *Investigation of the Crash of the X-15-3 Aircraft on November 15, 1967*, January 1968, pp. 8-15, and 25. email, Johnny G. Armstrong to Dennis R. Jenkins, 26 July 2002; Radio Transcript for Flight 3-65-97;
2. Emails, Robert G. Hoey to Dennis R. Jenkins, 24 August and 20 November 2002.
3. Bellman, *Investigation of the Crash*, p. 4; emails, Johnny G. Armstrong to Dennis R. Jenkins, 26 July and 23 November 2002; email, Robert G. Hoey to Dennis R. Jenkins, 20 November 2002.
4. To date, this is the only hypersonic spin that has been encountered during manned flight research. See Donald R. Bellman, et al., NASA report (no number), *Investigation of the Crash*, January 1968, pp. 8-15; letter, Robert G. Hoey to Dennis R. Jenkins, 12 August 2002.
5. Radio Transcript for Flight 3-65-97; Bellman *Investigation of the Crash*, pp. 4 and 8-15.
6. Bellman *Investigation of the Crash*, pp. 31-32.
7. Emails, Johnny G. Armstrong to Dennis R. Jenkins, 26 July and 23 November 2002.
8. Bellman, *Investigation of the Crash*, pp. 8-15.
9. Aeronautical Order 130, awarding the rating of Command Pilot Astronaut, to Major Michael J. Adams, 15 November 1967. In the author's collection.
10. USAF Headquarters Development Directive No. 32, 5 March 1964, reprinted in System Package Program, System 653A, 18 May 1964, p. 13-7; memorandum, John V. Becker and R. E. Supp, subject: Report of Meeting of USAF/NASA Working Groups on Hypersonic Aircraft Technology, 21-22 September 1966; James E. Love and William R. Young, NASA technical note D-3732, "Survey of Operation and Cost Experience of the X-15 Airplane as a Reusable Space Vehicle," November 1966, pp. 7.
11. "X-15 Program," a briefing prepared by the AFFTC in late October 1968. In the files at the AFFTC History Office.
12. Ibid.
13. Ibid.
14. USAF Headquarters Development Directive No. 32, 5 March 1964, reprinted in System Package Program, System 653A, 18 May 1964, p. 13-7; memorandum, John V. Becker and R. E. Supp, subject: Report of Meeting of USAF/NASA Working Groups on Hypersonic Aircraft Technology, 21-22 September 1966; Love and Young, "Survey of Operation and Cost Experience of the X-15 Airplane as a Reusable Space Vehicle," pp. 7.
15. Letter, Robert G. Hoey to Dennis R. Jenkins, 13 August 2002.
16. Milton O. Thompson, *At the Edge of Space: The X-15 Flight Program*, (Washington and London: Smithsonian Institution Press, 1992), p. 223.
17. At the 3rd Eugen Sänger Memorial Lecture in 1968, John Becker stated that 109 flights exceeded Mach 5. A reevaluation of the flight data shows that only 108 actually did. See John V. Becker, "The X-15 Program in Retrospect," 3rd Eugen Sänger Memorial Lecture, Bonn, Germany, 5 December 1968, p. 3 for Becker's original numbers.
18. TWX 632136Z Jan 69, subject: Termination XB-70, X-15 program, 4 January 1969. This TWX also requested instruction for the reassignment of the remaining XB-70A (62-0001); TWX 202041Z Feb 69, subject: Transfer of X-15 SN56-6670 to the Smithsonian Museum.
19. Email, F. Robert van der Linden/X-15 Curator for the NASM to Dennis R. Jenkins, 6 May 2002. It is not unusual for the NASM to begin the process of obtaining a significant vehicle much earlier than would seem appropriate. For instance, they began attempts to acquire the Space Shuttle *Columbia* as early as 1982, barely a year after it had made its first flight.
20. NASA DFRC Press Release 02-21, " NASA's Historic B-52B and 'New' B-52H Participating in 50th Anniversary Activities, 11 April 2002.

Chapter 10 – The Research Program

1. Letter, Gerald M. Truszynski to Dennis R. Jenkins, 9 May 2002; Kenneth C. Sanderson, NASA technical memorandum X-56000, "The X-15 Flight Test Instrumentation," 21 April 1964, pp. 2-3. A similar paper was presented by Sanderson at the Third International Flight Test Instrumentation Symposium in Buckinghamshire, England, 13-16 April 1964; Lieutenant Colonel Burt Rowen, "Human-Factors Support of the X-15 Program," *Air University Quarterly Review*, Air War College, Volume X, Number 4, Winter 1958-59, pp. 31-39.
2. A. Scott Crossfield, *Always Another Dawn: The Story of a Rocket Test Pilot*, (New York: The World Publishing Company, 1960), pp. 263-264; telephone conversation, Charles H. Feltz to Dennis R. Jenkins, 12 May 2002.
3. Lieutenant Colonel Burt Rowen, "Human-Factors Support of the X-15 Program," *Air University Quarterly Review*, Air War College, Volume X, Number 4, Winter 1958-59, pp. 31-39; North American report NA58-190, "X-15 Research Airplane NAA Model NA-240 Flight Test Program," 1 August 1958, pp. II-2 through II-3. In the AFFTC Access to Space Office Project Files; Kenneth C. Sanderson, NASA technical memorandum X-56000, "The X-15 Flight Test Instrumentation," 21 April 1964, p. 4.
4. James E. Love (manager), "X-15 Program," NASA FRC, October 1961. pp. 14-15. In the AFFTC Access to Space Office Project Files. Richard D. Banner, Albert E. Kuhl, and Robert D. Quinn, "Preliminary Results of Aerodynamic Heating Studies on the X-15," (a paper in the *Research Airplane Committee Report on the Conference on the Progress of the X-15 Project*, A Compilation of the Papers presented at the Flight Research Center, 20-21 November 1961), p. 13; Sanderson, "The X-15 Flight Test Instrumentation," pp. 11-12.
The instrumentation number varied widely over the course of the program, and among the three airplanes. For instance, in early 1961, the X-15-1 had 750 thermocouples installed: 293 surface units, 191 located in the substructure, and 266 located in various compartments. The telemetered data included such things as control surface positions (right stabilizer, left stabilizer, vertical stabilizer, upper dive brake, lower dive brake, right wing flap – since the flaps were mechanically connected there was no sensor on the left one), stability augmentation system servo shaft positions (left/right pitch and roll, yaw), airplane attitude (pitch, roll, yaw – all from the stable platform), altitude (three precisions; 0-30 in. Hg, 0-3 in. Hg, and 0-1 in. Hg), airspeed (again, in three precisions: 0-2500 psf, 0-1000 psf, and 0-100 psf), horizontal velocity (0-7000 fps), vertical velocity (0-6000 psf), pilot control positions (longitudinal trim, all three control sticks plus the rudder pedals), accelerations (+8/-1-g normal, ±1-g transverse, and ±5-g longitudinal), and various cameras.
5. Banner, Kuhl, and Quinn, "Preliminary Results of Aerodynamic Heating Studies on the X-15," p. 13; North American report NA58-190, "X-15 Research Airplane NAA Model NA-240 Flight Test Program," 1 August 1958, pp. II-2 through II-3. In the AFFTC Access to Space Office Project Files; "Advanced development Plan for X-15 Research Aircraft, Advanced Technology Program 653A," 17 November 1961, pp. 40-41. In the files at the AFFTC History Office; James E. Love (manager), "X-15 Program," NASA FRC, October 1961. pp. 14-15, and 22. In the AFFTC Access to Space Office Project Files.
6. Minutes of Meeting, X-15 Human Factors Subcommittee, 30 December 1960; Vincent N. Capasso/X-15 Project Engineer, "X-15 Operations Flight Report for Flight 3-58-87," 3 May 1967; X-15 Status Report, Paul F. Bikle/FRC to J. Martin/NASA Headquarters, 5 May 1967, pp. 5-6; "X-15 Semi-Annual Status Report No. 7," 10 May 1967, p. 29. All in the files at the DFRC History Office. At the end of 1960 this subcommittee changed its name to the Bioastronautics Subcommittee because of "the obsolescence of the term human factors" (emphasis in the original).
7. Jack Fischel and Lannie D. Webb, NASA technical note D-2407, "Flight-Informational Sensors, Display, and Space Control of the X-15 Airplane for Atmospheric and Near-Space Flight Missions," August 1964, p. 4 (this TN was a reproduced copy of a paper presented by the authors at the Aviation and Space Travel Congress on Interrelations Between Air and Space Navigation and Aerospace in Berlin on 22-27 August 1963; presented by the Deutsche Gesellschaft für Ortung und Navigation E.V.); Terry J. Larson and Lannie D. Webb, NASA technical note D-1724, "Calibrations and Comparisons of Pressure-Type Airspeed-Altitude Systems of the X-15 Airplane from Subsonic to High Supersonic Speeds," February 1963; "Advanced development Plan for X-15 Research Aircraft, Advanced Technology Program 653A," 17 November 1961, pp. 43-44. In the files at the AFFTC History Office
8. Letter, Robert G. Hoey to Dennis R. Jenkins, 13 August 2002.
9. Harry R. Bratt and M. J. Kuramoto, "Biomedical Flight Data Collection," *ISA Journal*, October 1963, pp. 57-58; Bratt, "Biomedical Aspects of the X-15 Program, 1959-1964," p. 3.
10. X-15 Status Report, Paul F. Bikle/FRC to H. Brown/NASA Headquarters, 2 October 1961, p. 4. In the files at the DFRC History Office; Burt Rowen, Ralph N. Richardson, and Garrison P. Layton, Jr., "Bioastronautics Support of the X-15 Program," (a paper in the *Research Airplane Committee Report on the Conference on the Progress of the X-15 Project*, A Compilation of the Papers presented at the Flight Research Center, 20-21 November 1961), p. 257; Bratt, "Biomedical Aspects of the X-15 Program, 1959-1964," p. 3. Axilla; of or relating to the armpit. The skin temperature sensors would make a return on later versions of the biomed instrumentation.
11. Rowen, Richardson, and Layton, "Bioastronautics Support of the X-15 Program," pp. 258 and 264.
12. Air Force contract AF04(611)6344.
13. Bratt and Kuramoto, "Biomedical Flight Data Collection," pp. 58-59; Bratt, "Biomedical Aspects of the X-15 Program, 1959-1964," p. 4.
14. Bratt, "Biomedical Aspects of the X-15 Program, 1959-1964," p. 3.
15. Ibid., pp. 4-5, and 12. The Korotkoff sounds are audible vibrations generated by the turbulent flow of blood beyond an abrupt constriction in an artery, such as produced by an occlusive cuff on the upper arm. As the occlusive cuff pressure is lowered, the pressure at the first audible sound is taken as the systolic pressure (peak pressure at the passage of the pulse wave). The pressure at the last audible sound, or the point at which the amplitude and frequency of the sounds changes abruptly, is taken as the diastolic pressure (relaxation pressure between pulse waves).
16. Bratt, "Biomedical Aspects of the X-15 Program, 1959-1964," p. 2.
17. Statement of Work for the Micrometeorite Collection experiment (#13). In the AFFTC Access to Space Office Project Files; "X-15 Semi-Annual Status Report No. 3," 1 December 1964, p. 5; X-15 Status Report, Paul F. Bikle/FRC to J. Martin/NASA Headquarters, 10 January 1967, p. 6. In the files at the DFRC History Office. Interestingly, the weight of the pods often differed from side to side. For instance, on Flight 3-57-86 the right pod weighed 72.4 pounds with the longitudinal center of gravity at 34 percent of the wing-tip chord; the left pod weighed 97.2 pounds at 33-percent chord.
18. Trip Report, Captain Hugh D. Clark/X-15 Project Office, describing a trip on 20-24 August 1962 to the Flight Research Center to discuss the Follow-On Experiments Program, report dated 17 September 1962. In the files of the Air Force Historical Research Agency; "X-15 Semi-Annual Status Report No. 3," 1 December 1964, p. 5; X-15 Status Report, Paul F. Bikle/FRC to J. Martin/NASA Headquarters, 1 December 1965, p. 4; Ronald S. Waite/X-15 Project engineer, "X-15 Operations Flight Report for Flight 1-45-72," 15 April 1964. In the files at the DFRC History Office.
19. "X-15 Semi-Annual Status Report No. 3," 1 December 1964, p. 5; X-15 Status Report, Paul F. Bikle/FRC to J. Martin/NASA Headquarters, 1 December 1965, p. 4. In the files at the DFRC History Office.
20. Trip Report, Captain Hugh D. Clark/X-15 Project Office, describing a trip on 20-24 August 1962 to the Flight Research Center to discuss the Follow-On Experiments Program, report dated 17 September 1962. In the files of the Air Force Historical Research Agency.
21. Ibid.
22. Ibid.
23. Elmor J. Adkins and Johnny G. Armstrong, "Development and Status of the X-15A-2 Airplane," (a paper in the *Progress of the X-15 Research Airplane Program*, A Compilation of the Papers presented at the Flight Research Center, 7 October 1965, NASA SP-90, (Washington, D.C.: NASA, 1965), p. 105; Johnny G. Armstrong, AFFTC technology document FTC-TD-69-4, "Flight Planning and Conduct of the X-15A-2 Envelope Expansion Program, July 1969, p. 7.
24. X-15 Status Report, Paul F. Bikle/FRC to J. Martin/NASA Headquarters, 5 May 1967; Ronald S. Waite/X-15 Project Engineer, "X-15 Flight Operations Report for Flight 1-63-104," 20 May 1966.
25. See a variety of status reports, for example, X-15 Status Report, Paul F. Bikle/FRC to H. Brown/NASA Headquarters, 15 January 1962, p. 3. In the files at the DFRC History Office.
26. Captain Ronald G. Boston, "The X-15's Role in Aerospace Progress," a paper prepared at the Department of History of the Air Force Academy, August 1978, p. 36.
27. North American report NA61-295 "Development of Coating Materials for Reduction of the Infrared Emission of the YB-70 Air Vehicle," 16 March 1961, no page numbers. See also, for example, North American report NA-59-53-1, "Thermal Radiation Characteristics of the B-70 Weapon System," 31 July 1959 and North American report NA-59-1887, "B-70 Radar Cross Section, Infrared Radiation, and Infrared Countermeasures," 31 December 1959. Both originally classified secret.
28. Ibid.
29. X-15 Status Reports, Paul F. Bikle/FRC to H. Brown/NASA Headquarters, 15 February 1961, p. 6; Bratt, "Biomedical Aspects of the X-15 Program, 1959-1964," p. 16. This data was directly applicable to Project Mercury, and helped ease some anxiety over the astronauts health on the first manned flights.
30. "Advanced Development Plan for X-15 Research Aircraft, Advanced Technology Program 653A," 17 November 1961, pp. 45-46. In the files at the AFFTC History Office. X-15 Status Reports, Paul F. Bikle/FRC to H. Brown/NASA Headquarters, 1 August 1961, p. 4 and 1 September 1961, p. 4. In the files at the DFRC History Office.
31. Ibid.
32. James E. Love, "History and Development of the X-15 Research Aircraft," not dated, p. 23. In the files at the DFRC History Office.
33. Memorandum of Understanding, "X-15 Flight Research Program, signed on 15 August 1961 by the Research Airplane Committee; letter, Hugh L. Dryden to Major General Marvin C. Demler, no subject (but referencing the MoU), 12 July 1961. Both in the AFFTC Access to Space Office Project Files; "Advanced Development Plan for X-15 Research Aircraft, Advanced Technology Program 653A," 17 November 1961, pp. 2-3. In the files at the AFFTC History Office; System Package Program, System 653A, 18 May 1964, 6-37 through 6-48; NASA news release 62-98; X-15 news release 62-91; letter, Hugh L. Dryden to Lieutenant General James Ferguson, 15 July 1963; NASA news release 64-42. All in the files of the DFRC History Office. At this point the Research Airplane Committee included Hugh L Dryden from NASA, Major General Marvin C. Demler from the Air Force, and Rear Admiral John T. Hayward from the Navy.
34. News release 62-91, "X-15 Assigned New Follow-On Research Role," 13 April 1962; System Package Program, System 653A, 18 May 1964, 6-37 through 6-48; NASA news release 62-98; X-15 news release 62-91; letter, Hugh L. Dryden to Lieutenant General James Ferguson, 15 July 1963; NASA news release 64-42. All in the files of the DFRC History Office. At this point the Research airplane Committee consisted of Hugh L. Dryden, Major General Marvin C. Demler, and Vice Admiral William F. Raborn.
35. "Advanced Development Plan for X-15 Research Aircraft, Advanced Technology Program 653A," 17 November 1961, p. 47. In the files at the AFFTC History Office; X-15 Status Report, Paul F. Bikle/FRC to H. Brown/NASA Headquarters, 16 April 1962, p. 3; System Package Program, System 653A, 18 May 1964, p. 6-37; "X-15 Semi-Annual Status Report No. 1," October 1963, p. 34; "X-15 Semi-Annual Status Report No. 3," 1 December 1964, p. 16. In the files at the DFRC History Office.
36. "X-15 Semi-Annual Status Report No. 1," October 1963, p. 34; "X-15 Semi-Annual Status Report No. 3," 1 December 1964, p. 16; X-15 Status Reports, Paul F. Bikle/FRC to J. Martin/NASA Headquarters, 9 July 1965, 1 April, and 8 August 1966; "X-15 Semi-Annual Status Report No. 6," 1 November 1966, p. 15. In the files at the DFRC History Office; Captain Ronald G. Boston, "The X-15's Role in Aerospace Progress," a paper prepared at the Department of History of the Air Force Academy, August 1978, pp. 36-37; email, Marilyn Meade/University of Wisconsin to Dennis R. Jenkins, 5 June 2002. Ms. Meade indicates that the original X-15 film was reflown onboard Spacelab 1 during STS-9 on 28 November 1983 to commemorate the original event.
37. "Advanced Development Plan for X-15 Research Aircraft, Advanced Technology Program 653A," 17 November 1961, p. 48. In the files at the AFFTC History Office; Statement of Work for the Ultraviolet Earth Background Experiment (#2). In the AFFTC Access to Space Office Project Files; "X-15 Semi-Annual Status Report No. 1," October 1963, p. 35; "X-15 Semi-Annual Status Report No. 3," 1 December 1964, p. 16; X-15 Status Report, Paul F. Bikle/FRC to J. Martin/NASA Headquarters, 1 April 1966, p. 8. In the files at the DFRC History Office.
38. "X-15 Semi-Annual Status Report No. 1," October 1963, p. 35; "X-15 Semi-Annual Status Report No. 3," 1 December 1964, p. 16. In the files at the DFRC History Office; X-15 Status Reports, Paul F. Bikle/FRC to J. Martin/NASA Headquarters, 4 February 1965 and 1 April 1966; "X-15 Semi-Annual Status Report No. 6," 1 November 1966, p. 15. In the files at the DFRC History Office.
39. "X-15 Semi-Annual Status Report No. 1," October 1963, p. 35; "X-15 Semi-Annual Status Report No. 3," 1 December 1964, p. 16. In the files at the DFRC History Office; Anthony Jalink, Jr., "Radiation Measurements of the Earth's Horizon," (a paper in the *Progress of the X-15 Research Airplane Program*, A Compilation of the Papers presented at the Flight Research Center, 7 October 1965, NASA SP-90, (Washington, D.C.: NASA, 1965), pp. 96-98.
40. "X-15 Semi-Annual Status Report No. 1," October 1963, p. 35; "X-15 Semi-Annual Status Report No. 3," 1 December 1964, p. 16; X-15 Status Report No. 66-4, Paul F. Bikle/FRC to J. Martin/NASA Headquarters, 1 April 1966, pp. 8-9. In the files at the DFRC History Office; Anthony Jalink, Jr., "Radiation Measurements of the Earth's Horizon," (a paper in the *Progress of the X-15 Research Airplane Program*, A Compilation of the Papers presented at the Flight Research Center, 7 October 1965, NASA SP-90, (Washington, D.C.: NASA, 1965), pp. 98-99; Captain Ronald G. Boston, "The X-15's Role in Aerospace Progress," a paper prepared at the Department of History of the Air Force Academy, August 1978, p. 38. A horizon profile – usually called a "limb" in astronomy – is the apparent edge of the disk of a solar-system body as projected on the sky or the apparent

edge of the Sun, Moon, or a planet or any other celestial body with a detectable disc. A hypothesis that atmospheric phenomena are sufficiently stable to serve as space navigation aids fostered interest in establishing and examining horizon profiles, and provided the basis for this experiment.

41. Donald I. Groening, "Investigation of High-Speed High-Altitude Photography," (a paper in the *Progress of the X-15 Research Airplane Program*, A Compilation of the Papers presented at the Flight Research Center, 7 October 1965, NASA SP-90, (Washington, D.C.: NASA, 1965), p. 85.
42. Trip Report, Captain Hugh D. Clark/X-15 Project Office, describing a trip on 20-24 August 1962 to the Flight Research Center to discuss the Follow-On Experiments Program, report dated 17 September 1962. In the files of the Air Force Historical Research Agency.
43. Air Force report AL-TR-64-328, "Influence of High-Speed Flight on Photography," 8 January 1965, pp. 7-9. In the AFFTC Access to Space Office Project Files.
44. Air Force report AL-TR-64-328, pp. 8, 11-17, and 27; Statement of Work for the Induced Turbulence Experiments (#5 and #6). In the AFFTC Access to Space Office Project Files. The X-15 modifications were performed under ECP X-15-155.
45. Air Force report AL-TR-64-328, pp. 8, 11-17, and 27.
46. "X-15 Semi-Annual Status Report No. 1," October 1963, pp. 33 and 41; "X-15 Semi-Annual Status Report No. 3," 1 December 1964, pp. 16 and 20. In the files at the DFRC History Office; Air Force report AL-TR-64-328, "Influence of High-Speed Flight on Photography," 8 January 1965, p. iii. In the AFFTC Access to Space Office Project Files.
47. Groening, "Investigation of High-Speed High-Altitude Photography," pp. 85-86.
48. Air Force report AL-TR-64-328, pp. xiv and 11-21; letter, Richard J. Harer to Dennis R. Jenkins 125 October 2002.
49. Groening, "Investigation of High-Speed High-Altitude Photography," pp. 86-88.
50. Boston, "The X-15's Role in Aerospace Progress," pp. 42-43.
51. "X-15 Semi-Annual Status Report No. 3," 1 December 1964, p. 16. In the files at the DFRC History Office.
52. "Advanced Development Plan for X-15 Research Aircraft, Advanced Technology Program 653A," 17 November 1961, p. 51. In the files at the AFFTC History Office; Trip Report, Captain Hugh D. Clark/X-15 Project Office, describing a trip on 20-24 August 1962 to the Flight Research Center to discuss the Follow-On Experiments Program, report dated 17 September 1962. In the files of the Air Force Historical Research Agency; "X-15 Semi-Annual Status Report No. 3," 1 December 1964, p. 16. In the files at the DFRC History Office.
53. "X-15 Semi-Annual Status Report No. 1," October 1963, p. 36; "X-15 Semi-Annual Status Report No. 3," 1 December 1964, p. 16; System Package Program, System 653A, 18 May 1964, p. 6-39; X-15 Status Report, Paul F. Bikle/FRC to J. Martin/NASA Headquarters, 1 April 1966, p. 9. In the files at the DFRC History Office.
54. Ronald P. Banas, NASA technical memorandum X-1136, "Comparison of Measured and Calculated Turbulent Heat Transfer in a Uniform and Nonuniform Flow Field on the X-15 Upper Vertical Fin at Mach Numbers of 4.2 and 5.3," 28 May 1965, pp. 25-26. Often the leading edge profile is quoted as a diameter instead of a radius; the original leading edge had a diameter of 1.0 inch, the new one was 0.030-inch.
55. Banas, "Comparison of Measured and Calculated Turbulent Heat Transfer in a Uniform and Nonuniform Flow Field on the X-15 Upper Vertical Fin at Mach Numbers of 4.2 and 5.3," pp. 9-10.
56. "Advanced Development Plan for X-15 Research Aircraft, Advanced Technology Program 653A," 17 November 1961, p. 51. In the files at the AFFTC History Office; "X-15 Semi-Annual Status Report No. 3," 1 December 1964, p. 16. In the files at the DFRC History Office.
57. "Advanced Development Plan for X-15 Research Aircraft, Advanced Technology Program 653A," 17 November 1961, p. 51; "X-15 Semi-Annual Status Report No. 1," October 1963, p. 34; "X-15 Semi-Annual Status Report No. 3," 1 December 1964, p. 16. In the files at the DFRC History Office; Statement of Work for the Infrared Exhaust Signature experiment (#10). In the AFFTC Access to Space Office Project Files. The Cambridge Research Laboratory and Geophysics Research Directorate at Hanscom Field, Massachusetts are now part of the Space Vehicles Directorate (VS) with headquarters located at Kirtland AFB, New Mexico, at the site of the former Phillips Laboratory.
58. "X-15 Semi-Annual Status Report No. 1," October 1963, p. 34; "X-15 Semi-Annual Status Report No. 3," 1 December 1964, p. 16. In the files at the DFRC History Office; Statement of Work for the Infrared Exhaust Signature experiment (#10). In the AFFTC Access to Space Office Project Files.
59. System Package Program, System 653A, 18 May 1964, p. 6-39; "X-15 Semi-Annual Status Report No. 1," October 1963, pp. 36-37; "X-15 Semi-Annual Status Report No. 3," 1 December 1964, p. 17.
60. "Advanced Development Plan for X-15 Research Aircraft, Advanced Technology Program 653A," 17 November 1961, p. 49; Earl J. Montoya and Terry J. Larson, NASA technical memorandum X-56009, "Stratosphere and Mesosphere Density-Height Profiles Obtained with the X-15 Airplane."
61. "X-15 Semi-Annual Status Report No. 1," October 1963, p. 34; "X-15 Semi-Annual Status Report No. 3," 1 December 1964, p. 17. In the files at the DFRC History Office; Statement of Work for the Atmospheric Density Measurements experiment (#12). In the AFFTC Access to Space Office Project Files; Jack J. Horvath and Gary F. Rupert, University of Michigan report 06093-1-F, "Pitot Measurements on an X-15 Rocket Plane," August 1968, pp. 38-39. Air Force contract number AF19(628)-3313 (Project 6020, Task 606002).
62. X-15 Status Report 66-5, Paul F. Bikle/FRC to J. Martin/NASA Headquarters, 4 May 1966, p. 7; "X-15 Semi-Annual Status Report No. 6," 1 November 1966, p. 15; Jack J. Horvath and Gary F. Rupert, University of Michigan report 06093-1-F, "Pitot Measurements on an X-15 Rocket Plane," August 1968, pp. 2 and 38.
63. "X-15 Semi-Annual Status Report No. 1," October 1963, p. 33; "X-15 Semi-Annual Status Report No. 3," 1 December 1964, p. 17; "X-15 Semi-Annual Status Report No. 6," 1 November 1966, p. 21. All in the files at the DFRC History Office; Statement of Work for the Micrometeorite Collection experiment (#13). In the AFFTC Access to Space Office Project Files; X-15 Status Report 66-8, Paul F. Bikle/FRC to J. Martin/NASA Headquarters, 8 August 1966, p. 6. In the files at the DFRC History Office. Boston, "The X-15's Role in Aerospace Progress," p. 37.

    Initially, NASA and North American studied installing some sort of bulge on or near the wingtip; subsequently analysis indicated that this had unexpected aero-thermo problems and was abandoned. Next came a study of an external store that could be suspended beneath the X-15 wing, but this too had aero-thermo problems. The wingtip solution had the fewest problems and was the easiest to implement, although the wings did have to be largely disassembled in order to run wires through them to connect to the pods.
64. X-15 Status Report, Paul F. Bikle/FRC to J. Martin/NASA Headquarters, 1 April 1966, p. 10. In the files at the DFRC History Office.
65. X-15 Status Reports, Paul F. Bikle/FRC to J. Martin/NASA Headquarters, 3 March 1967, p. 4 and 10 May 1967, p. 4; memorandum, Elmor J. Adkins/X-15 Project Office to Assistant Division Chief, Research Projects, subject: Preliminary report on X-15 flight 3-58-87, 10 May 1967; memorandum, Elmor J. Adkins/X-15 Project Office to Assistant Division Chief, Research Projects, subject: Preliminary report on X-15 flight 3-64-95, 3 November 1967. All in the files at the DFRC History Office; Melvin E. Burke and Robert J. Basso, "Résumé of X-15 Experience Related to Flight Guidance Research," (a paper in the *Progress of the X-15 Research Airplane Program*, A Compilation of the Papers presented at the Flight Research Center, 7 October 1965, NASA SP-90, (Washington, D.C.: NASA, 1965), p. 79-80.
66. "X-15 Semi-Annual Status Report No. 1," October 1963, p. 34; "X-15 Semi-Annual Status Report No. 3," 1 December 1964, pp. 17-18. In the files at the DFRC History Office.
67. X-15 Status Report, Paul F. Bikle/FRC to J. Martin/NASA Headquarters, 1 April 1966, pp. 10-11. In the files at the DFRC History Office.
68. System Package Program, System 653A, 18 May 1964, pp. 6-40 and 6-41.
69. "X-15 Semi-Annual Status Report No. 1," October 1963, p. 36. These balloons were 30-inches in diameter; each was folded, packaged, and housed with its own gas expansion bottle in a very small space. The balloons had been used on Mercury for various experiments in space. See Lloyd S. Swenson, Jr., James M. Greenwood, and Charles C. Alexander, *This New Ocean: A History of Project Mercury*, (Washington DC: NASA, 1966), pp. 444 and others.
70. X-15 Status Reports, Paul F. Bikle/FRC to J. Martin/NASA Headquarters, 1 April and 4 May 1966; "X-15 Semi-Annual Status Report No. 3," 1 December 1964, p. 18; "X-15 Semi-Annual Status Report No. 6," 1 November 1966, p. 21. In the files at the DFRC History Office.
71. Boston, "The X-15's Role in Aerospace Progress," pp. 38-39.
72. Carlton R. Gray, "An Horizon Definition Experiment," AIAA paper No. 69-869, presented at the AIAA Guidance, Control, and Flight Mechanics Conference, Princeton, New Jersey, 18-20 November 1969, p. 1; "X-15 Semi-Annual Status Report No. 3," 1 December 1964, p. 18. In the files at the DFRC History Office.
73. Gray, "An Horizon Definition Experiment," pp. 1-3; X-15 Status Report, Paul F. Bikle/FRC to J. Martin/NASA Headquarters, 1 April 1966, p. 11. In the files at the DFRC History Office.
74. X-15 Status Reports, Paul F. Bikle/FRC to J. Martin/NASA Headquarters, 1 April 1966, pp. 8-9, 3 March 1967, p. 1, 6 September 1968, p. 4, and 7 October 1968, p. 2; Gray, "An Horizon Definition Experiment," p. 2; "X-15 Semi-Annual Status Report No. 1," October 1963, p. 35. All in the files at the DFRC History Office. The Manned Spacecraft Center was subsequently renamed the Johnson Space Center.
75. Gray, "An Horizon Definition Experiment," pp. 8-12; Boston, "The X-15's Role in Aerospace Progress," pp. 38-39.
76. "Advanced Development Plan for X-15 Research Aircraft, Advanced Technology Program 653A," 17 November 1961, p. 56; System Package Program, System 653A, 18 May 1964, p. 6-41; "X-15 Semi-Annual Status Report No. 1," October 1963, p. 36 "X-15 Semi-Annual Status Report No. 3," 1 December 1964, p. 19; "X-15 Semi-Annual Status Report No. 4," 1 April 1965, p. 13; X-15 Status Report, Paul F. Bikle/FRC to J. Martin/NASA Headquarters, 1 April 1966, p. 11. In the files at the DFRC History Office.
77. System Package Program, System 653A, 18 May 1964, p. 6-41; Letter, Ralph H. Becker/Navigation & Guidance Laboratory, to Ted Little/AMC, subject: High Altitude Daytime Sky Background Radiation Measurement Program, 29 October 1962; "X-15 Semi-Annual Status Report No. 1," October 1963, p. 33; "X-15 Semi-Annual Status Report No. 3," 1 December 1964, p. 19. In the files at the DFRC History Office; Boston, "The X-15's Role in Aerospace Progress," p. 39; letter, Ralph H. Becker/Navigation & Guidance Laboratory, to Ted Little/AMC, subject: High Altitude Daytime Sky Background Radiation Measurement Program, 29 October 1962; "X-15 Semi-Annual Status Report No. 1," October 1963, p. 33; "X-15 Semi-Annual Status Report No. 3," 1 December 1964, p. 19; X-15 Status Report 66-5, Paul F. Bikle/FRC to J. Martin/NASA Headquarters, 4 May 1966, p. 8; "X-15 Semi-Annual Status Report No. 6," 1 November 1966, p. 23. In the files at the DFRC History Office. The Original Nortronics contract was AF33(694)-291 for the Sky Radiation Measurement Program (for use on the Lockheed U-2).
78. "X-15 Semi-Annual Status Report No. 1," October 1963, p. 41; X-15 Semi-Annual Status Report No. 3," 1 December 1964, p. 19; X-15 Status Reports, Paul F. Bikle/FRC to J. Martin/NASA Headquarters, 1 March, 1 April 1966, and 5 May 1967; memorandum, James R. Welsh for E. James Adkins, Subject: Preliminary report on X-15 flight 1-71-121, 16 May 1967. In the files at the DFRC History Office. There seems to a great deal of confusion in the official documentation concerning the experiment number assigned to the Western Test Range Launch Monitoring Experiment. Most documentation calls it Experiment #20, however many Air Force documents refer to it as Experiment #28. Since most documents use #20 that is what will be used here.
79. Memorandum, Jack L. Kolf/FRC to James E. Love/X-15 Program Manager, subject: WTR Experiment Coordination, 23 May 1968. Most likely, the "other reasons" for launching the missiles were operational training; real missiles were routinely removed from operational silos, transported to Vandenberg, and launched by operational crews. On several occasions Vandenberg has launched multiple Minuteman ICBMs during operational testing; no multiple Titan launches were ever conducted.
80. X-15 Status Reports, Paul F. Bikle/FRC to J. Martin/NASA Headquarters, 6 September 1968, p. 2 and 4 November 1968, pp. 1-2. In the files at the DFRC History Office.
81. Memorandum, James R. Welsh to Assistant Chief, Research Projects, Subject: Preliminary report on X-15 flight 1-79-139, 5 September 1968; memorandum, Jack L. Kolf to Assistant Chief, Research Projects, Subject: Preliminary report on X-15 flight 1-81-141, 5 November 1968; email between Jeffery Geiger, 30th Space Wing Historian, and Dennis R. Jenkins, 8 April 2002; "X-15 Program," a briefing prepared by the AFFTC in late October 1968. In the files at the AFFTC History Office.
82. System Package Program, System 653A, 18 May 1964, p. 6-42; "X-15 Semi-Annual Status Report No. 1," October 1963, p. 37-40; "X-15 Semi-Annual Status Report No. 3," 1 December 1964, p. 19. In the files at the DFRC History Office.
83. "X-15 Semi-Annual Status Report No. 1," October 1963, p. 40.
84. John V. Becker, "A Hindsight Study of the NASA Hypersonic Research Engine Project" (Washington D.C., NASA/OAST, 1 July 1976), p. 9. In the files at the NASA History Office.
85. Memorandum, Paul F. Bikle to the NASA Office of Aeronautical Research, subject: Repairs to the X-15-2 Airplane, 27 December 1962. In the files at the NASA History Office; Ronald G. Boston, "Outline of the X-15's Contributions to Aerospace Technology," 21 November 1977. Unpublished preliminary version of the typescript available in the NASA Dryden History Office, p. 12.
86. "X-15 Semi-Annual Status Report No. 1," October 1963, p. 40; Marquardt report MP1209, "Hypersonic Airbreathing Propulsion Systems for Testing on the X-15: Feasibility and Preliminary Design Study," prepared under contract NAS4-382, 3 December 1963.
87. Marquardt report MP1209, "Hypersonic Airbreathing Propulsion Systems for Testing on the X-15: Feasibility and Preliminary Design Study," prepared under contract NAS4-382, 3 December 1963.
88. Ibid.
89. "X-15 Semi-Annual Status Report No. 3," 1 December 1964, p. 19. In the files at the DFRC History Office; Kennedy F. Rubert, "Hypersonic Air-Breathing Propulsion-System Testing," (a paper in the *Progress of the X-15 Research Airplane Program*, A Compilation of the Papers presented at the Flight Research Center, 7 October 1965, NASA SP-90, (Washington, D.C.: NASA, 1965)), p. 128.
90. Rubert, "Hypersonic Air-Breathing Propulsion-System Testing," p. 128.
91. Frank W. Burcham, Jr., and Jack Nugent, NASA technical note D-5638, "Local Flow Field Around a Pylon-Mounted Dummy Ramjet Engine on the X-15A-2 Airplane for Mach Numbers From 2.0 to 6.7," February 1970, pp. 3-5 and 22-28.
92. Burcham and Nugent, "Local Flow Field Around a Pylon-Mounted Dummy Ramjet Engine on the X-15A-2 Airplane for Mach Numbers From 2.0 to 6.7," pp. 3-4 and 22-28.
93. Ibid., pp. 3, 16-17, and 22-28.
94. Becker, "A Hindsight Study of the NASA Hypersonic Research Engine Project," pp. 27-28 and 54-58.
95. Ronald S. Waite/X-15 Project Engineer, "X-15 Operations Flight Report for Flight 1-53-86," 13 April 1965; "X-15 Semi-Annual Status Report No. 1," October 1963, p. 41; "X-15 Semi-Annual Status Report No. 3," 1 December 1964, p. 20. Both in the files at the DFRC History Office.
96. System Package Program, System 653A, 18 May 1964, p. 6-43; "X-15 Semi-Annual Status Report No. 3," 1 December 1964, p. 20; X-15 Status Report, Paul F. Bikle/FRC to J. Martin/NASA Headquarters, 1 April 1966, p. 12. In the files at the DFRC History Office.
97. Letter, Albert J. Evans to Hugh L. Dryden, subject: Notification of Approval of Additions to the X-15 Test-Bed Program, 30 March 1964. In the files at the NASA History Office; X-15 Status Report, Paul F. Bikle/FRC to J. Martin/NASA Headquarters, 1 April 1966, p. 13; "X-15 Semi-Annual Status Report No. 6," 1 November 1966, p. 25. In the files at the DFRC History Office.
98. X-15 Status Report, Paul F. Bikle/FRC to J. Martin/NASA Headquarters, 1 April 1966, p. 12. In the files at the DFRC History Office; memorandum, James R. Welsh (for Elmor J. Adkins, Chief/X-15 Project Office) to Assistant Chief, Research Projects, subject: Preliminary report on X-15 flight 3-61-91, 2 August 1967.
99. Memorandum, Elmor J. Adkins, Chief/X-15 Project Office to Assistant Chief, Research Projects, subject: Preliminary report on X-15 flight 3-62-92, 14 September 1967; memorandum, Elmor J. Adkins, Chief/X-15 Project Office to Assistant Chief, Research Projects, subject: Preliminary report on X-15 flight 3-63-94, 2 November 1967.
100. "X-15 Semi-Annual Status Report No. 1," October 1963, p. 37; "X-15 Semi-Annual Status Report No. 3," 1 December 1964, p. 19. In the files at the DFRC History Office.
101. "X-15 Semi-Annual Status Report No. 1," October 1963, p. 41; "X-15 Semi-Annual Status Report No. 3," 1 December 1964, p. 20. In the files at the DFRC History Office.
102. Groening, "Investigation of High-Speed High-Altitude Photography," pp. 85, 88, and 93; Air Force report AL-TR-64-328, "Influence of High-Speed Flight on Photography," 8 January 1965, p. 18. In the AFFTC Access to Space Office Project Files. IR Ektachrome differs from normal film in that the spectral sensitivity of each emulsion layer is shifted toward the infrared. The blue light was removed by filtering and, in the final reversed image that was printed, naturally green objects were blue, yellow objects were green, and red objects were yellow. Objects radiating or reflecting strongly in the near infrared, such as healthy vegetation, were red.
103. X-15 Status Reports, Paul F. Bikle/FRC to J. Martin/NASA Headquarters, 3 January and 1 April 1966; "X-15 Semi-Annual Status Report No. 6," 1 November 1966, p. 25; William P. Albrecht/X-15 Project Engineer, "X-15 Operations Flight Report for Flight 2-52-96," 25 August 1967; William P. Albrecht/X-15 Project Engineer, "X-15 Operations Flight Report for Flight 2-53-97," 9 October 1967.
104. X-15 Status Report, Paul F. Bikle/FRC to J. Martin/NASA Headquarters, 1 April 1966, p. 13; "X-15 Semi-Annual Status Report No. 6," 1 November 1966, p. 25. In the files at the DFRC History Office. There seems to be a great deal of confusion in the official documentation concerning the number assigned to the Western Test Range Launch Monitoring experiment. Most documentation calls it Experiment #20, however many Air Force documents refer to it as experiment #28. Since most documents use #20 that is what will be used here. To further confuse matters, very late in the program the X-Ray Air Density Experiment was called #28, as reflected here.
105. "X-15 Semi-Annual Status Report No. 7," 10 May 1967, p.27; James E. Love and Jack Fischel, "Summary of X-15 Program," (a paper in the *Progress of the X-15 Research Airplane Program*, A Compilation of the Papers presented at the Flight Research Center, 7 October 1965, NASA SP-90, (Washington, D.C.: NASA, 1965), p. 14; X-15 Status Reports, Paul F. Bikle/FRC to J. Martin/NASA Headquarters, 1 April and 4 May 1966. In the files at the DFRC History Office.
106. X-15 Status Report 66-10, Paul F. Bikle/FRC to J. Martin/NASA Headquarters, 6 October 1966, p. 6. In the files at the DFRC History Office.
107. X-15 Status Report, Paul F. Bikle/FRC to J. Martin/NASA Headquarters, 1 April 1966, p. 13. In the files at the DFRC History Office.
108. Rodney K. Bogue, FRC working paper 30, "X-15 Fixed Ball Nose Flight Test Results, July 1972. Typescript in the files at the DFRC History Office. Several clarifications to the original narrative were provided in an email between Rodney K. Bogue and Dennis R. Jenkins, 6 June 2002.
109. For more on the SEADS experiment, see Dennis R. Jenkins, *Space Shuttle: The History of the National Space Transportation System – The First 100 Flights*, (Cape Canaveral, FL: the author, 2001), pp. 436-437.
110. X-15 Status Report, Paul F. Bikle/FRC to J. Martin/NASA Headquarters, 8 November 1967, p. 2; Vincent N. Capasso, "X-15 Operations Flight Report for Flight 1-75-133," 9 April 1968; memorandum, James R. Welsh/X-15 Research Project Office to Assistant Chief, Research Projects, subject: Preliminary report on X-15 flight 1-75-133, 17 April 1968; Vincent N. Capasso, "X-15 Operations Flight Report for Flight 1-76-134," 30 April 1968. All in the files at the DFRC History Office.
111. "X-15 Semi-Annual Status Report No. 1," October 1963, p. 35; "X-15 Semi-Annual Status Report No. 3," 1 December 1964, pp. 8-9; Ronald J. Wilson, NASA technical note D-3331, "Drag and Wear Characteristics of Various Skid Materials on Dissimilar Lakebed Surfaces During the Slideout of the X-15 Airplane," March 1966. Data in the table comes mainly from Wilson. The cermet process was interesting, and involved (1) coating a standard 4130 steel skid by copper-brazing a 0.1865-inch screen of tungsten-carbide chips to the skid surface after precoating the surface with a flux, (2) flame-spraying a 0.020-inch to 0.040-inch thick matrix of tungsten (35-percent), chrome, nickel, and boron (65-percent) on top of the copper-brazed carbide chips, then fusing and grit blasting; and (3) flame-spraying with a copper-nickel matrix. The surface was then ground to a nominal thickness of 0.20-inch.
112. L. J. McLain and Murray Palitz, NASA technical note D-4813, "Flow-Field Investigations on the X-15 Airplane and Model up to Hypersonic Speeds," 22 March 1968, pp. 4-6.
113. Robert D. Quinn and Frank V. Olinger, NASA confidential technical memorandum X-1921, "Flight-Measured Heat Transfer and Skin Friction at a Mach Number of 5.25 and at Low Wall Temperatures," 19 August 1969, pp 1-20. For data on earlier heat-transfer and skin-friction studies, see, for example, Richard D.

Banner and Albert E. Kuhl, "A Summary of X-15 Heat-Transfer and Skin-Friction Measurements, NASA technical memorandum X-1210, 1966.
114. X-15 Status Report, Paul F. Bikle/FRC to J. Martin/NASA Headquarters, 4 April 1967, p. 2; Robert D. Quinn and Frank V. Olinger, NASA confidential technical memorandum X-1921, "Flight-Measured Heat Transfer and Skin Friction at a Mach Number of 5.25 and at Low Wall Temperatures," 19 August 1969, pp 5-8.
115. X-15 Status Report, Paul F. Bikle/FRC to J. Martin/NASA Headquarters, 4 April 1967, p. 4; Karen S. Green and Terrill W. Putnam, NASA technical memorandum X-3126, "Measurements of Sonic Booms Generated by an Airplane Flying at Mach 3.5 and 4.8," 5 September 1974. Note that the X-15 flight program had been over nearly 6 years when this report was issued.
116. X-15 Status Report, Paul F. Bikle/FRC to J. Martin/NASA Headquarters, 4 April 1967, p. 4. In the files at the DFRC History Office.
117. Karen S. Green and Terrill W. Putnam, NASA technical memorandum X-3126, "Measurements of Sonic Booms Generated by an Airplane Flying at Mach 3.5 and 4.8," 5 September 1974, passim.
118. Ibid.
119. Aeronutronic (a Division of Ford Motor Company) report number 12121U, "X-15 Recoverable Booster System," 11 December 1961, pp. 1-3. In the files at the DFRC History Office.
120. Ibid., pp. 5-6 and 21.
121. Ibid., p. 10 and drawings attached to the back of the report.
122. Ibid., pp. 10-11.
123. Ibid., pp. 12-16 and 25.
124. X-15 Status Report, Paul F. Bikle/FRC to H. Brown/NASA Headquarters, 15 March 1962, p. 3. In the files at the DFRC History Office.
125. Marquardt report (no number), "A Study of the Ejector Ramjet Engine for X-15 Propulsion," 3 January 1967, originally classified confidential, no page numbers.
126. Ibid.
127. Ibid.
128. Ibid.
129. North American report NA-60-1, "X-15 Research Capability," 11 November 1960, no page numbers. In the files at the USAF Test Pilot School, Edwards AFB.
130. Ibid.
131. Ibid.

Chapter 11 – Technical Description

1. C. L. Davis, "X-15 Structure and Structural Development," (a paper in the *Research Airplane Committee Report on the Conference on the Progress of the X-15 Project*, A Compilation of the Papers presented in Los Angeles, California, 28-30 July 1958), pp. 213-214.
2. Richard L. Schleicher, "Structural Design of the X-15," North American Aviation, 1963, pp. 9-10. Copy provided courtesy of Gerald H. Balzer Collection.
3. Ibid., pp. 10-11.
4. Ibid., pp. 27-29.
5. Ibid., pp. 27-29.
6. Davis, "X-15 Structure and Structural Development," pp. 213-214; X-15 Interim Flight Manual, FHB-23-1, 18 March 1960, changed 12 May 1961, pp. 1-3–1-6.
7. Schleicher, "Structural Design of the X-15," pp. 7 and 22.
8. Davis, "X-15 Structure and Structural Development," pp. 216 and 219; Richard L. Schleicher, "Structural Design of the X-15," a paper presented to the Royal Aeronautical Society on 18 April 1963, and printed in the *Journal of the Royal Aeronautical Society*, Vol. 67, October 1963, pp. 622. In the files at the Armstrong Memorial Library, Edwards AFB; Richard L. Schleicher, "Structural Design of the X-15," North American Aviation, 1963, pp. 7 and 24; Robert D. Reed and Joe D. Watts, "Skin and Structural Temperatures Measured on the X-15 Airplane During a Flight to Mach Number of 3.3," NASA Confidential Technical Memorandum X-468, January 1961, pp. 2-3; Richard L. Schleicher, "Structural Design of the X-15," *Journal of the Royal Aeronautical Society*, Vol. 67, October 1963, pp. 622.
9. George R. Mellinger, "The X-15," *Aerospace Engineering*, August 1961, p. 29.
10. X-15 Interim Flight Manual, FHB-23-1, 18 March 1960, changed 12 May 1961, various pages.
11. X-15 Interim Flight Manual, pp. 1-7–1-8; John W. Gibb, "X-15 Propellant System description," (a paper in the *Research Airplane Committee Report on the Conference on the Progress of the X-15 Project*, A Compilation of the Papers presented in Los Angeles, California, 28-30 July 1958), pp. 285-286.
12. Elmor J. Adkins and Johnny G. Armstrong, "Development and Status of the X-15A-2 Airplane," (a paper in the *Progress of the X-15 Research Airplane Program*, A Compilation of the Papers presented at the Flight Research Center, 7 October 1965, NASA SP-90, (Washington, D.C.: NASA, 1965), pp. 104-105.
13. Gibb, "X-15 Propellant System description," pp. 285-286.
14. Ibid., p. 286.
15. X-15 Interim Flight Manual. Other sources list these engines as having either 7,000-lbf or 8,000-lbf each. It is likely that these thrust values are at some altitude, not sea level.
16. "Handbook: Operation, Service, and Overhaul Instructions, with Parts Catalog, for Liquid Rocket Engines Model XLR11," 1 April 1955; X-15 Interim Flight Manual; email, Bill Arnold (Reaction Motors) to Dennis R. Jenkins, 4 November 2002.
17. X-15 Interim Flight Manual; Purchase Order L-96-233(G), 6 October 1961. Although called a purchase order, this was actually a disposal form that showed "unlisted excess experimental project support property." Bill Arnold remembers "The XLR11 engines that were used in the X-15 program were recovered from various locations. The old NACA had, what I consider to be a virtue, the ability to never throw things away. They had stored a number of the engines deep in some warehouse along with a bunch of residual spare parts left over from the completion of flight testing of the X-1E. It did not require too much effort to reactivate these engines for use in the X-15. My observation now is that some people at the NACA may have had the foresight to think that Reaction Motors would not have a big engine in time for the flight testing of the X-15 and that the -11s would be needed." Many of these XLR11 engines would go on to power the heavyweight lifting bodies as they began their test program.
18. Email, Scott Crossfield to Dennis R. Jenkins, 7 February 2002.
19. Telephone conversation, Charles H. Feltz to Dennis R. Jenkins, 19 February 2002.
20. All of the airframe competitors had noted this, as had Douglas in the D-558-III study.
21. Charles H. Feltz, "Description of the X-15 Airplane, Performance, and Design Mission" (a paper presented at the NACA Conference on the Progress of the X-15 Project, Langley Aeronautical Laboratory, 25-26 October 1956), pp. 28.
22. Captain K. E. Weiss and First Lieutenant R. G. Leiby, Air Force report AFFTC-TR-60-36, "Preliminary Flight Test Rating Test XLR99-RM-1 Rocket Engine, October 1960. In the files of the AFFTC Access to Space Office Project Files; Richard G. Leiby, Donald R. Bellman, and Norman E. DeMar, "XLR99 Engine Operating Experience," (a paper in the *Research Airplane Committee Report on the Conference on the Progress of the X-15 Project*, A Compilation of the Papers presented at the Flight Research Center, 20-21 November 1961), p. 216; C. Wayne Ottinger and James F. Maher, "YLR99-1 Rocket Engine Operating Experience in the X-15 Research Aircraft," a proposed, but apparently unpublished, NASA Technical Note prepared during May 1963. Typescript in the Files at the DFRC History Office.
23. Email, Bill Arnold (Reaction Motors) to Dennis R. Jenkins, 8 October 2002.
24. It was decided that a 6 percent increase in thrust and efficiency could be achieved through the addition of a nozzle extension to expand the gases to an altitude equivalent pressure of 45,000 feet rather than the 19,000 feet represented by the 9.8:1 nozzle; however, the change would add considerable weight to the engine and upset the center of gravity of the X-15. The basic concept was proposed for various follow-on vehicles, but no actual engines were ever built to this configuration. See Richard G. Leiby, Donald R. Bellman, and Norman E. DeMar, "XLR99 Engine Operating Experience," (a paper in the *Research Airplane Committee Report on the Conference on the Progress of the X-15 Project*, A Compilation of the Papers presented at the Flight Research Center, 20-21 November 1961), p. 216.
25. Lawrence N. Hjelm and Bernard R. Bornhorst, "Development of Improved Ceramic Coatings to Increase the Life of the XLR99 Thrust Chamber," (a paper in the *Research Airplane Committee Report on the Conference on the Progress of the X-15 Project*, A Compilation of the Papers presented at the Flight Research Center, 20-21 November 1961), pp. 217-218.
26. William Beller, "Turbopump Key to New X-15 Engine," *Missiles and Space*, 15 August 1960, pp. 33-34; email Bill Arnold (Reaction Motors) to Dennis R. Jenkins, 8 October 2002; email Jerry Brandt to Dennis R. Jenkins, 4 October 2002.
27. Richard G. Leiby, Donald R. Bellman, and Norman E. DeMar, "XLR99 Engine Operating Experience," (a paper in the *Research Airplane Committee Report on the Conference on the Progress of the X-15 Project*, A Compilation of the Papers presented at the Flight Research Center, 20-21 November 1961), pp. 217-218.
28. System Package Program, System 653A, 18 May 1964, p. 6-14, In the files at the DFRC History Office; email, Bill Arnold (Reaction Motors) to Dennis R. Jenkins, 5 October 2002. Arnold remembers, " The change in designation of the XLR99 to a YLR99 was a matter of formality. I believe that the change from X (experimental) to Y (production ready) meant that the item could be listed in Federal supply codes as available for purchase and for use as a standard stock item. This was more or less a status symbol for the engine and Reaction Motors as a significant accomplishment in the rocket industry."
29. Utility Flight Manual.
30. Ibid.
31. Ibid; X-15 Status Report, Paul F. Bikle/FRC to J. Martin/NASA Headquarters, 8 November 1967, p. 1. In the files at the DFRC History Office.
32. Carl Taylor/Vickers, Inc., "Emergency stability for the X-15," *Hydraulics & Pneumatics*, December 1962, P. 74; Utility Flight Manual.
33. Robert J. Culleton/North American Aviation, "X-15 Hydraulic-System Development," (a paper in the *Research Airplane Committee Report on the Conference on the Progress of the X-15 Project*, A Compilation of the Papers presented in Los Angeles, California, 28-30 July 1958), p. 293; Robert J. Culleton/North American Aviation, "To 250,000 feet and 4,100 mph – a study of fluid power on the X-15," *Hydraulics & Pneumatics*, December 1962, pp. 69-70; C. J. Hohmann/Vickers, Inc., "Designing a hydraulic pump for the X-15," *Hydraulics & Pneumatics*, December 1962, pp. 75-77.
34. Culleton "X-15 Hydraulic-System Development," pp. 294-295.
35. Ibid., pp. 294-295.
36. Scholer Bangs, "X-15 pilot evaluates hydraulic system performance," *Hydraulics & Pneumatics*, December 1962, pp. 82-84 (this was an interview with Neil A. Armstrong and James E. Love).
37. Utility Flight Manual.
38. Ibid.
39. C. L. Davis, "X-15 Structure and Structural Development," (a paper in the *Research Airplane Committee Report on the Conference on the Progress of the X-15 Project*, A Compilation of the Papers presented in Los Angeles, California, 28-30 July 1958), p. 219; Richard L. Schleicher, "Structural Design of the X-15," North American Aviation, 1963, pp. 7-8. Copy provided courtesy of Gerald H. Balzer Collection.
40. Richard L. Schleicher, "Structural Design of the X-15," North American Aviation, 1963, pp. 8-9. Copy provided courtesy of Gerald H. Balzer Collection.
41. Wendell H. Stillwell, *X-15 Research Results*, NASA SP-60, (Washington DC: NASA, 1965), pp. 51-52; Utility Flight Manual.
42. Utility Flight Manual.
43. Ibid.
44. Ibid.
45. Ibid.
46. Ibid.
47. Ibid.
48. Ibid.
49. X-15 Interim Flight Manual; X-15 Status Report, Paul F. Bikle/FRC to H. Brown/NASA Headquarters, 15 March 1961, p. 2. In the files at the DFRC History Office.
50. Utility Flight Manual.
51. Ibid. For some reason, on the X-15A-2 this switch was labeled DAMPER LANDING DISENGAGE.
52. X-15 Status Report, Paul F. Bikle/FRC to H. Brown/NASA Headquarters, 16 April 1962, pp. 3; "X-15 Semi-Annual Status Report No. 2," April 1964, p. 6; Utility Flight Manual; "X-15 Semi-Annual Status Report No. 6," 1 November 1966, p. 13; "X-15 Semi-Annual Status Report," 10 May 1967, p. 34.
53. Today this would be called a reaction control system, and often was even in the 1960s. But officially it was the ballistic control system.
54. Utility Flight Manual.
55. George B. Merrick, North American, "X-15 Controlled in space by reaction-control rocket system," *SAE Journal*, August 1960, pp. 38-41; Robert D. Reed and Joe D. Watts, "Skin and Structural Temperatures Measured on the X-15 Airplane During a Flight to Mach Number of 3.3," NASA confidential technical memorandum X-468, January 1961, pp. 2-3; Bruce O. Wagner, "X-15 Auxiliary Power Units and Reaction Controls," (a paper in the *Research Airplane Committee Report on the Conference on the Progress of the X-15 Project*, A Compilation of the Papers presented in Los Angeles, California, 28-30 July 1958), p. 303; Utility Flight Manual. The Bell Aircraft-developed "ring-slot pintle" nozzles had a relatively high heat capacity and caused local heat-sink effects in the skin around them. But they were the only nozzles that were thin enough to fit in the wing without some sort of fairing and its attendant aero-thermal problems.
56. Utility Flight Manual.
57. Ibid.
58. Ibid; email, Robert G. Hoey to Dennis R. Jenkins, 25 August 2002.
59. Utility Flight Manual; Richard L. Schleicher, "Structural Design of the X-15," North American Aviation, 1963, pp. 7-8. Copy provided courtesy of Gerald H. Balzer Collection.
60. Utility Flight Manual.
61. Ibid.
62. North American report NA-58-824B, "Operating and Maintenance Instructions for B-52A Carrier Airplane AF52003 and B-52B Carrier Airplane AF52008," 15 May 1959 (changed 18 August 1961), pp. 1-30 through 1-48.
63. James E. Love, "History and Development of the X-15 Research Aircraft," not dated, p. 14. In the files at the DFRC History Office.
64. William P. Albrecht/X-15 Project Engineer, "X-15 Operations Flight Report for Flight 1-70-119," 27 March 1967.
65. Ibid; "X-15 Semi-Annual Status Report," 10 May 1967, p. 33.
66. James M. McKay and Eldon E. Kordes, "Landing Loads and Dynamics of the X-15 Airplane," (a paper in the *Research Airplane Committee Report on the Conference on the Progress of the X-15 Project*, A Compilation of the Papers presented at the Flight Research Center, 20-21 November 1961), pp. 61-62; Richard L. Schleicher, "Structural Design of the X-15," North American Aviation, 1963, pp. 11 and 33. Copy provided courtesy of Gerald H. Balzer Collection; Utility Flight Manual. It should be noted that the main gear touched down at roughly 9 fps; by the time the large moment arm was factored in, the nose gear touched down at 18 fps, providing a somewhat jarring landing (about 3.9-g vertical) for the pilots.
67. Utility Flight Manual.
68. X-15 Status Report, Paul F. Bikle/FRC to H. Brown/NASA Headquarters, 16 October 1961, p. 1. In the files at the DFRC History Office.
69. William D. Mace and Jon L. Ball, "Flight Characteristics of X-15 Hypersonic Flow-Direction Sensor," (a paper in the *Research Airplane Committee Report on the Conference on the Progress of the X-15 Project*, A Compilation of the Papers presented at the Flight Research Center, 20-21 November 1961), pp. 196-197; Nortronics report NORT-60-46, pp. 3-6. Unfortunately the copy of the report in the DFRC History Office is missing the first two pages, so the title and exact date (the "60" in the report number probably establishes 1960 as the year) could not be ascertained; Kenneth C. Sanderson, NASA technical memorandum X-56000, "The X-15 Flight Test Instrumentation," 21 April 1964, pp. 8-9.
70. Mace and Ball, "Flight Characteristics of X-15 Hypersonic Flow-Direction Sensor," pp. 196-197; Nortronics report NORT-60-46, pp. 3-6.
71. Jack Fischel and Lannie D. Webb, NASA technical note D-2407, "Flight-Informational Sensors, Display, and Space Control of the X-15 Airplane for Atmospheric and Near-Space Flight Missions," August 1964, p. 5; Nortronics report NORT-60-46, pp. 3-10.
72. X-15 Status Report, Paul F. Bikle/FRC to H. Brown/NASA Headquarters, 15 May 1960, p. 8; X-15 Status Report, Paul F. Bikle/FRC to H. Brown/NASA Headquarters, 1 June 1960, p. 10. In the files at the DFRC History Office.
73. "X-15 Semi-Annual Status Report No. 6," 1 November 1966, p. 15; X-15 Status Report, Paul F. Bikle/FRC to J. Martin/NASA Headquarters, 5 May 1967, p. 10; telephone conversation, Rodney K. Bogue/DFRC to Dennis R. Jenkins, 6 June 2002. The status report says that the new nose was tested in the exhaust of a Lockheed F-104 Starfighter, but photographic evidence shows it was really just the J79 engine (probably from an F-104) on the test stand.
74. "Advanced development Plan for X-15 Research Aircraft, Advanced Technology Program 653A," 17 November 1961, pp. 43-44.
75. Johnny G. Armstrong, AFFTC technology document FTC-TD-69-4, "Flight Planning and Conduct of the X-15A-2 Envelope Expansion Program, July 1969, p. 26; X-15 Status Report, Paul F. Bikle/FRC to J. Martin/NASA Headquarters, 12 July 1966, p. 9. In the files at the DFRC History Office.
76. See various memoranda and letters in the files at the NASA History Office and Air Force Historical Research Agency. For example, see memorandum, Arthur W. Vogeley to Hartley A. Soulé/Research Airplane Project Leader, no subject, 30 November 1955; memorandum, Walter C. Williams to Hartley A. Soulé/Research Airplane Project Leader, no subject, 27 January 1956. In the files at the NASA History Office; memorandum, Brigadier General Victor R. Haugen, WADC, to Chief, Aerospace Equipment Division, Director of Procurement and Production, AMC, subject: Flight Data System for the X-15, 22 April 1957; purchase request DE-7-S-4184. In the files at the AFMC History Office; Contract AF33(600)-35397, 5 June 1957. In the files at the Air Force Historical Research Agency.
77. M. L. Lipscomb and John A. Dodgen, "All-Attitude Flight-Date System for the X-15 Research Airplane," (a paper in the *Research Airplane Committee Report on the Conference on the Progress of the X-15 Project*, A Compilation of the Papers presented in Los Angeles, California, 28-30 July 1958), p. 161; Jay V. Christensen and John A. Dodgen, "Flight Experience with X-15 Inertial Data System," (a paper in the *Research Airplane Committee Report on the Conference on the Progress of the X-15 Project*, A Compilation of the Papers presented at the Flight Research Center, 20-21 November 1961), p. 204. Quote from the 1958 paper; Jack Fischel and Lannie D. Webb, NASA technical note D-2407, "Flight-Informational Sensors, Display, and Space Control of the X-15 Airplane for Atmospheric and Near-Space Flight Missions," August 1964, p. 5; Sanderson, "The X-15 Flight Test Instrumentation," pp. 10-11. The 1965 flight manual says that the corridor was 240 miles wide and 720 miles long.
78. Jay V. Christensen and John A. Dodgen, "Flight Experience with X-15 Inertial Data System," (a paper in the *Research Airplane Committee Report on the Conference on the Progress of the X-15 Project*, A Compilation of the Papers presented at the Flight Research Center, 20-21 November 1961), p. 203-204.
79. Lipscomb and Dodgen, "All-Attitude Flight-Date System for the X-15 Research Airplane," p. 159; Christensen and Dodgen, "Flight Experience with X-15 Inertial Data System," p. 203-213.
80. James E. Love and Jack Fischel, "Status of X-15 Program," (a paper in the *Progress of the X-15 Research Airplane Program*, A Compilation of the Papers presented at the Flight Research Center, 7 October 1965, NASA SP-90, (Washington, D.C.: NASA, 1965), p. 6; Melvin E. Burke and Robert J. Basso, "Résumé of X-15 Experience Related to Flight Guidance Research," (a paper in the *Progress of the X-15 Research Airplane Program*, A Compilation of the Papers presented at the Flight Research Center, 7 October 1965, NASA SP-90, (Washington, D.C.: NASA, 1965), p. 76-77 and 83; X-15 Status Reports, Paul F. Bikle/FRC to J. Martin/NASA Headquarters, 4 May and 12 July 1966. In the files at the DFRC History Office.
81. X-15 Status Report, Paul F. Bikle/FRC to J. Martin/NASA Headquarters, 3 January 1966, p. 3. In the files at the DFRC History Office.
82. Love and Fischel, "Status of X-15 Program," p. 6; Burke and Basso, "Résumé of X-15 Experience Related to Flight Guidance Research," p. 77-78 and 84; letter, Robert G. Hoey to Dennis R. Jenkins, 13 August 2002.
83. Burke and Basso, "Résumé of X-15 Experience Related to Flight Guidance Research," p. 77-78 and 84; X-15 Status Reports, Paul F. Bikle/FRC to J. Martin/NASA Headquarters, 12 January, 4 February, 1 April 1965 and 3 January 1966. In the files at the DFRC History Office.
84. Interim Flight Manual; Utility Flight Manual; North American report NA58-190, "X-15 Research Airplane NAA Model NA-240 Flight Test Program," 1 August 1958, pp. II-2 through II-3. In the AFFTC Access to Space Office Project Files; email, A. Scott Crossfield to Dennis R. Jenkins, 28 May 2002.
85. Ibid; email, Robert G. Hoey to Dennis R. Jenkins, 24 August 2002.
86. Utility Flight Manual; email, Robert G. Hoey to Dennis R. Jenkins, 24 August 2002.
87. Email, Robert G. Hoey to Dennis R. Jenkins, 24 August 2002

88. Utility Flight Manual; email, Robert G. Hoey to Dennis R. Jenkins, 24 August 2002.
89. Utility Flight Manual.
90. Utility Flight Manual; email, Robert G. Hoey to Dennis R. Jenkins, 24 August 2002
91. Email, Robert G. Hoey to Dennis R. Jenkins, 24 August 2002.
92. Ibid.
93. X-15 Interim Flight Manual.
94. Utility Flight Manual; letter, Robert G. Hoey to Dennis R. Jenkins, 12 August 2002, with comments to a draft version of this manuscript.
95. X-15 Status Report, Paul F. Bikle/FRC to H. Brown/NASA Headquarters, 15 December 1960, p. 5; Minneapolis-Honeywell report MH-2373-TM1, "Operation and Maintenance Manual, MH-96 Flight Control System for the X-15 Aircraft," Volume V, System Description and Bench Test Procedure (Preliminary), 31 May 1961, provided under Air Force contract number AF33(616)-6610, pp. 3-6.
96. Minneapolis-Honeywell report MH-2373-TM1, pp. 3-6.
97. Ibid.
98. Robert P. Johannes, Neil A. Armstrong, and Thomas C. Hays, "Development of X-15 Self-Adaptive Flight Control System," (a paper in the *Research Airplane Committee Report on the Conference on the Progress of the X-15 Project*, A Compilation of the Papers presented at the Flight Research Center, 20-21 November 1961), pp. 183-184. On the X-15 the attitude reference was provided by the stable platform (and later the Honeywell IFDS); the alpha and beta information was provided by the ball nose.
Bob Hoey provided this observation, "Limit cycle is a natural phenomenon associated with high feedback gains. The frequency is primarily a function of the amount of friction and slop in the control linkage. Frequency CAN be tailored to some degree by lead compensation, as mentioned. The key point is that limit cycle occurs VERY, VERY close to the stability boundary of the system. Controlling the gain to a specified limit cycle amplitude is like walking on the edge of a cliff. The slightest miscue that might cause the gain to get a little too high can result in loss of stability and loss of control. We saw that on the simulator often when we were a little ham-fisted with the controls. Milt [Thompson] had a wild few seconds on one of his heating flights, and of course, Mike really saw the dark side of the MH-96 system [on Flight 3-65-97]." Letter, Robert G. Hoey to Dennis R. Jenkins, 13 August 2002, with comments to a draft version of this manuscript.
99. Johannes, Armstrong, and Hays, "Development of X-15 Self-Adaptive Flight Control System," pp. 186-187; letter, Robert G. Hoey to Dennis R. Jenkins, 13 August 2002.
100. Johannes, Armstrong, and Hays, "Development of X-15 Self-Adaptive Flight Control System," p. 188.
101. Minneapolis-Honeywell report MH-2373-TM1, pp. 7-8; Johannes, Armstrong, and Hays, "Development of X-15 Self-Adaptive Flight Control System," p. 188.
102. Utility Flight Manual.
103. Ibid.
104. Eldon E. Kordes, Robert D. Reed, and Alpha L. Dawdy, "Structural Heating Experiences of the X-15," (a paper in the *Research Airplane Committee Report on the Conference on the Progress of the X-15 Project*, A Compilation of the Papers presented at the Flight Research Center, 20-21 November 1961), pp. 33-34; Lawrence P. Greene and Rolland L. Benner, "X-15 Experience from the Designer's Viewpoint," (a paper in the *Research Airplane Committee Report on the Conference on the Progress of the X-15 Project*, A Compilation of the Papers presented at the Flight Research Center, 20-21 November 1961), pp. 318-319.
105. Richard L. Schleicher, "Structural Design of the X-15," North American Aviation, 1963, pp. 37-38. Copy provided courtesy of Gerald H. Balzer Collection.
106. Kordes, Reed, and Dawdy, "Structural Heating Experiences of the X-15," pp. 33-34; Greene and Benner, "X-15 Experience from the Designer's Viewpoint," pp. 318-319; James E. Love and Jack Fischel, "Status of X-15 Program," (a paper in the *Progress of the X-15 Research Airplane Program*, A Compilation of the Papers presented at the Flight Research Center, 7 October 1965, NASA SP-90, (Washington, D.C.: NASA, 1965), p. 6.
107. Elmor J. Adkins and Johnny G. Armstrong, "Development and Status of the X-15A-2 Airplane," (a paper in the *Progress of the X-15 Research Airplane Program*, A Compilation of the Papers presented at the Flight Research Center, 7 October 1965, NASA SP-90, (Washington, D.C.: NASA, 1965), p. 105.
108. http://users.bestweb.net/~kcoyne/x15seat.htm, accessed 1 April 2002.
109. Utility Flight Manual.
110. Minutes of Meeting, X-15 Human Factors Subcommittee, 30 December 1960; J. F. Hegenwald, "Development of X-15 Escape System," (a paper in the *Research Airplane Committee Report on the Conference on the Progress of the X-15 Project*, A Compilation of the Papers presented in Los Angeles, California, 28-30 July 1958), p. 132.
111. X-15 Status Report, Paul F. Bikle/FRC to J. Martin/NASA Headquarters, 2 June 1965, p. 7.
112. Utility Flight Manual.
113. Lieutenant Colonel Burt Rowen, AFFTC report TN-61-4, "Biomedical Monitoring of the X-15 Program," May 1961, pp. 2-3; Edwin G. Vail and Richard G. Willis, "Pilot Protection for the X-15 Airplane," (a paper in the *Research Airplane Committee Report on the Conference on the Progress of the X-15 Project*, A Compilation of the Papers presented in Los Angeles, California, 28-30 July 1958), pp. 117-118.
114. Vail and Willis, "Pilot Protection for the X-15 Airplane," p. 119.
115. Ibid., p. 119.
116. Ibid., p. 119; corrections to the MA-3 description supplied by Jack Bassick at the David Clark Company in a letter to Dennis R. Jenkins 3 June 2002
117. Vail and Willis, "Pilot Protection for the X-15 Airplane," pp. 119-120. The method to pressurize the MC-2 in the X-15 was slightly different from other MC-2 suits used in other aircraft.
118. Lieutenant Colonel Harry R. Bratt, AFFTC technical report FTC-TR-65-24, "Biomedical Aspects of the X-15 Program: 1959-1964," August 1965, pp. 6-7. In the AFFTC Access to Space Office Project Files.
119. Ibid., pp. 7-8; corrections to the A/P22S-2 description supplied by Jack Bassick at the David Clark Company in a letter to Dennis R. Jenkins 3 June 2002
120. James E. Love, "History and Development of the X-15 Research Aircraft," not dated, p. 13; X-15 Status Reports, Paul F. Bikle/FRC to H. Brown/NASA Headquarters, 15 July 1960, p. 6 and 29 July 1960 p. 7. In the files at the DFRC History Office; Lieutenant Colonel Burt Rowen, Major Ralph N. Richardson, and Garrison P. Layton, Jr., "Bioastronautics Support of the X-15 Program," (a paper in the *Research Airplane Committee Report on the Conference on the Progress of the X-15 Project*, A Compilation of the Papers presented at the Flight Research Center, 20-21 November 1961), p. 255. A slightly expanded version of this paper was subsequently republished as AFFTC technical report FTC-TDR-61-61, "Bioastronautics Support of the X-15 Program," December 1961.
121. Rowen, Richardson, and Layton, "Bioastronautics Support of the X-15 Program," pp. 255-256.
122. Ibid., pp. 256-257.
123. Rowen, Richardson, and Layton, "Bioastronautics Support of the X-15 Program;" Lieutenant Colonel Harry R. Bratt, AFFTC technical report FTC-TR-65-24, "Biomedical Aspects of the X-15 Program: 1959-1964," August 1965, pp. 8-9. In the AFFTC Access to Space Office Project Files.
124. Christopher T. Carey, "Supporting Life at 80,000 feet: Evolution of the American High Altitude Pressure Suit." http://www.lanset.com/aeolusaero/Articles/Suits.htm, accessed on 9 April 2002.
125. X-15 Interim Flight Manual; Utility Flight Manual.

Chapter 12 – Stillborn Concepts

1. House Report 1228, Project Mercury, First Interim Report, 86th Congress, 2nd Session, p. 2; comments by Clotaire Wood, NACA, 26 January 1960, on Draft, NIS Meeting at ARDC Headquarters, 19 June 1958; memorandum, Maxime A. Faget, NACA Langley, to Hugh L. Dryden, Director, NACA, no subject, 5 June 1958; comments by Maxime A. Faget on "Outline of History of USAF Man-in-Space R&D Program," *Missiles and Rockets*, Volume 10, Number 13 26 March 1962, pp. 148-149; Mark Wade, http://www.astronautix.com/craftfam/mercury.htm, accessed 7 April 2002; Lloyd S. Swenson, Jr., James M. Greenwood, and Charles C. Alexander, *This New Ocean: A History of Project Mercury*, (Washington DC: NASA, 1966), pp. 77-78.
2. Email, A. Scott Crossfield to Dennis R. Jenkins, 28 June 2002; Mark Wade, http://www.astronautix.com/craft/x15b.htm, accessed 7 April 2002; "Outline of History of USAF Man-in-Space R&D Program," *Missiles and Rockets*, Volume 10, Number 13, 26 March 1962, pp. 148-149; memorandum, Clarence A. Syvertson to Director, Langley Aeronautical Laboratory, subject: Visit to WADC, Wright-Patterson AFB, Ohio, to Attend Conference on January 29-31, 1958, Concerning Research Problems Associated with Placing a Man in a Satellite Vehicle, Moffett Field, 18 February 1958.
3. Lloyd S. Swenson, Jr., James M. Greenwood, and Charles C. Alexander, *This New Ocean: A History of Project Mercury*, (Washington DC: NASA, 1966), pp. 78-81.
4. A. Scott Crossfield, *Always Another Dawn: The Story of a Rocket Test Pilot*, (New York: The World Publishing Company, 1960), pp. 280-281. Unfortunately, a copy of the report could not be located, and neither Scott Crossfield nor Charlie Feltz had any particular memories of the concept. The X-15B designation was rather arbitrarily used by Storms and was not an official Air Force designation.
5. Crossfield, *Always Another Dawn*, pp. 281-282, and 287.
6. Ibid., pp. 374-375.
7. Memorandum, John V. Becker to Floyd L. Thompson, 29 October 1964; letter, Paul F. Bikle to C. W. Harper, 13 November 1964.
8. Paul F. Bikle and John S. McCollom, "X-15 Research Accomplishments and Future Plans," (a paper in the *Progress of the X-15 Research Airplane Program*, A Compilation of the Papers presented at the Flight Research Center, 7 October 1965, NASA SP-90, (Washington, D.C.: NASA, 1965), p. 139.
9. Draft Statement of Work, "Feasibility Study and Cost Analysis of Modifying an X-15 Aircraft to a Slender Hypersonic Configuration," January 1965, no page numbers. In the files at the DFRC History Office.
10. Ibid.
11. Project Development Plan, "Delta Wing X-15," second draft, December 1965, pp. 1-2. In the files at the DFRC History Office.
12. Ibid., pp. 2-3. In addition to 37 powered flights, planners envisioned two captive and one glide flight.
13. Ibid., p. 33.
14. North American report NA-67-344, "Technical Proposal for a Conceptual Design Study for the Modification of an X-15 Air Vehicle to a Hypersonic Delta-Wing Configuration," 17 May 1967, volume I, p. 4. In the files at the JSC History Office.
15. Ibid., passim; North American report NA-67-344, "Technical Proposal for a Conceptual Design Study for the Modification of an X-15 Air Vehicle to a Hypersonic Delta-Wing Configuration," 17 May 1967, volume I, p. 42. In the files at the JSC History Office.
16. Ibid., volume I, pp. 2-3 and 28.
17. Ibid., p. 86.
18. Ibid., p. 34.
19. Ibid., p. 34.
20. Ibid., pp. 104-108.
21. Ibid., p. 38.
22. Ibid., p. 128.
23. Ibid., pp. 15 and 142. At some point North American had also proposed installing the YLR91 in the X-15A-2 as a means of increasing its performance.
24. Ibid., pp. 197-199.
25. Paul F. Bikle and John S. McCollom, "X-15 Research Accomplishments and Future Plans," (a paper in the *Progress of the X-15 Research Airplane Program*, A Compilation of the Papers presented at the Flight Research Center, 7 October 1965, NASA SP-90, (Washington, D.C.: NASA, 1965), pp. 138-139; Paul Gwozdz, Reaction Motors report number TR-4085-1, "A Study to Determine Modifications Which Extend the Low and High Thrust Range of the YLR99 Turborocket Engine," undated (but signed on 11 October 1966), p. 2. In the files at the DFRC History Office. The modified XLR99 (called a YLR99 in the report) would theoretically be capable of 87,000-lbf at 100,000 feet, but Reaction Motors recommended slightly derating it to increase reliability.
26. North American report NA-67-344, volume I, pp. 131-132.
27. Ibid., pp. 176-180.
28. North American news release GHH031067, 17 March 1967. Provided courtesy of Mike Lombardi, Boeing Historical Archives.
29. It is sometimes difficult to figure which factor had the most effect on the decision not to proceed with the delta-wing program. The MH-96 and other advanced flight control equipment on X-15-3 could have been replaced; there were spare parts and complete systems procured for Dyna-Soar available if somebody had wanted to use them, although there would have been integration costs to bring them up to the X-15 configuration. The loss of political support for the program had been ongoing for some time; Apollo had siphoned off too much budget, but was obviously going to succeed despite the disastrous Apollo 1 fire in January 1967. It was probably more a case that too many things were going against the program, and the easiest answer was simply not to request continued funding.
30. For a better description of the Aerospaceplane program, see Dennis R. Jenkins, *Space Shuttle: The History of the National Space Transportation System – The First 100 Missions*, (Cape Canaveral, FL: the author, 2001), pp. 52-55.
31. See for example, Convair report GD/C-DCJ-65-004, "Reusable Space Launch Vehicle Study, 18 May 1965.

Appendix A – Selected Biographies

1. Jonathan McDowell, "The X-15 Spaceplane," *Quest*, Volume 3, Number 1, Spring 1994, p. 5.
2. Jacqueline Cochran received her pilot license in 1932, set three major flying records in 1937 and won the prestigious Bendix Race in 1938. In 1941, Cochran selected a group of highly qualified women pilots to ferry aircraft for the British Air Transport Auxiliary. In 1942, Cochran, at the request of Army General Henry "Hap" Arnold, organized the Women's Flying Training Detachment (WFTD) which was subsequently merged with Nancy Love's Women's Auxiliary Ferry Squadron (WAFS) to form the Women Airforce Service Pilots (WASPS) with Cochran as director. Following the war, Cochran continued to establish speed records into the 1960s. She was the first woman to break the sound barrier, doing so in 1953 in an F-86 Sabre. She was a fourteen-time winner of the Harmon Trophy, awarded to the best female pilot of the year. Cochran also became the first woman to break Mach 2 in the Lockheed F-104 Starfighter. Cochran authored two autobiographies – *The Stars at Noon* and *Jackie Cochran* with Mary Ann Bucknam Brinley.
3. Biography of Major Michael J. Adams, Air Force Systems Command, Edwards AFB, 12 November 1965; letter, Colonel Clyde S. Charry/AFFTC to Paul Bikle/FRC, subject: Selection of Crew Member for X-15 Program, 14 July 1966; letter, William H. Dana to Dennis R. Jenkins, 14 June 2002, containing comments to a draft of this manuscript.
4. http://www.dfrc.nasa.gov/PAO/PAIS/HTML/bd-dfrc-p001.html, accessed on 29 April 2002; http://www.jsc.nasa.gov/Bios/htmlbios/armstrong-na.html, accessed on 29 April 2002.
5. Biography, John V. Becker, 8 April 1959. In the files at the NASA History Office.
6. Ibid.
7. Richard P. Hallion, *On the Frontier: Flight Research at Dryden, 1946-1981*, NASA SP-4303 (Washington, D.C., 1984), p. 104; letter, Richard J. Harer to Dennis R. Jenkins, 15 October 2002.
8. Telephone conversation, A. Scott Crossfield with Dennis R. Jenkins, 8 August 2002.
9. Thompson quote from Milton O. Thompson, *At the Edge of Space: The X-15 Flight Program*, (Washington DC: Smithsonian Institution Press, 1992), p. 4.
10. http://www.edwards.af.mil/history/docs_html/people/pilot_crossfield.html, accessed on 29 April 2002; http://www.dfrc.nasa.gov/PAO/PAIS/HTML/bd-dfrc-p021.html, accessed on 29 April 2002.
11. Letter, William H. Dana to Dennis R. Jenkins, 14 June 2002.
12. http://www.edwards.af.mil/history/docs_html/people/pilot_dana.html, accessed on 29 April 2002; http://www.dfrc.nasa.gov/PAO/PAIS/HTML/bd-dfrc-p002.html, accessed on 29 April 2002.
13. http://www.hq.nasa.gov/office/pao/History/Biographies/dryden.html, accessed on 2 May 2002.
14. Thompson quote from *At the Edge of Space*, p. 16.
15. http://www.edwards.af.mil/history/docs_html/people/pilot_engle.html, accessed on 29 April 2002; http://www.jsc.nasa.gov/Bios/htmlbios/engle-jh.html, accessed 29 April 2002.
16. Resume provided to Dennis R. Jenkins by Charles H. Feltz, 15 May 2002.
17. http://icdweb.cc.purdue.edu/~ivenc/who.html, accessed 25 April 2002.
18. http://www.kinsella.org/director/iven.htm, accessed 25 April 2002.
19. http://www.edwards.af.mil/history/docs_html/people/bio_kincheloe.html, accessed on 29 April 2002.
20. Total flight time from telephone conversation with William J. Knight to Dennis R. Jenkins, 24 June 2002.
21. http://www.edwards.af.mil/history/docs_html/people/pilot_knight.html, accessed on 29 April 2002.
22. Thompson, *At the Edge of Space*, p. 11.
23. http://www.af.mil/news/biographies/rushworth_ra.html, accessed on 24 June 2002; telephone conversation with William J. Knight to Dennis R. Jenkins, 24 June 2002.
24. http://www.af.mil/news/biographies/rushworth_ra.html, accessed on 24 June 2002; Thompson, *At the Edge of Space*, p. 13.
25. http://www.af.mil/news/biographies/rushworth_ra.html, accessed on 24 June 2002.
26. Eve Dumovich, "Harrison Storms: The Quarterback for the Race to the Moon," *Manager* (Boeing internal magazine), Issue 5/6, 2000. Copy provided by Charles H. Feltz.
27. http://www.dfrc.nasa.gov/PAO/PAIS/HTML/bd-dfrc-p018.html, accessed 29 April 2002.
28. Thompson, *At the Edge of Space*, p. 5.
29. http://www.dfrc.nasa.gov/PAO/PAIS/HTML/bd-dfrc-p019.html, accessed on 29 April 2002.
30. Letter, Alvin S. White to Dennis R. Jenkins, 18 June 2002.
31. Letter, Alvin S. White to Dennis R. Jenkins, 8 June 2002.
32. http://www.edwards.af.mil/history/docs_html/people/white_biography.html, accessed on 29 April 2002.
33. Letter, Major General Robert M. White (USAF, Retired) to Dennis R. Jenkins, 13 June 2002, with comments on a draft copy of this manuscript.
34. Biography, Walter C. Williams, 11 October 1995. In the files at the NASA History Office.

Abbott, Ira, 32
Ablator, *See* X-15: ablator
Accident Boards, 120
Adams, Michael J., viii, 123, 125 (ills.), 127, 149-151, 149 (ills.), 152 (ills.), 155, 215, 217, 217 (ills.)
Adaptive flight control system, *See* Minneapolis-Honeywell: MH-96
Adelsback, LeRoy "Lee", viii (ills.), 114 (ills.)
Adkins, Elmore J., 45
Aerojet: XLR73-AJ-1, 20, 30
Aeronautics and Astronautics Coordinating Board, 122
Air Force Flight Test Center, *See* U.S. Air Force: Air Force Flight Test Center
Air Force Museum, *See* U.S. Air Force: Air Force Museum
Air Research and Development Command, *See* U.S. Air Force: Air Research and Development Command
Albrecht, William, 145
Allavie, John E. "Jack", 70, 71, 116
Allen, Bob, Sr., 154 (ills.)
Allen, H. Julian, 10, 12, 251 (note #20)
Alternate stability augmentation system, 83, 111-112, 189-190
Ames boost guidance display, 149, 168-169
Ames, Milton, 19
Anderson, Clarence E. "Bud", 60
AP-76, *See* Republic: AP-76
Apt, Milburn G., 6, 44
Armstrong, Johnny G., 45, 87, 136, 145, 151
Armstrong, Neil A., viii, 48, 66, 81, 85, 89 (ills.), 91 (ills.), 93, 109 (ills.), 111 (ills.), 116, 217, 218, 218 (ills.)
Arnold Engineering Development Center, *See* U.S. Air Force: Arnold Engineering Development Center
Astronaut Memorial, 155
Astronaut rating, 117, 120, 152 (ills.), 225 (note #92)
Atwood, John Leland "Lee", 33
Auxiliary power units, 49, 97, 120, 125, 127, 186

B-36, *See* Convair: B-36
B-52, *See* Boeing: B-52 and NB-52
B-58, *See* Convair: B-58
B-70, *See* North American: B-70
Bailey, Clyde, 114 (ills.)
Baker, Charlie, 154 (ills.)
Baker, Tom, 101 (ills.)
Ball nose, 49, 158, 158 (ills.), 168, 174, 179, 193-194, 193 (ills.), 194 (ills.)
Ballarat Lake, 58 (ills.), 150
Ballistic Control System: early concepts, 16, 21, 26, 27, 37 (ills.), 92
Barnett, Lorenzo "Larry", viii (ills.), 114 (ills.), 154 (ills.)
Bastow, William, 114 (ills.)
Beatty, Nevada, *See* High Range
Becker, John V., vi, viii, 2, 8 (ills.), 9, 12, 14, 20, 26, 36, 173, 210, 215, 218, 218 (ills.)
Beeler, De Elroy, 19
Beilman, Jack, 81
Bell Aircraft Company
    BoMi, 12, 13, 14, 22
    D171, 21-24
    X-1, vii, xii (ills.), 1, 1 (ills.), 3, 4, 6, 51, 250 (note #1)
    X-1, origin of, 3
    X-1A, 3 (ills.), 4 (ills.), 5, 13
    X-1B, 5, 7 (ills.)
    X-1C, 5
    X-1D, 5
    X-1E, 6 (ills.), 7
    X-2, 5 (ills.), 6, 7, 7 (ills.), 11, 44, 51
    XLR81-BA-1, 20, 21, 28, 30 (ills.), 30-31, 214
Bell, Lawrence D., 5
Bellman, Donald R., 120, 151
Benner, Roland L. "Bud", 35, 101

Bergner, Chester, 114 (ills.)
Berkowitz, William, 70, 97 (ills.)
Beta dot technique, 82
Bikle, Paul F., 52, 62, 108, 112, 114, 114 (ills.), 122, 127, 129, 159, 177, 210, 218, 218 (ills.)
Biomedical research, 114, 157-158
Blair, Richard L., 249 (ills.) Blue Scout, *See* Experiments, on X-15: Recoverable booster system
Blue Scout, use on X-15, 176
Blunt body concept, 10, 12
Bock, Charles C., Jr., 70, 71
Boeing Company, The
    B-52 as a carrier aircraft, 39, 67, 67-68, 67-68 (ills.)
    KC-135 as a carrier aircraft, 66-67
    NB-52 flight tests, 70-76
    NB-52 modifications, 69-70
BoMi, *See* Bell: BoMi
Boyd, Albert, 51
Bridgeman, William B., 6
British Advisory Committee for Aeronautics, 2
Brown, Frank, 114 (ills.)
Bryan, G. H., 1
Bryan, Harold, 114 (ills.)
Bryant, Roy G., vii (ills.), ix, 101 (ills.)
BuAer, *See* U.S. Navy: Bureau of Aeronautics
Bug-eye camera bays, *See* X-15: Bug-eye camera bays
Butchart, Stan, 37 (ills.)

C-130, *See* Lockheed: C-130
C-47, *See* Douglas: R4D
Caldwell, Frank W., 2
Cannon, Joseph, 4
Capasso, Vincent N., Jr., 249 (ills.)
Carl, Marion E., 4, 6
Carman, L. Robert, 11, 35
Caruso, Hank, 90 (ills.)
Castor solid rocket boosters, 177, 215
Centrifuge (human), *See* U.S. Navy: Naval Aviation Medical Acceleration Laboratory
Chase aircraft, definition, 77-78, 90
Chenoweth, Paul L., 45
Clark, David, 43 (caption)
Clark, William, viii (ills.)
Clousing, Lawrence A., 11
Collier Trophy, 5, 117, 117 (ills.)
Committee on Aerodynamics, *See* National Advisory Committee on Aeronautics
Convair: B-36 as a carrier aircraft, 21, 22, 23 (ills.), 28, 29 (ills.), 30, 33, 39, 65-67, 65-66 (ills.)
Cooney, Tom, 101 (ills.)
Cooper, Marcus F., 85, 110
Cooper, Norm, 82-83
Cornell Aeronautical Laboratory, 80
Craft, James B. 249 (ills.)
Crossfield, A. Scott, vi, vii, viii, 6, 7, 17, 19, 35, 43, 43 (ills.), 47, 48, 71, 76, 80, 85, 87 (ills.), 90, 91 (ills.), 96, 97 (ills.), 99, 100 (ills.), 101, 105, 107-110, 111 (ills.), 117, 117 (ills.), 183, 217, 218-219, 218 (ills.)
Crossfield, A. Scott: "Chief son-of-a-bitch", 35
Crowley, Gus, 19, 20, 32
Cuddeback Lake, 57, 58, 58(ills.), 59, 121, 122, 135, 150, 151
Cupp, Ira O., viii (ills.), 249 (ills.)
Curtis, Merle, viii (ills.), 114 (ills.)

D-558-I, *See* Douglas: D-558-I
D-558-II, *See* Douglas: D-558-II
D-558-III, *See* Douglas: D-558-III

D171, *See* Bell: D171
Damberg, Carl F., 33
Dampers, *See* stability augmentation system
Dana, William H., vii, viii, 46 (ills.), 81, 113 (ills.), 114 (ills.), 123, 124 (ills.), 127, 150, 153, 153 (ills.), 217, 219, 219 (ills.)
Daniels, James, 114 (ills.)
David Clark Company
    A/P22S-2 suit, 89, 110, 124, 206-207, 206 (ills.)
    Full-pressure suits, 89, 204
    MC-2 suit, 43 (ills.), 49, 49 (ills.), 89 (ills.), 96, 204-205, 205 (ills.)
    S1023/S1024 suits, 206, 207
Day, Richard E., 45, 46, 48, 82, 87, 111-112
DC-3, *See* Douglas: R4D
de Havilland: DH.108 Swallow, 1, 250 (note #2)
Delamar Lake, 57, 58, 59 (ills.), 121 (ills.), 122, 149, 168
Delta-wing, *See* North American: X-15 with delta wings
Dives, Willard E., 151
Dixon, R. E., 32
Dome, Cecil, 114 (ills.)
Donaldson, Coleman duP., 9
Donlan, Charles J., 11
Dornberger, Walter R., 11, 12
Dorr, Paschal "Herm", 114 (ills.), 154 (ills.), 249 (ills.)
Douglas Aircraft Company
    D-558, origins, 3
    D-558-I Skystreak, 2 (ills.), 3, 4, 6
    D-558-II Skyrocket, vii, xii (ills.), 6, 12
    D-558-III, 14, 36, 66, 251 (note #57)
    Model 671, 14-17, 24
    Model 684, 17, 24-26
    R4D Skytrain (Gooney Bird), 53 (ills.), 62, 80, 83 (ills.)
Dow, Norris, 13
Drake, Hubert M. "Jake", 11, 35
Dry lakes, 57-63, 253-254 (note #32), *See also* each lake name.
Dry lakes: Markings of, 62
Dryden Flight Research Center, *See* National Aeronautics and Space Administration: Dryden Flight Research Center
Dryden, Hugh L., 6, 12, 14, 20, 32, 51, 52, 114 (ills.), 219
Dustin, Allen F., viii (ills.), 249 (ills.)

Edgerton, Harold, 151
Edwards AFB, map of, 92 (ills.)
Edwards Creek Valley Dry Lake, 62
Edwards, Glen W., 51
Eggers, Alfred J., Jr., 10
Eglin AFB, trip to, 73, 116
Electrocardiogram, use on X-15, 158-159
Electronic Engineering Company, 52-56
Elkin, Hugh, 26
Ely, Nevada, *See* High Range
Emergency preparations, 119
Engle, Joe H., 112 (ills.), 113 (ills.), 121, 125 (ills.), 133, 217, 220, 220 (ills.)
Escape concepts, early, 25, 27, 28, 34, 35
Escape concepts, after contract award, 36, 43, 203
ESO-7487, *See* North American: ESO-7487
Estes, Howell M., Jr., 33
Evans, Howard, 209 (ills.)
Everest, Frank K., Jr., 5, 6
Experiment accommodations, 160
Experiments, on X-15
    Air-breathing propulsion (#22), 171
    Atmospheric-density measurements (#12), 168
    B-70 emission coatings, 119 (ills.), 157, 163
    Cold wall, 175, 175 (ills.)
    Detachable high-temperature leading edge (#8), 167, 175, 188 (ills.)

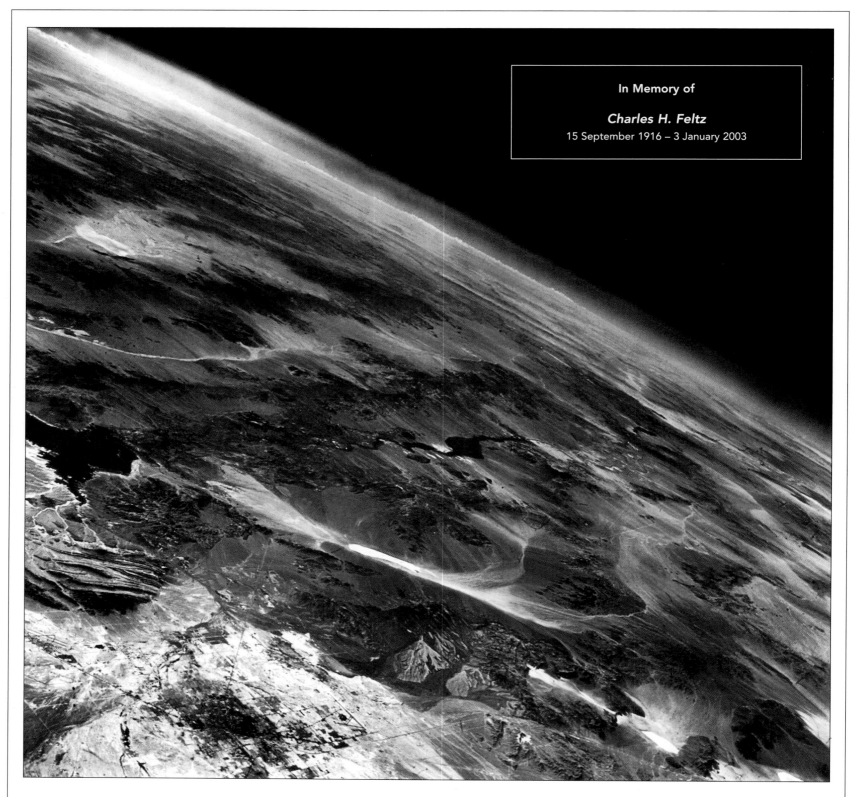

In Memory of

Charles H. Feltz

15 September 1916 – 3 January 2003

A view of the southwestern United States taken by the Hycon camera in X-15-2. Before the manned space programs began, the X-15 flights were by far the highest Man had ever gone and provided some of the first photos that showed the curvature of the Earth. (NASA Dryden)

THE END